Mario Puzo

FOOLS DIE

THE FOURTH K

This edition published in 1999 by Cresset Editions,
an imprint of Random House UK Ltd,
20 Vauxhall Bridge Road, London SW1V 2SA

Printed and bound in Germany

ISBN 0 09187 276 6

FOOLS DIE

For Erika

BOOK ONE

1

'LISTEN to me. I will tell you the truth about a man's life. I will tell you the truth about his love for women. That he never hates them. Already you think I'm on the wrong track. Stay with me. Really—I'm a master of magic.

'Do you believe a man can truly love a woman and constantly betray her? Never mind physically, but betray her in his mind, in the very "poetry of his soul". Well, it's not easy, but men do it all the time.

'Do you want to know how women can love you, feed you that love deliberately to poison your body and mind simply to destroy you? And out of passionate love choose not to love you any more? And at the same time dizzy you with an idiot's ecstasy? Impossible? That's the easy part.

'But don't run away. This is not a love story.

'I will make you feel the painful beauty of a child, the animal horniness of the adolescent male, the yearning suicidal moodiness of the young female. And then (here's the hard part) show you how time turns man and woman around full circle, exchanged in body and soul.

'And then of course there is TRUE LOVE. Don't go away! It exists or I will make it exist. I'm not a master of magic for nothing. Is it worth what it costs? And how about sexual fidelity? Does it work? Is it love? Is it even human, that perverse passion to be with only one person? And if it doesn't work, do you still get a bonus for trying? Can it work both ways? Of course not, that's easy. And yet—

'Life is a comical business, and there is nothing funnier than love travelling through time. But a true master of magic can make his audience laugh and cry at the same time. Death is another story. I will never make a joke about death. It is beyond my powers.

'I am always alert for death. He doesn't fool me. I spot him right away. He loves to come in his country-bumpkin disguise; a comical wart that suddenly grows and grows; the dark, hairy mole that sends its roots to the very bone; or hiding behind a pretty little fever blush. Then suddenly that grinning skull appears to take the victim by surprise. But never me. I'm waiting for him. I take my precautions.

'Parallel to death, love is a tiresome, childish business, though men believe more in love than death. Women are another story. They have a powerful secret. They don't take love seriously and never have.

'But again, don't go away. Again; this is not a love story. Forget about love. I will show you all the stretches of power. First the life of a poor struggling writer. Sensitive. Talented. Maybe even some genius. I will show you the artist getting the shit kicked out of him for the sake of his art. And why he so richly deserves it. Then I will show him as a cunning criminal and having the time of his life. Ah, what joy the true artist feels when he finally becomes a crook. It's out in the open now, his essential nature. No more kidding around about his honour. The son of a bitch is a hustler. A conniver. An enemy of society right out in the clear instead of hiding behind his whore's cunt of art. What a relief. What pleasure. Such sly delight. And then how he becomes an honest man again. It's an awful strain being a crook.

'But it helps you to accept society and forgive your fellowman. Once that's done no person should be a crook unless he really needs the money.

'Then on to one of the most amazing success stories in the history of literature. The intimate lives of the giants of our culture. One crazy bastard especially. The classy world. So now we have the poor struggling genius world, the crooked world and the classy literary world. All this laced with plenty of sex, some complicated ideas you won't be hit over the head with and may even find interesting. And finally on to a full-blast ending in Hollywood with our hero gobbling up all its rewards, money, fame, beautiful women. And . . . don't go away—don't go away— how it all turns to ashes.

'That's not enough? You've heard it all before? But remember I'm a master of magic. I can bring all these people truly alive. I can show you what they truly think and feel. You'll weep for

3

them, all of them, I promise you that. Or maybe just laugh. Anyway, we're going to have a lot of fun. And learn something about life. Which is really no help.

'Ah, I know what you're thinking. That conning bastard trying to make us turn the page. But wait, it's only a tale I want to tell. What's the harm? Even if I take it seriously, you don't have to. Just have a good time.

'I want to tell you a story, I have no other vanity. I don't desire success or fame or money. But that's easy, most men, most women don't, not really. Even better, I don't want love. When I was young, some women told me they loved me for my long eyelashes. I accepted. Later it was for my wit. Then for my power and money. Then for my talent. Then for my mind—deep. OK, I can handle all of it. The only woman who scares me is the one who loves me for myself alone. I have plans for her. I have poisons and daggers and dark graves in caves to hide her head. She can't be allowed to live. Especially if she is sexually faithful and never lies and always puts me ahead of everything and everyone.

'There will be a lot about love in this book, but it's not a love book. It's a war book. The old war between men who are true friends. The great "new" war between men and women. Sure it's an old story, but it's out in the open now. The Women's Liberation warriors think they have something new, but it's just their armies coming out of their guerrilla hills. Sweet women ambushed men always: at their cradles, in the kitchen, the bedroom. And at the graves of their children, the best place not to hear a plea for mercy.

'Ah well, you think I have a grievance against women. But I never hated them. And they'll come out better people than men, you'll see. But the truth is that only women have been able to make me unhappy, and they have done so from the cradle on. But most men can say that. And there's nothing to be done.

'What a target I've given here. I know—I know—how irresistible it seems. But be careful. I'm a tricky storyteller, not just one of your vulnerable sensitive artists. I've taken my precautions. I've still got a few surprises left.

'But enough. Let me get to work. Let me begin and let me end.'

BOOK TWO

2

ON the luckiest day of Jordan Hawley's life he betrayed his three best friends. But yet unknowing, he wandered through the dice pit of the huge gambling casino in the Hotel Xanadu, wondering what game to try next. Still early afternoon, he was a ten-thousand-dollar winner. But he was tired of the glittering red dice skittering across green felt.

He moved out of the pit, the purple carpet sinking beneath his feet, and moved toward the hissing wheel of a roulette table, pretty with red and black boxes, punishing green zero and double zero. He made some foolhardy bets, lost and moved into the blackjack pit.

The small horseshoe blackjack tables ran down in double rows. He walked between them like a captive through an Indian gauntlet. Blue-backed cards flashed on either side. He made it through safely and came to the huge glass doors that led out into the streets of the city of Las Vegas. From here he could see down the Strip sentinelled by luxury hotels.

Under the blazing Nevada sun, a dozen Xanadus glittered with million-watt neon signs. The hotels seemed to be melting down into a shimmering golden haze, an unreachable mirage. Jordan Hawley was trapped inside the air-conditioned casino with his winnings. It would be madness to go out to where only other casinos awaited him, with their strange unknown fortunes. Here he was a winner, and soon he would see his friends. Here he was shielded from the burning yellow desert.

Jordan Hawley turned away from the glass door and sat down at the nearest blackjack table. Black hundred-dollar chips, tiny cindered suns, rattled in his hands. He watched a dealer sliding cards from his freshly made shoe, the oblong wooden box that held the cards.

Jordan bet heavy on each of two small circles, playing two hands. His luck was good. He played until the shoe ran out. The dealer busted often, and when he shuffled up, Jordan moved on. His pockets bulged chips everywhere. But that was no sweat because he was wearing a specially designed Sy Devore Vegas Winner sports coat. It had red crimson trim on sky blue cloth and specially zippered pockets that were optimistically capacious. The inside of the jacket also held special zippered cavities so deep no pickpocket could get at them. Jordan's winnings were safe, and he had plenty of room for more. Nobody had ever filled the pockets of a Vegas Winner jacket.

The casino, lit by many huge chandeliers, had a bluish haze, neon reflected by the deep purple carpeting. Jordan stepped out of this light and into the darkened area of the bar lounge with its lowered ceiling and small platform for performers. Seated at a small table, he could look out on the casino as a spectator looks on a lighted stage.

Mesmerized, he watched afternoon gamblers drift in intricate choreographed patterns from table to table. Like a rainbow flashing across a clear blue sky, a roulette wheel flashed its red, black numbers to match the table layout. Blue white-backed cards skittered across green felt tables. White-dotted red square dice were dazzling flying fish over the whale-shaped crap tables. Far off, down the rows of blackjack tables, those dealers going off duty washed their hands high in the air to show they were not palming chips.

The casino stage began to fill up with more actors: sun wor- shippers wandering in from the outdoor pool, others from tennis courts, golf courses, naps and afternoon free and paid love- making in Xanadu's thousand rooms. Jordan spotted another Vegas Winner jacket coming across the casino floor. It was Merlyn. Merlyn the Kid. Merlyn wavered as he passed the roulette wheel, his weakness. Though he rarely played because he knew its huge five and a half percent cut like a sharp sword. Jordan from the darkness waved a crimson-striped arm, and Merlyn took up his stride again as if he were passing through flames, stepped off the lighted stage of the casino floor and sat down. Merlyn's zippered pockets did not bulge with chips, nor did he have any in his hands.

They sat there without speaking, easy with each other. Merlyn looked like a burly athlete in his crimson and blue jacket. He was younger than Jordan by at least ten years, and his hair was jet

7

black. He also looked happier, more eager for the coming battle against fate, the night of gambling.

Then from the baccarat pit in the far corner of the casino they saw Cully Cross and Diane step through the elegant royal grey railing and move over the casino floor coming toward them. Cully too was wearing his Vegas Winner jacket. Diane was in a white summer frock, low-cut and cool for her day's work, the top of her breasts dusted pearly white. Merlyn waved, and they came forward through the casino tables without swerving. And when they sat down, Jordan ordered the drinks. He knew what they wanted.

Cully spotted Jordan's bulging pockets. 'Hey,' he said, 'you went and got lucky without us?'

Jordan smiled. 'A little.' They all looked at him curiously as he paid for the drinks and tipped the cocktail waitress with a red five-dollar chip. He noticed their glances. He did not know why they looked at him so oddly. Jordan had been in Vegas three weeks and had changed fearsomely in that three weeks. He had lost twenty pounds. His ash-blond hair had grown long, whiter. His face, though still handsome, was now haggard; the skin had a greyish tinge. He looked drained. But he was not conscious of this because he felt fine. Innocently, he wondered about these three people, his friends of three weeks and now the best friends he had in the world.

The one Jordan liked best was the Kid. Merlyn. Merlyn prided himself on being an impassive gambler. He tried never to show emotion when he lost or won and usually succeeded. Except that an exceptionally bad losing streak gave him a look of surprised bewilderment that delighted Jordan.

Merlyn the Kid never said much. He just watched everybody. Jordan knew that Merlyn the Kid kept tabs on everything he did, trying to figure him out. Which also amused Jordan. He had the Kid faked out. The Kid was looking for complicated things and never accepted that he, Jordan, was exactly what he presented to the world. But Jordan liked being with him and the others. They relieved his loneliness. And because Merlyn seemed more eager, more passionate, in his gambling, Cully had named him the Kid.

Cully himself was the youngest, only twenty-nine, but oddly enough seemed to be the leader of the group. They had met three weeks ago here in Vegas, in this casino, and they had only one thing in common. They were degenerate gamblers. Their three-week-long debauch was considered extraordinary because the

8

casino percentage should have ground them into the Nevada desert sands in their first few days.

Jordan knew that the others, Cully 'Countdown' Cross and Diane, were also curious about him, but he didn't mind. He had very little curiosity about any of them. The Kid seemed young and too intelligent to be a degenerate gambler, but Jordan never tried to nail down why. It was really of no interest to him.

Cully was nothing to wonder about or so it seemed. He was your classical degenerate gambler with skills. He could count down the cards in a four-deck blackjack shoe. He was an expert on all the gambling percentages. The Kid was not. Jordan was a cool, abstracted gambler where the Kid was passionate. And Cully professional. But Jordan had no illusions about himself. At this moment he was in their class. A degenerate gambler. That is, a man who gambled simply to gamble and must lose. As a hero who goes to war must die. Show me a gambler and I'll show you a loser, show me a hero and I'll show you a corpse, Jordan thought.

They were all at the end of their bankrolls, they would all have to move on soon, except maybe Cully. Cully was part pimp and part tout. Always trying to work a con to get an edge on the casinos. Sometimes he got a blackjack dealer to go partners against the house, a dangerous game.

The girl, Diane, was really an outsider. She worked as a shill for the house and she was taking her break from the baccarat table. With them, because these were the only three men in Vegas she felt cared about her.

As a shill she played with casino money, lost and won casino money. She was subject not to fate but to the fixed weekly salary she received from the casino. Her presence was necessary to the baccarat table only in slack hours because gamblers shied away from an empty table. She was the flypaper for the flies. She was, therefore, dressed provocatively. She had long jet black hair she used as a whip, a sensuous full mouth and an almost perfect long-legged body. Her bust was on the small side, but it suited her. And the baccarat pit boss gave her home phone number to big players. Sometimes the pit boss or a ladderman would whisper that one of the players would like to see her in his room. She had the option to refuse, but it was an option to be used carefully. When she complied, she was not paid directly by the customer. The pit boss gave her a special chit for fifty or a hundred dollars that she could cash at the casino cage. This she hated to do. So she would pay one of the other girl shills five dollars to cash her chit for her. When Cully heard this, he became her friend. He liked soft women, he could manipulate them.

Jordan signalled the cocktail waitress for more drinks. He felt relaxed. It gave Jordan a feeling of virtue to be so lucky and so early in the day. As if some strange God had loved him, found him good and were rewarding him for the sacrifices he had offered up to the world he had left behind him. And he had this sense of comradeship with Cully and Merlyn.

They ate breakfast together often. And always had this late-afternoon drink before starting their big gambling action that would destroy the night. Sometimes they had a midnight snack to celebrate a win, the lucky man picking up the tab and buying keno tickets for the table. In the last three weeks they had become buddies, though they had absolutely nothing in common and their friendship would die with their gambling lust. But now, still not busted out, they had a strange affection for each other. Coming off a winning day, Merlyn the Kid had taken the three of them into the hotel clothing store and bought their crimson and blue Vegas Winner jackets. That day all three had been winners and had worn their jackets superstitiously ever since.

Jordan had met Diane on the night of her deepest humiliation, the same night he first met Merlyn. The day after meeting her he had bought her coffee on one of her breaks, and they had talked but he had not heard what she was saying. She sensed his lack of interest and had been offended. So there had been no action. He was sorry afterward, sorry that night in his ornately decorated room, alone and unable to sleep. As he was unable to sleep every night. He had tried sleeping pills, but they gave him nightmares that frightened him.

The jazz combo would be coming on soon, the lounge filled up. Jordan noticed the look they had given him when he had tipped the waitress with a red five-dollar chip. They thought he was generous. But it was simply because he didn't want to be bothered figuring out what the tip should be. It amused him to see how his values had changed. He had always been meticulous and fair but never recklessly generous. At one time his part of the world had been scaled and metered out. Everyone earned rewards. And finally it hadn't worked. He was amazed now at the absurdity of having once based his life on such reasoning.

The combo was rustling through the darkness up to the

stage. Soon they would be playing too loud for anyone to talk, and this was always the signal for the three men to start their serious gambling.

'Tonight's my lucky night,' Cully said. 'I got thirteen passes in my right arm.'

Jordan smiled. He always responded to Cully's enthusiasm. Jordan knew him only by the name of Cully Countdown, the name he had earned at the blackjack tables. Jordan liked Cully because the man never stopped talking and his talk rarely required answers. Which made him necessary to the group because Jordan and Merlyn the Kid never talked much. And Diane, the baccarat shill, smiled a lot but didn't talk much either.

Cully's small-featured, dark, neat face was glowing with confidence. 'I'm going to hold the dice for an hour,' he said. 'I'm going to throw a hundred numbers and no sevens. You guys get on me.'

The jazz combo gave their opening flourish as if to back Cully up.

Cully loved craps, though his best skill was at blackjack where he could count down the shoe. Jordan loved baccarat because there was absolutely no skill or figuring involved. Merlyn loved roulette because it was to him the most mythical, magical game. But Cully had declared his infallibility tonight at craps and they would all have to play with him, ride his luck. They were his friends, they couldn't jinx him. They rose to go to the dice pit and bet with Cully, Cully flexing his strong right arm that magically concealed thirteen passes.

Diane spoke for the first time. 'Jordy had a lucky streak at baccarat. Maybe you should bet on him.'

'You don't look lucky to me,' Merlyn said to Jordan.

It was against the rules for her to mention Jordan's luck to fellow gamblers. They might tap him for a loan or he might feel jinxed. But by this time Diane knew Jordan well enough to sense he didn't care about any of the usual superstitions gamblers worried about.

Cully Countdown shook his head. 'I have the feeling.' He brandished his right arm, shaking imaginary dice.

The music blared; they could no longer hear each other speak. It blew them out of their sanctuary of darkness into the blazing stage that was the casino floor. There were many more players now, but they could move fluidly. Diane, her coffee break over, went back to the baccarat table to bet the house money, to fill up space. But without passion. As a house shill, winning and losing house money, she was boringly immortal. And so she walked more slowly than the others.

Cully led the way. They were the Three Musketeers in their crimson and blue Vegas Winner sports coats. He was eager and confident. Merlyn followed almost as eagerly, his gambling blood up. Jordan followed more slowly, his huge winnings making him appear heavier than the other two. Cully was trying to sniff out a hot table, one of his signposts being if the house racks of chips were low. Finally he led them to an open railing and the three lined up so that Cully would get the dice first coming around the stickman. They made small bets until Cully finally had the red cubes in his loving rubbing hands.

The Kid put twenty on the line. Jordan two hundred. Cully Countdown fifty. He threw a six. They all backed up their bets and bought all the numbers. Cully picked up the dice, passionately confident, and threw them strongly against the far side of the table. Then stared with disbelief. It was the worst of catastrophes. Seven out. Wiped. Without even catching another number. The Kid had lost a hundred and forty, Cully a big three fifty. Jordan had gone down the drain for fourteen hundred dollars.

Cully muttered something and wandered away. Thoroughly shaken, he was now committed to playing very careful blackjack. He had to count every card from the shoe to get an edge on the dealer. Sometimes it worked, but it was a long grind. Sometimes he would remember every card perfectly, figure out what was left in the shoe, get a ten percent edge on the dealer and bet a big stack of chips. And even then sometimes with that big ten percent edge he got unlucky and lost. And then count down another shoe. So now, his fantastic right arm having betrayed him, Cully was down to case money. The night before him was a drudgery. He had to gamble very cleverly and still not get unlucky.

Merlyn the Kid also wandered away, also down to his case money, but with no skills to back up his play. He had to get lucky.

Jordan, alone, prowled around the casino. He loved the feeling of being solitary in the crowd of people and the gambling hum. To be alone without being lonely. To be friends with strangers for an hour and never see them again. Dice clattering.

He wandered through the blackjack pit, the horseshoe tables in straight rows. He listened for the tick, of a second carder. Cully had taught him and Merlyn this trick. A crooked dealer with fast hands was impossible to spot with the eye. But if you listened very carefully, you could hear the slight rasping tick when he slid out the second card from beneath the top card of his deck. Because the top card was the card the dealer needed to make his hand good.

A long queue was forming for the dinner show though it was only seven. There was no real action in the casino. No big betters. No big winners. Jordan clicked the black chips in his hand, deliberating. Then he stepped up to an almost empty crap table and picked up the red glittering dice.

Jordan unzipped the outside pocket of his Vegas Winner sports jacket and heaped black hundred-dollar chips into his table rack. He bet two hundred on the line, backed up his number and then bought all the numbers for five hundred dollars each. He held the dice for almost an hour. After the first fifteen minutes the electricity of his hot hand ran through the casino and the table jammed full. He pressed his bets to the limit of five hundred, and the magical numbers kept rolling out of his hand. In his mind he banished the fatal seven to hell. He forbade it to appear. His table rack filled to overflowing with black chips. His jacket pockets bulged to capacity. Finally his mind could no longer hold its concentration, could no longer banish the fatal seven, and the dice passed from his hands to the next player. The gamblers at the table gave him a cheer. The pit boss gave him metal racks to carry his chips to the casino cage. Merlyn and Cully appeared. Jordan smiled at them.

'Did you get on my roll?' he asked.

Cully shook his head. 'I got in on the last ten minutes,' he said. 'I did a little good.'

Merlyn laughed. 'I didn't believe in your luck. I stayed off.'

Merlyn and Cully escorted Jordan to the cashier's cage to help him cash in. Jordan was astonished when the total of the metal racks came to over fifty thousand dollars. And his pockets bulged with still more chips.

Merlyn and Cully were awestricken. Cully said seriously, 'Jordy, now's the time for you to leave town. Stay here and they'll get it back.'

Jordan laughed. 'The night's young yet.' He was amused that his two friends thought it such a big deal. But the strain told on him. He felt enormously tired. He said, 'I'm going up to my

13

room for a nap. I'll meet you guys and buy a big dinner maybe about midnight. OK?'

The case teller had finished counting and said to Jordan, 'Sir would you like cash or a cheque? Or would you like us to hold it for you here in the cage?'

Merlyn said, 'Get a cheque.'

Cully frowned with thoughtful greed, but then noticed that Jordan's secret inner pockets still bulged with chips, and he smiled. 'A cheque is safer,' he said.

The three of them waited, Cully and Merlyn flanking Jordan, who looked beyond them to the glittering casino pits. Finally the cashier reappeared with the saw-toothed yellow cheque and handed it to Jordan.

The three men turned together in an unconscious pirouette; their jackets flashed crimson and blue beneath the keno board lights above them. Then Merlyn and Cully took Jordan by the elbows and thrust him into one of the spokelike corridors toward his room.

A plushy, expensive, garish room. Rich gold curtains, a huge silver quilted bed. Exactly right for gambling. Jordan took a hot bath and then tried to read. He couldn't sleep. Through the windows the neon lights of the Vegas Strip sent flashes of rainbow colour, streaking the walls of his room. He drew the curtains tighter, but in his brain he still heard the faint roar that diffused through the huge casino like surf on a distant beach. Then he put out the lights in the room and got into bed. It was a good fake, but his brain refused to be fooled. He could not fall asleep.

Then Jordan felt the familiar fear and terrible anxiety. If he fell asleep, he would die. He desperately wanted to sleep, yet he could not. He was too afraid, too frightened. But he could never understand why he was so terribly frightened.

He was tempted to try the sleeping pills again; he had done so earlier in the month and he had slept, but only with nightmares that he couldn't bear. And left him depressed the next day. He preferred going without sleep. As now.

Jordan snapped on the light, got out of bed and dressed. He emptied out all his pockets and his wallet. He unzipped all the outside and inside pockets of his Vegas Winner sports coat and shook it upside down so that all the black and green and red chips poured down on the silk coverlet. The hundred-dollar bills formed a huge pile, the black and reds forming curious spirals and chequered patterns. To pass the time he started to count the money and sort out the chips. It took him almost an hour.

He had over five thousand dollars in cash. He had eight thousand dollars in black hundred-dollar chips and another six thousand dollars in twenty-five-dollar greens, almost a thousand dollars in five-dollar reds. He was astonished. He took the big jagged-edged Hotel Xanadu cheque out of his wallet and studied the black and red script and the numbered amount in green. Fifty thousand dollars. He studied it carefully. There were three different signatures on the cheque. One of the signatures he particularly noticed because it was so large and the script so clear. Alfred Gronevelt.

And still he was puzzled. He remembered turning in some chips for cash several times during the day, but he hadn't realized it was for more than five thousand. He shifted on the bed and all the carefully stacked piles collapsed into each other.

And now he was pleased. He was glad that he had enough money to stay in Vegas, that he would not have to go on to Los Angeles to start his new job. To start his new career, his new life, maybe a new family. He counted all the money again and added the cheque. He was worth seventy-one thousand dollars. He could gamble forever.

He switched off the bedside light so that he could lie there in the darkness with his money surrounding and touching his body. He tried to sleep to fight off the terror that always came over him in this darkened room. He could hear his heart beating faster and faster until finally he had to switch the light back on and get up from the bed.

High above the city in his penthouse suite, the hotel owner, Alfred Gronevelt, picked up the phone. He called the dice pit and asked how much Jordan was ahead. He was told that Jordan had killed the table profits for the night. Then he called back the operator and told her to page Xanadu Five. He held on. It would take a few minutes for the page to cover all the areas of the hotel and penetrate the minds of the players. Idly he gazed out the penthouse window and could see the great thick red and green python of neon that wound down the Las Vegas Strip. And further off, the dark surrounding desert mountains enclosing, with him, thousands of gamblers trying to beat the house, sweating for those millions of dollars of greenbacks lying so mockingly in cashier cages. Over the years these gamblers had left their bones on that gaudy neon Strip.

Then he heard Cully's voice come over the phone. Cully was Xanadu Five. (Gronevelt was Xanadu One.)

'Cully, your buddy hit us big,' Gronevelt said. 'You sure he's legit?'

Cully's voice was low. 'Yeah, Mr Gronevelt. He's a friend of mine and he's square. He'll drop it back before he leaves.'

Gronevelt said, 'Anything he wants, lay it on him. Don't let him go wandering down the Strip, giving our money to other joints. Lay a good broad on him.'

'Don't worry,' Cully said. But Gronevelt caught something funny in his voice. For a moment he wondered about Cully. Cully was his spy, checking the operation of the casino and reporting the blackjack dealers who were going partners with him to beat the house. He had big plans for Cully when this operation was over. But now he wondered.

'What about that other guy in your gang, the Kid?' Gronevelt said. 'What's his angle, what the hell is he doing here three weeks?'

'He's small change,' Cully said. 'But a good kid. Don't worry, Mr Gronevelt. I know what I got riding with you.'

'OK,' Gronevelt said. When he hung up the phone, he was smiling. Cully didn't know that pit bosses had complained about Cully's being allowed in the casino because he was a countdown artist. That the hotel manager had complained about Merlyn and Jordan being allowed to keep desperately needed rooms for so long despite fresh loaded gamblers who came in every weekend. What no one knew was that Gronevelt was intrigued by the friendship of the three men; how it ended would be Cully's true test.

In his room Jordan fought the impulse to go back down into the casino. He sat in one of the stuffed armchairs and lit a cigarette. Everything was OK now. He had friends, he had gotten lucky, he was free. He was just tired. He needed a long rest someplace far away.

He thought, Cully and Diane and Merlyn. Now his three best friends, he smiled at that.

They knew a lot of things about him. They had all spent hours in the casino lounge together, gossiping, resting between bouts of gambling. Jordan was never reticent. He would answer any question, though he never asked any. The Kid always asked questions so seriously, with such obvious interest, that Jordan never took offence.

Just for something to do he took his suitcase out of the closet to pack. The first thing that hit his eye was the small handgun he had bought back home. He had never told his friends about the gun. His wife had left him and taken the children. She had left him for another man, and his first reaction had been to kill the other man. A reaction so alien to his true nature that even now he was constantly surprised. Of course, he had done nothing. The problem was to get rid of the gun. The best thing to do was to take it apart and throw it away piece by piece. He didn't want to be responsible for anybody's getting hurt by it. But right now he put it to one side and threw some clothes in the suitcase, then sat down again.

He wasn't that sure he wanted to leave Vegas, the brightly lit cave of his casino. He was comfortable there. He was safe there. His not caring really about winning or losing was his magic cloak against fate. And most of all, his casino cave closed out all the other pains and traps of life itself.

He smiled again, thinking about Cully's worrying about his winnings. What, after all, would he do with the money? The best thing would be to send it to his wife. She was a good woman, a good mother, a woman of quality and character. The fact that she had left him after twenty years to marry her lover did not, could not, change those facts. For at this moment, now that the months had passed, Jordan saw clearly the justice of her decision. She had a right to be happy. To live her life to its fullest potential. And she had been suffocating living with him. Not that he had been a bad husband. Just an inadequate one. He had been a good father. He had done his duty in every way. His only fault was that after twenty years he no longer made his wife happy.

His friends knew his story. The three weeks he had spent with them in Vegas seemed like years, and he could talk to them as he could never talk to anyone back home. It had come out over drinks in the lounge, after midnight meals in the coffee shop.

He knew they thought him cold-blooded. When Merlyn asked him what the visitation rights were with his children, Jordan shrugged. Merlyn asked if he would ever see his wife and kids again, and Jordan tried to answer honestly. 'I don't think so,' he said. 'They're OK.'

And Merlyn the Kid shot back at him, 'And you, are you OK?'

And Jordan laughed without faking it, laughing at the way Merlyn the Kid zeroed in on him. Still laughing, he said, 'Yeah, I'm OK.' And then just once he paid the Kid off for being so nosy. He looked him right in the eye and said coolly, 'There's nothing more to see. What you see is it. Nothing complicated. People are not that important to other people. When you get older, that's the way it is.'

Merlyn looked back at him and lowered his eyes and then said very softly, 'It's just that you can't sleep at night, right?'

Jordan said, 'That's right.'

Cully said impatiently, 'Nobody sleeps in this town. Just get a couple of sleeping pills.'

'They give me nightmares,' Jordan said.

'No, no,' Cully said, 'I mean them.' He pointed to three hookers seated around a table, having drinks. Jordan laughed. It was the first time he had heard the Vegas idiom. Now he understood why sometimes Cully broke off gambling with the announcement he was going to take on a couple of sleeping pills.

If there was ever a time for walking sleeping pills, it was to-night, but Jordan had tried that the first week in Vegas. He could always make it, but he never really felt the relief from tension afterward. One night a hooker, a friend of Cully's, had talked him into 'twins', taking her girlfriend with her. Only another fifty and they would really shoot the works because he was a nice guy. And he'd said OK. It had been sort of cheery and comforting with so many breasts surrounding him. An infantile comfort. One girl finally cradled his head in her breast while the other one rode him astride. And at the final moment of tension, as finally he came, surrendering at least his flesh, he caught the girl astride giving a sly smile to the girl on whose breasts he rested. And he understood that now that he was finally out of the way, finished off, they could get down to what they really wanted. He watched while the girl who had been astride went down on the other girl with a passion far more convincing than she had shown with him. He wasn't angry. He'd just as soon they got something out of it. It seemed in some way more natural to be so. He had given them an extra hundred. They thought it was for being so good, but really it was for that sly secret smile—for that comforting, sweetly confirming betrayal. And yet the girl lying back in the final exaltation of her Judas climax had reached out her hand blindly for Jordan to hold, and he had been moved to tears.

And all the walking sleeping pills had tried their best for him.

They were the cream of the country, these girls. They gave you affection, they held your hand, they went to a dinner and a show, they gambled a little of your money, never cheated or rolled you. They made believe they truly cared and they fucked your brains out. All for a solitary hundred-dollar bill, a single Honeybee in Cully's phrase. They were a bargain. Ah, Christ, they were a bargain. But he could never let himself be faked out even for the tiny bought moment. They washed him down before leaving him: a sick, sick man on a hospital bed. Well, they were better than the regular sleeping pills, they didn't give him nightmares. But they couldn't put him to sleep either. He hadn't really slept for three weeks.

Wearily Jordan sagged against the headboard of his bed. He didn't remember leaving his chair. He should put out the lights and try to sleep. But the terror would come back. Not a mental fear, but a physical panic that his body could not fight off even as his mind stood by and wondered what was happening. There was no choice. He had to go back down into the casino. He threw the cheque for fifty thousand into his suitcase. He would just gamble his cash and chips.

Jordan scooped everything off the bed and stuffed his pockets. He went out of the room and down the hall into the casino. The real gamblers were at the tables now, in these early-morning hours. They had made their business deals, finished their dinners in the gourmet rooms, taken their wives to the shows and put them to bed or stuck them with dollar chips at the roulette wheel. Out of traffic. Or they had gotten laid, blown, attended a necessary civic function. All now free to battle fate. Money in hand, they stood in the front rank at crap tables. Pit bosses with blank markers waited for them to run out of chips so they could sign for another grand or two or three. During the coming dark hours men signed away fortunes. Never knowing why. Jordan looked away to the far end of the casino.

An elegantly royal grey railed enclosure nestled the long oval baccarat table from the main casino floor. An armed security guard stood at the gate because the baccarat table dealt mostly in cash, not chips. The green felt table was guarded at each end by high towered chairs. Seated in these chairs were the two laddermen, checking the croupiers and payouts, their hawkish concentration only thinly disguised by the evening dress all casino employees wore inside the baccarat enclosure. The laddermen watched every motion of the three croupiers and pit boss who ran the action. Jordan started walking toward them until he could see the distinct figures of the croupiers in their formal evening dress.

Four Saints in black tie, they sang hosannas to winners, dirges to losers. Handsome men, their motions quick, their charm continental, they graced the game they ruled. But before Jordan could get through the royal grey gate, Cully and Merlyn stepped before him.

Cully said softly, 'They only have fifteen minutes to go. Stay out of it.' Baccarat closed at 3 A.M.

And then one of the Saints in black tie called out to Jordan, 'We're making up the last shoe, Mr J. A. Banker shoe.' He laughed. Jordan could see the cards all dumped out on the table, blue-backed, then scooped to be stacked before the shuffle, their inner white pale faces showing.

Jordan said, 'How about you two guys coming in with me? I'll put up the money and we'll bet the limit in each chair.' Which meant that with the two-thousand limit Jordan would be betting six thousand on each hand.

'Are you crazy?' Cully said. 'You can go to hell.'

'Just sit there,' Jordan said. 'I'll give you ten percent of everything your chair wins.'

'No,' Cully said and walked away from him and leaned against the baccarat railing.

Jordan said, 'Merlyn, sit in a chair for me?'

Merlyn the Kid smiled at him and said quietly. 'Yeah, I'll sit in the chair.'

'You get ten percent,' Jordan said.

'Yeah, OK,' Merlyn said. They both went through the gate and sat down. Diane had the newly made up shoe, and Jordan sat down in the chair beside her so that he could get the shoe next. Diane bent her head to him.

'Jordy, don't gamble any more,' she said. He didn't bet on her hand as she dealt blue cards out of the shoe. Diane lost, lost her casino's twenty dollars and lost the bank and passed the shoe on to Jordan.

Jordan was busy emptying out all the outside pockets of his Vegas Winner sports coat. Chips, black and green, hundred-dollar notes. He placed a stack of bills in front of Merlyn's chair six. Then he took the shoe and placed twenty black chips in the Banker's slot. 'You too,' he said to Merlyn. Merlyn counted twenty hundred-dollar bills from the stack in front of him and placed them on his Banker's slot.

The croupier held up one palm high to halt Jordan's dealing. Looked around the table to see that everyone had made his bet. His palm fell to a beckoning hand, and he sang out to Jordan, 'A card for the Player.'

Jordan dealt out the cards. One to the croupier, one to himself. Then another one to the croupier and another one to himself. The croupier looked around the table and then threw his two cards to the man betting the highest amount on Player's. The man peeked at his cards cautiously and then smiled and flung his two cards face up. He had a natural, invincible nine. Jordan tossed his cards face up without even looking at them. He had two picture cards. Zero. Bust-out. Jordan passed the shoe to Merlyn. Merlyn passed the shoe on to the next player. For one moment Jordan tried to halt the shoe, but something about Merlyn's face stopped him. Neither of them spoke.

The golden brown box worked itself slowly around the table. It was chopping. Banker won. Then Player. No consecutive wins for either. Jordan riding the Banker all the way, pressing, had lost over ten thousand dollars from his own pile, Merlyn still refusing to bet. Finally Jordan had the shoe once again.

He made his bet, the two-thousand-dollar limit. He reached over into Merlyn's money and stripped off a sheaf of bills and threw them onto the Banker's slot. He noticed briefly that Diane was no longer beside him. Then he was ready. He felt a tremendous surge of power, that he could will the cards to come out of the shoe as he wished them to.

Calmly and without emotion Jordan hit twenty-four straight passes. By the eighth pass the railing around the baccarat table was crowded and every gambler at the table was betting Bank, riding with luck. By the tenth pass the croupier in the money slot reached down and pulled out the special five-hundred-dollar chips. They were a beautiful creamy white with gold threads running through.

Cully was pressed against the rail, watching. Diane standing with him. Jordan gave them a little wave. For the first time he was excited. Down at the other end of the table a South American gambler shouted, 'Maestro', as Jordan hit his thirteenth pass. And then the table became strangely silent as Jordan pressed on.

He dealt effortlessly from the shoe, his hands seemed to flow. Never once did a card stumble or slip as he passed it out from his

21

hiding place in the wooden box. Never did he accidentally show a card's pale white face. He flipped over his own cards with the same rhythmic movement each time, without looking, letting the head croupier call numbers and hits. When the croupier said, 'A card for the Player,' Jordan slipped it out easily with no emphasis to make it good or bad. When the croupier called, 'A card for the Banker,' again Jordan slipped it out smoothly and swiftly, without emotion. Finally going for the twenty-fifth pass, he lost to Player's, the Player's hand being played by the croupier because everyone was betting Bank.

Jordan passed the shoe on to Merlyn, who refused it and passed it on to the next chair. Merlyn, too, had stacks of gold five-hundred dollar chips in front of him. Since they had won on Bank, they had to pay the five percent house commission. The croupier counted out the commission plaques against their chair numbers. It was over five thousand dollars. Which meant that Jordan had won a hundred thousand dollars on that one hot hand. And every gambler around the table had bailed out.

Both laddermen high up in their chairs were on the phone calling the casino manager and the hotel owner with the bad news. An unlucky night at the baccarat table was one of the few serious dangers to the casino profit margin. Not that it meant anything in the long run, but an eye was always kept on natural disasters. Gronevelt himself came down from his penthouse suite and quietly stepped into the baccarat enclosure, standing in the corner with the pit boss, watching. Jordan saw him out of the corner of his eye and knew who he was, Merlyn had pointed him out one day.

The shoe travelled around the table and remained a coyly Banker's shoe. Jordan made a little money. Then he had the shoe in his hand again.

This time effortlessly and easily, his hands balletic, he accomplished every baccarat player's dream. He ran out the shoe with passes. There were no more cards left. Jordan had stack on stack of white gold chips in front of him.

Jordan threw four of the gold and white chips to the head croupier. 'For you, gentlemen,' he said.

The baccarat pit boss said, 'Mr Jordan, why don't you just sit here and we'll get all this money turned into a cheque?'

Jordan stuffed the huge wad of hundred-dollar bills in his jacket, then the black hundred-dollar chips, leaving endless stacks of gold and white five-hundred-dollar chips on the table.

22

'You can count them for me,' he said to the pit boss. He stood up to stretch his legs, and then he said casually, 'Can you make up another shoe?'

The pit boss hesitated and turned to the casino manager standing with Gronevelt. The casino manager shook his head for a no. He had Jordan tabbed as a degenerate gambler. Jordan would surely stay in Vegas until he lost. But tonight was his hot night. And why buck him on *his* hot night? Tomorrow the cards would fall differently. He could not be lucky forever and then his end would be swift. The casino manager had seen it all before. The house had an infinity of nights and every one of them with the edge, the percentage. 'Close the table,' the casino manager said.

Jordan bowed his head. He turned to look at Merlyn and said, 'Keep track, you get ten percent of your chair's win,' and to his surprise he saw a look almost of grief in Merlyn's eyes and Merlyn said, 'No.'

The money croupiers were counting up Jordan's gold chips and stacking them so that the laddermen, the pit boss and the casino manager could also keep track of their count. Finally they were finished. The pit boss looked up and said with reverence, 'You got two hundred and ninety thousand dollars here, Mr J. You want it all in a cheque?' Jordan nodded. His inside pockets were still lumpy with other chips, paper money. He didn't want to turn them in.

The other gamblers had left the table and the enclosure when the casino manager said there would not be another shoe. Still the pit boss whispered. Cully had come through the railing and stood beside Jordan, as did Merlyn, the three of them looking like members of some street gang in their Vegas Winner sports coats.

Jordan was really tired now, too tired for the physical exertion of craps and roulette. And blackjack was too slow with its five-hundred-dollar limit. Cully said. 'You're not playing any more. Jesus, I never saw anything like this. You can only go down. You can't get that lucky any more.' Jordan nodded in agreement.

The security guard took trays of Jordan's chips and the signed receipts from the pit boss to the cashier's cage. Diane joined their group and gave Jordan a kiss. They were all tremendously excited. Jordan at that moment felt happy. He really was a hero. And without killing or hurting anyone. So easily. Just by betting a huge amount of money on the turning of cards. And winning.

They had to wait for the cheque to come back from the cashier's cage. Merlyn said mockingly to Jordan. 'You're rich, you can do anything you want.'

Cully said, 'He has to leave Vegas.'

Diane was squeezing Jordan's hand. But Jordan was staring at Gronevelt, standing with the casino manager and the two laddermen, who had come down from their chairs. The four men were whispering together. Jordan said suddenly, 'Xanadu Number One, how about dealing up a shoe?'

Gronevelt stepped away from the other men, and his face was suddenly in the full glare of the light. Jordan could see that he was older than he had thought. Maybe about seventy, though ruddy and healthy. He had iron grey hair, thick and neatly combed. His face was redly tanned. His figure was sturdy, not yet willowing away with age. Jordan could see that he had reacted only slightly to being addressed by his telephone code name.

Gronevelt smiled at him. He wasn't angry. But something in him responded to the challenge, brought back his youth, when he had been a degenerate gambler. Now he had made his world safe, his life was under control. He had many pleasures, many duties, some dangers but very rarely a pure thrill. It would be sweet to taste one again, and besides, he wanted to see just how Jordan would go, what made him tick.

Gronevelt said softly, 'You have a cheque for two hundred ninety grand coming from the cage, right?'

Jordan nodded.

Gronevelt said, 'I'll have them make up a shoe. We play one hand. Double or nothing. But you have to bet Player's, not Banker's.'

Everyone in the baccarat enclosure seemed stunned. The croupiers looked at Gronevelt in amazement. Not only was he risking a huge sum of money, contrary to all casino laws, he was also risking his casino licence if the State Gaming Commission got tough about this bet. Gronevelt smiled at them. 'Shuffle those cards,' he said. 'Make up the shoe.'

At that moment the pit boss came through the gate of the enclosure and handed Jordan the yellow oblong ragged-edged piece of paper that was the cheque. Jordan looked at it for just one moment, then put it down on the Player's slot and said smiling to Gronevelt, 'You got a bet.'

Jordan saw Merlyn back away and lean up against the royal grey railing. Merlyn again was studying him intently. Diane took

24

a few steps to the side in bewilderment. Jordan was pleased with their astonishment. The only thing he didn't like was betting against his own luck. He hated the idea of dealing the cards out of the shoe and betting against his own hand. He turned to Cully.

'Cully, deal the cards for me,' he said.

But Cully shrank away, horrified. Then Cully glanced at the croupier, who had dumped the cards from the canister under the table and was stacking them for the shuffle. Cully seemed to shudder before he turned to face Jordan.

'Jordy, it's a sucker bet,' Cully said softly as if he didn't want anyone to hear. He shot a quick glance at Gronevelt, who was staring at him. But he went on. 'Listen, Jordy, the Bank has a two and a half percent edge on the Player all the time. Every hand that's dealt. That's why the guy who bets Bank has to pay five percent commission. But now the house has Bank. On a bet like this the commission doesn't mean anything. It's better to have the two and a half percent edge in the odds on how the hand comes out. Do you understand that, Jordy?' Cully kept his voice in an even tone. As if he were reasoning with a child.

But Jordan laughed. 'I know that,' he said. He almost said that he had counted on that, but it wasn't really true. 'How about it, Cully, deal the cards for me. I don't want to go against my luck.'

The croupier shuffled the huge deck in sections, put them all together. He held out the blank yellow plastic card for Jordan to cut. Jordan looked at Cully. Cully backed away without another word. Jordan reached out and cut the deck. Everyone now advanced toward the edge of the table. Gamblers outside the enclosure, seeing the new shoe tried to get in and were barred by the security guard. They started to protest. But suddenly they fell silent. They crowded around outside the railing. The croupier turned up the first card he slid out of the shoe. It was a seven. He slid seven cards out of the shoe, burying them in the slot. Then he shoved the shoe across the table to Jordan. Jordan sat down in his chair. Suddenly Gronevelt spoke. 'Just one hand,' he said.

The croupier held up his arm and said carefully, 'Mr J., you are betting Player's, you understand? The hand I turn up will be the hand you are betting on. The hand you turn up as the Banker will be the hand you are betting against.'

Jordan smiled. 'I understand.'

The croupier hesitated and said, 'If you prefer, I can deal from the shoe.'

'No,' Jordan said. 'That's OK.' He was really excited. Not only for the money but because of the power flowing from him to cover the people and the casino.

The croupier said, holding up his palm, 'One card to me, one card to yourself. Then one card to me and one card to yourself. Please.' He paused dramatically, held up his hand nearest Jordan and said, 'A card for the Player.'

Jordan swiftly and effortlessly slid the blue-backed cards from the slotted shoe. His hands, again extraordinarily graceful, did not falter. They travelled the exact distance across the green felt to the waiting hands of the croupier, who quickly flipped them face up and then stood stunned by the invincible nine. Jordan couldn't lose. Cully behind him let out a roar, 'Natural nine.'

For the first time Jordan looked at his two cards before turning them over. He was actually playing Gronevelt's hand and so hoping for losing cards. Now he smiled and turned up his Banker's cards. 'Natural nine,' he said. And so it was. The bet was a standoff. A draw. Jordan laughed. 'I'm too lucky,' he said.

Jordan looked up at Gronevelt. 'Again?' he asked.

Gronevelt shook his head. 'No,' he said. And then to the croupier and the pit boss and the laddermen. 'Close down the table.' Gronevelt walked out of the enclosure. He had enjoyed the bet, but he knew enough not to stretch life to a dangerous limit. One thrill at a time. Tomorrow he would have to square the unorthodox bet with the Gaming Commission. And he would have to have a long talk with Cully the next day. Maybe he had been wrong about Cully.

Like bodyguards, Cully, Merlyn and Diane surrounded Jordan and herded him out of the baccarat enclosure. Cully picked up the yellow jagged-edged cheque from the green felt table and stuffed it into Jordan's left breast pocket and then zipped it up to make it safe. Jordan was laughing with delight. He looked at his watch. It was 4 A.M. The night was almost over. 'Let's have coffee and breakfast,' he said. He led them all to the coffee shop with its yellow upholstered booths.

When they were seated, Cully said, 'OK, he's got close to four hundred grand. We have to get him out of here.'

'Jordy, you have to leave Vegas. You're rich. You can do anything you want.' Jordan saw that Merlyn was watching him intently. Damn, that was getting irritating.

Diane touched Jordan on his arm and said, 'Don't play any

more. Please.' Her eyes were shining. And suddenly Jordan realized that they were acting as if he had escaped or been pardoned from some sort of exile. He felt their happiness for him, and to repay it he said, 'Now let me stake you guys, you too, Diane. Twenty grand apiece.'

They were all a little stunned. Then Merlyn said, 'I'll take the money when you get on that plane leaving Vegas.'

Diane said. 'That's the deal, you have to get on the plane, you have to leave here. Right, Cully?'

Cully was not that enthusiastic. What was wrong with taking the twenty grand now, then putting him on the plane? The gambling was over. They couldn't jinx him. But Cully had a guilty conscience and couldn't speak his mind. And he knew this would probably be the last romantic gesture of his life. To show true friendship, like those two assholes Merlyn and Diane. Didn't they know Jordan was crazy? That he could sneak away from them and lose the whole fortune?

Cully said, 'Listen, we have to keep him away from the tables. We got to guard him and hogtie him until that plane leaves tomorrow for LA.'

Jordan shook his head, 'I'm not going to Los Angeles. It has to be farther away. Any place in the world.' He smiled at them. 'I've never been out of the United States.'

'We need a map,' Diane said. 'I'll call the bell captain. He can get us a map of the world. Bell captains can do anything.' She picked up the phone on the ledge of the booth and made the call. The bell captain had once gotten her an abortion on ten minutes' notice.

The table became covered with platters of food, eggs, bacon, pancakes and small breakfast steaks. Cully had ordered like a prince.

While they were eating, Merlyn said, 'You sending the cheques to your kids?' He didn't look at Jordan, who studied him quietly, then shrugged. He really hadn't thought about it. For some reason he was angry with Merlyn for asking the question, but just for a moment.

'Why should he give the money to his kids?' Cully said. 'He took care of them pretty good. Next thing you'll be saying he should send the cheques to his wife.' He laughed as if it were beyond the realm of possibility, and again Jordan was a little angry. He had given a wrong picture of his wife. She was better than that.

27

Diane lit a cigarette. She was just drinking coffee, and she had a slight reflective smile on her face. For just one moment her hand brushed Jordan's sleeve in some act of complicity or understanding as if he too were a woman and she were allying herself with him. At that moment the bell captain came personally with an atlas. Jordan reached into a pocket and gave him a hundred-dollar bill. The bell captain almost ran away before Cully, outraged, could say anything. Diane started to unfold the atlas.

Merlyn the Kid was still intent on Jordan. 'What does it feel like?' he asked.

'Great,' Jordan said. He smiled, amused at their passion.

Cully said, 'You go near a crap table and we're gonna climb all over you. No shit.' He slammed his hand down on the table. 'No more.'

Diane had the map spread out over the table, covering the messy dishes of half-eaten food. They pored over it, except Jordan. Merlyn found a town in Africa. Jordan said calmly he didn't want to go to Africa.

Merlyn was leaning back, not studying the map with the others. He was watching Jordan. Cully surprised them all when he said, 'Here's a town in Portugal I know, Mercedas.' They were surprised because for some reason they had never thought of him as living in any place but Vegas. Now suddenly he knew a town in Portugal.

'Yeah, Mercedas,' Cully said. 'Nice and warm. Great beach. It has a small casino with a fifty-dollar top limit and the casino is only open six hours a night. You can gamble like a big shot and never even get hurt. How does that sound to you, Jordan? How about Mercedas?'

'OK,' Jordan said.

Diane began to plan the itinerary. 'Los Angeles over the North Pole to London. Then a flight to Lisbon. Then I guess you go by car to Mercedas.'

'No,' Cully said. 'There's planes to some big town near there, I forget which. And make sure he gets out of London fast. Their gambling clubs are murder.'

Jordan said, 'I have to get some sleep.'

Cully looked at him. 'Jesus, yeah, you look like shit. Go up to your room and conk out. We'll make all the arrangements. We'll wake you up before your plane leaves. And don't try coming back down into the casino. Me and the Kid will be guarding the joint.'

Diane said, 'Jordan, you'll have to give me some money for the tickets.' Jordan took a huge wad of hundred-dollar bills from his pocket and put them on the table. Diane carefully counted out thirty of them.

'It can't cost more than three thousand first class all the way, could it?' she asked. Cully shook his head.

'Tops, two thousand,' Cully said. 'Book his hotels too.' He picked the rest of the bills up from the table and stuffed them back into Jordan's pocket.

Jordan got up and said, trying for the last time, 'Can I stake you now?'

Merlyn said quickly, 'No, it's bad luck, not until you get on the plane.' Jordan saw the look of pity and affection on Merlyn's face. Then Merlyn said, 'Get some sleep. When we call you, we'll help you pack.'

'OK,' Jordan said and left the coffee shop and went down the corridor that led to his room. He knew Cully and Merlyn had followed him to where the corridor started, to make sure that he didn't stop to gamble. He vaguely remembered Diane kissing him good-bye, and even Cully had gripped his shoulder with affection. Who would have thought that a guy like Cully had ever been in Portugal.

When Jordan entered his room, he double bolted the door and put the interior chain on it. Now he was absolutely secure. He sat down on the edge of the bed. And suddenly he was terribly angry. He had a headache and his body was trembling uncontrollably.

How dare they feel affection for him? How dare they show him compassion? They had no reason—no reason. He had never complained. He had never sought their affection. He had never encouraged any love from them. He did not desire it. It disgusted him.

He slumped back against the pillows, so tired he could not undress. The jacket, lumpy with chips and money, was too uncomfortable, and he wriggled out of it and let it drop to the carpeted floor. He closed his eyes and thought he would fall asleep instantly, but again that mysterious terror electrified his body, forcing him upward. He couldn't control the violent trembling of his legs and arms.

The darkness of the room began to run with tiny ghosts of dawn. Jordan thought he might call his wife and tell her of the fortune he had won. But knew he could not. And could not tell his children. Or any of his old friends. In the last grey shreds of

29

this night there was not a person in the world he wished to dazzle with his good luck. There was not one person in the world to share his joy in winning this great fortune.

He got up from the bed to pack. He was rich and must go to Mercedas. He began to weep; an overwhelming grief and rage drowned out everything. He saw the gun lying in the suitcase and then his mind was confused. All the gambling he had done in the last sixteen hours tumbled through his brain, the dice flashing winning numbers, the blackjack tables with their winning hands, the oblong baccarat table strewn with the pale white faces of turned dead cards. Shadowing those cards, a croupier, in black tie and dazzling white shirt, held up a palm, calling softly, 'A card for the Player.'

In one smooth, swift motion Jordan scooped the gun up in his right hand. His mind icily clear. And then, as surely and swiftly as he had dealt his fabulous twenty-four winning hands in baccarat, he swung the muzzle up into the soft line of his neck and pulled the trigger. In that eternal second he felt a sweet release from terror. And his last conscious thought was that he would never go to Mercedas.

3

MERLYN the Kid stepped out of the casino glass doors. He loved to watch the rising sun while it was still a cold yellow disc, to feel the cool desert air blowing gently from mountains that rimmed the desert city. It was the only time of day he ever stepped out of the air-conditioned casino. They had often planned a picnic in those mountains. Diane had one day appeared with a lunch hamper. But Cully and Jordan refused to leave the casino.

He lit a cigarette, enjoyed it with long, slow puffs, though he rarely smoked. Already the sun was beginning to glow a little redder, a round grill plugged into an infinite neon galaxy. Merlyn turned to go back into the casino, and as he passed through the glass doors, he could spot Cully in his Vegas Winner sports coat hurrying through the dice pit, obviously looking for him. They met in front of the baccarat enclosure. Cully leaned against one of the ladder chairs. His lean dark face was contorted with hatred, fright and shock.

'That son of a bitch, Jordan,' Cully said, 'he cheated us out of our twenty grand.' Then he laughed. 'He blew his head off. He beat the house for over four hundred grand and he blew his fucking brains out.'

Merlyn didn't even look surprised. He leaned back wearily against the baccarat enclosure, the cigarette slipped out of his hand. 'Oh, shit,' he said. 'He never looked lucky.'

'We better wait here and catch Diane when she gets back from the airport,' Cully said. 'We can split the money from the ticket refund.'

Merlyn looked at him, not with amazement, but with curiosity. Was Cully that unfeeling? He didn't think so. He saw the sickly smile on Cully's face, a face trying to be tough but filled with dismay that was close to fear. Merlyn sat down at the closed baccarat table. He felt a little dizzy from lack of sleep and from exhaustion. Like Cully, he felt rage, but for a different reason. He had studied Jordan carefully, watched his every movement. Had cunningly led him on to tell his story, his life history. He had sensed that Jordan did not wish to leave Las Vegas. That there was something wrong with him. Jordan had never told them about the gun. And Jordan had always reacted perfectly when he saw Merlyn watching him. Merlyn realized that Jordan had faked him out. Every fucking time. He had faked them out. What made Merlyn dizzy was that he had figured Jordan perfectly all the time they had known each other in Vegas. He'd put all the pieces together but simply through lack of imagination had failed to see the completed picture. Because, of course, now that Jordan was dead, Merlyn knew that there could have been no other ending. From the very beginning Jordan was to have died in Las Vegas.

Only Gronevelt was not surprised. High up in his penthouse suite, long night after night through the years, he never pondered the evil that lurked in the heart of man. He planned against it. Far below his cashier's cage hid a million cash dollars the whole world plotted to steal, and he lay awake night after night, spinn-

31

ing spells to foil those plots. And so coming to know all the boring evil, some hours of the night he pondered other mysteries and was more afraid of the good in the soul of man. That it was the greater danger to his world and even to himself.

When security police reported the shot, Gronevelt immediately called the sheriff's office and let them force entry into the room. But with his own men present. For an honest inventory. There were two casino cheques totalling three hundred and forty thousand dollars. And there was close to one hundred thousand in bills and chips stuffed in that ridiculous linen duster jacket Jordan wore. Its zippered pockets held chips not dumped on the bed.

Gronevelt looked out the windows of his penthouse, at the reddening desert sun climbing over the sandy mountains. He sighed. Jordan could never lose his winnings back, the casino had forever lost that particular bankroll. Well, that was the only way a degenerate gambler could ever keep his lucky win. The only way.

But now Gronevelt had to get to work. The papers had to hush the suicide. How bad it would look, a four-hundred-grand winner blowing his brains out. And he didn't want rumours spreading that there had been a murder so that the casino could recover its losses. Steps had to be taken. He placed the necessary calls to his Eastern offices. A former United States senator, a man of irreproachable integrity, was detailed to bring the sad news to the freshly made widow. And to tell her that her husband had left a fortune in winnings she could collect for the estate when she collected the body. Everyone would be discreet, nobody cheated, justice done. Finally it would only be a tale that gamblers told each other on bust-out nights, in the coffee shops on neon Vegas Strip. But to Gronevelt it was really not that interesting. He had stopped trying to figure out gamblers a long time ago.

The funeral was simple, the burial in a Protestant cemetery surrounded by the golden desert. Jordan's widow flew in and took care of everything. She was also briefed by Gronevelt and his staff as to what Jordan had won. Every cent was meticulously paid. The cheques were turned over to her, and all the cash found on the corpse. The suicide was hushed up. With the cooperation of the authorities and the newspapers. It would look so bad for the image of Las Vegas, a four-hundred-grand winner being found dead. Jordan's widow signed a receipt for the cheques and money. Gronevelt asked her discretion but had no worries on that score. If this good-looking broad was burying her husband in Vegas, not bringing him home, not letting Jordan's kids come to the funeral, then she had a few jokers to hide.

Gronevelt, the ex-senator and the lawyers escorted the widow out of the hotel to her waiting limousine (Xanadu's courtesy, as everything was its courtesy). The Kid, who had been waiting for her, stepped in front of them. He said to the good-looking woman, 'My name is Merlyn, your husband and I were friends. I'm sorry.'

The widow saw that he was watching her intently, studying her. She knew immediately he had no ulterior motive, that he was sincere. But he looked just a little too interested. She had seen him in the funeral chapel with a young girl whose face had been swollen with weeping. She wondered why he had not approached her then. Probably because the girl had been Jordan's.

She said quietly, 'I'm glad he had a friend here.' She was amused by the young man staring at her. She knew she had a special quality that attracted men, not so much her beauty as the intelligence superimposed on that beauty which enough men had told her was a very rare combination. For she had been unfaithful to her husband many times before she had found the one man she had decided she would live with. She wondered if this young man, Merlyn, knew about her and Jordan and what had happened that final night. But she was not concerned, she felt no guilt. His death, she knew, as no one else could know, had been an act of self-will and self-choice. An act of malice by a gentle man.

She felt just a little flattered by the intensity, the obvious fascination with which the young man stared at her. She could not know that he saw not only the fair skin, the perfect bones beneath, the red, delicately sensual mouth, he saw too and would always see, her face as the mask of the angel of death.

4

WHEN I told Jordan's widow that my name was Merlyn, she gave me a cool, friendly stare, without guilt or grief. I recognized a woman who had complete control of her life, not from bitchiness or self-indulgence, but out of intelligence. I understood why Jordan had never said a harsh word against her. She was a very special woman, the kind a lot of men love. But I didn't want to know her. I was too much on Jordan's side. Though I had always sensed his coldness, his rejection of all of us beneath his courtesy and seeming friendliness.

The first time I met Jordan I knew there was something out of sync. with him. It was my second day in Vegas and I had hit it lucky playing percentage blackjack, so I jumped in for a crack at the baccarat table. Baccarat is strictly a luck game with a twenty-dollar minimum. You were completely in the hands of fate, and I always hated that feeling. I always felt I could control my destiny if I tried hard enough.

I sat down at the long oval baccarat table, and I noticed Jordan at the other end. He was a very handsome guy of about forty, maybe even forty-five. He had this thick white hair but not white from age. A white that he was born with, from some albino gene. There was just me and him and another player, plus three house shills to take up space. One of the shills was Diane, sitting two chairs down from Jordan, dressed to advertise that she was in action, but I found myself watching Jordan.

He seemed to me that day an admirable gambler. He never showed elation when he won. He never showed disappointment when he lost. When he handled the shoe, he did it expertly, his hands elegant, very white. But as I watched him making piles of

34

hundred-dollar bills, it suddenly dawned on me that he really didn't care whether he won or lost.

The third player at the table was a 'steamer', a bad gambler who chased losing bets. He was small and thin and would have been bald except that his jet black hair was carefully streaked across his pate. His body was packed with enormous energy. Every movement he made was violent. The way he threw his money down to bet, the way he picked up a winning hand, the way he counted the bills in front of him and angrily scrambled them into a heap to show he was losing. Handling the shoe, he dealt without control so that often a card would flip over or fly past the outstretched hand of the croupier. But the croupier running the table was impassive, his courtesy never varied. A Player card sailed through the air, tilting to one side. The mean-looking guy tried to add another black hundred-dollar chip to his bet. The croupier said, 'Sorry, Mr A., you can't do that.'

Mr A.'s angry mouth got even meaner. 'What the fuck, I only dealt one card. Who says I can't?'

The croupier looked up to the ladderman on his right, the one sitting high above Jordan. The ladderman gave a slight nod, and the croupier said politely, 'Mr A., you have a bet.'

Sure enough, the first card for the Player was a four, bad card. But Mr A. lost anyway when Player drew out on him. The shoe passed to Diane.

Mr A. bet Player's against Diane's Bank. I looked down the table at Jordan. His white head was bowed, he was paying no attention to Mr A. But I was. Mr A. put five one-hundred-dollar bills on Player's. Diane dealt out the cards mechanically. Mr A. got the Player's cards. He squeezed them out and threw the hand down violently. Two picture cards. Nothing. Diane had two cards totalling five. The croupier called, 'A card for the Player.' Diane dealt Mr A. another card. It was another picture. Nothing. The croupier sang out, 'The Bank wins.'

Jordan had bet Bank. I had been about to bet Player's, but Mr A. pissed me off, so I bet Bank. Now I saw Mr A. lay down a thousand dollars on Player's. Jordan and I let our money ride on Bank.

She won the second hand with a natural nine over Mr A.'s seven. Mr A. gave Diane a malevolent stare as if to scare her out of winning. The girl's behaviour was impeccable.

She was very carefully neutral, very carefully a nonparticipant, very carefully a mechanical functionary. But despite all this, when Mr A. bet a thousand dollars on Player's and Diane threw over a winning natural nine, Mr A. slammed his fist down on the table and said, 'Fucking cunt,' and looked at her with hatred. The croupier running the game stood straight up, not a muscle in his face changing. The ladderman leaned forward like Jehovah ducking His head out of the heavens. There was now some tension at the table.

I was watching Diane. Her face crumpled a little. Jordan stacked his money as if unaware of what was happening. Mr A. got up and went over to the pit boss at the desk used for writing markers. He whispered. The pit boss nodded. Everyone at the table was up to stretch his legs while a new shoe was being assembled. I saw Mr A. leave through the royal grey gate toward the corridors that led to the hotel rooms. I saw the pit boss go over to Diane and talk to her, and then she too left the baccarat enclosure. It wasn't hard to figure out. Diane was going to turn a trick with Mr A. and change his luck.

It took the croupiers about five minutes to make up the new shoe. I ducked out to make a few roulette bets. When I got back, the shoe was running. Jordan was still in the same seat, and there were two male shills at the table.

The shoe went around the table three times just chopping before Diane came back. She looked terrible, her mouth sagged, her whole face looked as if it would fall apart, despite the fact that it had been freshly made up. She took a seat between me and one of the money croupiers. He too noticed something wrong. For a moment he bent his head down and I heard him whisper, 'You OK, Diane?' It was the first time I heard her name.

She nodded. I passed her the shoe. But her hands dealing the cards out of the shoe were trembling. She kept her head down to hide the tears glistening in her eyes. Her whole face was 'shamed', I could think of no other word for it. Whatever Mr A. had done to her in his room was sure enough punishment for her luck against him. The money croupier made a slight motion to the pit boss, and he came over and tapped Diane on the arm. She left her seat at the table and a male shill took her place. Diane sat at one of the seats alongside of the rail, with another girl shill.

The shoe was still chopping from Bank to Player to Bank to Player. I was trying to switch my bets at the right time to catch the chopping rhythm. Mr A. came back to the table, to the very seat where he had left his money and cigarettes and lighter.

He looked like a new man. He had showered and recombed his

36

hair. He had even shaved. He didn't look that mean any more. He had on a fresh shirt and trousers and some of his furious energy had been drained away. He wasn't relaxed by any means, but at least he didn't occupy space like one of those whirling cyclones you see in comic strips.

As he sat down, he spotted Diane seated alongside the railing and his eyes gleamed. He gave her a malicious, admonitory grin. Diane turned her head.

But whatever he had done, no matter how terrible, had changed not only his humour but his luck. He bet Player's and won constantly. Meanwhile, nice guys like Jordan and me were getting murdered. That pissed me off, or the pity I felt for Diane, so I deliberately spoiled Mr A.'s good day.

Now there are guys who are a pleasure to gamble with around a casino table and guys who are a pain in the ass. At the baccarat table the biggest pain in the ass is the guy, Banker or Player, who when he gets his first two cards takes a long drawn-out minute to squeeze them out as the table waits impatiently for the determination of their fate.

This is what I started doing to Mr A. He was in chair two and I was in chair five. So we were on the same half of the table and could sort of look into each other's eyes. Now I was a head taller than Mr A. and better built. I looked twenty-one years old. Nobody could guess I was over thirty and had three kids and a wife back in New York that I had run away from. So outwardly I was a pretty soft touch to a guy like Mr A. Sure, I might be physically stronger, but he was a legitimate bad guy with an obvious rep. in Vegas. I was just a dopey kid turning degenerate gambler.

Like Jordan, I nearly always bet Bank in baccarat. But when Mr A. got the shoe, I went head to head against him and bet Player's. When I got the Player's two cards, I squeezed them out with exquisite care before showing them face up. Mr A. buzzed his body around in his seat; he won, but he couldn't contain himself and on the next hand said, 'Come on, jerk, hurry up.'

I kept my cards face down on the table and looked at him calmly. For some reason my eyes caught Jordan down at the other end of the table. He was betting Bank with Mr A., but he was smiling. I squeezed my cards very slowly.

The croupier said, 'Mr M., you're holding up the game. The table can't make any money.' He gave me a brilliant smile, friendly. 'They don't change no matter how hard you squeeze.'

37

'Sure,' I said and threw the cards face up with the disgusted expression of a loser. Again Mr A. smiled in anticipation. Then, when he saw my cards, he was stunned. I had an unbeatable natural nine.

Mr A. said, 'Fuck.'

'Did I throw up my cards fast enough?' I said politely.

He gave me a murderous look and shuffled his money. He still hadn't caught on. I looked down to the other end of the table and Jordan was smiling, a really delighted smile, even though he too had lost riding with Mr A. I jockeyed Mr A. for the next hour.

I could see Mr A. had juice in the casino. The ladderman had let him get away with a couple of 'claim agent' tricks. The croupiers treated him with careful courtesy. This guy was making five-hundred and thousand-dollar bets. I was betting mostly twenties. So if there was any trouble, I was the one the house'd bounce on.

But I was playing it just right. The guy had called me a jerk and I hadn't got mad or tough. When the croupier told me to turn over my cards faster, I had done so amiably. The fact that Mr A. was now 'steaming' was his gambler's fault. It would be a tremendous loss of face for the casino to take his side. They couldn't let Mr A. get away with anything outrageous because it would humiliate them as well as me. As a peaceful gambler I was, in a sense, their guest, entitled to protection from the house.

Now I saw the ladderman opposite me reach down the side of his chair to the phone attached to it. He made two calls. While watching him, I missed betting when Mr A. got the shoe. I stopped betting for a while and just relaxed in the chair. The baccarat chairs were plush and very comfortable. You could sit in them for twelve hours, and many people did.

The tension at the table relaxed when I refused to bet Mr A.'s shoe. They figured I was being prudent or chickenshit. The shoe kept chopping. I noticed two very big guys in suits and ties came through the baccarat gate. They went over to the pit boss, who obviously told them the heat was off and they could relax because I could hear them laughing and telling jokes.

The next time Mr A. got the shoe, I shoved a twenty-dollar bet on Player's. Then to my surprise the croupier receiving the Player's two cards didn't toss them to me but to the other end of the table, near Jordan. That was the first time I ever saw Cully.

Cully had this lean, dark Indian face, yet affable because of his

38

unusually thickened nose. He smiled down the table at me and Mr A. I noticed he had bet forty dollars on Player's. His bet outranked my twenty, so he got the Player's cards to flip over. Cully turned them over immediately. Bad cards, and Mr A. beat him. Mr A. noticed Cully for the first time and smiled broadly.

'Hey, Cully, what you doing playing baccarat, you fucking countdown artist?'

Cully smiled. 'Just giving my feet a rest.'

Mr A. said, 'Bet with me, you jerkoff. This shoe is ready to turn Bank.'

Cully just laughed. But I noticed he was watching me. I put down my twenty bet on Player's. Cully immediately put down forty on Player's to make sure he would get the cards. Again he immediately turned up his cards, and again Mr A. beat him.

Mr A. called, 'Attaboy, Cully, you're my lucky charm. Keep betting against me.'

The money croupier paid off the Banker's slots and then said respectfully, 'Mr A., you're up to the limit.'

Mr A. considered for a moment. 'Let it ride,' he said.

I knew that I would have to be very careful. I kept my face impassive. The slot croupier running the game had his palm up to halt the dealing of the shoe until all bets had been made. He glanced down inquiringly at me. I didn't make a move. The croupier looked to the other end of the table. Jordan made a bet on the Bank, riding with Mr A. Cully put a hundred-dollar bet on Player's, watching me all the time.

The slot croupier let his hand fall, but before Mr A. could get a card out of the shoe, I threw the stack of bills in front of me on Player's. Behind me the buzz of voices of the pit boss and his two friends stopped. Opposite me the ladderman inclined his head from the heavens.

'The money plays,' I said. Which meant that the croupier could count it out only after the bet was decided. The Player's cards must come to me.

Mr A. dealt them to the slot croupier. The slot croupier threw the two cards face down across the green felt. I gave them a quick squeeze and threw them over. Only Mr A. could see how I made my face fall slightly as if I had lousy cards. But what I turned over was a natural nine. The croupier counted out my money. I had bet twelve hundred dollars and won.

Mr A. leaned back and lit up a cigarette. He was really steaming. I could feel his hatred. I smiled at him. 'Sorry,' I said.

Exactly like a nice young kid. He glared at me.

At the other end of the table Cully got up casually and sauntered down to my side of the table. He sat in one of the chairs between me and Mr A. so that he would get the shoe. Cully slapped the box and said, 'Hey, Cheech, get on me. I feel lucky. I got seven passes in my right arm.'

So Mr A. was Cheech. An ominous-sounding name. But Cheech obviously liked Cully, and just as obviously Cully was a man who made a science of being liked. Because he now turned to me as Cheech made a bet on the Bank. 'Come on, Kid,' he said. 'Let's all break this fucking casino together. Ride with me.'

'You really feel lucky?' I asked, just a little wide-eyed.

'I may run out the shoe,' Cully said. 'I can't guarantee it, but I may just run out the shoe.'

'Let's go,' I said. I put a twenty on the Bank. We were all riding together. Me, Cheech, Cully, Jordan down on the other far side of the table. One of the shills had to take the Player's hand and promptly turned up a cold six. Cully turned over two picture cards and on his draw got another picture for a total of zip, zero, the worst hand in baccarat. Cheech had lost a thousand. Cully had lost a hundred. Jordan had lost five hundred. I had lost a measly twenty. I was the only one to reproach Cully. I shook my head ruefully. 'Gee,' I said, 'there goes my twenty.' Cully grinned and passed me the shoe. Looking past him, I could see Cheech's face darkening with rage. A jerkoff kid who lost a twenty, daring to bitch. I could read his mind as if it were a deck of cards face up on the green felt.

I bet twenty on my Bank, waited to slide the cards out. The croupier in the slot was the young handsome one who had asked Diane if she was OK. He had a diamond ring on the hand he held upraised to halt my deal until all the bets were made. I saw Jordan put down his bet. On the Bank as usual. He was riding with me.

Cully slapped a twenty on Bank. He turned to Cheech and said, 'Come on, ride with us. This kid looks lucky.'

'He looks like he's still jerking off,' Cheech said. I could see all the croupiers watching me. On his high chair the ladderman sat very still and straight. I looked big and strong; they were just a little disappointed in me.

Cheech put three hundred down on Player's. I dealt and won. I kept hitting passes and Cheech kept upping his bet against me. He called for a marker. Well, there wasn't much left of the shoe, but I ran it out with perfect gambling manners, no squeezing of the cards, no joyous exclamations. I was proud of myself. The croupiers emptied the canisters and assembled the cards for a new shoe. Everybody paid his commissions. Jordan got up to stretch his legs. So did Cheech, so did Cully. I stuffed my winnings into my pocket. The pit boss brought the marker over to Cheech to sign. Everything was fine. It was the perfect moment.

'Hey, Cheech,' I said. '*I'm* a jerkoff?' I laughed. Then I started walking around the table to leave the baccarat pit and made sure to pass close to him. He could no more resist taking a swing at me than a crooked croupier palm a stray hundred-dollar chip.

And I had him cold. Or I thought I did. But Cully and the two big hoods had miraculously come between us. One hood caught Cheech's fist in his big hand as if it were a tiny ball. Cully shoved his shoulder into me, knocking me off stride.

Cheech was screaming at the big guy. 'You son of a bitch. Do you know who I am? Do you know who I am?'

To my surprise the big hood let Cheech's hand go and stepped back. He had served his purpose. He was a preventive force, not a punitive one. Meanwhile, nobody was watching me. They were cowed by Cheech's venomous fury, all except the young croupier with the diamond ring. He said very quietly, 'Mr A., you are out of line.'

With incredible whiplike fury Cheech struck out and hit the young croupier right smack on the nose. The croupier staggered back. Blood came billowing out onto his frilly white shirtfront and disappeared into the blue-black of his tuxedo. I ran past Cully and the two hoods and hit Cheech a punch that caught him in the temple and bounced him off the floor. And he bounced right up again. I was astonished. It was all going to be very serious. This guy ran on nuclear venom.

And then the ladderman descended from his high chair, and I could see him clearly in the bright lamp of the baccarat table. His face was seamed and parchment pale as if his blood had been frozen white by countless years of air conditioning. He held up a ghostly hand and said quietly, 'Stop.'

Everybody froze. The ladderman pointed a long, bony finger and said, 'Cheech, don't move. You are in very big trouble. Believe me.' His voice was quietly formal.

Cully was leading me through the gate, and I was more than willing to go. But I was really puzzled by some of the reactions.

There was something very deadly about the young croupier's face even with the blood flowing from his nose. He wasn't scared, or confused, or badly hurt enough not to fight back. But he had never raised a hand. Also, his fellow croupiers had not come to his aid. They had looked on Cheech with a sort of awestricken horror that was not fear but pity.

Cully was pushing me through the casino through the surflike hum of hundreds of gamblers muttering their voodoo curses and prayers over dice, blackjack, the spinning roulette wheel. Finally we were in the relative quiet of the huge coffee shop.

I loved the coffee shop, with its green and yellow chairs and tables. The waitresses were young and pretty in spiffy short-skirted uniforms of gold. The walls were all glass; you could see the outside world of expensive green grass, the blue-sky pool, the specially grown huge palm trees. Cully led me to one of the large special booths, a table big enough for six people, equipped with phones. He took the booth as a natural right.

As we were drinking coffee, Jordan came walking by us. Cully immediately jumped up and grabbed him by the arm. 'Hey, fellah,' he said, 'have coffee with your baccarat buddies.' Jordan shook his head and then saw me sitting in the booth. He gave me an odd smile, amused by me for some reason, and changed his mind. He slid into the booth.

And that's how we first met, Jordan, Cully and I. That day in Vegas when I first saw him, Jordan didn't look too bad, in spite of his white hair. There was an almost impenetrable air of reserve about him which intimidated me, but Cully didn't notice. Cully was one of those guys who would grab the Pope for a cup of coffee.

I was still playing the innocent kid. 'What the hell did Cheech get sore about?' I said. 'Jesus, I thought we were all having a good time.'

Jordan's head snapped up, and for the first time he seemed to be paying attention to what was going on. He was smiling too, as at a child trying to be clever beyond its years. But Cully was not so charmed.

'Listen, Kid,' he said. 'The ladderman was on to you in two seconds. What the hell do you think he sits way up there for? To pick his fucking nose? To watch pussy walk by?'

'Yeah, OK,' I said. 'But nobody can say it was my fault. Cheech got out of line. I was a gentleman. You have to admit that. The hotel and the casino have no complaint about me.'

42

Cully gave an amiable smile. 'Yeah, you worked that pretty good. You were really clever. Cheech never caught on and fell right into the trap. But one thing you didn't figure. Cheech is a dangerous man. So now my job is to get you packed and put you on a plane. What the fuck kind of a name is that anyway, Merlyn?'

I didn't answer him. I pulled my sports shirt up and showed him the bare front of chest and belly. I had a long, very ugly purple scar on it. I grinned at Cully and said to him, 'You know what that is?' I asked him.

He was wary now, alert. His face really hawklike.

I gave it to him slow. 'I was in the war,' I said. 'I got hit by machine-gun bullets and they had to sew me up like a chicken. You think I give a shit about you and Cheech both?'

Cully was not impressed. But Jordan was smiling still. Not everything I said was true. I had been in the war, I had been in combat, but I never got hit. What I was showing Cully was my gallbladder operation. They had tried a new way of cutting that left this very impressive scar.

Cully sighed and said, 'Kid, maybe you're tougher than you look, but you're still not tough enough to stay here with Cheech.'

I remembered Cheech bouncing up from that punch so quickly and I started worrying. I even thought for a minute about letting Cully put me on a plane. But I shook my head.

'Look, I'm trying to help,' Cully said. 'After what happened Cheech will be looking for you, and you're not in Cheech's league, believe me.'

'Why not?' Jordan asked.

Cully gave it back very quick. 'Because this Kid is human and Cheech ain't.'

It's funny how friendships start. At this point we didn't know we were going to be close Vegas buddies. In fact, we were all getting to be slightly pissed off with each other.

Cully said, 'I'll drive you to the airport.'

'You're a very nice guy,' I said. 'I like you. We're baccarat buddies. But the next time you tell me you're going to drive me to the airport you'll wake up in the hospital.'

Cully laughed gleefully. 'Come on,' he said. 'You hit Cheech a clean shot and he bounced right up. You're not a tough guy. Face it.'

At that I had to laugh because it was true. I was out of my natural character. And Cully went on. 'You show me where bullets hit you, that doesn't make you a tough guy. That makes you the victim of a tough guy. Now if you showed me a guy who had scars because of bullets *you* put into *him*, I'd be impressed. And if Cheech hadn't bounced up so quick after you hit him, I'd be impressed. Come on, I'm doing you a favour. No kidding.'

Well, he was right all the way. But it didn't make any difference. I didn't feel like going home to my wife and my three kids and the failure of my life. Vegas suited me. The casino suited me. Gambling was right down my alley. You could be alone without being lonely. And something was always happening just like now. I wasn't tough, but what Cully missed was that almost literally nothing could scare me because at this particular time of my life I didn't give a shit about anything.

So I said to Cully, 'Yeah, you're right. But I can't leave for a couple of days.'

Now he really looked me over. Then he shrugged. He picked up the bill and signed it and got up from the table. 'See you guys around,' he said. And left me alone with Jordan.

We were both uneasy. Neither of us wanted to be with the other. I sensed that we were both using Vegas for a similar purpose, to hide out from the real world. But we didn't want to be rude, Jordan because he was essentially an enormously gentle man. And though I usually had no difficulty getting away from people, there was something about Jordan I instinctively liked, and that happened so rarely I didn't want to hurt his feelings by just leaving him alone.

Then Jordan said, 'How do you spell your name?'

I spelled it out for him. M-e-r-l-y-n. I could see his loss of interest in me and I grinned at him. 'That's one of the archaic spellings,' I said.

He understood right away and he gave me his sweet smile. 'Your parents thought you would grow up to be a magician?' he asked. 'And that's what you were trying to be at the baccarat table?'

'No,' I said. 'Merlyn's my last name. I changed it. I didn't want to be King Arthur, and I didn't want to be Lancelot.'

'Merlin had his troubles,' Jordan said.

'Yeah,' I said. 'But he never died.'

And that's how Jordan and I became friends, or started our friendship with a sort of sentimental schoolboy confidence.

The morning after the fight with Cheech, I wrote my daily

44

short letter to my wife telling her that I would be coming home in a few days. Then I wandered through the casino and saw Jordan at a crap table. He looked haggard. I touched him on the arm, and he turned and gave me that sweet smile that affected me always. Maybe because I was the only one he smiled at so easily. 'Let's eat breakfast,' I said. I wanted him to get some rest. Obviously he had been gambling all night. Without a word Jordan picked up his chips and went with me to the coffee shop. I still had my letter in my hand. He looked at it and I said, 'I write my wife every day.'

Jordan nodded and ordered breakfast. He ordered a full meal, Vegas style. Melon, eggs and bacon, toast and coffee. But he ate little, a few bites, and then coffee. I had a rare steak, which I loved in the morning but never had except in Vegas.

While we were eating, Cully came breezing in, his right hand full of red five-dollar chips.

'Made my expenses for the day,' he said, full of confidence. 'Counted down on one shoe and caught my percentage bet for a hundred.' He sat down with us and ordered melon and coffee.

'Merlyn, I got good news for you,' he said. 'You don't have to leave town. Cheech made a big mistake last night.'

Now for some reason that really pissed me off. He was still going on about that. He was like my wife, who keeps telling me I have to adjust. I don't have to do *anything*. But I let him talk. Jordan as usual didn't say a word, just watched me for a minute. I felt that he could read my mind.

Cully had a quick nervous way of eating and talking. He had a lot of energy, just like Cheech. Only his energy seemed to be charged with goodwill, to make the world run smoother. 'You know the croupier that Cheech punched in the nose and all that blood? Ruined the kid's shirt. Well, that kid is the favourite nephew of the deputy police chief of Las Vegas.'

At that time I had no sense of values. Cheech was a genuine tough guy, a killer, a big gambler, maybe one of the hoods who helped run Vegas. So what was a deputy police chief's nephew? *And* his lousy bloody nose? I said as much. Cully was delighted at this chance to instruct.

'You have to understand,' Cully said, 'that the deputy police chief of Las Vegas is what the old kings used to be. He's a big fat guy who wears a Stetson and a holster with a forty-five. His family has been in Nevada since the early days. The people elect him every year. His word is law. He gets paid off by every hotel in this

45

town. Every casino begged to have the nephew working for them and pay him top baccarat croupier money. He makes as much as the ladderman. Now you have to understand the chief considers the Constitution of the United States and the Bill of Rights as an aberration of milksop Easterners. For instance, any visitor with any kind of criminal record has to register as soon as he comes to town. And believe me he'd better. Our chief also doesn't like hippies. You notice there're no long-haired kids in this town? Black people, he's not crazy about them. Or bums and panhandlers. Vegas may be the only city in the United States where there are no panhandlers. He likes girls, good for casino business, but he doesn't like pimps. He doesn't mind a dealer living off his girlfriend hustling or stuff like that. But if some wise guy builds up a string of girls, look out. Prostitutes are always hanging themselves in their cells, slashing their wrists. Bust-out gamblers commit suicide in prison. Convicted murderers, bank embezzlers. A lot of people in prison do themselves in. But have you ever heard of a pimp committing suicide? Well, Vegas has the record. Three pimps have committed suicide in our chief's jail. Are you getting the picture?'

'So what happened to Cheech?' I said. 'Is he in jail?'

Cully smiled. 'He never got there. He tried to get Gronevelt's help.'

Jordan murmured, 'Xanadu Number One?'

Cully looked at him, a little startled.

Jordan smiled. 'I listen to the telephone pages when I'm not gambling.'

For just a minute Cully looked a little uncomfortable. Then he went on.

'Cheech asked Gronevelt to cover him and get him out of town.'

'Who's Gronevelt?' I asked.

'He owns the hotel,' Cully said. 'And let me tell you, his ass was in a sling. Cheech isn't alone, you know.'

I looked at him. I didn't know what that meant.

'Cheech, he's connected,' Cully said significantly. 'Still and all Gronevelt had to give him to the chief. So now Cheech is in the Community Hospital. He has a skull fracture, internal injuries, and he'll need plastic surgery.'

'Jesus,' I said.

'Resisting arrest,' Cully said. 'That's our chief. And when Cheech recovers, he's barred forever from Vegas. Not only that, the baccarat pit boss got fired. He was responsible for watching out for the nephew. The chief blames him. And now that pit boss can't work in Vegas. He'll have to get a job in the Caribbean.'

'Nobody else will hire him?' I asked.

'It's not that,' Cully said. 'The chief told him he doesn't want him in town.'

'And that's it?' I asked.

'That's it,' Cully said. 'There was one pit boss that sneaked back into town and got another job. The chief happened to walk in and just dragged him out of the casino. Beat the shit out of him. Everybody got the message.'

'How the hell can he get away with that shit?' I said.

'Because he's a duly appointed representative of the people,' Cully said. And for the first time Jordan laughed. He had a great laugh. It washed away the remoteness and coldness you always felt coming off him.

Later that evening Cully brought Diane over to the lounge where Jordan and I were taking a break from our gambling. She had recovered from whatever Cheech had done to her the night before. It was obvious she knew Cully pretty well. And it became obvious that Cully was offering her as bait to me and Jordan. We could take her to bed whenever we wanted to.

Cully made little jokes about her breasts and legs and her mouth, how lovely they were, how she used her mane of jet black hair as a whip. But mixed in the crude compliments were solemn remarks on her good character, things like: 'This is one of the few girls in this town who won't hustle you.' And 'she never hustles for a free bet. She's such a good kid, she doesn't belong in this town.' And then to show his devotion he held out the palm of his hand for Diane to tip her cigarette ash into so that she wouldn't have to reach for the ashtray. It was primitive gallantry, the Vegas equivalent of kissing the hand of a duchess.

Diane was very quiet, and I was a little put out that she was more interested in Jordan than me. After all, hadn't I avenged her like the gallant knight that I was? Hadn't I humiliated the terrible Cheech? But when she left for her tour of duty shilling baccarat, she leaned over and kissed my cheek and, smiling a little sadly, said, 'I'm glad you're OK. I was worried about you. But you shouldn't be so silly.' And then she was gone.

In the weeks that followed we told each other our stories and got to know each other. An afternoon drink became a ritual, and most of the time we had dinner together at one in the morning, when Diane finished her shift on the baccarat table. But it all depended on our gambling patterns. If one of us got hot, he'd skip eating until his luck turned. This happened most often with Jordan.

But then there were long afternoons when we'd sit around out by the pool and talk under the burning desert sun. Or take midnight walks along the neon-drowned Strip, the glittering hotels planted like mirages in the surrounding desert. And so we told each other our lives.

Jordan's story seemed the most simple and the most banal, and he seemed the most ordinary person in the group. He'd had a perfectly happy life and a common, ordinary destiny. He was some sort of executive genius and by the age of thirty-five had his own company dealing in the buying and selling of steel. Some sort of middleman, it made him a handsome living. He married a beautiful woman, and they had three children and a big house and everything they wanted. Friends, money, career and true love. And that lasted for twenty years. And then, as Jordan put it, his wife grew out of him. He had concentrated all his energies on making his family safe from the terrors of a jungle economy. It had taken all his will and his energies. His wife had done her duty as a wife and mother. But there came a time when she wanted more out of life. She was a witty woman, curious, intelligent, well read. She devoured novels and plays, went to museums, joined all the town cultural groups, and she eagerly shared everything with Jordan. He loved her even more. Until the day she told him she wanted a divorce. Then he ceased loving her and he ceased loving his kids or his family and his work. He had done everything in the world for his nuclear family. He had guarded them from all the dangers of the outside world, built fortresses of money and power, never dreaming the gates could be opened from within.

Which was not how he told it, but how I listened to it. He just said quite simply that he didn't 'grow with his wife'. That he had been too immersed in his business and hadn't paid proper attention to his family. That he didn't blame her at all when she divorced him to marry one of his friends. Because that friend was just like her; they had the same tastes, the same kind of wit, the same flair for enjoying life.

So he, Jordan, had agreed to everything his wife wanted. He had sold his business and given her all the money. His lawyer told him he was being too generous, that he would regret it later. But Jordan said it really wasn't generous because he could make a lot more money and his wife and her husband couldn't. 'You wouldn't think it to watch me gamble,' Jordan said, 'but I'm supposed to be a great businessman. I got job offers from all over the country. If my plane hadn't landed in Vegas, I'd be working toward my first million bucks in Los Angeles right now.'

It was a good story, but to me it had a phony ring to it. He was just *too* nice a guy. It was all *too* civilized.

One of the things wrong with it was that I knew that he never slept nights. Every morning I went to the casino to work up an appetite for breakfast by throwing dice. And I'd find Jordan at the crap table. It was obvious he'd been gambling all night. Sometimes when he was tired, he'd be in the roulette or blackjack pits. And as the days went by, he looked worse and worse. He lost weight and his eyes seemed to be filled with red pus. But he was always gentle, very low-key. And he never said a word against his wife.

Sometimes, when Cully and I were alone in the lounge or at dinner, Cully would say, 'Do you believe that fucking Jordan? Can you believe that a guy would let a dame put him out of whack like that? And can you believe how he talks about her like she's the greatest cunt built?'

'She wasn't a dame,' I said. 'She was his wife for a lot of years. She was the mother of his children. She was the rock of his faith. He's an old-time Puritan who got a knuckleball thrown at him.'

It was Jordan who got me started talking. One day he said, 'You ask a lot of questions, but you don't say much.' He paused for a moment as if he were debating whether he was really interested enough to ask the question. Then he said, 'Why are you here in Vegas for so long?'

'I'm a writer,' I told him. And went on from there. The fact that I had published a novel impressed both of them and that reaction always amused me. But what really amazed them was that I was thirty-one years old and had run away from a wife and three kids.

'I figured you most to be twenty-five,' Cully said. 'And you don't wear a ring.'

'I never wore a ring,' I said.

Jordan said kiddingly, 'You don't need a ring. You look guilty without it.' For some reason I couldn't imagine him making that kind of joke when he was married and living in Ohio. Then he would have felt it rude. Or maybe his mind hadn't been that free. Or maybe it was something his wife would have said and he would let her say and just sit back and enjoy it because she could get away with it and maybe he couldn't. It was fine with me. Anyway, I told them the story about my marriage, and in the process it came out that the scar on my belly I had shown them was the scar of a gallbladder operation, not a war wound. At that point of the story Cully laughed and said, 'You bullshit artist.'

I shrugged, smiled and went on with my story.

5

I HAVE no history. No remembered parents. I have no uncles, no cousins, no city or town. I have only one brother, two years older than me. At the age of three, when my brother, Artie, was five, we were both left in an orphanage outside New York. We were left by my mother. I have no memory of her.

I didn't tell this to Cully and Jordan and Diane. I never talked about those things. Not even to my brother, Artie, who is closer to me than anyone in the world.

I never talk about it because it sounds so pathetic, and it wasn't really. The orphanage was fine, a pleasant, orderly place with a good school system and an intelligent administrator. It did well by me until Artie and I left it together. He was eighteen and found a job and an apartment. I ran away to join him. After a few months I left him too, lied about my age and joined the Army to fight in WW II. And now here in Vegas sixteen years later I told Jordan and Cully and Diane about the war and my life that followed.

The first thing I did after the war was to enrol in writing

courses in the New School for Social Research. Everybody then wanted to be a writer, as twenty years later everyone hoped to be a filmmaker.

I had found it hard to make friends in the Army. It was easier at the school. I also met my future wife there. Because I had no family, except for my older brother, I spent a lot of time at the school, hanging out in the cafeteria rather than going back to my lonely rooms in Grove Street. It was fun. Every once in a while I got lucky and talked a girl into living with me for a few weeks. The guys I made friends with, all out of the Army and going to school under the GI Bill, talked my language. The trouble was that they were all interested in the literary life and I was not. I just wanted to be a writer because I was always dreaming stories. Fantastic adventures that isolated me from the world.

I discovered that I read more than anyone else, even the guys going for PhD's in English. I didn't really have much else to do, though I always gambled. I found a bookie on the East Side near Tenth Street and bet every day on ball games, football, basketball and baseball. I wrote some short stories and started a novel about the war. I met my wife in one of the short-story classes.

She was a tiny Irish-Scotch girl with a big bust and large blue eyes and very very serious about everything. She criticized other people's stories carefully, politely, but very toughly. She hadn't had a chance to judge me because I had not yet submitted a story to the class. She read a story of her own. And I was surprised because the story was very good and very funny. It was about her Irish uncles who were all drunks.

So when the story was over, the whole class jumped on her for supporting the stereotype that the Irish drank. Her pretty face contorted in hurt astonishment. Finally she was given a chance to answer.

She had a beautiful soft voice, and plaintively she said, 'But I've grown up with the Irish. All of them drink. Isn't that true?' She said this to the teacher, who also happened to be Irish. His name was Maloney and he was a good friend of mine. Though he didn't show it, he was drunk at that very moment.

Maloney leaned back in his chair and said solemnly, 'I wouldn't know, I'm Scandinavian myself.' We all laughed and poor Valerie bowed her head, still confused. I defended her because though it was a good story, I knew she would never be a real writer. Everybody in the class was talented, but only a few had the energy and desire to go a long way, to give up their life for writing. I was one of them. I felt she was not. The secret was simple. Writing was the only thing I wanted to do.

Near the term end I finally submitted a story. Everybody loved it. After class Valerie came up to me and said, 'How come I'm so serious and everything I write comes out sounding so funny? And you always make jokes and act as if you're not serious and your story makes me cry?'

She was serious. As usual. She wasn't coming on. So I took her for coffee. Her name was Valerie O'Grady, a name she hated for its Irishness. Sometimes I think she married me just to get rid of the O'Grady. And she made me call her Vallie. I was surprised when it took me over two weeks to get her in bed. She was no free-swinging village girl and she wanted to be sure I knew it. We had to go through a whole charade of my getting her drunk first so that she could accuse me of taking advantage of a national or racial weakness. But in bed she surprised me.

I hadn't been that crazy about her before. But in bed she was great. I would guess that there are some people who fit sexually, who respond to each other on a primary sexual level. With us I think we were both so shy, so withdrawn into ourselves, that we couldn't relax with other partners sexually. And that we responded to each other fully for some mysterious reason springing out of that mutual shyness. Anyway, after that first night in bed we were inseparable. We went to all the little movie houses in the village and saw all the foreign films. We'd eat Italian or Chinese and go back to my room and make love, and about midnight I'd walk her to the subway so that she could go home to her family in Queens. She still didn't have the nerve to stay overnight. Until one weekend she couldn't resist. She wanted to be there Sunday to make me breakfast and read the Sunday papers with me in the morning. So she told the usual daughterly lies to her parents and stayed over. It was a beautiful weekend. But when she got home she ran into a clan fire fight. Her family jumped all over her, and when I saw her Monday night, she was in tears.

'Hell,' I said. 'Let's get married.'

She said in surprise, 'I'm not pregnant.' And was even more surprised when I burst out laughing. She really had no sense of humour, except when she wrote.

Finally I convinced her that I meant it. That I really wanted to marry her, and she blushed and then started to cry.

So on the following weekend I went out to her family's house in Queens for Sunday dinner. It was a big family, father, mother, three brothers and three sisters, all younger than Vallie. Her father was an old Tammany Hall worker and earned his living with some political job. There were some uncles there and they all got drunk. But in a cheerful happy-go-lucky way. They got drunk as other people stuff themselves at a big dinner. It was no more offensive than that. Though I didn't usually drink, I had a few and we all had a good time.

The mother had dancing brown eyes. Vallie obviously got her sexuality from the mother and lack of humour from her father. I could see the father and uncles watching me with shrewd drunken eyes, trying to judge whether I was just a sharpie screwing their beloved Vallie, kidding her about marriage.

Mr O'Grady finally got to the point. 'When are you two planning to get hitched?' he asked. I knew if I gave the wrong answer, I could get punched in the mouth by a father and three uncles right then and there. I could see the father hated me for screwing his little girl before marrying her. But I understood him. That was easy. Also, I wasn't hustling. I never hustled people, or so I thought. So I laughed and said, 'Tomorrow morning.'

I laughed because I knew it was an answer that would reassure them but one they could not accept. They could not accept because all their friends would think that Vallie was pregnant. We finally settled on a date two months ahead, so that there would be formal announcements and a real family wedding. And that was OK with me too. I don't know whether I was in love. I was happy and that was enough. I was no longer alone, I could begin my true history. My life would extend outward, I would have a family, wife, children, my wife's family would be my family. I would settle in a portion of the city that would be mine. I would no longer be a single solitary unit. Holidays and birthdays could be celebrated. In short, I would be 'normal' for the first time in my life. The Army really didn't count. And for the next ten years I worked at building myself into the world.

The only people I knew to invite to the wedding were my brother, Artie, and some guys from the New School. But there was a problem. I had to explain to Vallie that my real name wasn't Merlyn. Or rather that my original name was not Merlyn. After the war I changed my name legally. I had to explain to the judge that I was a writer and that Merlyn was the name I wanted to write under. I gave him Mark Twain as an example. The judge nodded as if he knew a hundred writers who had done the same thing.

The truth was that at that time I felt mystical about writing. I wanted it to be pure, untainted. I was afraid of being inhibited if anybody knew anything about me and who I really was. I wanted to write universal characters. (My first book was heavily symbolic). I wanted to be two absolutely separate identities.

It was through Mr O'Grady's political connections that I got my job as federal Civil Service employee. I became a GS-6 clerk administrator to Army Reserve Units.

After the kids, married life was dull but still happy. Vallie and I never went out. On holidays we'd have dinner with her family or at my brother Artie's house. When I worked nights, she and her friends in the apartment house would visit each other. She made a lot of friends. On weekend nights she'd visit their apartments when they had a little party and I'd stay in our apartment to watch the kids and work on my book. I'd never go. When it was her turn to entertain, I hated it, and I guess I didn't hide that too well. And Vallie resented it. I remember one time I went into the bedroom to look at the kids and I stayed in there reading some pages of manuscript. Vallie left our guests and came looking for me. I'll never forget the hurt look when she found me reading, so obviously reluctant to come back to her and her friends.

It was after one of these little affairs that I got sick for the first time. I woke up at two in the morning and felt an agonizing pain in my stomach and all over my back.

I couldn't afford a doctor so the next day I went to the Veterans Administration hospital, and then they took all kinds of X-rays and made some other tests over a period of a week. They couldn't find anything, but I had another attack and just from the symptoms they diagnosed a diseased gallbladder.

A week later I was back in the hospital with another attack, and they shot me full of morphine. I had to miss two days' work. Then about a week before Christmas, just as I was about to finish up work on my night job, I got a hell of an attack. (I didn't mention that I was working nights in a bank to get extra money for Christmas.) The pain was excruciating. But I figured I could make it to the VA hospital on twenty-third Street. I took a cab that let me off about a half block from the entrance. It was now after midnight. When the cab pulled away, the pain hit me an agonizing solar plexus blow. I fell to my knees in the dark street. The pain radiated all over my back. I flattened out onto the ice-cold pavement. There wasn't a soul around, no one that could help me. The entrance to the hospital was a hundred feet away. I was so paralyzed by pain I couldn't move. I wasn't

54

even scared. In fact, I was wishing I would just die, so that the pain would go away. I didn't give a shit for my wife or my kids or my brother. I just wanted out. I thought for a moment about the legendary Merlin. Well, I was no fucking magician. I remember rolling over once to stop the pain and rolling off the ledge of the sidewalk and into the gutter. The edge of the curb was a pillow for my head.

And now I could see the Christmas lights decorating a nearby store. The pain receded a little. I lay there thinking I was a fucking animal. Here I was an artist, a book published and one critic had called me a genius, one of the hopes of American literature, and I was dying like a dog in the gutter. And through no fault of my own. Just because I had no money in the bank. Just because I had nobody who really gave a shit about whether I lived or not. That was the truth of the whole business. The self-pity was nearly as good as morphine.

I don't know how long it took me to crawl out of the gutter. I don't know how long it took me to crawl through to the entrance of the hospital, but I was finally in an arc of light. I remember people putting me in a wheelchair and taking me to the emergency room and I answered questions and then magically I was in a warm white bed and feeling blissfully sleepy, without pain, and I knew they had shot me with morphine.

When I awoke, a young doctor was taking my pulse. He had treated me the other time and I knew his name was Cohn. He grinned at me and said, 'They called your wife, she'll be down to see you when the kids go to school.'

I nodded and said, 'I guess I can't wait until Christmas for that operation.'

Dr Cohn looked a little thoughtful and then said cheerily, 'Well, you've come this far, why don't you wait until Christmas? I'll schedule it for the twenty-seventh. You can come Christmas night and we'll get you ready.'

'OK,' I said. I trusted him. He had talked the hospital into treating me as an outpatient. He was the only guy who seemed to understand when I said that I didn't want the operation until after Christmas. I remember his saying, 'I don't know what you're trying to do, but I'm with you.' I couldn't explain that I had to keep working the two jobs until Christmas so my kids would get toys and still believe in Santa Claus. That I was totally responsible for my family and its happiness, and it was the only thing I had.

I'll always remember that young doctor. He looked like your

55

movie actor doctor except that he was so unpretentious and easy. He sent me home loaded up with morphine. But he had his reasons. A few days after the operation he told me, and I could see how happy it made him to tell me, 'Listen, you're a young guy to have gallbladder and the tests didn't show anything. We went on your symptoms. But that's all it was, gallbladder, big stones. But I want you to know there was nothing else in there. I took a real good look. When you go home, don't worry. You'll be as good as new.'

At that time I didn't know what the hell he meant. In my usual style it only came to me a year later that he had been afraid of finding cancer. And that's why he hadn't wanted to operate before Christmas with just a week to go.

6

I TOLD Jordan and Cully and Diane how my brother, Artie, and my wife, Vallie, came to see me every day. And how Artie would shave me and drive Vallie back and forth from the hospital while Artie's wife took care of my kids. I saw Cully smiling slyly.

'OK,' I said. 'That scar I showed you was my gallbladder scar. No machine guns. If you had any fucking brains you'd know I would never be alive if I got hit like that.'

Cully was still smiling. He said, 'Did it ever cross your mind that when your brother and your wife left the hospital maybe they fucked before going home? Is that why you left her?'

I laughed like hell, and I knew I'd have to tell them about Artie.

'He's a very good-looking guy,' I said. 'We look alike, but he's older.' The truth is that I'm a sort of charcoal sketch of my brother, Artie. My mouth is too thick. My eye sockets are too hollow. My nose is too big. And I look too strong, but you should see Artie. I told them that the reason I married Vallie was that she was the only one of my girlfriends who didn't fall in love with my brother.

My brother, Artie, is incredibly handsome on a delicate scale. His eyes are like those eyes in the Greek statues. I remember when we both were bachelors how girls used to fall in love with him, cry over him, threaten to kill themselves over him. And how distressed he'd be about that. Because he really didn't know what the hell it was all about. He could never see his beauty. He was a little self-conscious about being small, and his hands and feet were tiny. 'Just like a baby's,' one girl had said adoringly.

But what distressed Artie was the power he had over them. He finally came to hate it. Ah, how I would have loved it, girls never fell in love with me like that. How I would like it now, that sheer senseless falling in love with externals, the love never earned by qualities of goodness, of character, of intelligence, of wit, of charm, of life-force. In short, how I would like to be loved in a way never earned so that I would never have to keep earning it or work for it. I love that love the way I love the money I win when I get lucky gambling.

But Artie took to wearing clothes that didn't fit. He dressed conservatively in a way that didn't suit his looks. He deliberately tried to hide his charm. He could only relax and be his natural self with people he really cared about and felt safe with. Otherwise he developed a colourless personality that in an inoffensive way kept everyone at a distance. But even so he kept running into trouble. So he married young and was maybe the only faithful husband in the city of New York.

On his job as a research chemist with the federal Food and Drug Administration his female associates and assistants fell in love with him. His wife's best friend and her husband won his trust, and they had a great friendship for about five years. Artie let his guard down. He trusted them. He was his natural self. The wife's best friend fell in love with him and broke up her marriage and announced her love to the world, causing a lot of trouble and suspicion from Artie's wife. Which was the only time I ever saw him angry with her. And his anger was deadly. She accused him of encouraging the infatuation. He said to her in the coldest tone I ever heard any man use to a woman, 'If you believe that, get the hell out of my life.' Which was so unnatural of him that his wife almost had a breakdown from remorse. I really think she hoped he was guilty so she could get a hold over him. Because she was completely in his power.

She knew something about him that I knew and very few other people knew. He could not bear to inflict pain. On anyone or anything. He could never reproach anyone. That's why he hated women being in love with him. He was, I think, a sensual man, he would have loved a great many women easily and enjoyed it, but he could never have borne the conflicts. In fact, his wife said the one thing she missed in their relationship was that she could use a real fight or two. Not that she never had fights with Artie. They were married after all. But she said that all their fights were one-punch affairs, figuratively, of course. She'd fight and fight and fight, and then he'd wipe her out with one cold remark so devastating she would burst into tears and quit.

But with me he was different; he was older and he treated me as a kid brother. And he knew me, he could read me better than my wife. And he never got angry with me.

It took me two weeks to recover from the operation before I was well enough to go home. On the final day I said good-bye to Dr Cohn and he wished me luck.

The nurse brought my clothes and told me I'd have to sign some papers before I could leave the hospital. She escorted me to the office. I really felt shitty that nobody had come to take me home. None of my friends. None of my family. Artie. Sure, they didn't know I was going home alone. I was feeling like a little kid, nobody loved me. Was it right that I had to go home after a serious operation, alone, in the subway? What if I got weak? Or fainted? Jesus, I felt shitty. Then I burst out laughing. Because I was really full of shit.

The truth was that Artie had asked who was taking me home, and I had said Valerie. Valerie had said she would come down to the hospital, and I told her it was OK, I would take a cab if Artie couldn't make it. So she assumed I had told Artie. My friends had, of course, assumed that somebody in my family would take me home. The fact of the matter is that I wanted to hold a grudge in some funny kind of way. Against everybody.

Except that somebody should have known. I'd always prided myself on being self-sufficient. That I never needed anyone to care about me. That I could live completely alone and inside myself. But this was one time that I wanted some excessive sentimentality that the world dishes out in such abundance.

And so when I got back to the ward and found Artie holding my suitcase, I almost burst into tears. My spirits went way up and I gave him a hug, one of the few times I'd ever done that. Then I asked happily, 'How the hell did you know I was leaving the hospital today?'

Artie gave me a sad, tired smile. 'You shit, I called Valerie. She said she thought I was picking you up, that's what you told her.'

'I never told her that,' I said.

'Oh, come on,' Artie said. He took my arm, leading the way out of the ward. 'I know your style,' he said. 'But it's not fair to people who care about you. What you do is not fair to them.'

I didn't say anything until we were out of the hospital and in his car. 'I told Vallie you might come down,' I said. 'I didn't want her to bother.'

Artie was driving through traffic now, so he couldn't look at me. He spoke quietly, reasonably. 'You can't do what you do with Vallie. You can do it with me. But you can't do it with Vallie.'

He knew me as no one else did. I didn't have to explain to him how I felt like such a fucking loser. My lack of success as an artist had done me in, the shame of my failure to take care of my wife and kids had done me in. I couldn't ask anyone to do anything for me. I literally couldn't bear to ask anyone to take me home from the hospital. Not even my wife.

When we got home, Vallie was waiting for me. She had a bewildered, scared look on her face when she kissed me. The three of us had coffee in the kitchen. Vallie sat near me and touched me. 'I can't understand,' she said. 'Why couldn't you tell me?'

'Because he wanted to be a hero,' Artie said. But he said it to throw her off the track. He knew I wouldn't want her to know how really beat I was mentally. I guess he thought it would be bad for her to know that. And besides, he had faith in me. He knew I'd bounce back. That I'd be OK. Everybody gets a little weak once in a while. What the hell. Even heroes get tired.

After coffee, Artie left. I thanked him and he gave me his sardonic smile, but I could see that he was worried about me. There was, I noticed, a look of strain on his face. Life was beginning to wear him down. When he was out of the house, Vallie made me go to bed and rest. She helped me undress and lay down in bed beside me, naked too.

I fell asleep immediately. I was at peace. The touch of her warm body, her hands that I trusted, her untreacherous mouth and eyes and hair made sleep the sweet sanctuary it could never be with the deep drugs of pharmacology. When I woke up, she was gone. I could hear her voice in the kitchen and the voices of the children home from school. Everything seemed worth it.

Women, for me, were a sanctuary, used selfishly it is true, but making everything else bearable. How could I or any man suffer all the defeats of everyday life without that sanctuary? Jesus, I'd come home hating the day I had just put in on my job, worried to death about the money I owed, sure of my final defeat in life because I would never be a successful writer. And all the pain would vanish because I'd have supper with my family, I'd tell stories to the kids and at night I would make completely confident and trusting love with my wife. And it would seem a miracle. And of course, the real miracle was that it was not just Vallie and me but countless other millions of men with their wives and children. And for thousands of years. When all that goes, what will hold men together? Never mind that it wasn't all love and that sometimes it was even pure hatred. I had a history now.

And then it all goes away anyway.

In Vegas I told all this in fragments, sometimes over drinks in the lounge, sometimes at an after-midnight supper in the coffee shop. And when I was finished, Cully said, 'We still don't know why you left your wife.' Jordan looked at him with mild contempt. Jordan had already made the rest of the voyage and gone far past me.

'I didn't leave my wife and kids,' I said. 'I'm just taking a break. I write to her every day. Some morning I'll feel like going home and just get on the plane.'

'Just like that?' Jordan asked. Not sardonically. He really wanted to know.

Diane hadn't said anything, she rarely did. But now she patted me on the knee and said, 'I believe you.'

Cully said to her, 'Where do you come off believing in any guy?'

'Most men are shitty,' Diane said. 'But Merlyn isn't; not yet anyway.'

'Thanks,' I said.

'You'll get there,' Diane said coolly.

I couldn't resist. 'How about Jordan?' I knew she was in love with Jordan. So did Cully. Jordan didn't know because he didn't want to know and he didn't care. But now he turned a politely inquiring face toward Diane as if he were interested in her opinion. On that night he really looked like hell. The bones of his face were beginning to show through the skin in sickly white planes.

'No, not you,' she said to him. And Jordan turned his head away from her. He didn't want to hear it.

Cully, who was so outgoing and amiable, was the last to tell his story, and then, like all of us, he held back the most important part, which I didn't find out until years later. Meanwhile, he gave an honest picture of his true character, or so it seemed. We all knew that he had some mysterious connection with the hotel and its owner, Gronevelt. But it was also true that he was a degenerate gambler and general lowlife. Jordan was not amused by Cully, but I have to admit that I was. Everything out of the ordinary or caricatures of types interested me automatically. I made no moral judgments. I felt that I was above that. I just listened.

Cully was an education. And an inspiration. Nobody would ever do him in. *He* would do *them* in. He had an instinct for survival. A zest for life, based on immorality and a complete disregard for ethics. And yet he was enormously likable. He could be funny. He was interested in everything, and he could relate to women in a completely unsentimental, realistic way that women loved.

Despite the fact that he was always short of money, he could get to bed with any of the show girls working in the hotel with romantic sweet talk. If she held out, he might pull his fur coat routine.

It was slick. He would bring her to a fur shop farther down the Strip. The owner was a friend of his, but the girl didn't know this. Cully would have the owner show the girl his stock of furs, in fact, have the guy lay all the pelts out on the floor so that he and the girl could pick out the finest. After they made the selection, the furrier would measure the girl and tell her the coat would be ready in two weeks. Then Cully would write out a cheque for two or three thousand dollars as a down payment and tell the owner to give the girl the coat and send him the bill. He'd give the girl the receipt.

That night Cully would take the girl out to dinner and after dinner he'd let her bet a few bucks on roulette, then take her to his room where as he said, she had to come across because she had the receipt worth a couple of grand in her pocketbook. Since Cully was so madly in love with her, how could she not? Just the fur coat might not do it. Just Cully's being in love might not do it. But put both of them together and, as Cully explained, you had an ego-greed parlay that was a winner every time.

Of course, the girl never got the fur coat. During the two-week love affair, Cully would pick a fight and they'd break up. And Cully said, not once, never, not one time, had the girl given him back the receipt for the fur coat. In every case she rushed down to the fur store and tried to collect the deposit or even the coat. But of course, the owner blandly told all of them that Cully had already picked up his deposit and cancelled the order. His payoff was some of Cully's rejects.

Cully had another trick for the soft hookers in the chorus line. He would have a drink with them a few nights in a row, listen attentively to their troubles and be enormously sympathetic. Never making a bad move or a come-on. Then maybe on the third night he would take out a hundred-dollar bill in front of them, put it in an envelope and put the envelope into the inside pocket of his jacket. Then he would say, 'Listen, I don't usually do this, but I really like you. Let's get comfortable in my room and I'll give you this for cab fare home.'

The girl would protest a little. She wanted that C note. But she didn't want to be thought a hooker. Cully would turn on the charm. 'Listen,' he would say, 'it's gonna be late when you leave. Why should you pay your cab fare home? That's the least I can do. And I really like you. What's the harm?' Then he would take out the envelope and give it to her, and she would slip it into her purse. He would immediately escort her to his room and screw her for hours before he let her go home. Then came, he said, the funny part. The girl, on her way down in the elevator, would rip open the envelope for her C note and find a ten-dollar bill. Because naturally, Cully had had two envelopes inside his jacket.

Very often the girl would ride the elevator back up and start hammering on Cully's door. He would go into the bathroom and run a tub to drown out the noise, shave leisurely and wait for her to go away. Or, if she were shyer and less experienced, she would call him from the lobby phone and explain that maybe he had made a mistake, that there was only a ten-dollar bill in the envelope.

Cully loved this. He'd say, 'Yeah, right. What can the cab fare be, two, three dollars? But I just wanted to make sure, so I gave you ten.'

The girl would say, 'I saw you put a hundred dollars in the envelope.'

Cully would positively get indignant. 'A hundred bucks for a cab fare,' he'd say. 'What the hell are you, a goddamn hooker? I never paid a hooker in my life. Listen, I thought you were a nice girl. I really liked you. Now you pull this shit. Listen, don't call me any more.' Or sometimes, if he thought he could get away with it, he'd say, 'Oh, no, sweetheart. You're mistaken.' And he'd con her for another shot. Some girls believed it was an honest mistake, or as Cully was smart enough to point out, they had to make believe that they had made a mistake not to look foolish. Some even made another date to prove they weren't hookers, that they hadn't gone to bed with him for the hundred dollars.

And yet this was not to save money, Cully gambled his money away. It was the feeling of power, that he could 'move' a beautiful girl. He was especially challenged if a girl had a reputation for only putting out for guys she really liked.

If the girls were really straight, Cully got a little more complicated. He would try to get into their heads, pay them extravagant compliments. Complain about his own inability to get sexually aroused unless he had a real interest in or real knowledge of the girl. He would send them little presents, give them twenty-dollar bills for a cab fare. But still, some smart girls wouldn't let him get his foot in the door. Then he would switch them. He would start talking about a friend of his, a wealthy man who was the best guy in the world. Who took care of girls out of friendship, they didn't even have to come across. This friend would join them for a drink and it would really be a wealthy friend of Cully's, usually a gambler with a big dress business in New York or an auto agency in Chicago. Cully would talk the girl into going to dinner with his friend, the friend being well briefed. The girl had nothing to lose. A free dinner with a likable, wealthy man.

They would have dinner. The man would lay a couple of hundreds on her or send an expensive gift to her the next day. The man would be charming all the way, never pressing. But there were portents of fur coats, automobiles, diamond rings of many carats perceived in the future. The girl would go to bed with the rich friend. And after the rich friend moved on, the beautiful girl who could not be 'moved' would fall into Cully's lap for a cab fare.

Cully had no remorse. His position was that women not married were all soft hustlers, out to hook you with one gimmick or another, including true love, and that you were within your rights to hustle them back. The only time he showed a little pity was when the girls didn't hammer on his door or call him from the lobby. He knew then that the girls were straight, humiliated that they had been tricked. Sometimes he would look them up and if they needed money for rent or to get through the month he would tell them it had been a joke and he would slip them a hundred or two.

And for Cully it was a joke. Something to tell his fellow thieves and hustlers and gamblers. They would all laugh and congratulate him on not getting robbed. These hustlers were all keenly aware of women as an enemy, true, an enemy that had fruits necessary to men, but they were indignant about paying a stickup price, which meant money, time and affection. They needed the company of women, they needed the softness of women around them. They would pay air fares in the thousands to take girls with them from Vegas to London just to have them around. But that was OK. After all, the poor kid had to pack and travel. She was earning the money. And she had to be ready at all times for a quick screw or a before-lunch·blow job without preamble or the usual courtesies. No hassles. Above all, no hassles. Here was the cock. Take care of it. Never mind do you love me. Never mind let's eat first. Never mind I want to sightsee first. Never mind a little nap, later, not now, tonight, next week, the day after Christmas. Right now. Quick service all the way down the line. Big gamblers, they wanted first class.

Cully's wooing seemed, to me, profoundly malicious, but women like him a hell of a lot better than other men. It seemed as if they understood him, saw through all his tricks but were pleased that he went to all that trouble. Some of the girls he tricked became good friends, always ready to screw him if he felt lonely. And Jesus, once he got sick, and there was a whole regiment of floozy Nightingales passing through his hotel room, washing him, feeding him and, as they tucked him in, blowing him to make sure he was relaxed enough to get a good night's sleep. Rarely did Cully get angry with a girl, and then he would say with a really deadly loud contempt, 'Take a walk,' the words having a devastating effect. Maybe it was the switch from complete sympathy and respect he showed them before he became ugly, and maybe it was because to the girl there was no reason for him to turn ugly. Or that he used it quite cruelly for shock when the charm didn't work.

Yet given all this, still Jordan's death affected him. He was terribly angry at Jordan. He took the suicide as a personal affront. He bitched about not having taken the twenty grand, but I could sense that it didn't really bother him. A few days later I came into the casino and found him dealing blackjack for the house. He had taken a job, he had given up gambling. I couldn't believe he was serious. But he was. It was as if he had entered the priesthood as far as I was concerned.

7

A WEEK after Jordan's death I left Vegas, forever I thought, and headed back for New York.

Cully took me to the plane and we had coffee in the terminal while I waited to board. I was surprised to see that Cully was really affected by my leaving. 'You'll come back,' he said. 'Everybody comes back to Vegas. And I'll be here. We'll have some great times.'

'Poor Jordan,' I said.

'Yeah,' Cully said. 'I'll never in my whole life be able to figure that out. Why did he do it? Why the hell did he do it?'

'He never looked lucky,' I said.

We shook hands when my boarding was announced. 'If you get jammed up back home, give me a call,' Cully said. 'We're buddies. I'll bail you out.' He even gave me a hug. 'You're an action guy,' he said. You'll always be in action. So you'll always be in trouble. Give me a call.'

I really didn't believe that he was sincere. Four years later he was a success, and I was in big trouble appearing before a grand jury looking to indict me. And when I called Cully, he flew to New York to help me.

8

FLEEING Western daylight, the huge jet slid into the spreading darkness of the Eastern time zones. I dreaded the moment when the plane would land and I'd have to face Artie and he'd drive me home to the Bronx housing project where my wife and kids were waiting. Craftily I had presents for them, miniature toy slot machines, for Valerie a pearl inset ring which had cost me two hundred dollars. The girl in the Xanadu Hotel gift shop wanted five hundred dollars, but Cully muscled a special discount.

But I didn't want to think about the moment I would have to walk through the door of my home and meet the faces of my wife and three children. I felt too guilty. I dreaded the scene I would have to go through with Valerie. So I thought about what had happened to me in Vegas.

I thought about Jordan. His death didn't distress me. Not now anyway. After all, I had known him for only three weeks, and not really known him. But what, I wondered, had been so touching in his grief? A grief I had never felt and hoped I never would feel. I had always suspected him, studied him as I would a chess problem. Here was a man who had lived an ordinary happy life. A happy childhood. He talked about that sometimes, how happy he had been as a child. A happy marriage. A good life. Everything went right for him until that final year. Then why didn't he recover? Change or die, he said once. That was what life was all about. And he simply couldn't change. The fault was his.

During those three weeks his face became thinner as if the bones underneath were pushing themselves outward to give some sort of warning. And his body began shrinking alarmingly for so short a time. But nothing else betrayed him and his desire. Going back over those days, I could see now that everything he said and did was to throw me off the track. When I refused his offer to stake me and Cully and Diane, it was simply to show my affection was genuine. I thought that might help him. But he had lost the capacity for what Austen called 'the blessing of affection'.

I guess he thought it was shameful, his despair or whatever it was. He was solid American, it was disgraceful for him to feel it pointless to stay alive.

His wife killed him. Too simple. His childhood, his mother, his father, his siblings? Even if the scars of childhood heal, you never grow out of being vulnerable. Age is no shield against trauma.

Like Jordan, I had gone to Vegas out of a childish sense of betrayal. My wife put up with me for five years while I wrote a book, never complained. She wasn't too happy about it, but what the hell, I was home nights. When my first novel was turned down and I was heartbroken, she said bitterly, 'I knew you would never sell it.'

I was stunned. Didn't she know how I felt? It was one of the most terrible days of my life and I loved her more than anyone else in the world. I tried to explain. The book was a good book. Only it had a tragic ending and the publisher wanted an upbeat ending and I refused. (How proud I was of that. And how right I was. I was always right about my work, I really was.) I thought my wife would be proud of me. Which shows how dumb writers are. She was enraged. We were living so poor, I owed so much money, where the fuck did I come off, who the fuck did I think I was, for Christ sake? (Not those words, she never in her life said 'fuck'.) She was so mad she just took the kids and left the house and didn't come back home until it was time to cook supper. And she had wanted to be a writer once.

My father-in-law helped us out. But one day he ran into me coming out of a secondhand bookstore with an armload of books and he was pissed off. It was a beautiful spring day, sunshiny yellow. He had just come out of his office, and he looked wilted and strained. And there I was walking along, grinning with anticipation at devouring the printed goodies under my arm. 'Jesus,' he said, 'I thought you were writing a book. You're just fucking off.' He could say the word pretty well.

A couple of years later the book was published my way, got great reviews but made just a few grand. My father-in-law, instead of congratulating me, said, 'Well, it didn't make any money. Five years' work. Now you concentrate on supporting your family.'

Gambling in Vegas, I figured it out. Why the hell *should* they be sympathetic? Why should they give a shit about this crazy eccentricity I had about creating art? Why the fuck should they care? They were absolutely right. But I never felt the same about them again.

The only one who understood was my brother, Artie, and even he, over the last year, I felt, was a little disappointed in me, though he never showed it. And he was the human being closest to me in my life. Or had been until he got married.

Again my mind shied away from going home and I thought about Vegas. Cully had never spoken about himself, though I asked him questions. He would tell you about his present life but seldom anything about himself before Vegas. And the funny thing was that I was the only one who seemed to be curious. Jordan and Cully rarely asked any questions. If they had, maybe I would have told them more.

Though Artie and I grew up as orphans, in an asylum, it was no worse and probably a hell of a lot better than military schools and fancy boarding schools to rich people ship their kids just to get them out of the way. Artie was my older brother, but I was always bigger and stronger; physically anyway. Mentally he was stubborn as hell and a lot more honest. He was fascinated by science and I loved fantasy. He read chemistry and maths books and worked out chess problems. He taught me chess, but I was always too impatient; it's not a gambling game. I read novels. Dumas and Dickens and Sabatini, Hemingway, Fitzgerald and later on Joyce and Kafka and Dostoevsky.

I swear being an orphan had no effect on my character. I was just like any other kid. Nobody later in life could guess we had never known our mother or father. The only unnatural or warping effect was that instead of being brothers, Artie and I were mother and father to each other. Anyway, we left the asylum in our teens, Artie got a job and I went to live with him. Then Artie fell in love with a girl and it was time for me to leave. I joined the Army to fight the big war, WW II. When I came out five years later, Artie and I had changed back into brothers. He was the father of a family and I was a war veteran. And that's all there was to it. The only time I thought of us as having been orphans was when Artie and I stayed up late in his house and his wife got tired and went to bed. She kissed Artie good-night before she left us. And I thought that Artie and I were special. As children we were never kissed good-night.

But really we had never lived in that asylum. We both escaped through books. My favourite was the story of King Arthur and his Round Table. I read all the versions, all the popularizations, and the original Malory version. And I guess it's obvious that I thought of King Arthur as my brother, Artie. They had the same names, and in my childish mind I found them very similar in the sweetness of their characters. But I never identified with any of the brave knights like Lancelot. For some reason they struck me as dumb. And even as a child I had no interest in the Holy Grail. I didn't want to be Galahad.

But I fell in love with Merlin, with his cunning magic, his turning himself into a falcon or any animal. His disappearing and reappearing. His long absences. Most of all, I loved when he told King Arthur that he could no longer be the king's right hand. And the reason. That Merlin would fall in love with a girl and teach her his magic. And that she would betray Merlin and use his own magic spells against him. And so he would be imprisoned in a cave for a thousand years before the spell wore off. And then he would come back into the world again. Boy, that was some lover, that was some magician. He'd outlive them all. And so as a child I tried to be a Merlin to my brother, Artie. And when we left the asylum, we changed our last name to Merlyn. And we never talked about being orphans again. Between ourselves or to anyone.

The plane was dipping down. Vegas had been my Camelot, an irony that the great Merlin could have easily explained. Now I was returning to reality. I had some explaining to do to my brother and to my wife. I got my packages of presents together as the plane taxied to its bay.

9

IT all turned out to be easy. Artie didn't ask me questions about why I had run off from Valerie and the kids. He had a new car, a big station wagon, and he told me his wife was pregnant again. That would be the fourth kid. I congratulated him on becoming a father. I made a mental note to send his wife flowers in a few days. And then I cancelled the note. You can't send flowers to a guy's wife when you owe that guy thousands of dollars. And when you might have to borrow more money off him in the future. It wouldn't bother Artie, but his wife might think it funny.

On the way to the Bronx housing project I lived in I asked Artie the important question 'How does Vallie feel about me?'

'She understands,' Artie said. 'She's not mad. She'll be glad to see you. Look, you're not that hard to understand. And you wrote every day. And you called her a couple of times. You just needed a break.' He made it sound normal. But I could see that my running off for a month had frightened him about me. He was really worried.

And then we were driving through the housing project that always depressed me. It was a huge area of buildings built in tall hexagons, erected by the government for poor people. I had a five-room apartment for fifty bucks a month, including utilities. And the first few years it had been OK. It was built by government money and there had been screening processes. The original settlers had been the hardworking law-abiding poor. But by their virtues they had moved up in the economic scale and moved out to private homes. Now we were getting the hard-core poor who could never make an honest living or didn't want to. Drug addicts, alcoholics, fatherless families on welfare, the father having taken off. Most of these new arrivals were blacks, so Vallie felt she couldn't complain because people would think she was a racist. But I knew we had to get out of there soon, that we had to move into a white area. I didn't want to get stuck in another asylum. I didn't give a shit whether anybody thought it was racial. All I knew was I was getting outnumbered by people who didn't like the colour of my skin and who had very little to lose no matter what they did. Common sense told me that was a dangerous situation. And that it would get worse. I didn't like white people much, so why should I love blacks? And of course, Vallie's father and mother would put a down payment on a house for us. But I wouldn't take money from them. I would take money only from my brother, Artie. Lucky Artie.

The car had stopped. 'Come up and rest and have some coffee,' I said.

'I have to get home,' Artie said. 'Besides, I don't want to see the scene. Go take your lumps like a man.'

I reached into the back seat and swung my suitcase out of the car. 'OK,' I said. 'Thanks a lot for picking me up. I'll come over to see you in a couple of days.'

'OK,' Artie said. 'You sure you got some dough?'

'I told you I came back a winner,' I said.

'Merlyn the Magician,' he said. And we both laughed. I walked away from him down the path that led to my apartment house door. I was waiting for his motor to hum up as he took off, but I guess he watched me until I entered the building. I didn't look back. I had a key, but I knocked. I don't know why. It was as if I had no right to use that key. When Vallie opened the door, she waited until I entered and put my suitcase in the kitchen before she embraced me. She was very quiet, very pale, very subdued. We kissed each other very casually as if it were no big deal having been separated for the first time in ten years.

'The kids wanted to wait up,' Vallie said. 'But it was too late. They can see you in the morning before they go to school.'

'OK,' I said. I wanted to go into their bedrooms to see them, but I was afraid I would wake them and they'd stay up and wear Vallie out. She looked very tired now.

I lugged the suitcase into our bedroom and she followed me. She started unpacking and I sat on the bed. Watching her. She was very efficient. She sorted out the boxes she knew were presents and put them on the dresser. The dirty clothes she sorted into piles for laundry and dry cleaning. Then took the dirty clothes into the bathroom to throw them into the hamper. She didn't come out, so I followed her in there. She was leaning against the wall, crying.

'You deserted me,' she said. And I laughed. Because it wasn't true and because it wasn't the right thing for her to say. She could have been witty or touching or clever, but she had simply told me what she felt, without art. As she used to write her stories at the New School. And because she was so honest, I laughed. And I guess I laughed because now I knew I could handle her and the whole situation. I could be witty and funny and tender and make her feel OK. I could show her that it didn't mean anything, my leaving her and the kids.

'I wrote you every day,' I said. 'I called you at least four or five times.'

She buried her face in my arms. 'I know,' she said. 'I was just never sure you were coming back. I don't care about anything, I just love you. I just want you with me.'

'Me too,' I said. It was the easiest way to say it.

She wanted to make me something to eat and I said no. I took a quick shower and she was waiting for me in bed. She always wore her nightgown to bed even though we were going to make love and I would have to take it off. That was her Catholic childhood and I liked it. It gave our lovemaking a certain ceremony. And seeing her lying there, waiting for me, I was glad I had been faithful to her. I had plenty of other guilts to handle, but that at least was one I wouldn't have. And it was worth something, in that time and that place. I don't know if it did her any good.

With the lights out, careful not to make noise so as not to wake the children, we made love as we always had for the more than ten years we had known each other, and had children together, and I guess loved each other. She had a lovely body, lovely breasts, and she was naturally and innocently orgasmic. All the parts of her body were responsive to touch and she was sensibly passionate. Our lovemaking was nearly always satisfying, and so it was tonight. And afterwards she fell into a deep sleep, her hand holding mine until she rolled on her side and the connection broke.

But I or my body clock had flown three hours faster in time. Now that I was safe home with my wife and children I could not imagine why I had run away. Why I had stayed nearly a month in Vegas, so solitary and cut off. I felt the relaxation of an animal that has reached sanctuary. I was happy to be poor and trapped in marriage and burdened by children. I was happy to be un-successful as long as I could lie in a bed beside my wife, who loved me and would support me against the world. And then I thought, this was how Jordan must have felt before he got the bad news. But I wasn't Jordan. I was Merlyn the Magician, I would make it all come out right.

The trick is to remember all the good things, all the happy times. Most of the ten years had been happy. In fact, at one time I had gotten pissed off because I was too happy for my means and circumstances and my ambitions. I thought of the casino burning brightly in the desert, and Diane gambling as a shill without any chance of winning or losing, of being happy or unhappy. And Cully behind the table in his green apron, dealing for the house. And Jordan dead.

But lying now in my bed, the family I had created breathing around me, I felt a terrible strength. I would make them safe against the world and even against myself.

I was sure I could write another book and get rich. I was sure that Vallie and I would be happy forever, that the strange neutral zone that separated us would be destroyed; I would never betray her or use my magic to sleep for a thousand years. I would never be another Jordan.

10

IN Gronevelt's penthouse suite, Cully stared through huge windows. The red and green python neon Strip ran out to the black desert mountains. Cully was not thinking of Merlyn or Jordan or Diane. He was nervously waiting for Gronevelt to come out of the bedroom, preparing his answers, knowing that his future was at stake.

It was an enormous suite, with a built-in bar for the living room, big kitchen to service the formal dining room; all open to the desert and encircling mountains. As Cully moved restlessly to another window, Gronevelt came through the archway of the bedroom.

Gronevelt was impeccably dressed and barbered, though it was after midnight. He went to the bar and asked Cully, 'You want a drink?' His Eastern accent was New York or Boston or Philadelphia. Around the living room were shelves filled with books. Cully wondered if Gronevelt really read them. The newspaper reporters who wrote about Gronevelt would have been astonished to think so.

Cully went over to the bar and Gronevelt made a gesture for him to help himself. Cully took a glass and poured some scotch into it. He noticed Gronevelt was drinking plain club soda.

'You've been doing good work,' Gronevelt said. 'But you helped that guy Jordan at the baccarat table. You went against me. You take my money and you go up against me.'

'He was a friend of mine,' Cully said. 'It wasn't a big deal. And I knew he was the kind of guy that would take care of me good if he was winners.'

'Did he give you anything,' Gronevelt asked, 'before he knocked himself off?'

'He was going to give us all twenty grand, me and that kid that hung out with us and Diane, the raven-haired baccarat shill.'

Cully could see that Gronevelt was interested and didn't seem too pissed off because he had helped Jordan out.

Gronevelt walked over to the huge window and gazed at the desert mountains shining blackly in the moonlight.

'But you never got the money,' Gronevelt said.

'I was a jerk,' Cully said. 'The Kid said he'd wait until we put Jordan on the plane, so me and Diane said we'd wait too. That's a mistake I'll never make again.'

Gronevelt said calmly, 'Everybody makes mistakes. It's not important unless the mistake is fatal. You'll make more.' He finished off his drink. 'Do you know why that guy Jordan did it?'

Cully shrugged. 'His wife left him. Took him for everything he had, I guess. But maybe there was something wrong with him physically, maybe he had cancer. He looked like hell the last few days.'

Gronevelt nodded. 'That baccarat shill, she a good fuck?'

Cully shrugged. 'Fair.'

At that moment Cully was surprised to see a young girl come

out of the bedroom area into the living room. She was all made up and dressed to go out. She had her purse slung jauntily over her shoulder. Cully recognized her as one of the seminudes in the hotel stage show. Not a dancer but a show girl. She was beautiful and he remembered that her bare breasts on the stage had been knockouts.

The girl gave Gronevelt a kiss on the lips. She ignored Cully, and Gronevelt did not introduce her. He walked her to the door, and Cully saw him take out his money clip and slip a one-hundred-dollar bill from it. He held the girl's hand as he opened the door and the hundred-dollar bill disappeared. When she was gone, Gronevelt came back into the room and sat down on one of the two sofas. Again he made a gesture and Cully sat down in one of the stuffed chairs facing him.

'I know all about you,' Gronevelt said. 'You're a countdown artist. You're a good mechanic with a deck of cards. From the work you've done for me I know you're smart. And I've had you checked out all the way down the line.'

Cully nodded and waited.

'You're a gambler but not a degenerate gambler. In fact, you're ahead of the game. But you know, all countdown artists eventually get barred from the casinos. The pit bosses here wanted to throw you out long ago. I stopped them. You know that.'

Cully just waited.

Gronevelt was staring him straight in the eye. 'I've got you all taped except for one thing. That relationship you had with Jordan and the way you acted with him and that other kid. The girl I know you didn't give a fuck about. So before we go any further, explain that to me.'

Cully took his time and was very careful. 'You know I'm a hustler,' he said. 'Jordan was a strange wacky kind of guy. I had a hunch I could make a score with him. The kid and girl fell into the picture.'

Gronevelt said, 'That kid, who the hell was he? That stunt he pulled with Cheech, that was dangerous.'

Cully shrugged. 'Nice kid.'

Gronevelt said almost kindly. 'You liked him. You really liked him and Jordan or you never would have stood with them against me.'

Suddenly Cully had a hunch. He was staring at the hundreds of volumes of books stacked around the room. 'Yeah, I liked them. The Kid wrote a book, didn't make much money. You can't go through life never liking anybody. They were really sweet guys. There wasn't a hustler bone in either of them. You could trust them. They'd never try to pull a fast one on you. I figured it would be a new experience for me.'

Gronevelt laughed. He appreciated the wit. And he was interested. Though few people knew it, Gronevelt was extremely well read. He treated it as a shameful vice. 'What's the Kid's name?' He asked it offhand, but he was genuinely interested. 'What's the name of the book?'

'His name is John Merlyn,' Cully said. 'I don't know the book.'

Gronevelt said, 'I never heard of him. Funny name.' He mused for a while, thinking it over. 'That his real name?'

'Yeah,' Cully said.

There was a long silence as if Gronevelt were pondering something, and then he finally sighed and said to Cully, 'I'm going to give you the break of your life. If you do your job the way I tell you to and if you keep your mouth shut, you'll have a good chance of making some big money and being an executive in this hotel. I like you and I'll gamble on you. But remember, if you fuck me, you're in big trouble. I mean big trouble. Do you have a general idea of what I'm talking about?'

'I do,' Cully said. 'It doesn't scare me. You know I'm a hustler. But I'm smart enough to be straight when I have to.'

Gronevelt nodded. 'The most important thing is a tight mouth.' And as he said this, his mind wandered back to the early evening he had spent with the show girl. A tight mouth. It seemed to be the only thing that helped him these days. For a moment he had the sense of weariness, a failing of his powers, that had seemed to come more often in the past year. But he knew that just by going down and walking through his casino he would be recharged. Like some mythic giant, he drew power from being planted on the life-giving earth of his casino floor, from all the people working for him, from all the people he knew, rich and famous and powerful who came to be whipped by his dice and cards, who scourged themselves at his green felt tables. But he had paused too long, and he saw Cully watching him intently, with curiosity and intelligence working. He was giving this new employee of his an edge.

'A tight mouth,' Gronevelt repeated. 'And you have to give up all the cheap hustling, especially with broads. So what, they want presents? So what if they clip you for a hundred here, a thousand there? Remember then they are paid off. You are evened out. You never want to owe a woman anything. *Anything*. You always want to be evened out with broads: Unless you're a pimp or a jerk. Remember that. Give them a Honeybee.'

'A hundred bucks?' Cully asked kiddingly. 'Can't it be fifty? I don't own a casino.'

Gronevelt smiled a little. 'Use your own judgment. But if she has anything at all going, make it a Honeybee.'

Cully nodded and waited. So far this was bullshit. Gronevelt had to get down to the real meat. And Gronevelt did.

'My biggest problem right now,' Gronevelt said, 'is beating taxes. You know you can only get rich in the dark. Some of the other hotel owners are skimming in the counting room with their partners. Jerks. Eventually the Feds will catch up with them. Somebody talks and they get a lot of heat. A lot of heat. The one thing I don't like is heat. But skimming is where the real money is. And that is where you are going to help.'

'I'll be working in the counting room?' Cully asked.

Gronevelt shook his head impatiently. 'You'll be dealing,' he said. 'At least for a while. And if you work out, you'll move up to be my personal assistant. That's a promise. But you have to prove yourself to me. All the way. You get what I mean?'

'Sure,' Cully said. 'Any risk?'

'Only from yourself,' Gronevelt said. And suddenly he was staring at Cully very quietly and intently and as if he were saying something without words that he wanted Cully to grasp. Cully looked him in the eye and Gronevelt's face sagged a little with an expression of weariness and distaste, and suddenly Cully understood. If he didn't prove himself, if he fucked up, he had a good chance of being buried in the desert. He knew that this distressed Gronevelt, and he felt a curious bond with the man. He wanted to reassure him.

'Don't worry, Mr Gronevelt,' he said. 'I won't fuck up. I appreciate what you're doing for me. I won't let you down.'

Gronevelt nodded his head slowly. His back was turned to Cully, and he was staring out the huge window to the desert and mountains beyond.

'Words don't mean anything,' he said. 'I'm counting on your being smart. Come up to see me tomorrow at noon and I'll lay everything out. And one other thing.'

Cully made himself look attentive.

Gronevelt said harshly, 'Get rid of that fucking jacket you and your buddies always wore. That Vegas Winner shit. You don't know how that jacket irritated me when I saw you three guys walking through my casino wearing it. And that's the first thing you can remind me of. Tell that fucking store owner not to order any more of those jackets.'

'OK,' Cully said.

'Let's have another drink and then you can go,' Gronevelt said. 'I have to check the casino in a little while.'

They had another drink, and Cully was astonished when Gronevelt clicked their glasses together as if to celebrate their new relationship. It encouraged him to ask what had happened to Cheech.

Gronevelt shook his head sadly. 'I might as well give you the facts of life in this town. You know Cheech is in the hospital. Officially he got hit by a car. He'll recover, but you'll never see him in Vegas again until we get a new deputy police chief.'

'I thought Cheech was connected,' Cully said. He sipped his drink. He was very alert. He wanted to know how things worked on Gronevelt's level.

'He's connected very big back East,' Gronevelt said. 'In fact, Cheech's friends wanted me to help him get out of Vegas. I told them I had no choice.'

'I don't get it,' Cully said. 'You have more muscle than the deputy police chief.'

Gronevelt leaned back and drank slowly. As an older and wiser man he always found it pleasant to instruct the young. And even as he did so, he knew that Cully was flattering him, that Cully probably had all the answers. 'Look,' he said, 'we can always handle trouble with the federal government with our lawyers and the courts; we have judges and we have politicians. One way or another we can fix things with the governor or the gambling control commissions. The deputy's office runs the town the way we want it. I can pick up the phone and get almost anybody run out of town. We are building an image of Vegas as an absolute safe place for gamblers. We can't do that without the deputy. Now to exercise that power he has to have it and we have to give it to him. We have to keep him happy. He also has to be a certain kind of very tough guy with certain values. He can't let a hood like Cheech punch his nephew and get away with it. He has to break his legs. And we have to let him. I have to let him. Cheech has to let him. The people back in New York have to let him. A small price to pay.'

'The deputy is that powerful?' Cully asked.

'Has to be,' Gronevelt said. 'It's the only way we can make this town work. And he's a smart guy, a good politician. He'll be deputy for the next ten years.'

'Why just ten?' Cully asked.

Gronevelt smiled. 'He'll be too rich to work,' Gronevelt said. 'And it's a very tough job.'

After Cully left, Gronevelt prepared to go down to the casino floor. It was now nearly two in the morning. He made his special call to the building engineer to pump pure oxygen through the casino air-conditioning system to keep the gamblers from getting sleepy. He decided to change his shirt. For some reason it had become damp and sticky during his talk with Cully. And as he changed, he gave Cully some hard thought.

He thought he could read the man. Cully had believed that the incident with Jordan was a mark against him with Gronevelt. On the contrary, Gronevelt had been delighted when Cully stuck up for Jordan at the baccarat table. It proved that Cully was not just your run-of-the-mill, one-shot hustler, that he wasn't one of your fake, scroungy, crooked shafters. It proved that he was a hustler in his heart of hearts.

For Gronevelt had been a sincere hustler all his life. He knew that the true hustler could come back to the same mark and hustle him two, three, four, five, six times and still be regarded as a friend. The hustler who used up a mark in one shot was bogus, an amateur, a waster of his talent. And Gronevelt knew that the true hustler had to have his spark of humanity, his genuine feeling for his fellowman, even his pity of his fellowman. The true genius of a hustler was to love his mark sincerely. The true hustler had to be generous, compassionately helpful and a good friend. This was not a contradiction. All these virtues were essential to the hustler. They built up his almost rocklike credibility. And they were all to be used for the ultimate purpose. When as a true friend he stripped the mark of those treasures which he, the hustler, coveted or needed for his own life. And it wasn't that simple. Sometimes it was for money. Sometimes it was to acquire the other man's power or simply the leverage that the other man's power generated. Of course, a hustler had to be cunning and ruthless, but he was nothing, he was transparent, he was a one-shot winner, unless he had a heart. Cully had a heart. He had shown that when he had stood by Jordan at the baccarat table and defied Gronevelt.

But now the puzzle for Gronevelt was: did Cully act sincerely or cunningly? He sensed that Cully was very smart. In fact, so smart that Gronevelt knew he would not have to keep a check on Cully for a while. Cully would be absolutely faithful and honest for the next three years. He might cut a few tiny corners because he knew that such liberties would be a reward for doing his job well. But no more than that. Yes, for the next few years Cully would be his right-hand man on an operational level, Gronevelt thought. But after that he would have to keep a check on Cully no matter how hard Cully worked to show honesty and faithfulness and loyalty and even his true affection for his master. That would be the biggest trap. A true hustler, Cully would have to betray him when the time was ripe. Gronevelt knew that and knew that it would be very hard to prepare himself against it.

BOOK THREE

11

VALERIE'S father fixed it so that I didn't lose my job. My time away was credited as vacation and sick time, so I even got paid for my month's goofing off in Vegas. But when I went back, the Regular Army major, my boss, was a little pissed off. I didn't worry about that. If you're in the federal Civil Service of the United States of America and you are not ambitious and you don't mind a little humiliation, your boss has no power.

I worked as a GS-6 administrative assistant to Army Reserve units. Since the units met only once a week for training, I was responsible for all administrative work of the three units assigned to me. It was a cinch racket job. I had a total of six hundred men to take care of, make out their payrolls, mimeograph their instruction manuals, all that crap. I had to check the administrative work of the units done by Reserve personnel. They made up morning reports for their meetings, cut promotion orders, prepared assignments. All this really wasn't as much work as it sounded except when the units went off to summer training camp for two weeks. Then I was busy.

Ours was a friendly office. There was another civilian named Frank Alcore who was older than me and belonged to a Reserve unit he worked for as an administrator. Frank, with impeccable logic, talked me into going crooked. I worked alongside him for two years and never knew he was taking graft. I found out only after I came back from Vegas.

The Army Reserve of the United States was a great pork barrel. By just coming to a meeting for two hours a week you got a full day's pay. An officer could pick up over twenty bucks. A top-ranking enlisted man with his longevity ten dollars. Plus pension rights. And during the two hours you just went to meetings of instruction or fell asleep at a film.

Most civilian administrators joined the Army Reserve. Except me. My magician hat divined the thousand-to-one-shot kicker. That there might be another war and the Reserve units would be the first guys called into the Regular Army.

Everybody thought I was crazy. Frank Alcore begged me to join. I had been a private in WW II for three years, but he told me he could get me appointed sergeant major based on my civilian experience as an Army unit administrator. It was a ball, doing your patriotic duty, earning double pay. But I hated the idea of taking orders again even if it was for two hours a week and two weeks in the summer. As a working stiff I had to follow my superior's instructions. But there's a big difference between orders and instructions.

Every time I read newspaper reports about our country's well-trained Reserve force I shook my head. Over a million men just fucking off. I wondered why they didn't abolish the whole thing. But a lot of small towns depended on Army Reserve payrolls to make their economies go. A lot of politicians in the state legislatures and Congress were very high-ranking Reserve officers and made a nice bundle.

And then something happened that changed my whole life. Changed it only for a short time, but changed it for the better both economically and psychologically. I became a crook. Courtesy of the military structure of the United States.

Shortly after I came back from Vegas the young men in America became aware that enlisting in the newly legislated six months' active duty programme would net them a profit of eighteen months' freedom. A young man eligible for the draft simply enlisted in the Army Reserve programme and did six months' Regular Army time in the States. After that he did five and a half years in the Army Reserve. Which meant going to one two-hour meeting a week and one two-week summer camp active duty. If he waited and got drafted, he'd serve two full years, and maybe in Korea.

But there were only so many openings in the Army Reserve. A hundred kids applied for each vacancy, and Washington had a quota system put into effect. The units I handled received a quota of thirty a month, first come, first served.

Finally I had a list of almost a thousand names. I controlled the list administratively, and I played it square. My bosses, the Regular Army major adviser and a Reserve lieutenant colonel commanding the units, had the official authority. Sometimes they slipped some favourite to the top. When they told me to do that, I never protested. What did I give a shit? I was working on my book. The time I put into the job was just to get a pay-cheque.

Things started getting tighter. More and more young men were getting drafted. Cuba and Vietnam were far off on the horizon. About this time I noticed something fishy going on. And it had to be very fishy for me to notice because I had absolutely no interest in my job or its surroundings.

Frank Alcore was older and married with a couple of kids. We had the same Civil Service grade, we operated on our own, he had his units and I had mine. We both made the same amount of money, about a hundred bucks a week. But he belonged to his Army Reserve unit as a master sergeant and earned another extra grand a year. Yet he was driving to work in a new Buick and parking it in a nearby garage which cost three bucks a day. He was betting all the ball games, football, basketball and baseball, and I knew how much that cost. I wondered where the hell he was getting the dough. I kidded him and he winked and told me he could really pick them. He was killing his bookmaker. Well, that was my racket, he was on my ground—and I knew he was full of shit. Then one day he took me to lunch in a good Italian joint on Ninth Avenue and showed his hole card.

Over coffee, he asked, 'Merlyn how many guys do you enlist a month for your units? What quota do you get from Washington?'

'Last month thirty,' I said. 'It goes from twenty-five to forty depending how many guys we lose.'

'Those enlistment spots are worth money,' Frank said. 'You can make a nice bundle.'

I didn't answer. He went on. 'Just let me use five of your spaces a month,' he said. 'I'll give you a hundred bucks a spot.'

I wasn't tempted. Five hundred bucks a month was a hundred percent income jump for me. But I just shook my head and told him to forget it. I had that much ego. I had never done anything dishonest in my adult life. It was beneath me to become a common bribe-taker. After all, I was an artist. A great novelist waiting to be famous. To be dishonest was to be a villain. I would have muddied my narcissistic image of myself. It didn't matter that my wife and children lived on the edge of poverty. It didn't matter that I had to take an extra job at night to make ends meet. I was a hero born. Though the idea of kids *paying* to get into the Army tickled me.

Frank didn't give up. 'You got no risk,' he said. 'Those lists can be faked. There's no master sheet. You don't have to take money from the kids or make deals. I'll do all that. You just enlist them when I say OK. Then the cash goes from my hand to yours.'

Well, if he was giving me a hundred, he had to be getting two hundred. And he had about fifteen slots of his own to enlist, and at the rate of two hundred each that was three grand a month. What I didn't realize was that he couldn't use the fifteen slots for himself. The commanding officers of his units had people to be taken care of. Political bosses, congressmen, United States senators sent kids in to beat the draft. They were taking the bread out of Frank's mouth and he was properly pissed off. He could sell only five slots a month. But still, a grand a month tax-free? Still, I said no.

There are all kinds of excuses you can make for finally going crooked. I had a certain image of myself. That I was honourable and would never tell a lie or deceive my fellowman. That I would never do anything underhand for the sake of money. I thought I was like my brother, Artie. But Artie was down-to-the-bone honest. There was no way for him ever to go crooked. He used to tell me stories about the pressures brought on him in his job. As a chemical engineer testing new drugs for the federal Food and Drug Administration he was in a position of power. He made fairly good money, but when he ran his tests, he disqualified a lot of the drugs that the other federal chemists passed. Then he was approached by the huge drug companies and made to understand that they had jobs which paid a lot more money than he could ever make. If he were a little more flexible, he could move up in the world. Artie brushed them off. Then finally one of the drugs he had vetoed was approved over his head. A year later the drug had to be recalled and banned because of the toxic effects on patients, some of whom died. The whole thing got into the papers, and Artie was a hero for a while. He was even promoted to the highest Civil Service grade. But he was made to understand that he could never go higher. That he would never become the head of the agency because of his lack of understanding of the political necessities of the job. He didn't care and I was proud of him.

I wanted to live an honourable life, that was my big hang-up. I prided myself on being a realist, so I didn't expect myself to be perfect. But when I did something shitty, I didn't approve of it or kid myself, and usually I did stop doing the same kind of shitty

85

thing again. But I was often disappointed in myself since there was such a great variety of shitty things a person can do, and so I was always caught by surprise.

Now I had to sell myself the idea of turning crook. I wanted to be honourable because I felt more comfortable telling the truth than lying. I felt more at ease innocent than guilty. I had thought it out. It was a pragmatic desire, not a romantic one. If I had felt more comfortable being a liar and a thief, I would have done so. And therefore was tolerant of those who did so behave. It was, I thought, their métier, not necessarily a moral choice. I claimed that morals had nothing to do with it. But I did not really believe that. In essence I believed in good and evil as values.

And then if truth were told, I was always in competition with other men. And therefore, I wanted to be a better man, a better person. It gave me a satisfaction not to be greedy about money when other men abased themselves for it. To disdain glory, to be honest with women, to be an innocent by choice. It gave me pleasure not to be suspicious of the motives of others and to trust them in almost anything. The truth was I never trusted myself. It was one thing to be honourable, another to be foolhardy.

In short, I would rather be cheated than to cheat someone; I would rather be deceived than be a deceiver; I gladly accepted being hustled as long as I did not become a hustler. I would rather be faked out than be a fake-out artist. And I understood that this was an armour I sheathed myself in, that it was not really admirable. The world could not hurt me if it could not make me feel guilty. If I thought well of myself, what did it matter that others thought ill of me? Of course, it didn't always work. The armour had chinks. And I made a few slips over the years.

And yet—and yet—I felt that even this, smugly upright as it sounded, was, in a funny kind of way, the lowest kind of cunning. That my morality rested on a foundation of cold stone. That quite simply there was nothing in life I desired so much that it could corrupt me. The only thing I wanted to do was create a great work of art. But not the fame or money or power, or so I thought. Quite simple to benefit humanity. Ah. Once as an adolescent, beset with guilt and feelings of unworthiness, hopelessly at odds with the world, I stumbled across the Dostoevsky novel *The Brothers Karamazov*. That book changed my life. It gave me strength. It made me see the vulnerable beauty of all

86

people no matter how despicable they might outwardly seem. And I always remembered the day I finally gave up the book, took it back to the asylum library and then walked out into the lemony sunlight of an autumn day. I had a feeling of grace.

And so all I wished for was to write a book that would make people feel as I felt that day. It was to me the ultimate exercise of power. And the purest. And so when my first novel was published, one that I worked on for five years, one that I suffered great hardship to publish without any artistic compromise, the first review that I read called it dirty, degenerate, a book that should never have been written and once written should never have been published.

The book made very little money. It received some superlative reviews. It was agreed that I had created a genuine work of art, and indeed, I had to some extent fulfilled my ambition. Some people wrote letters to me that I might have written to Dostoevsky. I found that the consolation of these letters did not make up for the sense of rejection that commercial failure gave me.

I had another idea for a truly great novel, my *Crime and Punishment* novel. My publisher would not give me an advance. No publisher would. I stopped writing. Debts piled up. My family lived in poverty. My children had nothing that other children had. My wife, my responsibility, was deprived of all material joys of society, etc., etc. I had gone to Vegas. And so I couldn't write. Now it became clear. To become the artist and good man I yearned to be, I had to take bribes for a little while. You can sell yourself anything.

Still, it took Frank Alcore six months to break me down, and then he had to get lucky. I was intrigued by Frank because he was the complete gambler. When he bought his wife a present, it was always something he could put in the pawnshop if he ran short of cash. And what I loved was the way he used his cheque account.

On Saturdays, Frank would go out to do the family shopping. All the neighbourhood merchants knew him and they cashed his cheques. In the butcher's he'd buy the finest cuts of veal and beef and spend a good forty dollars. He'd give the butcher a cheque for a hundred and pocket the sixty bucks' change. The same story at the grocery and the vegetable man. Even the liquor store. By noon Saturday he'd have about two hundred bucks' change from his shopping, and he would use that to make his bets on the baseball games. He didn't have a penny in his cheque account to cover. If he lost his cash on Saturday, he'd get credit at his bookmakers to bet the Sunday games, doubling up. If he won, he'd rush to the bank on Monday morning to cover his cheques. If he lost, he'd let the cheques bounce. Then during the week he would hustle bribes for recruiting young draft dodgers into the six months' programme to cover the cheques when they came around the second time.

Frank would take me to the night ball games and he'd pay for everything, including the hot dogs. He was a naturally generous guy, and when I tried to pay, he'd push my hand aside and say something like: 'Honest men can't afford to be sports.' I always had a good time with him, even at work. During lunch hour we'd play gin and I would usually beat him for a few dollars, not because I played better cards but because his mind was on his sports action.

Everybody has an excuse for his breakdown in virtue. The truth is you break down when you are prepared to break down.

I came in to work one morning when the hall outside my office was crowded with young men to be enlisted in the Army six months' programme. In fact, the whole armoury was full. All the units were busy enlisting on all eight floors. And the armoury was one of those old buildings that had been built to house whole battalions to march around in. Only now half of each floor was partitioned off for storerooms, classrooms and our administrative offices.

My first customer was a little old man who had brought in a young kid of about twenty-one to be enlisted. He was way down on my list.

'I'm sorry, we won't be calling you for at least six months,' I said.

The old guy had startlingly blue eyes that radiated power and confidence. 'You had better check with your superior,' he said.

At that moment I saw my boss, the Regular Army major signalling frantically to me through his glass partition. I got up and went into his office. The major had been in combat in the Korean War and WW II, with ribbons all over his chest. But he was sweating and nervous.

'Listen,' I said, 'that old guy told me I should talk to you. He wants his kid ahead of everybody on the list. I told him I couldn't do it.'

The major said angrily, 'Give him anything he wants. That old guy is a congressman.'

'What about the list?' I said.

'Fuck the list,' the major said.

I went back to my desk where the congressman and his young protégé were seated. I started making out the enlistment forms. I recognized the kid's name now. He would be worth over a hundred million bucks someday. His family was one of the great success stories in American history. And here he was in my office enlisting in the six months' programme to avoid doing a full two years' active duty.

The congressman behaved perfectly. He didn't lord it over me, didn't rub it in that his power made me subvert the rules. He talked quietly, friendly, hitting just the right note. You had to admire the way he handled me. He tried to make me feel I was doing him a favour and mentioned that if there was anything he could ever do for me, I should call his office. The kid kept his mouth shut except to answer my questions when I was typing out his enlistment form.

But I was a little pissed off. I don't know why. I had no moral objection to the uses of power and its unfairness. It was just that they had sort of run me over and there was nothing I could do about it. Or just maybe the kid was so fucking rich, why couldn't he do his two years in the Army for a country that had done so well by his family?

So I slipped in a little zinger that they couldn't know about. I gave the kid a critical MOS recommendation. MOS stands for Military Occupational Specialty, the particular Army job he would be trained for. I recommended him for one of the few electronic specialties in our units. In effect I was making sure that this kid would be one of the first guys called up for active duty in case there was some sort of national emergency. It was a long shot, but what the hell.

The major came out and swore the kid in, making him repeat the oath which included the fact that he did not belong to the Communist party or one of its fronts. Then everybody shook hands all around. The kid controlled himself until he and his congressman started out of my office. Then the kid gave the congressman a little smile.

Now that smile was a child's smile when he puts something over on his parents and other adults. It is disagreeable to see it on the faces of children. And was more so now. I understood that the smile didn't really make him a bad kid, but that smile absolved me of any guilt for giving him the booby-trapped MOS.

Frank Alcore had been watching the whole thing from his desk on the other side of the room. He didn't waste any time. 'How long are you going to be a jerk?' Frank asked. 'That congressman took a hundred bucks out of your pocket. And God knows what he got out of it. Thousands. If that kid had come in to us, I could have milked him for at least five hundred.' He was indignant. Which made me laugh.

'Ah, you don't take things seriously enough,' Frank said. 'You could get a big jump in money, you could take care of a lot of your problems if you'd just listen.'

'It's not for me,' I said.

'OK, OK,' Frank said. 'But you gotta do me a favour. I need an open spot bad. You notice that red-headed kid at my desk? He'll go five hundred. He's expecting his draft notice any day. Once he gets the notice he can't be enlisted in the six months' programme. Against regulations. So I have to enlist him today. And I haven't got a spot in my units. I want you to enlist him in yours and I'll split the dough with you. Just this one time.'

He sounded desperate so I said, 'OK, send the guy in to see me. But you keep the money. I don't want it.'

Frank nodded. 'Thanks. I'll hold your share. Just in case you change your mind.'

That night, when I went home, Vallie gave me supper and I played with the kids before they went to bed. Later Vallie said she would need a hundred dollars for the kids' Easter clothes and shoes. She didn't say anything about clothes for herself, though like all Catholics, for her buying a new outfit for Easter was almost a religious obligation.

The following morning I went into the office and said to Frank, 'Listen, I changed my mind. I'll take my half.'

Frank patted me on the shoulder. 'That a boy,' he said. He took me into the privacy of the men's room and counted out five fifty-dollar bills from his wallet and handed them over. 'I'll have another customer before the end of the week.' I didn't answer him.

It was the only time in my life I had done anything really dishonest. And I didn't feel so terrible. To my surprise I actually felt great. I was cheerful as hell, and on the way home I bought Vallie and the kids presents. When I got there and gave Vallie the hundred dollars for the kids' clothes, I could see she was relieved that she wouldn't have to ask her father for the money. That night I slept better than I had for years.

I went into business for myself, without Frank. My whole personality began to change. It was fascinating being a crook. It brought out the best in me. I gave up gambling and even gave up writing; in fact, I lost all interest in the new novel I was working on. I concentrated on my government job for the first time in my life.

I started studying the thick volumes of Army regulations, looking for all the legal loopholes through which draft victims could escape the Army. One of the first things I learned was that medical standards were lowered and raised arbitrarily. A kid who couldn't pass the physical one month and was rejected for the draft might easily pass six months later. It all depended on what draft quotas were established by Washington. It might even depend on budget allocations. There were clauses that anyone who had had shock treatments for mental disorders was physically ineligible to be drafted. Also homosexuals. Also if he was in some sort of technical job in private industry that made him too valuable to be used as a soldier.

Then I studied my customers. They ranged in age from eighteen to twenty-five, and the hot items were usually about twenty-two or twenty-three, just out of college and panicked at wasting two years in the United States Army. They were frantic to enlist in the Reserve and just do six months' active duty.

These kids all had money or came from families with money. They all had trained to enter a profession. Someday they would be the upper middle class, the rich, the leaders in many different walks of American life. In wartime they would have fought to get into Officers Candidate School. Now they were willing to settle for being bakers and uniform repair specialists or truck maintenance crewmen. One of them at age twenty-five had a seat on the New York Stock Exchange; another was a securities specialist. At that time Wall Street was alive with new stocks that went up ten points as soon as they were issued, and these kids were getting rich. Money rolled in. They paid me, and I paid my brother, Artie, the few grand I owed him. He was surprised and a little curious. I told him that I had gotten lucky gambling. I was too ashamed to tell him the truth, and it was one of the few times I ever lied to him.

Frank became my adviser. 'Watch out for these kids,' he said. 'They are real hustlers. Stick it to them and they'll respect you more.'

I shrugged. I didn't understand his fine moral distinctions.

'They're all a fuckin' bunch of crybabies,' Frank said. 'Why can't they go and do their two years for their country instead of fucking off with this six months' bullshit? You and me, we fought in the war, we fought for our country and we don't own shit. We're poor. These guys, the country did good by them. Their families are all well-off. They have good jobs, big futures. And the pricks won't even do their service.'

I was surprised at his anger, he was usually such an easygoing guy, not a bad word for anybody. And I knew his patriotism was genuine. He was fiercely conscientious as a Reserve master sergeant, he was only crooked as a civil servant.

In the following months I had no trouble building up a clientele. I made up two lists: one was the official waiting roster; the other was my private list of bribers. I was careful not to be greedy. I used ten slots for pay and ten slots from the official lists. And I made my thousand a month like clockwork. In fact, my clients began to bid, and soon my going price was three hundred dollars. I felt guilty when a poor kid came in and I knew he would never work his way up the official list before he got drafted. That bothered me so much that finally I disregarded the official list entirely. I made ten guys a month pay, and ten lucky guys got in free. In short, I exercised power, something I had always thought I would never do. It wasn't bad.

I didn't know it, but I was building up a corps of friends in my units that would help save my skin later on. Also, I made another rule. Anybody who was an artist, a writer, an actor or a fledgling theatre director got in for nothing. That was my tithe because I was no longer writing, had no urge to write, and felt guilty about that too. In fact, I was piling up guilts as fast as I was piling up money. And trying to expiate my guilts in a classical American way, doing good deeds.

Frank bawled me out for my lack of business instinct. I was too nice a guy, I had to be tougher or everybody would take advantage of me. But he was wrong. I was not as nice a guy as he thought or the rest of them thought.

Because I was looking ahead. Just using any kind of minimum intelligence, I knew that this racket had to blow up someday. There were too many people involved. Hundreds of civilians with jobs like mine were taking bribes. Thousands of reservists were being enlisted in the six months' programme only after paying a substantial entrance fee. That was something that still tickled me, everybody paying to get into the Army.

One day a man of about fifty came in with his son. He was a wealthy businessman, and his son was a lawyer just starting his practice. The father had a bunch of letters from politicians. He talked to the Regular Army major, then he came in again on the night of the unit's meeting and met the Reserve colonel. They were very polite to him but referred him to me with the usual quota crap. So the father came over with his son to my desk to put the kid's name down on the official waiting list. His name was Hiller and his son's name was Jeremy.

Mr Hiller was in the automobile business, he had a Cadillac dealership. I made his son fill out the usual questionnaire and we chatted.

The kid didn't say anything, he looked embarrassed. Mr Hiller said, 'How long does he have to wait on this list?'

I leaned back in my chair and gave him the usual answer. 'Six months,' I said.

'He'll be drafted before then,' Mr Hiller said. 'I'd appreciate it if you could do something to help him.'

I gave him my usual answer. 'I'm just a clerk,' I said. 'The only people that can help you are the officers you talked to already. Or you could try your congressman.'

He gave me a long, shrewd look, and then he took out his business card. 'If you ever buy a car, come to see me, I'll get it for you at cost.'

I looked at his card and laughed. 'The day I can buy a Cadillac,' I said, 'I won't have to work here any more.'

Mr Hiller gave me a nice friendly smile. 'I guess that's right,' he said. 'But if you can help me, I'd really appreciate it.'

The next day I had a call from Mr Hiller. He had the ersatz friendliness of the salesman con artist. He asked after my health, how I was doing and remarked on what a fine day it was. And then he said how impressed he was with my courtesy, so unusual in a government employee dealing with the public. So impressed and overcome with gratitude that when he heard about a year-old Dodge being offered for sale, he had bought it and would be willing to sell it to me at cost. Would I meet him for lunch to discuss it?

I told Mr Hiller I couldn't meet him for lunch but I would drop over to his automobile lot on my way home from work. He was located out in Roslyn, Long Island, which wasn't more than a half hour away from my housing project in the Bronx. And it was still light when I got there. I parked my car and wandered around the grounds looking at the Cadillacs, and I was smitten by middle-class greed. The Cadillacs were beautiful, long, sleek and heavy; some burnished gold, others creamy white, dark blue, fire engine red. I peeked into the interiors and saw the lush carpeting, the rich-looking seats. I had never cared much about cars, but at that moment I hungered for a Cadillac.

I walked toward the long brick building and passed a robin's-egg blue Dodge. It was a very nice car that I would have loved before I walked through those miles of fucking Cadillacs. I looked inside. The upholsters was comfortable-looking but not rich. Shit.

In short, I was reacting in the style of the classically nouveau riche thief. Something very funny had happened to me the past months. I was very unhappy taking my first bribe. I had thought I would think less of myself, I had always so prided myself on never being a liar. Then why was I so enjoying my role as a sleazy small-time bribe-taker and hustler?

The truth was that I had become a happy man because I had become a traitor to society. I loved taking money for betraying my trust as a government employee. I loved hustling the kids who came in to see me. I deceived and dissembled with the lip-smacking relish of a peasant penny ante Iago. Some nights, lying awake, thinking up new schemes, I also wondered at this change in myself. And I figured out that I was getting my revenge for having been rejected as an artist, that I was compensating for my worthless heritage as an orphan. For my complete lack of worldly success. And my general uselessness in the whole scheme of things. Finallly I had found something I could do well; finally I was a success as a provider for my wife and children. And oddly enough I became a better husband and father. I helped the kids with their homework. Now that I had stopped writing I had more time for Vallie. We went out to the movies, I could afford a baby-sitter and the price of admission. I bought her presents. I even got a couple of magazine assignments and dashed off the pieces with ease. I told Vallie that I got all this fresh money from doing the magazine work.

I was a happy, happy thief, but in the back of my mind I knew there would come a day of reckoning. So I gave up all thoughts of buying a Cadillac and settled for the robin's-egg blue Dodge.

Mr Hiller had a large office with pictures of his wife and children on his desk. There was no secretary and I hoped it was because he was smart enough to get rid of her so that she wouldn't see me. I liked dealing with smart people. I was afraid of stupid people.

Mr Hiller made me sit down and take a cigar. Again he inquired after my health. Then he got down to brass tacks. 'Did you see that blue Dodge? Nice car. Perfect shape. I can give you a real buy on it. What do you drive now?'

'A 1950 Ford,' I said.

'I'll let you use that as a trade-in,' Mr Hiller said. 'You can have the Dodge for five hundred dollars cash and your car.'

I kept a straight face. Taking the five hundred bucks out of my wallet, I said, 'You got a deal.'

Mr Hiller looked just a little surprised. 'You'll be able to help my son, you understand.' He really was a little worried that I hadn't caught on.

Again I was astonished at how much I enjoyed these little transactions. I knew I could stick him up. That I could get the Dodge just by giving him my Ford. I was really making about a thousand dollars on this deal even by paying him the five hundred. But I didn't believe in a crook driving hard bargains. I still had a little bit of Robin Hood in me. I still thought of myself as a guy who took money from the rich only by giving them their money's worth. But what delighted me most was the worry on his face that I hadn't caught on that this was a bribe. So I said very calmly, without a smile, very matter-of-fact, 'Your son will be enlisted in the six months' programme within a week.'

Relief and a new respect showed on Mr Hiller's face. He said, 'We'll do all the papers tonight, and I'll take care of the license plates. It's all set to go.' He leaned over to shake my hand. 'I've heard stories about you,' he said. 'Everybody speaks highly about you.'

I was pleased. Of course, I knew what he meant. That I had a good reputation as an honest crook. After all, that was something. It was an achievement.

While the papers were being drawn up by the clerical staff, Mr Hiller chatted to some purpose. He was trying to find out if I acted alone or whether the major and colonel were in on it. He was clever, his business training, I guess. First he complimented me on how smart I was, how I caught on quickly to everything. Then he started to ask me questions. He was worried that the two officers would remember his son. Didn't they have to swear his son into the Reserve six months' programme? Yes, that was true, I said.

'Won't they remember him?' Mr Hiller said. 'Won't they ask about how he jumped so quickly on the list?'

He had a point but not much of one. 'Did I ask you any questions about the Dodge?' I said.

Mr Hiller smiled at me warmly. 'Of course,' he said. 'You know your business. But it's my son. I don't want to see him get in trouble for something I did.'

My mind began to wander. I was thinking how pleased Vallie would be when she saw the blue Dodge: blue was her favourite colour and she hated the beat-up old Ford.

I forced myself to think about Mr Hiller's question. I remembered his Jeremy had long hair and wore a well-tailored suit with waistcoat, shirt and tie.

'Tell Jeremy to get a short haircut and wear sports clothes when I call him into the office,' I said. 'They won't remember him.'

Mr Hiller looked doubtful. 'Jeremy will hate that,' he said.

'Then he doesn't have to,' I said. 'I don't believe in telling people to do what they don't feel like doing. I'll take care of it.' I was just a little impatient.

'All right,' Mr Hiller said. 'I'll leave it in your hands.'

When I drove home with the new car, Vallie was delighted and I took her and the kids for a drive. The Dodge rode like a dream and we played the radio. My old Ford didn't have a radio. We stopped off and had pizza and soda, routine now but something we had rarely done before in our married life because we had had to watch every penny. Then we stopped off in a candy store and had ice-cream sodas and I bought a doll for my daughter and war games for the two boys. And I bought Vallie a box of Schrafft chocolates. I was a real sport, spending money like a prince. I sang songs in the car as we were driving home, and after the kids were in bed, Vallie made love to me as if I were the Aga Khan and I had just given her a diamond as big as the Ritz.

I remembered the days when I had hocked my typewriter to get us through the week. But that had been before I ran away to Vegas. Since then my luck had changed. No more two jobs; twenty grand stashed away in my old manuscript folders on the bottom of the clothes closet. A thriving business which could make my fortune unless the whole racket blew up or there was some worldwide accommodation that made the big powers stop spending so much money on their armies. For the first time I understood how the war industry bigwigs and industrialists and the Army generals felt. The threat of a stabilized world could plunge me back into poverty. It was not that I wanted another war, but I couldn't help laughing when I realized that all my so-called liberal attitudes were dissolving in the hope that Russia and the United States didn't get too friendly, not for a while at least.

Vallie was snoring a little, which didn't bother me. She worked hard with the kids and taking care of the house and me. But it was curious that I was always awake late at night no matter how exhausted I was. She always fell asleep before I did. Sometimes I would get up and work on my novel in the kitchen and cook myself something to eat and not go back to bed until three or four in the morning. But now I wasn't working on a novel, so I had no work to do. I thought vaguely that I should start writing again. After all, I had the time and money. But the truth was I found my life too exciting, wheeling and dealing and taking bribes and for the first time spending money on little foolish things.

But the big problem was where to stash my cash permanently. I couldn't keep it in the house. I thought of my brother, Artie. He could bank it for me. And he would if I asked him to do it. But I couldn't. He was so painfully honest. And he would ask me where I got the dough and I'd have to tell him. He had never done a dishonest thing for himself or his wife and kids. He had a real integrity. He would do it for me, but he would never feel the same about me. And I couldn't bear that. There are some things you can't do or shouldn't do. And asking Artie to hold my money was one of them. It wouldn't be the act of a brother or a friend.

Of course, some brothers you wouldn't ask because they'd steal it. And that brought Cully into my mind. I'd ask him about the best way to stash the money the next time he came to town. That was my answer. Cully would know, that was his métier. And I had to solve the problem. I had a hunch the money was going to roll in faster and faster.

The next week I got Jeremy Hiller into the Reserves without any trouble, and Mr Hiller was so grateful that he invited me to come to his agency for a new set of tyres for my blue Dodge. Naturally I thought this was out of gratitude, and I was delighted that he was such a nice guy. I forgot he was a business-man. As the mechanic put new tyres on my car, Mr Hiller in his office gave me a new proposition.

He started off dishing out some nice strokes. With an admiring smile he told me how smart I was, how honest, so absolutely reliable. It was a pleasure to have dealings with me, and if I ever left the government, he would get me a good job. I swallowed it all up, I had had very little praise in my life, mostly from my brother, Artie, and some obscure book reviewers. I didn't even guess what was coming.

'There is a friend of mine who needs your help very badly,' Mr Hiller said. 'He has a son who needs desperately to get in the six months' Reserve programme.'

'Sure,' I said. 'Send the kid in to see me and have him mention your name.'

'There's a big problem,' Mr Hiller said. 'This young man has already received his draft notice.'

I shrugged. 'Then he's shit out of luck. Tell his folks to kiss him good-bye for two years.'

Mr Hiller smiled. 'Are you sure there's nothing a smart young man like you can do? It could be worth a lot of money. His father is a very important man.'

'Nothing,' I said. 'The Army regulations are specific. Once a guy receives his draft notice he can no longer be enlisted in the Army Reserve six months' programme. Those guys in Washing-ton are not that dumb. Otherwise everybody would wait for his draft notice before enlisting.'

Mr Hiller said, 'This man would like to see you. He's willing to do anything, you know what I mean?'

'There's no point,' I said. 'I can't help him.'

Then Mr Hiller leaned on me a little. 'Go see him just for me,' he said. And I understood. If I just went to see this guy, even if I turned him down, Mr Hiller was a hero. Well, for four brand-new tyres I could spend a half hour with a rich man.

'OK,' I said.

Mr Hiller wrote on a slip of paper and handed it to me. I looked at it. The name was Eli Hemsi, and there was a phone number. I recognized the name. Eli Hemsi was the biggest man in the garment industry, in trouble with the unions, involved with the mobs. But he also was one of the social lights of the city. A buyer of politicians, a pillar of support to charitable causes, etc. If he was such a big wheel, why did he have to come to me? I asked Mr Hiller that question.

'Because he's smart,' Mr Hiller said. 'He's a Sephardic Jew. They are the smartest of all the Jews. They have Italian, Spanish and Arab blood, and that mixture makes them real killers, besides being smart. He doesn't want his son as a hostage to some politician who can ask him for a big favour. It's a lot cheaper and a lot less dangerous for him to come to you. And besides, I told him how good you were. To be absolutely honest, right now you're the only person who can help him. Those big shots don't dare step in on something like the draft. It's too touchy. Politicians are scared to death of it.'

I thought about the congressman who had come in to my office. He'd had balls then. Or maybe he was at the end of his political career and didn't give a shit. Mr Hiller was watching me carefully.

'Don't get me wrong,' he said. 'I'm Jewish. But the Sephardic you have to be careful with or they'll just outwit you. So when you get to see him, just use your head.' He paused and anxiously asked, 'You're not Jewish, are you?'

'I don't know,' I said. I thought then how I felt about orphans. We were all freaks. Not knowing our parents, we never worried about the Jews or the blacks, whatever.

The next day I called Mr Eli Hemsi at his office. Like married men having an affair, my clients' fathers gave me only their office numbers. But they would have my home number, just in case they had to get in touch with me right away. I was already getting a lot of calls which made Vallie wonder. I told her it was gambling and magazine work calls.

Mr Hemsi asked me to come down to his office during my lunch hour and I went. It was one of the garment centre buildings on Seventh Avenue just ten minutes away from the armoury. A nice little stroll in the spring air. I dodged guys pushing hand trucks loaded with racks of dresses and reflected a little smugly on how hard they were working for their paltry wages while I collected hundreds for a little dirty paperwork at the crossroads. Most of them were black guys. Why the hell weren't they out mugging people like they were supposed to? Ah, if they only had the proper education, they could be stealing like me, without hurting people.

In the building the receptionist led me through showrooms that exhibited the new styles for the coming seasons. And then I was ushered through a little grubby door into Mr Hemsi's office suite. I was really surprised at how plush it was, the rest of the building was so grubby. The receptionist turned me over to Mr Hemsi's secretary, a middle-aged no-nonsense woman, but impeccably dressed, who took me into the inner sanctum.

Mr Hemsi was a great big guy who would have looked like a Cossack if it had not been for his perfectly tailored suit, rich-looking white shirt and dark red tie. His face was powerfully craggy and had a look of melancholy. He looked almost noble and certainly honest. He rose from his desk and grasped my hands in both of his to greet me. He looked deep into my eyes. He was so close to me that I could see through the thick, ropy grey hair. He said gravely, 'My friend is right, you have a good heart. I know you will help me.'

'I really can't help. I'd like to, but I can't,' I said. And I explained the whole draft board thing to him as I had to Mr Hiller. I was colder than I meant to be. I don't like people looking deep into my eyes.

He just sat there nodding his head gravely. Then, as if he hadn't heard a word I'd said, he just went on, his voice really melancholy now.

'My wife, the poor woman, she is in very bad health. It will kill her if she loses her son now. He is the only thing she lives for. It will kill her if he goes away for two years. Mr Merlyn, you must help me. If you do this for me, I will make you happy for the rest of your life.'

It wasn't that he convinced me. It wasn't that I believed a word he'd said. But that last phrase got to me. Only kings and emperors can say to a man, 'I will make you happy for the rest of your life.' What confidence in his powers he had. But then, of course, I realized he was talking about money.

'Let me think about it,' I said, 'maybe I can come up with something.'

Mr Hemsi was nodding his head up and down very gravely. 'I know you will, I know you have a good head and a good heart,' he said. 'Do you have children?'

'Yes,' I said. He asked me how many and how old they were and what sex. He asked about my wife and how old she was. He was like an uncle. Then he asked me for my home address and phone number so that he could get in touch with me if necessary.

When I left him, he walked me to the elevator himself. I figured I had done my job. I had no idea how I could get his son off the hook with the draft board. And Mr Hemsi was right, I did have a good heart. I had a good enough heart not to try to hustle him and his wife's anxieties and then not deliver. And

I had a good enough head not to get mixed up with a draft board victim. The kid had had his notice and would be in the Regular Army in another month. His mother would have to live without him.

The very next day Vallie called me at work. Her voice was very excited. She told me that she just received special delivery service of about five cartons of clothing. Clothes for all the kids, winter and fall outfits, and they were beautiful. There was also a carton of clothes for her. All of it more expensive than we could ever buy.

'There's a card,' she said. 'From a Mr Hemsi. Who is he? Merlyn, they are just beautiful. Why did he give them to you?'

'I wrote some brochures for his business,' I said. 'There wasn't much money in it, but he did promise to send the kids some stuff. But I thought he just meant a few things.'

I could hear the pleasure in Vallie's voice. 'He must be a nice man. There must be over a thousand dollars' worth of clothes in the boxes.'

'That's great,' I said. 'I'll talk to you about it tonight.'

After I hung up, I told Frank what had happened and about Mr Hiller, the Cadillac dealer.

Frank squinted at me. 'You're on the hook,' he said. 'That guy will be expecting you to do something for him now. How are you going to come across?'

'Shit,' I said, 'I can't figure out why I even agreed to go see him.'

'It was those Cadillacs you saw on Hiller's lot,' Frank said. 'You're like those coloured guys. They'd go back to those huts in Africa if they could drive around in a Cadillac.'

I noticed a little hitch in his speech. He had almost said 'niggers' but switched to 'coloured'. I wondered if it was because he was ashamed of saying the ugly word or because he thought I might be offended. As for the Harlem guys liking Cadillacs I always wondered why people got pissed off about that. Because they couldn't afford it? Because they should not go into debt for something not useful? But he was right about those Cadillacs getting me on the hook. That's why I had agreed to see Hemsi and do Hiller the favour. Way back in my head I hoped for a shot at one of those luxurious sleek cars.

That night, when I got home, Vallie put on a fashion show for me with her and the kids. She had mentioned five cartons, but she hadn't mentioned their size. They were enormous, and

Vallie and the kids had about ten outfits each. Vallie was more excited than I had seen her in a long time. The kids were pleased, but they didn't care too much about clothes at that age, not even my daughter. The thought flashed through my mind that maybe I'd get lucky and find a toy manufacturer whose kid had ducked the draft.

But then Vallie pointed out that she would have to buy new shoes to go with the outfits. I told her to hold off for a while and made a note to keep an eye out for a shoe manufacturer's son.

Now the curious thing was that I would have felt that Mr Hemsi was patronizing me if the clothes had been of ordinary quality. There would have been the touch of the poor receiving the hand-me-downs of the rich. But his stuff was top-rate, quality goods I could never afford no matter how much bribe money I raked in. Five thousand bucks, not a thousand. I took a look at the enclosed card. It was a business card with Hemsi's name and title of president and the name of the firm and its address and phone printed on it. There was nothing written. No message of any kind. Mr Hemsi was smart all right. There was no direct evidence that he had sent the stuff, and I had nothing that I could incriminate him with.

At the office I had thought that maybe I could ship the stuff back to Mr Hemsi. But after seeing how happy Vallie was, I knew that was not possible. I lay awake until three in the morning, figuring out ways for Mr Hemsi's son to beat the draft.

The next day, when I went into the office, I made one decision. I wouldn't do anything on paper that could be traced back to me a year or two later. This could be very tricky. It was one thing to take money to put a guy ahead on a list for the six months' programme, it was another to get him out of the draft, after he had received his induction notice.

So the first thing I did was to call up Hemsi's draft board. I got one of the clerks there, a guy just like me. I identified myself and gave him the story I had thought out. I told him that Paul Hemsi had been on my list for the six months' programme and that I had meant to enlist him two weeks ago but that I had sent his letter to the wrong address. That it had been all my fault and I felt guilty about it and also that maybe I could get in trouble on my job if the kid's family started to holler. I asked him if the draft board could cancel the induction notice so that I could enlist him. I would then send the usual official form to the draft board, showing that Paul Hemsi was in the six months' programme of the Army Reserve, and they could take him off their draft rolls. I used what I thought was exactly the right tone, not too anxious. Just a nice guy trying to right a wrong. While I was doing this, I slipped in that if the guy at the draft board could do me this favour, I would help him get a friend of his in the six months' programme.

This last gimmick I had thought about while lying awake the previous night. I figured that the clerks at the draft board probably were contacted by kids on their last legs, about to be drafted, and that the draft board clerks probably got propositioned a lot. And I figured if a draft board clerk could place a client of his in the six months' programme it could be worth a thousand bucks.

But the guy at the draft board was completely casual and accommodating. I don't even think he caught on that I was propositioning him. He said sure, he'd withdraw the induction notice, that it was no problem and I suddenly got the impression that smarter guys than I had already pulled this dodge. Anyway, the next day I got the necessary letter from the draft board and called Mr Hemsi and told him to send his son into my office to be enlisted.

It all went off without a hitch. Paul Hemsi was a nice soft-spoken kid, very shy, very timid, or so it seemed to me. I had him sworn in, stashed his papers until he got his active-duty orders. I drew his supply stuff for him myself, and when he left for his six months' active duty, nobody in his outfit had seen him. I'd turned him into a ghost.

By now I realized that all this action was getting pretty hot and implicating powerful people. But I wasn't Merlyn the Magician for nothing. I put on my star-spangled cap and started to think it all out. Someday it would blow up. I had myself pretty well covered except for the money stashed in my house. I had to hide the money. That was the first thing. And then I had to show another income so I could spend money openly.

I could stash my money with Cully in Las Vegas. But what if Cully got cute or got killed? As for making money legit, I had had offers to do book reviews and magazine work, but I had always turned them down. I was a pure storyteller, a fiction writer. It seemed demeaning to me and my art to write anything else. But what the hell, I was a crook, nothing was beneath me now.

Frank asked me to go to lunch with him and I said OK. Frank

was in great form. Happy-go-lucky, top-of-the-world. He'd had a winning week gambling and the money was rolling in. With no sense of what the future could bring, he believed he'd keep winning, the whole bribe sham would last forever. Without even thinking of himself as a magician, he believed in a magic world.

12

IT was nearly two weeks later that my agent arranged an appointment for me with the editor-in-chief of Everyday Magazines. This was a group of publications that drowned the American public with information, pseudoinformation, sex and pseudosex, culture and hard-hat philosophy. Movie mags, adventure mags for blue-collar workers, a sport monthly, fishing and hunting comics. Their 'class' leader, top-of-the-line magazine was slanted to swinging bachelors with a taste for literature and avant-garde cinema.

A real smorgasbord, Everyday gobbled up free-lance writers because they had to publish a half million words a month. My agent told me that the editor in chief knew my brother, Artie, and that Artie had called him to prepare the way.

At Everyday Magazines all the people seemed to be out of place. Nobody seemed to belong. And yet they put out profitable magazines. Funny, but in the federal government we all seemed to fit, everybody was happy and yet we all did a lousy job.

The chief editor, Eddie Lancer, had gone to school with my brother at the University of Missouri, and it was my brother who first mentioned the job to my agent. Of course, Lancer knew I was completely unqualified after the first two minutes of the interview. So did I. Hell, I didn't even know what the backyard of a magazine was. But with Lancer this was a plus. He didn't give a shit about experience. What Lancer was looking for was guys touched with schizophrenia. And later he told me that I had qualified highly on that score.

Eddie Lancer was a novelist too; he had published a hell of a book that I loved just a year ago. He knew about my novel and said he liked it and that carried a lot of weight in getting the job. On his bulletin board was a big newspaper headline ripped out of the morning *Times*: ATOM BOMB WAR SEEN BAD FOR WALL STREET.

He saw me staring at the clipping and said, 'Do you think you could write a short fiction piece about a guy worrying about that?'

'Sure,' I said. And I did. I wrote a story about a young executive worrying about his stocks going down after the atom bomb's fall. I didn't make the mistake of poking fun at the guy or being moral. I wrote it straight. If you accepted the basic premise, you accepted the guy. If you didn't accept the basic premise, it was a very funny satire.

Lancer was pleased with it. 'You're made to order for our magazine,' he said. 'The whole idea is to have it both ways. The dummies like it and the smart guys like it. Perfect.' He paused for a moment. 'You're a lot different from your brother, Artie.'

'Yeah, I know,' I said. 'So are you.'

Lancer grinned at me. 'We were best friends in college. He's the most honest guy I ever met. You know when he asked me to interview you, I was surprised. It was the first time I ever knew him to ask a favour.'

'He does that only for me,' I said.

'Straightest guy I ever knew in my life,' Lancer said.

'It will be the death of him,' I said. And we laughed.

Lancer and I knew we were both survivors. Which meant we were not straight, that we were hustlers to some degree. Our excuse was that we had books to write. And so we had to survive. Everybody had his own particular and valid excuse.

Much to my surprise (but not to Lancer's) I turned out to be a hell of a magazine writer. I could write the pulp adventure and war stories. I could write the soft-porn love stories for the top-of-the-line magazine. I could write a flashy, snotty film review and a sober, snotty book review. Or turn the other way and write an enthusiastic review that would make people want to go out and see or read for themselves what was so good. I never signed my real name to any of this stuff. But I wasn't ashamed of it. I knew it was schlock, but still I loved it. I loved it because all my life I had never had a skill to be proud of. I had been a lousy soldier, a losing gambler. I had no hobby, no mechanical skills. I couldn't fix a car, I couldn't grow a plant. I was a lousy typist, and not a really first-rate bribe-taker government clerk. Sure, I was an artist, but that's nothing to brag about. That's just a religion or a hobby. But now I really had a skill, I was an expert schlock writer, and loved it. Especially since for the first time in my life I was making a good living. Legitimately.

The money from the stories averaged four hundred dollars a month and with my regular Army Reserve job brought me to about two hundred bucks a week. And as if work sparked more energy, I found myself starting my second novel. Eddie Lancer was on a new book too, and we spent most of our working time together talking about our novels rather than articles for the magazine.

We finally became such good friends that after six months of free-lance work he offered me a magazine editor slot. But I didn't want to give up the two to three grand a month in graft that I was still making on my Army Reserve job. The bribe-taking sham had geen going on for nearly two years without any kind of hitch. I now had the same attitude as Frank. I didn't think anything would ever happen. Also, the truth was that I liked the excitement and the intrigue of being a thief.

My life settled down into a happy groove. My writing was going well, and every Sunday I took Vallie and the kids for rides out in Long Island, where family houses were springing up like weeds and inspected models. We had already picked out our house. Four bedrooms, two baths and only a ten percent down payment on the twenty-six-thousand-dollar price with a twelve-month wait. In fact, now was the time to ask Eddie Lancer for a small favour.

'I've always loved Las Vegas,' I told Eddie. 'I'd like to do a piece on it.'

'Sure, anytime,' he said. 'Just make sure you get something in it on hookers.' And he arranged for the expenses. Then we talked about the colour illustration for the story. We always did this together because it was a lot of fun, and we got a lot of laughs. As usual Eddie finally came up with the effective idea. A gorgeous girl in scanty costume in a wild pelvic dance. And out of her navel rolled red dice showing the lucky eleven. The cover line would read 'Get Lucky with Las Vegas Girls'.

One assignment had to come first. It was a plum. I was going to interview the most famous writer in America, Osano.

Eddie Lancer gave me the assignment for his flagship magazine, *Everyday Life*, the class magazine of the chain. After that one I could do the Las Vegas piece and trip.

Eddie Lancer thought Osano was the greatest writer in America, but was too awed to do the interview himself. I was the only one on the staff not impressed. I didn't think Osano was all that good. Also, I distrusted any writer who was an extrovert. And Osano had appeared on TV a hundred times, been the judge at the Cannes Film Festival, got arrested for leading protest marchers no matter what they were protesting against. And gave blurbs for every new novel written by one of his friends.

Also, he had come up the easy way. His first novel, published when he was twenty-five, made him world-famous. He had wealthy parents, a law degree from Yale. He had never known what it was to struggle for his art. Most of all, I had sent him my first published novel, hoping for a blurb, and he never acknowledged receiving it.

When I went to interview Osano, his stock as a writer was just slipping with editors. He could still command a hefty advance for a book, he still had critics buffaloed. But most of his books were nonfiction. He had not been able to finish a fiction book in the last ten years.

He was working on his masterpiece, a long novel that would be the greatest thing since *War and Peace*. All the critics agreed about that. So did Osano. One publishing house advanced him over a hundred grand and was still whistling for its money and the book ten years later. Meanwhile, he wrote nonfiction books on hot subjects that some critics claimed were better than most novels. He turned them out in a couple of months and picked up a fat cheque. But each one sold less. He had worn his public out. So finally he accepted an offer to be editor-in-chief of the most influential Sunday book review section in the country.

The editor before Osano had been in the job twenty years. A guy with great credentials. All kinds of degrees, the best colleges, an intellectual, wealthy family. Class. And a left-handed swinger all his life. Which was OK except that as he aged, he got more outrageous. One sunny, horny afternoon he was caught going down on the office boy behind a ceiling-high stack of books that he had built as a screen in his office. If the office boy had been a famous English author, maybe nothing would have happened. And if the books he used to build that wall had been reviewed, it wouldn't have been so bad. But the books used to build that wall never got out to his staff of readers or to the free-lance reviewers. So he was retired as editor emeritus.

With Osano, the management knew it was home free. Osano was right-handed all the way. He loved women, all sizes and shapes, any age. The smell of cunt turned him on like a junkie. He fucked broads as devotedly as a heroin addict taking a fix. If Osano didn't get his piece of ass that day or at least a blow job, he'd get frantic. But he wasn't an exhibitionist. He'd always lock his office door. Sometimes a bookish teenybopper. Other times a society broad who thought he was the greatest living American writer. Or a starving female novelist who needed some books to review to keep body and soul and ego together. He was shameless in using his leverage as editor, his fame as a world-renowned novelist and what proved to be the busiest bee in his bonnet, a contender for the Nobel Prize in literature. He said it was the Nobel Prize that got the really intellectual ladies. And for the last three years he had mounted a furious campaign for the Nobel with the help of all his literary friends, he could show these ladies articles in classy quarterlies touting him for the prize.

Oddly enough Osano had no ego about his own physical charms—his personal magnetism. He dressed well, spent good money on clothes, yet it was true he was not physically attractive. His face was all lopsided bone, and his eyes were a pale, sneaky green. But he discounted his vibrant aliveness that was magnetic to all people. Indeed, a great deal of his fame rested not on his literary achievement but on his personality, which included a quick, brilliant intelligence that was attractive to men as well as women.

But the women went crazy for him, bright college girls, well-read society matrons, Women's Lib fighters who cursed him out and then tried to get him in the sack so they could have it on him, so they said, the way men used to have it on women in Victorian days. One of his tricks was to really address himself to women in his books.

I never liked his work, and I didn't expect to like him. The work is the man. Except that it proved not to be true. After all, there are some compassionate doctors, curious teachers, honest lawyers, idealistic politicians, virtuous women, sane actors, wise writers. And so Osano, despite his fishwife style, the spite in his work, was in reality a great guy to hang out with and not too much of a pain in the ass to listen to, even when he talked about his writing.

Anyway, he had quite an empire as editor of the book review. Two secretaries. Twenty staff readers. And a great outdoors of free-lance critics from top-name authors to starving poets, unsuccessful novelists, college professors and jet-set intellectuals. He used them all and hated them all. And he ran the review like a lunatic.

Page one of the Sunday review is something an author kills for. Osano knew that. He got the first page automatically when he published a book, in all the book reviews in the country. But he hated most fiction writers, he was jealous of them. Or he would have a grudge against the publisher of the book. So he would get a biography of Napoleon or Catherine the Great written by a heavyweight college professor and put it on page one. Book and review usually were both equally unreadable, but Osano was happy. He had infuriated everybody.

The first time I ever saw Osano he lived up to all the literary party stories, all the gossip, all the public images he had ever created. He played the role of the great writer for me with a natural gusto. And he had the props to suit the legend.

I went out to the Hamptons, where Osano took a summer house, and found him ensconced (his word) like an old sultan. At fifty years of age, he had six kids from four different marriages and at that time had not gotten his fifth, sixth and terminal seventh notch. He had on long blue tennis shorts and blue tennis jacket specially tailored to hide his bulging beer gut. His face was already craggily impressive, as befitted the next winner of the Nobel Prize for literature. Despite his wicked green eyes, he could be naturally sweet. Today he was sweet. Since he was head of the most powerful Sunday literary review, everybody kissed his ass with the utmost devotion every time he published. He didn't know I was out to kill him, because I was an unsuccessful writer with one flop novel published and the second coming hard. Sure, he'd written one big almost great novel. But the rest of his work was bullshit, and if *Everyday Life* let me, I'd show the world what this guy was really made of.

I wrote the article all right, and I caught him dead to rights. But Eddie Lancer turned it down. They wanted Osano to do a big political story, and they didn't want him to get mad. So it was a day wasted. Except that it really wasn't. Because two years later Osano called me up and offered me a job working for him as assistant on a new big literary review. Osano remembered me, had read the story the magazine killed, and he liked my guts, or so he said. He said it was because I was a good writer and I liked the same things about his work that he liked.

That first day we sat in his garden and watched his kids play tennis. I have to say right now he really loved his kids and he was perfect with them. Maybe because he was so much a child himself. Anyway, I got him talking about women and Women's Lib and sex. And he threw in love with it. He was pretty funny. And though in his writings he was the great all-time left-winger, he could be pretty Texas chauvinistic. Talking about love, he said that once he fell in love with a girl he always stopped being jealous of his wife. Then he put on his big writer-statesman look and said, 'No man is allowed to be jealous of more than one woman at a time—unless he's Puerto Rican.' He felt he was allowed to make jokes about Puerto Ricans because his radical credentials were impeccable.

The housekeeper came out to yell at the children fighting for a game on the tennis court. She was a pretty bossy housekeeper and pretty snotty with the kids, as if she were their mother. She also was a handsome woman for her age, which was about Osano's. For a moment I wondered. Especially when she gave us both a contemptuous look before she went back into the house.

I got him talking about women, which was easy. He took the cynic's stance, which is always a great stance to take when you're not crazy about some particular lady. He was very authoritative, as befitted a writer who had had more gossip written about him than any novelist since Hemingway.

'Listen, kid,' he said, 'love is like the little red toy wagon you get for Christmas on your sixth birthday. It makes you deliriously happy and you just can't leave it alone. But sooner or later the wheels come off. Then you leave it in a corner and forget it. Falling in love is great. Being in love is a disaster.'

Asking quietly and with the respect he thought due, I said, 'What about women, do you think they feel the same way since they claim to think as men think?'

He flashed me a quick look of those surprisingly green eyes. He was on to my act. But it was OK. That was one of the great things about Osano even then. So he went on.

'Women's Lib thinks we have power and control over their lives. In its way that's as stupid as a guy's thinking women are purer sexually than men. Women will fuck anybody, anytime, any place, except that they're afraid of talk. Women's Lib bull-shits about the fraction of a percent of men who have power. Those guys are not men. They're not even human. That's whose place women have to take. They don't know you have to kill to get there.'

I interrupted. 'You're one of those men.'

Osano nodded. 'Yeah. And metaphorically I had to kill. What women will get is what men have. Which is shit, ulcers and heart attacks. Plus a lot of shitty jobs men hate to do. But I'm all for equality. I'll kill those cunts then. Listen, I'm paying alimony to four healthy broads who can earn their own living. All because they are not equal.'

'Your affairs with women are almost as famous as your books,' I said. 'How do you handle women?'

Osano grinned at me. 'You're not interested in how I write books.'

I said smooth as shit, 'Your books speak for themselves.'

He gave me another long, thoughtful look, then went on.

'Never treat a woman too good. Women stick with drunks, gamblers, whoremasters and even beater-uppers. They can't stand a sweet, good guy. Do you know why? They get bored. They don't want to be happy. It's boring.'

'Do you believe in being faithful?' I asked.

'Sure I do. Listen, being in love means making another person the central thing in your life. When that no longer exists, it's not love any more. It's something else. Maybe something better, more practical. Love is basically an unfair, unstable, paranoid relationship. Men are worse than women at it. A woman can screw a hundred times, not feel like it once and he holds it against her. But it's true that the first step downhill is when she doesn't want to fuck when you do. Listen, there's no excuse. Never mind the headaches. No shit. Once a broad starts turning you down in bed it's all over. Start looking for your backer-upper. Never take an excuse.'

I asked him about orgasmic women who could have ten orgasms to a man's one. He waved it aside.

'Women don't come like men,' he said. 'For them it's a little *phitt*. Not like a guy's. Guys really blow their brains with their nuts. Freud was close, but he missed it. Men really *fuck*. Women don't.'

Well, he didn't really believe that all the way, but I knew what he was saying. His style was exaggeration.

I switched him on to helicopters. He had this theory that in twenty years the auto would be obsolete, that everybody would have his own chopper. All it needed were some technical improvements as when auto power steering and brakes enabled every woman to drive and put railroads out of business. 'Yeah,' he said, 'that's obvious.' What was also obvious was that on this particular morning he was wound up on women. So he switched back.

'The young guys today are on the right track. They say to their broads, sure, you can fuck anybody you want, I'll still love you. They are so full of shit. Listen, any guy who knows a broad will fuck strangers thinks of her as a geek.'

I was offended by the comparison and astonished. The great Osano, whose writings women were particularly crazy about. The most brilliant mind in American letters. The most open mind. Either I was missing his point or he was full of shit. I saw his housekeeper slapping some of the little kids around. I said, 'You sure give your housekeeper a lot of authority.'

Now he was so sharp that he caught everything without even trying. He knew exactly how I felt about what he'd been saying. Maybe that's why he told me the truth, the whole story about his housekeeper. Just to needle me.

'She was my first wife,' he said. 'She's the mother of my three oldest kids.'

He laughed when he saw the look on my face. 'No, I don't screw her. And we get along fine. I pay her a damn good salary but no alimony. She's the one wife I don't pay alimony.'

He obviously wanted me to ask why not. I did.

'Because when I wrote my first book and got rich, it went to her head. She was jealous of me being famous and getting a lot of attention. *She* wanted attention. So some young guy, one of the admirers of my work, gave her the business, and she fell for it. She was five years older than him, but she was always a sexy broad. She really fell in love, I'll give her that. What she didn't realize was that he was fucking her just to put the great novelist Osano down. So she asked for a divorce and half the money my book made. That was OK with me. She wanted the kids, but I didn't want my kids around that creep she was in love with. So

I told her when she married the guy, she'd get the kids. Well, he fucked her brains out for two years and blew all her dough. She forgot about her kids. She was a young broad again. Sure, she came to see them a lot, but she was busy travelling all over the world on my dough and chewing the young guy's cock to shreds. When the money runs out, he takes off. She comes back and wants the kids. But by now she has no case. She deserted them for two years. She puts on a big scene how she can't live without them. So I gave her a job as a housekeeper.'

I said coolly, 'That's maybe the worst thing I ever heard of.'

The startling green eyes flashed for a moment. But then he smiled and said musingly, 'I guess it looks that way. But put yourself in my place. I love having my kids around me. How come the father never gets the kids? What kind of bullshit is that? Do you know men never recover from that bullshit? The wife gets tired of being married, so men lose their kids. And men stand still for it because they got their balls chopped off. Well, I didn't stand still for it. I kept the kids and got married again right away. And when that wife started pulling bullshit, I got rid of her too.'

I said quietly, 'How about her children? How do they feel about their mother being a housekeeper?'

The green eyes flashed again. 'Oh, shit. I don't put her down. She's only my housekeeper between wives; otherwise she's more like a free-lance governess. She has her own house. I'm her landlord. Listen, I thought of giving her more dough, of buying her a house and making her independent. But she's a dizzy cunt like all of them. She'd become obnoxious again. She'd go down the drain. Which is OK, but she'd make more trouble for me and I've got books to write. So I control her with money. She has a damn good living from me. And she knows if she gets out of line, she's out on her ass and scratching to make a living. It works out.'

'Could it be you're antiwoman?' I said, smiling.

He laughed. 'You say that to a guy who's been married four times, he doesn't even have to deny it. But OK. I'm really anti-Women's Lib in one sense. Because right now most women are just full of shit. Maybe it's not their fault. Listen, any broad who doesn't want to fuck two days in a row, get rid of her. Unless she has to go to the hospital in an ambulance. Even if she has forty stitches in her cunt. I don't care whether she enjoys it or not. Sometimes I don't enjoy it and I do it and I have to get a hard-on. That's your job if you love somebody, you gotta fuck their brains out. Jesus, I don't know why I keep getting married. I swore I wouldn't do it any more, but I always get conned. I always believe it's not getting married that makes them unhappy. They are so full of shit.'

'With the proper conditioning don't you think women can become equal?'

Osano shook his head. 'They forget they age worse than men. A guy at fifty can get a lot of young broads. A broad at fifty finds it rough. Sure, when they get political power, they'll pass a law so that men of forty or fifty get operated on to look older and equal things out. That's how democracy works. That's full of shit too. Listen, women have it good. They shouldn't complain.

'In the old days they didn't know they had union rights. They couldn't be fired no matter how lousy a job they did. Lousy in bed. Lousy in the kitchen. And who ever had fun with his wife after a couple of years? And if he did, she was a cunt. And now they want to be equal. Let me at 'em. I'll give them equality. I know what I'm talking about; I've been married four times. And it cost me every penny I made.'

Osano really hated women that day. A month later I picked up the morning paper and read that he'd married for the fifth time. An actress in a little theatre group. She was half his age. So much for the common sense of America's foremost man of letters. I never dreamed that I would be working for him someday and be with him until he died, miraculously a bachelor but still in love with a woman, with women.

I caught it that day through all the bullshit. He was crazy about women. That was his weakness, and he hated it.

13

I WAS finally ready for my trip to Las Vegas to see Cully again. It would be the first time in over three years, three years since Jordan had blown himself away in his room, a four-hundred-grand winner.

We had kept in touch, Cully and I. He phoned me a couple of times a month and sent Christmas presents for me and my wife and kids, stuff I recognized that came from the Xanadu Hotel gift shop, where I knew he got them for a fraction of their selling price or, knowing Cully, even for nothing. But still, it was nice of him to do it. I had told Vallie about Cully but never told her about Jordan.

I knew Cully had a good job with the hotel because his secretary answered his phone with 'Assistant to the President.' And I wondered how in a few years he had managed to climb so high. His telephone voice and manner of speaking had changed; he spoke in a lower tone; he was more sincere, more polite, warmer. An actor playing a different part. Over the phone it would be just idle chitchat and gossip about big winners and big losers and funny stories about the characters staying in the hotel. But never anything about himself. Eventually one of us would mention Jordan, usually near the end of the call, or maybe the mention of Jordan would end the call. He was our touchstone.

Vallie packed my suitcase. I was going over the weekend, so I would only have to miss a day's work at my Army Reserve job. And in the far-off distant future, which I smelled, the magazine story would give me the cover for the cops about why I went to Vegas.

The kids were in bed while Vallie was packing my bag because I was leaving early the next morning. She gave me a little smile.

'God, it was terrible the last time you went. I thought you wouldn't come back.'

'I just had to get away then,' I said. 'Things were going bad.'

'Everything's changed since,' Vallie said musingly. 'Three years ago we didn't have money at all. Gee, we were so broke I had to ask my father for some money and I was afraid you'd find out. And you acted as if you didn't love me any more. That trip changed everything. You were different when you came back. You weren't mad at me any more and you were more patient with the kids. And you got work with the magazines.'

I smiled at her. 'Remember, I came back a winner. A few extra grand. Maybe if I'd come back a loser, it would have been a whole different story.'

Vallie snapped the suitcase shut. 'No,' she said. 'You were different. You were happier, happier with me and the kids.'

'I found out what I was missing,' I said.

'Oh, yeah,' she said. 'With all those beautiful hookers in Vegas.'

'They cost too much,' I said. 'I needed my money to gamble.'

It was all kidding around, but part of it was serious. If I told her the truth, that I never looked at another woman, she wouldn't believe me. But I could give good reasons. I had felt so much guilt about being such a lousy husband and father who couldn't give his family anything, who couldn't even make a decent living for them, that I couldn't add to that guilt by being unfaithful to her. And the overriding fact was that we were so lucky in bed together. She was really all I wanted, perfect for me. I thought I was for her.

'Are you going to do some work tonight?' she asked. She was really asking if we were going to make love first so that she could get ready. Then, after we'd made love, usually I would get up to work on my writing and she would fall so soundly asleep she would not stir until morning. She was a great sleeper. I was lousy at it.

'Yes,' I said. 'I want to work. I'm too excited about the trip to sleep anyway.'

It was nearly midnight, but she went into the kitchen to make me a fresh pot of coffee and some sandwiches. I would work until three or four in the morning and then still wake up before she did in the morning.

The worst part about being a writer, anyway for me when I was working well, was the inability to sleep. Lying in bed, I could never turn off the machine in my brain that kept thinking about the novel I was working on. As I lay in the dark, the characters became so real to me that I forgot my wife and my kids and everyday life. But tonight I had another less literary reason. I wanted Vallie to go to sleep so that I could get my big stash of bribe money from its hiding place.

From the bedroom closet way back from its darkest corner I took my old Las Vegas Winner sports jacket and carried it into the kitchen. I had never worn it since I had come home from Las Vegas three years ago. Its bright colours had faded in the darkness of the closet, but it was still pretty garish. I put it on and went into the kitchen. Vallie took one look at it and said, 'Merlyn, you're not going to wear that.'

'My lucky jacket,' I said. 'Besides, it's comfortable for the plane ride.' I knew she had hidden it way back in the closet so that I would never see it and never think to wear it. She hadn't dared throw it out. Now the jacket would come in handy.

Vallie sighed. 'You're so superstitious.'

She was wrong. I was rarely superstitious even though I thought I was a magician, and its really not the same thing.

After Vallie kissed me good-night and went to bed, I had some coffee and looked over the manuscript I had taken from my desk in the bedroom. I did mostly editing for an hour. I took a peek into the bedroom and saw Vallie was sound asleep. I kissed her very lightly. She didn't stir. Now I loved it when she kissed me good-night. The simple, dutiful, wifely kiss that seemed to seal us away from all the loneliness and treacherousness of the outside world. And often lying in bed, in the early-morning hours, Vallie asleep and I not able to sleep, I would kiss her lightly on the mouth, hoping she would wake up to make me feel less lonely by making love. But this time I was aware that I had given her a Judas kiss, partly out of affection, but really to make sure she would not awaken when I dug out the hidden money.

I closed the bedroom door and then went to the hall closet which held the big trunk with all my old manuscripts, the carbon copies of my novel and the original manuscript of the book I had worked on for five years and had earned me three thousand dollars. It was a hell of a lot of paper, all the rewrites and carbons, paper I had thought would make me rich and famous and honoured. I dug underneath to the big reddish folder with its stringed cover. I pulled it out and brought it into the kitchen. Sipping my coffee, I counted out the money.

A little over forty thousand dollars. The money had come rolling in very fast lately. I had become the Tiffany's of bribe-takers, with rich, trusting customers. The twenties, about seven thousand dollars' worth, I left in the envelope. There were thirty-three thousand in hundreds. I put these in five long envelopes I had brought from my desk. Then I crammed the money-filled envelopes into the different pockets of the Vegas Winner sports coat. I zipped up the pockets and hung the jacket on the back of my chair.

In the morning, when Vallie hugged me good-bye, she would feel something in the pockets, but I would just tell her it was some notes for the article I was taking with me to Vegas.

14

WHEN I got off the plane, Cully was waiting for me at the door of the terminal. The airport was still so small I had to walk from the plane, but construction was under way to build another wing to the terminal—Vegas was growing. And so was Cully.

He looked different, taller and slimmer. And he was smartly dressed in a Sy Devore suit and sports shirt. His hair had a different cut. I was surprised when he gave me a hug and said, 'Same old Merlyn.' He laughed at the Vegas Winner sports coat and told me I had to get rid of it.

He had a big suite for me at the hotel with a bar stocked with booze and flowers on the tables. 'You must have a lot of juice,' I said.

'I'm doing good,' Cully said. 'I've given up gambling. I'm on the other side of the tables. You know.'

'Yeah,' I said. I felt funny about Cully now, he seemed so different. I didn't know whether to follow through with my original plan and trust him. In three years a guy could change.

And after all, we had only known each other a few weeks.

But as we were drinking together, he said with real sincerity, 'Kid, I'm really glad to see you. Ever think about Jordan?'

'All the time,' I said.

'Poor Jordan,' Cully said. 'He went out a four-hundred-grand winner. That's what made me give up gambling. And you know, ever since he died, I've had tremendous luck. If I play my cards right, I could wind up top man in this hotel.'

'No shit,' I said. 'What about Gronevelt?'

'I'm his number one boy,' Cully said. 'He trusts me with a lot of stuff. He trusts me like I trust you. While we're at it, I could use an assistant. Anytime you want to move your family to Vegas you got a good job with me.'

'Thanks,' I said. I was really touched. At the same time I wondered about his affection for me. I knew he was not a man who cared about anyone easily. I said, 'About the job I can't answer you now. But I came out here to ask a favour. If you can't do it for me, I'll understand. Just tell me straight, and whatever the answer is, we'll at least have a couple of days together and have a good time.'

'You got it,' Cully said. 'Whatever it is.'

I laughed. 'Wait until you hear,' I said.

For a moment Cully seemed angry. 'I don't give a shit what it is. You got it. If I can do it, you got it.'

I told him about the whole graft operation. That I was taking bribes and that I had thirty-three grand in my jacket that I had to stash in case the whole operation blew up. Cully listened to me intently, watching my face. At the end he was smiling broadly.

'What the hell are you smiling at?' I said.

Cully laughed. 'You sound like a guy confessing to a priest that he committed murder. Shit, what you're doing everybody does if he ever gets the chance. But I have to admit I'm surprised. I can't picture you telling a guy he has to pay blackmail.'

I could feel my face getting red. 'I never asked any of those guys for money,' I said. 'They always come to me. And I never take the money upfront. After I do it for them, they can pay me what they promised or they can stiff me. I don't give a shit.' I grinned at him. 'I'm a soft hustler, not a hooker.'

'Some crook,' Cully said. 'First thing, I think you're too worried. It sounds like the kind of operation that can go on indefinitely. And even if it blows up, the worst that can happen to you is that you lose your job and get a suspended sentence. But you're right, you have to stash the dough in a good place. Those Feds are real bloodhounds, and when they find it, they'll take it all away from you.'

I was interested in the first part of what he said. One of my nightmares was that I would go to jail and Vallie and the kids would be without me. That's why I had kept everything from my wife. I didn't want her to worry. Also, I didn't want her to think less of me. She had an image of me as the pure, uncorrupted artist.

'What makes you think I won't go to jail if I'm caught?' I asked Cully.

'It's a white-collar crime,' Cully said. 'Hell, you didn't stick up a bank or shoot some poor bastard store owner or defraud a widow. You just took dough from some young punks who were trying to get an edge and cut down their Army time. Jesus, that's some unbelievable sham. Guys paying to get *into* the Army. Nobody would believe it. A jury would laugh themselves sick.'

'Yeah, it strikes me funny too,' I said.

Cully was all business suddenly. 'OK, tell me what you want me to do right now. It's done. And if the Feds nail you, promise you'll call me right away. I'll get you out. OK?' He smiled at me affectionately.

I told him my plan. That I would turn in my cash for chips a thousand dollars at a time and gamble but for small stakes. I'd do that in all the casinos in Vegas, and then, when I cashed in my chips for cash, I would just take a receipt and leave the money in the cashier's cages as a gambling credit. The FBI would never think to look in the casinos. And the cash receipts I could stash with Cully and pick up whenever I needed some ready money.

Cully smiled at me. 'Why don't you let me hold your money? Don't you trust me?'

I knew he was kidding, but I handled the crack seriously. 'I thought about that,' I said. 'But what if something happens to you? Like a plane crash. Or you get your gambling bug? I trust you now. But how do I know you won't go crazy tomorrow or next year?'

Cully nodded his head approvingly. Then he asked, 'What about your brother, Artie? You and he are so close. Can't he hold the money for you?'

'I can't ask him to do that for me,' I said.

Cully nodded again. 'Yeah, I guess you can't. He's too honest, right?'

'Right,' I said. I didn't want to go into any long explanation about how I felt. 'What's wrong with my plan? Don't you think it's any good?'

Cully got up and began pacing up and down the room. 'It's not bad,' he said. 'But you don't want to have credits in all the casinos. That looks fishy. Especially if the money stays there a long time. That is really fishy. People only leave their money in the cage until they gamble it away or they leave Vegas. Here's what you do. Buy chips in all the casinos and check them into our cage here. You know, about three or four times a day cash in for a few thousand and take a receipt. So all your cash receipts will be in our cage. Now if the Feds do nose around or write to the hotel, it has to go through me. And I'll cover you.'

I was worried about him. 'Won't that get you into trouble?' I asked him.

Cully sighed patiently. 'I do that stuff all the time. We get a lot of inquiries from Internal Revenue. About how much guys have lost. I just send them old files. There's no way they can check me out. I make sure files don't exist that will help them.'

'Jesus,' I said. 'I don't want my cage record to disappear. I won't be able to collect on my receipts.'

Cully laughed. 'Come on, Merlyn,' he said. 'You're just a two-bit bribe-taker. The Feds don't come in here with a gang of auditors for you. They send a letter or subpoena. Which they will never even think of doing, by the way. Or look at it another way. If you spend the dough and they find out your income exceeded what you earned on your pay, you can say you won it gambling. They can't prove otherwise.'

'And I can't prove I did,' I said.

'Sure you can,' Cully said. 'I'll testify for you, and so will a pit boss and a stickman at the crap table. That you had a tremendous roll with the dice. So don't worry about the deal, no matter how it falls. Your only problem is where to hide the casino cage receipts.'

We both thought that over for a while. Then Cully came up with an answer. 'Do you have a lawyer?' he asked.

'No,' I said, 'but my brother, Artie, has a friend who is a lawyer.'

'Then make out your will,' Cully said. 'In your will you put in that you have cash deposits in this hotel to the amount of thirty-three thousand dollars and you leave it to your wife. No, never mind your brother's lawyer. We'll use a lawyer I know here in Vegas that we can trust. Then the lawyer will mail your copy of the will to Artie in a specially legally sealed envelope. Tell Artie not to open it. That way he won't know anything and he won't be involved. He'll never know. All you have to tell him is that he is not to open the envelope but hold it for you. The lawyer will send a letter to that effect also. There's no way Artie can get into trouble. And he won't know anything. You just dream up a story why you want him to have the will.'

'Artie won't ask me for a story,' I said. 'He'll just do it and never ask a question.'

'That's a good brother you got there,' Cully said. 'But now what do you do with the receipts? The Feds will sniff out a bank vault if you get one. Why don't you just bury it with your old manuscripts like you did the cash? Even if they get a search warrant, they'll never notice those pieces of paper.'

'I can't take that chance,' I said. 'Let me worry about the receipts. What hapens if I lose them?'

Cully didn't catch on or made believe he didn't. 'We'll have records in our file,' he said. 'We just make you sign a receipt certifying that you lost your receipts when you get your money. You just have to sign when you get your cash.'

Of course, he knew what I was going to do. That I would tear up the receipts but not tell him so he could never be sure, so that he couldn't mess with the records of the casino owing me money. It meant that I didn't completely trust him, but he accepted that easily.

Cully said, 'I've got a big dinner laid on tonight for you with some friends. Two of the nicest-looking ladies in the show.'

'No woman for me,' I said.

Cully was amazed. 'Jesus, aren't you tired of just screwing your wife yet? All these years.'

'No,' I said. 'I'm not tired.'

'You think you're going to be faithful to her all your life?' Cully said.

'Yep,' I said, laughing.

Cully shook his head, laughing too. 'Then you'll really be Merlyn the Magician.'

'That's me,' I said.

So we went to dinner, just the two of us. And then Cully came around with me to all the casinos in Vegas as I bought chips in thousand-dollar lots. My Vegas Winner sports jacket really came in handy. At the different casinos we had drinks with pit bosses and shift managers of the casinos and the girls from the shows. They all treated Cully like an important man, and they all had great stories to tell about Vegas. It was fun. When we got back to the Xanadu, I pushed my chips into the cashier's cage and got a receipt for fifteen thousand dollars. I tucked it into my wallet. I hadn't made a bet all night. Cully was hanging all over me.

'I have to do a little gambling,' I said.

Cully smiled crookedly. 'Sure you do, sure you do. As soon as you lose five hundred bucks, I'm going to break your fucking arm.'

At the crap table I pulled out five one-hundred dollar bills and changed them into chips. I made five-dollar bets and bet all the numbers. I won and I lost. I drifted into my old gambling patterns, moving from craps to blackjack and roulette. Soft, easy, dreamy gambling, betting small, winning and losing, playing loose percentages. It was one in the morning when I reached into my pocket and took out two thousand dollars and bought chips. Cully didn't say anything.

I put the chips into my jacket pocket and walked over to the cashier's cage and turned them in for another cash receipt. Cully was leaning against an empty crap table, watching me. He nodded his head approvingly.

'So you've got it licked,' he said.

'Merlyn the Magician,' I said. 'Not one of your lousy degenerate gamblers.' And it was true. I had felt none of the old excitement. There was no urge to take a flyer. I had enough money to buy my family a house and a bankroll for emergencies. I had good sources of income. I was happy again. I loved my wife and was working on a novel. Gambling was fun, that was all. I had lost only two hundred bucks the whole evening.

Cully took me into the coffee shop for a nightcap of milk and hamburgers. 'I have to work during the day,' he said. 'Can I trust you not to gamble?'

'Don't worry,' I said. 'I'll be busy turning the cash into chips all over town. I'll go down to five-hundred-dollar buys so I won't be so noticeable.'

'That's a good idea,' Cully said. 'This town has more FBI agents than dealers.'

He paused for moment. 'You sure you don't want a sleeping

partner? I have some beauties.' He picked up one of the house phones on the ledge of our booth.

'I'm too tired,' I said. And it was true. It was after one in the morning here in Vegas, but New York time was 4 A.M. and I was still on New York time.

'If you need anything, just come up to my office,' he said. 'Even if you just want to kill some time and bullshit.'

'OK, I will,' I said.

The next day I woke up about noon and called Vallie. There was no answer. It was 3 P.M. New York time and it was Saturday. Vallie had probably taken the kids to her father and mother's house out on Long Island. So I called there and got her father. He asked a few suspicious questions about what I was doing in Vegas. I explained I was researching an article. He didn't sound too convinced, and finally Vallie got on the phone. I told her I would catch the Monday plane home and would take a cab from the airport.

We had the usual bullshit talk of husband and wife with such calls. I hated the phone. I told her I wouldn't call again since it was a waste of time and money, and she agreed. I knew she would be at her parents the next day too, and I didn't want to call her there. And I realized too that her going there made me angry. An infantile jealously. Vallie and the kids were my family. They belonged to me; they were the only family I had except Artie. And I didn't want to share them with grandparents. I knew it was silly, but still, I wasn't going to call again. What the hell, it was only two days and she could always call me.

I spent the day going through all the casinos in town on the Strip and the sawdust joints in the centre of town. There I traded my cash for chips in two- and three-hundred-dollar amounts. Again I'd do a little dollar-chip gambling before moving on to another casino.

I loved the dry, burning heat of Vegas, so I walked from casino to casino. I had a late-afternoon lunch in the Sands next to a table of pretty hookers having their before-going-to-work meal. They were young and pretty and high-spirited. A couple of them were in riding togs. They were laughing and telling stories like teenagers. They didn't pay any attention to me, and I ate my lunch as if I weren't paying any attention to them. But I tried to listen to their conversation. Once I thought I heard Cully's name mentioned.

I took a taxi back to the Xanadu. Vegas cabdrivers are friendly and helpful. This one asked me if I wanted some action, and I told him no. When I left the cab, he wished me a pleasant good day and told me the name of a restaurant where they had good Chinese food.

In the Xanadu casino I changed the other casino chips into a cash receipt, which I stuck into my wallet. I now had nine receipts and only a little over ten thousand in cash to convert. I emptied the cash out of my Vegas Winner sports jacket and put it into a regular suit jacket. It was all hundreds and fitted into two regular long white envelopes. Then I slung the Vegas Winner sports jacket over my arm and went up to Cully's office.

There was a whole wing of the hotel tacked on just for administration. I followed the corridor and took an offshoot corridor labelled 'Executive Offices'. I came to one of the shingles that read 'Executive Assistant to the President'. In the outer office was a very pretty young secretary. I gave her my name, and she buzzed the inner office and announced me. Cully came bouncing out with a big handshake and a hug. This new personality of his still threw me off. It was too demonstrative, too outgoing, not what we had been before.

He had a really stylish suite with couch and soft armchairs and low lighting and pictures on the wall, original oil paintings. I couldn't tell if they were any good. He also had three TV screens operating. One showed a corridor of the hotel. Another showed one of the crap tables in the casino in action. The third screen showed the baccarat table. As I watched the first screen, I could see a guy opening his hotel room door in the corridor and leading a young girl in with his hand on her ass.

'Better programmes than I get in New York,' I said.

Cully nodded. 'I have to keep an eye on everything in this hotel,' he said. He pushed buttons on a console on his desk, and the three pictures on the TV's changed. Now we saw a view of the hotel parking lot, a blackjack table in action and the cashier in the coffee shop ringing up money.

I threw the Vegas Winner sports jacket on Cully's desk. 'You can have it now,' I said.

Cully stared at the jacket for a long moment. Then he said absently, 'You converted all your cash?'

'Most of it,' I said. 'I won't need the jacket any more.' I laughed. 'My wife hated it as much as you do.'

Cully picked up the jacket. 'I don't hate it,' he said. 'Gronevelt

125

doesn't like to see it around. What do you think happened to Jordan's?'

I shrugged. 'His wife probably gave all his clothes to the Salvation Army.'

Cully was weighing the jacket in his hand. 'Light,' he said. 'But lucky. Jordan won over four hundred grand wearing it. And then he kills himself. Fucking dumb bastard.'

'Foolish,' I said.

Cully put the jacket gently down on his desk. Then he sat down and rocked back on his chair. 'You know, I thought you were crazy for turning down his twenty grand. And I was really pissed off when you talked me out of taking mine. But it was maybe the luckiest thing that ever happened to me. I would have gambled it away, and then I would have felt like shit. But you know, after Jordan killed himself and I didn't take that money, I got some pride. I don't know how to explain it. But I felt I didn't betray him. And you didn't. And Diane didn't. We were all strangers, and only the three of us cared something about Jordan. Not enough, I guess. Or it didn't mean that much to him. But finally it meant something to me. Didn't you feel that way?'

'No,' I said. 'I just didn't want his fucking money. I knew he was going to knock himself off.'

That startled Cully. 'Bullshit you did. Merlyn the Magician. Fuck you.'

'Not consciously,' I said. 'But way down underneath. I wasn't surprised when you told me. Remember?'

'Yeah,' Cully said. 'You didn't even give a shit.'

I passed that one. 'How about Diane?'

'She took it real hard,' Cully said. 'She was in love with Jordan. You know I fucked her the day of the funeral. Weirdest fuck I ever had. She was crazy wild and crying and fucking. Scared the shit out of me.'

He sighed. 'She spent the next couple of months getting drunk and crying on my shoulder. And then she met this square semi-millionaire, and now she's a straight lady in Minnesota someplace.'

'So what are you going to do with the jacket?' I asked him.

Suddenly Cully was grinning. 'I'm going to give it to Gronevelt. Come on, I want you to meet him anyway.' He got up out of his chair and grabbed the jacket and went out of the office. I followed him. We went down the corridor to another suite of

126

offices. The secretary buzzed us in to Gronevelt's huge private office.

Gronevelt rose from his chair. He looked older than I remembered him. He must be in his late seventies, I thought. He was immaculately dressed. His white hair made him look like a movie star in some character part. Cully introduced us.

Gronevelt shook my hand and then said quietly, 'I read your book. Keep it up. You'll be a big man someday. It's very good.'

I was surprised. Gronevelt went way back in the gambling business, he had been a very bad guy at one time and he was still a feared man in Vegas. For some reason I never thought he was a man who read books. Another cliché shot.

I knew that Saturdays and Sundays were busy times for men like Gronevelt and Cully who ran big Vegas hotels like the Xanadu. They had customer friends from all over the United States who flew in for weekends of gambling and who had to be entertained in many diverse ways. So I thought I would just say hello to Gronevelt and beat it.

But Cully threw the bright red and blue Vegas Winner sports coat on Gronevelt's huge desk and said, 'This is the last one. Merlyn finally gave it up.'

I noticed that Cully was grinning. The favourite nephew teasing the grouchy uncle he knew how to handle. And I noticed that Gronevelt played his role. The uncle who kidded around with his nephew who was the most trouble but in the long run the most talented and the most reliable. The nephew who would inherit.

Gronevelt rang the buzzer for his secretary, and when she came in, he said to her, 'Bring me a big pair of scissors.' I wondered where the hell a secretary for the president of the Xanadu Hotel would get a big pair of scissors at 6 P.M. on a Saturday night. She was back with them in two minutes flat. Gronevelt took the scissors and started cutting my Vegas Winner sports jacket. He looked at me deadpan and said, 'You don't know how much I hated you three guys when you used to walk through my casino wearing these fucking jackets. Especially that night when Jordan won all the money.'

I watched him turn my jacket into a huge pile of jagged pieces on his desk, and then I realized he was waiting for me to answer him. 'You really don't mind winners, do you?' I said.

'It had nothing to do with winning money,' Gronevelt said. 'It was so goddamn pathetic. Cully here wearing that jacket and

127

a degenerate gambler in his heart. He still is and always will be. He's in remission.'

Cully made a gesture of protest, said, 'I'm a businessman,' but Gronevelt waved him off, and Cully fell silent, watching the cut patches of material on the desk.

'I can live with luck,' Gronevelt said. 'But skill and cunning I can't abide.'

Gronevelt was working the cheap fake silk lining of the coat, scissoring it into tiny strips, but it was just to keep his hands busy while he was talking. He spoke directly to me.

'And you, Merlyn, you're one of the worst fucking gamblers I have ever seen and I've been in the business over fifty years. You're worse than a degenerate gambler. You're a romantic gambler. You think you're one of those characters like that Ferber novel where she has that asshole gambler for a hero. You gamble like an idiot. Sometimes you go with percentages, sometimes you go with hunches, another time you go with a system, then you switch to stabbing in thin air, or you're zigging and zagging. Listen you're one of the few people in this world I would tell to give up gambling completely.' And then he put down his scissors and gave me a genuinely friendly smile. 'But what the hell, it suits you.'

I was really a little hurt, and he had seen it. I thought myself a clever gambler, mixing logic with magic. Gronevelt seemed to read my mind. 'Merlyn,' he said. 'I like that name. It sort of suits you. From what I've read he wasn't that great a magician, and neither are you.' He picked up the scissors and started cutting again. 'But then why the hell did you pick that fight with that punk hit man?'

I shrugged. 'I didn't really pick a fight. But you know how it is. I was feeling lousy about leaving my family. Everything was going bad. I was just looking to take it out on somebody.'

'You picked the wrong guy,' Gronevelt said. 'Cully saved your ass. With a little help from me.'

'Thanks,' I said.

'I offered him the job, but he doesn't want it,' Cully said.

That surprised me. Obviously Cully had talked it over with Gronevelt before he offered me the job. And then suddenly I realized that Cully would have to tell Gronevelt all about me. And how the hotel would cover me if the Feds came looking.

'After I read your book, I thought we could use you as a PR man,' Gronevelt said. 'A good writer like you.'

I didn't want to tell him that they were two absolutely different things. 'My wife wouldn't leave New York, she has her family there,' I said. 'But thanks for the offer.'

Gronevelt nodded. 'The way you gamble maybe it's better not living in Vegas. The next time you come into town let's all have dinner together.' We took that for our dismissal and left.

Cully had a dinner date with some high rollers from California that he couldn't break, so I was on my own. He had left a reservation for me for the hotel dinner show that night, so I went. It was the usual Vegas stuff with almost nude chorus girls, dancing acts, a star singer and some vaudeville turns. The only thing that impressed me was a trained bear act.

A beautiful woman came out on the stage with six huge bears, and she made them do all kinds of tricks. After each bear completed a trick, the woman kissed the bear on the mouth and the bear would immediately shamble back into his position at the end of the line. The bears were so furry they looked as completely asexual as toys. But why had the woman made the kiss one of her command signals? Bears didn't kiss as far as I knew. And then I realized the kiss was for the audience, some sort of thrust at the onlookers. And then I wondered if the woman had done so consciously, as a mark of her contempt, a subtle insult. I had always hated the circus and refused to take my kids to see it. And so I never really liked animal acts. But this one fascinated me enough to watch it through to the end. Maybe one of the bears would pull a surprise.

After the show was over, I wandered out into the casino to convert the rest of my money into chips and then convert the chips into cash receipts. It was nearly eleven at night.

I started with craps, and instead of betting small to hold down my losses, I was, all of a sudden, making fifty- and hundred-dollar bets. I was losing about three thousand dollars when Cully came up behind me, leading his high rollers to the table and establishing their credit. He took one sardonic look at my green twenty-five-dollar chips and my bets on the green felt in front of me. 'You don't have to gamble any more, huh?' he said to me. I felt like a jerk, and when the dice sevened out, I took the remainder of my chips to the cashier's cage and turned them into receipts. When I turned around, Cully was waiting for me.

'Let's go have a drink,' he said. And he led me to the cocktail lounge where we used to booze with Jordan and Diane. From that darkened area we looked out at the brightly lit casino. When we sat down, the cocktail waitress spotted Cully and came over immediately.

'So you fell off the wagon,' Cully said. 'That fucking gambling. It's like malaria, always coming back.'

'You too?' I asked.

'A couple of times,' Cully said. 'I never got hurt, though. How much did you lose?'

'Just about two grand,' I said. 'I've turned most of the money into receipts. I'll finish it up tonight.'

'Tomorrow's Sunday,' Cully said. 'The lawyer friend of mine is available, so early in the morning you can make your will and have it mailed to your brother. Then I'm sticking to you like glue until I put you on the afternoon plane to New York.'

'We tried something like that once with Jordan,' I said jokingly.

Cully sighed. 'Why did he do it? His luck was changing. He was going to be a winner. All he had to do was hang in there.'

'Maybe he didn't want to push his luck,' I said. I had to be kidding, Cully said.

The next morning Cully rang my room, and we had breakfast together. After that he drove me down the Vegas Strip to a lawyer's office, where I had my will drawn up and witnessed. I repeated a couple of times that my brother, Artie, was to be mailed a copy of the will, and Cully finally cut in impatiently. 'That's all been explained,' he said. 'Don't worry. Everything will be done exactly right.'

When we left the office, Cully drove me around the city and showed me the new construction going on. The tower building of the Sands Hotel gleamed newly golden in the desert air. 'This town is going to grow and grow,' Cully said.

The endless desert stretched out to the far outlying mountains. 'It has plenty of room,' I said.

Cully laughed. 'You'll see,' he said. 'Gambling is the coming thing.'

We had a light lunch, and then for old times' sake we went down to the Sands and went partners for two hundred bucks each and hit the crap tables. Cully said self-mockingly, 'I have ten passes in my right arm,' so I let him shoot the dice. He was as unlucky as ever, but I noticed he didn't have his heart in it. He didn't enjoy gambling. He sure had changed. We drove to the airport, and he waited with me at the gate until boarding time.

'Call me if you run into any trouble,' Cully said. 'And the next time you come here we'll have dinner with Gronevelt. He likes you and he's a good guy to have on your side.'

I nodded. Then I took the cash receipts out of my pocket. The receipts good for thirty thousand dollars in the casino cage of the Xanadu Hotel. My expenses for the trip, gambling and air fare came to about the other three thousand. I handed the receipts to Cully.

'Keep these for me,' I said. I had changed my mind.

Cully counted the white slips. There were twelve of them. He checked the amounts. 'You trust me with your bankroll?' he asked. 'Thirty grand is a big number.'

'I have to trust somebody,' I said. 'And besides, I saw you turn down twenty grand from Jordan when you were flat on your ass.'

'Only because you shamed me into it,' Cully said. 'OK, I'll take care of this. And if things get real hot, I can loan you cash out of my roll and use these as security. Just so you don't leave any traces.'

'Thanks, Cully,' I said. 'Thanks for the hotel room and the meals and everything. And thanks for helping me out.' I felt a real rush of affection for him. He was one of my few friends. And yet I was surprised when he hugged me good-bye before I got on the plane.

And on the jet rushing through the light into the darker time zones of the East, fleeing so quickly from the descending sun in the West, as we plunged into darkness, I thought about the affection Cully had for me. We knew each other so little. And I thought it was because we both had so few people we could really get to know. Like Jordan. And we had shared Jordan's defeat and surrender into death.

I called from the airport to tell Vallie I had come home a day early. There was no answer. I didn't want to call her at her father's house, so I just caught a taxi to the Bronx. Vallie still wasn't home. I felt the familiar irritated jealousy that she had taken the kids to visit their grandparents in Long Island. But then I thought, what the hell. Why should she spend the Sunday alone in our project apartment when she could have the company of her happy-go-lucky Irish family, her brothers and sisters and their friends, where the kids could go out and play in fresh air and on country grass?

I would wait up for her. She had to be home soon. While I

waited, I called Artie. His wife came to the phone and said Artie had gone to bed early because he wasn't feeling good. I told her not to wake him, it wasn't important. And with a little feeling of panic I asked what was wrong with Artie. She said he just felt tired, he had been working too hard. It wasn't anything even to see the doctor about. I told her I would call Artie at work the next day, and then I hung up.

15

THE next year was the happiest time in my life. I was waiting for my house to be built. It would be the first time I'd own a house of my own, and I had a funny feeling about it. That now finally I would be just like everybody else. I would be separate and no longer dependent on society and other people.

I think this sprang from my growing distaste for the housing project I was living in. By their very good social qualities blacks and whites moved up in the economic scale and became ineligible to stay in the housing project when they earned too much money. And when they moved out, their places were taken by the not-so-well-adjusted. The blacks and whites moving in were the ones who would live there forever. Junkies, alcoholics, amateur pimps, small-scale thieves and spur-of-the-moment rapists.

Before this new invasion the housing project cops beat a strategic retreat. The new kids were wilder and started taking everything apart. Elevators stopped working; hall windows were smashed and never repaired. When I came home from work, there were empty whisky bottles in the hallway and some of the men sitting drunk on the benches outside the buildings. There were wild parties that brought in the regular city cops. Vallie made sure she picked up the kids at the bus stop when they came home from school. She even asked me once if we should move to her father's house until our own house was ready. This was after a ten-year-old black girl had been raped and thrown off the roof of one of the project buildings.

I said no, we'd sweat it out. We would stay. I knew what Vallie was thinking, but she was too ashamed to say it out loud. She was afraid of the blacks. Because she had been educated and conditioned as a liberal, a believer in equality, she couldn't bring herself to accept the fact that she feared all the black people moving in around her.

I had a different point of view. I was realistic, I thought, not a bigot. What was happening was that the city of New York was turning its housing projects into black slums, establishing new ghettos, isolating the blacks from the rest of the white community. In effect using projects as a *cordon sanitaire*. Tiny Harlems whitewashed with urban liberalism. And all the economic dregs of the white working class were being segregated here, the ones too badly educated to earn a living, too maladjusted to keep the family structure together. Those people with a little something on the ball would run for their lives to the suburbs or private homes or commercial apartments in the city. But the balance of power hadn't shifted yet. The whites still outnumbered the blacks two to one. The socially oriented families, black and white, still had a slim majority. I figured the housing project was safe at least for the twelve months we would have to stay there. I really didn't give a shit about anything else. I had, I guess, a contempt for all those people. They were like animals, without free will, content to live from one day to the other with booze and drugs and fucking just to kill time wherever they could find it. It was becoming another fucking orphan asylum. But then how come I was still there? What was I?

A young black woman with four kids lived on our floor. She was solidly built, sexy-looking, full of vibrant good humour and high spirits. Her husband had left her before she moved into the project, and I had never seen him. The woman was a good mother during the day; the kids were always neat, always sent off to school and met by the bus stop. But the mother was not so much on the ball at night. After supper we could see her all dressed up, going out on a date, while the kids were left home alone. Her oldest kid was only ten. Vallie used to shake her head and I told her it was none of her business.

But one night, late, when we were in bed, we heard the scream of fire engines. And we could smell smoke in our apartment. Our bedroom window looked directly across to the black woman's apartment, and like a tableau in a movie, we could see flames dancing in that apartment and the small children running through it. Vallie jumped up in her nightgown, tore a blanket off the bed and ran out of our apartment door. I followed her. We were just in time to see the other apartment door open down the long hallway and four children come running out. Behind them we could see flames in the apartment. Vallie was running down the hallway after them, and I wondered what the hell she was doing. She was running frantically, a blanket in her hand trailing the floor. Then I saw what she had seen. The biggest girl, coming out last, shooing the younger ones before her, had begun to fall. Her back was on fire. Then she was a torch of dark red flame. She fell. As she writhed on the cement floor in agony, Vallie jumped on her and wrapped her in the blanket. Dirty grey smoke rose above them as firemen poured into the hallway with hoses and axes.

The firemen took over, and Vallie was back with me in the apartment. Ambulances were clanging up onto the internal walks of the project. Then suddenly we saw the mother in the apartment opposite us. She was smashing at the glass with her hands, and screaming aloud. Blood poured over her finery. I didn't know what the hell she was doing, and then realized that she was trying to impale herself on the glass fragments. Firemen came up behind her, out of the smoke billowing from the dead flames, the charred furniture. They dragged her away from the window, and then we saw her strapped down on a stretcher being carried into the ambulance.

Again these low-income housing projects, built with no thought for profit, had been so made that the fire could not spread or the smoke become a hazard too quickly to other tenants. Just the one apartment was burned out. The little girl who was on fire would, they said, recover, though severely burned. The mother was already out of the hospital.

Saturday afternoon, a week later, Vallie took the kids to her father's house so that I could work on my book in peace. I was working pretty well when there was a knock at the apartment door. It was a timid knock I could barely hear from where I was working on the kitchen table.

When I opened the door, there was this skinny, creamy chocolate black guy at the door. He had a thin moustache and straightened hair. He murmured his name and I didn't catch it, but I nodded. Then he said, 'I just wanted to thank you and your wife for what you did for my baby.' And I understood that he was the father of the family down the hall, the one that had had the fire.

I asked him if he wanted to come in for a drink. I could see that he was almost close to tears, humiliated and ashamed to be making his thanks. I told him my wife was away, but I would tell her he had come by. He stepped just inside my door, to show that he wouldn't insult me by refusing to come into my house, but he wouldn't take a drink.

I tried my best, but it must have shown that I really hated him. That I had hated him ever since the night of the fire. He was one of the black guys who left their wives and children on welfare to go out and have a good time, to live their own lives. I had read the literature on the broken homes of black families in New York. And how the organization and torments of society made these men leave their wives and children. I understood it intellectually, but emotionally I reacted against it. Who the fuck were they to live their own lives? I wasn't leading my own life.

But then I saw that tears were streaming down that milk chocolate skin. And I noticed he had long eyelashes over soft brown eyes. And then I could hear his words. 'Oh, man,' he said. 'My little girl died this morning. She died in that hospital.' He started to fall away and I caught him and he said, 'She was supposed to get better, the burns weren't that bad, but she just died anyway. I came to visit her and everybody in that hospital looked at me. You know? I was her father? Where was I? What was I doing? Like they blame me. You know?'

Vallie kept a bottle of rye in the living room for her father and brothers when they came to visit. Neither Vallie nor I drank usually. But I didn't know where the hell she kept the bottle.

'Wait a minute,' I said to the man crying before me. 'You need a drink.' I found the bottle in the kitchen closet and got two glasses. We both drank it straight, and I could see he felt better, he composed himself.

And watching him, I realized that he had not come to give his thanks to the would-be saviours of his daughter. He had come to find someone to pour out his grief and his guilt. So I listened and wondered that he had not seen my judgment of him on his face.

He emptied his glass and I poured him more whisky. He slumped back on the sofa tiredly. 'You know, I never wanted to leave my wife and kids. But she was too lively and too strong. I worked hard. I work two jobs and save my money. I want to buy us a house and bring up my children right. But she wants fun, she wants a good time. She's too strong and I had to leave. I tried to see my kids more, she won't let me. If I give her extra money, she spends it on herself and not on the kids. And then, you know, we got further and further apart and I found a woman who liked to live the way I live and I became a stranger to my own children. And now everybody will blame me because my little girl died. Like I'm one of those flying dudes, who leave their old ladies just to follow their nose.'

'Your wife is the one that left them alone,' I said.

The man sighed. 'Can't blame her. She go crazy if she stay home every night. And she didn't have the money for a baby-sitter. I could have put up with her or I could have killed her, one or the other.'

I couldn't say anything, but I watched him and he watched me. I saw his humiliation at telling all this to a stranger and a white stranger. And then I realized that I was the only person to whom he could show his shame. Because I didn't really count and because Vallie had smothered the flames burning his daughter.

'She nearly killed herself that night,' I said.

He burst into tears again. 'Oh,' he said. 'She loves her kids. Leaving them alone don't mean nothing. She loves them all. And she ain't ever going to forgive herself, that's what I'm afraid of. That woman is going to drink herself to death, she's going down, man. I don't know what to do for her.'

There was nothing I could say to this. In the back of my head I was thinking, a day's work wasted, I'd never even get to go over my notes. But I offered him something to eat. He finished up his whisky and rose to go. Again that look of shame and humiliation in his face as he thanked me and my wife once again for what we had done for his daughter. And then he left.

When Vallie came home with the kids that night, I told her what had happened, and she went into the bedroom and wept while I made supper for the kids. And I thought of how I had condemned the man before I ever met him or knew anything about him. How I had just put him in a slot whittled out by the books I had read, the drunks and dopers who had come to live in the project with us. I thought of him fleeing from his own people into another world not so poor and black, escaping the doomed circle he had been born in. And left his daughter to die

136

by fire. He would never forgive himself, his judgment far harsher than that I in my ignorance had condemned him with.

Then a week later a lovey-dovey couple across the hall got into a fight and he cut her throat. They were white. She had a lover on the side who refused to stay on the side. But it wasn't fatal, and the errant wife looked dramatically romantic in her huge white neck bandages when she took her little kids to the school bus.

I knew we were getting out at the right time.

16

AT the Army Reserve office in the armoury the bribe business was booming. And for the first time in my Civil Service career I received an 'Excellent' rating. Because of my bribe rackets, I had studied all the complicated new regulations, and was finally an efficient clerk, the top expert in the field.

Because of this special knowledge, I had devised a shuttle system for my clients. When they finished their six months' active duty and came back to my Reserve unit for meetings and two weeks summer camp, I vanished them. I devised a perfectly legal system for them to beat it. In effect I could offer them a deal where after they did their six months' active duty, they became names on the Army Reserve inactive rosters to be called up only in case of war. No more weekly meetings, no more yearly summer camps. My price went up. Another plus: when I got rid of them, it opened up a valuable slot.

One morning I opened the *Daily News*, and there on the front page was a big photograph of three young men. Two of them were guys I had just enlisted the day before. Two hundred bucks each. My heart gave a big jump and I felt a little sick. What could it be but an exposé of the whole racket? The caper had blown up. I made myself read the caption. The guy in the middle was the son of the biggest politician in the state of New York. And the caption applauded the patriotic enlistment of the politician's son in the Army Reserve. That was all.

Still, that newspaper photo frightened me. I had visions of going to jail and Vallie and the kids being left alone. Of course, I knew her father and mother would take care of them, but I wouldn't be there. I'd lose my family. But then, when I got to the office and told Frank, he laughed and thought it was great. Two of my paying customers on page one of the *Daily News*. Just great. He cut out the photograph and put it on the bulletin board of his Army Reserve unit. It was a great inside joke for us. The major thought it was up on the board to boost unit morale.

That phony scare threw me off guard in a way. Like Frank, I started to believe that the racket could go on forever. And it might have, except for the Berlin crisis, which made President Kennedy decide to call up hundreds of thousands of Reserve troops. Which proved to be very unlucky.

The armoury became a madhouse when the news came out that our Reserve units were being called into the Army for a year's active duty. The draft dodgers who had connived and paid to get into the six months' programme went crazy. They were enraged. What hurt the worst was that here they were, the shrewdest young men in the country, budding lawyers, successful Wall Street operators, advertising geniuses, and they had been outwitted by that dumbest of all creatures, the United States Army. They had been bamboozled with the six months' programme, tricked, conned, sold, never paying attention to the one little catch. That they could be called up to active duty and be back in the Army again. City slickers being taken by the hicks. I wasn't too pleased by it either, though I congratulated myself for never having become a member of the Reserves for the easy money. Still, my racket was shot to hell. No more tax-free income of a thousand dollars a month. And I was to move into my new house on Long Island very soon. But still, I never realized that this would bring on the catastrophe I had long foreseen. I was too busy processing the enormous paperwork involved to get my units officially on active duty.

There were supplies and uniforms to be requisitioned, all kinds of training orders to be issued. And then there was the wild stampede to get out of the one-year recall. Everybody knew the Army had regulations for hardship cases. Those that had been in the Reserve programme for the last three or four years and had nearly finished their enlistment were especially stunned. During those years their careers had prospered, they had gotten married, they made kids. They had the military lords of America beat. And then it all became an illusion.

But remember, these were the sharpest kids in America, the future business giants, judges, show business whizbangs. They didn't take it lying down. One young guy, a partner in his father's seat on the Wall Street Exchange, had his wife committed to a psychiatric clinic, then put in papers for a hardship discharge on the grounds that his wife had had a nervous breakdown. I forwarded the documents complete with official letters from doctors and the hospital. It didn't work. Washington had received thousands of cases and taken a stand that nobody would get out on hardship. A letter came back saying the poor husband would be recalled to active duty and then the Red Cross would investigate his hardship claim. The Red Cross must have done a good job because a month afterward, when the guy's unit was shipped to Fort Lee, Virginia, the wife with the nervous breakdown came into my office to apply for necessary papers to join him down at camp. She was cheerful and obviously in good health. In such good health that she hadn't been able to go along with the charade and stay in the hospital. Or maybe the doctors wouldn't go that far out on a limb to keep the deception going.

Mr Hiller called me up about his son, Jeremy. I told him there was nothing I could do. He pressed me and pressed me, and I said jokingly that if his son was a homosexual, he might be discharged from the Army Reserve and not called to active duty. There was a long pause at the other end of the phone, and then he thanked me and hung up. Sure enough, two days later Jeremy Hiller came and filed the necessary papers to get out of the Army on the grounds he was a homosexual. I told him that it would always be on his record. That sometime later in life he might regret having such an official record. I could see that he was reluctant, and then he finally said, 'My father says it's better than being killed in a war.'

I sent the papers through. They were returned from Governors Island, First Army HQ. After Pfc. Hiller was recalled, his case would be evaluated by a Regular Army board. Another strikeout.

I was surprised that Eli Hemsi had not given me a call. The clothing manufacturer's son, Paul, had not even shown his face at the armoury since the recall to active duty notices had been sent out. But that mystery was solved when I received papers through the mail from a doctor famous for his book publications on psychiatry. These documents certified that Paul Hemsi had received electric shock treatments for a nervous condition over the past three months and could not be recalled to active duty, it would be disastrous to his health. I looked up the pertinent Army regulation. Sure enough, Mr Hemsi had found a way out of the Army. He must have been getting advice from people higher up than me. I forwarded the papers on to Governors Island. Sure enough, they finally came back. And with them special orders discharging Paul Hemsi from the United States Army Reserve. I wondered what that deal had cost Mr Hemsi.

I tried to help everybody who put in for a hardship discharge. I made sure the documents got down to Governors Island HQ and made special calls to check up on them. In other words, I was as cooperative as I could be to all my clients. But Frank Alcore was the opposite.

Frank had been recalled with his unit to active duty. And he felt it a point of honour to go. He made no effort to get a hardship discharge, though with his wife and kids and his old parents he had a good case. And he had very little sympathy for anybody in his units trying to get out of the one-year recall. As chief administrative officer of his battalion, both as a civilian and the battalion sergeant major, he sat on all the requests for hardship discharge. He made it as tough as he could for all of them. None of his men beat the recall to active duty, not even those who had legitimate grounds. And a lot of those guys he sat on were guys who had paid him top dollars to buy their enlistment in the six months' programme. By the time Frank and his units left the armoury and shipped to Fort Lee there was a lot of bad blood.

I got kidded about not having been caught in the Army Reserve programme, that I must have known something. But with that kidding there was respect. I had been the only guy in the armoury not to have been sucked in by the easy money and the absence of danger. I was sort of proud of myself. I had really thought it all out years ago. The monetary rewards were not enough to make up for the small percentage of danger involved. The odds were a thousand to one against being called to active duty, but I had still resisted. Or maybe I could see into the future. The irony was that a lot of WW II soldiers had been caught in the trap. And they couldn't believe it. Here they were, guys who had fought three or four years in the old war and now back in green fatigues. True, most of the oldtimers would never see combat or be in danger, but still, they were pissed off. It didn't seem fair. Only Frank Alcore didn't seem to mind. 'I took the gravy,' he said. 'Now I have to pay for it.' He smiled at me. 'Merlyn, I always thought you were a dummy, but you look pretty smart right now.'

At the end of the month, when everybody shipped out, I bought Frank a present. It was a wristwatch with all kinds of shit on it to show compass directions and time of day. Absolutely shockproof. It cost me two hundred bucks, but I really liked Frank. And I guess I felt a little guilty because he was going and I wasn't. He was touched by the gift and gave me an affectionate half hug. 'You can always hock it when your luck is running bad,' I said. And we both laughed.

For the next two months the armoury was strangely empty and quiet. Half the units had gone on active duty in the recall pro- gramme. The six months' programme was dead; didn't look like such a good deal any more. I was out of business, as far as my racket was concerned. There was nothing to do, so I worked on my novel at the office. The major was out a lot, and so was the Regular Army sergeant. And with Frank on active duty I was in the office all alone most of the time. On one of these days a young guy came in and sat at my desk. I asked him what I could do for him. He asked me if I remembered him. I did, vaguely, and then he said his name, Murray Nadelson. 'You took care of me as a favour. My wife had cancer.'

And then I remembered the scene. It had happened almost two years ago. One of my happy clients had arranged for me to meet with Murray Nadelson. The three of us had lunch together. The client was a sharpshooting Wasp Wall Street broker named Buddy Stove. A very soft-selling supersalesman. And he had told me the problem. Murray Nadelson's wife had cancer. Her treat- ment was expensive, and Murray couldn't afford to pay his way into the Army Reserve. Also, he was scared to death of getting inducted for two years and being shipped overseas. I asked why he didn't apply for a hardship deferment based on his wife's health. He had tried that, and it had been refused.

That didn't sound right, but I let it pass. Buddy Stove explained that one of the big attractions of the six months' active-duty programme was that the duty would be done in the States and Murray Nadelson could have his wife come down to live outside whatever training base he would be shipped to. After his six months they also wanted the deal where he would be transferred to the control group so that he wouldn't have to come to meetings. He really had to be with his wife as much as possible.

I nodded my head. OK, I could do it. Then Buddy Stove threw the curveball. He wanted all of it done for free. No charge. His friend Murray couldn't spend a penny.

Meanwhile, Murray couldn't look me in the eye. He kept his head down. I figured it was a hustle except that I couldn't imagine anybody laying that hex on his wife, saying that she had cancer, just to get out of paying some money. And then I had a vision. What if this whole thing blew up someday and the papers printed that I made a guy whose wife had cancer pay a bribe to take care of him? I would look like the worst villain in the world, even to myself. So I said, sure, OK, and said something to Murray about I hoped his wife would be OK. And that ended the lunch.

I had been just a little pissed off. I had made it a policy of enlisting anybody in the six months' programme who said he couldn't afford the money. That had happened a good many times. I charged it off to goodwill. But the transfer to a control group and beating five and a half years of Reserve duty was a special deal that was worth a lot of money. This was the first time I had been asked to give that away free. Buddy Stove himself had paid five hundred bucks for that particular favour, plus his two hundred for being enlisted.

Anyway, I had everything necessary done smoothly and efficiently. Murray Nadelson served his six months; then I vanished him into the control group, where he would be just a name on a roster. Now what the hell was Murray Nadelson doing at my desk? I shook his hand and waited.

'I got a call from Buddy Stove,' Murray said. 'He was recalled from the control group. They need his MOS in one of the units that went on active duty.'

'Tough luck for Buddy,' I said. My voice wasn't too sympathetic. I didn't want him to get the idea I was going to help.

But Murray Nadelson was looking me right in the eyes as if he were getting up the nerve to say something he found hard to say. So I leaned back in my chair and tilted it back and said, 'I can't do anything for him.'

Nadelson shook his head determinedly. 'He knows that.'

He paused a moment. 'You know I never thanked you properly for all the things you did for me. You were the only one who helped. I wanted to tell you that just one time. I'll never forget what you did for me. That's why I'm here. Maybe I can help you.'

Now I was embarrassed. I didn't want him offering me money at this late date. What was done was done. And I liked the idea of having some good deeds on the records I kept on myself.

'Forget it,' I said. I was still wary. I didn't want to ask how his wife was doing, I never had believed that story. And I felt uncomfortable, his being so grateful for my sympathy when it had been all public relations.

'Buddy told me to come see you,' Nadelson said. 'He wanted to warn you that there are FBI men all over Fort Lee questioning the guys in your units. You know, about paying to get in. They ask questions about you and about Frank Alcore. And your friend Alcore looks like he's in big trouble. About twenty of the men have given evidence that they paid him off. Buddy says there will be a grand jury in New York to indict him in a couple of months. He doesn't know about you. He wanted me to warn you to be careful about anything you say or do. And that if you need a lawyer, he'll get one for you.'

For a moment I couldn't even see him. The world had literally gone dark. I felt so sick that a wave of nausea almost made me throw up. My chair came forward. I had frantic visions of the disgrace, my being arrested, Vallie horrified, her father angry, my brother Artie's shame and disappointment in me. It was no longer a happy lark, my revenge against society. But Nadelson was waiting for me to say something.

'Jesus Christ,' I said. 'How did they get on to it? There hasn't been any action since the recall. What put them on the track?'

Nadelson looked a little guilty for his fellow bribe-givers. 'Some of them were so pissed off about getting recalled they wrote anonymous letters to the FBI about paying money to enlist in the six months' programme. They wanted to get Alcore into trouble, they blamed him. Some of them were pissed off because he fought them when they tried to beat the recall. And then down in camp he's a very gung-ho sergeant major, and they don't like that. So they wanted to get him into trouble, and they did.'

My mind was racing. It was nearly a year since I had seen

Cully in Vegas and stashed my money. Meanwhile, I had accumulated another fifteen thousand dollars. Also, I was due to move into my new house in Long Island very soon. Everything was breaking at the worst possible time. And if the FBI were talking to everybody down at Fort Lee, they would at least be talking to over a hundred guys I had taken money from. How many of them would admit to paying me off?

'Is Stove sure there's going to be a grand jury on Frank?' I asked Nadelson.

'There has to be,' Murray said. 'Unless the government covers the whole thing up, you know, kicks it under the rug.'

'Any chance of that?' I asked.

Murray Nadelson shook his head. 'No. But Buddy seems to think you may beat it. All the guys you had dealings with think you're a good guy. You never pushed for money, like Alcore did. Nobody wants to get you in trouble, and Buddy is spreading the word down there not to get you involved.'

'Thank him for me,' I said.

Nadelson stood up and shook my hand. 'I just want to thank you again,' he said. 'If you should need a character witness to testify for you, or you want to refer the FBI to me, I'll be waiting and do my best.'

I shook his hand. I really felt grateful. 'Is there anything I can do for you?' I said. 'Any chance of your being called up from the control group?'

'No,' Nadelson said. 'I have a baby son, you remember. And my wife died two months ago. So I'm safe.'

I'll never forget his face when he said this. The voice itself was filled with bitter self-loathing. And his face had on it a look of shame and hatred. He blamed himself for being alive. And yet there was nothing he could do except follow the course that life had laid out for him. To take care of his baby son, to go to work in the morning, to obey the request of a friend and come here to warn me and to speak a thanks to me for something I had done for him which he had felt important to him at the time and which really meant nothing to him now. I said I was sorry about his wife, I was a believer now all right, he was the real McCoy all right. I felt like shit for ever thinking that about him. And maybe he had saved that for the last because years ago, when he had kept his head down as Buddy Stove begged for him, he must have known that I thought they were both lying. It was a tiny revenge, and he was very welcome to it.

I spent a jittery week before the axe finally fell. It was on a Monday, and I was surprised when the major came into the office bright and early, for him, on a Monday. He gave me a funny look as he went on into his private office.

Punctually at ten two men walked in and asked for the major. I knew who they were right away. They were almost exactly according to literature and movies; dressed conservatively in suits and ties, wearing deadly Waspish fedoras. The older one was about forty-five with a craggy face that was calmly bored. The other one was just a little out of sync. He was much younger, and he had the tall, stringy physique of a nonathlete. Underneath his padded conservative suit was a very skinny frame. His face was just a little callow but handsome in a very good-natured way. I showed them into the major's office. They were with him for about thirty minutes; then they came out and stood in front of my desk. The older one asked formally, 'Are you John Merlyn?'

'Yes,' I said.

'Could we talk to you in a private room? We have your officer's permission.'

I got up and led them into one of the rooms that served as a Reserve unit HQ on meeting nights. Both of them immediately flipped open their wallets to show green ID cards. The older one introduced himself. 'I'm James Wallace of the Federal Bureau of Investigation. This is Tom Hannon.'

The guy named Hannon gave me a friendly smile. 'We want to ask you a few questions. But you don't have to answer them without consulting a lawyer. But if you do answer us, anything you say can be used against you. OK?'

'OK,' I said. I sat down at one end of the table, and they sat down, one on each side of the table so that I was sandwiched.

The older one, Wallace, asked, 'Do you have any idea why we're here?'

'No,' I said. I had made up my mind that I wouldn't volunteer even one word, that I wouldn't make any wisecracks. That I wouldn't put on any act. They would know I had an idea of why they were here, but so what?

Hannon said, 'Do you of your own personal knowledge have any information you can give about Frank Alcore taking bribes from reservists for any reason whatsoever?'

'No,' I said. There was no expression on my face. I had made up my mind not to be an actor. No starts of surprise, no smiles, nothing that could spur additional questions or attacks. Let them think I was covering for a friend. That would be normal even if I were not guilty.'

Hannon said, 'Have you ever taken money from any reservist for any reason whatsoever?'

'No,' I said.

Wallace said very slowly, very deliberately, 'You know all about this. You enlisted young men subject to the draft only when they paid you certains sums of money to do so. You know that you and Frank Alcore manipulated those lists. If you deny this, you are lying to a federal officer, and that is a crime. Now I ask you again, have you ever taken money or any other inducement to favour the enlistment of one individual over the other?'

'No,' I said.

Hannon laughed suddenly. 'We have your buddy Frank Alcore nailed. We have testimony that you two were partners. And that maybe you were in league with other civilian administrators or even officers in this building to solicit bribes. If you talk to us and tell us all you know, it could be a lot better for you.'

There hadn't been any question, so I just looked at him and didn't answer.

Suddenly Wallace said in his calm, even voice, 'We know you're the kingpin of this operation.' And then for the first time I broke my rules. I laughed. It was so natural a laugh that they couldn't take offence. In fact, I saw Hannon smile a little.

The reason I laughed was the word 'kingpin'. For the first time the whole thing struck me as something right out of a grade B movie. And I laughed because I had expected Hannon to say something like that, he looked callow enough. I had thought Wallace was the dangerous man, maybe because he was obviously in charge.

And I laughed because now I knew they were so obviously on the wrong track. They were looking for a really sophisticated conspiracy, an organized 'ring' with a 'mastermind'. Otherwise it wouldn't be worth the time of these heavy hitters from the FBI. They didn't know it was just a bunch of small-time clerks hustling to make an extra buck. They forgot and didn't understand that this was New York, where everybody broke a law every day in one form or another. They couldn't conceive of the notion that *everybody* would have the nerve to be crooked on his own. But I didn't want them to get pissed off about my laughing, so I looked Wallace right in the eye. 'I wish I were a kingpin of something,' I said ruefully, 'instead of a lousy clerk.'

Wallace looked at me intently and then said to Hannon, 'Do you have any more?' Hannon shook his head. Wallace stood up. 'Thank you for answering our questions.' At the same moment Hannon stood up, and so did I. For a moment we were all there standing close together, and without even thinking about it I stuck out my hand and Wallace shook it. I did the same thing with Hannon. And then we walked out of the room together and down the hall to my office. They nodded good-bye to me as they kept on going to the stairs that would lead them downstairs and out of the building, and I went into my office.

I was absolutely cool, not nervous. Not even a little bit. I wondered about my offering to shake hands. I think it was that act that broke the tension in me. But why did I do it? I think it was out of some sort of gratitude, that they hadn't tried to humiliate me or browbeat me. That they had kept the questioning within civilized limits. And I recognized that they had a certain pity for me. I was obviously guilty, but on such a small scale. A poor lousy clerk hustling a few extra bucks. Sure, they would have put me in jail if they could, but their hearts hadn't been in it. Or maybe it was just too small potatoes for them to exert themselves. Or maybe they couldn't help laughing at the crime itself. Guys paying to get *into* the Army. And then I laughed. Forty-five grand wasn't a few lousy bucks. I was letting self-pity carry me away.

As soon as I got back into my office, the major appeared in the doorway of the inner office and motioned me in to join him. The major had all his decorations on his uniform. He had fought in WW II and Korea, and there were at least twenty ribbons on his chest.

'How did you make out?' he asked. He was smiling a little.

I shrugged. 'OK, I guess.'

The major shook his head in wonderment. 'They told me it's been going on for years. How the hell did you guys do it?' He shook his head in admiration.

'I think it's bullshit,' I said. 'I never saw Frank take a dime off anybody. Just some guys pissed off about being recalled to active duty.'

'Yeah,' the major said. 'But down at Fort Lee they're cutting orders to fly about a hundred of those guys to New York to testify before a grand jury. That's not bullshit.' He gazed at me smilingly for a moment. 'What outfit were you in against the Germans?'

'Fourth Armoured,' I said.

'You've got a Bronze Star on your record,' the major said. 'Not much but something.' He had the Silver Star and Purple Heart among the ribbons on his chest.

'No, it wasn't,' I said. 'I evacuated French civilians under shellfire. I don't think I ever killed a German.'

The major nodded. 'Not much,' he agreed. 'But it's more than those kids ever did. So if I can help, let me know. OK?'

'Thanks,' I said.

And as I got up to go, the major said angrily almost to himself, 'Those two bastards started to ask me questions, and I told them to go fuck themselves. They thought I might be in on that shit.' He shook his head. 'OK,' he said, 'just watch your ass.'

Being an amateur criminal really doesn't pay. I started reacting to things like a murderer in a film showing the tortures of psychological guilt. Every time the doorbell to my apartment rang at an unusual time my heart really jumped. I thought it was the cops or the FBI. And of course, it was just one of the neighbours, one of Vallie's friends, dropping by to chat or borrow something. At the office the FBI agents dropped by a couple of times a week, usually with some young guy that they were obviously identifying me to. I figured it was some reservist who had paid his way into the six months' programme. One time Hannon came in to chat, and I went downstairs to a luncheonette to get coffee and sandwiches for us and the major. As we sat around chatting, Hannon said to me in the nicest way imaginable, 'You're a good guy, Merlyn, I really hate the idea of sending you to jail. But you know, I've sent a lot of nice guys to jail. I always think what a shame. If they'd just helped themselves a little bit.'

The major leaned back in his chair to watch my reaction. I just shrugged and ate my sandwich. My attitude was that it was pointless to give any answer to such remarks. It would lead to a general discussion about the whole bribe business. In any general discussion I might say something that in some way could help the investigation. So I said nothing. I asked the major if I could have a couple of days off to help my wife with the Christmas shopping. There was not really that much work and we had a new civilian in the office to replace Frank Alcore and he could mind the store while I was out. The major said sure. Also, Hannon had been dumb. His remark about sending a lot of nice guys to jail was dumb. He was too young to have sent a lot of nice guys or bad guys to jail. I had him tabbed for a rookie, a nice rookie,

148

but not the guy that was going to send me to jail. And if he did, I would be his first one.

We chatted a bit and Hannon left. The major was looking at me with a new respect. And then he said, 'Even if they can't pin anything on you, I suggest you look for a new job.'

Christmas was always a big thing with Vallie. She loved shopping for presents for her mother and father and the kids and me and her brothers and sisters. And this particular Christmas she had more money to spend than she had ever had before. The two boys had bicycles waiting for them in their closet. She had a great imported Irish wool buttoned sweater for her father and an equally expensive Irish lace shawl for her mother. I don't know what she had for me. She always kept that a secret. And I had to keep my present a secret from her. My present for her had been no problem. I had bought, for cash, a small diamond ring, the first piece of real jewelry I'd ever given her. I'd never given her an engagement ring. In those long ago years neither one of us believed in that kind of bourgeois nonsense. After ten years she had changed, and I didn't really give a damn one way or the other. I knew it would make her happy.

So on Christmas Eve the kids helped her decorate the tree while I did some work in the kitchen. Valerie still had no idea of the trouble I was in at my job. I wrote some pages on my novel and then went in to admire the tree. It was all silver with red and blue and golden bells gilded over with rough silvery braiding. On the top was a luminous star. Vallie never used electric lights. She hated them on a Christmas tree.

The kids were all excited, and it took us a long time to get them to bed and stay there. They kept sneaking out, and we didn't dare get tough with them, not Christmas Eve. Finally they wore out and fell asleep. I gave them a final check. They had on their fresh pyjamas for Santa Claus, and they had all been bathed and their hair brushed. They looked so beautiful that I couldn't believe they were my kids, that they belonged to me. At that moment I really loved Vallie. I felt that I was really lucky.

I went back into the living room. Vallie was stacking gaily wrapped Christmas packages bright with Christmas seals beneath the tree. There seemed to be an enormous number of them. I went and got my package for her and put it under the tree.

'I couldn't get you much,' I said slyly. 'Only one little present.'

I knew she would never suspect that she was getting a real diamond ring.

She smiled at me and gave me a kiss. She never cared really what she got for Christmas, she loved buying presents for others, for the kids especially and then for me and her family. Her father and mother and brothers and sisters. The kids got four or five presents. And there was one super-duper bicycle that I was sorry she had bought. It was a two-wheeled bike for my oldest son, and I was sorry because I would have to put it together. And I didn't have the faintest idea how.

Vallie opened a bottle of wine and made some sandwiches. I opened the huge carton that held the different parts of the bicycle. I spread everything out over the living-room floor, plus three sheets of printed instructions and diagrams. I took one look and said, 'I give up.'

'Don't be silly,' Vallie said. She sat down cross-legged on the floor, sipping wine and studying the diagrams. Then she started to work. I was the idiot helper. I went and got the screwdriver and the wrench and held the necessary parts so that she could screw them together. It was nearly three o'clock in the morning before we finally got the damn thing whole. By that time we had finished the wine and we were nervous wrecks. And we knew the kids would spring out of bed as soon as they woke up. We'd get only about four hours' sleep. And then we would have to drive to Vallie's parents' house for a long day of celebration and excitement.

'We'd better get to bed,' I said.

Vallie spread out on the floor. 'I think I'll just sleep here,' she said.

I lay down beside her, and then we both rolled over on our sides so that we could hug each other tight. We lay there blissfully tired and content. At that moment there was a loud knock on the door. Vallie got up quickly, a look of surprise on her face, and glanced at me questioningly.

In a fraction of a second my guilty mind built a whole scenario. It was, of course, the FBI. They had deliberately waited until Christmas Eve, until I was psychologically off guard. They were here with a search-and-arrest warrant. They would find the fifteen thousand dollars I had hidden in the house and take me away to jail. They would offer to let me spend Christmas with my wife and kids if I confessed. Otherwise I would be humiliated: Vallie would hate me for getting arrested on Christmas. The kids would cry, they would be traumatized forever.

I must have looked sick because Vallie said to me, 'What's wrong?' Again there was a loud knocking on the door. Vallie went out of the living room and down the hall to answer it. I could hear her talking to someone, and I went out to take my medicine. She was coming back down the hall and turning into the kitchen. In her arms were four bottles of milk.

'It was the milkman,' she said. 'He delivered early so that he could get back to his family before his kids woke up. He saw the lights under our door, so he knocked to wish us a Merry Christmas. He's a nice man.' She went into the kitchen.

I followed her in and sat weakly in one of the chairs. Vallie sat on my lap. 'I'll bet you thought it was some crazy neighbour or crook,' she said. 'You always think the worst will happen.' She kissed me fondly. 'Let's got to bed.' She gave me a more lingering kiss and so we went to bed. We made love and then she whispered, 'I love you.' 'Me too,' I said. And then I smiled in the darkness. I was easily the most chickenshit petty thief in the Western world.

But three days after Christmas a strange man came into my office and asked me if my name was John Merlyn. When I said yes, he handed me a folded letter. As I opened it he walked out. The letter had printed in Old English heavy letters:

UNITED STATES DISTRICT COURT

then in plain capital printing:

SOUTHERN DISTRICT OF NEW YORK

Then in block lines my name and address and off to the far end GREETING: in capital letters.

Then it read.

'WE COMMAND YOU, that all singular business and excuses being laid aside, you and each of you appear and attend before the GRAND INQUEST of the body of the people of the United States of America'—and then went on to give times and place and concluded 'alleged violation Title 18, U.S. Code.' It went on to say that if I didn't appear I would be in contempt of Court and liable to penalties of the law.

Well at least now I knew what law I had broken. Title 18, U.S. Code. I'd never heard of it. I read it over again. I was fascinated by the first sentence. As a writer I loved the way it

151

read. They must have taken it from the old English law. And it was funny how clear and concise lawyers could be when they wanted to be, no room for misunderstanding. I read that sentence over again 'WE COMMAND YOU, that all singular business and excuses being laid aside, you and each of you appear and attend before the GRAND INQUEST of the body of the people of the United States of America.'

It was great. Shakespeare could have written it. And now that it had finally happened I was surprised that I felt a sort of elation, an urgency to get it over with, win or lose. At the end of the working day, I called Las Vegas and got Cully in his office. I told him what had happened and that in a week I would appear before a grand jury. He told me to sit tight, not to worry. He would be flying in to New York the next day and he would call my house from his hotel in New York.

BOOK FOUR

17

IN the four years since Jordan's death, Cully had made himself Gronevelt's right-hand man. No longer a countdown artist, except in his heart, he seldom gambled. People called him by his real name, Cully Cross. His telephone page code was Xanadu Two. And most important of all, Cully now had 'The Pencil', that most coveted of Las Vegas powers. With the scribbling of his initials he could bestow free rooms, free food and free liquor to his favoured customers and friends. He did not have unrestricted use of 'The Pencil', a royal right reserved for hotel owners and the more powerful casino managers, but that too would come.

Cully had taken Merlyn's call on the casino floor, in the blackjack pit, where table number three was under suspicion. He promised Merlyn he would come to New York and help him. Then he went back to watching table three.

The table had been losing money every day for the last three weeks. By Gronevelt's percentage law this was impossible; there must be a sham. Cully had spied from the Eye in the Sky, rerun the videotapes monitoring the table, watched in person, but he still couldn't figure out what was happening. And he didn't want to report it to Gronevelt until he had solved the problem. He felt the table was having a run of bad luck, but he knew Gronevelt would never accept that explanation. Gronevelt believed that the house could not lose over the long run, that the laws of percentage were not subject to chance. As gamblers believed mystically in their luck so Gronevelt believed in percentages. His tables could never lose.

After taking Merlyn's call, Cully went by table three again.

Expert in all the shams, he made a final decision that the percentages had simply gone crazy. He would give a full report to Gronevelt and let him make the decision on whether to switch the dealers around or fire them.

Cully left the huge casino and took the staircase by the coffee shop to the second floor that led to the executive suites. He checked his own office for messages and then went on to Gronevelt's office. The secretary told him that Gronevelt had gone to his living suite in the hotel. He had the secretary call Gronevelt to see if it was OK to go to him and then he went.

He always marvelled at how Gronevelt had set himself up a home right there in the Xanadu Hotel. On the second floor was an enormous corner suite, but to get to it, you had to be buzzed into a huge outside terrace that had a swimming pool and a lawn of bright green artificial grass, a green so bright you knew it could never last for more than a week in the Vegas desert sun. There was another huge door into the suite itself, and again you had to be buzzed in.

Gronevelt was alone. He had on white flannels and an open shirt. The man looked amazingly healthy and youthful for his over seventy years. Gronevelt had been reading. His book lay opened on the velvet tan couch.

Gronevelt motioned Cully toward the bar and Cully made himself a scotch and soda and the same for Gronevelt. They sat facing each other.

'That losing table in the blackjack pit is straight,' Cully said. 'At least as far as I can see.'

'Not possible,' Gronevelt said. 'You've learned a lot in the last four years, but the one thing you refuse to accept is the law of percentages. It's not possible for that table to lose that amount of money over a three-week period without something fishy going on.'

Cully shrugged. 'So what do I do?'

Gronevelt said calmly, 'I'll give the order to the casino manager to fire the dealers. He wants to shift them to another table and see what happens. I know what will happen. It's better to fire them just like that.'

'OK,' Cully said. 'You're the boss.' He took a sip from his drink. 'You remember my friend Merlyn, the guy who writes books?'

Gronevelt nodded. 'Nice kid,' he said.

Cully put down his glass. He really didn't like booze, but

Gronevelt hated to drink alone. He said, 'That chickenshit caper he's involved in blew up. He needs my help. I have to fly into New York next week to see our collection people, so I thought I'd just go earlier and leave tomorrow if that's OK with you.'

'Sure,' Gronevelt said. 'If there's anything I can do, let me know. He's a good writer.' He said this as if he had to have an excuse to help. Then he added, 'We can always give him a job out here.'

'Thanks,' Cully said. 'Before you fire those dealers, give me one more shot. If you say it's a sham, then it is. It just pisses me off that I can't figure it out.'

Gronevelt laughed. 'OK,' he said. 'If I were your age, I'd be curious too. Tell you what, get the videotapes sent down here and we'll watch them together and go over a few things. Then you can catch the plane for New York tomorrow with a fresh mind. OK? Just have the tapes sent down for the night shifts, covering eight P.M. to two A.M. so we cover the busy times after the shows break.'

'Why do you figure those times?' Cully asked.

'Has to be,' Gronevelt said. When Cully picked up the phone, Gronevelt said, 'Call room service and order us something to eat.'

As the two of them ate, they watched the video films of the losing table. Cully couldn't enjoy his meal, he was so intent on the film. But Gronevelt hardly seemed to be glancing at the console screen. He ate calmly and slowly, relishing the half bottle of red wine that came with his steak. The film suddenly stopped as Gronevelt pushed the off button on his console panel.

'You didn't see it?' Gronevelt asked.

'No,' Cully said.

'I'll give you a hint,' Gronevelt said. 'The pit boss is clean. But not the floorwalker. One dealer on that table is clean, but the other two are not. It all happens after the dinner show breaks. Another thing. The crooked dealers give a lot of five-dollar reds for change or payoffs. A lot of times when they could give twenty-five-dollar chips. Do you see it now?'

Cully shook his head. 'Paint would show.'

Gronevelt leaned back and finally lit one of his huge Havana cigars. He was allowed one a day and always smoked it after dinner when he could. 'You didn't see it because it was so simple,' he said.

Gronevelt made a call down to the casino manager. Then he

flicked the video switch on to show the suspected blackjack table in action. On the screen Cully could see the casino manager come behind the dealer. The casino manager was flanked by two security men in plain clothes, not armed guards.

On the screen the casino manager dipped his hand into the dealer's money trays and took out a stack of red five-dollar chips. Gronevelt flicked off the screen.

Ten minutes later the casino manager came into the suite. He threw a stack of five-dollar chips on Gronevelt's desk. To Cully's surprise the stack of chips did not fall apart.

'You were right,' the casino manager said to Gronevelt.

Cully picked up the round red cylinder. It looked like a stack of five-dollar chips, but it was actually a five-dollar-chip-size cylinder with a hollow case. In the bottom the base moved inward on springs. Cully fooled around with the base and took it off with the scissors Gronevelt handed him. The red hollow cylinder, which looked like a stack of ten five-dollar red chips, disgorged five one-hundred-dollar black chips.

'You see how it works,' Gronevelt said. 'A buddy comes into the game and hands over this five stack and gets change. The dealer puts it in a rack in front of the hundreds, presses it, and the bottom gobbles up the hundreds. A little later he makes change to the same guy and dumps out five hundred dollars. Twice a night, a thousand bucks a day tax-free. They get rich in the dark!'

'Jesus,' Cully said. 'I'll never keep up with these guys.'

'Don't worry about it,' Gronevelt said. 'Go to New York and help your buddy and get our business finished there. You'll be delivering some money, so come see me about an hour before you catch the plane. And then when you get back here, I have some good news for you. You're finally going to get a little piece of the action, meet some important people.'

Cully laughed. 'I couldn't solve that little sham at blackjack and I get promoted?'

'Sure,' Gronevelt said. 'You just need a little more experience and a harder heart.'

18

ON the night plane to New York Cully sat in the first class section, sipping a plain club soda. On his lap was a metal briefcase covered with leather and equipped with a complicated locking device. As long as Cully held the briefcase, nothing could happen to the million dollars inside it. He himself could not open it.

In Vegas, Gronevelt had counted the money out in Cully's presence, stacking the case neatly before he locked it and handed it over to Cully. The people in New York never knew how or when it was coming. Only Gronevelt decided. But still, Cully was nervous. Clutching the briefcase beside him, he thought about the last years. He had come a long way, he had learned a lot and he would go further and learn more. But he knew that he was leading a dangerous life, gambling for big stakes.

Why had Gronevelt chosen him? What had Gronevelt seen? What did he foresee? Cully Cross, metal briefcase clutched to his lap, tried to divine his fate. As he had counted down the cards in the blackjack shoe, as he had waited for the strength to flow in his strong right arm to throw countless passes with the dice, he now used all his powers of memory and intuition to read what each chance in his life added up to and what could be left in the shoe.

Nearly four years ago, Gronevelt started to make Cully into his right-hand man. Cully had already been his spy in the Xanadu Hotel long before Merlyn and Jordan arrived and had performed his job well. Gronevelt was a little disappointed in him when he became friends with Merlyn and Jordan. And angry when Cully took Jordan's side in the now-famous baccarat table showdown. Cully had thought his career finished, but oddly enough, after that incident, Gronevelt gave him a real job. Cully often wondered about that.

For the first year Gronevelt made Cully a blackjack dealer, which seemed a hell of a way to begin a career as a right-hand man. Cully suspected that he would be used as a spy all over again. But Gronevelt had a more specific purpose in mind. He had chosen Cully as the prime mover in the hotel skimming operation.

Gronevelt felt that hotel owners who skimmed money in the casino counting room were jerks, that the FBI would catch up with them sooner or later. The counting room skimming was too obvious. The owners or their reps meeting there in person and each taking a packet of money before they reported to the Nevada Gaming Commission struck him as foolhardy. Especially when there were five or six owners quarrelling about how much they should skim off the top. Gronevelt had set up what he thought was a far superior system. Or so he told Cully.

He knew Cully was a 'mechanic'. Not a top-notch mechanic but one who could easily deal seconds. That is, Cully could keep the top card for himself and deal the second card from the top. And so an hour before his midnight-to-morning graveyard shift Cully would report to Gronevelt's suite and receive instructions. At a certain time, either I A.M. or 4 A.M. a blackjack player dressed in a certain coloured suit would make a certain number of sequence bets starting with one hundred dollars, then five hundred, then a twenty-five-dollar bet. This would identify the privileged customer, who would win ten or twenty thousand dollars in a few hours' gambling. The man would play with his cards face up, not unusual for big players in blackjack. Seeing the player's hand, Cully could save a good card for the customer by dealing seconds around the table. Cully didn't know how the money finally got back to Gronevelt and his partners. He just did his job without asking questions. And he never opened his mouth.

But as he could count down every card in the shoe, he easily kept track of these manufactured player winnings, and over the year he figured that he had on the average lost ten thousand dollars a week to these Gronevelt players. Over the year he worked as a dealer he knew close to the exact figure. It was around a half million dollars, give or take a ten grand. A beautiful sham without a tax bite and without cutting it up with the official point sharers in the hotel and casino. Gronevelt was also skimming some of his partners.

To keep the losses from being pinpointed, Gronevelt had Cully transferred to different tables each night. He also sometimes switched his shifts. Still, Cully worried about the casino manager's picking up on the whole deal. Except that maybe Gronevelt had warned the casino manager off.

So to cover his losses Cully used his mechanic's skill to wipe out the straight players. He did this for three weeks and then one day he received a phone call summoning him to Gronevelt's suite.

As usual Gronevelt made him sit down and gave him a drink. Then he said, 'Cully, cut out the bullshit. No cheating the customers.'

Cully said, 'I thought maybe that's what you wanted, without telling me.'

Gronevelt smiled. 'A good smart thought. But it's not necessary. Your losses are covered with paperwork. You won't be spotted. And if you are, I'll call off the dogs.' He paused for a moment. 'Just deal a straight game with the suckers. Then we won't get into any trouble we can't handle.'

'Is the second card business showing up on films?' Cully asked.

Gronevelt shook his head. 'No, you're pretty good. That's not the problem. But the Nevada Gaming Commission boys might send in a player that can hear the tick and link it up with your sweeping the table. Now true, that could happen when you're dealing to one of my customers, but then they would just assume you're cheating the hotel. So I'm clean. Also I have a pretty good idea when the Gaming Commission sends in their people. That's why I give you special times to dump out the money. But when you're operating on your own, I can't protect you. And then you're cheating the customer for the hotel. A big difference. Those Gaming Commission guys don't get too hot when *we* get beat, but the straight suckers are another story. It would cost a lot in political payoffs to set that straight.'

'OK,' Cully said. 'But how did you pick it up?'

Gronevelt said impatiently, 'Percentages. Percentages never lie. We built all these hotels on percentages. We stay rich on the percentage. So all of a sudden your dealer sheet shows you making money when you're dumping out for me. That can't happen unless you're the luckiest dealer in the history of Vegas.'

Cully followed orders, but he wondered about how it all worked. Why Gronevelt went to all the trouble. It was only later, when he had become Xanadu Two that he found out the details. That Gronevelt had been skimming not only to beat the government but most of the point owners of the casino. It was only years later he learned that the winning customers had been sent out of New York by Gronevelt's secret partner, a man named Santadio. That the customers thought that he, Cully, was a crooked dealer fixed by the partner in New York. That these customers thought they were victimizing Gronevelt. That Gronevelt and his beloved hotel were covered a dozen different ways.

Gronevelt had started his gambling career in Steubenville, Ohio, under the protection of the famous Cleveland mob with their control over local politics. He had worked the illegal joints and then finally made his way to Nevada. But he had a provincial patriotism. Every young man in Steubenville who wanted a dealing or croupier job in Vegas came to Gronevelt. If he couldn't place him in his own casino, he would place him in some other casino. You could run across Steubenville, Ohio, alumni in the Bahamas, Puerto Rico, on the French Riviera and even in London. In Reno and Vegas you could count them by the hundreds. Many of them were casino managers and pit bosses. Gronevelt was a green felt Pied Piper.

Gronevelt could have picked his spy from these hundreds; in fact, the casino manager at the Xanadu was from Steubenville. Then why had Gronevelt picked on Cully, a comparative stranger from another part of the country? Cully often wondered about that. And of course, later on, when he came to know the intricacies of the many controls, he understood that the casino manager had to be in on it. And it hit Cully full force. He had been picked because he was expendable if anything went wrong. He would take the rap one way or another.

For Gronevelt despite his bookishness, had come out of Cleveland into Vegas with a fearsome reputation. He was a man not to be trifled with, cheated or bamboozled. And he had demonstrated that to Cully in the last years. Once in a serious way and another time with high good humour, a special kind of Vegas gambling wit.

After a year Cully was given the office next to Gronevelt and named his special assistant. This involved driving Gronevelt around town and accompanying him to the floor of the casino at night when Gronevelt made his rounds to greet old friends and customers, especially those from out of town. Gronevelt also made Cully an aide to the casino manager so that he could learn the casino ropes. Cully got to know all the shift bosses well, the pit bosses, the floorwalkers, the dealers and croupiers in all the pits.

Every morning Cully had breakfast at about ten o'clock in Gronevelt's office suite. Before going up, he would get the win-loss figures for the casino's previous twenty-four hours of play from the cashier cage boss. He would give Gronevelt the little slip of paper as they sat down to breakfast, and Gronevelt would study the figures as he scooped out his first chunk of Crenshaw melon. The slip was made out very simply.

Dice Pit	$400,000 Drop	Hold	$60,000
Blackjack Pit	$200,000 Drop	Hold	$40,000
Baccarat			
Roulette	$100,000 Drop	Hold	$40,000
Others (wheel of fortune, keno included in above)			

The slot machines were totalled up only once a week, and those figures were given to Gronevelt by the casino manager in a special report. The slots usually brought in a profit of about a hundred thousand dollars a week. This was the real gravy. The casino could never get unlucky on slots. It was sure money because the machines were set to pay off only a certain percentage of the money played into them. When the figures on the slots went off, there could only be a sham going.

This was not true of the other games, like craps, blackjack and especially baccarat. In those games the house figures to hold sixteen percent of the drop. But even the house could get unlucky. Especially in baccarat, where the heavy gamblers sometimes plunged and caught a lucky streak.

Baccarat had wild fluctuations. There had been nights when the baccarat table lost enough money to wipe out the profits from all the other action in the casino that day. But then there would be weeks when the baccarat table won enormous amounts. Cully was sure that Gronevelt had a skim going on the baccarat table, but he couldn't figure out how it worked. Then he noticed one night when the baccarat table cleaned out some heavy players from South America that the next day's figures on the slip seemed to be less than they should be.

It was every casino's nightmare that the players would get a hot streak. In Las Vegas history there had been times when crap tables had gotten hot for weeks and the casino was lucky to break even only for the day. Sometimes even the blackjack players got smart and beat the house for three or four days running. In roulette it was extremely rare to have even one losing day a month. And the wheel of fortune and keno were straight bust-out operations, the players sitting ducks for the casino.

But these were all the mechanical things to know about running a gambling casino. Things you could learn by the book, that anyone could learn, given the right training and sufficient time. Under Gronevelt, Cully learned a good deal more.

Gronevelt made everybody know he did not believe in luck. That his true and infallible god was the percentage. And he backed it up. Whenever the casino keno game was hit for the big prize of twenty-five thousand dollars, Gronevelt fired all the personnel in the keno operation. Two years after the Xanadu Hotel had begun operating, it got very unlucky. For three weeks the casino never had a winning day and lost nearly a million dollars. Gronevelt fired everybody except the casino manager from Steubenville.

And it seemed to work. After the firings the profits would begin, the losing streak would end. The casino had to average fifty grand a day in winnings for the hotel to break even. And to Cully's knowledge the Xanadu had never had a losing year. Even with Gronevelt skimming off the top.

In the year he had been dealing and skimming for Gronevelt Cully had never been tempted into the error another man might make in his position: skimming on his own. After all, if it was so easy, why could not Cully have a friend of his drop around to win a few bucks? But Cully knew this would be fatal. And he was playing for bigger stakes. He sensed a loneliness in Gronevelt, a need for friendship, which Cully provided. And it paid off.

About twice a month Gronevelt took Cully into Los Angeles with him to go antique hunting. They would buy old gold watches, gilt-framed photographs of early Los Angeles and Vegas. They would search out old coffee grinders, ancient toy automobiles, children's savings banks shaped as locomotives and church steeples made in the 1880's, a gold set archaic money clip, into which Gronevelt would put a hundred-dollar black chip *casa* money for the recipient, or a rare coin. For special high rollers he picked up tiny exquisite dolls made in ancient China, Victorian jewel boxes filled with antique jewelry. Old lace scarves silky grey with age, ancient Nordic ale mugs.

These items would cost at least a hundred dollars each but rarely more than two hundred dollars. On these trips Gronevelt spent a few thousand dollars. He and Cully would have dinner in Los Angeles, and sleep over in the Beverly Hills Hotel and fly back to Vegas on an early-morning plane.

Cully would carry the antiques in his suitcase and back in the Xanadu would have them gift-wrapped and delivered to Gronevelt's suite. And Gronevelt every night or nearly every night would slip one in his pocket and take it down to the casino and present it to one of his Texas oil or New York garment centre high rollers who were good for fifty to a hundred grand a year at the tables.

Cully marvelled at Gronevelt's charm on these occasions. Gronevelt would unwrap the gift package and take out the gold watch and present it to the player. 'I was in LA and saw this and I thought about you,' he'd say to the player. 'Suits your personality. I've had it fixed up and cleaned, should keep perfect time.' Then he would add deprecatingly, 'They told me it was made in 1870, but who the hell knows? You know what hustlers those antique shops are.'

And so he gave the impression that he had given extraordinary care and thought to this one player. He insinuated the idea that the watch was extremely valuable. And that he had taken extra pains to put it in good working condition. And there was a grain of truth in it all. The watch would work perfectly, he had thought about the player to an extraordinary degree. More than anything else was the feeling of personal friendship. Gronevelt had a gift for exuding affection when he presented one of these tokens of his esteem which made it even more flattering.

And Gronevelt used 'The Pencil' liberally. Big players were, of course, comped, RFB—free room, food and beverage. But Gronevelt also granted this privilege to five-dollar chip bettors, who were wealthy. He was a master at turning these customers into big players.

Another lesson Gronevelt taught Cully was not to hustle young girls. Gronevelt had been indignant. He had lectured Cully severely. 'Where the fuck do you come off bullshitting those kids out of a piece of ass? Are you a fucking sneak thief? Would you go into their purses and snatch their small change? What kind of guy are you? Would you steal their car? Would you go into their house as a guest and lift their silverware? Then where do you come off stealing their cunt? That's their only capital, especially when they're beautiful. And remember once you slip them that Honeybee, you're evened out with them. You're free. No bullshit about a relationship. No bullshit about marriage or divorcing your wife. No asking for thousand-dollar loans. Or being faithful. And remember for five of those Honeybees, she'll always be available, even on her wedding day.'

Cully had been amused by this outburst. Obviously Gronevelt had heard about his operation with women, but just as obviously Gronevelt didn't understand women as well as he, Cully, did. Gronevelt didn't understand their masochism. Their willingness, their *need* to believe in a con job.

But he didn't protest. He did say wryly, 'It's not as easy as you make it out to be, even your way. With some of them a thousand Honeybees don't help.'

And surprisingly Gronevelt laughed and agreed. He even told a funny story about himself. Early in the Xanadu Hotel history a Texas woman worth many millions had gambled in the casino and he had presented her with an antique Japanese fan that cost him fifty dollars. The Texas heiress, a good-looking woman of forty and a widow, fell in love with him. Gronevelt was horrified. Though he was ten years older than she, he liked pretty young girls. But out of duty to the hotel bankroll he had taken her up to the hotel suite one night and went to bed with her. When she left, out of habit and perhaps out of foolish perversity or perhaps with the cruel Vegas sense of fun, he slipped her a Honeybee and told her to buy herself a present. To this day he didn't know why.

The oil heiress had looked down at the Honeybee and slipped it into her purse. She thanked him prettily. She continued to come to the hotel and gamble, but she was no longer in love with him.

Three years later Gronevelt was looking for investors to build additional rooms to the hotel. As Gronevelt explained, extra rooms were always desirable. 'Players gamble where they shit,' he said. 'They don't go wandering around. Give them a show room, a lounge show, different restaurants. Keep them in the hotel the first forty-eight hours. By then they're banged out.'

He had approached the oil heiress. She had nodded and said of course. She immediately wrote out a cheque and handed it to him with an extraordinarily sweet smile. The cheque was for a hundred dollars.

'The moral of that story,' Gronevelt said, 'is never treat a smart rich broad like a dumb poor cunt.'

Sometimes in LA Gronevelt would go shopping for old books. But usually, when he was in the mood, he would fly to Chicago to attend a rare books auction. He had a fine collection stored

165

in a locked glass-panelled bookcase in his suite. When Cully moved into his new office, he found a present from Gronevelt: a first edition of a book on gambling published in 1847. Cully read it with interest and kept it on his desk for a while. Then, not knowing what to do with it, he brought it into Gronevelt's suite and gave it back to him. 'I appreciate the gift, but it's wasted on me,' he said. Gronevelt nodded and didn't say anything. Cully felt that he had disappointed him, but in a curious way it helped cement their relationship. A few days later he saw the book in Gronevelt's special locked case. He knew then that he had not made a mistake, and he felt pleased that Gronevelt had tendered him such a genuine mark of affection, however misguided. From the man's history, though nothing in it showed in the mask he now wore.

But then he saw another side of Gronevelt that he had always known must exist. Cully had made it a habit to be present when the casino chips were counted three times a day. He accompanied the pit bosses as they counted the chips on all the tables, black-jack, roulette, craps, and the cash at baccarat. He even went into the casino cage to count the chips there. The cage manager was always a little nervous to Cully's eyes, but he dismissed this as his own suspicious nature because the cash and markers and chips in the safe always tallied correctly. And the casino cage manager was an old trusted member of Gronevelt's early days.

But one day, on some impulse, Cully decided to have the trays of chips pulled out of the safe. He could never figure out this impulse later. But once the scores of metal racks had been taken out of the darkness of the safe and closely inspected it became obvious that two trays of the black hundred-dollar chips were false. They were blank black cylinders. In the darkness of the safe, thrust far in the back where they would never be used, they had been passed as legitimate on the daily counts. The casino cage manager professed horror and shock, but they both knew that the sham could never have been attempted without his consent. Cully picked up a phone and called Gronevelt's suite. Gronevelt immediately came down to the cage and inspected the chips. The two trays amounted to a hundred thousand dollars. Gronevelt pointed a finger at the cage manager. It was a dreadful moment. Gronevelt's ruddy, tanned face was white, but his voice was composed. 'Get the fuck out of this cage,' he said. Then he turned to Cully. 'Make him sign over all his keys to you,' he said. 'And then have all the pit bosses on all three of the shifts in my office right away. I don't give a fuck where they are. The ones who are on vacation fly back to Vegas and check in with me as soon as they get here.' Then Gronevelt walked out of the cage and disappeared.

As Cully and the casino cage manager were doing the paper-work for signing over the keys, two men Cully had never seen before came in. The casino manager knew them because he turned very pale and his hands started shaking uncontrollably.

Both men nodded to him and he nodded back. One of the men said, 'When you're through, the boss wants to see you up in his office.' They were talking to the cage manager and ignored Cully. Cully picked up the phone and called Gronevelt's office. He said to Gronevelt, 'Two guys came down here, they say you sent them.'

Gronevelt's voice was like ice. 'That's right,' he said.

'Just checking,' Cully said.

Gronevelt's voice softened. 'Good idea,' he said. 'And you did a good job.' There was a slight pause. 'The rest of it is none of your business, Cully. Forget about it. Understand?' His voice was almost gentle now, and there was even a note of weary sadness in it.

The cage manager was seen for the next few days around Las Vegas and then disappeared. After a month Cully learned that his wife had put in a missing persons report on him. He couldn't believe the implication at first, despite the jokes he heard around town that the cage manager was now buried in the desert. He never dared mention anything to Gronevelt, and Gronevelt never spoke of the matter to him. Not even to compliment him upon his good work. Which was just as well. Cully didn't want to think that his good work might have resulted in the cage manager's being buried in the desert.

But in the last few months Gronevelt had shown his mettle in a less macabre way. With typical Vegas nimbleness of foot and quick-wittedness.

All the casino owners in Vegas had started making a big pitch for foreign gamblers. The English were immediately written off, despite their history of being the biggest losers of the nineteenth century. The end of the British Empire had meant the end of their high rollers. The millions of Indians, Australians, South Sea Islanders and Canadians no longer poured money into the coffers of the gambling milords. England was now a poor country, whose very rich scrambled to beat taxes and hold on to their estates. Those few who could afford to gamble preferred the aristocratic high-toned clubs in France and Germany and their own London.

The French were also written off. The French didn't travel and would never stand for the extra house double zero on the Vegas wheel.

But the Germans and Italians were wooed. Germany with its expanding postwar economy had many millionaires, and Germans loved to travel, loved to gamble and loved the Vegas women. There was something in the high-flying Vegas style that appealed to the Teutonic spirit, that brought back memories of *Oktoberfest* and maybe even *Götterdämmerung*. The Germans were also good-natured gamblers and more skilful than most.

Italian millionaires were big prizes in Vegas. They gambled recklessly while getting drunk; they let the soft hustlers employed by casinos keep them in the city a suicidal six or seven days. They seemed to have inexhaustible sums of money because none of them paid income tax. What should have gone into the public coffers of Rome slid into the hold boxes of air-conditioned casinos. The girls of Vegas loved the Italian millionaires because of their generous gifts and because for those six or seven days they fell in love with the same abandon they plunged on the sucker hard-way bets at the crap table.

The Mexican and South American gamblers were even bigger prizes. Nobody knew what was really going on down in South America, but special planes were sent there to bring the pampas millionaires to Vegas. Everything was free to these sporting gentlemen who left the hides of millions of cattle at the baccarat tables. They came with their wives and girlfriends, their adolescent sons eager to become gambling men. These customers too were favourites of the Las Vegas girls. They were less sincere than the Italians, perhaps a little less polished in their lovemaking according to some reports, but certainly with larger appetites. Cully had been in Gronevelt's office one day when the casino manager came with a special problem. A South American gambler, a premier player, had put in a request for eight girls to be sent to his suite, blondes, redheads but no brunettes and none shorter than his own five feet six inches.

Gronevelt took the request coolly. 'And what time today does he want this miracle to happen?' Gronevelt asked.

'About five o'clock,' the casino manager said. 'He wants to take them all to dinner afterward and keep them for the night.'

Gronevelt didn't crack a smile. 'What will it cost?'

'About three grand,' the casino manager said. 'The girls know they'll get roulette and baccarat money from this guy.'

'OK, comp it,' Gronevelt said. 'But tell those girls to keep him in the hotel as much as possible. I don't want him losing his dough down the Strip.'

As the casino manager started to leave, Gronevelt said. 'What the hell is he going to do with eight women?'

The casino manager shrugged. 'I asked him the same thing. He says he has his son with him.'

For the first time in the conversation, Gronevelt smiled. 'That's what I call real paternal pride,' he said. Then, after the casino manager left the room, he shook his head and said to Cully, 'Remember, they gamble where they shit *and* where they fuck. When the father dies, the son will keep coming here. For three grand he'll have a night he'll never forget. He'll be worth a million bucks to the Xanadu unless they have a revolution in his country.'

But the prize, the champions, the pearl without price that every casino owner coveted were the Japanese. They were hair-raising gamblers, and they always arrived in Vegas in groups. The top echelon of an industrial combine would arrive to gamble tax-free dollars, and their losses in a four-day stay many times went over a million dollars. And it was Cully who snared the biggest Japanese prize for the Xanadu Hotel and Gronevelt.

Cully had been carrying on a friendly go-to-the-movies-and-fuck-afterward love affair with a dancer in the Oriental Follies playing a Strip hotel. The girl was called Daisy because her Japanese name was unpronounceable, and she was only about twenty years old, but she had been in Vegas for nearly five years. She was a terrific dancer, cute as a pearl in its shell, but she was thinking about getting operations to make her eyes Occidental and her bust puffed to corn-fed American. Cully was horrified and told her she would ruin her appeal. Daisy finally listened to his advice only when he pretended an ecstasy greater than he felt for her budlike breasts.

They became such friends that she gave him lessons in Japanese while they were in bed and he stayed overnight. In the mornings she would serve him soup for breakfast, and when he protested, she told him that in Japan everyone ate soup for breakfast and that she made the best breakfast soup in her village outside Tokyo. Cully was astonished to find the soup delicious and tangy and easy on the stomach after a fatiguing night.

It was Daisy who alerted him to the fact that one of the great business tycoons of Japan was planning to visit Vegas. Daisy had Japanese newspapers airmailed to her by her family; she was homesick and enjoyed reading about Japan. She told Cully that a Tokyo tycoon, a Mr Fummiro, had given an interview stating that he would come to America to open up overseas branches of his television manufacturing business. Daisy said that Mr Fummiro was famous in Japan for being an outrageous gambler and would surely come to Vegas. She also told him that Mr Fummiro was a pianist of great skill, had studied in Europe and would almost certainly have become a professional musician if his father had not ordered his son to take over the family firm.

That day Cully had Daisy come over to his office at the Xanadu and dictated a letter for her to write on the hotel stationery. With Daisy's advice he constructed a letter that observed the, to Occidentals, subtle *politesse* of Japan and would not give Mr Fummiro offence.

In the letter he invited Mr Fummiro to be an honoured guest at the Xanadu Hotel for as long as he wished and at any time he wished. He also invited Mr Fummiro to bring as many guests as he desired, his whole entourage, including his business colleagues in the United States. In delicate language Daisy let Mr Fummiro know that all this would not cost him one cent. That even the theatre shows would be free. Before he mailed the letter, Cully got Gronevelt's approval since Cully still did not have the full authority of 'The Pencil'. Cully had been afraid that Gronevelt would sign the letter, but this did not happen. So now officially these Japanese were Cully's clients, if they came. He would be their 'Host'.

It was three weeks before he received an answer. And during that time Cully put in some more time studying with Daisy. He learned that he must always smile while talking to a Japanese client. That he always had to show the utmost courtesy in voice and gesture. She told him that when a slight hiss came into the speech of a Japanese man, it was a sign of anger, a danger signal. Like the rattle of a snake. Cully remembered that hiss in the speech of Japanese villains in WW II movies. He had thought it was just the mannerisms of the actor.

When the answer to the letter came, it was in the form of a

phone call from Mr Fummiro's overseas branch office in Los Angeles. Could the Xanadu Hotel have two suites ready for Mr Fummiro, the president of Japan Worldwide Sales Company and his executive vice-president, Mr Niigeta? Plus another ten rooms for other members of Mr Fummiro's entourage? The call had been routed to Cully since he had been specifically asked for, and he answered yes. Then, wild with joy, he immediately called Daisy, and told her he would take her shopping in the next few days. He told her he would get Mr Fummiro ten suites to make all the members of his entourage comfortable. She told him not to do so. That it would make Mr Fummiro lose face if the rest of his party had equal accommodations. Then Cully asked Daisy to go out that very day and fly to Los Angeles to buy kimonos that Mr Fummiro could wear in the privacy of his suite. She told him that this too would offend Mr Fummiro, who prided himself on being Westernized, though he surely wore the comfortable Japanese traditional garments in the privacy of his own home. Cully, desperately seeking for every angle to get an edge, suggested that Daisy meet Mr Fummiro and perhaps act as his interpreter and dinner companion. Daisy laughed and said that would be the last thing Mr Fummiro would want. He would be extremely uncomfortable with a Westernized Japanese girl observing him in this foreign country.

Cully accepted all her decisions. But one thing he insisted on. He told Daisy to make fresh Japanese soup during Mr Fummiro's three day stay. Cully would come to her apartment early every morning to pick it up and have it delivered to Mr Fummiro's suite when he ordered breakfast. Daisy groaned but promised to do so.

Late that afternoon Cully got a call from Gronevelt. 'What the hell is a piano doing in Suite four ten?' Gronevelt said. 'I just got a call from the hotel manager. He said you bypassed channels and caused a hell of a mess.'

Cully explained the arrival of Mr Fummiro and his special tastes. Gronevelt chuckled and said, 'Take my Rolls when you pick him up at the airport.' This was a car he used only for the richest of Texas millionaires or his favourite clients that he personally 'Hosted'.

The next day Cully was at the airport with three bellmen from the hotel, the chauffeured Rolls and two Cadillac limos. He arranged for the Rolls and the limousines to go directly onto the flying field so that his clients would not have to go through the terminal. And he greeted Mr Fummiro as soon as he came down the steps of the plane.

The party of Japanese was unmistakable, not only for their features, but because of the way they dressed. They were all in black business suits, badly tailored by Western standards, with white shirts and black ties. The ten of them looked like a band of very earnest clerks instead of the ruling board of Japan's richest and most powerful business conglomerate.

Mr Fummiro was also easy to pick out. He was the tallest of the band, very tall in comparison, a good five feet ten. And he was handsome with wide massive features, broad shoulders and jet black hair. He could have passed for a movie star out of Hollywood cast in an exotic role that made him look falsely Oriental. For a brief second the thought flashed through Cully's mind that this might be an elaborate sham.

Of the others only one stood close to Fummiro. He was slightly less tall than Fummiro, but much thinner. And he had the buck-teeth of the caricature Japanese. The remaining men were tiny and inconspicuous. All of them carried elegant black imitation samite briefcases.

Cully extended his hand with utmost assurance to Fummiro and said, 'I'm Cully Cross of the Xanadu Hotel. Welcome to Las Vegas.'

Mr Fummiro flashed a brilliantly polite smile. His white teeth were large and perfect, and he said in only slightly accented English, 'Very pleased to meet you.'

Then he introduced the buck-toothed man as Mr Niigeta, his executive vice-president. He murmured the names of the others, all of whom ceremoniously shook hands with Cully. Cully took their baggage tickets and assured them all luggage would be delivered to their rooms in the hotel.

He ushered them into the waiting cars. He and Fummiro and Niigeta into the Rolls, the others into the Cadillacs. On the way to the hotel he told his passengers that credit had been arranged. Fummiro patted Niigeta's briefcase and said in his slightly imperfect English, 'We have brought you cash money.' The two men smiled at Cully. Cully smiled back. He remembered to smile whenever he spoke as he told them all the conveniences of the hotel and how they could see any show in Vegas. For a fraction of a second he thought about mentioning the companionship of women, but some instinct made him hold back.

At the hotel he led them directly to their rooms and had a desk clerk bring up the registration forms for them to sign. All were on the same floor, Fummiro and Niigeta had adjoining suites with a connecting door. Fummiro inspected the living accommodations for his whole party, and Cully saw the glint of satisfaction in his eyes when he noted that his own suite was by far the best. But Fummiro's eyes really lit up when he saw the small piano in his suite. He immediately sat down and fingered the keys, listening. Cully hoped that it was in tune. He couldn't tell, but Fummiro vigorously nodded his head and, smiling broadly and face alight with pleasure, said, 'Very good, very kind,' and shook Cully's hand effusively.

Then Fummiro motioned to Niigeta to open the briefcase he was carrying. Cully's eyes bulged a little. There were neatly banded stacks of currency filling the case. He had no idea how much it might be. 'We would like to leave this on deposit in your casino cage,' Mr Fummiro said. 'Then we can just draw the money as we need it for our little vacation.'

'Certainly,' Cully said. Niigeta snapped the case shut, and the two of them went down to the casino, leaving Fummiro alone in his suite to freshen up.

They went into the casino manager's office, where the money was counted out. It came to five hundred thousand dollars. Cully made sure Niigeta was given the proper receipt and the necessary clerical work done so that the money could be drawn on demand at the tables. The casino manager himself would be on the floor with Cully and would identify Fummiro and Niigeta to the pit bosses and the floorwalkers. Then in every corner of the casino the two Japanese merely had to lift a finger and draw chips, then sign a marker. Without fuss, without showing identification. And they would get the royal treatment, the utmost deference. A deference especially pure since it related only to money.

For the next three days Cully was at the hotel early in the morning with Daisy's breakfast soup. Room service had orders to notify him as soon as Mr Fummiro called down for his breakfast. Cully would give him an hour to eat and then knock on his door to say good morning. He would find Fummiro already at his piano, playing soulfully, the serving bowl of soup empty on the table behind him. In these morning meetings Cully arranged show tickets and sightseeing trips for Mr Fummiro and his friends. Mr Fummiro was always smilingly polite and grateful, and Mr Niigeta would come through the connecting door from his own suite to greet Cully and compliment him on the breakfast soup, which he had obviously shared. Cully remembered to keep smiling and nodding his head as they did.

Meanwhile, in their three days' gambling in Vegas the band of ten Japanese terrorized the casinos of Vegas. They would travel together and gamble together at the same baccarat table. When Fummiro had the shoe, they all bet the limit with him on the bank. They had some hot streaks but luckily not at the Xanadu. They only bet baccarat, and they played with a *joie de vivre* more Italian than Oriental. Fummiro would whip the sides of the shoe and bang the table when he dealt himself a natural eight or nine. He was a passionate gambler and gloated over winning a two-thousand-dollar bet. This amazed Cully. He knew Fummiro was worth over half a billion dollars. Why should such paltry (though up to the Vegas limit) gambling excite him?

Only once did he see the steel behind Fummiro's handsome smiling façade. One night Niigeta placed a bet on Player's when Fummiro had the shoe. Fummiro gave him a long look, eyebrows arching, and said something in Japanese. For the first time Cully caught the slight hissing sound that Daisy had warned him against. Niigeta stuttered something in apology through his buck-teeth and immediately switched his money to ride with Fummiro.

The trip was a huge success for everybody. Fummiro and his band went back to Japan ahead over a hundred thousand dollars, but they had lost two hundred thousand to the Xanadu. They had made up for their losses at other casinos. And they had started a legend in Vegas. The band of ten men in their shiny black suits would leave one casino for another down the Strip. They were a frightening sight, marching ten strong into a casino, looking like undertakers come to collect the corpse of the casino's bankroll. The baccarat pit boss would learn from the Rolls driver where they were going and call that casino to expect them and give them red-carpet treatment. All the pit bosses pooled their information. It was in this way that Cully learned that Niigeta was a horny Oriental and getting laid by top-class hookers at the other hotels. Which meant that for some reason he didn't want Fummiro to know that he would rather fuck than gamble.

Cully took them to the airport when they left for Los Angeles. He had one of Gronevelt's antique gold fob watches which he presented to Fummiro with Gronevelt's compliments. Gronevelt himself had briefly stopped at the Japanese dining table to introduce himself and show the courtesies of the house.

Fummiro was genuinely effusive in his thanks, and Cully went through the usual rounds of handshakes and smiles before they got on their plane. Cully rushed back to the hotel, made a phone call to get the piano moved out of Fummiro's suite and then went into Gronevelt's office. Gronevelt gave him a warm handshake and a congratulatory hug.

'One of the best "Host" jobs I've seen in all my years in Vegas,' Gronevelt said. 'Where did you find out about that soup business?'

'A little girl named Daisy,' Cully said. 'OK if I buy her a present from the hotel?'

'You can go for a grand,' Gronevelt said. 'That's a very nice connection you made with those Japs. Keep after them. The special Christmas gifts and invitations. That guy Fummiro is a bust-out gambler if I ever saw one.'

Cully frowned. 'I was a little leery about laying on broads,' he said. 'You know Fummiro is a hell of a nice guy, and I didn't want to get too familiar first time out.'

Gronevelt nodded. 'You were right. Don't worry, he'll be back. And if he wants a broad, he'll ask for one. You don't make his kind of money by being afraid to ask.'

Gronevelt as usual was right. Three months later Fummiro was back and at the cabaret show asked about one of the leggy blonde dancers. Cully knew she was in action despite being married to a dealer at the Sands. After the show he called the stage manager and asked him if the girl would have a drink with Fummiro and him. It was arranged, and Fummiro asked the girl out for a late-night dinner. The girl looked questioningly at Cully and he nodded. Then he left them alone. He went to his office and called the stage manager to tell him to schedule a replacement for the midnight show. The next morning Cully did not go up to Fummiro's suite after breakfast was delivered. Later in the day he called the girl at her home and told her she could miss all her shows while Fummiro was in town.

On subsequent trips the pattern remained the same. By this time Daisy had taught one of the Xanadu chefs how to make the Japanese soup, and it was officially listed on the breakfast menu. One thing Cully learned was that Fummiro always watched the reruns of a certain long-lasting western TV show. He loved it. Especially the blonde ingenue who played a plucky but very feminine, yet innocent, dance hall girl. Cully had a brainstorm.

Through his movie contacts he got in touch with the ingenue, who was named Linda Parsons. He flew into Los Angeles, had lunch with her and told her about Fummiro's passion for her and her show. She was fascinated by Cully's stories about Fummiro's gambling. How he checked into the Xanadu with briefcases holding a million dollars in cash, which he would sometimes lose in three days of baccarat. Cully could see the childish, innocent greed in her eyes. She told Cully that she would love to come to Vegas the next time Fummiro arrived.

A month later Fummiro and Niigeta checked into the Xanadu Hotel for a four-day stay. Cully immediately told Fummiro about Linda Parsons' wishing to visit him. Fummiro's eyes lit up. Despite being over forty, he had an incredible boyish handsomeness, which his evident joy made even more charming. He asked Cully to call the girl immediately, and Cully said he would, not mentioning that he had already spoken to her and she had promised to come into town the next afternoon. Fummiro was so excited that he gambled like a madman that night and dropped over three hundred thousand dollars.

The next morning Fummiro went shopping for a new blue suit. For some reason he thought blue suits were the height of American elegance, and Cully arranged with the Sy Devore people at the Sands Hotel to measure and fit him out and specially tailor it for him that day. Cully sent one of his Xanadu 'Hosts' with Fummiro to make sure everything went smoothly.

But Linda Parsons caught an early plane and arrived in Vegas before noon. Cully met her plane and brought her to the hotel. She wanted to freshen up for Fummiro's arrival, so Cully put her in Niigeta's suite since he assumed that Niigeta was with his chief. It proved to be an almost fatal error.

Leaving her in the suite, Cully went back to his office and tried to locate Fummiro, but he had left the tailor shop and must have stopped off in one of the casinos along the way to gamble. He could not be traced. After about an hour he received a phone call from Fummiro's suite. It was Linda Parsons. She sounded a little upset. 'Could you come down?' she said. 'I'm having a language problem with your friend.'

Cully didn't wait to ask any questions. Fummiro spoke English well enough; for some reasons he was pretending not to be able to. Maybe he was disappointed in the girl. Cully had noticed that the ingenue, in person, had more mileage on her than appeared in the carefully photographed TV shows. Or maybe

Linda had said or done something that had offended his delicate Oriental sensibilities.

But it was Niigeta who let him into his suite. And Niigeta was preening himself with slightly drunken pride. Then Cully saw Linda Parsons come out of the bathroom clad in a Japanese kimono with golden dragons blazoned all over it.

'Jesus Christ,' Cully said.

Linda gave him a wan smile. 'You sure bullshitted me,' she said. 'He's not that shy and he's not that good-looking and doesn't even understand English. I hope he's rich at least.'

Niigeta was still smiling and preening, he even bowed toward Linda as she was talking. He had obviously not understood what she was saying.

'Did you fuck him?' Cully asked almost in despair.

Linda made a face. 'He kept chasing me around the suite. I thought at least we'd have a romantic evening together with flowers and violins, but I couldn't fight him off. So I figured what the hell. Let's get it over with if he's such a horny Jap. So I fucked him.'

Cully shook his head and said, 'You fucked the wrong Jap.'

Linda looked at him for a moment with a mixture of shock and horror. Then she burst out laughing. It was a genuine laughter that became her. She fell onto the sofa still laughing, her white thigh bared by the flopping of the kimono. For that moment Cully was charmed by her. But then he shook his head. This was serious. He picked up the phone and got Daisy at her apartment. The first thing Daisy said was, 'No more soup.' Cully told her to stop kidding around and to get down to the hotel. He told her it was terribly important and she had to be fast. Then he called Gronevelt and explained the situation. Gronevelt said he would come right down. Meanwhile, Cully was praying that Fummiro would not appear.

Fifteen minutes later Gronevelt and Daisy were in the suite with them. Linda had made Cully and Niigeta and herself a drink from the suite bar, and she still had a grin on her face. Gronevelt was charming with her. 'I'm sorry this happened,' he said. 'But just be a little patient. We'll get everything sorted out.' Then he turned to Daisy. 'Explain to Mr Niigeta exactly what happened. That he took Mr Fummiro's woman. That she thought he was Mr Fummiro. Explain that Mr Fummiro was madly in love with her and went out to buy a new suit for his meeting with her.'

Niigeta was listening intently with the same broad grin he always wore. But now there was a little alarm in his eyes. He asked Daisy a question in Japanese, and Cully noticed the little warning hiss in his speech. Daisy started talking to him rapidly in Japanese. She kept smiling as she talked, but Niigeta's smile kept fading as her words poured out, and when she finished, he fell to the floor of the suite in a dead faint.

Daisy took charge. She grabbed a whisky bottle and poured some down Niigeta's throat, then helped him up and to the sofa. Linda looked at him pityingly. Niigeta was wringing his hands and pouring out speech to Daisy. Gronevelt asked what he was saying. Daisy shrugged. 'He says it means the end of his career. He says that Mr Fummiro will get rid of him. That he made Mr Fummiro lose too much face.'

Gronevelt nodded. 'Tell him to just keep his mouth shut. Tell him I'm going to have him put into the hospital for a day because he's feeling ill, and then he'll fly back to Los Angeles for treatment. We'll make up a story for Mr Fummiro. Tell him never to tell a soul, and we'll make sure that Mr Fummiro never finds out what happened.'

Daisy translated and Niigeta nodded. His polite smile came back, but it was a ghastly grimace. Gronevelt turned to Cully. 'You and Miss Parsons wait for Fummiro. Act as if nothing happened. I'll take care of Niigeta. We can't leave him here; he'll faint again when he sees his boss. I'll ship him out.'

And that was how it worked. When Fummiro finally arrived an hour later, he found Linda Parsons, freshly dressed and made up, waiting for him with Cully. Fummiro was immediately enchanted, and Linda Parsons looked smitten with his handsomeness, but as innocently as the ingenue of the western TV movie could be.

'I hope you don't mind,' she said. 'But I took your friend's suite so that I could be right next to you. That way we can spend more time with each other.'

Fummiro grasped the implication. She was not just some slut who would move right in with him. She would have to fall in love first. He nodded with a broad smile and said, 'Of course, of course.' Cully heaved a sigh of relief. Linda was playing her cards just right. He said his good-byes and lingered for a moment in the hall. In a few minutes he could hear Fummiro playing the piano and Linda singing along with him.

In the three days that followed Fummiro and Linda Parsons

had the classical, almost geometrically perfect Las Vegas love affair. They were mad for each other and spent each minute together. In bed, at the gambling tables good luck or bad, shopping in the fancy arcades and boutiques of the Strip hotels. Linda loved Japanese soup for breakfast and loved Fummiro's piano playing. Fummiro loved Linda's blonde paleness, her milk-white and slightly heavy thighs, the longness of her legs, the soft, drooping fullness of her breasts. But most of all, he loved her constant good humour, her gaiety. He confided to Cully that Linda would have made a great geisha. Daisy told Cully that this was the highest compliment a man like Fummiro could give. Fummiro also claimed that Linda gave him luck when he gambled. When his stay was over, he had lost only two hundred thousand of the million in cash, American, that he had deposited in the casino cage. And that included a mink coat, a diamond ring, a palomino horse and a Mercedes car that he bought for Linda Parsons. He had gotten away cheap. Without Linda the chances were good he would have dropped at least half a million or maybe even the full million at the baccarat tables.

At first Cully thought of Linda as a high-class soft hooker. But after Fummiro left Vegas, he had dinner with her before she took the night plane to Los Angeles. She was really crazy about Fummiro. 'He's such an interesting guy,' she said. 'I loved that soup for breakfast and the piano playing. And he was just great in bed. No wonder the Japanese women do everything for their men.'

Cully smiled. 'I don't think he treats his women back home the way he treated you.'

Linda sighed. 'Yeah, I know. Still, it was great. You know, he took hundreds of pictures of me with his camera. You'd think I'd be tired of that, but I really loved him doing it. I took pictures of him too. He's a very handsome man.'

'And very rich,' Cully said.

Linda shrugged. 'I've been with rich guys before. And I make good money. But he was just like a little kid. I really don't like the way he gambles, though. God! I could live for ten years on what he loses in one day.'

Cully thought, is that so? And immediately made plans for Fummiro and Linda Parsons never to meet again. But he said with a wry smile, 'Yeah, I hate to see him get hurt like that. Might discourage him from gambling.'

Linda grinned at him. 'Yeah, I'll bet,' she said. 'But thanks for everything. I really had one of the best times of my life. Maybe I'll see you again.'

He knew what she was angling for, but instead, he said smoothly, 'Anytime you get the yen for Vegas just call me. Everything on the house except chips.'

Linda said a little pensively, 'Do you think Fummiro will call me the next time he comes in? I gave him my phone number in LA. I even said I'd fly to Japan on my vacation when we finish taping the show, and he said he'd be delighted and to let him know when I was coming. But he was a little cool about that.'

Cully shook his head. 'Japanese men don't like women to be so aggressive. They're a thousand years behind the times. Especially a big wheel like Fummiro. Your best bet is to lay back and play it cool.'

She sighed. 'I guess so.'

He took her to the airport and kissed her on the cheek before she boarded her plane. 'I'll give you a call when Fummiro comes in again,' he said.

When he got back to the Xanadu, he went up to Gronevelt's living suite and said wryly, 'There's such a thing as being too good to a player.'

Gronevelt said, 'Don't be disappointed. We didn't want his whole million this early in the game. But you're right. That actress is not the right girl to connect with a player. For one thing she's not greedy enough. For another, she's too straight. And worst of all, she's intelligent.'

'How do you know?' Cully asked.

Gronevelt smiled. 'Am I right?'

'Sure,' Cully said. 'I'll make sure to tout Fummiro off her when he comes in again.'

'You won't have to,' Gronevelt said. 'A guy like him has too much strength. He doesn't need what she can give him. Not more than once. Once is fun. But that's all it was. If it were more, he would have taken better care of her when he left.'

Cully was a little startled. 'A Mercedes, a mink coat and a diamond ring? That's not taking care of her?'

'Nope,' Gronevelt said. And he was right. The next time Fummiro came into Vegas he never asked about Linda Parsons. And this time he lost his million cash in the cage.

19

THE plane flew into morning light and the stewardess came around with coffee and breakfast. Cully kept the suitcase beside him as he ate and drank, and when he had finished, he saw New York's towers of steel on the horizon. The sight always awed him. As the desert stretched away from Vegas, so here the miles of steel and glass rooted and growing thickly toward the sky seemed limitless. And gave him a sense of despair.

The plane dipped and did a slow, graceful tilt to the left as it circled the city and then dropped down, white ceiling to blue ceiling, then to sunlit air with the cement grey runways and scattered green patches that formed the carpet earth. It touched down with a hard enough bump to wake those passengers who were still asleep.

Cully felt fresh and wide-awake. He was anxious to see Merlyn; the thought of it made him feel happy. Good old Merlyn, the original square, the only man in the world he trusted.

20

ON the day that I was to appear before the grand jury, my oldest son was graduating from the ninth grade and entering high school. Valerie wanted me to take off from work and go with her to the exercises. I told her I couldn't because I had to go to a special meeting on the Army recall programme. She still had no clue to the trouble I was in, and I didn't tell her. She couldn't help and she could only worry. If everything went OK, she'd never know. And that was how I wanted it. I really didn't believe in sharing troubles with marriage partners when they couldn't help.

Valerie was proud of her son's graduating day. Somewhere along the line a few years ago we realized he really couldn't read, yet was getting promoted each semester. Valerie was mad as hell and started teaching him to read, and she did a good job. Now he was getting top grades. Not that I wasn't mad. It was another grudge I had against New York City. We lived in a low-income area, all working stiffs and blacks. The school system didn't give a shit whether the kids learned anything or not. It just kept promoting them on to get rid of them, to get them out of the system without any trouble and with the least amount of effort.

Vallie was looking forward to moving into our new house. It was in a great school district, a Long Island community where the teacher made sure all their students qualified for college. And though she didn't say it, there were hardly any blacks. Her kids would grow up in the same kind of, to her, stable environment she had had as a Catholic schoolchild. That was OK with me. I didn't want to tell her that the problems she was trying to escape were rooted in the illnesses of our entire society and that we wouldn't escape them in the trees and lawns of Long Island.

And besides, I had other worries. I might be going to jail instead. It depended on the grand jury I would appear before today. Everything depended on that. I felt lousy when I got out of bed that morning. Vallie was taking the kids to school herself and staying there for the graduation exercises. I told her that I was going into work late, so they left before me. I got my own coffee, and as I drank it, I figured out all the things I had to do before the grand jury.

I had to deny everything. There was no way they could trace the bribe money I'd take, Cully had assured me of that. But the thing that worried me was that I had had to fill out a question-naire as to my assets. One question was did I own a house. And I had walked a thin line on that. The truth was that I had put a down payment on a Long Island home, a deposit, but there had not yet been a 'closing' on the house. So I just said no. I figured I didn't own a house and there was nothing said about a deposit. But I wondered if the FBI had found out about that. It seemed it must have.

So one of the questions I could expect the grand jury to ask would be if I had made a deposit on a house. And then I would have to answer yes. Then they would ask me why I hadn't put it down on the sheet and I would have to explain that. Then what if Frank Alcore cracked and pleaded guilty and told them about our dealings when we had been partners? I had already made up my mind to lie about that. It would be Frank's word against mine. He had always handled the deals by himself, nobody could back him up. And now I remembered one day when one of his customers had tried to pay me off with an envelope to deliver to Frank, because Frank was not in the office that day. I had refused. And that had been very lucky. Because that customer was one of the guys who had written the anonymous letter to the FBI that started the whole investigation. And that had been pure luck. I had refused simply because I didn't like the guy person-ally. Well, he would have to testify that I wouldn't take the money and that would be a point in my favour.

And would Frank crack and throw me to the grand jury? I didn't think so. The only way he could save himself would be to give evidence against someone higher up in the chain of com-mand. Like the major or the colonel. And the catch there was that they were not in it at all. And I felt Frank was too decent a guy to cause me grief just because he was caught. Besides, he had too much at stake. If he pleaded guilty, he would lose his government job and pension and his Reserve rank and pension. He had to brazen it out.

My only big worry was Paul Hemsi. The kid I had done the most for and whose father had promised to make me happy for the rest of my life. After I had taken care of Paul, I had never heard from Mr Hemsi again. Not even a package of stockings. I had expected a big score from that one, at least a couple of grand, but those initial cartons of clothing had been it, the whole thing. And I hadn't pushed it or asked for anything. After all, those cartons of clothes were worth thousands. They wouldn't 'make me happy for the rest of my life', but what the hell, I didn't mind being conned.

But when the FBI began its investigation, it got onto the gossip that Paul Hemsi had beaten the draft and been enlisted in the Reserves even after he got an induction notice. I knew that the letter from the draft board rescinding his induction notice had been pulled from our files and sent to higher headquarters. I had to assume that the FBI men had talked to the draft board clerk and that he had told them the story I had given him. Which would still have been OK. Nothing really illegal, a little administrative hocus-pocus that happened every day. But the word was out that Paul Hemsi had cracked under the FBI interrogation and had told them that I received a bribe from other friends of his.

I left the house and drove by my son's school. It had a huge playground with a basketball court of cement, the whole area fenced by high wire-mesh fences. And as I drove by, I could see that the graduation exercises were being held outside in the courtyard. I parked my car and stood outside the fence, clinging to the wire.

Young boys and girls barely in their teens stood in orderly rows, all neatly dressed for the ceremony, their hair combed, their faces scrubbed clean, waiting with childish pride for their ceremonial passing into the next step toward adulthood.

Stands had been erected for the parents. And a huge wooden platform for the dignitaries, the principal of the school, a precinct politician, an old grizzled guy wearing the blue braided overseas cap and 1920's-looking uniform of the American Legion. An American flag flew over the platform. I heard the principal saying something about not having enough time to give out the diplomas and honours individually, but that when he announced each class, the members of that class should turn and face the stands.

184

And so I watched them for a few minutes. After each announcement a row of the young boys and girls swung around to face the stand of mothers and fathers and other relatives to receive their applause. The faces were filled with pride and pleasure and anticipation. They were heroes this day. They had been praised by the dignitaries and applauded now by their elders. Some of the poor bastards still couldn't read. None of them had been prepared for the world or the trouble they would see. I was glad I couldn't see my son's face. I went back to the car and drove to New York and my meeting with the grand jury.

Near the federal courthouse building I put my car in the parking lot and went into the huge marble-floored hallways. I took an elevator to the grand jury room and stepped out of the elevator. And I was shocked to see benches filled with the young men who had been enlisted in our Reserve units. There were at least a hundred of them. Some nodded to me and a few shook my hand and we made jokes about the whole business. I saw Frank Alcore standing by himself near one of the huge windows. I went over to him and shook his hand. He seemed calm. But his face was strained.

'Isn't this a lot of shit?' he said as we shook hands.

'Yeah,' I said. Nobody was in uniform except Frank. He wore all his WW II campaign ribbons and his master sergeant stripes and longevity hash marks. He looked like a gung-ho career soldier. I knew he was gambling that a grand jury would refuse to indict a patriot called back to the defence of his country. I hoped it would work.

'Jesus,' Frank said. 'They flew about two hundred of us up from Fort Lee. All over a bunch of crap. Just because some of these little pricks couldn't take their medicine when they got recalled.'

I was impressed and surprised. It had seemed such a little thing we had done. Just taking some money for doing a harmless little hocus-pocus. It hadn't even seemed crooked. Just an accommodation, a meeting in terms of interest between two different parties beneficial to both and harmful to no one. Sure, we had broken a few laws, but we hadn't done anything really bad. And here the government was spending thousands of dollars to put us in jail. It didn't seem fair. We hadn't shot anybody, we hadn't stuck up a bank, we hadn't embezzled funds or forged cheques or received stolen goods or committed rape or even been spies for the Russians. What the hell was all the fuss about? I laughed. For some reason I was suddenly in really good spirits.

'What the hell are you laughing about?' Frank said. 'This is serious.'

There were people scattered all around us, some within ear-shot. I said to Frank cheerfully, 'What the hell do we have to worry about? We're innocent, and we know this is all a bunch of bullshit. Fuck them all.'

He grinned back at me, catching on. 'Yeah,' he said. 'But still, I'd like to kill a few of these little pricks.'

'Don't even say that kidding.' I gave him a warning look. They might have this hall bugged. 'You know you don't mean it.'

'Yeah, I guess so,' Frank said reluctantly. 'You'd think these guys would be proud to serve their country. I didn't squawk, and I've been through one war.'

Then we heard Frank's name being called out by one of the bailiffs near the two huge doors with the big black and white sign on them that read 'Grand Jury Room'. As Frank went in, I saw Paul Hemsi coming out. I went up to him and said, 'Hi Paul, how you doing?' I held out my hand and he shook it.

He seemed uncomfortable but didn't look guilty. 'How's your father?' I said.

'He's OK,' Paul said. He hesitated briefly. 'I know I'm not supposed to talk about my testimony. You know I can't do that. But my father said to tell you not to worry about anything.'

I felt a wild surge of relief. He had been my one real worry. But Cully had said he would fix the Hemsi family, and now it seemed to be done. I didn't know how Cully had managed it and I didn't care. I watched Paul go to the bank of elevators, and then another one of my customers, a young kid who was an apprentice theatre director I had enlisted at no charge, came up to me. He was really concerned about me, and he told me that he and his friends could testify that I had never asked for or received money from them. I thanked him and shook hands. I made some jokes and smiled a lot and it wasn't even acting. I was playing the role of the jolly slick bribe-taker thereby projecting his all-American innocence. I realized with some surprise that I was enjoying the whole thing. In fact, I was holding court with a lot of my cus-tomers, who were all telling me what a bunch of shit the whole business was, caused by a few soreheads. I even felt that Frank might beat the rap. Then I saw Frank come out of the grand jury room and heard my name called. Frank looked a little grim but mad, and I could tell he hadn't cracked, that he was going to fight it out. I went through the two huge doors and into the grand jury room. By the time I went through the doors I had wiped the smile off my face.

It was nothing like the movies. The grand just seemed to be a mass of people sitting in rows of folding chairs. Not in a jury box or anything. The district attorney stood by a desk with sheafs of paper he read from. There was a stenotype reporter sitting at a tiny desk with his machine on it. I was directed to sit on a chair that was on a little raised platform so that the jury could see me clearly. It was almost as if I were the ladderman in a baccarat pit.

The district attorney was a young guy dressed in a very conservative black suit with a white shirt and neatly knotted sky blue tie. He had thick black hair and very pale skin. I didn't know his name, and never knew it. His voice was very calm and very detached as he asked me questions. He was just putting information onto the record, not trying to impress the jury.

He didn't even come near me when he asked his questions, just stood by his desk. He established my identity and my job.

'Mr Merlyn,' he said, 'did you ever solicit money from anyone for any reason whatsoever?'

'No,' I said. I looked at him and the jury members right in the eye as I gave my answers. I kept my face serious, though for some reason I wanted to smile. I was still high.

The district attorney said, 'Did you receive any money from anyone in order for him to be enlisted in the six months' Army Reserve programme?'

'No,' I said.

'Do you have any knowledge of any other person's receiving money contrary to law in order to receive preferred treatment in any way?'

'No,' I said, still looking at him and the mass of people sitting so uncomfortably on their small folding chairs. The room was an interior room and dark with bad lighting. I couldn't really make out their faces.

'Do you have any knowledge of any superior officer or anyone else at all using special influences to get someone into the six months' programme when his name was not on the waiting lists kept by your office?'

I knew he would ask a question like that. And I had thought about whether I should mention the congressman who had come down with the heir of the steel fortune and made the major toe the line. Or tell how the Reserve colonel and some of the other Reserve officers had put their own friends' sons on the list out of turn. Maybe that would scare off the investigators or divert attention to those higher-ups. But then I realized that the reason the FBI was taking all this trouble was to uncover higher-ups, and if that happened, the investigation would be intensified. Also, the whole affair would acquire more importance to the newspapers if a congressman were involved. So I had decided to keep my mouth shut. If I were indicted and tried, my lawyer could always use that information. So now I shook my head and said, 'No.'

The district attorney shuffled his papers and then said, without looking at me, 'That will be all. You're excused.' I got out of my chair and stepped down and left the jury room. And then I realized why I was so cheerful, so high, almost delighted.

I had been a magician, really. All those years when everybody was sailing along, taking bribes without a worry in the world, I had peered into the future and foreseen this day. These questions, this courthouse, the FBI, the spectre of prison. And I had cast spells against them. I had hidden my money with Cully. I had taken great pains not to make enemies among all the people I had done illegal business with. I had never explicitly asked for any definite sum of money. And when some of my customers had stiffed me, I had never chased them. Even Mr Hemsi after promising to make me happy for the rest of my life. Well, he had made me happy just by getting his son not to testify. Maybe that's what had turned the trick, not Cully. Except that I knew better. It was Cully who had got me off the hook. But OK, even if I had needed a little help, I was still a magician. Everything had happened exactly as I knew it would. I was really proud of myself. I didn't care that maybe I was just a slick hustler who took intelligent precautions.

21

WHEN Cully got off the plane, he took a taxi to a famous bank in Manhattan. He looked at his watch. It was after 10 A.M. Gronevelt would be making his call right now to the vice-president of the bank that Cully was delivering the money to.

Everything was as planned. Cully was ushered into the vice-president's office, and behind closed, locked doors, he delivered the briefcase.

The vice-president opened it with his key and counted out the million dollars in front of Cully. Then he filled out a bank deposit slip, scribbled his signature on it and gave the slip of paper to Cully. They shook hands and Cully left. A block away from the bank he took a prepared, stamped envelope out of his jacket pocket and put the slip into it and sealed the envelope. Then he dropped it into a mailbox on the corner. He wondered how the whole thing worked, how the vice-president covered the drop and who picked up the money. Someday he would have to know.

Cully and Merlyn met in the Oak Room of the Plaza. They didn't talk about the problem until they had finished lunch and then walked through Central Park. Merlyn told Cully the whole story, and Cully nodded his head and made some sympathetic remarks. From what he could gather it was strictly a small-time grafter's operation that the FBI had stumbled onto. Even if Merlyn were convicted, he would get only a suspended sentence. There wasn't that much to worry about. Except that Merlyn was such a square guy he'd be ashamed of having a conviction on his record. That should be the worst of his worries, Cully thought.

When Merlyn mentioned Paul Hemsi, the name rang a bell in Cully's head. But now, as they walked through Central Park and

Merlyn told him about the meeting with Hemsi Senior in the garment centre, everything clicked. One of the many garment centre tycoons who came to Vegas for long weekends and the Christmas and New Year holidays, Charles Hemsi, was a big gambler and a devoted cunt man. Even when he came to Vegas with his wife, Cully had to arrange for Charlie Hemsi to get a piece. Right on the floor of the casino, with the Mrs Hemsi playing roulette, Cully would slip the key, its room-numbered wooden plaque attached, into Charlie Hemsi's hand. Cully would whisper what time the girl would be in the room.

Charlie Hemsi would wander out to the coffee shop to escape his wife's suspicious eye. From the coffee shop he would saunter down the long labyrinth of hotel corridors to the room numbered on the key plaque. Inside that room he would find a luscious girl waiting for him. It would take less than a half hour. Charlie would give the girl a black hundred-dollar chip, then, thoroughly relaxed, saunter down the blue-carpeted corridors into the casino. He would pass by the roulette table and watch his wife gamble, give her a few encouraging words, some chips, never the blacks, then plunge joyfully back into the wild mêlée of the crap tables. A big, bluff, good-natured guy, a lousy gambler who nearly always lost, a degenerate gambler who never quit when he was ahead. Cully had not remembered him immediately because Charlie Hemsi had been trying to take the cure.

Hemsi had markers out all over Vegas. The Xanadu casino cage alone held fifty grand of Charlie Hemsi's IOU's. Some of the casinos had already sent dunning letters. Gronevelt had told Cully to hold off. 'He may bail himself out,' Gronevelt said. 'Then he'll remember we were nice guys and we'll get most of his action. Money in the bank when that asshole gambles.'

Cully doubted it. 'That asshole owes over three hundred grand around town,' he said. 'Nobody has seen him in a year. I think he's going the claim agent route.'

'Maybe,' Gronevelt said. 'He's got a good business in New York. If he has a big year, he'll be back. He can't resist the gambling and the broads. Listen, he's sitting with his wife and kids, going to neighbourhood parties. Maybe he hits the hookers in the garment centre. But that makes him nervous, too many of his friends know. Here in Vegas it's all so clean. And he's a crap-shooter. They don't leave the table so easy.'

'And if his business doesn't have a big year?' Cully asked.

'Then he'll use his Hitler money,' Gronevelt said. He took note of Cully's politely inquiring and amused face. 'That's what the garment centre boys call it. During the war they all made a fortune in black-market deals. When materials were rationed by the government, a lot of money passed beneath the table. Money they didn't have to report to Internal Revenue. Couldn't report. They all got rich. But it's money they can't let show. If you want to get rich in this country, you have to get rich in the dark.'

It was that phrase Cully always remembered. 'You have to get rich in the dark.' The credo of Vegas, not only of Vegas, but of many of the businessmen who came to Vegas. Men who owned supermarkets, cash vending businesses, heads of construction firms, shady church officials of all denominations who collected cash in holy baskets. Big corporations with platoons of legal advisers who created a plain of darkness within the law.

Cully listened to Merlyn with only half an ear. Thank God Merlyn never talked much. It was soon over, and as they walked through the park in silence, Cully sorted everything out in his head. Just to make sure, he asked Merlyn to describe Hemsi Senior again. No, it wasn't Charlie. It must be one of his brothers, a partner in the business and, from the sound of it, the dominant partner. Charlie had never struck Cully as a hardworking executive. Counting down in his head, Cully could see all the steps he would have to take. It was beautiful, and he was sure Gronevelt would approve. He had only three days before Merlyn appeared before the grand jury, but that would be enough.

So now Cully could enjoy the walk through the park with Merlyn. They talked about old times. They asked the same old questions about Jordan. Why had he done it? Why would a man who had just won four hundred grand blow his brains out? Both of them were too young to dream of the emptiness of success, though Merlyn had read about it in novels and textbooks. Cully didn't buy that bullshit. He knew how happy 'The Pencil', the complete one, would make him. He would be an emperor. Rich and powerful men, beautiful women would be his guests. He could fly them from the ends of the world free, the Xanadu Hotel would pay. Just by his, Cully's, use of 'The Pencil'. He could bestow luxurious suites, the richest foods, fine wines, beautiful women one at a time, two at a time, three at a time. And really beautiful. He could transport the ordinary mortal into paradise for three, four, five days, even a week. All free.

Except, of course, that they had to buy chips, the greens and blacks, and they had to gamble. A small price to pay. They could win, after all, if they got lucky. If they gambled intelligently, they would not lose too much. Cully thought benevolently that he would use 'The Pencil' for Merlyn. Merlyn could have anything he wanted whenever he came to Vegas.

And now Merlyn was crooked. Or at least bent. Yet it was plain to Cully that it was a temporary aberration. Everybody gets bent at least one time in his life. And Merlyn showed his shame, at least to Cully. He had lost some of his serenity, some of his confidence. And this touched Cully. He had never been innocent and he treasured innocence in others.

So when he and Merlyn said their good-byes, Cully gave him a hug. 'Don't worry, I'll fix it. Go into that grand jury room and deny everything. OK?'

Merlyn laughed. 'What else can I do?' he said.

'And when you come out to Vegas, everything is on the house,' Cully said. 'You're my guest.'

'I don't have my lucky Winner jacket,' Merlyn said, smiling.

'Don't worry,' Cully said. 'If you sink too deep, I'll deal you a little blackjack personally.'

'That's stealing, not gambling,' Merlyn said. 'I gave up stealing ever since I got that notice to the grand jury.'

'I was only kidding,' Cully said. 'I wouldn't do that to Gronevelt. If you were maybe a beautiful broad, yes, but you're too ugly.' And he was surprised to see Merlyn flinch again. And it struck him that Merlyn was one of those people who thought of themselves as ugly. A lot of women felt that, but not men, he thought. Cully said his final good-bye by asking Merlyn if he needed some of his black cash stashed at the hotel, and Merlyn said not yet. And so they parted.

Back in his Plaza Hotel suite Cully made a series of calls to the casinos in Vegas. Yes, Charles Hemsi's markers were still outstanding. He made a call to Gronevelt to outline his plan and then changed his mind. Nobody in Vegas knew how many taps the FBI had around town. So he just mentioned casually to Gronevelt that he would stay in New York for a few days and ask for some markers from New York customers who were behind, a little late. Gronevelt was laconic. 'Ask them nice,' he said. And Cully said of course, what else could he do? They both understood they were talking for the FBI record. But Gronevelt had been alerted and would expect an explanation later in Vegas.

Cully would be in the clear, he had not tried to throw a fastball by Gronevelt.

The next day Cully got in touch with Charles Hemsi, not at the garment centre office, but on a golf course in Roslyn, Long Island. Cully rented a limo and got out there early. He had a drink at the clubhouse and waited.

It was two hours before he saw Charles Hemsi come off the links. Cully got up from his chair and strolled outside, where Charles was chatting with his partners before going into the lockers. He saw Hemsi hand over some money to one of the players; the sucker had just been hustled in golf, he lost everywhere. Cully sauntered up to them casually.

'Charlie,' he said with sincere Vegas 'Host' pleasure. 'Good to see you again.' He held out his hand and Hemsi shook it.

He could see that funny look on Hemsi's face which meant he recognized Cully but couldn't place him. Cully said, 'From the Xanadu Hotel. Cully. Cully Cross.'

Hemsi's face changed again. Fear mixed with irritation, then the salesman grimace. Cully gave his most charming smile, and slapping Hemsi on the back, he said, 'We've missed you. Haven't seen you in a long time. Jesus, what are the odds of me running into you like this? Like betting a number on the roulette wheel straight up.'

The golf partners were drifting into the clubhouse, and Charlie started to follow them. He was a big man, much bigger than Cully, and he just brushed past. Cully allowed it. Then he called after Hemsi, 'Charlie, give me a minute. I'm here to help.' He made his voice fill with sincerity, without pleading. And yet the notes of his words were strong, rang like iron.

The other man hesitated and Cully was quickly at his side. 'Charlie, listen, this will not cost you a dime. I can square all your markers in Vegas. And you don't pay a cent. All your brother has to do is a small favour.'

Charlie Hemsi's big bluff face went pale, and he shook his head. 'I don't want my brother to know about those markers. He's murder. No way can you tell my brother.'

Cully said softly, almost sorrowfully, 'The casinos are tired of waiting, Charlie. The collectors are going to be in the picture. You know how they operate. They go down to your place of business, make scenes. They scream for their money. When you see two seven-foot three-hundred-pound guys screaming for their money, it can be a little unnerving.'

'They can't scare my brother,' Charlie Hemsi said. 'He's tough and he has connections.'

'Sure,' Cully said. 'I don't mean they can make you pay if you don't want to. But your brother will know and he'll get involved and the whole thing will be messy. Look, I'll make you a promise. Get your brother to see me and I'll put a hold on all your markers at the Xanadu. And you can come there and gamble, and I'll comp you all the way just like before. You won't be able to sign markers, you'll have to play cash. If you win, you can make a little payment on the markers as you go along. That's a good deal. No?' Here Cully made a little gesture almost of apology.

He could see Charlie's light blue eyes get interested. The guy hadn't been to Vegas for a year. He must be missing the action. Cully recalled that in Vegas he had never asked to be comped for the golf course. Which meant, that he wasn't that crazy about golf. Because a lot of degenerate gamblers liked to put in a morning on the great golf course of the Xanadu Hotel. This guy was bored stiff. Still, Charlie hesitated.

'Your brother is going to know anyway,' Cully said. 'Better from me than the collectors. You know me. You know I'll never go over the line.'

'What's the small favour?' Charlie asked.

'Small, small,' Cully said. 'He'll do it once he hears the proposition. I swear to you. He won't mind. He'll be glad to do it.'

Charlie smiled a sad smile. 'He won't be glad,' he said. 'But come on into the clubhouse and we'll have a drink and talk.'

An hour later Cully was on his way back to New York. He had stood over Charlie when Charlie made the phone call to his brother and arranged the appointment. He had conned and hustled and charmed Charlie Hemsi a dozen different ways. That he would square all the markers in Vegas, that nobody would ever bother him for the money. That the next time Charlie came to Vegas he would have the best suite and be comped all the way. And also as a bonus, that there was a girl, tall, long-legged, blonde, from England with that great English accent, and the loveliest ass you ever saw, the best-looking dancer in the line at the Xanadu Hotel cabaret show. And Charlie could have her all night. Charlie would love her. And she would love Charlie.

So they had made arrangements for Charlie's trip at the end of the month. By the time Cully got through with him Charlie thought he was eating honey rather than getting castor oil poured down his throat.

Cully went back to the Plaza first to freshen up and change. He got rid of the limousine. He would walk down to the garment centre. In his room he put on his best Sy Devore suit, silk shirt and conservative brown plaid tie. He put cuff links into his shirt sleeves. He had a pretty good picture of Eli Hemsi from brother Charles, and he didn't want to make a bad first impression.

Walking through the garment centre, Cully felt disgust at the dirtiness of the city and the pinched, haggard faces walking its streets. Hand trucks, loaded with brightly coloured dresses gallowed from metal racks, were being pushed by black men or old-timers with the seamed red faces of alcoholics. They pushed the handtrucks through the streets like cowboys, stopping traffic, almost knocking down pedestrians. Like sand and tumbleweed of a desert, the garbage of discarded newspapers, remnants of food, empty pop bottles caught in the truck wheels, washed over their shoes and trouser cuffs. The sidewalks were so clogged with people you could hardly breathe, even in the open air. The buildings looked cancerous, grey tumours rising to the sky. Cully regretted for a moment his affection for Merlyn. He hated this city. He was amazed that anyone chose to live in it. And people made cracks about Vegas. And gambling. Shit. At least gambling kept the city clean.

The entranceway of the Hemsi building seemed neater than others; the skin of the foyer that held the elevator seemed to have a thinner coat of grime over the usual white tiles. Jesus, Cully thought, what a crummy business. But when he got off on the sixth floor, he had to change his mind. The receptionist and secretary were not up to Vegas standards, but Eli Hemsi's suite of offices was. And Eli Hemsi, Cully saw at a glance, was a man not to be fucked around with in any way.

Eli Hemsi was dressed in his usual dark silk suit with a pearly grey tie sitting on his startlingly white shirt. His massive head bowed in alert attention as Cully spoke. His deep-socketed eyes seemed sad. But his energy and force could not be contained. Poor Merlyn, Cully thought, getting mixed up with this guy.

Cully was as brief as could be under the circumstances, gravely businesslike. Charm would be wasted on Eli Hemsi. 'I've come here to help two people,' Cully said. 'Your brother, Charles, and a friend of mine named Merlyn. Believe me when I tell you that is my sole purpose. For me to help them you have to do a small favour. If you say no, there is nothing more I can do to help. But even if you say no, I will do nothing to hurt anyone. Everything will remain the same.' He paused for a moment to let Eli Hemsi say something, but that great buffalolike head was frozen with wary attention. The sombre eyes did not even flicker.

Cully went on. 'Your brother, Charles, owes my hotel in Vegas, the Xanadu, over fifty thousand dollars. He owes another two hundred and fifty thousand scattered around Vegas. Let me say right now that my hotel will never press him for his markers. He's been too good a customer and he's too nice a man. The other casinos may make things a little unpleasant for him, but they can't really make him pay if you use your connections, which I know you have. But then you owe your connections a favour which eventually may cost you more than what I ask.'

Eli Hemsi sighed and then asked in his soft but powerful voice, 'Is my brother a good gambler?'

'Not really,' Cully said. 'But that doesn't make any difference. Everybody loses.'

Hemsi sighed again. 'He's not much better in the business. I am going to buy him out, get rid of him, fire my own brother. He's nothing but trouble with his gambling and his women. When he was young, he was a great salesman, the best, but he's too old now and he's not interested. I don't know if I can help him. I know I won't pay his gambling debts. I don't gamble, I don't take that pleasure. Why should I pay for his?'

'I'm not asking you to,' Cully said. 'But here's what I can do. My hotel will buy all his markers from the other casinos. He won't have to pay for them unless he comes and gambles and wins at our casino. We won't give him any more credit, and I'll make sure no other casino in Vegas gives him credit. He can't get hurt if he just plays for cash. That's strength. For him. Just like letting people sign markers is our strength in our operation. I can give him that protection.'

Hemsi was still watching him very intently. 'But my brother keeps gambling?'

'You'll never be able to stop him,' Cully said simply. 'There are many men like him, very few men like yourself. Real life is not that exciting to him any more, he's not interested. Very common.'

Eli Hemsi nodded, thinking that over, rolling it around his

buffalolike head. 'But this isn't too bad a business deal for you,' he said to Cully. 'Nobody can collect my brother's debts, you said that yourself, so you're giving away nothing. And then my foolish brother comes with ten, twenty thousand dollars in his pocket and you win it from him: So you gain. No?'

Cully said very carefully, 'It could go another way. Your brother could sign more markers and owe a great deal more money. Enough money to make certain people think it worthwhile to collect them or try harder to collect them. Who knows how foolish a man can get? Believe me when I tell you that your brother won't be able to stay away from Vegas. It's in his blood. Men like him come from all over the world. Three, four, five times a year. I don't know why, but they come. It means something to them that you and I can't understand. And remember, I have to buy up his markers; that will cost me something.' As he said this, he wondered how he could make Gronevelt accept the proposition. But he would worry about that later.

'And what is the favour?' The question was finally asked in that same soft, yet powerful voice. It was really the voice of a saint, the voice seemed to give off a spiritual serenity. Cully was impressed and for the first time a little worried. Maybe this wouldn't work.

Cully said, 'Your son, Paul. He gave testimony against my friend Merlyn. You remember Merlyn. You promised to make him happy for the rest of his life.' And Cully let the steel come into his voice. He was annoyed by the power given off by this man. A power born of his tremendous success with money, the rise from poverty to millions in an adverse world, from the victorious wars of his life while carrying a foolish brother.

But Eli Hemsi did not rise to the bait of this ironic reproach. He did not even smile. He was still listening.

'Your son's testimony is the only evidence against Merlyn. Sure I understand, Paul was frightened.' Suddenly there was a dangerous flicker in those dark eyes watching him. Anger at this stranger knowing his son's first name and using it so familiarly and almost contemptuously. Cully gave back a sweet smile. 'A very nice boy you have, Mr Hemsi. Everybody is certain he was tricked, threatened, to make his statement to the FBI. I've consulted some very good lawyers. They say he can back off in the grand jury room, give his testimony in such a way so that he will not convince the jury and still not get in trouble with the FBI. Maybe he can retract the testimony altogether.' He studied the face opposite him. There was nothing to read. 'I assume your son has immunity,' Cully said. 'He won't be prosecuted. I also understand you probably have it arranged so he won't have to do his Army duty. He'll come out of it a hundred percent OK. I figure you have that all set. But if he does this favour, I promise you nothing will change.'

Eli Hemsi spoke now in a different voice. It was stronger, not so soft, yet persuasive, a salesman selling. 'I wish I could do that,' he said. 'That boy, Merlyn, he's a very nice boy. He helped me, I will be grateful to him forever.' Cully noted that here was a man who used the word 'forever' pretty often. No halfway gestures for him. He had promised Merlyn he would make him happy for the rest of his life. Now he was going to be grateful forever. A real fucking claim agent weaseling out of his obligations. For the second time Cully felt some anger that this guy was treating Merlyn like such a schmuck. But he continued to listen with an agreeable smile on his face.

'There is nothing I can do,' Hemsi said. 'I can't endanger my son. My wife would never forgive me. He is her whole life. My brother is a grown man. Who can help him? Who can guide him, who can make his life now? But my son has to be cared for. He is my first concern. Afterward, believe me, I will do anything for Mr Merlyn. Ten, twenty, thirty years from now. I will never forget him. Then, when this is all over, you can ask me anything.' Mr Hemsi rose from his desk and put out his hand, his powerful frame bent over with grateful solicitousness. 'I wish my son had a friend like you.'

Cully grinned at him, shook his hand. 'I don't know your son, but your brother is my friend. He's coming out to visit me in Vegas at the end of the month. But don't worry. I'll take care of him. I'll keep him out of trouble.' He saw the pondering look on Eli Hemsi's face. He might as well sock it to him all the way.

'Since you can't help me,' Cully said, 'I have to get Merlyn a really good lawyer. Now the district attorney has probably told you that Merlyn will plead guilty and get a suspended sentence. And everything will blow away so that your son not only will get immunity, but will never have to go back into the Army. That may be. But Merlyn will not plead guilty. There will be a trial. Your son will have to appear in an open court. Your son will have to testify. There will be a lot of publicity. I know that won't bother you, but the newspapers will get to know where your son, Paul, is and what he is doing. I don't care who promised you what. Your son will have to go into the Army. The newspapers will just put on too much pressure. And then, besides all that, you and your son will have enemies. To use your phrase, "I'll make you unhappy for the rest of your life." '

Now that the threat was out in the open, Hemsi leaned back in the chair and stared at Cully. His face, heavy and cragged, was more sad in its sombreness than angry. So Cully gave it to him again. 'You have connections. Call them and listen to their advice. Ask about me. Tell them I work for Gronevelt at the Xanadu Hotel. If they agree with you and call Gronevelt, there is nothing I can do. But you'll be in their debt.'

Hemsi leaned back in his chair. 'You say everything will come out right if my son does what you ask?'

'I guarantee it,' Cully said.

'He won't have to go back into the Army?' Hemsi asked again.

'I guarantee that too,' Cully said. 'I have friends in Washington, as you have. But my friends can do things your friends can't do, even if only because they can't be connected to you.'

Eli Hemsi was ushering Cully to the door. 'Thank you,' he said. 'Thank you very much. I have to think over everything you said. I'll be in touch with you.'

They shook hands again as he walked Cully to the door of his suite. 'I'm at the Plaza,' Cully said. 'And I'm leaving for Vegas tomorrow morning. So if you could call me tonight, I'd be grateful.'

But it was Charlie Hemsi who called him. Charlie was drunk and gleeful. 'Cully, you smart little bastard. I don't know how you did it, but my brother told me to tell you that everything is OK. He agrees with you completely.'

Cully relaxed. Eli Hemsi had made his phone calls to check him out. And Gronevelt must have backed the play. He felt an enormous affection and gratitude for Gronevelt. He said to Charlie, 'That's great. See you in Vegas at the end of the month, Charlie. You'll have the time of your life.'

'I wouldn't miss it,' Charlie Hemsi said. 'And don't forget that dancer.'

'I won't,' Cully said.

After that he dressed and went out for dinner. In the restaurant lobby he used the pay phone to call Merlyn. 'Everything is OK, it was all a misunderstanding. You're going to be all right.'

Merlyn's voice seemed far away, almost abstracted, and not as grateful as Cully would have liked it to be. 'Thanks,' Merlyn said. 'See you in Vegas soon.' And he hung up.

22

CULLY Cross squared everything for me, but poor patriotic Frank Alcore was indicted, released from active duty to civilian status, tried and convicted. A year in prison. A week later the major called me into his office. He wasn't mad at me or indignant; in fact, he had an amused smile on his face.

'I don't know how you did it, Merlyn,' he told me. 'But you beat the rap. Congratulations. And I don't give a shit, the whole business is a fucking joke. They should have put those kids in jail. I'm glad for you, but I've got my orders to handle this business and make sure it doesn't happen again. Now I'm talking to you as a friend. I'm not pressing. My advice is, resign from the government service. Right away.'

I was shocked and a little sick. I thought I was home free and here I was out of a job. How the hell would I meet all my bills? How would I support my wife and kids? How would I pay the mortgage on the new house on Long Island I would be moving into in just a few months?

I tried to keep a poker face when I said, 'The grand jury cleared me. Why do I have to quit?'

The major must have read me. I remember Jordan and Cully in Las Vegas kidding me about how anybody could tell what I was thinking. Because the major had a look of pity when he said, 'I'm telling you for your own good. The brass will have their CID people all over this armoury. The FBI may keep snooping around. All the kids in the Reserve will still try to use you, try to get you into deals. They'll keep the pot stirring. But if you quit, everything should blow over pretty quick. The investigators will cool off and go away with nothing to focus on.'

I wanted to ask about all the other civilians who had been

taking bribes, but the major anticipated me. 'I know of at least ten other advisers like you, unit administrators, who are going to resign. Some have already. Believe me, I'm on your side. And you'll be OK. You're wasting your time on this job. You should have done better for yourself at your age.'

I nodded. I was thinking that too. That I hadn't done much with my life so far. Sure, I'd had a novel published, but I was making a hundred bucks a week take-home pay from Civil Service. True, I earned another three or four hundred a month with free-lance articles for the magazines, but with the illegal gold mine closed down, I had to make a move.

'OK,' I said. 'I'll write a letter giving two weeks' notice.'

The major nodded and shook my hand. 'You have some paid sick leave coming,' he said. 'Use it up in those two weeks and look for a new job. I'll stand still for it. Just come in a couple of times a week to keep the paperwork going.'

I went back to my desk and wrote out my letter of resignation. Things weren't as bad as they looked. I had about twenty days of vacation pay coming to me, which was about four hundred dollars. I had, I figured, about fifteen hundred dollars in my government pension fund, which I could draw out, though I'd forfeit my rights to a pension when I was sixty-five. But that was more than thirty years away. I could be dead by then. A total of two grand. And then there was the bribe money I had stashed with Cully in Vegas. Over thirty grand there. For a moment I had an overwhelming sense of panic. What if Cully reneged on me and didn't give me my money? There would be nothing I could do about that. We were good friends, he had bailed me out of my troubles, but I had no illusions about Cully. He was a Vegas hustler. What if he said he had my money coming to him for the favour he had done me? I couldn't dispute it. I would have paid the money to keep out of jail. Christ, would I have paid it!

But the thing I dreaded most was having to tell Valerie I was out of a job. And having to explain to her father. The old man would ask around and get the truth anyway.

I didn't tell Valerie that night. The next day I took off from work and went to see Eddie Lancer at his magazines. I told him everything and he sat there, shaking his head and laughing. When I finished, he said, almost wonderingly, 'You know, I'm always getting surprised. I thought you were the straightest guy in the world next to your brother, Artie.'

I told Eddie Lancer about how taking the bribes, becoming a half-assed criminal had made me feel better psychologically. That in some way I had discharged a lot of the bitterness I felt. The rejection of my novel by the public, the drabness of my life, its basic failure, how I'd always really been unhappy.

Lancer was looking at me with that little smile on his face. 'And I thought you were the least neurotic guy I ever met,' he said. 'You're happily married, you have kids, you live a secure life, you earn a living. You're working on another novel. What the hell more do you want?'

'I'll need a job,' I told him.

Eddie Lancer thought that one over for a moment. Oddly enough I didn't feel embarrassed appealing to him.

'Just between you and me I'm leaving this place in about six months,' he said. 'They'll move another editor up to my place. I'll be recommending my successor and he'll owe me a favour. I'll ask him to give you enough free-lance to live on.'

'That would be great,' I said.

Eddie said briskly, 'I can load you up with work until then. 'Adventure stories, some of the love fiction crap and some book reviews I usually do. OK?'

'Sure,' I said. 'When do you figure you'll finish your book?'

'In a couple of months,' Lancer said. 'How about you?'

It was a question I always hated. The truth was that I had only an outline of a novel I wanted to write about a famous criminal case in Arizona. But I hadn't written anything. I had submitted the outline to my publisher, but he had refused to give me an advance. He said it was the kind of novel that wouldn't make money because it involved the kidnapping of a child who was murdered. There wouldn't be any sympathy for the kidnapper, the hero of the book. I was aiming at another *Crime and Punishment*, and that had scared the publisher off.

'I'm working on it,' I said. 'Still a long way to go.'

Lancer smiled sympathetically. 'You're a good writer,' he said. 'You'll make it big someday. Don't worry.'

We talked a while longer about writing and books. We both agreed we were better novelists than most of the famous novelists making their fortunes on the best-seller lists. When I left, I was in a confident mood. I always left Lancer that way. For some reason he was one of the few people I felt easy with, and because I knew he was smart and gifted, his good opinion of my talent cheered me up.

And so everything had turned out for the best. I was now a full-time writer, I would lead an honest life, I had escaped jail and in a few months I would move into my very own house, for the first time in my life. Maybe a little crime does pay.

Two months later I moved into my newly built house on Long Island. The kids all had their own bedrooms. We had three bathrooms and a special laundry room. I would no longer have to lie in my bath while newly washed clothes dripped down into my face. No longer have to wait for the kids to finish. I had the almost excruciating luxury of privacy. My own den to write in, my own garden, my own lawn. I was separate from other people. It was Shangri-La. And yet it was something so many people took for granted.

Most important of all, I felt that now my family was safe. We had left the poor and desperate behind us. They would never catch up; their tragedies would never cause ours. My children would never be orphans.

Sitting on my suburban back porch one day, I realized I was truly happy, maybe happier than I would ever be in my life again. And that made me a little pissed off. If I was an artist, why was I so happy with such ordinary pleasures, a wife I loved, children who delighted me, a cheap tract house in the suburbs? One thing was sure, I was no Gauguin. Maybe that was why I wasn't writing. I was too happy. And I felt a twinge of resentment against Valerie. She had me trapped. Jesus.

Except even this couldn't keep me feeling content. Everything was going so well. And the pleasure you took in children was so commonplace. They were so disgustingly 'cute'. When my son was five years old, I had taken him for a walk through the streets of the city and a cat had jumped out of a cellar and almost literally sailed in front of us. My son had turned to me and said, 'Is that a scaredy-cat?' When I told Vallie about it, she was delighted and wanted to send it in to one of those magazines that pay money for cute little stories. I'd had a different reaction. I wondered if one of his friends had taunted him with being a scaredy-cat and he had been puzzled by what the phrase meant rather than insulted. I thought of all the mysteries of language and experience my son was encountering for the first time. And I envied him the innocence of childhood as I envied him the luck he had in having parents he could say that to and then have them make a fuss over him.

And I remember one day when we had gone out for a family

Sunday-afternoon walk on Fifth Avenue, Valerie window-shopping for dresses she could never afford. Coming toward us was a woman about three feet tall but dressed elegantly in suede jerkin and white frilly blouse and dark tweed skirt. My daughter tugged at Valerie's coat and pointed to the dwarf lady and said, 'Mummy, what's that?'

Valerie was horrified with embarrassment. She was always terrified about hurting anyone's feelings. She shushed my daughter until the woman was safely past. Then she explained to our daughter that the woman was one of those people who had never grown taller. My daughter didn't really grasp the idea. Finally she asked, 'You mean she didn't grow up. You mean she's an old lady like you?'

Valerie smiled at me. 'Yes, dear,' she said. 'Now don't think about it any more. It only happens to very few people.'

At home that night, when I told my kids a story before sending them to bed, my daughter seemed to be lost in thought and not listening. I asked her what was wrong. Then, her eyes very wide, she said, 'Daddy, am I really a little girl or am I an old lady who didn't grow up?'

I knew that there were millions of people who had stories like this to tell about their kids. That it was all terribly common-place. And yet I couldn't help the feeling that sharing a part of my children's lives made me richer. That the fabric of my life was made up of these little things that seemed to have no importance.

Again my daughter. One evening at dinner she had infuriated Valerie by continuously misbehaving. She threw food at her brother, deliberately spilled a drink and then knocked over a gravy boat. Finally Valerie screamed at her, 'You do one more thing and I'll kill you.'

It was, of course, a figure of speech. But my daughter stared at her very intently and asked, 'Do you have a gun?'

It was funny because she so obviously believed that her mother couldn't kill her unless she had a gun. She knew nothing yet of wars and pestilence, of rapists and molesters, of automobile accidents and plane crashes, clubbings, cancer, poison, getting thrown out of a window. Valerie and I both laughed, and Valerie said, 'Of course I haven't got a gun, don't be silly.' And the knot of worried concentration disappeared from my daughter's face. I noticed that Valerie never made that kind of irritated remark again.

And Valerie astonished me too sometimes. She had become more and more Catholic and conservative with the years. She was no longer the bohemian Greenwich village girl who had wanted to become a writer. In the city housing project pets had been forbidden, and Vallie never told me she loved animals. Now that we owned a house Valerie bought a puppy and a kitten. Which didn't make me too happy, even though my son and daughter made a pretty picture playing with their pets on the lawn. The truth is that I had never liked house dogs and cats; they were caricatures of orphans.

I was *too* happy with Valerie. I had no idea then how rare this was and how valuable. And she was the perfect mother for a writer. When the kids fell and had to get stitched up, she never panicked or bothered me. She didn't mind doing all the work a man usually does around the house and which I had no patience for. Her parents now lived only thirty minutes away, and often in the evenings and on weekends she took the car and the kids and went there without even asking me if I wanted to go. She knew I hated that kind of visit and that I could use time alone to work on my book.

But for some reason she had nightmares, maybe because of her Catholic upbringing. During the night I would have to wake her up because she gave little cries of despair and wept even while sound asleep. One night she was terribly frightened and I held her close in my arms and asked her what was wrong, what she'd dreamed about and she whispered to me, 'Never tell me that I'm dying.'

Which scared the hell out of me. I had visions of her having gone to the doctor and receiving bad news. But the next morning, when I questioned her about it, she didn't remember anything. And when I asked her if she had been to see the doctor, she laughed at me. She said. 'It's my religious upbringing. I guess I just worry about going to hell.'

For two years I wrote free-lance articles for the magazines, watched my kids grow up, so happily married that it almost disgusted me. Valerie did a lot of visiting with her family, and I spent a lot of time in my basement writing den, so we really didn't see that much of each other. I had at least three assignments from the magazines every month, while working on a novel I hoped would make me rich and famous. The kidnapping and murder novel was my plaything; the magazines were my bread and butter. I figured I had another three years to go before I finished the book, but I didn't care. I read through the growing pile of manuscript whenever I became lonely. And it was lovely watching the kids grow older and Valerie happier and more content and less afraid of dying. But nothing lasts. It doesn't last because you don't want it to last, I think. If everything is perfect, you go looking for trouble.

After two years of living in my suburban house, writing ten hours every day, going to a movie once a month, reading everything in sight, I welcomed a call from Eddie Lancer asking me to have dinner with him in the city. For the first time in two years I would see New York at night. I had gone in during the day to talk over my magazine assignments with the editors, but I always drove home for dinner. Valerie had become a great cook, and I didn't want to miss the evening with my kids and my final nightcap of work in my den.

But Eddie Lancer was just back from Hollywood, and he promised me some great stories and some great food. And as usual he asked me how my novel was coming. He always treated me as if he knew I was going to be a great writer, and I loved that. He was one of the few people I knew who seemed to have a genuine kindness untouched by self-interest. And he could be very funny in a way I envied. He reminded me of Valerie when she had been writing stories at the New School. She had it in her writing and sometimes in everyday life. It flashed out every once in a while even now. And so I told Eddie I had to go into the magazines the next day to get an assignment and we could have dinner afterward.

He took me to a place called Pearl's that I had never heard of. I was so dumb that I didn't know it was New York's 'in' Chinese restaurant. It was the first time I had ever eaten Chinese food, and when I told Eddie that, he was amazed. He did a whole routine introducing me to different Chinese dishes while pointing out the celebrities and even opening up my fortune cookie and reading it for me. He also stopped me from eating the fortune cookie. 'No, no, you never eat them,' he said. 'That's terribly unsophisticated. If there's one valuable thing you'll get out of this night, it's learning never to eat your fortune cookie in a Chinese reataurant.'

It was a whole routine that was only funny between two friends in the context of their relationship with each other. But months later I read a story of his in *Esquire* in which he used that incident. It was a touching story, making fun of himself making fun of me. I knew him better after that story, how his good humour masked his essential loneliness and estrangement from the world and the people around him. And I got a hint of what he really thought about me. He painted a picture of me as a man in control of life and knowing where he was going. Which amused the hell out of me.

But he was wrong about the fortune cookie business being the only valuable thing I would get out of that night. Because after dinner he talked me into going to one of those New York literary parties, where again I met the great Osano.

We were having our dessert and coffee. Eddie made me order chocolate ice cream. He told me that it was the only dessert that went with Chinese food. 'Remember that,' he said. 'Never eat your fortune cookie and always order chocolate ice cream for dessert.' Then offhandedly he asked me to come to the party with him. I was a little reluctant. I had an hour and a half drive out to Long Island, and I was anxious to get home and maybe get in an hour's work before I went to bed.

'Come on,' Eddie said. 'You can't always be an uxorious hermit. Make a night out of it. There'll be some good booze, good talk and some nice-looking broads. And you might make some valuable contacts. It's harder for a critic to knock the shit out of you if he knows you personally. And your stuff may read better to some publisher if he's met you at a party and he thinks you're a nice guy.' Eddie knew that I had no publisher for my new book. The publisher of my first book never wanted to see me again because it had sold only two thousand copies and never got a paperback.

So I went to the party and met Osano. He never let on that he remembered that interview, and neither did I. But a week later I got a letter from him asking if I would come in and have lunch and see him about a job he had to offer me.

23

I TOOK the job with Osano for many different reasons. The job was interesting and prestigious. Since Osano had been appointed the editor of the most influential literary supplement in the country a few years ago, he had trouble with people working for him and so I would be his assistant. The money was good, and the work wouldn't interfere with my novel. And then I was too happy at home; I was becoming too much of a bourgeois hermit. I was happy, but my life was dull. I craved some excitement, some danger. I had vague fleeting memories of my running away to Vegas and how I had actually relished the loneliness and despair I felt then. Is that so crazy, to remember unhappiness with such delight and to despise happiness you hold in your hand?

But most of all, I took the job because of Osano himself. He was, of course, the most famous writer in America. Praised for his string of successful novels, notorious for his scrapes with the law and his revolutionary attitude toward society. Infamous for his scandalous sexual misbehaviour. He fought against everybody and everything. And yet at the party where Eddie Lancer had taken me to meet him he charmed and fascinated everyone. And the people at the party were the cream of the literary world and no slouches at being charming and difficult in their own right.

And I have to admit Osano charmed me. At the party he got into a furious argument with one of the most powerful literary critics in America, who was also a close friend and supporter of his work. But the critic had dared voice the opinion that non-fiction writers were creating art and that some critics were artists. Osano swarmed all over him. 'You bloodsucking cocksucker,' he shouted, drink balanced in one hand, his other hand

208

poised as if ready to throw a punch. 'You have the fucking nerve to make a living off real writers and then say you're the artist? You don't even know what art is. An artist creates out of nothing but himself, do you understand that, you fucking asshole? He's like a fucking spider, the cobwebs are packed away in his body. And you pricks just come along and blow them away with your fucking housewife brooms after he spins them out. You're good with a broom, you fucking jerkoff, that's all you are.' His friend was stunned because he had just praised Osano's nonfiction books and said they were art.

And Osano walked away to a group of women who were waiting to lionize him. There were a couple of feminists in the group, and he wasn't with them two minutes before his group again became the centre of attention. One of the women was shouting at him furiously as he listened to her with amused contempt, his sneaky green eyes glowing like a cat. Then he was off.

'You women want equality and you don't even understand power plays,' he said. 'Your hole card is your cunt, and you show it to your opponents face up. You give it away. And without your cunts you have no power at all. Men can live without affection but not without sex. Women have to have affection and can do without sex.' At this last statement the women swarmed over him with furious protests.

But he stood them off. 'Women are complaining about marriage when they are getting the best bargain they will ever get in their lives. Marriage is like those bonds you buy. There is inflation and there is devaluation. The value keeps going down and down for men. You know why? Women become less and less valuable as they grow older. And then we're stuck with them like an old car. Women don't age as well as men. Can you imagine a fifty-year-old broad being able to con a twenty-year-old kid into bed? And very few women have the economic power to buy youth as men do.'

One woman shouted, 'I have a twenty-year-old lover.' She was a good-looking woman of about forty.

Osano grinned at her wickedly. 'I congratulate you,' he said. 'But what about when you're fifty? With the young girls giving it away so easily you'll have to catch them coming out of grammar school and promise them a ten-speed bike. And do you think your young lovers fall in love with you as young women do with men? You haven't got that old Freudian father image working for you as we do. And I must repeat, a man at forty looks more attractive than he does at twenty. At fifty he can still be very attractive. It's biological.'

'Bullshit,' the attractive forty-year-old woman said. 'Young girls make fools out of you old guys and you believe their bullshit. You're not any more attractive, you just have more power. And you have all the laws on your side. When we change that, we'll change everything.'

'Sure,' Osano said. 'You'll get laws passed so that men will have to get operations to make themselves look uglier when they get older. In the name of fair play and equal rights. You may even get our balls cut off legally. That doesn't change the truth now.' He paused and said, 'You know the worst line of poetry? Browning. "Grow old along with me! The best is yet to be. . ."'

I just hung around and listened. What Osano was saying struck me as mostly bullshit. For one thing he had different ideas about writing. I hated literary talk, though I read all the critics and bought all the critical reviews.

What the hell was being an artist? It was not sensitivity. It was not intelligence. It was not anguish. Not ecstasy. That was all bullshit.

The truth was that you were like a safecracker fiddling with the dial and listening to the tumblers click into place. And after a couple of years the door might swing open and you could start typing. And the hell of it was that what was in the safe was most times not all that valuable.

It was just fucking hard work and a pain in the ass in the bargain. You couldn't sleep at night. You lost all your confidence with people and the outside world. You became a coward, a malingerer in everyday living. You ducked the responsibilities of your emotional life, but after all, it was the only thing you could do. And maybe that was why I was even proud of all the junk I wrote for pulp magazines and book reviews. It was a skill I had, finally a craft. I wasn't just a lousy fucking artist.

Osano never understood that. He had always striven to be an artist and turned out some art and near art. Just as years later he never understood the Hollywood thing, that the movie business was young, like a baby not yet toilet-trained, so you couldn't blame it for shitting all over everybody.

One of the women said, 'Osano, you have such a great track record with women. What's the secret of your success?' Everybody laughed, including Osano. I admired him even more, a guy with five ex-wives who could afford to laugh.

Osano said, 'I tell them it has to be a hundred percent my way and no percent their way before they move in with me. They understand my position and they accept. I always tell them that when they are no longer satisfied with the arrangement to just move out. No arguments, no explanations, no negotiations, just leave. And I can't understand it. They say yes when they move in, and then they break the rules. They try to get it ten percent their way. And when they don't get it, they start a fight.'

'What a marvellous proposition,' another woman said. 'And what do they get in return?'

Osano looked around, and with a perfectly straight face he said, 'A fair fuck.' Some of the women began to boo.

When I decided to take the job with him, I went back and read everything he'd written. His early work was first-rate, with sharp, precise scenes like etchings. The novels held together glued by character and story. And a lot of ideas working. His later books became deeper, more thoughtful, the prose more pompous. He was like an important man wearing his decorations. But all his novels invited the critics in, gave them a lot of material to work on, to interpret, to discuss, to stab around. But I thought his last three books were lousy. The critics didn't.

I started a new life. I drove to New York every day and worked from 11 A.M. to all hours. The offices of the review were huge, part of the newspaper which distributed it. The pace was hectic; books came in literally by the thousands every month, and we had space for only about sixty reviews each week. But all the books had to be at least skimmed. On the job Osano was genuinely kind to everybody who worked for him. He always asked me about my novel and volunteered to read it before publication and give me some editorial advice, but I was too proud to show it to him. Despite his fame and my lack of it, I thought I was the better novelist.

After long evenings working on the schedule of books to be reviewed and whom to give them to, Osano would drink from the bottle of whisky he kept in his desk and give me long lectures on literature, the life of a writer, publishers, women and anything else that was bugging him at that particular time. He had been working on his big novel, the one that he thought would win him the Nobel Prize, for the last five years. He had already collected an enormous advance on it, and the publisher was getting nervous and pushing him. Osano was really pissed off about that. 'That prick,' he said. 'He told me to read the classics for inspiration. That ignorant fuck. Have you ever tried to read the classics over again? Jesus, those old fuckers like Hardy and Tolstoy and Galsworthy had it made. They took forty pages to let out a fart. And you know why? They had their readers trapped. They had them by the balls. No TV, no radio, no movies. No travelling unless you wanted cysts over your asshole from bouncing around on stagecoaches. In England you couldn't even get fucked. Maybe that's why the French writers were more disciplined. The French at least were into fucking, not like those English Victorian jerkoffs. Now I ask you why should a guy with a TV set and a beach house read Proust?'

I'd never been able to read Proust, so I nodded. But I had read everybody else and couldn't see TV or a beach house taking their place.

Osano kept going. '*Anna Karenina*, they call it a masterpiece. It's a full-of-shit book. It's an educated upper-class guy condescending to women. He never shows you what that broad really feels or thinks. He gives us the conventional outlook of that time and place. And then he goes on for three hundred pages on how to run a Russian farm. He sticks that right in there as if anybody gives a shit. And who gives a shit about that asshole Vronsky and his soul? Jesus, I don't know who's worse, the Russians or the English. That fucking Dickens and Trollope, five hundred pages were nothing to them. They wrote when they had time off from tending their garden. The French kept it short at least. But how about that fucking Balzac? I defy! I defy! anybody to read him today.'

He took a slug of whisky and gave out a sigh. 'None of them knew how to use language. None of them except Flaubert, and he's not that great. Not that Americans are that much better. That fuck Dreiser doesn't even know what words mean. He's illiterate, I mean that. He's a fucking aborigine. Another nine-hundred-page pain in the ass. None of those fucking guys could get published today, and if they did, the critics would murder them. Boy, those guys had it made then. No competition.' He paused and sighed wearily. 'Merlyn, my boy, we're a dying breed, writers like us. Find another racket, hustle TV shit, do movies. You can do that stuff with your finger up your ass.' Then, exhausted, he would lie on the couch he kept in his office for his afternoon snooze. I tried to cheer him up.

'That could be a great idea for an *Esquire* article,' I told him. 'Take about six classics and murder them. Like that piece you did on modern novelists.'

Osano laughed. 'Jesus, that was fun. I was kidding and just using it for a power play to give myself more juice and everybody got pissed off. But it worked. It made me bigger and them smaller. And that's the literary game, only those poor assholes didn't know it. They jerked themselves off in their ivory towers and thought that would be enough.'

'So this should be easy,' I said. 'Except that the professor critics will jump on you.'

Osano was getting interested. He got up from the couch and went to his desk. 'What classic do you hate most?'

'*Silas Marner*,' I said. 'And they still teach it in schools.'

'Old dykey George Eliot,' Osano said. 'The school teachers love her. OK, that's one. I hate *Anna Karenina* most. Tolstoy is better than Eliot. Nobody gives a shit about Eliot any more, but the profs will come out screaming when I hit Tolstoy.'

'Dickens?' I said.

'A must,' Osano said. 'But not *David Copperfield*. I gotta admit I love that book. He was really a funny guy, that Dickens. I can get him on the sex stuff, though. He was some fucking hypocrite. And he wrote a lot of shit. Tons of it.'

We started making the list. We had the decency not to molest Flaubert and Jane Austen. But when I gave him Goethe's *Young Werther*, he clapped me on the back and howled. 'The most ridiculous book ever written,' he said. 'I'll make German hamburger out of it.'

Finally we had a list:

> *Silas Marner*
> *Anna Karenina*
> *Young Werther*
> *Dombey and Son*
> *The Scarlet Letter*
> *Lord Jim*
> *Moby Dick*
> Proust (Everything)
> Hardy (Anything)

'We need one more for an even ten,' Osano said.

'Shakespeare,' I suggested.

Osano shook his head. 'I still love Shakespeare. You know it's ironic; he wrote for money, he wrote fast, he was an ignorant lowlife, yet nobody could touch him. And he didn't give a shit whether what he wrote was true or not, just so long as it was beautiful or touching. How about "Love is not love which alters when it alteration finds"? And I could give you tons. But he's too great. Even though I always hated that fucking phony Macduff and that moron Othello.'

'You still need one more,' I said.

'Yeah,' said Osano, grinning with delight. 'Let's see. *Dostoevsky*. He's the guy. How about *Brothers Karamazov*?'

'I wish you luck,' I said.

Osano said thoughtfully. 'Nabokov thinks he's shit.'

'I wish him luck too,' I said.

So we were stuck, and Osano decided to go with just nine. That would make it different from the usual ten of anything anyway. I wondered why we couldn't get up to ten.

He wrote the article that night and it was published two months later. He was brilliant and infuriating, and all through it he dropped little hints how his great novel in progress would have none of the faults of these classics and would replace them all. The article started a furious uproar, and there were articles all over the country attacking him and insulting his novel in progress, which was just what he wanted. He was a first-rate hustler, Osano. Cully would be proud of him. And I made a note that the two of them should meet someday.

In six months I became Osano's right-hand man. I loved the job. I read a lot of the books and gave notes on them to Osano so that he could assign them for review to the free-lancers we used. Our offices were an ocean of books; you were swamped with them, you tripped over them, they covered our desks and chairs. They were like those masses of ants and worms covering a dead carcass. I had always loved and revered books, but now I could understand the contempt and disdain of some intellectual reviewers and critics; they served as valets to heroes.

But I loved the reading part, especially novels and biographies. I couldn't understand the science books or philosophy or the more erudite critics, so Osano shovelled them off to other specialized assistants. It was his pleasure to take on the heavyweight literary critics who came out with books, and he usually murdered them. When they called or wrote to protest, he told them that he 'umpired the ball, not the player', which lowbrow chatter inflamed them the more. But always keeping his Nobel

Prize in mind, he treated some critics very respectfully, gave a lot of space for their articles and books. There were very few of these exceptions. He especially hated English novelists and French philosophers. And yet as time went on, I could see that he hated the job and goofed off from it as much as he could.

And he used his position shamelessly. The publishers' public relations girls soon learned that if they had a 'hot' book they wanted to get reviewed, they had only to take Osano out to lunch and lay a big line of bullshit on him. If the girls were young and pretty, he would kid around and make them understand in a nice way that he would trade space for a piece of ass. He was that upfront about it. Which to me was shocking. I thought that happened only in the movie business. He used the same bargaining techniques on reviewers looking for free-lance work. He had a big budget and we commissioned a lot of reviews that we would pay for but never use. And he always kept his bargains. If they came across, he came across. By the time I arrived he had a nice long string of girlfriends who had access to the most influential literary review in America on the strength of their sexual generosity. I loved the contrast of this with the high intellectual and moral tone of the review.

I often stayed late with him in the office on our deadline nights and we would go out for dinner and a drink together, after which he would go get shacked. He would always want to fix me up, but I kept telling him I was happily married. This developed into a standing joke. 'You still not tired of fucking your *wife*?' he would ask. Just like Cully. I wouldn't answer, just ignore him. It was none of his business. He would shake his head and say, 'You're the tenth wonder. Married a hundred years and still like fucking your wife.' Sometimes I would give him an irritated look, and he'd say, quoting from some writer I'd never read, 'No villain need be. Time is the enemy.' It was his favourite quote. He used it often.

And working there, I got a taste of the literary world. I had always dreamed about being part of it. I thought of it as a place where no one quarrelled or bargained about money. That since these were the people who created the heroes you loved in their books, the creators were like them. And of course, I found out that they were the same as anybody else, only crazier. And I found out that Osano hated all these people too. He'd give me lectures.

'The only special person is the novelist,' Osano would say.

'Not like your fucking short story writers and screenwriters and poets and playwrights and those fucking flyweight literary journalists. All fancy dress. All thin. Not a heavy bone in them. You have to have heavy bones in your work when you write a novel.' He mused about that and then wrote it on a piece of paper, and I knew there would be an essay about heavy bones in next Sunday's review.

Then other times he would rant about the lousy writing in the review. Circulation was going down, and he blamed the dullness of the critical profession.

'Sure, those fuckers are smart, sure, they have interesting things to say. But they can't write a decent sentence. They're like guys who stutter. They break your feet as you try to hang onto every word coming out between those clenched teeth.'

Every week Osano had his own essay on the second page. His writing was brilliant, witty and slanted to make as many enemies as possible. One week he published an essay in favour of the death penalty. He pointed out that in any national referendum the death penalty would be approved by an overwhelming vote. That it was only the elitist class like the readers of the review that had managed to bring the death penalty to a standstill in the United States. He claimed this was a conspiracy of the upper echelons of government. He claimed that it was government policy to give the criminal and poverty-stricken elements a licence to steal, assault, burglarize, rape and murder the middle class. That this was an outlet provided for the lower classes so that they would not turn revolutionary. That the higher echelons of government had estimated the cost to be less this way. That the elitists lived in safe neighbourhoods, sent their children to private schools, hired private security forces and so were safe from the revenge of the misled proletariat. He mocked the liberals who claimed that human life was sacred and that a government policy of putting citizens to death had a brutalizing effect on humanity in general. We were only animals, he said, and should be treated no better than the rogue elephants that were executed in India when they killed a human being. In fact, he asserted, the executed elephant had more dignity and would go to a higher heaven than the heroin-crazed murderers who were allowed to live in a comfortable prison for five or six years before they were let out to murder more middle-class citizens. When he dealt with whether the death penalty was a deterrent, he pointed out that the English were the most law-abiding people on earth, policemen didn't even carry guns. And he attributed this solely to the fact that the English had executed eight-year-old children for stealing lace handkerchiefs as late as the nineteenth century. Then he admitted that though this had wiped out crime and protected property, it had finally turned those more energetic of the working classes into political animals rather than criminal ones and so had brought socialism to England. One Osano line particularly enraged his readers. 'We don't know if capital punishment is a deterrent, but we know that men we execute will not murder again.'

He finished the essay by congratulating the rulers of America for having the ingenuity to give their lower classes a licence to steal and kill so that they would not become political revolutionists.

It was an outrageous essay, but he wrote it so well that the whole thing appeared logical. Letters of protest rolled in by the hundreds from the most famous and important social thinkers of our liberal intellectual readership. A special letter composed by a radical organization and signed by the most important writers in America was sent to the publisher asking that Osano be removed as editor of the review. Osano printed it in the next issue.

He was still too famous to be fired. Everybody was waiting for his 'great' novel to be finished. The one that would assure him of the Nobel Prize. Sometimes when I went into his office, he would be writing on long yellow sheets, which he would put into a desk drawer when I entered and I knew this was the famous work in progress. I never asked him about it and he never volunteered anything.

A few months later he got into trouble again. He wrote a page two essay in the review in which he quoted studies to show that stereotypes were perhaps true. That Italians were born criminals, that Jews were better at making money than anybody else and better violin players and medical students, that worst of all, more than any other people, they put their parents into old folks' homes. Then he quoted studies to show that the Irish were drunks owing perhaps to some unknown chemical deficiency or diet or that the fact that they were repressed homosexuals. And so on. That really brought the screams. But it didn't stop Osano.

In my opinion he was going crazy. One week he took the front page for his own personal review of a book on helicopters. That crazy bee in his bonnet was still buzzing. Helicopters would replace the automobile, and when that happened, all the millions of miles of concrete highways would be torn up and replaced by farmland. The helicopter would help return families to their nuclear structure because then it would be easy for people to visit far-flung relatives. He was convinced the automobile would become obsolete. Maybe because he hated cars. For his weekends in the Hamptons he always took a seaplane or a helicopter specially chartered.

He claimed that only a few more technical inventions would make the helicopter as easy to handle as the automobile. He pointed out that the automatic shift had made millions of women drivers who couldn't handle shifting gears. And this little aside brought down the wrath of Women's Liberation groups. What made it worse, in that very same week a serious study of Hemingway had been published by one of the most respected literary scholars in America. This scholar had a powerful network of influential friends, and he had spent ten years on the study. It got front-page reviews in every publication but ours. Osano gave it page five and three columns instead of the full page. Later that week the publisher sent for him, and he spent three hours in the big office suite on the top floor, explaining his actions. He came down, grinning from ear to ear, and said to me cheerfully, 'Merlyn, my boy, I'll put some life in this fucking rag yet. But I think you should start looking for another job. I don't have to worry, I'm nearly finished with my novel and then I'll be home free.'

By that time I had been working for him for nearly a year and I couldn't understand how he got any work done at all. He was screwing everything he could get his hands on, plus he went to all the New York parties. During that time he had knocked out a quickie short novel for a hundred grand advance. He wrote it in the office on the review's time, and it took him two months. The critics were crazy about it, but it didn't sell very much though it was nominated for the National Book Award. I read the book, and the prose was brilliantly obscure, the characterizations ridiculous, the plotting lunatic. To me it was a foolish book despite some complicated ideas. He had a first-rate mind, no question of that. But to me the book was a total failure as a novel. He never asked if I had read it. He obviously didn't want my opinion. He knew it was full of shit, I guess. Because one day he said, 'Now that I've got a bankroll I can finish the big book.' A sort of apology.

I got to like Osano, but I was always just a little afraid of him. He could draw me out as nobody else could. He made me talk about literature and gambling and even women. And then, when he had measured me, he would lay me out. He had a keen eye for pretentiousness in everyone else but himself. When I told him about Jordan's killing himself in Vegas and everything that had happened afterwards and how I felt it had changed my life, he thought that over for a long time and then he gave me his insights combined with a lecture.

'You hold onto that story, you always go back to it, do you know why?' he asked me. He was wading through the piles of books in his office, waving his arms around. 'Because you know that's the one area you're not in danger. You'll never knock yourself off. You'll never be that shattered. You know I like you, you wouldn't be my right-hand man if I didn't. And I trust you more than anybody I know. Listen, let me confess something to you. I had to redraw my will last week because of that fucking Wendy.' Wendy had been his third wife and still drove him crazy with her demands though she had remarried since their divorce. When he just mentioned her, his eyes went a little crazy. But then he calmed down. He gave me one of his sweet smiles that made him look like a little kid, though he was well into his fifties by now.

'I hope you don't mind,' he said. 'But I've named you as my literary executor.'

I was stunned and pleased, and with all that I shrank away from the whole thing. I didn't want him to trust me that much or like me that much. I didn't feel that way about him. I had come to enjoy his company, indeed, to be fascinated by how his mind worked. And though I tried to deny it, I was impressed by his literary fame. I thought of him as rich and famous and powerful, and the fact that he had to trust me so much showed me how vulnerable he was, and that dismayed me. It shattered some of my illusions about him.

But then he went on about me. 'You know, underneath everything, you have a contempt for Jordan you don't dare admit to yourself. I've listened to that story of yours I don't know how many times. Sure, you liked him, sure, you felt sorry for him; maybe you even understood him. Maybe. But you can't accept the fact that a guy that had so much going for him knocked himself off. Because you know you had a ten times worse life than he had and you would never do such a thing. You're even happy. You're living a shitty life, you never had anything, you knocked your balls off working, you've got a limited bourgeois marriage and you're an artist with half your life gone and no real success. And you're basically happy. Christ, you still enjoy fucking your wife and you've been married—what?—ten, fifteen years. You're either the most insensitive prick I ever met or the most together. One thing I know, you're the toughest. You live in your own world, you do exactly what you want to do. You control your life. You never get into trouble, and when you do, you don't panic; you get out of it. Well, I admire you, but I don't envy you. I've never seen you do or say a really mean thing, but I don't think you really give a shit about anybody. You're just steering your life.'

And then he waited for me to react. He was grinning, the sneaky green eyes challenging. I knew he was having fun just laying it on, but I also knew he meant it a little and I was hurt.

There were a lot of things I wanted to say. I wanted to tell him how it was growing up an orphan. That I had missed what was basic, the core of almost every human being's experience. That I had no family, no social antennae, nothing to bind myself to the rest of the world. I had only my brother, Artie. When people talked about life, I couldn't really grasp what they meant until after I had married Vallie. That was why I had volunteered to fight in the war. I had understood that war was another universal experience, and I hadn't wanted to be left out of it. And I had been right. The war had been my family, no matter how dumb that sounds. I was glad now I hadn't missed it. And what Osano missed or didn't bother saying because he assumed I knew it was that it wasn't that easy to exercise control over your own life. And what he couldn't know was that the coin of happiness was a currency I could never understand. I had spent most of my early life being unhappy purely because of external circumstance. I had become relatively happy again because of external circumstance. Marrying Valerie, having kids, having a skill or art or the ability to produce written matter that earned me a living made me happy. It was a controlled happiness built on what I had gained from a dead loss. And so, very valuable to me. I knew I lived a limited life, what seemed to be a life that was bare, bourgeois. That I had very few friends, no sociability, little interest in success. I just wanted to make it through life, or so I thought.

And Osano, watching me, was still smiling. 'But you're the

toughest son of a bitch I've ever seen. You never let anybody get near you. You never let anybody know what you really think.'

At this I had to protest. 'Listen, you ask me my opinion about anything and I'll give it to you. Don't even ask. Your last book was a piece of shit, and you run this review like a lunatic.'

Osano laughed. 'I don't mean that kind of stuff. I never said you weren't honest. But let it go. You'll know what I'm talking about someday. Especially if you start chasing broads and wind up with somebody like Wendy.'

Wendy came around to the review offices once in a while. She was a striking brunette with crazy eyes and a body loaded with sexual energy. She was very bright, and Osano would give her books to review. She was the only one of his ex-wives who was not afraid of him, and she had made his life miserable ever since they were divorced. When he fell behind in his alimony payments, she tried to have him arrested. Whenever he published a new book, she went to court to get her child support and alimony raised. She had taken a twenty-year-old writer into her apartment and supported him. The writer was heavy on drugs, and Osano worried about what he might do to the kids.

Osano told stories about their marriage that were to me incredible. That once, going to a party, they had gotten into the elevator and Wendy refused to tell him the floor the party was on simply because they had quarrelled. He became so infuriated that he had started to choke her to make her tell him, playing a game, as he called it, of 'choke the chicken'. A game that was his fondest memory of the marriage. Her face turning black, she shook her head, still refusing to answer his question about where the party was being held. He had to release her. He knew she was crazier than he was.

Sometimes when they had minor arguments, she would call the police to have him thrown out of the apartment and the police would come and be stunned by her unreasonableness. They would see Osano's clothes scissored to pieces on the floor. She admitted doing it, but that didn't give Osano a right to hit her. What she left out was that she had sat on the pile of scissored suits and shirts and ties and masturbated over them with a vibrator.

And Osano had stories to tell about the vibrator. She had gone to a psychiatrist because she could not achieve orgasms. After six months she had admitted to Osano that the psychiatrist was

221

fucking her as part of the therapy. Osano wasn't jealous; by this time he really loathed her, 'loathe' he said, 'not hate. There's a difference.'

But Osano would get furious every time he got the bill from the psychiatrist and he would rage to her, 'I pay a guy a hundred dollars a week to fuck my wife and they call that modern medicine?' He told the story when his wife gave a cocktail party, and she was so mad that she stopped going to the psychiatrist and bought a vibrator. Every evening before dinner she locked herself into the bedroom to shut out the kids and masturbated with the machine. She always achieved orgasm. But she laid down the strict rule that she was never to be disturbed during that hour, by the children or her husband. The whole family, even the children, referred to it as 'The Happy Hour'.

What made Osano finally leave her, as he told the story, was when she started carrying on about how F. Scott Fitzgerald had stolen all his best stuff from his wife, Zelda. That she would have become a great novelist if her husband had not done this. Osano grabbed her by the hair of her head and shoved her nose into *The Great Gatsby*.

'Read this, you dumb cunt,' he said. 'Read ten sentences, then read his wife's book. Then come and tell me that shit.'

She read both and came back to Osano and told him the same thing. He punched her in the face and blackened both her eyes and then left for good.

Just recently Wendy had won another infuriating victory over Osano. He knew she was giving the child-support payments to her young lover. But one day his daughter came to him and asked for money for clothes. She explained that her gynaecologist had told her not to wear jeans any more because of a vaginal irritation, and when she had asked her mother for money for dresses, her mother said, 'Ask your father.' This was after they had been divorced for five years.

To avoid an argument, Osano gave his daughter's support money to her directly. Wendy didn't object. But after a year she took Osano to court for the year's money. The daughter testified for her father. Osano had been sure he would win when the judge knew all the circumstances. But the judge told him sternly not only to pay the money directly to the mother but also to pay the support money for the past year in a lump sum. So in effect he paid twice.

Wendy was so delighted with her victory that she tried to be friendly with him afterwards. In front of their children he brushed off her affectionate advances and said coldly, 'You are the worst cunt I've ever seen.' The next time Wendy came around to the review he refused her entrance to his office and cut off all the work he had given her. And what amazed him was that she couldn't understand why he loathed her. She raged about him to her friends and spread the word that he had never satisfied her in bed, that he couldn't get it up. That he was a repressed homosexual who really liked little boys. She tried to keep him from having the kids for the summer, but Osano won that battle. Then he published a maliciously witty short story about her in a national magazine. Maybe he couldn't handle her in life, but in fiction he painted a truly terrible portrait, and since everybody in the literary world of New York knew her, she was recognized immediately. She was shaken, as much as it was possible for her to be, and she left Osano alone after that. But she rankled in him like some poison. He couldn't bear to think about her without his face flushing and his eyes going a little crazy.

One day he came into the office and told me that the movies had bought one of his old novels to make into a picture and he had to go out there for a conference on the script, all expenses paid. He offered to take me along. I said OK but that I would like to drop off in Las Vegas to visit an old friend for a day or two while we were out there. He said that would be OK. He was between wives and he hated to travel alone or be alone and he felt he was going into enemy territory. He wanted a friend along with him. Anyway, that was what he said. And since I'd never been to California and I'd get paid while I was away, it looked like a good deal. I didn't know that I would more than earn my way.

24

I WAS in Vegas when Osano finished up on the conferences for that movie script of his book. So I took the short flight to LA to fly home with him, keep him company from LA to New York. Cully wanted me to bring Osano to Vegas just to meet him. I couldn't talk Osano into it, so I went to LA.

In his suite at the Beverly Hills Hotel Osano was more pissed off than I had ever seen him. He felt the movie industry had treated him like shit. Didn't they know that he was world-famous, the darling of literary critics from London to New Delhi, from Moscow to Sydney, Australia? He was famous in thirty languages, including the different variations of the Slavic. What he left out was that every movie made from one of his books had lost money for some strange reason.

And Osano was pissed off about other things. His ego couldn't stand the director of the film's being more important than the writer. When Osano tried to get a girlfriend of his a small part in the film, he couldn't swing it, and that pissed him off. It pissed him even more when the cameraman and the supporting actor got their girlfriends into the movie. The fucking cameraman and a lousy supporting actor had more clout than the great Osano. I just hoped I could get him on the plane before he went crazy and started tearing the whole studio apart and wound up in the clink. And we had a whole day and night to wait in LA for the plane the next morning. To quiet him down, I brought him around to his West Coast agent, a very hip, tennis-playing guy who had a lot of clients in show business. He also had some of the best-looking girlfriends I had ever seen. His name was Doran Rudd.

Doran did his best, but when disaster waits, nothing helps. 'You need a night out,' Doran said, 'a little relaxation, a good dinner with a beautiful companion, a little tranquillizer so you can sleep tonight. Maybe a blow job pill.' Doran was absolutely charming with women. But alone with men he insulted the female species.

Well, Osano had to go into a little act before he gave the OK. After all, a world-famous writer, a future Nobel literary prize-winner, doesn't want to be fixed up like some teenage kid. But the agent had handled guys like Osano before. Doran Rudd had fixed up a secretary of state, a President, the biggest evangelist in America who drew millions of believers to the Holy Tabernacle and was the horniest big-cocked son of a bitch in the world, so Doran said.

It was a pleasure to watch the agent smooth Osano's ruffled ego. This wasn't a Vegas operation, where girls were sent to your room like a pizza. This was class.

'I've got a really intelligent girl who's dying to meet you,' Doran told Osano. 'She's read all your books. She thinks you're the greatest writer in America. No shit. And she's not one of your starlets. She has a psychology degree from the University of California, and she takes bit parts in movies so that she can make contacts to write a script. Just the girl for you.'

Of course, he didn't fool Osano. Osano knew the joke was on him, that he was to be conned into what he really wanted. So he couldn't resist saying as Doran picked up the phone, 'That's all very well, but do I get to fuck her?'

The agent was already dialling with a gold-headed pencil.

'You got a ninety percent chance,' he said.

Osano asked quickly, 'How do you get that figure?' He always did that whenever somebody pulled a statistic on him. He hated statistics. He even believed the *New York Times* made up its stock market quotations just because one of his IBM stocks had been listed at 295 and, when he tried to sell it, he could get only 290.

Doran was startled. He stopped dialling. 'I sent her out with five guys since I've known her. Four of them scored.'

'That's eighty percent,' Osano said. Doran started dialling again. When a voice answered, he leaned back in his swivel chair and gave us a wink. Then he went into his dance.

I admired it. I really admired it. He was so good. His voice was so warm, his laugh so infectious.

'Katherine,' the agent crooned. 'My favourite, favourite client. Listen, I was talking to the director who's going to make that Western with Clint Eastwood. Would you believe he remembered you from that one interview last year? He said you gave the best reading of anybody, but he had to go with a name and after the picture he was sorry he did. Anyway, he wants to see you tomorrow at eleven or three. I'll call you later to get the exact time. OK? Listen I have a really good feeling about this one. I think this is the big break. I think your time has come. No, no kidding.'

He listened for a while. 'Yeah, yeah, I think you'd be great in that. Absolutely marvellous.' He rolled his eyes at us comically which made me dislike him. 'Yeah, I'll sound them out and get back to you. Hey, listen, guess who I've got in my office right now. Nope. Nope. Listen, it's a writer. Osano. Yeah, no kidding. No, honest. Yes, he really is. And believe it or not he happened to mention you not by name, but we were talking about movies and he mentioned that part you did, that cameo role, in *City Death*. Isn't that funny? Yeah, he's a fan of yours. Yeah, I told him you love his work. Listen, I've got a great idea. I'm going out to dinner with him tonight, Chasen's, why don't you come beautify our table? Great. I'll have a limo pick you up at eight. OK, sweetheart. You're my baby. I know he'll like you. He doesn't want to meet any starlets. He doesn't like the starlet type. He needs conversation and I just realized that you two were made for each other. Right, good-bye, honey.'

The agent hung up and leaned back and gave us his charming smile. 'She's really a nice cunt,' he said.

I could see Osano was a little depressed by the whole scene. He really liked women, and he hated to see them hustled. He often said he'd rather be hustled by a woman than hustle her. In fact, he once gave me his whole philosophy about being in love. How it was better to be the victim.

'Look at it this way,' Osano had said. 'When you're in love with a broad, you're getting the best of it even though she's hustling you. You're the guy who's feeling great, you're the guy who's enjoying every minute. She's the one who's having a lousy time. She's working . . . you're playing. So why complain when she finally dumps you and you know you've been conned?'

Well, his philosophy was put to the test that night. He got home before midnight and called my room and then came in for a drink to tell me what happened with Katherine. Katherine's percentage for scores had gone down that night. She had been a charming vibrant little brunette and swarmed all over Osano.

226

She loved him. She adored him. She was thrilled to death that she was having dinner with him. Doran got the message and disappeared after coffee. Osano and Katherine were having a final loosening-up bottle of champagne before going back to the hotel to get down to business. That's when Osano's luck turned bad, though he could still have bailed out if it hadn't been for his ego.

What screwed it up was one of the most unusual actors in Hollywood. His name was Dickie Sanders, and he had won an Oscar and had been in six successful movies. What made him unique was that he was a dwarf. That's not as bad as it sounds. He just missed being a very short man. And he was a very handsome guy, for a dwarf. You could say he was a miniature James Dean. He had the same sad, sweet smile which he used with devastating and calculated effect on women. They couldn't resist him. And as Doran said later, all bullshit aside, what balling broad could resist going to bed with a handsome dwarf?

So when Dickie Sanders walked into the restaurant, it was no contest. He was alone and he stopped at their table to say hello to Katherine; it seemed they knew each other, she'd had a bit part in one of his movies. Anyway, Katherine adored him twice as much as she adored Osano. And Osano got so pissed off he left her with the dwarf and went back to the hotel alone.

'What a fucking town,' he said. 'A guy like me loses out to a fucking dwarf.' He was really sore. His fame didn't mean anything. The Nobel Prize coming didn't mean anything. His Pulitzers and National Book Awards cut no ice. He came second to a dwarf actor, and he couldn't stand it. I had to carry him to his room finally and pour him into his bed. My final words of consolation to him were: 'Listen, he's not a dwarf, he's just a very short guy.'

Next morning, when Osano and I got on that 747 to New York, he was still depressed. Not only because he'd brought Katherine's average down, but because they'd botched the movie version of his book. He knew it was a lousy script, and he was right. So he was really in a bad mood on the plane and bullied a scotch off the stewardess even before takeoff.

We were in the very front seats near the bulkhead, and in the two seats across the aisle were one of those middle-aged couples, very thin, very elegant. The man had a beaten-down, unhappy look on his face that was sort of appealing. You got the impression that he was living in a private hell, but one that he deserved.

Deserved because of his outward arrogance, the richness of his dress, the spitefulness of his eyes. He was suffering, and by Christ he was going to make everybody else around him suffer too, if he thought they would stand for it.

His wife looked like the classic spoiled woman. She was obviously rich, richer than her husband, though possibly they were both rich. The stamp was on them in the way they took the menu from the stewardess. The way they glanced at Osano sipping his technically illegal drink.

The woman had that bold handsomeness preserved by top-notch plastic surgery and glossed over with the even tan of daily sunlamps and Southern sun. And had that discontented mouth that is perhaps the ugliest thing in any woman. At her feet and up against the bulkhead wall was a wire-mesh box which held maybe the prettiest French poodle in the whole world. It had curly silver fur which fell into ringlets over its eyes. It had a pink mouth and pink ribbon bow over its head. It even had a beautiful tail with a pink bow on it that wagged around. It was the happiest little dog you ever saw and the sweetest-looking. The two miserable human beings that owned it obviously took pleasure from owning such a treasure. The man's face softened a little as he looked at the poodle. The woman didn't show pleasure, but a proprietary pride, like an older ugly woman in charge of her beautiful virginal daughter that she is preparing for the marketplace. When she reached out her hand for the poodle to lick lasciviously, it was like a Pope extending his ring to be kissed.

The great thing about Osano was that he never missed anything even when he seemed to be looking the other way. He had paid strict attention to his drink, slouched down in his seat. But now he said to me, 'I'd rather get a blow job from that dog than that broad.' The jet engines made it impossible for the woman across the aisle to hear, but I felt nervous anyway. She gave us a coldly dirty look, but maybe that's the way she always looked at people.

Then I felt guilty at having condemned her and her husband. They were, after all, two human beings. Where did I come off putting them down on sheer speculation? So I said to Osano, 'Maybe they're not as bad as they look.'

'Yes, they are,' he said.

That wasn't worthy of him. He could be chauvinistic, racist and narrow-minded but only off the top of his head. It really didn't mean anything. So I let it go, and as the pretty stewardess imprisoned us in our seats for dinner, I told him stories about Vegas. He couldn't believe I had once been a degenerate gambler.

Ignoring the people across the aisle, forgetting about them, I said to him, 'You know what gamblers call suicide?'

'No,' Osano said.

I smiled. 'They call it the Big Ace.'

Osano shook his head. 'Isn't that marvellous?' he said dryly.

I saw he was a little contemptuous of the melodrama of the phrase, but I kept on. 'That's what Cully said to me that morning when Jordan did it. Cully came down and he said, "You know what that fucking Jordy did? He pulled the Big Ace out of his sleeve. The prick used his Big Ace." ' I paused, remembering it more clearly now years later. It was funny. I had never remembered that phrase before or Cully using it that night. 'He capitalized it in his voice, you know. The Big Ace.'

'Why do you think he really did it?' Osano asked. He was not too interested, but he saw I was upset.

'Who the hell knows?' I said. 'I thought I was so smart. I thought I had him figured. I nearly had him figured, but then he faked me out. That's what kills me. He made me disbelieve in his humanity, his tragic humanity. Never let anybody make you disbelieve in anybody's humanity.'

Osano grinned, nodded his head at the people across the aisle. 'Like them?' he said. And then I realized that this was what made me tell him the story.

I glanced at the woman and man. 'Maybe.'

'OK,' he said. 'But sometimes it goes against the grain. Especially rich people. You know what's wrong with rich people? They think they're as good as anybody else just because they got lots of dough.'

'They're not?' I asked.

'No,' Osano said. 'They're like hunchbacks.'

'Hunchbacks are not as good as anybody else?' I asked. I nearly said dwarfs.

'No,' Osano said. 'Nor are people with one eye, basket cases, and critics and ugly broads and chickenshit guys. They gotta work at being as good as other people. Those two people didn't work at it. They never got there,'

He was being a little irrational and illogical, not at his most brilliant. But what the hell, he'd had a bad week. And it's not everybody who gets his love life ruined by a dwarf. I let it ride.

We finished our dinner, Osano drinking the lousy champagne and eating the lousy food that even in first class you would trade in for a Coney Island hot dog. As they lowered the movie screen, Osano bolted out of his chair and went up the steps to the 747 dome lounge. I finished my coffee and followed him up there.

He was seated in a long-backed chair and had lit up one of his long Havana cigars. He offered me one and I took it. I was developing a taste for them, and that delighted Osano. He was always generous but a little careful with his Havanas. If you got one from him, he watched you closely to see if you enjoyed it enough to deserve it. The lounge was beginning to fill up. The stewardess on duty was busy making drinks. When she brought Osano his martini, she sat on the arm of his lounge chair and he put one hand in her lap to hold her hand.

I could see that one of the great things about being as famous as Osano was that you get away with stuff like that. In the first place, you had the confidence. In the second place, the young girl, instead of thinking you a dirty old man, is usually enormously flattered that somebody so important could think her that attractive. If Osano wanted to screw her, she must be something special. They didn't know that Osano was so horny he would screw anything with skirts. Which is not as bad as it sounds since a lot of guys like him screwed anything in pants and skirts.

The young girl was charmed by Osano. Then a good-looking woman passenger started coming on to him, an older woman with a crazy, interesting face. She told us about how she had just recovered from heart surgery and hadn't fucked for six months and was now ready to go. That's the kind of thing women always told Osano. They felt they could tell him anything because he was a writer and so would understand anything. Also, because he was famous and that would make them interesting to him.

Osano took out his heart-shaped Tiffany pillbox. It was filled with white tablets. He took one and offered the box to the heart lady and the stewardess. 'Come on,' he said. 'It's an upper. We'll really be flying high.' Then he changed his mind. 'No, not you,' he said to the heart lady. 'Not in your condition.' That's when I knew the heart lady was out of it.

Because the pills were really penicillin pills Osano always took before sexual contact so that he would be immunized against VD. And he always used this trick to make a prospective partner take them to double the insurance. He popped one in his mouth and washed it down with Scotch. The stewardess laughingly took one, and Osano watched her with a cheerful smile. He offered me the box and I shook my head.

The stewardess was really a pretty young thing, but she couldn't handle Osano and the heart lady. Trying to get the attention back to her, she said sweetly to Osano, 'Are you married?'

Now she knew, as everybody knew, that not only was Osano married, but he had been married at least five times. She didn't know that a question like that irritated Osano because he always felt a little guilty about cheating—on all his wives, even the ones he'd divorced. Osano grinned at the stewardess and said coolly, 'I'm married, I got a mistress and I got a steady girlfriend. I'm just looking for a dame I can have some fun with.'

It was insulting. The young girl flushed and took off to serve the other passengers drinks.

Osano settled down to enjoy the conversation with the heart lady, giving advice on her first fuck. He was putting her on a little.

'Listen,' he said. 'You don't want to straight fuck for the first time out. It won't be a good fuck for the guy because you'll be a little scared. The thing to do is have the guy go down on you while you're half asleep. Take a tranquillizer and then, just as you're dozing off, he eats you up, you know? And get a guy who's good at it. A real gentleman blow job artist.'

The woman turned a little red. Osano grinned. He knew what he was doing. I got a little embarrassed too. I always fall a little in love with strange women who hit me right. Usually after the first hour I fall out of love again, which I knew would happen with this lady. I could see her thinking how she could get Osano to do the job for her. She didn't know that she was too old for him and he was just playing his cards very coolly to nail the young stewardess.

There we were speeding along at six hundred miles an hour and not feeling a thing. But Osano was getting drunker, and things started going bad. The heart lady was boozy, maudlin about dying and how to find the right guy to go down on her the right way. That made Osano nervous. He said to her, 'You can always play the Big Ace.' Of course, she didn't know what he was talking about. But she knew she was being dismissed, and the hurt look on her face irritated Osano even more. He ordered another drink, and the stewardess, jealous and pissed off that he

231

had ignored her, gave him the drink and slipped away in the cool, insulting way the young can always use to put older people down. Osano showed his age that day.

At that moment the couple with the poodle came up the steps into the lounge. Well, she was one woman I would never fall in love with. The discontented mouth, that artificially tinted nut-brown face with all the lines of life excised by a surgeon's knife, were too repellent, no fantasies could be spun around them unless you were into sadomaso stuff.

The man carried the beautiful little poodle, the dog's tongue hanging out with happiness. Carrying the poodle gave the sour-faced man a touching air of vulnerability. As usual Osano seemed not to notice them, though they gave him glances that showed they knew who he was. Probably from TV. Osano had been on TV a hundred times and always making himself interesting in a foolish way that lessened his real worth.

The couple ordered drinks. The woman said something to the man and he obediently dropped the poodle to the floor. The poodle stayed close to them, then wandered around a bit, sniffing at all the people and at all the chairs. I knew Osano hated animals, but he didn't seem to notice the poodle sniffing at his feet. He kept talking to the heart lady. The heart lady leaned over to fix the pink ribbon over the poodle's head and get her hand licked by the poodle's little pink tongue. I never could understand the animal thing, but this poodle was, in a funny kind of way, sexy. I wondered what went on with that sour-faced couple. The poodle pattered around the lounge, wandered back to its owners and sat on the feet of the woman. She put on dark glasses, which for some reason seemed ominous, and when the stewardess brought her drink, she said something to the young girl. The stewardess looked at her in astonishment.

I guess it was at this moment that I got a little nervous. I knew Osano was all jazzed up. He hated being trapped in a plane, he hated being trapped in a conversation with a woman he didn't really want to screw. What he was thinking about was how to get the young stewardess into a toilet and give her a quick, savage fuck. The young stewardess came to me with my drink and leaned over to whisper in my ear. I could see Osano getting jealous. He thought the girl was coming on to me, and that was an insult to his fame more than anything else. He could understand the girl wanting a younger, better-looking guy but not turning down his fame.

But the stewardess was whispering a different kind of trouble.

232

She said, 'That woman wants me to tell Mr Osano to put out his cigar. She says it's bothering her dog.'

Jesus Christ. The dog wasn't even supposed to be up in the lounge running around. It was supposed to be in its box. Everybody knew that. The girl whispered worriedly. 'What should I do?'

I guess what happened next was partly my fault. I knew Osano could go crazy at any time and that this was a prime time. But I was always curious about how people react. I wanted to see if the stewardess would really have the nerve to tell a guy like Osano to put out one of his beloved Havana cigars because of a fucking dog. Especially when Osano had paid for a first class ticket just to smoke it in the lounge. I also wanted to see Osano put the hard-faced snotty woman in her place. I would have ditched my cigar and let it ride. But I knew Osano. He would send the plane down into hell first.

The stewardess was waiting for an answer. I shrugged. 'Whatever your job makes you do,' I said. And it was a malicious answer.

I guess the stewardess felt the same way. Or maybe she just wanted to humiliate Osano because he was no longer paying any attention to her. Or maybe, because she was just a kid, she took what she thought was the easy way out. Osano, if you didn't know him, looked easier to handle than the bitch lady.

Well, we all made a bad mistake. The stewardess stood next to Osano and said, 'Sir, would you mind putting out your cigar? That lady says the smoke is bothering her dog.'

Osano's startling green eyes went cold as ice. He gave the stewardess a long, hard look.

'Let me hear that again,' he said.

Right then I was ready to jump out of the plane. I saw the look of maniacal rage form over Osano's face. It was no longer a joke. The woman was staring at Osano with distaste. She was dying for an argument, a real uproar. You could see she'd love a fight. The husband glanced out the window, studying the limitless horizon. Obviously this was a familiar scene and he had every confidence that his wife would prevail. He even had a slight, satisfied smile. Only the sweet-looking poodle was distressed. It was gasping for air and giving delicate little hiccups. The lounge was smoky but not from just Osano's cigar. Nearly everybody had cigarettes going, and you got the feeling that the poodle owners would make everybody stop smoking.

The stewardess, frightened by Osano's face, was paralysed—

233

she couldn't speak. But the woman was not intimidated. You could see that she just loved seeing that look of maniacal rage on Osano's face. You could also see that she never in her life had been punched in the mouth, that she had never gotten a few teeth knocked out. The thought had never occurred to her. So she even leaned towards Osano to speak to him, putting her face in range. I almost closed my eyes. In fact, I did close my eyes for a fraction of a second and I could hear the woman in her cultured, cold voice saying very flatly to Osano, 'Your cigar is distressing my dog. Could you please just stop?'

The words were snotty enough, but the tone was insulting beyond any mere words. I could see she was waiting for an argument about her dog's not being allowed in the lounge, how the lounge was for smoking. How she realized that if she had said the smoke was distressing her personally, Osano would get rid of the cigar. But she wanted him to put out the cigar for her dog. She wanted a scene.

Osano grasped all this in a second. He understood everything. And I think that was what drove him crazy. I saw that smile come over his face, a smile that could be infinitely charming but for the cold green eyes that were pure maniac.

He didn't yell at her. He didn't punch her in the face. He gave her husband one look to see what he would do. The husband smiled faintly. He liked what his wife was doing, or so it seemed. Then with a deliberate motion Osano put out his cigar in the welled tray of his seat. The woman watched him with contempt. Then Osano reached out his arm across the table and you could see the woman thought he was going to pet the poodle. I knew better. Osano's hand went down over the poodle's head and around its neck.

What happened next was too quick for me to stop. He lifted the poor dog up, rising out of his seat, and strangled it with both hands. The poodle gasped and choked, its pink-beribboned tail wagging in distress. Its eyes started bulging out of its mattress of silky ringed fur. The woman screamed and sprang up and clawed at Osano's face. The husband didn't move out of his seat. At that moment the plane hit a small air pocket and we all lurched. But Osano, drunk, all his balance concentrated on strangling the poodle, lost his footing and went sprawling down the aisle, his hands still tight around the dog's throat. To get up he had to turn the dog loose. The woman was screaming something about killing him. The stewardess was screaming out of shock. Osano, standing straight up, smiled around the lounge and then advanced towards the woman, still screaming at him. She thought that now he would be ashamed of what he had done, that she could abuse him. She didn't know that he had already made up his mind to strangle her as he had the dog. Then she caught on. . . . She shut up.

And Osano said with maniacal quiet, 'You cunt, now you get it.' And he lunged for her. He was really crazy. He hit her in the face. I ducked in front and grabbed him. But he had his hands around her throat and she screamed. And then it became a madhouse. The plane must have had security guards in plain clothes because two men took Osano very professionally by the arms and peeled his coat back to form a straitjacket. But he was wild and he was throwing them around anyway. Everybody watched, horrified. I tried to quiet Osano down, but he couldn't hear anything. He was berserk. He was screaming curses at the woman and her husband. The two security men were trying to gentle him down, addressing him by name, and one, a good-looking strong boy, was asking him if they let him go would he behave. Osano still fought. Then the strong boy lost his temper.

Now Osano was in an uncontrollable rage because partly it was his nature and partly because he was famous and knew he would be insulated against any retaliations for his rage. The young strong boy understood this by instinct, but now he was affronted that Osano didn't respect his superior youthful strength. And he got mad. He took a handful of Osano's hair and yanked his head back so hard he nearly snapped his neck. Then he put his arm around Osano's neck and said, 'You son of a bitch, I'll break it.' Osano went still.

Jesus, it was a mess after that. The captain of the plane wanted to put Osano in a straitjacket, but I talked him out of it. The security cleared out the lounge, and Osano and I sat there with them for the rest of the trip. They didn't let us off in New York until the plane was empty, so we never saw the woman again. But that last glimpse of her was enough. They had washed the blood off her face, but she had one eye almost shut and her mouth was mashed to pulp. The husband carried the poodle still alive, wagging its tail desperately for affection and protection. Later there were some legal complaints that the lawyers handled. Of course, it got in all the papers. The great American novelist and prime candidate for the Nobel Prize had almost murdered a little French poodle. Poor dog. Poor Osano. The cunt had turned out to be a large stockholder in the airline plus having millions of other dollars, and of course, she couldn't even threaten never to fly that airline again. As for Osano he was perfectly happy. He had no feelings about animals. He said, 'As long as I can eat them, I can kill them.' When I pointed out that he had never eaten dog meat, he just shrugged and said, 'Cook it right and I'll eat it.'

One thing Osano missed. That crazy woman had her humanity too. OK, she was crazy. OK, she deserved a bloody mouth, it might even have done her good. But she really didn't deserve what Osano did to her. She really couldn't help the kind of person she was, I thought then. The earlier Osano would have seen all that. For some reason he couldn't now.

25

THE sexy poodle didn't die, so the lady didn't press charges. She didn't seem to mind getting her face smashed or it wasn't important to her or to her husband. She might even have enjoyed it. She sent Osano a friendly note, leaving the door open for them to get together. Osano gave a funny little growl and tossed the note into his wastepaper basket. 'Why don't you give her a try,' I said. 'She might be interesting.'

'I don't like hitting women,' Osano said. 'That bitch wants me to use her as a punching bag.'

'She could be another Wendy,' I said. I knew Wendy always had some sort of fascination for him despite their being divorced all these years and despite all the aggravation she caused him.

'Jesus,' Osano said. 'That's all I need.' But he smiled. He knew what I meant. That maybe beating women didn't displease him that much. But he wanted to show me I was wrong.

'Wendy was the only wife I had that made me hit her,' he said. 'All my other wives, they fucked my best friends, they stole my money, they beat me for alimony, they lied about me, but I never hit them, I never even disliked them. I'm good friends with all my other wives. But that fucking Wendy is some piece of work. A class by herself. If I'd stayed married to her, I'd have killed her.'

But the poodle strangling had got around in the literary circles of New York. Osano worried about his chances of getting the Nobel Prize. 'Those fucking Scandinavians love dogs,' he said. He fined up his active campaign for the Nobel by writing letters to all his friends and professional acquaintances. He also kept publishing articles and reviews on the most important critical works to appear in the review. Plus essays on literature which I always thought were full of shit. His great novel, because it was the only thing he wrote in longhand. The rest of his stuff he banged out with two fingers on the typewriter he could swivel to from his executive desk piled with books. He was the fastest typist I have ever seen even with just two fingers. He sounded like a machine gun, literally. And with that machine-gun typing he wrote the definition of what the great American novel should be, explained why England no longer produced great fiction except in the spy genre, took apart the latest works and sometimes the body of work of guys like Faulkner, Mailer, Styron, Jones, anybody who could give him competition for the Nobel. He was so brilliant, the language so charged that he convinced you. By publishing all that crap, he demolished his opponents and left the field clear for himself. The only trouble was that when you went to his own work, he had only his first two novels published twenty years ago that could give him serious claim to a literary reputation. The rest of his novels and nonfiction work were not that good.

The truth was that over the last ten years he had lost a great deal of his popular success and his literary reputation. He had published too many books done off the top of his head, made too many enemies with the high-handed way he ran the review. Even when he did some ass kissing by praising powerful literary figures he did it with such arrogance and condescension, did it with himself mixed up with it in some way (as his Einstein article had been as much about himself as about Einstein) that he made enemies of the people he was stroking. He wrote one line that really caused an uproar. He said the huge difference between French literature of the nineteenth century and English literature was that French writers had plenty of sex and the English didn't. Our review clientele boiled with rage.

On top of this his personal behaviour was scandalous. The publishers of the review had learned of the airplane incident, and it had leaked into the gossip columns. On one of his lectures at a California college he met a young nineteen-year-old literary student who looked more like a cheerleader or starlet than a lover of books, which she really was. He brought her to New York to live with him. She lasted about six months, but during that time he took her to all the literary parties. Osano was in his middle fifties, not yet grey but definitely paunchy. When you saw them together, you got a little uncomfortable. Especially when Osano was drunk and she had to carry him home. Plus he was drinking while he was working in the office. Plus he was cheating on his nineteen-year-old girlfriend with a forty-year-old female novelist who had just published a best-seller. The book wasn't really that good, but Osano wrote a full-page essay in the review hailing her as a future great of American literature.

And he did one thing I really hated. He would give a quote to any friend who asked. So you saw novels coming out that were lousy but with a quote from Osano saying something like: 'This is the finest Southern novel since Styron's *Lie Down in Darkness*.' Or, 'A shocking book that will dismay you,' which was kind of sly because he was trying to play both ends against the middle, doing his friend the favour and yet trying to warn the reader off the book with an ambiguous quote.

It was easy for me to see that he was coming apart in some way. I thought maybe he was going crazy. But I didn't know from what. His face looked unhealthy, puffy; his green eyes had a glitter that was not really normal. And there was something wrong with his walk, a hitch in his stride or a little waver to the left sometimes. I worried about him. Because despite my disapproval of his writings, his striving for the Nobel with all his cutthroat manoeuvres, his trying to screw every dame he came into contact with, I had an affection for him. He would talk to me about the novel I was working on, encourage me, give me advice, try to lend me money though I knew he was in hock up to his ears and spent money at an enormous rate supporting his five ex-wives and eight or nine children. I was awe-stricken by the amount of work he published, flawed though it was. He always appeared in one of the monthlies, sometimes in two or three; every year he published a nonfiction book on some subject the publishers thought was 'hot'. He edited the review and did a long essay for it every week. He did some movie work. He earned enormous sums, but he was always broke. And I knew he owed a fortune. Not only from borrowing money but drawing advances on future books. I mentioned this to him, that he was digging a hole he'd never get out of, but he just waved the idea away impatiently.

'I've got my ace in the hole,' he said. 'I got the big novel nearly finished. Another year maybe. And then I'll be rich again. And then on to Scandinavia for the Nobel Prize. Think of all those big blonde broads we can fuck.' He always included me on the trip for the Nobel.

The biggest fights we had were when he'd ask me about what I thought of one of his essays on literature in general. And I would infuriate him with my by now familiar line that I was just a storyteller. 'You're an artist with divine inspiration,' I'd tell him. 'You're the intellectual, you've got a fucking brain that could squirt out enough bullshit for a hundred courses on modern literature. I'm just a safecracker. I put my ear to the wall and wait to hear the tumblers fall in place.'

'You and your safecracker bullshit,' Osano said. 'You're just reacting away from me. You have ideas. You're a real artist. But you like the idea of being a magician, a trickster, that you can control everything, what you write, your life in general, that you can beat all the traps. That's how you operate.'

'You have the wrong idea of a magician,' I told him. 'A magician does magic. That's all.'

'And you think that's enough?' Osano asked. He had a slightly sad smile on his face.

'It's enough for me,' I said.

Osano nodded his head. 'You know, I was a great magician once, you read my first book. All magic, right?'

I was glad that I could agree. I had an affection for that book. 'Pure magic,' I said.

'But it wasn't enough,' Osano said. 'Not for me.'

Then too bad for you, I thought. And he seemed to read my mind. 'No, not how you think,' he said. 'I just couldn't do it again because I don't want to do it or I can't do it maybe. I wasn't a magician any more after that book. I became a writer.'

I shrugged a little unsympathetically, I guess. Osano saw it and said, 'And my life went to shit, but you can see that. I envy you your life. Everything is under control. You don't drink, you don't smoke, you don't chase broads. You just write and gamble and play the good father and husband. You're a very unflashy magician, Merlyn. You're a very safe magician. A safe life, safe books; you've made despair disappear.'

He was pissed off at me. He thought he was driving into the bone. He didn't know he was full of shit. And I didn't mind, that meant my magic was working. That was all he could see, and that was fine with me. He thought I had my life under control, that I didn't suffer or permit myself to, that I didn't feel the bouts of loneliness that drove him on to different women, to booze, to his snorts of cocaine. Two things he didn't realize. That he was suffering because he was actually going crazy, not suffering. The other was that everybody else in the world suffered and was lonely and made the best of it. That it was no big deal. In fact, you could say that life itself wasn't a big deal, never mind his fucking literature.

And then suddenly I had troubles from an unexpected quarter. One day at the review I got a call from Artie's wife, Pam. She said she wanted to see me about something important, and she wanted to see me without Artie. Could I come over right away? I felt a real panic. In the back of my mind I was always worried about Artie. He was really frail and always looked tired. His fine-boned handsomeness showed stress more clearly than most. I was so panicky I begged her to tell me what it was over the phone, but she wouldn't. She did tell me that there was nothing physically wrong, no medical reports of doom. It was a personal problem she and Artie were having, and she needed my help.

Immediately, selfishly, I was relieved. Obviously she had a problem, not Artie. But still I took off early from work and drove out to Long Island to see her. Artie lived on the North Shore of Long Island and I lived on the South Shore. So it really wasn't much out of my way. I figured I could listen to her and be home for dinner, just a little late. I didn't bother to call Valerie.

I always liked going to Artie's house. He had five kids, but they were nice kids who had a lot of friends who were always around and Pam never seemed to mind. She had big jars of cookies to feed them and gallon jugs of milk. There were kids watching television and other kids playing on the lawn. I said hi to the kids, and they gave me a brief hi back Pam took me into the kitchen with its huge bay window. She had coffee ready and poured some. She kept her head down and then suddenly looked up at me and said, 'Artie has a girlfriend.'

240

Despite her having had five kids, Pam was still very young-looking with a fine figure, tall, slender, lanky before the kids, and one of those sensual faces that had a Madonna kind of look. She came from a Midwest town, Artie had met her in college and her father was president of a small bank. Nobody in the last three generations of her family had ever had more than two kids, and she was a hero-martyr to her parents because of the five births. They couldn't understand it, but I did. I had once asked Artie about it and he had said, 'Behind that Madonna face is one of the horniest wives on Long Island. And that suits me fine.' If any other husband had said that about his wife, I would have been offended.

'Lucky you,' I had said.

'Yeah,' Artie said. 'But I think she feels sorry for me, you know, the asylum business. And she wants to make sure I never feel lonely again. Something like that.'

'Lucky, lucky you,' I had said.

And so now, when Pam made her accusation, I was a little angry. I knew Artie. I knew it wasn't possible for him to cheat on his wife. That he would never endanger the family he had built up or the happiness it gave him.

Pam's tall form was drooping; tears were in her eyes. But she was watching my face. If Artie were having an affair, the only one he would ever tell was me. And she was hoping I would give away the secret by some expression on my face.

'It's not true,' I said. 'Artie always had women running after him and he hated it. He's the straightest guy in the world. You know I wouldn't try to cover for him. I wouldn't rat on him, but I wouldn't cover for him.'

'I know that,' Pam said. 'But he comes home late at least three times a week. And last night he had lipstick on his shirt. And he makes phone calls after I go up to bed, late at night. Does he call you?'

'No,' I said. And now I felt shitty. It might be true. I still didn't believe it, but I had to find out.

'And he's spending extra money he never spent before,' Pam said. 'Oh, shit.' She was crying openly now.

'Will he be home for dinner tonight?' I asked. Pam nodded. I picked up the kitchen phone and called Valerie and told her I was eating at Artie's house. I did that once in a while on the spur of the moment when I had an urge to see him, so she didn't ask any questions. When I hung up the phone, I said to Pam, 'You got enough to feed me?'

241

She smiled and nodded her head. 'Of course,' she said.

'I'll go down and pick him up at the station,' I said. 'And we'll have this all straightened out before we eat dinner.' I burlesqued it a bit and said, 'My brother is innocent.'

'Oh, sure,' Pam said. But she smiled.

Down at the station, as I waited for the train to come in, I felt sorry for Pam and Artie. There was a little smugness in my pity. I was the guy Artie always had to bail out and finally I was going to bail him out. Despite all the evidence, the lipstick on the shirt, the late hours and phone calls, the extra money, I knew that Artie was basically innocent. The worst it could be was some young girl being so persistent that he finally weakened a little, maybe. Even now I couldn't believe it. Mixed with the pity was the envy I always felt about Artie's being so attractive to women in a way I could never be. With just a touch of satisfaction I felt it was not all that bad being ugly.

When Artie got off the train, he wasn't too surprised to see me. I had done this before, visiting him unexpectedly and meeting his train. I always felt good doing it, and he was always glad to see me. And it always made me feel good to see that he was glad to see me waiting for him. This time, watching him carefully, I noticed he wasn't quite that glad to see me today.

'What the hell are you doing here?' he said, but he gave me a hug and he smiled. He had an extraordinarily sweet smile for a man. It was the smile he had as a child and it had never changed.

'I came to save your ass,' I said cheerfully. 'Pam finally got the goods on you.'

He laughed. 'Jesus, not that shit again.' Pam's jealousy was always good for a laugh

'Yep,' I said. 'The late hours, the late phone calls and now, finally, the classic evidence: lipstick on your shirt.' I was feeling great because just by seeing Artie and talking to him I knew it was all a mistake.

But suddenly Artie sat down on one of the station benches. His face looked very tired. I was standing over him and beginning to feel just a little uneasy.

Artie looked up at me. I saw a strange look of pity on his face. 'Don't worry,' I said. 'I'll fix everything.'

He tried to smile. 'Merlyn the Magician,' he said. 'You'd better put on your fucking magic hat. At least sit down.' He lit up a cigarette. I thought again that he smoked too much. I sat down next to him. Oh, shit, I thought. And my mind was racing onto how to square things between him and Pam. One thing I knew, I didn't want to lie to her or have Artie lie to her.

'I'm not cheating on Pam,' Artie said. 'And that's all I want to tell you.'

There was no question about my believing him. He would never lie to me. 'Right,' I said. 'But you have to tell Pam what's going on or she'll go crazy. She called me at work.'

'If I tell Pam, I have to tell you,' Artie said. 'You don't want to hear it.'

'So tell me,' I said. 'What the hell's the difference? You always tell me everything. How can it hurt?'

Artie dropped his cigarette to the stone cement floor of the train platform. 'OK,' he said. He put his hand on my arm and I felt a sudden sense of dread. When we were children alone together, he always did that to comfort me. 'Let me finish, don't interrupt,' he said.

'OK,' I said. My face was suddenly very warm. I couldn't think of what was coming.

'For the last couple of years I've been trying to find our mother,' Artie said. 'Who she is, where she is, what we are. A month ago I found her.'

I was standing up. I pulled my arm away from his. Artie stood up and tried to hold me again. 'She's a drunk,' he said. 'She wears lipstick. She looks pretty good. But she's all alone in the world. She wants to see you, she says that she couldn't help—'

I broke in on him. 'Don't tell me any more,' I said. 'Don't ever tell me any more. You do what you want, but I'll see her in hell before I'll see her alive.'

'Hey, come on, come on,' Artie said. He tried to put his hand on me again and I broke away and walked towards the car. Artie followed me. We got in and I drove him to the house. By this time I was under control and I could see that Artie was distressed, so I said to him, 'You'd better tell Pam.'

Artie said, 'I will.'

I stopped in the driveway of the house. 'You coming in for dinner?' Artie asked. He was standing by my open window, and again he reached in to put his hand on my arm.

'No,' I said.

I watched him as he went into the house, shooing the last of the kids still playing on the lawn into the house with him. Then I drove away. I drove slowly and carefully, I had trained myself all my life to be more careful when most people became more

243

reckless. When I got home, I could see by Vallie's face that she knew about what happened. The kids were in bed, and she had dinner for me on the kitchen table. While I ate, she ran her hand over the back of my head and neck when she went by to the stove. She sat opposite, drinking coffee, waiting for me to open the subject. Then she remembered. 'Pam wants you to call her.'

I called. Pam was trying to make some apology for having gotten me into such a mess. I told her it was no mess, and did she feel better now that she knew the truth? Pam giggled and said, 'Christ, I think I'd rather it were a girlfriend.' She was cheerful again. And now our roles were reversed. Early that day I had pitied her, she was the person in terrible danger and I was the one who would rescue or try to help her. Now she seemed to think it was unfair that the roles were reversed. That was what the apology was about. I told her not to worry.

Pam stumbled over what she wanted to say next. 'Merlyn, you didn't really mean it, about your mother, that you won't see her?'

'Does Artie believe me?' I asked her.

'He says he always knew it,' Pam said. 'He wouldn't have told you until he'd softened you up. Except for me causing the trouble. He was teed off at me for bringing it all on.'

I laughed. 'See,' I said, 'it started off as a bad day for you and now it's a bad day for him. He's the injured party. Better him than you.'

'Sure,' Pam said. 'Listen, I'm sorry for you, really.'

'It has nothing at all to do with me,' I said. And Pam said OK and thanks and hung up.

Valerie was waiting for me now. She was watching me intently. She'd been briefed by Pam and maybe even by Artie on how to handle this, and she was being careful. But I guess she hadn't really grasped it. She and Pam were really good women, but they didn't understand. Both their parents had made trouble and objections about them marrying orphans with no traceable lineage. I could imagine the horror stories told about similar cases. What if there had been insanity or degeneracy in our family? Or black blood or Jewish blood or Protestant blood, all that fucking shit. Well, now here was a nice piece of evidence turned up when it was no longer needed. I could figure out that Pam and Valerie were not too happy about Artie's romanticism, his digging up the lost link of a mother.

'Do you want her here to the house so that she can see the children?' Valerie asked.

244

'No,' I said.

Valerie looked troubled and a little terrified. I could see how she was thinking what if her children rejected her some day.

'She's your mother,' Valerie said. 'She must have had a very unhappy life.'

'Do you know what the word "orphan" means?' I said. 'Have you looked it up in the dictionary? It means a child who has lost both parents through death. Or a young animal that has been deserted or has lost its mother. Which one do you want?'

'OK,' Valerie said. She looked terrified. She went to look in on the kids and then went into our bedroom. I could hear her going into the bathroom and preparing for bed. I stayed up late reading and making notes, and when I went to bed, she was sound asleep.

It was all over in a couple of months. Artie called me up one day and told me his mother had disappeared again. We arranged to meet in the city and have dinner together so that we could talk alone. We could never talk about it with our wives present, as if it were too shameful for their knowledge. Artie seemed cheerful. He told me she had left a note. He told me that she drank a lot and always wanted to go to bars and pick up men. That she was a middle-aged floozy but that he liked her. He had made her stop drinking, he had bought her new clothes, he had rented her a nicely furnished apartment, given her an allowance. She had told him everything that had happened to her. It hadn't really been her fault. I stopped him there. I didn't want to hear about that.

'Are you going to look for her again?' I asked him.

Artie smiled his sad, beautiful smile. 'No,' he said. 'You know, I was a pain in the ass to her even now. She really didn't like having me around. At first, when I found her, she played the role I wanted her to play, I think, out of a sense of guilt that maybe she could make things up to me by letting me take care of her. But she really didn't like it. She even made a pass at me one day, I think, just to get some excitement.' He laughed. 'I wanted her to come to the house, but she never would. It's just as well.'

'How did Pam take the whole business?' I asked.

Artie laughed out loud. 'Jesus, she was even jealous of my mother. When I told her it was all over, you should have seen the look of relief on her face. One thing I have to say for you, brother, you took the news without cracking a muscle.'

'Because I don't give a shit one way or the other,' I said.

245

'Yeah,' Artie said. 'I know. It doesn't matter. I don't think you would have liked her.'

Six months later Artie had a heart attack. It was a mild one, but he was in the hospital for weeks and off from work another month. I went to see him in the hospital every day, and he kept insisting that it had been some sort of indigestion, that it was a borderline case. I went down to the library and read everything I could about heart attacks. I found out that his reaction was a common one with heart attack victims and that sometimes they were right. But Pam was panic-stricken. When Artie came out of the hospital, she put him on a strict diet, threw all the cigarettes out of the house and stopped smoking so that Artie could quit. It was hard for him, but he did. And maybe the heart attack did scare him because now he took care of himself. He took the long walks the doctor prescribed, ate carefully and never touched tobacco. Six months later he looked better than he had ever looked in his life and Pam and I stopped giving each other panicky looks whenever he was out of the room. 'Thank God, he's stopped smoking,' Pam said. 'He was up to three packs a day. That's what did him in.'

I nodded, but I didn't believe it. I always believed it was that two months he spent trying to claim his mother that did him in.

And as soon as Artie was OK, I got into trouble. I lost my job on the literary review. Not through any fault of mine but because Osano got fired and as his right-hand man I was fired with him.

Osano had weathered all the storms. His contempt of the most powerful literary circles in the country, the political intelligentsia, the culture fanatics, the liberals, the conservatives, Women's Liberation, the radicals, his sexual escapades, his gambling on sports, his use of his position to lobby for the Nobel Prize. Plus a nonfiction book he published in defence of pornography, not for its redeeming social value, but as anti-elitist pleasure of the poor in intellect. For all these things the publishers would have liked to fire him, but the circulation of the review had doubled since he became editor.

By this time I was making good money. I wrote a lot of Osano's articles for him. I could imitate his style pretty well, and he would start me off with a fifteen-minute harangue on how he felt about a particular subject, always brilliantly crazy. It was easy for me to write the article based on his fifteen minutes of ranting. Then he'd go over and put in a few of his masterful touches and we'd split the money. Just half his money was twice what I got paid for an article.

Even that didn't get us fired. It was his ex-wife Wendy who did us in. Though that's maybe unfair; Osano did us in, Wendy handed him the knife.

Osano had spent four weeks in Hollywood while I ran the review for him. He was completing some sort of movie deal, and during the four weeks we used a courier to fly out and give him review articles to OK before I ran it. When Osano finally came back to New York, he gave a party for all his friends to celebrate his homecoming and the big chunk of money he had earned in Hollywood.

The party was held at his East Side brownstone which his latest ex-wife used with their batch of three kids. Osano was living in a small studio apartment in the Village, the only thing he could afford, but too small for the party.

I went because he insisted that I go. Valerie didn't come. She didn't like Osano and she didn't like parties outside her family circle. Over the years we had come to an unspoken agreement. We excused each other from each other's social lives whenever possible. My reason was that I was too busy working on my novel, my job and free-lance writing assignments. Her excuse was that she had to take care of the kids and didn't trust baby-sitters. We both enjoyed the arrangement. It was easier for her than it was for me since I had no social life except for my brother, Artie, and the review.

Anyway, Osano's party was one of the big events of the literary set in New York. The top people of the *New York Times Book Review* came, the critics for most of the magazines and novelists that Osano was still friendly with. I was sitting in a corner talking with Osano's latest-ex-wife when I saw Wendy come in and I thought immediately, Jesus, trouble. I knew she had not been invited.

Osano spotted her at the same time and started walking towards her with the peculiar lurching gait he'd acquired in the last few months. He was a little drunk, and I was afraid he might lose his temper and cause a scene or do something crazy, so I got up and joined them. I arrived just in time to hear Osano greet her.

'What the fuck do you want?' he said. He could be frightening when he was angry, but from what he had told me about Wendy I knew she was the one person who enjoyed making him mad. But I was still surprised at her reaction.

Wendy was dressed in jeans and sweater and a scarf over her

head. It made her thin dark face Medea-like. Her wiry black hair escaped from the scarf like thin black snakes.

She looked at Osano with a deadly calm which held malevolent triumph. She was consumed with hatred. She took a long look around the room as if drinking in what she now no longer could claim any part of, the glittering literary world of Osano that he had effectively banished her from. It was a look of satisfaction. Then she said to Osano, 'I have something very important to tell you.'

Osano downed his glass of Scotch. He gave her an ugly grin. 'So tell me and get the fuck out.'

Wendy said very seriously, 'It's bad news.'

Osano laughed uproaringly and genuinely. That really tickled him. 'You're always bad news,' he said and laughed again.

Wendy watched him with quiet satisfaction. 'I have to tell you in private.'

'Oh, shit,' Osano said. But he knew Wendy, she would delight in a scene. So he took her up the stairs to his study. I figured later that he didn't take her to one of the bedrooms because deep down he was afraid he would try to fuck her, she still had that kind of hold on him. And he knew she would delight in refusing him. But it was a mistake to bring her into the study. It was his favourite room, still kept for him as a place to work. It had a huge window which he loved to stare out of while he was writing and watch the goings-on in the street below.

I hung around at the bottom of the stairs. I really don't know why, but I felt that Osano was going to need help. So I was the first one to hear Wendy scream in terror and the first one to act on that scream. I ran up the stairs and kicked in the door of the study.

I was just in time to see Osano reach Wendy. She was flailing her thin arms at him, trying to keep him away. Her bony hands were curled, the fingers extended like claws to scratch his face. She was terrified, but she was enjoying it too. I could see that. Osano's face was bleeding from two long furrows on his right cheek. And before I could stop him, he had hit Wendy in the face so that she swayed towards him. In one terrible swift motion he picked her up as if she were a weightless doll and threw her through the picture window with tremendous force. The window shattered, and Wendy sailed through it to the street below.

I don't know whether I was more horrified by the sight of Wendy's tiny body breaking through the window or Osano's completely maniacal face. I ran out of the room and shouted, 'Call an ambulance.' I snatched up a coat from the hallway and ran out in the street.

Wendy was lying on the cement like an insect whose legs had been broken. As I came out of the house, she was teetering up on her arms and legs but had only gotten to her knees. She looked like a spider trying to walk, and then she collapsed again.

I knelt beside her and covered her with the coat. I took off my jacket and folded it beneath her head. She was in pain, but there was no blood trickling out of her mouth or ears and there was not that deadly film over the eyes that long ago during the war I had recognized as a danger signal. Her face finally was calm and at peace with itself. I held her hand, it was warm, and she opened her eyes. 'You'll be OK,' I said. 'An ambulance is coming. You'll be OK.'

She opened her eyes and smiled at me. She looked very beautiful and for the first time I understood Osano's being fascinated by her. She was in pain but actually grinning, 'I fixed that son of a bitch this time,' she said.

When they got her to the hospital, they found that she had suffered a broken toe and a fracture of the clavicle. She was conscious enough to tell what had happened, and the cops went looking for Osano and took him away. I called Osano's lawyer. He told me to keep my mouth shut as much as I possibly could and that he would straighten everything out.. He had known Osano and Wendy a long time and he understood the whole thing before I did. He told me to stay where I was until he called.

Needless to say, the party broke up after detectives questioned some of the people, including myself. I said I hadn't seen anything except Wendy falling through the window. No, I hadn't seen Osano near her, I told them. And they left it at that. Osano's ex-wife gave me a drink and sat next to me on the sofa. She had a funny little smile on her face. 'I always knew this would happen,' she said.

It took almost three hours for the lawyer to call me. He said he had Osano out on bail but that it would be a good idea for someone to be with him a couple of days. Osano would be going to his studio apartment in the Village. Could I go down there to keep him company and keep him from talking to the press? I said I would. Then the laywer briefed me. Osano had testified that Wendy had attacked him and that he had flung her away from him and she had lost her balance and went through the

249

window. That was the story given to the newspapers. The lawyer was sure that he could get Wendy to go along with the story out of her own self-interest. If Osano went to jail, she would lose out on alimony and child-support. It would all be smoothed over in a couple of days if Osano could be kept from saying something outrageous. Osano should be at his apartment in an hour, the lawyer would bring him there.

I left the brownstone and took a taxi down to the Village. I sat on the stoop of the apartment house until the lawyer's chauffeured limo rolled up. Osano got out.

He looked dreadful. His eyes were bulging out of his head, and his skin was dead white with strain. He walked right past me, and I got into the elevator with him. He took his keys out, but his hands were shaking and I knew he could never get it into the lock. I did it for him.

When we were in his tiny studio apartment, Osano flopped down on the couch that opened out into a bed. He still hadn't said a word to me. He was lying there now, his face covering his hands out of weariness, not despair. I looked around the studio apartment and thought, here was Osano, one of the most famous writers in the world and he lived in this hole. But then I remembered that he rarely lived here. That he was usually living in his house in the Hamptons or up in Provincetown. Or with one of the rich divorced women he would have a love affair with for a few months.

I sat down in a dusty armchair and kicked a pile of books into a corner. 'I told the cops I didn't see anything,' I said to Osano.

Osano sat up and his hands were away from his face. To my amazement I could see that wild grin on his face.

'Jesus, how did you like the way she sailed through the air. I always said she was a fucking witch. I didn't throw her that hard. She was flying on her own.'

I stared at him. 'I think you're going fucking crazy,' I said. 'I think you'd better see a doctor.' My voice was cold. I couldn't forget Wendy lying in the street.

'Shit, she's going to be OK,' Osano said. 'And you don't ask why. Or do you think I throw all my ex-wives out the window?'

'There's no excuse,' I said.

Osano grinned. 'You don't know Wendy. I'll bet twenty bucks when I tell you what she said to me, you'll agree you'd have done the same thing.'

'Bet,' I said. I went into the bathroom and wet a facecloth and threw it to him. He wiped his face and neck and sighed with pleasure as the cold water refreshed his skin.

Osano hunched forward on the couch. 'She reminded me how she had written me letters the last two months begging for money for our kid. Of course, I didn't send her any money, she'd spend it on herself. Then she said that she hadn't wanted to bother me while I was busy in Hollywood, but that our youngest boy had gotten sick with spinal meningitis and because she didn't have enough money she had to put him in the charity ward in the city hospital, Bellevue no less. Can you imagine that fucking cunt? She didn't call me that he was sick because she wanted to lay all that shit on me, all that guilt on me.'

I knew how Osano loved all his kids from his different wives. I was amazed at this capacity in him. He always sent them birthday presents and always had them with him for the summers. And he dropped in to see them sporadically to take them to the theatre or to dinner or a ball game. I was astonished now that he didn't seem worried about his kid being sick. He understood what I was feeling.

'The kid only had a high fever, some sort of respiratory infection. While you were being so gallant about Wendy, I was calling the hospital before the cops came. They told me there was nothing to worry about. I called my doctor and he's having the kid taken to a private hospital. So everything's OK.'

'Do you want me to hang around?' I asked him.

Osano shook his head. 'I have to go see my kid and take care of the other kids now that I've deprived them of their mother. But she'll be out tomorrow, that bitch.'

Before I left him, I asked Osano one question. 'When you threw her out that window, did you remember that it was really only two storeys above the street?'

He grinned at me again. 'Sure,' he said. 'And besides, I never figured she'd sail that far. I tell you she's a witch.'

All the New York newspapers had front-page stories the next day. Osano was still famous enough for that kind of treatment. At least Osano didn't go to jail because Wendy didn't press charges. She said that maybe she had stumbled and gone through the window. But that was the next day and the damage had been done. Osano was made to resign gracefully from the review and I resigned with him. One columnist, trying to be funny, speculated that if Osano won the Nobel Prize, he would be the first one to win who had ever thrown his wife out of the window. But the truth was that everybody knew that this little comedy would end all Osano's hopes in that direction. You couldn't give the sober respectable Nobel to a sordid character like Osano. And Osano didn't help matters much when a little later he wrote a satirical article on the ten best ways to murder your wife.

But right now we both had a problem. I had to earn a living free-lance without a job. Osano had to lie low some place where the press couldn't keep hounding him. I could solve Osano's problem. I called Cully in Las Vegas and explained what had happened. I asked Cully if he could stash Osano in the Xanadu Hotel for a couple of weeks. I knew nobody would be looking for him there. And Osano was agreeable. He had never been to Las Vegas.

26

WITH Osano safely stashed in Vegas I had to fix my other problem. I had no job, so I took on as much free-lance work as I could get. I did book reviews for *Time* magazine, the *New York Times*, and the new editor of the review gave me some work. But for me it was too nerve-racking. I never knew how much money was going to come in at any particular time. And so I decided that I would go all-out to finish my novel and hope that it would make a lot of money. For the next two years my life was very simple. I spent twelve to fifteen hours a day in my workroom. I went with my wife to the supermarket. I took my kids to Jones Beach in the summer, on Sundays, to give Valerie a rest. Sometimes at midnight I took Dexamyls to keep me awake so that I could work until three or four in the morning.

During that time I saw Eddie Lancer for dinner a few times in New York. Eddie had become primarily a screenwriter in Hollywood, and it was clear that he would no longer write novels. He enjoyed the life out there, the women, the easy money, and swore he would never write another novel again. Four of his screenplays had become hit movies and he was much in demand. He offered to get me a job working with him if I was willing to come out there, and I told him no. I couldn't see myself working in the movie business. Because despite the funny stories Eddie told me, what was very clear was that being a writer in the movies was no fun. You were no longer an artist. You were just a translator of other people's ideas.

During those two years I saw Osano about once a month. He had stayed a week in Vegas and then disappeared. Cully called me to complain that Osano had run away with his favourite girlfriend, a girl named Charlie Brown. Cully hadn't been mad. He had just been astonished. He told me the girl was beautiful, was making a fortune in Vegas under his guidance and was living a great life, and she had abandoned all this to go with a fat old writer who not only had a beer gut but was the craziest guy Cully had ever seen.

I told Cully that that was another favour I owed him and if I saw the girl with Osano in New York, I would buy her a plane ticket back to Vegas.

'Just tell her to get in touch with me,' Cully said. 'Tell her I miss her, tell her I love her, tell her anything you want. I just want to get her back. That girl is worth a fortune to me in Vegas.'

'OK,' I said. But when I met Osano in New York for dinner, he was always alone and he didn't much look like anybody who could hold the affections of a young, beautiful girl with the advantages that Cully had described.

It's funny when you hear of somebody's success, of his fame. That fame, like a shooting star that has appeared out of nowhere. But the way it happened to me was surprisingly tame.

I lived the life of a hermit for two years and at the end the book was finished and I turned it into my publisher and I forgot about it. A month later my editor called me into New York and told me they had sold my novel to a paperback house for reprint for over half a million dollars. I was stunned. I really couldn't react. Everybody, my editor, my agent, Osano, Cully, had warned me that a book about kidnapping a child where the kidnapper is a hero would not appeal to a mass public. I expressed my astonishment to my editor, and he said, 'You told such a great story that it doesn't matter.'

When I went home to Valerie that night and told her what had happened, she seemed not to be surprised either. She merely said calmly, 'We can buy a bigger house. The kids are getting bigger, they need more room.' And then life simply went on as before, except that Valerie found a house only ten minutes from her parents and we bought it and moved in.

By that time the novel was published. It made all the best-seller lists all over the country. It was a big best-seller, and yet it really didn't seem to change my life in any way. In thinking about this I realized that it was because I had such few friends. There was Cully, there was Osano, there was Eddie Lancer and that was it. Of course, my brother, Artie, was terribly proud of me and wanted to give a big party until I told him he could give the party but I wouldn't come. What really touched me was a review of the book by Osano which appeared on the front page of the literary review. He praised me for the right reasons and pointed out the true flaws. In his usual fashion he overrated the book because I was a friend of his. And then, of course, he went on and talked about himself and his novel in progress.

I called his apartment, but there was no answer. I wrote him a letter and got a letter in return. We had dinner together in New York. He looked terrible, but he had a great-looking young blonde who rarely spoke but ate more than Osano and I put together. He introduced her as 'Charlie Brown', and I realized she was Cully's girl, but I never gave her Cully's message. Why should I hurt Osano?

There was one funny incident I always remembered. I told Valerie to go out shopping and buy herself some new clothes, whatever she wanted, and that I would mind the kids for that day. She went with some of her girlfriends and came back with an armful of packages.

I was trying to work on a new book but really couldn't get into it, so she showed me what she had bought. She unwrapped a package and showed me a new yellow dress.

'It cost ninety dollars,' Valerie said. 'Can you imagine ninety dollars for a little summer dress?'

'It looks beautiful,' I said dutifully. She was holding it against her neck.

'You know,' she said, 'I really couldn't make up my mind whether I liked the yellow one or the green one. Then I decided on the yellow. I think I look better in the yellow, don't you?'

I laughed. I said, 'Honey, didn't it occur to you that you could buy both?'

254

She looked at me stunned for a moment, and then she too laughed. And I said, 'You can buy a yellow and a green and a blue and a red.'

And we both smiled at each other, and for the first time we realized, I think, that we had entered some sort of new life. But on the whole I found success not to be as interesting or as satisfying as I had thought it would be. So, as I usually did, I read up on the subject and I found that my case was not unusual, that in fact, many men who had fought all their lives to reach the top of their professions immediately celebrated by throwing themselves out of a high window.

It was wintertime, and I decided to take the whole family down to Puerto Rico for a vacation. It would be the first time in our married life that we had been able to afford to go away. My kids had never even been to summer camp.

We had a great time swimming, enjoying the heat, enjoying the strange streets and food, the delight of leaving the cold winter one morning and that afternoon being in the broiling sun, enjoying the balmy breezes. At night I took Valerie to the hotel gambling casino while the children dutifully sat in the great wicker chairs of the lobby, waiting for us. Every fifteen minutes or so Valerie would run down and see if they were OK, and finally she took them all to our suite of rooms and I gambled until four o'clock in the morning. Now that I was rich, naturally I was lucky, and I won a few thousand dollars and in a funny way I enjoyed winning in the casino more than the success and the huge sums of money I had made so far on the book.

When we got back home, there was an even greater surprise waiting for me. A movie studio, Malomar Films, had spent a hundred thousand dollars for the film rights to my book and another fifty thousand dollars, plus expenses for me to go out to Hollywood to write the screenplay.

I talked it over with Valerie. I really didn't want to write movie scripts. I told her I would sell the book but turn down the screenwriting contract. I thought she would be pleased, but instead, she said, 'I think it would be good for you to go out there. I think it would be good for you to meet more people, to know more people. You know I worry about you sometimes because you're so solitary.'

'We could all go out,' I said.

'No,' Valerie said. 'I'm really happy here with my family and we can't take the children out of school and I wouldn't want them to grow up in California.'

Like everybody else in New York, Valerie regarded California as an exotic outpost of the United States filled with drug addicts, murderers and mad preachers who would shoot a Catholic on sight.

'The contract is for six months,' I said, 'but I could work for a month and then go back and forth.'

'That sounds perfect,' Valerie said, 'and besides, to tell you the truth, we could use a rest from each other.'

That surprised me. 'I don't need a rest from you,' I said.

'But I need a rest from you,' Valerie said. 'It's nerve-racking to have a man working at home. Ask any woman. It just upsets the whole routine of my keeping house. I never could say anything before because you couldn't afford an outside studio to work in, but now that you can, I wish you wouldn't work at home any more. You can rent a place and leave in the morning and come home at night. I'm sure you'd work better.'

I don't know even now why her saying this offended me so much. I had been happy staying and working at home, and I was really hurt that she didn't feel the same way, and I think it was this that made me decide to do the screenplay of my novel. It was a childish reaction. If she didn't want me home, I'd leave and see how she liked it. At that time I would swear that what would have thrilled any other writer didn't thrill me. Hollywood was a nice place to read about, but I didn't even want to visit it.

I realized a part of my life was over. In his review Osano had written, 'All novelists, bad and good, are heroes. They fight alone, they must have the faith of saints. They are more often defeated than victorious and they are shown no mercy by a villainous world. Their strength fails (that's why most novels have weak spots, are an easy target for attack); the troubles of the real world, the illness of children, the betrayal by friends, the treacheries of wives must all be brushed aside. They ignore their wounds and fight on, calling on miracles for fresh energy.'

I disapproved of his melodramatics, but it was true that I felt as if I were deserting the company of heroes. I didn't give a damn if that was a typical writer's sentimentality.

BOOK FIVE

27

MALOMAR Films, though a subsidiary of Moses Wartberg's Tri-Culture Studios, operated on a completely independent basis, creatively, and had its own small lot. And so Bernard Malomer had free rein for his planned picture of the John Merlyn novel.

All Malomer wanted to do was make good movies, and that was never easy, not with Wartberg's Tri-Culture Studios hovering over his every move. He hated Wartberg. They were acknowledged enemies, but Wartberg, as an enemy, was interesting, fun to deal with. Also, Malomar respected Wartberg's financial and management genius. He knew that moviemakers like himself could not exist without it.

Malomar in his plush suite of offices nestled in a corner of his own lot had to put up with a bigger pain in the ass than Wartberg, though a less deadly one. If Wartberg has cancer of the rectum, as Malomar jokingly said, Jack Houlinan has haemorrhoids and, on a day-to-day basis, far more irritating.

Jack Houlinan, vice-president in charge of creative public relations, played his role of the number one PR genius with a killing sincerity. When he asked you to do something outrageous and was refused, he acknowledged with violent enthusiasm your right to refuse. His favourite line was: 'Anything you say is OK with me. I would never, never try to persuade you to do anything you don't want to do. I only asked.' This would be after an hour's pitch of why you had to jump off the Empire State Building to make sure your new picture got some space in the *Times*.

But with his bosses, like the VP in charge of production at Wartberg's Tri-Culture International Studios, with this Merlyn picture for Malomar Films and his own personal client, Ugo

Kellino, he was much more frank, more human. And now he was talking frankly to Bernard Malomar, who really didn't have time for bullshit.

'We're in trouble,' Houlinan said. 'I think this fucking picture can be the biggest bomb since Nagasaki.'

Malomar was the youngest studio chief since Thalberg and liked to play a dumb genius role. With a straight face he said, 'I don't know that picture, and I think you're full of shit. I think you're worried about Kellino. You want us to spend a fortune just because that prick decided to direct himself and you want to get him insurance.'

Houlinan was Ugo Kellino's personal PR rep with a retainer of fifty grand a year. Kellino was a great actor but almost certifiably insane with ego, a not uncommon disease in top actors, actresses, directors and even script girls who fancied themselves screenplay writers. Ego in movie land was like TB in a mining town. Endemic and ravaging but not necessarily fatal.

In fact, their egos made many of them more interesting than they would otherwise be. This was true of Kellino. His dynamism on screen was such that he had been included in a list of the fifty most famous men in the world. The laminated news story living in his den with his own legend in red crayon that said, 'For fucking'. Houlinan always said, his voice emphatic, admiring, 'Kellino would fuck a *snake*.' Accenting the word as if the phrase were not an old macho cliché but coined now especially for his client.

A year ago Kellino had insisted on directing his next picture. He was one of the few stars who could get away with such a demand. But he had been put on a strict budget, his upfront money and percentages pledged for a completion bond. Malomar Films was in for a top two million and then off the hook. Just in case Kellino went crazy and started shooting a hundred takes of each scene with his latest girlfriend opposite him or his latest boyfriend under him. Both of which he had proceeded to do with no visible harm to the picture. But then he had fucked around with the script. Long monologues, the lights soft and shadowy on his despairing face, he had told the story of his tragic boyhood in excruciating flashbacks, to explain why he was fucking boys and girls on the screen. The implication was that if he had had a decent childhood, he would never have fucked anybody. And he had final cut, the studio couldn't doctor up the picture in the editing room legally. Except that they would anyway if necessary.

Malomar wasn't too worried. A Kellino starrer would get the studio's two million back. That was certain. Everything else was gravy. And if worst came to worst, he could bury the picture in distribution; nobody would see it. And he had come out of the deal with his main objective. That Kellino would star in John Merlyn's blockbuster best-selling novel that Malomar felt in his bones would make the studio a fortune.

Houlinan said, 'We have to get a special campaign. We have to spend a lot of money. We have to sell it on its class.'

'Jesus Christ,' Malomar said. He was usually more polite. But he was tired of Kellino, he was tired of Houlinan and he was tired of motion pictures. Which didn't mean anything. He was tired of beautiful women and charming men. He was tired of California weather. To divert himself he studied Houlinan. He had a long-standing grudge against him and Kellino.

Houlinan was beautifully dressed. Silk suit, silk tie, Italian shoes, Piaget watch. His eyeglass frames were specially made, black and gold-flecked. He had the benign sweet Irish face of the leprechaun preachers that filled the California TV screens on Sunday mornings. It was hard to believe he was a black-hearted son of a bitch and proud of it.

Years ago Kellino and Malomar had quarrelled in a public restaurant, a vulgar shouting match that had become a humiliating story in the columns and trades. And Houlinan had masterminded a campaign to make Kellino come out of the argument as the hero and Malomar the craven villain, the weakling studio chief bending to the heroic movie star. Houlinan was a genius all right. But a little short-sighted. Malomar had made him pay ever since.

For the last five years not a month had gone by that the papers had not carried a story about Kellino's helping somebody less fortunate than himself. Did a poor girl with leukaemia need a special blood transfusion from a donor who lived in Siberia? Page five of any newspaper would tell you Kellino had sent his private jet to Siberia. Did a black go to a Southern jail for protesting? Kellino posted bail. When an Italian policeman with seven kids got chopped down by a Black Panther ambush in Harlem, did not Kellino send a cheque for ten thousand dollars to the widow and set up a scholarship for all seven children? When a Black Panther was accused of murdering a cop, Kellino sent ten thousand dollars to his defence fund. Whenever a famous old-time movie star became ill, the papers noted that

Kellino picked up his hospital tab and assured him of a cameo role in his next film so that the old codger would have something to live for. One of the old codgers with ten million stashed and a hatred for his profession gave an interview insulting Kellino's generosity, spitting on it in fact, and it was so funny that even the great Houlinan couldn't get it squashed.

And Houlinan had more hidden talents. He was a pimp whose fine nose for new fresh starlets made him the Daniel Boone of Hollywood's celluloid wilderness. Houlinan often boasted of his technique. 'Tell any actress she was great in her bit part. Tell her that three times in one evening and she pulls down your pants and tears your cock off by the roots.' He was Kellino's advance scout, many times testing the girl's talents in bed before passing her on. Those who were too neurotic, even by the lenient industry standards, never got past him to Kellino. But as Houlinan often said, 'Kellino's rejects are worth picking up options on.'

Malomar said with the first pleasure he had felt that day, 'Forget about any big advertising budgets. It's not that kind of picture.'

Houlinan looked at him thoughtfully. 'How about doing a little private promoting with some of the more important critics? You have a couple of big ones that owe you a favour.'

Malomar said dryly, 'I'm not wasting it on this.' He didn't say that he was going to call in all his IOU's on the big picture next year. He already had that one mapped out, and Houlinan was not going to run that show. He wanted the next picture to be the star, not Kellino.

Houlinan looked at him thoughtfully. Then said, 'I guess I'll have to build my own campaign.'

Malomar said wearily, 'Just remember it's still a Malomar Films' production. Clear everything with me. OK?'

'*Of course*,' Houlinan said with his special emphasis as if it had never occurred to him to do anything else.

Malomar said evenly, 'Jack, remember there's a line you don't go over with me. No matter who you are.'

Houlinan said with his dazzling smile, 'I never forget that. Have I ever forgotten that? Listen, there's a great looking broad from Belgium. I got her stashed in the Beverly Hills Hotel bungalow. Shall we have a breakfast conference tomorrow?'

'Another time,' Malomar said. He was tired of women flying in from all over the world to be fucked. He was tired of all the slender, beautiful, chiselled faces, the thin, elegant bodies perfectly dressed, the beauties he was constantly photographed with at parties and restaurants and premières. He was famous not only as the most talented producer in Hollywood, but as the one who had the most beautiful women. Only his closest friends knew he preferred sex with plump Mexican maids who worked in his mansion. When they kidded him about his perverseness, Malomar always told them that his favourite relaxation was going down on a woman and that those beautiful women in the magazines had nothing to go down on but bone and hair. The Mexican maid had meat and juice. Not that all this was always true; it was just that Malomar, knowing how elegant he looked, wanted to show his distaste for that elegance.

At this time in his life all Malomar wanted to do was make a good movie. The happiest hours for him were after dinner when he went into the cutting room and worked until the early-morning hours editing a new film.

As Malomar ushered Houlinan out of the door, his secretary murmured that the writer of the novel was waiting with his agent, Doran Rudd. Malomar told her to bring them in. He introduced them to Houlinan.

Houlinan gave both men a quick appraisal. Rudd he knew. Sincere, charming, in short a hustler. He was a type. The writer also was a type. The naïve novelist who comes out to work on his film script, gets dazzled by Hollywood, faked out of his shoes by producers, directors and studio heads and then falls for a starlet and wrecks his life by divorcing his wife of twenty years for a broad who had screwed every casting director in town just for openers. And then gets indignant at the way his half-assed novel gets mutilated on the screen. This one was no different. He was quiet and obviously shy and dressed like a slob. Not a fashionable slob, which was the new fad even among producers like Malomar and stars who sought specially patched and faded blue jeans that were exquisitely fitted by top tailors—but real slob. And ugly to boot like that fucking French actor who grossed so high in Europe. Well, he, Houlinan, would do his little bit to grind this guy into sausage right now.

Houlinan gave the writer, John Merlyn, a big hello and told him that his book was the very best book he had ever read in his life. He hadn't read it.

Then he stopped at the door and turned around and said to the writer, 'Listen, Kellino would love to have his picture taken with you this afternoon. We have a conference with Malomar later, and it would be great publicity for the movie. OK for about three o'clock? You should be through here, right?'

Merlyn said OK. Malomar grimaced. He knew Kellino wasn't even in town, that he was sunning himself in Palm Springs and wouldn't arrive until six. Houlinan was going to make Merlyn hang around for a no-show just to teach him where the muscle was in Hollywood. Well, he might as well learn.

Malomar, Doran Rudd, and Merlyn had a long session on the writing of the movie. Malomar noted that Merlyn seemed reasonable and cooperative rather than the usual pain in the ass. He gave the agent the usual bullshit about bringing in the picture for a million when everybody knew that eventually they'd have to spend five. It was only when they left that Malomar got his first surprise. He mentioned to Merlyn that he could wait for Kellino in the library. Merlyn looked at his watch and said mildly, 'It's ten after three. I never wait more than ten minutes for anybody, not even my kids.' Then he walked out.

Malomar smiled at the agent. 'Writers,' he said. But he often said, 'Actors,' in the same tone of voice. And 'Directors' and 'Producers'. He never said it about actresses because you couldn't put down a human being who had to contend with a menstrual cycle and wanting to be an actress both. That made them fucking crazy just for openers.

Doran Rudd shrugged. 'He doesn't even wait for doctors. We both had to take a physical together, and we had ten A.M. appointments. You know doctor's offices. You gotta wait a few minutes. He told the receptionist, "I'm on time, why isn't the doctor on time?" Then he walked out.'

'Jesus,' Malomar said.

He was getting pains in his chest. He went into the bathroom and swallowed an angina pill and then went to take a nap on the couch as his doctor had ordered. One of his secretaries would wake him up when Houlinan and Kellino arrived.

'*The Stone Woman is Kellino's debut as director. As an actor he is always marvellous; as a director he is less than competent; as a philosopher he is pretentious and despicable. This is not to say that* Stone Woman *is a bad film. It isn't really trashy, merely hollow.*

'*Kellino dominates the screen, we always believe the character he plays, but here the character he plays is a man we do not care about. How can we care about a man who throws away his life for an empty-headed doll like Selina Denton whose personality appeals to men satisfied* with women whose breasts and rear are extravagantly rounded in the cliché style of male chauvinistic fantasy? Selina Denton's acting, her usual wooden-Indian style, insipid face contorted in grimaces of ecstasy, is just plain embarrassing. When will Hollywood casting directors learn that the audience is interested in seeing real women on the screen? An actress like Billie Stroud with her commanding presence, her intelligent and forceful technique, her striking appearance (she is truly beautiful if one can forget all the deodorant commercial stereotypes the American male has idolized since the invention of television) might have salvaged the film, and it is surprising that Kellino, whose acting is so intelligent and intuitive, did not realize this when he was casting. Presumably he had enough clout as star and director and co-producer to call this shot, at least.

'The script by Hascom Watts is one of those pseudoliterary exercises that read well on paper but don't make any sense at all on film. We are expected to feel a sense of tragedy for a man to whom nothing tragic happens, a man who finally commits suicide because his comeback as an actor fails (everyone fails) and because an empty-headed, selfish woman uses her beauty (all in the eyes of the beholder) to betray him in the most banal fashion since the heroines of Dumas the Younger.

'The counterpart of Kellino trying to save the world by being on the right side of every social question is good-hearted but essentially fascist in concept. The embattled liberal hero evolves into the fascist dictator, as Mussolini did. The treatment of women in this film is also basically fascist; they do nothing except manipulate men with their bodies. When they do take part in political movements, they are shown as destroyers of men striving to better the world. Can't Hollywood believe for a moment that there is a relationship between men and women in which sex does not play a part? Can't it show just one goddamn time that women have the "manly" virtues of a belief in humanity and its terrible struggle to go forward? Don't they have the imagination to foresee that women might, just might, love a movie that portrays them as real human beings, rather than those familiar rebellious puppets that break the strings men attach to them?

'Kellino is not a gifted director; he is less than competent. He places the camera where it should be; the only trouble is that he never gets the lead out of it. But his acting saves the film from the complete disaster the whoremongering script dooms it to be. Kellino's directing doesn't help, but it doesn't destroy the film. The rest of the cast is simply dreadful. It's not fair to dislike an actor because of his looks, but George Fowles is physically too slimy even for the slimy role he plays here. Selina Denton is too empty-looking even for the empty woman she plays here. It's not a bad idea sometimes to cast against the role, and maybe that's what Kellino should have done in this film. But maybe it wasn't worth the trouble. The

264

fascist philosophy of the script, its male chauvinistic conception of what constitutes a "lovable" woman, doomed the whole project before they loaded film into the camera.'

'That fucking cunt,' Houlinan said not in anger but with bewildered helplessness. 'What the fuck does she want from a movie anyway? And Jesus Christ, why does she keep going on about Billie Stroud being a good-looking broad? In all my forty years in movies I've never seen an uglier movie star. It's beyond me.'

Kellino said thoughtfully, 'All those other fucking critics follow her. We can forget about this movie.'

Malomar listened to both of them. A matched pair of pain in the asses. What the hell did it matter what Clara Ford said? The picture with Kellino as star would make its money back and help pay some studio overhead. That's all he'd ever expected from it. And now he had Kellino on the hook for the important picture, from the novel by John Merlyn. And Clara Ford, brilliant as she was, didn't know that Kellino had a backup director doing all the work without credit.

The critic was a particular hate of Malomar's. She spoke with such authority, she wrote so well, she was so influential but she had no idea at all about what went into the making of a movie. She complained about casting. Didn't she know that it depended on whom Kellino was fucking in the major female role and then it depended on who was fucking the casting director for the smaller parts? Didn't she know these were the jealously guarded prerogatives of many people in power in certain movies? There were a thousand broads for each bit part and you could fuck half of them without even giving them anything, just letting them read for it and saying you might call them back for another read. And all those fucking directors building up their own private harems, more powerful than the greatest money-makers in the world as far as beautiful, intelligent women were concerned. Not that you even bothered to do that. Even that was too much trouble and not worth it. What amused Malomar was that the critic was the only one who got the unflappable Houlinan upset.

Kellino was angry about something else. 'What the hell does she mean it's fascist? I've been antifascist all my life.'

Malomar said tiredly, 'She's just a pain in the ass. She uses the word "fascist" the way we use the word "cunt". She doesn't mean anything by it.'

Kellino was mad as hell. 'I don't give a shit about my acting.

But nobody compares me with fascists and gets away with it.'

Houlinan paced up and down the room, almost dipped into Malomar's box of Monte Cristo cigars, then thought better of it. 'That broad is killing us,' he said. 'She's always killing us. And your barring her from previews doesn't help, Malomar.'

Malomar shrugged. 'It's not supposed to help, I do it for my bile.'

They both looked at him curiously. They knew what bile meant but knew it wasn't in character for him to say it. Malomar had read it in a script that morning.

Houlinan said, 'No shit, it's too late for this picture, but what the hell are we going to do about Clara on the next one?'

Malomar said, 'You're Kellino's personal press agent, do what you want. Clara's your baby.'

He was hoping to end this conference early. If it had been just Houlinan, it would have ended in two minutes. But Kellino was one of the truly great stars, and his ass had to be kissed with infinite patience and extreme shows of love.

Malomar had the rest of the day and evening scheduled for the cutting room. His greatest pleasure. He was one of the greatest film editors in the business and he knew it. And besides, he loved cutting a film so that all the starlet heads dropped on the floor. It was easy to recognize them. The unnecessary close-ups of a pretty girl watching the main action. The director had banged her, and that was his pay-off. Malomar in his cutting room chopped her right out unless he liked the director or the one-in-a-million times the shot worked. Jesus, how many broads had put out to see themselves up there on the screen for one split second, thinking that one split second would send them on the way to fame and fortune. That their beauty and talent would flash out like lightning. Malomar was tired of beautiful women. They were a pain in the ass, especially if they were bright. Which didn't mean he didn't get hooked once in a while. He'd had his share of disastrous marriages, three, all with actresses. Now he was looking for any broad who wasn't hustling him for something. He felt about pretty girls as a lawyer feels hearing his phone ring. It can mean only trouble.

'Get one of your secretaries in here,' Kellino said. Malomar rang the buzzer on his desk, and a girl appeared in the door as if by magic. As she better had. Malomar had four secretaries: two guarding the outer door of his offices and another two guarding the inner sanctum door, one on each side like dragons. No matter

what disasters happened—when Malomar rang his buzzer, somebody appeared. Three years ago the impossible had happened.
He had pressed the buzzer and nothing happened. One secretary
was having a nervous breakdown in a nearby executive office,
and a free-lance producer was curing her with some head.
Another had dashed upstairs to accounting to get some figures on
the grosses of a film. The third was out sick that day. The fourth
and last had been overcome with a painful desire to take a leak,
and gambled. She established a woman's record for taking a leak,
but it was not enough. In that fatal few seconds Malomar rang
his buzzer and four secretaries were not insurance enough.
Nobody appeared. All four were fired.

Now Kellino dictated a letter to Clara Ford. Malomar
admired his style. And knew what he was getting to. He didn't
bother to tell Kellino that there was no chance.

'Dear Miss Ford,' Kellino dictated. 'Only my admiration for
your work impels me to write this letter and point out a few areas
where I disagree with you in your review of my new film. Please
don't think this is a complaint of any kind. I respect your
integrity enough and revere your intelligence too much to voice
an idle complaint. I just want to state that the failure of the film,
if indeed it is a failure, is entirely due to my inexperience as a
director. I still think it was a beautifully written script. I think
the people who worked with me in the film were very good and
handicapped by me as a director. That is all I have to say except
that I am still one of your fans and maybe someday we can get
together for lunch and a drink and really talk about film and art.
I feel that I have a great deal to learn before I direct my next
film (which won't be for quite a long time, I assure you) and what
better person to learn than from you?
                                        Sincerely, Kellino.'

'It won't work,' Malomar said.

'Maybe,' Houlinan said.

'You'll have to go after her and fuck her brains out,' Malomar
said. 'And she's too smart a broad to fall for your line of bullshit.'

Kellino said, 'I really admire her. I really want to learn from
her.'

'Never mind that,' Houlinan almost yelled. 'Fuck her. Jesus.
That's the answer. Fuck her brains out.'

Malomar suddenly found them both unbearable. 'Don't do it
in my office,' he said. 'Get out of here and let me work.'

They left. He didn't bother to walk them to the door.

The next morning in his special suite of offices in Tri-Culture Studios, Houlinan was doing what he liked to do best. He was preparing press releases that would make one of his clients look like God. He had consulted Kellino's contract to make sure that he had the legal authority to do what he had to do, and then he wrote:

TRI-CULTURE STUDIOS & MALOMAR FILMS
PRESENT
A MALOMAR-KELLINO PRODUCTION
STARRING
UGO KELLINO
FAY MEADOWS
IN A UGO KELLINO FILM
'JOYRIDE'
DIRECTED BY BERNARD MALOMAR

... Also starring, and then he scribbled a few names very small to indicate the small type. Then he put: 'Executive Producers: Ugo Kellino and Hagan Cord.' Then: 'Produced by Malomar and Kellino.' And then he indicated much smaller type: 'Screenplay by John Merlyn from the novel by John Merlyn.' He leaned back in his chair and admired his work. He buzzed his secretary to type it up and then asked his secretary to bring in the Kellino obituary file.

He loved to look at that file. It was thick with the operations that would be put into effect on Kellino's death. He and Kellino had worked for a month up in Palm Springs perfecting the plan. Not that Kellino expected to die, but he wanted to make sure that when he did, everybody would know what a great man he had been. There was a thick folder which contained all the names of everybody he knew in show business who would be called for quotes upon his death. There was a complete outline on a television tribute. A two-hour special.

All the movie star friends would be asked to appear. There were specific clips of film in another folder of Kellino in his best roles that would be shown on that special. There was a film clip of him accepting his two Academy Awards as best actor. There was a fully written comedy sketch in which friends of his would poke fun at his aspirations to be a director.

There was a list of everybody Kellino had helped so that some of them could tell little anecdotes about how Kellino has rescued

268

them from the depths of despair on condition they never let anyone know.

There was a note on those ex-wives who would be approached for a quote and those who would not be. There were plans for one wife in particular: to fly her out of the country to a safari in Africa on the day Kellino died so no one in the media could get in touch with her. There was an ex-President of the United States who had already given his quote.

In the file was a recent letter to Clara Ford asking for a contribution to Kellino's obituary. It was written on the letterhead of the Los Angeles *Times* and was legitimate but inspired by Houlinan. He had gotten his copy of Clara Ford's reply but never showed it to Kellino. He read it again. 'Kellino is a gifted actor who has done some marvellous work in films, and it's a pity that he passed away too soon to achieve the greatness that might have been in store for him with the proper role and the proper direction.'

Every time that Houlinan read that letter he had to have another drink. He didn't know whom he hated more, Clara Ford or John Merlyn. Houlinan hated snotty writers on sight, and Merlyn was one of them. Who the fuck was that son of a bitch he couldn't wait to have his picture taken with Kellino? But at least he could fix Merlyn's wagon, Ford was beyond his reach. He tried getting her fired by organizing a campaign of hate mail from fans, by using all the pressure of Tri-Culture Studios, but she was simply too powerful for him. He hoped Kellino was having better luck with her than he had, but he would soon know. Kellino had been on a date with her. He'd taken her to dinner the night before and was sure to call him and report everything that happened.

28

IN my first weeks in Hollywood I began to think of it as the Land of Empidae. An amusing conceit, at least to me, even if a bit condescending.

The empid is an insect. The female is cannibalistic, and the act of sex whets her appetite so that in the last moment of the male's ecstasy he finds himself without a head.

But in one of those marvellous evolutionary processes the male empid learned to bring a tiny bit of food wrapped in a web spun from his own body. While the murderous female peels away the web, he mounts her, copulates and makes his getaway.

A more highly developed male empid figured out that all he had to do was spin a web around a tiny stone or pebble, any little bit of junk. In a great evolutionary jump the male empid fly became a Hollywood producer. When I mentioned this to Malomar, he grimaced and gave me a dirty look; then he laughed.

'OK,' he said, 'do you want to get your fucking head bit off for a piece of ass?'

At first nearly everyone I met struck me as a person who would eat off somebody's ear or foot or elbow to become successful. And yet, as I stayed on, I was struck by the passion of people involved in film-making. They really loved it. Script girls, secretaries, studio accountants, cameramen, propmen, the technical crews, the actors and actresses, the directors and even the producers. They all said 'the movie I made'. They all considered themselves artists. I noticed that the only ones concerned with films that did not speak this way were usually screenwriters. Maybe that was because everyone rewrote their scripts. Everybody put his fucking two cents in. Even the script girl would change a line or two, or a character actor's wife would rewrite her husband's part, and he'd bring it in the next day and say that was the way he thought it should be played. Naturally the rewrite showed off his talents rather than forwarded the movie's purpose. It was an irritating business for a writer. Everyone wanted his job.

It occurred to me that moviemaking is a dilettante art form to an extreme degree and this innocently enough because the medium itself is so powerful. By using a combination of photographs, costumes, music and a simple story line, people with absolutely no talent could actually create works of art. But maybe that was going too far. They could at least produce something good enough to give themselves a sense of importance, some value.

Movies can give you great pleasure and move you emotionally. But they can teach you very little. They couldn't plumb the depths of a character the way a novel could. They couldn't teach you as books could teach you. They could only make you feel; they could not make you understand life. Film is so magical it can give some value to almost anything. For many people it could be a form of drug, a harmless cocaine. For others it could be a form of valuable therapy. Who doesn't want to record his past life or future traits as he would want them to be so that he could love himself?

Anyway that was as close as I could figure the movie world out, at that time. Later on, bitten a little by the bug himself, I felt that it was maybe a too cruel and snobbish view.

I wondered about the powerful hold making films seemed to have on everyone. Malomar passionately loved making films. All the people who worked in films struggled to control them. The directors, the stars, the chief photographers, the studio wheels.

I was aware that cinema was the most vital art of our time, and I was jealous. On every college campus, students, instead of writing novels, were making their own films. And suddenly it occurred to me that maybe the use of film was not even an art. That it was a form of therapy. Everyone wanted to tell his own life story, his own emotions, his own thoughts. Yet how many books had been published for that reason? But the magic was not that strong in books or painting or music. Movies combined all the arts; movies should be irresistible. With that powerful arsenal of weapons it should be impossible to make a bad movie. You could be the biggest asshole in the world and still make an interesting film. No wonder there was so much nepotism in moviemaking. You literally could let a nephew write a screen-play, take a girlfriend and make her a star, make your son the head of a studio. Movies could make a successful artist out of anyone. Mute Miltons no longer.

And how come no actor had ever murdered a director or a producer? Certainly over the years there had been plenty of cause, financial and artistic. How come a director had never murdered the head of a studio? How come a writer had never murdered a director? It must be that the making of a film purged people of violence, was therapeutic.

Could it be that some day one of the most effective treatments for the emotionally disturbed would be to let them make their own motion pictures? Christ, think of all the professional people in films who were crazy or near crazy anyway. Actors and actresses were certifiable certainly.

So that would be it. In the future everybody would stay home and watch films his friends made to keep from going crazy. The films would save his life. Think of it that way. And finally every asshole could be an artist. Certainly, if the people in this business could turn out good pictures, anybody could. Here you had bankers, garment makers, lawyers, etc., deciding what movies would be made. They didn't even have that craziness which might help create art. So what would be lost if every asshole made a film? The only problem was to get the cost down. You wouldn't need psychiatrists any more or talent. Every body could be an artist.

All those people, unlovable, never understood you had to work at being loved, yet despite their narcissism, infantilism, their self-love, they could now project their internal image of themselves to a lovable exterior on the screen. Make themselves lovable as shadows. Without having earned it in real life. And of course, you could say that all artists do that; think of the image of the great writer as a self-indulgent prick in his personal life. Osano. But at least they had to have some gift, some talent in their art that gave pleasure or learning or deeper understanding.

But with film everything was possible without talent, without any gift. You could get a really rich prick making the story of his life, and without the help of a great director, great writer, great star, etc., etc., just with the magic of film make himself a hero. The great future of film for all these people was that it could work with no talent, which didn't mean that talent could not make it better.

Because we were working so closely on the script, Malomar and I spent a lot of time together, sometimes late at night in his movie mogul home where I felt uncomfortable. It was too much for one person, I thought. The huge, heavily furnished rooms, the tennis court, the swimming pool and the separate house that held the screening room. One night he offered to screen a new movie, and I told him I wasn't that crazy about movies. I guess my snottiness showed because he got a little pissed off.

'You know we'd be doing a lot better on this script if you didn't have such contempt for the movie business,' he said.

That stung me a little. For one thing I prided myself that my manners were too good to show such a thing. For another I had a professional pride in my work and he was telling me I was fucking off. For still another I had come to respect Malomar. He was the producer-director and he could have ridden right over me while we were working together, but he never did. And when he made a suggestion to change the script, he was usually right. When he was wrong and I could prove it by argument, he deferred to me. In short, he did not fit all my preconceived notions of the Land of Empidae.

So instead of watching the movie or working on the script, we fought that night. I told him how I felt about the movie business and the people in it. The more I talked, the less angry Malomar became, and finally he was smiling.

'You talk like some cunt who can't get guys any more,' Malomar said. 'Movies are the new art form, you worry your racket is becoming obsolete. You're just jealous.'

'Movies can't compare with novels,' I said. 'Movies can never do what books do.'

'That's irrelevant,' Malomar said. 'Movies are what people want now and in the future. And all your bullshit about producers and the empid fly. You came here for a few months and you pass judgment on everybody. You put us all down. But every business is the same, they all wave that carrot on a stick. Sure, movie people are fucking crazy, sure, they hustle, sure, they use sex like barter beads, but so what? What you ignore is, all of them, producers and writers, directors and actors, go through a lot of pain. They study their trade or craft for years and work harder than any people I know. They are truly dedicated, and no matter what you say, it takes talent and even genius to make a good movie. Those actors and actresses are like the fucking infantry. They get killed. And they don't get the important roles by fucking. They have to be proven artists, they have to know their craft. Sure there are assholes and maniacs in this business that ruin a five-million-dollar picture by casting their boyfriend or girlfriend. But they don't last long. And then you go on about producers and directors. Well, directors I don't have to defend. It's the toughest job in the business. But producers have a function too. They're like lion tamers in a zoo. You know what it is to make a picture? First you have to kiss ten asses on the financial board of a studio. Then you have to be mother and father to some crazy fucking stars. You have to keep the crews happy or they murder you with malingering and overtime. And then you have to keep them all from murdering each other. Look, I hate Moses Wartberg, but I recognize that he has a financial genius that helps keep the movie business going. I respect that genius as much as I despise his artistic taste. And I have to fight him all the time as a producer and a director. And I think even you will admit that a couple of my movies could be called art.'

'That's at least half bullshit,' I said.

Malomar said, 'You keep putting down producers. Well, they are the guys who get pictures together. And they do it by spending two years kissing a hundred different babies, financial babies, actor babies, director babies, writer babies. And producers have to change their diapers, get tons of shit up their nose into their brain. Maybe that's why they usually have such lousy taste. And yet a lot of them believe in art more than the talent. Or in its fantasy. You never see a producer not appear at the Academy Awards to pick up his Oscar.'

'That's just ego,' I said, 'not a belief in art.'

'You and your fucking art,' Malomar said. 'Sure, only one movie out of a hundred is worth something, but what about books?'

'Books have a different function,' I said defensively. 'Movies can only show the outside.'

Malomar shrugged. 'You really are a pain in the ass.'

'Movies are not art,' I said. 'It's magic tricks for kids.' I only half believed that.

Malomar sighed. 'Maybe you have the right idea. In every form, it's all magic, not art. It's a fake-out so that people forget about dying.'

That wasn't true, but I didn't argue. I knew Malomar had trouble since his heart attack and I didn't want to say that this was what influenced him. For my money it was art that made you understand how to live.

` Well, OK, he didn't convince me, but after that I did look around me in a less prejudiced way. But he was right in one thing. I was jealous of the movies. The work was so easy, the rewards so rich, the fame dizzying. I hated the idea of going back to writing novels alone in a room. Underneath all my contempt was a childish envy. It was something I could never really be a part of; I didn't have the talent or the temperament. I would always in some way despise it but for reasons more snobbish than moral.

I had read all about Hollywood, and by Hollywood I really mean the movie business. I had heard writers, especially Osano, come back East and curse the studios, call the producers the worst cocksucking meddlers in the world, the studio chiefs the crudest, rudest men this side of the apes, the studios so crooked, overbearing and criminal that they made the Black Hand look like the Sweet Sisters of Charity. Well, how they came back from Hollywood, that's how I went in.

I had all the confidence in the world that I could handle it. When Doran took me into my first meeting with Malomar and Houlinan, I spotted them right away. Houlinan was easy. But Malomar was more complicated then I expected. Doran, of course, was a caricature. But to tell the truth I liked Doran and Malomar. I detested Houlinan on sight. And when Houlinan told me to have my picture taken with Kellino, I almost told him to go fuck himself. When Kellino didn't show up on time, I had my out. I hate waiting for anybody. I don't get mad at them for being late, so why should they get mad at me for not waiting?

What made Hollywood fascinating was all the difference species of empid fly.

Young guys with vasectomy cards, cans of film under their arms, scripts and cocaine in their studio apartments, hoping to make movies, searching for talented young girls and guys to read for parts and fuck to pass time. Then there were the bona fide producers with offices on the studio lots and a secretary, plus a hundred thousand dollars in development money. They called agents and casting agencies to send people over. These producers had at least one picture to their credit. Usually a low-budget dumb picture that never made back the cost of the negative and wound up being shown on airplanes or at drive-ins. These producers paid off a Californian weekly for a quote that called their film one of the ten best pictures of the year. Or a planted *Variety* report that the picture had outgrossed *Gone with the Wind* in Uganda, which really meant *Gone with the Wind* had never played there. These producers usually had signed pictures of big stars on their desks inscribed with 'LOVE'. They spent the day interviewing beautiful, struggling actresses who were deadly serious about their work and had no idea that for the producers it was just a way to kill an afternoon and maybe get lucky with a blow job that would give them a better appetite for dinner. If they were really hot for a particular actress, they would take her for lunch in the studio commissary and introduce her to the heavyweights who went by. The heavyweights, having gone through the same routine in their salad days, stood still for this if you didn't push it too far. The heavyweights had outgrown this kid stuff. They were too busy unless the girl was something special. Then she might get a shot.

The girls and boys knew the game, knew it was partly a fixed wheel, but they also knew that you could get lucky. So they took their chances with a producer, a director, a star, but if they really knew their stuff and had some brains, they would never pin their hopes on a writer. I realized now how Osano must have felt.

But again I always understood this was part of the trap. Along with the money and the plush suites and the flattery and heady atmosphere of studio conferences and the feeling of importance in making a big film. So I never really got hooked. If I got a little horny, I flew to Vegas and gambled it cold. Cully would always try to send a class hooker to my room. But I always refused. Not that I was priggish, and of course, I was tempted. But I liked gambling more and had too much guilt.

I spent two weeks in Hollywood playing tennis, going out to dinner with Doran and Malomar, going to parties. The parties were interesting. At one I met a faded star who had been my masturbation fantasy when I was a teenager. She must have been fifty, but she still looked pretty good with face-lifts and all kinds of beauty aids. But she was just a little fat and her face was puffy with alcohol. She got drunk and tried to fuck every male and female at the party but couldn't find a taker. And this was a girl that millions of young red-blooded Americans had fantasized about. I found that sort of interesting. I guess the truth is that it depressed me too. The parties were OK. Familiar faces of actors and actresses. Agents brimming over with confidence. Charming producers, forceful directors. I have to say they were a hell of a lot more charming and interesting than I ever was at a party.

And then I loved the balmy climate. I loved the palm tree streets of Beverly Hills, and I loved goofing around Westwood with all its movie theatres and young college kids who were film aficionados with really great-looking girls. I understood why all those 1930 novelists had 'sold out'. Why spend five years writing a novel that made two grand when you could live this life and make the same money in a week?

During the day I would work in my office, have conferences on the script with Malomar, lunch in the commissary, wander over to a set and watch a picture being shot. On the set the intensity of the actors and actresses always fascinated me. One time I was really awed. A young couple played a scene in which the boy murdered his girlfriend while they made love. After the scene the two of them fell into each other's arms and wept as if they had been part of a real tragedy. They walked off the set hugging each other.

Lunch at the commissary was fun. You met all the people acting in films, and it seemed as if everybody had read my book, at least they said they did. I was surprised that actors and actresses really didn't talk much. They were good listeners. Producers talked a lot. Directors were preoccupied, usually accompanied by three or four assistants. The crew seemed to have the best time. But to watch shooting a picture was boring. It wasn't a bad life, but I missed New York. I missed Valerie and the kids, and I missed my dinners with Osano. Those were nights I'd hop on a plane to Vegas for the evening, sleep over and come back in the early morning.

Then one day at the studio, after I had been back and forth a few times, NY to LA, LA to NY, Doran asked me to come to a party at his rented house in Malibu. A goodwill party where movie critics, scriptwriters and production people mixed it up with actors and actresses and directors. I didn't have anything better to do, I didn't feel like going to Vegas, so I went to Doran's party, and there I met Janelle for the first time.

29

IT was one of those Sunday informal gatherings thrown in a Malibu house that had a tennis court plus a big Jacuzzi pool, with steaming hot water. The house was divided from the ocean by only a thin strip of sand. Everybody was dressed casually. I noticed that most of the men threw their car keys on the table in the first receiving room, and when I asked Eddie Lancer about that, he told me that in Los Angeles male trousers were tailored so perfectly that you couldn't put anything into your pockets.

As I moved through the different rooms, I heard interesting conversations. A tall, thin, aggressive-looking dark woman was falling all over a handsome producer type wearing a yachting cap. A very short little blonde rushed up to them and said to the woman, 'Lay another hand on my husband and I'll punch you right in the cunt.' The man in the yachting cap had a stutter and very deadpan said, 'Th-th-that's OK. She doesn't use it mu-u-u-ch anyway.'

Going through a bedroom, I saw a couple head to toe and I heard a woman's very schoolmarm voice say, 'Get *up* here.'

I heard a guy I recognized as a New York novelist saying, 'The movie business. If you make a reputation as a great dentist, they'll let you do brain surgery.' And I thought, another pissed-off writer.

I wandered out into the parking area near the Pacific Coast Highway and I saw Doran with a group of friends admiring a Stutz Bearcat. Somebody had just told Doran the car cost sixty thousand dollars. Doran said, 'For that kind of money it should be able to give head.' And everybody laughed. Then Doran said, 'How do you get the nerve to just park it? It's like having a night job while being married to Marilyn Monroe.'

I really went to the party just to meet Clara Ford, for my money the best American film reviewer who ever lived. She was smart as hell, wrote great sentences, read a lot of books, saw every movie and agreed with me on ninety-nine films out of a hundred. When she praised a film, I knew I could go see it and probably love it, or at the very least would be able to sit through the damn thing. Her reviews were the closest a critic could come to being an artist, and I liked the fact that she never claimed to be creative. She was content to be a critic.

At the party I didn't get much chance to talk to her, which was OK with me. I just wanted to see what kind of lady she really was. She came with Kellino, and he kept her busy. And since most of the people clustered around Kellino, Clara Ford got a lot of attention. So I sat in the corner and just watched.

Clara Ford was one of those small, sweet-looking women who are usually called plain, but her face was so alive with intelligence that, in my eyes anyway, she was beautiful. What made her fascinating was that she could be both tough and innocent at the same time. She was tough enough to take on all the other major movie critics in New York and show them up as top-notch assholes. She did it A-B-C, like a prosecuting DA with an airtight case. She showed up as an idiot one guy whose humourous Sunday columns on movies were embarrassing. She took on the voice of the Greenwich Village avant-garde movie buffs and showed him for the dull bastard he was, yet she was smart enough to see him as an idiot savant, the dumbest guy who ever put words on paper, with a real feeling for certain movies. By the time she was through she had all their balls in her unfashionable J. C. Penney handbag.

I could see she was having a good time at the party. And that she was aware that Kellino was conning her with his romancing. Through the uproar I could hear Kellino say, 'An agent is an idiot savant *manqué*.' That was an old trick of his with critics, male and female. In fact, he had scored a great success with an astringent male critic by calling another critic a fag *manqué*.

Now Kellino was being so fucking charming with Clara Ford that it was a scene in a movie. Kellino showed his dimples like muscles and Clara Ford, for all her intelligence, was beginning to wilt and hang onto him a little.

Suddenly a voice next to me said, 'Do you think Kellino will let her fuck him on the first date?'

The voice came from a really good-looking blond girl, or

rather a woman because she wasn't a kid. I guessed she was about thirty. Like Clara Ford, what gave her face some of its beauty was its intelligence.

She had great sharp-planed bones in her face with lovely white skin over those bones, you couldn't notice the skin owed something to makeup. She had vulnerable brown eyes that could be delighted as a child's and tragic as a Dumas heroine. If this sounds like a lover's description out of Dumas, that's OK. Maybe I didn't feel this way when I first saw her. That came later. Right now the brown eyes looked mischievous. She was having a good time standing outside the party storm centre. What she had, which was unusual in beautiful women, was the delighted, happy air that children have when they are being left alone, doing what is to them amusing. I introduced myself and she said her name was Janelle Lambert.

I recognized her now. I'd seen her in small parts in different movies and she'd always been good. She gave her part second effort. You always liked her on screen, but you never thought of her as great. I could see she admired Clara Ford and had hoped the critic would say something to her. She hadn't, so now Janelle was being funny malicious. In another woman it would have been a catty remark about Ford, but with her it was OK.

She knew who I was and said the usual things about the book that people say. And I put on my usual absentminded act as if I had barely heard the compliment. I liked the way she dressed, modest, yet stylish as hell without being high fashion.

'Let's go over,' she said. I thought she wanted to meet Kellino, but when we got there, I saw her trying to get Clara Ford into a conversation. She said intelligent things, but you could see Ford putting the ice on her because she was so beautiful, or so I thought then.

Suddenly Janelle turned and walked away from the group. I followed her. She had her back to me, but when I caught her at the door, I found that she was crying.

Her eyes were magnificent with tears in them. They were golden brown flecked with black dots that were maybe just darker brown (later I found out they were contact lenses), and the tears made the eyes bigger, with more gold. It also betrayed the fact that she'd given the eyes a little help with makeup that was now running.

'You're beautiful when you cry,' I said. I was imitating Kellino in one of his charming roles.

'Oh, fuck you, Kellino,' she said.

I hate women using words like 'fuck' and 'cunt' and 'mother-fucker'. But she was the only woman I ever heard who made the word 'fuck' sound humorous and friendly. The f and the k were Southern slurry soft.

Maybe it was obvious that she had never said the word until lately. Maybe it was because she grinned at me to let me know she knew I was imitating Kellino. She had a great grin, not a charming smile.

'I don't know why I'm so silly,' she said. 'But I never go to parties. I just came because I knew she'd be here. I admire her so much.'

'She's a good critic,' I said.

'Oh, she's so smart,' Janelle said. 'She once wrote something nice about me. And you know, I thought she'd like me. Then she put me down. For no reason.'

'She had plenty of reason,' I said. 'You're beautiful and she's not. And she's got plans for Kellino tonight, and she was not going to have him distracted by you.'

'That's silly,' she said. 'I don't like actors.'

'But you're beautiful,' I said. 'Also, you were talking intelligently. She has to hate you.'

For the first time she looked at me with something like real interest. I was way ahead of her. I liked her because she was beautiful. I liked her because she never went to parties. I liked her because she didn't go for actors like Kellino, who were so goddamn handsome and charming and dressed so beautifully in exquisitely tailored suits, with haircut by a scissored Rodin. And because she was intelligent. Also, she could cry over a critic putting her down at a party. If she was that tenderhearted, maybe she wouldn't kill me. It was the vulnerability finally that made me ask her to have dinner and a movie. I didn't know what Osano could have told me. A vulnerable woman will kill you all the time.

The funny thing is, I didn't see her sexually. I just liked her a hell of a lot. Because despite the fact that she was beautiful and had that wonderfully happy grin even with tears, she was not really a sexy woman at first glance. Or I was too inexperienced to notice. Because later, when Osano met her, he said he felt the sexuality in her like an exposed electric wire. When I told Janelle about Osano, she said that must have happened to her after I met her. Because before she met me, she had been off sex.

281

When I kidded her about that and didn't believe her, she gave me that happy grin and asked if I had ever heard about vibrators.

It's funny that a grown woman telling you that she masturbated with a vibrator can turn you on to her. But it's easy to figure out. The implication is that she is not promiscuous, though she is beautiful and lives in a milieu where men are after women as quickly as a cat after a mouse and mostly for the same reason.

We went out with each other for two weeks, about five times, before we finally got to bed together. And maybe we had a better time before we slept together than we did afterward.

I would go to work at the studio during the day and work on the script and have some drinks with Malomar and then go back to the suite at the Beverly Hills Hotel and read. Sometimes I'd go to a movie. On the nights I'd have a date with Janelle she'd meet me at the suite, and then she would drive me around to the movies and a restaurant and then back to the suite. We'd have a few drinks and talk, and she'd go home about one in the morning.

She told me why she divorced her husband. When she was pregnant, she'd been horny as hell, but he didn't care for her pregnant. Then when the baby came, she'd loved nursing it. She was delighted by the milk flowing from her breast and the baby enjoying it. She wanted her husband to taste the milk, to suck her breast and feel the flow. She thought it would be so great. Her husband turned away in disgust. And that finished him for her.

'I've never told anybody that before,' she said.

'Jesus,' I said. 'He was crazy.'

Late one night in the suite she sat beside me on the sofa. We necked like kids and I got her panties down around her legs and then she balked and stood up. By this time I had my pants down in anticipation, and she was laughing and half crying, and she said, 'I'm sorry. I'm an intelligent woman. But I just can't.' We looked at each other and we both started laughing. We just looked too funny, both of us, with our bare legs and crotches and her white panties over her bare feet. Me with my pants and shorts snagging my ankles.

By that time I liked her too much to get mad. And oddly enough I didn't feel rejected. 'It's OK,' I said. I pulled up my trousers. She pulled up her panties and we hugged each other on the sofa again. When she left, I asked her if she would come around the next night. When she said she would, I knew she would go to bed with me.

The next night she came into the suite and kissed me. Then she said, with a shy smile, 'Shit, guess what happened.'

I knew enough, innocent as I was, that when a prospective bed mate says something like that, you're out in the cold. But I wasn't worried.

'My period started,' she said.

'That doesn't bother me if it doesn't bother you,' I said. I took her by the hand and led her to the bedroom. In two seconds we were naked in bed except for her panties and I could feel the pad underneath. 'Take all that stuff off,' I said. She did. We kissed and just held each other.

We weren't in love that first night. We just liked each other a hell of a lot. We made love like kids. Just kissing and fucking straight. And holding each other and talking and feeling comfortable and warm. She had satinlike skin and a lovely soft ass that wasn't mushy. She was one of those women who had an ass that could never be mistaken for a man's. Not that I've seen that many men's or women's. But from photos in magazines I've often been struck by the fact that only as an ass, an ass could be any gender. Otherwise why all the fancy underclothes?

She had small breasts that had a really great feel to them and big red nipples. We made love twice in the space of an hour, and it had been a long time since I had done that. Finally we got thirsty, and I went into the other room to open a bottle of champagne I had waiting. When I got back into the bedroom, she had her panties back on. She was sitting cross-legged on the bed with a wet towel in her hand, and she was scrubbing out the dark bloodstains on the white sheets. I stood watching her, naked, champagne glasses in my hand, and it was then I first got that overwhelming feeling of tenderness that is the signal of doom. She looked up and smiled at me, her blond hair tousled, her huge brown eyes myopically serious.

'I don't want the maid to see,' she said.

'No, we don't want her to know what we did,' I said.

Very seriously she kept scrubbing, peering nearsightedly at the sheets to make sure that she hadn't missed any spots. Then she dropped the wet towel on the floor and took a glass of champagne from my hand. We sat on the bed together, drinking and smiling foolishly at each other in a delighted sort of way. As if we had both made the team, passed some sort of important test. But we still weren't in love with each other. The sex had been good but not great. We were just happy to be together, and when she had to go home, I asked her to sleep over but she said she couldn't and I didn't question her. I thought maybe she was living with a guy and she could stay out late on him but not stay overnight. And it didn't bother me. That was the great thing about not being in love.

One good thing about Women's Lib is that maybe it will make falling in love less corny. Because, of course, when we did fall in love, it was in the corniest tradition. We fell in love by having a fight.

Before that we had a little trouble. One night in bed I couldn't quite get there. Not that I was impotent, but I couldn't finish. And she was trying like hell for me to make it. Finally she started to yell and scream that she would never have sex again, that she hated sex and why did we ever start. She was crying with frustration and failure. I laughed her out of it. I explained to her that it was no big deal. That I was tired. That I had a lot of things on my mind like a five-million-dollar movie, plus all the usual guilts and hang-ups of a conditioned twentieth-century American male who had led a square life. I held her in my arms and we talked for a while and then after that we both came—no sweat. Still not great but good.

OK. There came a time when I had to be back to New York to take care of family business, and then, when I came back to California, we had a date for my first night back. I was so anxious that on the way to the hotel in my rented car, I went through a red light and got smashed by another car I didn't get hurt, but I had to get a new car and I guess I was in a mild sort of shock. Anyway, when I called Janelle, she was surprised She had misunderstood. She thought it was for the next night. I was mad as hell. I'd nearly gotten myself killed so I could see her, and she was pulling this routine on me. But I was polite.

I told her I had some business the next night, but I would call her later on in the week when I knew I would be free. She had no idea I was angry, and we chatted for a while. I never called her. Five days later she called me. Her first words were: 'You son of a bitch, I thought you really liked me. And then you pulled that old Don Juan shit of not calling me. Why the hell didn't you just come out and say you don't like me anymore.'

'Listen,' I said. 'You're the phony one. You knew goddamn well we had a date that night. You cancelled out because you had something better to do.'

She said very quietly, very convincingly. 'I misunderstood, or you made the mistake.'

'You're a goddamn liar,' I said. I couldn't believe the infantile rage I felt. But maybe it was more than that. I'd trusted her. I thought she was great. And she had pulled one of the oldest female tricks. I knew, because before I married, I'd been on the other end when girls broke their dates that way to be with me. And I hadn't thought much of those girls.

That was that. It was over and I really didn't give a shit. But two nights later she called me.

We said hello to each other, and then she said, 'I thought you really liked me.'

And I found myself saying, 'Honey, I'm sorry.' I don't know why I said 'honey'. I never use that word. But it loosened her all up.

'I want to see you,' she said.

'Come on over,' I said.

She laughed. 'Now?' It was one in the morning.

'Sure,' I said.

She laughed again. 'OK,' she said.

She got there about twenty minutes later. I had a bottle of champagne ready and we talked and then I said, 'Do you want to go to bed?' She said, 'Yes.'

Why is it so hard to describe something that is completely joyful? It was the most innocent sex in the world and it was great. I hadn't felt so happy since I was a kid playing ball all day in the summer. And I realized that I could forgive Janelle everything when I was with her and forgive her nothing when I was away from her.

I had told Janelle once before that I loved her, and she had told me not to say something like that, that she knew that I didn't mean it. I wasn't sure I meant it, so I said OK. I didn't say it now. But sometime during the night we both woke up and we made love and she said very seriously in the darkness, 'I love you.'

Jesus Christ. The whole business is so goddamn cornball. It's so much bullshit that they use to make you buy a new kind of shaving cream or fly a special airline. But then why is it so effective? After that everything changed. The act of sex became special. I literally never even saw another woman, and it was enough just to see her to get sexually excited. When she met me at the plane, I'd grab her behind the cars in the parking lot to touch her breasts and legs and kiss her twenty times before we drove to the hotel.

I couldn't wait. Once, when she protested laughingly, I told

285

her about the polar bears. About how a male polar bear could react only to the scent of one particular female polar bear and sometimes had to wander over a thousand square miles of Arctic ice before he could fuck her. And that was why there were so few polar bears. She was surprised at that, and then she caught on that I was kidding and punched me. But I told her really that was the effect she had on me. That it was not love or that she was so great-looking and smart and everything that I had ever dreamed about in a woman since I was a kid. It was not that at all. I was not vulnerable to that corny bullshit of love and soul mates and all that. It was quite simply that she had the right smell; her body gave off the right odour for me. It was simple and nothing to brag about.

The great thing was that she understood. She knew I wasn't being cute. That I was rebelling against my surrender to her and to the cliché of romantic love. She just hugged me and said. 'OK, OK.' And when I said, 'Don't take too many baths,' she just hugged me again and said, 'OK.'

Because really it was the last thing in the world I wanted. I was happily married. I loved my wife more than anyone else in the world at one time, and still liked her better than any female I ever met even when I started being unfaithful. So now for the first time I felt guilty with both of them. And stories about love had always irritated me.

Well, we were more complicated than polar bears. And the catch in my fairy tale, which I didn't point out to Janelle, was that the female polar bear did not have the same problem as the male.

And then, of course, I pulled the usual shitty things that people in love do. I slyly asked around about her. Did she date producers and stars to get parts? Did she have other affairs? Did she have another boyfriend? In other words, was she a cunt and fucking a million other guys at the drop of a hat? It's funny the things you do when you fall for a woman. You would never do it with a guy you liked. There you always trusted your own judgment, your own gut feeling. With women you were always mistrustful. There is something really shitty about being in love.

And if I had gotten some real dirt on her, I wouldn't have fallen in love. How is it that for a shitty romanticism? No wonder so many women hate men now. My only excuse was that I had been a writing hermit so many years and not smart about women to begin with. And then I couldn't get any scandal on her. She

286

didn't go out to parties. She wasn't linked with any actors. In fact, for a girl who had appeared and worked in movies pretty often, very little was known about her. She didn't run with any of the movie crowds or go to any of the eating places where everybody went. She never appeared in the gossip columns. In short, she was the girl of a square hermit's dream. She even liked to read. What more could I want?

Asking around, I found out to my surprise that Doran Rudd had grown up with her in some hick town in Tennessee. He told me she was the straightest girl in Hollywood. He also told me not to waste my time, that I'd never get laid. This delighted me. I asked him what he thought of her, and he said she was the best woman he had ever known. It was only later, and it was Janelle who told me, that I learned that they had been lovers, had lived together, that it was Doran who had brought her to Hollywood.

Well, she was very independent. Once I tried to pay for the gas when we were riding around in her car. She laughed and refused. She didn't care how I dressed and she liked it when I didn't care how she dressed. We went to movies together in jeans and sweaters and even ate in some of the fancy joints that way. We had enough status for that. Everything was perfect. The sex became great. As good as when you're a kid, and with innocent foreplay that was more erotic than any porno jazz.

Sometimes we'd talk about getting her fancy-undergarments, but we never got around to it. A couple of times we tried to use the mirrors to catch any reflections, but she was too nearsighted and she was too vain to put on her glasses. Once we even read a book on anal sex together. We got all excited and she said OK. We worked very carefully, but we didn't have any Vaseline. So we used her cold cream. It was really funny because to me it felt lousy, as if the temperature had gone down. As for her, the cold cream didn't work and she screamed bloody murder. And then we quit. It was not for us, we were too square. Giggling like kids, we took a bath; the book had been very stern about cleaning up after anal sex. What it came down to was that we didn't need any help. It was just great. And so we lived happily ever after. Until we became enemies.

And during that happy time, a blonde Scheherazade, she told me the story of her life. And so I lived not two but three lives. My family life in New York with my wife and children, with Janelle in Los Angeles and Janelle's life before she met me. I used the 747 planes like magic carpets. I was never so happy in my life. Working on movies was like shooting pool or gambling, relaxing. Finally I had found the crux of what life should be. And I was never more charming. My wife was happy, Janelle was happy, my kids were happy. Artie didn't know what was going on, but one night, when we were having dinner together, he said suddenly, 'You know for the first time in my life I don't worry about you any more.'

'When did that start?' I said, thinking it was because of my success with the book and my working in movies.

'Just now,' Artie said. 'Just this second.'

I was instantly on the alert. 'What does that mean exactly?' I said.

Artie thought it over. 'You were never really happy,' he said. 'You were always a grim son of a bitch. You never had any real friends. All you did was read books and write books. You couldn't stand parties, or movies, or music, or anything. You couldn't even stand it when our families had holiday dinners together. Jesus, you never even enjoyed your kids.'

I was shocked and hurt. It wasn't true. Maybe I seemed that way, but it wasn't really true. I felt a sick feeling in my stomach. If Artie thought of me this way, what did other people think? I had that familiar feeling of desolation.

'It's not true,' I said.

Artie smiled at me. 'Of course it's not. I just mean that now you show things more to other people besides me. Valerie says you're a hell of a lot easier to live with.'

Again I was stung. My wife must have complained all these years and I never knew it. She never reproached me. But at this moment I knew I had never really made her happy, not after the first few years of our marriage.

'Well, she's happy now,' I said.

And Artie nodded. And I thought how silly that was, that I had to be unfaithful to my wife to make her happy. And I realized suddenly that I loved Valerie more now than I ever had. That made me laugh. It was all very convenient, and it was in the textbooks I had been reading. Because as soon as I found myself in the classical unfaithful-husband position, I naturally started to read all the literature on it. 'Valerie doesn't mind my going out to California so much?' I asked.

Artie shrugged. 'I think she likes it. You know I'm used to you, but you are a tough guy on the nerves.'

Again I was a little stunned, but I could never get mad at my brother.

'That's good,' I said. 'I'm leaving for California tomorrow to work on the movie again.'

Artie smiled. He understood what I was feeling. 'As long as you keep coming back,' he said. 'We can't live without you.' He never said anything so sentimental, but he'd caught on that my feelings were hurt. He still babied me.

'Fuck you,' I said but I was happy again.

It seems incredible that only twenty-four hours later I was three thousand miles away, alone with Janelle, in bed, and listening to her life story.

One of the first things she told me was that she and Doran Rudd were old friends, had grown up in the same Southern town of Johnson City, Tennessee, together. And that finally they had become lovers and moved to California, where she became an actress and Doran Rudd an agent.

30

WHEN Janelle went to California with Doran Rudd, she had one problem. Her son. Only three years old and too young to cart around. She left him with her ex-husband. In California she lived with Doran. He promised her a start in movies and did get her a few small parts or thought he did. Actually he made the contacts, and Janelle's charm and wit did the rest. During that time she remained faithful to him, but he obviously cheated with anyone in sight. Indeed, once he tried to talk her into going to bed with another man and him at the same time. She was repelled by the idea. Not because of any morality, but because it was bad enough to feel used by one man as a sexual object and the thought of two men feasting off her body was repugnant to her. At that time, she said, she was too unsophisticated to realize that she would get a chance to watch the two men making love together. If she had, she might have considered it—just to see Doran get it up the ass, as he richly deserved.

She always believed the Californian climate was more responsible for what happened to her life than anything else. People there were weird, she said to Merlyn often, when telling him stories. And you could see she loved their being weird, no matter how much damage they had done to her.

Doran was trying to get his foot in the door as a producer, trying to put a package together. He had bought a terrible script from an unknown writer, whose only virtue was that he agreed to take a net percentage instead of cash upfront. Doran persuaded a former big-time director to direct it and a washed-up male star to play the lead.

Of course, no studio would touch the project. It was one of those packages that sounded good to innocents. Doran was a terrific salesman and hunted outside money. One day he brought home a good prospect, a tall, shy, handsome man of about thirty-five. Very soft-spoken. No bullshitter. But he was an executive in a solid financial institution that dealt with investments. His name was Theodore Lieverman, and he fell in love with Janelle over the dinner table.

They dined in Chasen's. Doran picked up the bill and then left early for an appointment with his writer and director. They were working on the script, Doran said, frowning with concentration. Doran had given Janelle her instructions.

'This guy can get us a million dollars for the movie. Be nice to him. Remember you play the second female lead.'

That was Doran's technique. He promised the second female lead so he could have some bargaining power. If Janelle became difficult, he would up the ante to the first female lead. Not that that meant anything. He would, if necessary, renege on both promises.

Janelle had no intention of being nice in Doran's sense. But she was surprised to find that Theodore Lieverman was a very sweet guy. He didn't make leering jokes about starlets. He didn't come on to her. He was genuinely shy. And he was overcome by her beauty and her intelligence, which gave her a heady feeling of power. When he took her home to Doran's and her apartment after dinner, she invited him in for a drink. Again he was the perfect gentleman. So Janelle liked him. She was always interested in people, found everybody fascinating. And she knew from Doran that Ted Lieverman would inherit twenty million dollars someday. What Doran had not told her was that he was married and had two children. Lieverman told her. Quite diffidently he said, 'We're separated. Our divorce is being held up because her lawyers are asking too much money.'

Janelle grinned, her infectious grin which always disarmed most men except Doran. 'What's too much money?'

Theodore Lieverman said, grimacing, 'A million dollars. That's OK. But she wants it in cash, and my lawyers feel this is the wrong time to liquidate.'

Janelle said laughingly, 'Hell, you have twenty million. What's the difference?'

For the first time Lieverman became really animated. 'You don't understand. Most people don't. It's true I'm worth about sixteen, maybe eighteen million, but my cash flow isn't too good. You see, I own real estate and stocks and corporations, but you have to keep the money investing going back in. So I really have very little liquid capital. I wish I could spend money like Doran. And you know, Los Angeles is a terribly expensive place to live.'

Janelle realized she had met that familiar type in literature, the stingy millionaire. And since he was not witty, not charming, not sexually magnetic, since, in short, he had no bait except his sweetness and his money, which he made clear he didn't part with easily, she got rid of him after the next drink. When Doran came home that night, he was angry.

'Goddamn, that could have been our meal ticket,' Doran told her. It was then she decided to leave him.

The next day she found a small apartment in Hollywood near the Paramount lot and on her own got a bit part in a movie. After her few days' work was done. homesick for her child and Tennessee she went back for a visit of two weeks. And that was all she could stand of Johnson City.

She debated bringing her son back with her. but that would be impossible, so she left him with her ex-husband again. She felt miserable leaving him, but she was determined to make some money and some sort of career before setting up a household.

Her ex-husband was still obviously smitten by her charm. Her looks were better, more sophisticated. She turned him on deliberately and then brushed him off when he tried to get her to bed. He left in an ugly mood. She was contemptuous of him. She had truly loved him, and he had betrayed her with another woman when she was pregnant. He had refused the milk from her breast that she had wanted him to share with the baby.

'Wait a minute,' Merlyn said. 'Give me that again.'

'What?' Janelle said. She grinned. Merlyn waited.

'Oh, I had great tits when I had the baby. And I was fascinated by the milk. I wanted him to taste it. I told you about it once.'

When she filed for divorce, she refused to accept alimony out of sheer contempt.

When she got back to her apartment in Hollywood, she found two messages on her phone service. One from Doran and the other from Theodore Lieverman.

She called Doran first and got him in. He was surprised that she had gone back to Johnson City, but didn't ask a single question about their mutual friends. He was too intent, as usual, on what was important to him.

'Listen,' he said. 'That Ted Lieverman is really gone on you. I'm not kidding. He's madly in love, not just after your ass. If you play your cards right, you can marry twenty million dollars. He's been trying to get in touch with you and I gave him your number. Call him back. You can be a queen.'

'He's married,' Janelle said.

'The divorce comes through next month,' Doran said. 'I checked him out. He's a very straight, square guy. He gets one taste of you in bed and you got him and his millions forever.' All this was off the top of his head. Janelle was just one of his cards.

'You're disgusting,' Janelle said.

Doran was at his most charming. 'Ah, honey, come on. Sure we split. Still, you are the best piece of ass I ever had in my life. Better than all those Hollywood broads. I miss you. Believe me, I understand why you split. But that doesn't mean we can't stay friends. I'm trying to help, you have to grow up. Give this guy a chance, that's all I ask.'

'OK, I'll call him,' Janelle said.

She had never been concerned about money in the sense that she wanted to be rich. But now she thought about what money could do. She could bring her son to live with her and have servants to take care of him when she was working. She could study with the best teachers of drama. Gradually she had come to love acting. She knew finally that it was what she wanted to do with her life.

The love for acting was something she had not even told Doran, but he sensed it. She had taken countless plays and books on drama and film from the library and read them all. She enrolled in a little theatre workshop whose director gave himself such airs of importance that she was amused, yet charmed. When he told her she was one of the best natural talents he had ever seen, she almost fell in love with him and quite naturally went to bed with him.

Charmless, stingy, rich, Theodore Lieverman held a golden key to so many doors that she called him. And arranged to meet him that night for dinner.

Janelle found Lieverman sweet, quiet and shy; she took the initiative. Finally she got him to talk about himself. Little things came out. He had had twin sisters, a few years younger than he, who had both died in a plane crash. He had had a nervous breakdown from that tragedy. Now the wife wanted a divorce, a million dollars in cash and part of his holdings. Gradually he bared an emotionally deprived life—an economically rich boyhood which had left him weak and vulnerable. The only thing he was good at was making money. He had a scheme to finance Doran's movie that was foolproof. But the time had to be ripe, the investors played like fish. He, Lieverman, would throw in the pump-priming cash, the development money.

They went out nearly every night for two or three weeks, and he was always so nice and shy that Janelle finally became impatient. After all, he sent her flowers after each date. He bought her a pin from Tiffany's, a lighter from·Gucci's and an antique gold ring from Roberto's. And he was madly in love with her. She tried to get him into bed and was astonished when he proved reluctant. She could only show her willingness, and then finally he asked her to go to New York and Puerto Rico with him. He had to go on a business trip for his firm. She understood that for some reason he could not make love to her, initially, in Los Angeles. Probably because of guilt feelings. Some men were like that. They could only be unfaithful when they were a thousand miles from their wives. The first time anyway. She found this amusing and interesting.

They stopped in New York, and he brought her to his business meetings. She saw him negotiating for the movie rights for a new novel coming out and a script written by a famous writer. He was shrewd, very low-key, and she saw here was his strength. But that first night they finally got to bed together in their suite at the Plaza and she learned one of the truths about Theodore Lieverman.

293

He was almost totally impotent. She was angry at first, feeling the lack in herself. She did everything she could and finally she made him get there. The next night was a little better. In Puerto Rico he was a little better still. But he was easily the most incompetent and boring lover she had ever had. She was glad to get back to Los Angeles. When he dropped her off at her apartment, he asked her to marry him. She said she'd think it over.

She had no intention of marrying him until Doran gave her a tongue-lashing. 'Think it over? Think it over? Use your head,' he said. 'The guy is crazy about you. You marry him. So you stick with him for a year. You come out with at least a million and he'll still be in love with you. You'll call your own shots. Your career has a hundred times better chance of going. Besides, through him, you'll meet other rich guys. Guys that you'll like better and maybe love. You can change your whole life. Just be bored for a year, hell, that's not suffering. I wouldn't ask you to suffer.'

It was like Doran to think that he was being very clever. That he was really opening Janelle's eyes to the verities of life every woman knows or is taught from her cradle. But Doran recognized that Janelle really hated to do anything like that not because it was immoral but because she could not betray another human being in such a fashion. So cold-bloodedly. And also because she had such a zest for life that she couldn't bear being bored for a year. But as Doran quickly pointed out, the chances were good that she would be bored that year even without Theodore to bring her down. And also she would really make poor Theodore happy for that year.

'You know, Janelle,' Doran said, 'having you around on your worst day is better than having most people around on their best day.' It was one of the very few things he had said since his twelfth birthday that was sincere. Though self-serving.

But it was Theodore acting with uncommon aggressiveness who tipped the balance. He bought a beautiful two-hundred-fifty-thousand-dollar house in Beverly Hills, with swimming pool, tennis court, two servants. He knew Janelle loved to play tennis, she had learned to play in California, had had a brief affair as a matter of course with her tennis teacher, a slim, beautiful blond young man who had to her astonishment billed her for his teaching. Later other women told her about California men. How they would have drinks in a bar, let you pay for your own drinks and then ask you to go to their apartments for the night. They wouldn't even spring for the cab fare home. She enjoyed the tennis pro in bed and on the tennis court, and he had improved her performance in both areas. Eventually she tired of him because he dressed better than she did. Also, he batted right and left and he vamped her male as well as her female friends, which even Janelle, open-minded as she was, felt was stretching it.

She had never played tennis with Lieverman. He had casually mentioned once that he had beaten Arthur Ashe in high school, so she assumed he was out of her class and like most good tennis players would rather not play with hackers. But when he persuaded her to move into the new house, they gave an elaborate tennis party.

She loved the house. It was a luxurious Beverly Hills mansion with guest rooms, a den, a cabana for the pool, an outdoor Jacuzzi. She and Theodore went over plans to decorate and put in some special wood panelling. They went shopping together. But now in bed he was a complete bust, and Janelle didn't even try him any more. He promised her that when his divorce came through next month and they married, he would be OK. Janelle devoutly hoped so because feeling guilty, she had decided the least she could do, since she was going to marry him for his money, was to be a faithful wife. But going without sex was getting on her nerves. It was on the day of the tennis party that she knew it was all down the drain. She had felt there was something fishy about the whole deal. But Theodore Lieverman inspired so much confidence in her, her friends and even the cynical Doran that she thought it was her guilty conscience looking for a way out.

On the day of the tennis party, Theodore finally got on the court. He played well enough, but he was a hacker. There was no way he could have beaten Arthur Ashe even in his bassinet. Janelle was astonished. The one thing she was sure of was that her lover was not a liar. And she was no innocent. She had always assumed lovers were liars. But Theodore never bullshitted, never bragged, never mentioned his money or his high standing in investment circles. He never really talked to other people except Janelle. His low key approach was extremely rare in California, so much so that Janelle had been surprised that he had lived his whole life in that state. But seeing him on the tennis court, she knew he had lied in one respect. And lied well. A casual deprecatory remark that he had never repeated, never lingered on. She had never doubted him. As she had never doubted anything he said really. There was no question that he loved her. He had shown that in every way, which of course didn't mean too much when he couldn't get it up.

That night after the tennis party was over he told her that she should get her little boy from Tennessee and move him to the house. If it had not been for his lie about beating Arthur Ashe, she would have agreed. It was well she did not. The next day when Theodore was at work she received a visitor.

The visitor was Mrs Theodore Lieverman, the heretofore invisible wife. She was a pretty little thing, but frightened and obviously impressed by Janelle's beauty, as if she couldn't believe her husband had come up with such a winner. As soon as she announced who she was, Janelle felt an overwheming relief and greeted Mrs Lieverman so warmly the woman was further confused.

But Mrs Lieverman surprised Janelle too. She wasn't angry. The first thing she said was startling. 'My husband is nervous, very sensitive,' she said. 'Please don't tell him I came to see you.'

'Of course,' Janelle said. Her spirits were soaring. She was elated. The wife would demand her husband and she would get him back so fast her head would swim.

Mrs Lieverman said cautiously, 'I don't know how Ted is getting all this money. He makes a good salary. But he hasn't any savings.'

Janelle laughed. She already knew the answer. But she asked anyway. 'What about the twenty million dollars?'

'Oh, God. Oh, God,' Mrs Lieverman said. She put her head down in her hands and started to weep.

'And he never beat Arthur Ashe in tennis in high school,' Janelle said reassuringly.

'Oh, God, God,' Mrs Lieverman wailed.

'And you're not getting divorced next month,' Janelle said.

Mrs Lieverman just whimpered.

Janelle went to the bar and mixed two stiff Scotches. She made the other woman drink through the sniffles.

'How did you find out?' Janelle asked.

Mrs Lieverman opened her purse as if looking for a handkerchief for her sniffles. Instead, she brought out a sheaf of letters and handed them to Janelle. They were bills. Janelle looked at them thoughtfully. And she got the whole picture. He had written a twenty-five-thousand-dollar cheque as down payment on the beautiful house. With it was a letter requesting that he be allowed to move in until the final closing. The cheque had bounced. The builder was now threatening to put him in jail. The cheques for hired help had bounced. The caterer's cheque for the tennis party had bounced.

'Wow,' Janelle said.

'He's too sensitive,' Mrs Lieverman said.

'He's sick,' Janelle said.

Mrs Lieverman nodded.

Janelle said thoughtfully, 'Is it because of his two sisters who died in the plane crash?'

There was a scream from Mrs Lieverman, a shriek finally of outrage and exasperation. 'He never had any sisters. Don't you understand? He's a pathological liar. He lies about everything. He has no sisters, he has no money, he's not divorcing me, he used the firm's money to take you to Puerto Rico and New York and to pay the expenses of this house.'

'Then why the hell do you want him back?' Janelle asked.

'Because I love him,' Mrs Lieverman said.

Janelle thought that over for at least two minutes, studying Mrs Lieverman. Her husband was a liar, a cheat, had a mistress, couldn't get it up in bed, and that's only what *she* knew about him, plus the fact, of course, that he was a lousy tennis player. Then what the hell was Mrs Lieverman? Janelle patted the other woman on the shoulder, gave her another drink and said, 'Wait here for five minutes.'

That's all it took her to throw all her things into two Vuitton suitcases Theodore had bought her, probably with bum cheques. She came down with the suitcases and said to the wife, 'I'm leaving. You can wait here for your husband. Tell him I never want to see him again. And I'm truly sorry for the pain I've caused you. You have to believe me when I tell you that he said you had left him. That you didn't care.'

Mrs Lieverman nodded miserably.

Janelle left in the bright new baby blue Mustang Theodore had bought her. No doubt it would be repossessed. She could have it driven back to the house. Meanwhile, she had no place to go. She remembered the director and costume designer, Alice De Santis, who had been so friendly, and she decided to drive to her house and ask her advice. If Alice was not at home, she would go to Doran. She knew he would always take her in.

Janelle loved the way Merlyn enjoyed the story. He didn't laugh. His enjoyment was not malicious. He just smiled, closing

297

his eyes, savouring it. And he said the right thing—wonderingly, almost admiringly.

'Poor Lieverman,' he said. 'Poor, poor Lieverman.'

'What about me, you bastard?' Janelle said with mock rage. She flung herself naked on his naked body and put her hands around his neck. Merlyn opened his eyes and smiled.

'Tell me another story.'

She made love to him instead. She had another story to tell him, but he wasn't ready for it yet. He had to fall in love with her first, as she was in love with him. He couldn't take more stories yet. Especially about Alice.

31

I HAD come to the point now that lovers always come to. They are so happy they can't believe they deserve it. And so they start thinking that maybe it's all a fake. So with me jealousy and suspicion haunted the ecstasies of our lovemaking. Once she had to read for a part and couldn't meet my plane. Another time I understood she would spend the night and she had to go home to sleep because she had to get up for an early-morning call at the studio. Even when she made love to me in the early afternoon so that I wouldn't be disappointed and I would believe her, I thought she lied. And now, expecting she would lie, I said to her, 'I had lunch with Doran this afternoon. He says you had a fourteen-year-old lover when you were just a Southern belle.'

Janelle raised her head slightly and gave the sweet, tentative smile that made me forget how I hated her.

'Yes,' she said. 'That was a long time ago.'

She bowed her head then. Her face had an absentminded, amused look as she remembered that love affair. I knew she always remembered her love affairs with affection, even when they ended very badly. She looked up again.

'Does that bother you?' she said.

'No,' I said. But she knew it did.

'I'm sorry,' she said. She looked at me for a moment, then turned her head away. She reached out with her hands, slid them under my shirt and caressed my back. 'It was innocent,' she said.

I didn't say anything, just moved away because the remembered touch made me forgive her everything.

Again expecting her to lie, I said, 'Doran told me because of the fourteen-year-old kid you stood trial for impairment of the morals of a minor.'

With all my heart I wanted her to lie. I didn't care if it was true. As I would not blame or reproach her if she were an alcoholic or hustler or murderess. I wanted to love her, and that was all. She was watching me with that quiet, contemplative look as if she would do anything to please me.

'What do you want me to say?' she asked, looking directly into my face.

'Just tell me the truth,' I said.

'Well, then it's true,' she said. 'But I was acquitted. The judge dismissed the case.'

I felt an enormous relief. 'Then you didn't do it.'

'Do what?' she asked.

'You know,' I said.

She gave me that sweet half-smile again. But it was touched with a sad mockery.

'You mean, did I make love to a fourteen-year-old boy?' she asked. 'Yes, I did.'

She waited for me to walk out of the room. I remained still. Her face became more mocking. 'He was very big for his age,' she said.

That interested me. It interested me because of the boldness of the challenge. 'That makes all the difference,' I said dryly. And watched her when she gave a delighted laugh. We had both been angry with each other. Janelle because I dared judge her. I was going to leave, so she said, 'It's a good story, you'll like it.' And she saw me bite. I always loved a story almost as much as making love. Many nights I'd listened to her for hours, fascinated as she told her life story, making guesses at what she left out or edited for my tender male ears as she would have edited a horror story for a child.

It was the thing she loved me most for, she told me once. The

299

eagerness for stories. And my refusal to make judgements. She could always see me shifting it around in my head, how I would tell it or how I would use it. And I had never really condemned her for anything she'd done. As she knew now I would not when she told her story.

After her divorce Janelle had taken a lover, Doran Rudd. He was a disc jockey on the local radio station. A rather tall man, a little older than Janelle. He had a great deal of energy, was always charming and amusing and finally got Janelle a job as the weather girl of the radio station. This was a fun job and well paid for a town like Johnson City.

Doran was obsessed with being the town character. He had an enormous Cadillac, bought his clothes in New York and swore he would make it big some day. He was awed and enchanted by performers. He went to see all the road companies of all the Broadway plays and always sent notes back to one of the actresses, followed up by flowers, followed up by offers of dinner. He was surprised to find how easy it was to get them to bed. He gradually realized how lonely they were. Glamorous onstage, they were a little pathetic-looking back in their second-rate hotel rooms stocked with old-model refrigerators. He would always tell Janelle about his adventures. They were more friends than lovers.

One day he got his break. A father and son duo were booked into the town concert hall. The father was a pickup piano player who had earned a steady living unloading freight cars in Nashville until he discovered his nine-year-old son could sing. The father, a hardworking Southern man who hated his job, immediately saw his son as the impossible dream come true. He might escape from a life of dull, backbreaking toil.

He knew his son was good, but he didn't really know how good. He was quite content with teaching the young boy all the gospel songs and making a handsome living touring the Bible Belt. A young cherub praising Jesus in pure soprano was irresistible to that regional audience. The father found his new life extremely agreeable. He was gregarious, had an eye for a pretty girl and welcomed vacations from his already worn-out wife, who, of course, remained home.

But the mother, too, dreamed of all the luxuries her son's pure voice would bring her. They were both greedy but not greedy as the rich are greedy, as a way of life, but greedy as a starving man on a desert island who is suddenly rescued and can finally realize all his fantasies.

So when Doran went backstage to rave about the lad's voice, then proposition the parents, he found a willing audience. Doran knew how good the boy was and soon realized that he was the only one. He reassured them that he did not want any percentage of the gospel-singing earnings. He would manage the boy and take only thirty percent of anything the boy earned over twenty-five thousand dollars a year.

It was, of course, an irresistible offer. If they got twenty-five thousand dollars a year, an incredible sum, why worry if Doran got thirty percent of the rest? And how could their boy, Rory, make more than that amount? Impossible. There was not that much money. Doran also assured Mr Horatio Bascombe and Mrs Edith Bascombe that he would not charge them for any expenses. So a contract was prepared and signed.

Doran immediately went into furious action. He borrowed money to produce an album of gospel songs. It was an enormous hit. In that first year the boy Rory earned over fifty thousand dollars. Doran immediately moved to Nashville and made connections in the music world. He took Janelle with him and made her administrative assistant in his new music company. The second year Rory made more than a hundred thousand dollars, most of it on a single of an old religious ballad Janelle found in Doran's disc jockey files. Doran had absolutely no creative taste in any sense; he would never have recognized the worth of the song.

Doran and Janelle were living together now. But she didn't see that much of him. He was travelling to Hollywood for a movie deal or to New York to get an exclusive contract with one of the big recording companies. They would all be millionaires. Then the catastrophe. Rory caught a bad cold and seemed to lose his voice. Doran took him to the best specialist in New York. The specialist cured Rory completely but then casually, just in passing, said to Doran, 'You know his voice will change as he goes into puberty.'

It was something that Doran had not thought of. Maybe because Rory was big for his age. Maybe because Rory was a totally innocent young boy, unworldly. He had been shielded from girlfriends by his mother and father. He loved music and was indeed an accomplished musician. Also, he had always been sickly until his eleventh year. Doran was frantic. A man who has the location of a secret gold mine and misplaced the map. He had plans to make millions out of Rory; now he saw it all going down the drain. Millions of dollars at stake. Literally millions of dollars!

Then Doran got one of his greater ideas. He checked it out medically. After he had all the dope, he tried his scheme out on Janelle. She was horrified.

'You are a terrible son of a bitch,' she said, almost in tears.

Doran couldn't understand her horror. 'Listen,' he said, 'the Catholic Church used to do it.'

'They did it for God,' Janelle said. 'Not for a gold album.'

Doran shook his head. 'Please stick to the point. I have to convince the kid and his mother and father, that's going to be a hell of a job.'

Janelle laughed. 'You really are crazy. I won't help you, and even if I did, you'll never convince one of them.'

Doran smiled at her. 'The father is the key. I was thinking you could be nice to him. Soften him up for me.'

It was before Doran had acquired the creamy, sunlit, extra smoothness of California. So when Janelle threw the heavy ashtray at him, he was too surprised to duck. It chipped one of his teeth and made his mouth bleed. He didn't get angry. He just shook his head at Janelle's squareness.

Janelle would have left him then, but she was too curious. She wanted to see if Doran could really pull it off.

Doran was, in general, a good judge of character, and he was really sharp on finding the greed threshold. He knew one key was Mr Horatio Bascombe. The father could swing his wife and son. Also, the father was the most vulnerable to life. If his son failed to make money, it was back to going to church for Mr Bascombe. No more travelling around the country, playing piano, tickling pretty girls, eating exotic foods. Just his worn-out wife. The father had most at stake; the loss of Rory's voice was more important to him than anyone.

Doran softened Mr Bascombe up with a pretty little singer from a sleazy Nashville jazz club. Then a fine dinner with cigars the following evening. Over cigars he outlined Rory's career. A Broadway musical, an album with special songs written by the famous Dean brothers. Then a big role in a movie that might turn Rory into another Judy Garland or Elvis Presley. You wouldn't be able to count the money. Bascombe was drinking it all in, purring like a cat. Not even greedy because it was all there.

It was inevitable. He was a millionaire. Then Doran sprang it on him.

'There's only one thing wrong,' Doran said. 'The doctors say his voice is about to change. He's going into puberty.'

Bascombe was a little worried. 'His voice will get a little deeper. Maybe it will be better.'

Doran shook his head. 'What makes him a superstar is that high, clear sweetness. Sure he might be better. But it will take him five years to train it and break through with a new image. And then it's a hundred to one shot he'll make it big. I sold him to everybody on the voice he has now.'

'Well, maybe his voice won't change,' Bascombe said.

'Yeah, maybe it won't,' Doran said and left it at that.

Two days later Bascombe came around to his apartment. Janelle let him in and gave him a drink. He looked her over pretty carefully, but she ignored him. And when he and Doran started talking, she left the room.

That night in bed, after making love, Janelle asked Doran, 'How is your dirty little scheme coming?'

Doran grinned. He knew Janelle despised him for what he was doing, but she was such a great broad she had still given him her usual great piece of ass. Like Rory, she still didn't know how great she was. Doran felt content. That's what he liked, good service. People who didn't know their value.

'I've got the greedy old bastard hooked,' he said. 'Now I've got to work on the mother and the kid.'

Doran, who thought he was the greatest salesman east of the Rockies, attributed his final success to those powers. But the truth was that he was lucky. Mr Bascombe had been softened up by the extremely hard life he had led before the miracle of his son's voice. He could not give up the golden dream and go back to slavery. That was not so unusual. Where Doran got really lucky was with the mother.

Mrs Bascombe had been a small-town Southern belle, mildly promiscuous in her teens and swept off her feet into matrimony by Horatio Bascombe's piano playing and Southern small-town charm. As her beauty faded year by year, she succumbed to the swampy miasma of Southern religiosity. As her husband became more unlovable, Mrs Bascombe found Jesus more attractive. Her son's voice was her love offering to Jesus. Doran worked on that. He kept Janelle in the room while he talked to Mrs Bascombe, knowing the delicate subject matter would make the older woman nervous if she were alone with a male.

Doran was respectfully charming and attentive to Mrs Bascombe. He pointed out that in the years to come a hundred million people all over the world would hear her son, Rory, singing the glories of Jesus. In Catholic countries, in Moslem countries, in Israel, in the cities of Africa. Her son would be the most powerful evangelist for the Christian religion since Luther. He would be bigger than Billy Graham, bigger than Oral Roberts, two of Mrs Bascombe's saints on earth. And her son would be saved from the most grievous and easiest-to-fall-into sin on this earth. It was clearly the will of God.

Janelle watched them both. She was fascinated by Doran. That he could do such a thing without being evil, merely mercenary. He was like a child stealing pennies from his mother's pocket book. And Mrs Bascombe after an hour of Doran's feverish pleading was weakening. Doran finished her off.

'Mrs Bascombe, I just know you'll make this sacrifice for Jesus. The big problem is your son, Rory. He's just a boy, and you know how boys are.'

Mrs Bascombe gave him a grim smile. 'Yes,' she said, 'I know.' She darted a quick venomous look at Janelle. 'But my Rory is a good boy. He'll do what I say.'

Doran heaved a sigh of relief. 'I knew I could count on you.'

Then Mrs Bascombe said coolly, 'I'm doing this for Jesus. But I'd like a new contract drawn up. I want fifteen percent of your thirty percent as his co-manager.' She paused for a moment. 'And my husband needn't know.'

Doran sighed. 'Give me some of that old-time religion all the time,' he said. 'I just hope you can swing it.'

Rory's mama did swing it. Nobody knew how. It was all set. The only one who didn't like the idea was Janelle. In fact, she was horrified, so horrified she stopped sleeping with Doran, and he considered getting rid of her. Also, Doran had one final problem. Getting a doctor who would cut off a fourteen-year-old kid's balls. For that was the idea. What was good enough for the old Popes was good enough for Doran.

It was Janelle who blew the whole thing up. They were all gathered in Doran's apartment. Doran was working out how to screw Mrs Bascombe out of her co-manager's fifteen percent, so he wasn't paying attention. Janelle got up, took Rory by the hand and led him to the bedroom.

Mrs Bascombe protested. 'What are you doing with my boy?'

Janelle said sweetly, 'We'll be right out. I just want to show him something.' Once inside the bedroom she locked the door. Then very firmly she led Rory to the bed, unbuckled his belt, stripped down his trousers and shorts. She put his hand between her legs and his head between her now bare breasts.

In three minutes they were finished, and then the boy surprised Janelle. He pulled on his trousers, forgetting his shorts. He unlocked the bedroom door and flew into the living room. His first punch caught Doran square in the mouth, and then he was throwing punches like a windmill until his father restrained him.

Naked on the bed, Janelle smiled at me. 'Doran hates me, even though it's six years later. I cost him millions of dollars.'

I was smiling too. 'So what happened at the trial?'

Janelle shrugged. 'We had a civilized judge. He talked to me and the kid in chambers, and then he dismissed the case. He warned the parents and Doran they were subject to prosecution but advised everybody to keep their mouths shut.'

I thought that over. 'What did he say to you?'

Janelle smiled again. 'He told me that if he were thirty years younger, he'd give anything if I were his girl.'

I sighed. 'Jesus, you make everything sound right. But now I want you to answer truthfully. Swear?'

'Swear,' Janelle said.

I paused for a moment, watching her. Then I said, 'Did you enjoy fucking that fourteen-year-old kid?'

Janelle didn't hesitate. 'It was terrific,' she said.

'OK,' I said. I was frowning with concentration, and Janelle laughed. She loved these times best when I was really interested in figuring her out. 'Let's see,' I said. 'He had curly hair and a great build. Great skin, no pimples yet. Long eyelashes and choirboy virginity. Wow.' I thought a little longer.

'Tell me the truth. You were indignant, but deep down you knew here was your excuse to fuck a fourteen-year-old kid. You couldn't have done it otherwise, even though that was what you really wanted to do. That the kid turned you on from the beginning. And so you could have it both ways. You saved the kid by fucking him. Great. Right?'

'No,' Janelle said, smiling sweetly.

I sighed again and then laughed. 'You're such a phony.' But I was licked and I knew it. She had performed an unselfish act, she had saved the manhood of a budding boy. That she had a hell of a thrill along the way was, after all, a bonus the virtuous deserved. Down South everybody serves Jesus—in his own way.

And Jesus, I really loved her more.

32

MALOMAR had had a hard day and a special conference with Moses Wartberg and Jeff Wagon. He had fought for Merlyn's and his movie. Wartberg and Wagon had hated it after he had shown them a first draft. It became the usual argument. They wanted to turn it into schlock, put in more action, coarsen the characters. Malomar stood fast.

'It's a good script,' he said. 'And remember this is just a first draft.'

Wartberg said, 'You don't have to tell us. We know that. We've judged it on that basis.'

Malomar said coolly, 'You know I'm always interested in your opinions and I weigh them very carefully. But everything you've said so far strikes me as irrelevant.'

Wagon said appeasingly, with his charming smile, 'Malomar, you know we believe in you. That's why we gave you your original contract. Hell, you have full control over your pictures. But we have to back our judgment with advertising and publicity. Now we've let you project a million dollars over budget. That gives us, I think, a moral right to have some say in the final shape of this picture.'

Malomar said, 'That was a bullshit budget to begin with and we all knew it and we all admitted it.'

Wartberg said, 'You know that in all our contracts, when we go over budget, you start losing your points in the picture. Are you willing to take that risk?'

'Jesus,' Malomar said. 'I can't believe that if this makes a lot of money, you guys would invoke that clause.'

Wartberg gave his shark grin. 'We may or may not. That's the chance you will have to take if you insist on your version of the film.'

Malomar shrugged. 'I'll take that risk,' he said. 'And if that's all you guys have to say, I'll get back to the cutting room.'

When he left Tri-Culture Studios to be driven back to his own lot, Malomar felt drained. He thought of going home and taking a nap, but there was too much work to be done. He wanted to put in at least another five hours. He felt the slight pains in his chest starting again. Those bastards will kill me yet, he thought. And then he suddenly realized that since his heart attack Wartberg and Wagon had been less afraid of him, had argued with him more, had harried him about costs more. Maybe the bastards *were* trying to kill him.

He sighed. The fucking things he had to put up with, and that fucking Merlyn always bitching about producers and Hollywood and how they all weren't artists. And here he was risking his life to save Merlyn's conception of the picture. He felt like calling Merlyn up and making him go to the arena with Wartberg and Wagon to do his own fighting, but he knew that Merlyn would just quit and walk away from the picture. Merlyn didn't believe as he, Malomar, did. Didn't have his love for film and what film could do.

Well, the hell with it, Malomar thought. He'd make the picture his way and it would be good and Merlyn would be happy, and when the picture made money, the studio would be happy, and if they tried to take away his percentage because of the overbudget, he'd take his production company elsewhere.

As the limousine pulled up to a stop, Malomar felt the elation he'd always felt. The elation of an artist coming to his work knowing that he would fashion something beautiful.

He laboured with his film editors for almost seven hours, and when the limousine dropped him at his home, it was nearly midnight. He was so tired he went directly to bed. He almost groaned with weariness. The pains in his chest came and spread to his back, but after a few minutes they went away and he lay there quietly, trying to fall asleep. He was content. He had done a good day's work. He had fought off the sharks and he had cut film.

Malomar loved to sit in the cutting room with the editors and the director. He loved to sit in the dark and make decisions on

307

what the tiny flickering images should do and not do. Like God, he gave them a certain kind of soul. If they were 'good', he made them physically beautiful by telling the editor to cut an unflattering image so that a nose was not too bony; a mouth not too mean. He could make a heroine's eyes more doelike with a better lighted shot, her gestures more graceful and touching. He would not send the good down to despair and defeat. He was more merciful.

Meanwhile, he kept a sharp eye on the villains. Did they wear the right colour tie and the right cut of jacket to enhance their villainy? Did they smile too trustingly? Were the lines in their faces too decent? He blotted out that image with the cutting machine. Most of all, he refused to let them be boring. The villain had to be interesting. Malomar in his cutting room truly watched every feather that fell from the tail of the sparrow. The world he created must have a sensible logic, and when he finished with that particular world, you usually were glad to have seen it exist.

Malomar had created hundreds of these worlds. They lived in his brain forever and ever as the countless galaxies of God must exist in His brain. And Malomar's feat was as astounding to him. But it was different when he left the darkened cutting room and emerged into the world created by God which made no sense at all.

Malomar had suffered three heart attacks over the past few years. From overwork, the doctor said. But Malomar always felt that God had fucked up in the cutting room. He, Malomar, was the last man who should have a heart attack. Who would oversee all those worlds to be created? And he took such good care of himself. He ate sparingly and correctly. He exercised. He drank little. He fornicated regularly but not to excess. He never drugged. He was still young, handsome; he looked like a hero. And he tried to behave well, or as well as possible in the world God was shooting. In Malomar's cutting room a character like Malomar would never die from a heart attack. The editor would excise the frame, the producer call for a rewrite of the script. He would command the directors and all the actors to the rescue. Such a man would not be allowed to perish.

But Malomar could not excise the chest pains. And often at night, very late, in his huge house, he popped angina pills in his mouth. And then he would lie in bed petrified with fear. On really bad nights he called his personal physician. The doctor would come and sit with him through the night, examine him, reassure him, hold his hand until dawn broke. The doctor would never refuse him because Malomar had written the script for the doctor's life. Malomar had given him access to beautiful actresses so that he could become their doctor and sometimes their lover. When Malomar in his early days indulged in more strenuous sex, before his first heart attack, when his huge home was filled with overnight guests of starlets and high-fashion models, the doctor had been his dinner companion and they had sampled together the smorgasbord of women prepared for the evening.

Now on this midnight, Malomar alone in his bed, in his home, phoned the doctor. The doctor came and examined him and assured him the pains would go away. That there was no danger. That he should let himself fall asleep. The doctor brought him water for his angina pills and tranquillizers. And the doctor measured his heart with his stethoscope. It was intact; it was not breaking into pieces as Malomar felt it was. And after a few hours, resting more easily, Malomar told the doctor he could go home. And then Malomar fell asleep.

He dreamed. It was a vivid dream. He was at a railroad station, enclosed. He was buying a ticket. A small but burly man pushed him aside and demanded his ticket. The small man had a huge dwarf's head and screamed at Malomar. Malomar reassured him. He stepped aside. He let the man buy his ticket. He told the man, 'Look, whatever is bothering you is OK with me.' And as he did so, the man grew taller, his features more regular. He was suddenly an older hero, and he said to Malomar, 'Give me your name; I'll do something for you.' He loved Malomar. Malomar could see that. They were both very kind to each other. And the railroad agent selling the tickets now treated the other man with enormous respect.

Malomar came awake in the vast darkness of his huge bedroom. His eye lenses narrowed down, and with no peripheral vision, he fixed on the white rectangular light from the open bathroom door. For just a moment he thought the images on the cutting-room screen had not ended, and then he realized it had only been a dream. At that realization his heart broke away from his body in a fatal arhythmic gallop. The electrical impulses of his brain snarled together. He sat up, sweating. His heart went into a final thundering rush, shuddered. He fell back, eyes closing, all light fading on the screen that was his life. The last thing he ever heard was a scraping noise like celluloid breaking against steel, and then he was dead.

33

IT was my agent, Doran Rudd, who called me with the news of Malomar's death. He told me there was going to be a big conference on the picture at Tri-Culture Studios the next day. I had to fly out and he would meet my plane.

At Kennedy Airport I called Janelle to tell her I was coming into town, but I got her answering machine with her French-accented machine voice, so I left a message for her.

Malomar's death shocked me. I had developed an enormous respect for him during the months we had worked together. He never gave out any bullshit, and he had an eagle eye for any bullshit in a script or a piece of film. He tutored me when he showed me films, explaining why a scene didn't play or what to watch for in an actor who might be showing talent even in a bad role. We argued a lot. He told me that my literary snobbishness was defensive and that I hadn't studied film carefully enough. He even offered to teach me how to direct a film, but I refused. He wanted to know why.

'Listen,' I said, 'just by existing, just by standing still and not bothering anybody, man is a fate-creating agent. That's what I hate about life. And a movie director is the worst fate-creating agent on earth. Think of all those actors and actresses you make miserable when you turn them down. Look at all the people you have to give orders to. The money you spend, the destinies you control. I just write books, I never hurt anybody, I only help. They can take it or leave it.'

'You're right,' Malomar said. 'You'll never be a director. But I think you're full of shit. Nobody can be that passive.' And of course, he was right. I just wanted to control a more private world.

But still I felt saddened by his death. I had some affection for him though we did not really know each other well. And then too I was a little worried about what was going to happen to our movie.

Doran Rudd met me at the plane. He told me that Jeff Wagon would now be the producer and that Tri-Culture had swallowed up Malomar Studios. He told me to expect a lot of trouble. On the way over to the studio he briefed me on the whole Tri-Culture operation. On Moses Wartberg, on his wife, Bella, on Jeff Wagon. Just for openers he told me that though they were not the most powerful studio in Hollywood, they were the most hated, often called 'Tri-Vulture Studios'. That Wartberg was a shark and the three VPs were jackals. I told him that you couldn't mix up your symbols like that, that if Wartberg was a shark, the others had to be pilot fish. I was kidding around, but my agent wasn't even listening. He just said, 'I wish you were wearing a tie.'

I looked at him. He was in his slick black leather jacket over a turtleneck sweater. He shrugged.

'Moses Wartberg could have been a Semitic Hitler,' Doran said. 'But he would have done it a little differently. He would have sent all the adult Christians to the gas chamber and then set up college scholarships for their children.'

Comfortably slouched down in Doran Rudd's Mercedes 450SL, I barely listened to Doran's chatter. He was telling me that there was going to be a big fight over the picture. That Jeff Wagon would be producer and Wartberg would be taking a personal interest in it. They had killed Malomar with their harassment, Doran said. I wrote that off as typical Hollywood exaggeration. But the essence of what Doran was telling me was that the fate of the picture would be decided today. So in the long ride to the studio I tried to remember everything I knew or had heard about Moses Wartberg and Jeff Wagon.

Jeff Wagon was the essence of a schlock producer. He was schlock from the top of his craggy head to the tiptoes of his Bally shoes. He had made his mark in TV, then muscled his way into feature films by the same process with which a blob of ink spreads on a linen tablecloth and with the same aesthetic effect. He had made over a hundred TV feature films and twenty theatrical films. Not one of them had had a touch of grace, of quality, of art. The critics, the workers and artists in Hollywood had a classic joke that compared Wagon with Selznick, Lubitsch, Thalberg. They would say of one of his pictures that it had the Dong imprint because a young malicious actress called him the Dong.

A typical Jeff Wagon picture was loaded with stars a bit frayed by age and celluloid wear and tear, desperate for a paycheque. The talent knew it was a schlock picture. The directors were handpicked by Wagon. They were usually run-of-the-mill with a string of failures behind them so that he could twist their arms and make them shoot the picture his way. The odd thing was that though all the pictures were terrible, they either broke even or made money simply because the basic idea was good in a commercial way. It usually had a built-in audience, and Jeff Wagon was a fierce bulldog on cost. He was also terrific on contracts that screwed everybody out of his percentage if the picture became a big hit and made a lot of cash. And if that didn't work, he would have the studio start litigation so that a settlement could be made on percentages. But Moses Wartberg always said that Jeff Wagon came up with sound ideas. What he presumably didn't know was that Wagon stole even these ideas. He did this by what could only be called seduction.

In his younger days Jeff Wagon had lived up to his nickname by knocking over every starlet on the Tri-Culture lot. He was very much on the line with his approach. If they came across, they became girls in TV movies who were bartenders or receptionists. If they played their cards right, they could get enough work to carry them through the year. But when he went into feature films, this was not possible. With three-million-dollar budgets you didn't fuck around handing out parts for a piece of ass. So then he got away with letting them read for a part or promising to help them as much as he could but never a firm commitment. And of course, some of them were talented, and with his foot in the door for them they got some nice parts in feature films. A few became stars. In the Land of Empidae, Jeff Wagon was the ultimate survivor.

But one day out of the northern rain forests of Oregon a breathtaking beauty of eighteen appeared. She had everything going for her. Great face, great body, fiery temperament, even talent. But the camera refused to do right by her. In that idiotic magic of film her looks didn't work.

She was also a little crazy. She had grown up beautiful as a woodsman and hunter in the Oregon forests. She could skin a deer and fight a grizzly bear. She had reluctantly let Jeff Wagon fuck her once a month because her agent gave her a little heart-to-heart talk. But she came from a place where the people were straight shooters, and she expected Jeff Wagon to keep his word and get her the part. When it didn't happen, she went to bed with Jeff Wagon with a deer-skinning knife and, at the crucial moment, stuck it into one of Jeff Wagon's balls.

It didn't turn out badly. For one thing she only took a nick off his right ball, and everybody agreed that with his big balls a little chip wouldn't do him any harm. Jeff Wagon himself tried to cover up the incident, refused to press charges. But the story got out. The girl was shipped home to Oregon with enough money for a log cabin and a new deer-hunting rifle. And Jeff Wagon had learned his lesson. He gave up seducing starlets and devoted himself to seducing writers out of their ideas. It was both more profitable and less dangerous. Writers were dumber and more cowardly.

And so he seduced writers by taking them to expensive lunches. By dangling jobs before their eyes. A rewrite of a script in production, a couple of thousand dollars for a treatment. Meanwhile, he let them talk about their ideas for future novels or screenplays. And then he would steal their ideas by switching them to other locales, changing the characters, but always preserving the central idea. And then it was his pleasure to screw them by giving them nothing. And since writers did not usually have a clue to the worthiness of their ideas, they never protested. Not like those cunts who gave you a piece of their ass and expected the moon.

It was the agents that got on to Jeff Wagon and forbade their writer clients to go to lunch with him. But there were fresh young writers coming into Hollywood from all over the country. All hoping for that one foot in the door that would make them rich and famous. And it was Jeff Wagon's genius that he could let them see the door crack open just enough to jam toes black and blue when he slammed the door shut.

Once when I was in Vegas, I told Cully that he and Wagon mugged their victims the same way. But Cully disagreed.

'Listen,' Cully said. 'Me and Vegas are after your money, true. But Hollywood wants your balls.'

He didn't know that Tri-Culture Studios had just bought one of the biggest casinos in Vegas.

Moses Wartberg was another story. On one of my early visits to Hollywood I had been taken to Tri-Culture Studios to pay my respects.

I met Moses Wartberg for a minute. And I knew who he was right away. There was that sharklike look to him that I had seen in top military men, casino owners, very beautiful and very rich women and top Mafia bosses. It was the cold steel of power, the iciness that ran through the blood and brain, the chilling absence of mercy or pity in all the cells of the organism. People who were absolutely dedicated to the supreme drug power. Power already achieved and exercised over a long period of time. And with Moses Wartberg it was exercised down to the smallest square inch.

That night, when I told Janelle that I had been to Tri-Culture Studios and met Wartberg, she said casually, 'Good old Moses. I know Moses.' She gave me a challenging look, so I took the bait. 'OK,' I said. 'Tell me how you know Moses.'

Janelle got out of bed to act out the part. 'I had been in town for about two years and wasn't getting anyplace, and then I was invited to a party where all the big wheels would be, and like a good little would-be star, I went to make contacts. There were a dozen girls like me. All walking around, looking beautiful, hoping that some powerful producer would be struck by our talent. Well, I got lucky. Moses Wartberg came over to me, and he was charming. I didn't know how people could say such terrible things about him. I remember his wife came up for a minute and tried to take him away, but he didn't pay any attention to her. He just kept on talking to me and I was at my most fascinating Southern belle best and, sure enough, by the end of the evening I had an invitation from Moses Wartberg to have dinner at his house the next night. In the morning I called up all my girl-friends and told them about it. They congratulated me and told me I would have to fuck him and I said of course I would not, not on my first date and I also thought he'd respect me more if I held him off a little.'

'That's a good technique,' I said.

'I know,' she said. 'It worked with you, but that's the way I felt. I hadn't ever gone to bed with a man unless I really liked him. I'd never gone to bed with a man just to make him do something for me. I told my girlfriends that, and they told me I was crazy. That if Moses Wartberg was really in love with me or really liked me, I would be on my way to being a star.'

For a few minutes she gave a charming pantomime of false virtue arguing itself into honest sinning.

'And so what happened?' I said.

Janelle stood proud, her hands on her hips, her head tilted dramatically. 'At five o'clock that afternoon I made the greatest decision of my life. I decided I would fuck a man I didn't know just to get ahead. I thought I was so brave and I was delighted that finally I had made a decision that a man would make.'

She came out of her role for just a moment.

'Isn't that what men do?' she said sweetly. 'If they can make a business deal, they'd give anything, they demean themselves. Isn't that business?'

I said, 'I guess so.'

She said to me, 'Didn't you have to do that?'

I said, 'No.'

'You never did anything like that to get your books published, to get an agent or to get a book reviewer to treat you better?'

I said, 'No.'

'You have a good opinion of yourself, don't you?' Janelle said. 'I've had affairs with married men before, and the one thing I have noticed is that they all want to wear that big white cowboy hat.'

'What does that mean?'

'They want to be fair to their wives and girlfriends. That's the one impression they want to make, so you can't blame them for anything, and you do that too.'

I thought that over a minute. I could see what she meant. 'OK,' I said. 'So what?'

'So what?' Janelle said. 'You tell me you love me, but you go back to your wife. No married man should tell another woman he loves her unless he's willing to leave his wife.'

'That's romantic bullshit,' I said.

For a moment she became furious. She said, 'If I went to your house and told your wife you loved me, would you deny me?'

I laughed and I really laughed. I pressed my hand across my chest and said, 'Would you say that again?'

And she said, 'Would you deny me?'

And I said, 'With all my heart.'

She looked at me a moment. She was furious, and then she started to laugh. She said, 'I regressed with you, but I won't regress anymore.'

And I understood what she was saying.

'OK,' I said. 'So what happened with Wartberg?'

She said, 'I took my best bath with all my turtle oil. I anointed myself, dressed in my best outfit and drove myself to the sacrificial altar. I was let into the house and there was Moses Wartberg and we sat down and had a drink and he asked about my career and we were talking for about an hour and he was being very clever, letting me know that if the night turned out OK, he would do a lot of things for me and I was thinking, the son of a bitch isn't going to fuck me, he's not even going to feed me.' Janelle stopped and looked at me.

'That's something I never did to you,' I said.

She gave me a long look, and she went on. 'And then he said, "There's dinner waiting upstairs in the bedroom. Would you like to go up?" And I said, in my Southern belle voice, "Yes, I think I'm a little hungry." He escorted me up the stairs, a beautiful staircase just like the movies, and opened the bedroom door. He closed it behind me, from the outside, and there I was in the bedroom with a little table set up with some nice snacks on it.'

She struck another pose of the innocent young girl, bewildered.

'Where's Moses?' I said.

'He's outside. He's in the hallway.'

'He made you eat alone?' I said.

'No,' Janelle said. 'There was Mrs Bella Wartberg in her sheerest négligée waiting for me.'

I said, 'Jesus Christ.'

Janelle went into another act. 'I didn't know I was going to fuck a woman. It took me eight hours to decide to fuck a man, and now I find out I had to fuck a woman. I wasn't ready for that.'

I said I wasn't ready for that either.

She said, 'I really didn't know what to do. I sat down and Mrs Wartberg served some sandwiches and tea and then she pushed her breasts out of her gown and said, "Do you like these, my dear?" And I said, "They're very nice." '

And then Janelle looked me in the eye and hung her head, and I said, 'Well, what happened? What did she say after you said they're nice?'

Janelle made her eyes look wide open, startled. 'Bella Wartberg said to me, "Would you like to suck on these, my dear?" '

And then Janelle collapsed on the bed with me. She said, 'I ran out of the room, I ran down the stairs, out of the house, and it took me two years to get another job.'

'It's a tough town,' I said.

'Nay,' Janelle said. 'If I had talked to my girlfriends another eight hours, that would have been OK too. It's just a matter of getting your nerve up.'

I smiled at her, and she looked me in the eye, challengingly. 'Yeah,' I said, 'what's the difference?'

As the Mercedes sped over the freeways, I tried to listen to Doran.

'Old Moses is the dangerous guy,' Doran was saying, 'watch out for him.' And so I thought about Moses.

Moses Wartberg was one of the most powerful men in Hollywood. His studio, Tri-Culture Studios, was financially sounder than most companies but made the worst movies. Moses Wartberg had created a money-making machine in a field of creative endeavour. And without a creative bone in his body. This was recognized as sheer genius.

Wartberg was a sloppily fat man, carelessly tailored in Vegas-style suits. He spoke little, never showed emotion, he believed in giving you everything you could take away from him. He believed in giving you nothing you could not force from him and his battery of studio lawyers. He was impartial. He cheated producers, stars, writers and directors out of their percentages of successful films. He was never grateful for a great directing job, a great performance, a great script. How many times had he paid big money for lousy stuff? So why should he pay a man what his work was worth if he could get it for less?

Wartberg talked about movies as generals talk about making war. He said things like: 'You can't make an omelette without breakings eggs.' Or when a business associate made claims to their social relationship, when an actor told him how much they loved each other personally and why was the studio screwing him, Wartberg gave a thin smile and said coldly, 'When I hear the word "love", I reach for my wallet.'

He was scornful of personal dignity, proud when accused of having no sense of decency. He was not ambitious to be known as a man whose word was his bond. He believed in contracts with fine print, not handshakes. He was never too proud to cheat his fellowman out of an idea, a script, a rightful percentage of a movie's profits. When reproached, usually by an overwrought artist (producers knew better), Wartberg would simply answer, 'I'm a moviemaker,' in the same tone that Baudelaire might have answered a similar reproach with 'I am a poet.'

317

He used lawyers as a hood used guns, used affection as a prostitute used sex. He used good works as the Greeks used the Trojan Horse, supported the Will Rogers home for retired actors, Israel, the starving millions of India, Arab refugees from Palestine. It was only personal charity to individual human beings that went against his grain.

Tri-Culture Studios had been losing money when Wartberg took charge. He immediately put it on a strict computer with a bottom-line basis. His deals were the toughest in town. He never gambled on truly creative ideas until they had been proved at other studios. And his big ace in the hole was small budgets.

When other studios were going down the drain with ten-million-dollar pictures, Tri-Culture Studios never made one that went over three million. In fact, over two million and Moses Wartberg or one of his three assistant vice-presidents was sleeping with you twenty-four hours a day. He made producers post completion bonds, directors pledge percentages, actors swear their souls away, to bring in a picture on budget. A producer who brought a picture in on budget or below budget was a hero to Moses Wartberg and knew it. It didn't matter if the picture just made its cost. But if the picture went over budget, even if it grossed twenty million and made the studio a fortune, Wartberg would invoke the penalty clause in the producer's contract and take away his percentage of the profits. Sure, there would be lawsuits, but the studio had twenty salaried lawyers sitting around on their asses who needed practice in court. So a deal could usually be made. Especially if the producer or actor or writer wanted to make another picture at Tri-Culture.

The one thing everybody agreed upon was that Wartberg was a genius at organization. He had three vice-presidents who were in charge of separate empires and competing with each other for Wartberg's favour and the day when they would succeed him. All three had palatial homes, big bonuses and complete power within their own spheres subject only to Wartberg's veto. So the three of them hunted down talent, scripts, thought out special projects. Always knowing that they had to keep the budget low, the talent tractable, and to stamp out any spark of originality before they dared bring it up to Wartberg's suite of offices on the top floor of the studio building.

His sexual reputation was impeccable. He never had fun and games with starlets. He never put pressure on a director or producer to hire a favourite in a film. Part of this was his ascetic nature, a low sexual vitality. The other was his own sense of personal dignity. But the main reason was that he had been happily married for thirty years to his childhood sweetheart.

They had met in a Bronx high school, married in their teens and lived together forever after.

Bella Wartberg had lived a fairy-tale life. A zaftig teenager in a Bronx high school, she had charmed Moses Wartberg with the lethal combination of huge breasts and excessive modesty. She wore loose heavy wool sweaters, dresses a couple of sizes too large, but it was like hiding a glowing radioactive piece of metal in a dark cave. You knew they were there, and the fact that they were hidden made them even more aphrodisiacal. When Moses became a producer, she didn't really know what it meant. She had two children in two years and was quite willing to have one a year for the rest of her fertile life, but it was Moses who called a halt. By that time he had channelled most of his energy into his career, and also, the body that he thirsted for was marred by childbirth scars, the breasts he had sucked had drooped and become veined. And she was too much the good little Jewish housewife for his taste. He got her a maid and forgot about her. He still valued her because she was a great laundress, his white shirts were impeccably starched and ironed. As soon as he put them on, they became wilted. She was a fine housekeeper. She kept track of his Vegas suits and gaudy ties, rotating them to the dry cleaner's at exactly the right time, not so often as to wear them out prematurely, not too seldom as to make them appear soiled. Once she had bought a cat that sat on the sofa, and Moses had sat down on that sofa, and when he rose, his trouser leg had cat hairs on it. He picked up the cat and threw it against the wall. He screamed at Bella hysterically. She gave away the cat the next day.

But power flows magically from one source to another. When Moses became head of Tri-Culture Studios, it was as if Bella Wartberg had been touched by the magic wand of a fairy. The California-bred executive wives took her in hand. The 'in' hairdresser shaped her a crown of black curls that made her look regal. The exercise class at the Sanctuary, a spa to which all the show people belonged, punished her body unmercifully. She went down from a hundred and fifty pounds to a hundred and ten. Even her breasts shrank, shrivelled. But not enough to conform to the rest of her body. A plastic surgeon cut them down into two small perfectly proportioned rosebuds. While he was at it, he whittled down her thighs and took a chunk out of her ass. The studio fashion experts designed a wardrobe to fit her new body and her new status. Bella Wartberg looked into her mirror and saw there, not a zaftig Jewish princess lushly fleshed, vulgarly handsome, but a slim, Waspy, forty-year-old ex-debutante, peppy, vivacious, brimming full of energy. What she did not see mercifully was that her appearance was a distortion of what she had been, that her old self, like a ghost, persisted through the bones of her body, the structure of her face. She was a skinny fashionable lady built on the heavy bones she had inherited. But she believed she was beautiful. And so she was quite ready when a young actor on the make pretended to be in love with her.

She returned his love passionately, sincerely. She went to his grubby apartment in Santa Monica and for the first time in her life was thoroughly fucked. The young actor was virtile, dedicated to his profession and threw himself into his role so wholeheartedly that he almost believed he was in love. So much so that he bought her a charm bracelet from Gucci's that she would treasure the rest of her life as proof of her first great passion. And so, when he asked for her help in getting a role in one of Tri-Culture's big feature films, he was thoroughly confounded when she told him she never interfered in her husband's business. They quarrelled bitterly, and the actor disappeared from her life. She missed him, she missed the grubby apartment, his rock records, but she had been a level-headed girl and had grown to be a levelheaded woman. She would not make the same mistake. In the future she would pick her lovers as carefully as a comedian picks his hat.

In the years that followed she became an expert negotiator in her affairs with actors, discriminating enough to seek out talented people rather than untalented ones, and indeed, she enjoyed the talented ones more. It seemed that general intelligence went with talent. And she helped them in their careers. She never made the mistake of going directly to her husband. Moses Wartberg was too Olympian to be concerned with such decisions. Instead, she went to one of the three vice-presidents. She would rave about the talent of an actor she had seen in a little art group giving Ibsen and insist that she didn't know the actor personally but she was sure he would be an asset to the studio. The vice-president would put the name down and the actor would get a small part. Soon enough the word got around. Bella Wartberg became so notorious for fucking anybody, anywhere, that whenever she stopped by one of the vice-president's offices, that VP would make sure that one of his secretaries was present, as a gynaecologist would make sure a nurse was present when examining a patient.

The three VP's jockeying for power had to accommodate Wartberg's wife, or felt they had to. Jeff Wagon became good friends with Bella and would even introduce her to some especially upstanding young fellow. When all this failed, she prowled the expensive shops of Rodeo for women, took long lunches with pretty starlets at exclusive restaurants, wearing ominously huge macho sunglasses.

Because of his close relationship with Bella, Jeff Wagon was the odds-on favourite to get Moses Wartberg's spot when he retired. There was one catch. What would Moses Wartberg do when he learned that his wife, Bella, was the Messalina of Beverly Hills? Gossip columnists planted Bella's affairs as 'blind items' Wartberg couldn't fail to see. Bella was notorious.

As usual Moses Wartberg surprised everyone. He did so by doing absolutely nothing. Only rarely did he take his revenge on the lover; he never took reprisals against his wife.

The first time he took his revenge was when a young rock and roll star boasted of his conquest, called Bella Wartberg 'a crazy old cunt'. The rock and roll star had meant it as a supreme compliment, but to Moses Wartberg it was as insulting as one of his vice-presidents coming to work in blue jeans and turtleneck sweater. The rock and roll star made ten times as much money from a single album as he was being paid for the featured part in his movie. But he was infected with the American dream; the narcissism of playing himself on film entranced him. On the night of the first preview he had assembled his entourage of fellow artists and girlfriends and taken them to the Wartberg private screening room crammed with the top stars of Tri-Culture Studios. It was one of the big parties of the year.

The rock and roll star sat and sat and sat. He waited and waited and waited. The film ran on and on. And on screen he was nowhere to be seen. His part was on the cutting-room floor. He had immediately gotten stoned out of his mind and had to be taken home.

Moses Wartberg had celebrated his transformation from producer to head of a studio with a great coup. Over the years he had noticed that the studio moguls were furious with all the attention given actors, writers, directors and producers at the

Academy Awards. It infuriated them that their employees were the ones who received all the credit for the movies that they had created. It was Moses Wartberg who years before first supported the idea for an Irving Thalberg award to be given at the Academy ceremonies. He was clever enough to have included in the plan that the award would not be a yearly one. That it would be given to a producer for constantly high quality over the years. He was also clever enough to have the clause put in that no one would be eligible to receive the Thalberg Award more than once. In effect many producers, whose pictures never won Academy Awards, but who had a lot of clout in the movie industry, got their share of publicity by winning the Thalberg. But still, this left out the actual studio heads and the real money-making stars whose work was never good enough. It was then that Wartberg supported a Humanitarian Award to be given to the person in the movie industry of the highest ideals, who gave of himself for the betterment of the industry and mankind. Finally, two years ago, Moses Wartberg had been given this award and accepted it on television in front of one hundred million admiring American *viewers*. The award was presented by a Japanese director of international renown for the simple reason that no American director could be found who could give the award with a straight face. (Or so Doran said when telling me this particular story.)

On the night when Moses Wartberg received his award, two screenwriters had heart attacks from outrage. An actress threw her television set out of the fourth-floor suite of the Beverly Wilshire Hotel. Three directors resigned from the Academy. But that award became Moses Wartberg's most prized possession. One screenwriter commented that it was like members of a concentration camp voting for Hitler as their most popular politician.

It was Wartberg who developed the technique of loading a rising star with huge mortgage payments on a Beverly Hills mansion to force him to work hard in lousy movies. It was Moses Wartberg whose studio continually fought in the courts to the bitter end to deprive creative talent of the monies due them. It was Wartberg who had the connections in Washington. Politicians were entertained with beautiful starlets, secret funds, paid-for expensive vacations at the studio facilities all over the world. He was a man who knew how to use lawyers and the law to do financial murder; to steal and cheat. Or so Doran said. To me he sounded like·any red-blooded American businessman.

Apart from his cunning, his fix in Washington was the most important asset that Tri-Culture Studios possessed.

His enemies spread many scandalous stories about him that were not true because of his ascetic life. They started rumours that with careful secrecy he flew to Paris every month to indulge himself with child prostitutes. They spread the rumour that he was a voyeur. That he had a peephole to his wife's bedroom when she entertained her lovers. But none of this was true.

Of his intelligence and force of character there could be no doubt. Unlike the other movie moguls, he shunned the publicity limelight, the one exception being his seeking the Humanitarian Award.

When Doran drove into the Tri-Culture Studios lot, it was hate at second sight. The buildings were concrete, the grounds land-scaped like those industrial parks that make Long Island look like benign concentration camps for robots. When we went through the gates, the guards didn't have a special parking spot for us, and we had to use the metred lot with its red-and-white-striped wooden arm that raised automatically. I didn't notice that I would need a quarter coin to get out through the exit arm.

I thought this was an accident, a secretarial slipup, but Doran said it was part of the Moses Wartberg technique to put talent like me in its place. A star would have driven right back off the lot. They would never put it over with directors or even a big featured player. But they wanted writers to know that they were not to get delusions of grandeur. I thought Doran was paranoid and I laughed, but I guess it irritated me, just a little.

In the main building our identities were checked by a security guard, who then made a call to make sure we were expected. A secretary came down and took us up in the elevator to the top floor. And that top floor was pretty spooky. Classy but spooky.

Despite all this, I have to admit I was impressed with Jeff Wagon's charm and movie business bottom line. I knew he was a phony and hustler, but that seemed natural somehow. As it is not unnatural to find an exotic-looking inedible fruit on a tropical island. We sat down in front of his desk, my agent and I, and Wagon told his secretary to stop all calls. Very flattering. But he obviously had not given the secret code word really to stop all calls because he took at least three during our conference.

We still had a half hour to wait for Wartberg before the conference would start. Jeff Wagon told some funny stories, even the one about how the Oregon girl took a slice out of his balls. 'If she'd done a better job,' Wagon said, 'she would have saved me a lot of money and trouble these past years.'

Wagon's phone buzzed, and he led me and Doran down the hall to a luxurious conference room that could serve as a movie set.

At the long conference table sat Ugo Kellino, Houlinan and Moses Wartberg chatting easily. Farther down the table was a middle-aged guy with a head of fuzzy white hair. Wagon introduced him as the new director for the picture. His name was Simon Bellfort, a name I recognized. Twenty years ago he had made a great war film. Right afterward he had signed a long-term contract with Tri-Culture and became the ace schlockmaster for Jeff Wagon.

The young guy with him was introduced as Frank Richetti. He had a sharp, cunning face and was dressed in a combo Polo Lounge-rock star-Californian hippie style. The effect was stunning to my eyes. He fitted perfectly Janelle's description of the attractive men who roamed Beverly Hills as Don Juan-hustler-semipimps. She called them Slime City. But maybe she just said that to cheer me up. I didn't see how any girl could resist a guy like Frank Richetti. He was Simon Bellfort's executive producer on the film.

Moses Wartberg wasted no time on any bullshit. His voice laden with power, he put everything right on the line.

'I'm not happy with the script Malomar left us,' he said. 'The approach is all wrong. It's not a Tri-Culture film. Malomar was a genius, he could have shot this picture. We don't have anybody on this lot in his class.'

Frank Richetti broke in, suave, charming. 'I don't know, Mr Wartberg. You have some fine directors here.' He smiled fondly at Simon Bellfort.

Wartberg gave him a very cold look. We would hear no more from Richetti. And Bellfort blushed a little and looked away.

'We have a lot of money budgeted for this picture,' Wartberg went on. 'We have to insure that investment. But we don't want the critics jumping all over us, that we ruined Malomar's work. We want to use his reputation *for* the picture. Houlinan is going to issue a press release signed by all of us here that the picture will be made as Malomar wanted it to be made. That it will be

324

Malomar's picture, a final tribute to his greatness and his contribution to the industry.'

Wartberg paused as Houlinan handed out copies of the press release. Beautiful letterhead, I noticed, with the Tri-Culture logo in slashing red and black.

Kellino said easily, 'Moses, old boy, I think you'd better mention that Merlyn and Simon will be working with me on the new script.'

'OK, it's mentioned,' Wartberg said. 'And, Ugo, let me remind you that you can't fuck with the production or the directing. That's part of our deal.'

'Sure,' Kellino said.

Jeff Wagon smiled and leaned back in his chair. 'The press release is our official position,' he said, 'but, Merlyn, I must tell you that Malomar was very sick when he helped you with this script. It's terrible. We'll have to rewrite it, I have some ideas. There's a lot of work to be done. Right now we fill up the media with Malomar. Is that OK with you, Jack?' he asked Houlinan. And Houlinan nodded.

Kellino said to me very sincerely, 'I hope you'll work with me on this picture to make it the great movie that Malomar wanted it to be.'

'No,' I said. 'I can't do that. I worked on the script with Malomar, I think it's fine. So I can't agree to any changes or rewriting, and I won't sign any press release to that effect.'

Houlinan broke in smoothly. 'We all know how you feel. You were very close to Malomar in this picture. I approve of what you just said, I think it's marvellous. It's rare that there's such loyalty in Hollywood, but remember, you have a percentage in the film. It's in your interest to make the film a success. If you are not a friend of the picture, if you are an enemy of the picture, you're taking money out of your pocket.'

I really had to laugh when he said that line. 'I'm a friend of the picture. That's why I don't want to rewrite it. You're the guys that are the enemy of this picture.'

Kellino said abruptly, harshly, 'Fuck him. Let him go. We don't need him.'

For the first time I looked directly at Kellino, and I remembered Osano's description of him. As usual, Kellino was dressed beautifully, perfectly cut suit, a marvellous shirt, silky brown shoes. He looked beautiful, and I remembered Osano's use of the Italian peasant word *cafone*. A '*cafone*,' he said, 'is a peasant who

325

has risen to great riches and great fame and tries to make himself a member of the nobility. He does everything right. He learns his manners, he improves his speech and he dresses like an angel. But no matter how beautifully he dresses, no matter how much care he takes, no matter how much time he cleans, there clings to his shoe one tiny piece of shit.'

And looking at Kellino, I thought how perfectly he fitted this definition.

Wartberg said to Wagon, 'Straighten this out,' and he left the room. He couldn't be bothered fucking around with some half-assed writer. He had come to the meeting as a courtesy to Kellino.

Wagon said smoothly, 'Merlyn is essential to this project, Ugo. I'm sure when he thinks it over, he'll join us. Doran, why don't we all meet again in a few days?'

'Sure,' Doran said. 'I'll call you.'

We got up to leave. I handed my copy of the press release to Kellino. 'There's something on your shoe,' I said. 'Use this to wipe it off.'

When we left Tri-Culture Studios, Doran told me not to worry. He told me he could get everything straightened out within the week, that Wartberg and Wagon could not afford to have me as an enemy of the picture. They would compromise. And not to forget my percentage.

I told him that I didn't give a shit and I told him to drive faster. I knew that Janelle would be waiting for me at the hotel, and it seemed as if the thing I wanted most in the world was to see her again. To touch her body and kiss her mouth and lie with her and hear her tell me stories.

I was glad to have an excuse to stay in Los Angeles for a week to be with her for six or seven days. I really didn't give a shit about the picture. With Malomar dead I knew it would just be another piece of schlock from Tri-Culture Studios.

When Doran left me off at the Beverly Hills Hotel, he put his hand on my arm and said, 'Wait a minute. There's something I have to talk to you about.'

'OK,' I said impatiently.

Doran said, 'I've been meaning to tell you for a long time, but I felt maybe it wasn't my business.'

'Jesus,' I said. 'What the hell are you talking about? I'm in a hurry.'

Doran smiled a little sadly, 'Yeah, I know. Janelle is waiting for you, right? It's Janelle I want to talk to you about.'

'Look,' I said to Doran, 'I know all about her and I don't care what she did, what she was. It doesn't make any difference to me.'

Doran paused for a moment. 'You know that girl, Alice, she lives with?'

'Yeah,' I said. 'She's a sweet girl.'

'She's a little dykey,' Doran said.

I felt a strange sense of recognition as if I were Cully counting down a shoe. 'Yeah,' I said. 'So what?'

'So is Janelle,' Doran said.

'You mean she's a lesbian?' I said.

'Bisexual is the word,' Doran said. 'She likes men and women.'

I thought that over for a moment, and then I smiled at him and said, 'Nobody's perfect.' And I got out of the car and went up to my suite, where Janelle was waiting for me, and we made love together before going out to supper. But this time I didn't ask her for any stories. I didn't mention what Doran said. There was no need. I had caught on a long time ago and made my peace with it. It was better than her fucking other men.

BOOK SIX

34

OVER the years Cully Cross had counted down the shoe perfectly and finally caught the loaded winning hand. He was really Xanadu Two, loaded with 'juice', and had full power of 'The Pencil'. A 'Gold Pencil'. He could comp everything, not only room, food and beverage, the standard RFB, but air fares from all over the world, top-price call girls, the power to make customer markers disappear. He could even dispense free gambling chips to the top-rank entertainers who played the Xanadu Hotel.

During those years Gronevelt had been more like a father to him than a boss. Their friendship had become stronger. They had battled against hundreds of scams together, repelled the pirates, inside and out, who tried to buccaneer the Hotel Xanadu's sacred bankroll. Claim agents reneging on markers, magnet toters trying to empty slot machines against all the laws of chance, junket masters who sneaked in bad-credit artists with phoney ID's, house dealers dumping out, keno ticket forgers, computer boys at blackjack tables, dice switchers by the thousand. Cully and Gronevelt had fought them off.

During those years Cully had won Gronevelt's respect with his flair for attracting new customers to the hotel. He had organized a worldwide backgammon tournament to be held at the Xanadu. He had kept a million-dollar-a-year customer by giving him a new Rolls-Royce every Christmas. The hotel charged the car off to public relations, a tax deduction. The customer was happy to receive a sixty-thousand-dollar car which would have cost him a hundred eighty thousand dollars in tax dollars, a twenty percent cut of his losses. But Cully's finest coup had been with Charles Hemsi. Gronevelt bragged about his protégé's cunning for years after that.

Gronevelt had had his reservations about Cully's buying up all of Hemsi's markers around Vegas for ten cents on the dollar. But he had given Cully his head. And sure enough, Hemsi came to Vegas at least six times a year and always stayed at the Xanadu. On one trip he had had a fantastic roll at the crap table and won seventy thousand dollars. He used that money to pay off some of his markers, and so the Xanadu was already ahead of the game. But then Cully showed his genius.

On one trip Charlie Hemsi mentioned that his son was being married to a girl in Israel. Cully was overjoyed for his friend and insisted on the Hotel Xanadu's picking up the whole tab for the wedding. Cully told Hemsi that the Hotel Xanadu jet plane (another Cully idea, the plane bought to steal business from the junkets) would fly the whole wedding party to Israel and pay for their hotels there. The Xanadu would pay for the wedding feast, the orchestra, all expenses. There was only one catch. Since the wedding guests were from all over the United States, they would have to board the plane in Las Vegas. But no sweat, they could all stay at the Xanadu, free of charge.

Cully calculated the cost to the hotel at two hundred thousand dollars. He convinced Gronevelt that it would pay off, and if it didn't, they at least would have Charlie Hemsi and son as players for life. But it proved to be a great 'Host' coup. Over a hundred wedding guests came to Vegas, and before they left for the wedding in Israel, they left nearly a million dollars·in the hotel's cashier cage.

But today Cully planned to present Gronevelt with an even greater money-making scheme, one that would force Gronevelt and his partners to name him general manager of the Hotel Xanadu, the most powerful open official position next to Gronevelt. He was waiting for Fummiro. Fummiro had piled up markers in his last two trips; he was having trouble paying. Cully knew why and Cully had the solution. But he knew that he had to let Fummiro take the initiative, that he would shy away if Cully himself suggested the solution. Daisy had taught him that.

Fummiro finally came to town, played his piano in the morning and drank his soup for breakfast. He wasn't interested in women. He was intent on gambling, and in three days he had lost all his cash and signed another three hundred thousand in markers. Before he left, he summoned Cully to his hotel room. Fummiro was very polite and just a little nervous. He didn't want to lose face. He was afraid that Cully would think that he did not wish to pay his gambling debts, but very carefully he explained to Cully that though he had plenty of money in Tokyo and the million dollars was a mere trifle to him, the problem was getting the cash out of Japan, turning the Japanese yen into American dollars.

'So, Mr Cross,' he said to Cully, 'if you could come to Japan, I will pay you there in yen, and then I'm sure that you can find a way to get the money to America.'

Cully wanted to assure Fummiro of the hotel's complete trust and faith in him. 'Mr Fummiro,' he said, 'there's really no rush, your credit is good. The million dollars can wait until the next time you can come to Vegas. It's really no problem. We're always delighted to have you here. Your company is such a pleasure to us. Please don't concern yourself. Just let me put myself at your service, and now, if there's anything you would like, please tell me and I will arrange anything you wish. It's an honour for us to have you owe us this money.'

Fummiro's handsome face relaxed. He was not dealing with a barbarian American, but one who was almost as polite as a Japanese. He said, 'Mr Cross, why don't you come to visit me? We will have a wonderful time in Japan. I will take you to a geisha house, you will have the best of food, the best of liquor, the best of women. You will be my personal guest and I can repay you for some of the hospitality you have always shown me and I can give you the million dollars for the hotel.'

Cully knew that the Japanese government had a tough law about smuggling yen out of the country. Fummiro was proposing a criminal act. He waited and just nodded his head, remembering to smile continuously.

Fummiro went on. 'I would like to do something for you. I trust you with all my heart, and that is the only reason I am saying this to you. My government is very strict on the exporting of yen. I would like to get my own money out. Now when you pick up a million for the Hotel Xanadu, if you could take one million out for me and deposit it in your cage, you receive fifty thousand dollars.'

Cully felt the sweet satisfaction of counting down the shoe perfectly. He said sincerely, 'Mr Fummiro, I will do it out of my friendship for you. But of course, I must speak to Mr Gronevelt.'

'Of course,' Fummiro said. 'I will also speak to him.'

Immediately afterward Cully called Gronevelt's suite and was

332

told by his special operator that Gronevelt was busy and not taking any calls that afternoon. He left a message that the matter was urgent. He waited in his office. Three hours later the phone rang, and it was Gronevelt telling him to come down to the suite.

Gronevelt had changed a great deal over the last few years. The red had drained from his skin, leaving it a ghostly white. His face was like that of a fragile hawk. He had very suddenly become old, and Cully knew that he rarely had a girl to while away his afternoons. He seemed more and more immersed in his books and left most of the detail of running the hotel to Cully. But every evening he still made his tour of the casino floor, checking all the pits, watching the dealers and the stickmen and the pit bosses with his hawklike eyes. He still had that capacity to draw the electric energy of the casino into his small-framed body.

Gronevelt was dressed to go down to the casino floor. He fiddled with the control panel that would flood the casino pits with pure oxygen. But it was still too early in the evening. He would push the button sometime in the early-morning hours when the players were tiring and thinking of going to bed. Then he would revive them as if they were puppets. It was only in the past year that he had the oxygen controls wired directly to his suite.

Gronevelt ordered dinner to be brought up to the suite. Cully was tense. Why had Gronevelt kept him waiting for three hours? Had Fummiro spoken to him first? And he knew instantly that this was what had happened. He felt resentment; the two of them were so strong, he was not yet at their eminence and so they had consulted together without him.

Cully said smoothly, 'I guess Fummiro told you about his idea. I told him I'd have to check it out with you.'

Gronevelt smiled at him. 'Cully, my boy, you're a wonder. Perfect. I couldn't have done better myself. You let that Jap come to you. I was afraid you might get impatient with all those markers piling up in the cage.'

'That's my girlfriend, Daisy,' Cully said. 'She made a Japanese citizen out of me.'

Gronevelt frowned a little. 'Women are dangerous,' he said. 'Men like you and I can't afford to let them get too close. That's our strength. Women can get you killed over nothing. Men are more sensible and more trustworthy.' He sighed. 'Well, I don't have to worry about you in that area. You spread the Honeybees around pretty good.' He sighed, gave his head a little shake and returned to business.

'The only trouble with this whole deal is that we've never found a safe way to get money out of Japan. We have a fortune in markers there, but I wouldn't give a nickel for them. We have a whole set of problems. One, if the Japanese government catches you, you'll do years in the clink. Two, once you pick up the money you'll be a target for hijackers. Japanese criminals have very good intelligence. They'll know right away when you pick up the money. Three, two million dollars in yen will be a big, big suitcase. In Japan they X-ray baggage. How do you get it turned into U.S. dollars once you get it out? How do you get into the United States, and then, though I think I can guarantee you it won't happen, how about hijackers on this end? People in this hotel will know we are sending you there to pick up the money. I have partners, but I can't guarantee the discretion of all of them. Also, by sheer accident, you could lose the money. Cully, here's the position you will be in. If you lose the money, we will always suspect you of being guilty unless you get killed.'

Cully said, 'I thought of all that. I checked the cage, and I see we have at least another million or two million dollars in markers with other Japanese players. So I would be bringing out four million dollars.'

Gronevelt laughed. 'In one trip that would be an awful gamble. Bad percentage.'

Cully said, 'Well, maybe one trip, maybe two trips, maybe three trips. First I have to find out how it could be done.'

Gronevelt said, 'You're taking all the risk in every way. As far as I can see, you're getting nothing out of it. If you win, you win nothing. If you lose, you lose everything. If you take a position like that, then the years I've spent teaching you have been wasted. So why do you want to do this? There's no percentage.'

Cully said, 'Look, I'll do it on my own without help, I'll take all the blame if it goes wrong. But if I bring back four million dollars, I would expect to be named general manager of the hotel. You know that I'm your man. I would never go against you.'

Gronevelt sighed, 'It's an awful gamble on your part. I hate to see you do it.'

'Then it's OK?' Cully asked. He tried to keep the jubilation out of his voice. He didn't want Gronevelt to know how eager he was.

'Yeah,' Gronevelt said. 'But just pick up Fummiro's two million, never mind the money the other people owe us. If something goes wrong, then we only lose the two million.'

Cully laughed, playing the game. 'We only lose one million, the other million is Fummiro's. Remember?'

Gronevelt said completely serious. 'It's all ours. Once that money is in our cage, Fummiro will gamble it away. That's the strength of this deal.'

The next morning Cully took Fummiro to the airport in Gronevelt's Rolls-Royce. He had an expensive gift for Fummiro, an antique coin bank made in the days of the Italian Renaissance. The bank was filled with gold coins. Fummiro was ecstatic, but Cully sensed a sly amusement beneath his effusions of delight.

Finally Fummiro said, 'When are you coming to Japan?'

'Between two weeks and a month from now,' Cully said. 'Even Mr Gronevelt will not know the exact day. You understand why.'

Fummiro nodded. 'Yes, you must be very careful. I will have the money waiting.'

When Cully got back to the hotel, he put in a call to Merlyn in New York. 'Merlyn, old buddy, how about keeping me company on a trip to Japan, all expenses paid and geisha girls thrown in?'

There was a long pause on the other end, and then he heard Merlyn's voice say, 'Sure.'

35

GOING to Japan struck me as a good idea. I had to be in Los Angeles the following week to work on the movie anyway, so I'd be partway there. And I was fighting so much with Janelle that I wanted to take a break from her. I knew she would take my going to Japan as a personal insult, and that pleased me.

Vallie asked me how long I would be in Japan and I said about a week. She didn't mind my going, she never did mind. In fact, she was always happy to see me leave, I was too restless around the house, too nerve-racking. She spent a lot of time visting her parents and other members of her family, and she took the kids with her.

When I got off the plane in Las Vegas, Cully met me with the Rolls-Royce, right on the landing field, so that I wouldn't have to walk through the terminal. That set off alarm bells in my head.

A long time ago Cully had explained to me why he sometimes met people right on the landing field. He did this to escape FBI camera surveillance of all incoming passengers.

Where all the gate corridors converged into the central waiting room of the terminal there was a huge clock. Behind this clock, in a specially constructed booth, were movie cameras that recorded the throngs of eager gamblers rushing to Las Vegas from every part of the world. At night the FBI team on duty would run all the film and check it against their wanted lists. Happy-go-lucky bank robbers, on-the-run embezzlers, counterfeit money artists, successful kidnappers and extortionists were astonished when they were picked up before they had a chance to gamble away their ill-gotten gains.

When I asked Cully how he knew about this, he told me he had a former top FBI agent working as chief of security for the hotel. It was that simple.

Now I noticed that Cully had driven the Rolls himself. There was no chauffeur. He guided the car around the terminal to the baggage area, and we sat in the car while we waited for my luggage to come down the chute. While we waited, Cully briefed me.

First he warned me not to tell Gronevelt that we were going to Japan the following morning. To pretend that I had come in just for a gambling holiday. Then he told me about our mission, the two million dollars in yen he'd have to smuggle out of Japan and the hazards involved. He said very sincerely, 'Look, I don't think there's any danger, but you may not feel the same way. So if you don't want to go, I'll understand.'

He knew there was no way I could refuse him. I owed him the favour; in fact, I owed him two favours. One for keeping me out of jail. The other for handing me back my thirty-thousand-dollar stash when the troubles were all over. He had given me

336

back my thirty grand in cash, twenty-dollar bills, and I had put the money in a savings bank account in Vegas. The cover story would be that I had won it gambling, and Cully and his people were prepared to back the cover. But it never came to that. The whole Army Reserve scandal died away.

'I always wanted to see Japan,' I said. 'I don't mind being your bodyguard. Do I carry a gun?'

Cully was horrified. 'Do you want to get us killed? Shit, if they want to take the money away from us, let them take it. Our protection is secrecy and moving very fast. I have it all worked out.'

'Then why do you need me?' I asked him. I was curious and a little wary. It didn't make sense.

Cully sighed. 'It's a hell of a long trip to Japan,' Cully said. 'I need some company. We can play gin on the plane and hang out in Tokyo and have some fun. Besides, you're a big guy, and if some small-time snatch-and-run artists lock onto us, you can scare them off.'

'OK,' I said. But it still sounded fishy.

That night we had dinner with Gronevelt. He didn't look well, but he was in great form telling stories about his early days in Vegas. How he had made his fortune in tax-free dollars before the federal government sent an army of spies and accountants to Nevada.

'You have to get rich in the dark,' Gronevelt said. It was the bee in his bonnet, buzzing around as crazily as Osano's Nobel Prize hornet. 'Everybody in this country has to get rich in the dark. Those thousands of little stores and business firms skimming off the top, big companies creating a legal plain of darkness.' But none of them was so plentiful in opportunity as Vegas. Gronevelt tapped the edge of his Havana cigar and said with satisfaction, 'That's what makes Vegas so strong. You can get rich in the dark here easier than any place else. That's the strength.'

Cully said, 'Merlyn is just staying the night. I figure I'll go into Los Angeles with him tomorrow morning and pick up some antiques. And I can see some of those Hollywood people about their markers.'

Gronevelt took a long puff on his Havana. 'Good idea,' he said, 'I'm running out of presents.' He laughed. 'Do you know where I got that idea about giving presents? From a book published in 1870 about gambling. Education is a great thing.'

337

He sighed and rose, a signal for us to leave. He shook my hand and then courteously escorted us to the door of his suite. As we went out the door, Gronevelt said gravely to Cully, 'Good luck on your trip.'

Outside on the false green grass of the terrace, I stood with Cully in the desert moonlight. We could see the Strip with its millions of red and green lights, the dark desert mountains far away. 'He knows we're going,' I said to Cully.

'If he does, he does,' Cully said. 'Meet me for breakfast at eight A.M. We have to get an early start.'

The next morning we flew from Las Vegas to San Francisco. Cully carried a huge suitcase of rich brown leather, its corners made of dull shining brass. Strips of brass bound the case. The locking plate was also heavy. It was formidable-looking and strong. 'It won't bust open,' Cully said. 'And it will be easy for us to keep track of it on the baggage trucks.'

I had never seen a suitcase like it and said so. 'Just an antique I picked up in LA,' Cully said smugly.

We jumped on a Japan Airlines 747 with just fifteen minutes to spare. Cully had deliberately timed it very close. On the long flight we played gin, and when we landed in Tokyo, I had him beaten for six thousand dollars. But Cully didn't seem to mind; he just slapped me on the back and said, 'I'll get you on the trip home.'

We took a taxi from the airport to our Tokyo hotel. I was eager to see the fabulous city of the Far East. But it looked like a shabbier and smokier New York. It also seemed smaller in scale, the people shorter, the buildings flatter, the dusky skyline a miniaturization of the familiar and overpowering skyline of New York City. When we entered the heart of the city, I saw men wearing white surgical gauze masks. It made them look eerie. Cully told me that the Japanese in urban centres wore these masks to guard against lung infections from the heavily polluted air.

We passed buildings and stores that seemed to be made of wood, as if they were sets on a movie lot, and intermingled with them were modern skyscrapers and office buildings. The streets were full of people, many of them in Western dress, others, mainly women, in some sort of kimono outfit. It was a bewildering collage of styles.

The hotel was a disappointment. It was modern and American.

338

The huge lobby had a chocolate-coloured rug and a great many black leather armchairs. Small Japanese men in black American business suits sat in most of these chairs clutching briefcases. It could have been a Hilton hotel in New York.

'This is the Orient?' I said to Cully.

Cully shook his head impatiently. 'We're getting a good night's snooze. Tomorrow I'll do my business, and tomorrow night I'll show you what Tokyo is really made of. You'll have a great time. Don't worry.'

We had a big suite together, a two-bedroom suite. We unpacked our suitcases and I noticed that Cully had very little in his brassbound monster. We were both tired from the trip, and though it was only six o'clock Tokyo time, we went to bed.

The next morning there was a knock at the door of my bedroom and Cully said, 'Come on, time to get up.' Dawn was just breaking outside my window.

He ordered breakfast in the suite, which disappointed me. I began to get the idea that I wasn't going to see much of Japan. We had eggs and bacon, coffee and orange juice and even some English muffins. The only thing Oriental were some pancakes. The pancakes were huge and twice as thick as a pancake should be. They were more like huge slabs of bread, and they were a very funny sickly yellow colour rather than brown. I tasted one and I could swear that it tasted like fish.

I said to Cully, 'What the hell are these?'

He said, 'They're pancakes but cooked in fish oil.'

'I'll pass,' I said, and I pushed the dish over to him.

Cully finished them off with gusto. 'All you have to do is get used to it,' he said.

Over our coffee I asked him, 'What's the programme?'

'It's a beautiful day out,' Cully said. 'We'll take a walk and I'll lay it out for you.'

I understood that he didn't want to talk in the room. That he was afraid it might be bugged.

We left the hotel. It was still very early in the morning, the sun just coming up. We turned down a side street and suddenly I was in the Orient. As far as the eye could see there were little ramshackle houses, small buildings and along the curb stretched huge piles of green-coloured garbage so high that it formed a wall.

There were a few people out in the streets, and a man went by us riding a bicycle, his black kimono floating behind him. Two wiry men in khaki work pants and khaki shirts, white gauze masks covering their faces, suddenly appeared before us. I gave a little jump and Cully laughed as the two men turned into another side street.

'Jesus,' I said, 'those masks are spooky.'

'You'll get used to them,' Cully said. 'Now listen close. I want you to know everything that's going on, so you don't make any mistakes.'

As we walked along the wall of grey-green garbage, Cully explained to me that he was smuggling out two million dollars in Japanese yen and that the government had very strict laws about exporting the national currency.

'If I get caught, I go to jail,' Cully said. 'Unless Fummiro can put the fix in. Or unless Fummiro goes to jail with me.'

'How about me?' I said. 'If you get caught, don't I get caught?'

'You're an eminent writer,' Cully said. 'The Japanese have a great respect for culture. You'll just get thrown out of the country. Just keep your mouth shut.'

'So I'm just here to have a good time,' I said. I knew he was full of shit and I wanted him to know I knew it.

Then another thing occurred to me. 'How the hell do we get through customs in the States?' I said.

'We don't,' Cully said. 'We dump the money in Hong Kong. It's a free port. The only people who have to go through customs there are the ones travelling on Hong Kong passports.'

'Jesus,' I said. 'Now you tell me we're going to Hong Kong. Where the fuck do we go after that, Tibet?'

'Be serious,' Cully said. 'Don't panic. I did this a year ago with a little money, just for a trial run.'

'Get a gun for me,' I said. 'I got a wife and three kids, you son of a bitch. Give me a fighting chance.' But I was laughing. Cully had really roped me in.

But Cully didn't know I was kidding. 'You can't carry a gun,' he said. 'Every Japanese airline has their electronic security check of your person and your hand luggage. And most of them X-ray any baggage you check in.' He paused for a moment and then said, 'The only airline that doesn't X-ray checked baggage is the Cathay. So if something happens to me, you know what to do.'

'I can just picture myself alone in Hong Kong with two million bucks,' I said. 'I'd have a million fucking hatchets in my neck,' I said.

'Don't worry,' Cully said soothingly. 'Nothing's going to happen. We'll have a ball.'

I was laughing, but I was also worried. 'But if something does happen,' I said, 'what do I do in Hong Kong?'

Cully said, 'Go to the Futaba Bank and ask for the vice-president. He'll take the money and change it into Hong Kong dollars. He'll give you a receipt and charge you maybe twenty grand. Then he'll change the Hong Kong dollars into American dollars and charge you another fifty thousand dollars. The American dollars will be sent to Switzerland and you'll get another receipt. A week from now the Hotel Xanadu will receive a draft from the Swiss bank for two million minus the Hong Kong bank charges. See how simple it is?'

I thought this over as we walked back to the hotel. Finally I came back to my original question. 'Why the hell do you need me?'

'Don't ask me any more questions, just do what I tell you,' Cully said. 'You owe me a favour, right?'

'Right,' I said. And I didn't ask any more questions.

When we got back to the hotel, Cully made some phone calls, talking Japanese, and then told me he was going out. 'I should be back around five P.M.,' he said. 'But I may be a little late. Just wait in this room for me. If I'm not back tonight, you hop the morning plane for home. OK?'

'OK,' I said.

I tried reading in the bedroom of the suite and then imagined noises in the living room, so I went there to read. I ordered lunch in the suite, and after I had finished eating, I called the States. The connection went through in only a few minutes, which surprised me. I thought it would take at least a half hour.

Vallie picked up the phone right away, and I could tell from her voice that she was pleased that I'd called.

'How is the mysterious Orient?' she asked. 'Are you having a good time? Have you gone to a geisha house yet?'

'Not yet,' I said. 'So far all I've seen is the morning Tokyo garbage. Since then I've been waiting for Cully. He's out doing business. At least I've got him beat for six grand in gin.'

'Good,' Valerie said. 'You can buy me and the kids some of those fabulous kimonos. Oh, by the way, you got a call yesterday from some man who claimed he was a friend of yours in Vegas. He said he expected to see you out there. I told him you were in Tokyo.'

My heart stopped a little. Then I said casually, 'Did he give his name?'

'No,' Valerie said. 'Don't forget our presents.'

'I won't,' I said.

I spent the rest of the afternoon worrying. I called the airline for a reservation back to the States for the next morning. Suddenly I wasn't so sure that Cully would be back. I checked his bedroom. The big brassbound suitcase was gone.

Darkness was beginning to fall when Cully came into the suite. He was rubbing his hands, excited and happy. 'Everything is all set,' he said. 'Nothing to worry about. Tonight we have fun and tomorrow we wind things up. The day after that we'll be in Hong Kong.'

'I called my wife,' I said. 'We had a nice little chat. She told me some guy called from Vegas and asked where I was. She told him Tokyo.'

That cooled him off. He thought about it. Then shrugged. 'That sounds like Gronevelt,' Cully said. 'Just making sure his hunch was right. He's the only one who has your phone number.'

'Do you trust Gronevelt on a deal like this?' I asked Cully. And right away I knew I had stepped over the line.

'What the hell do you mean?' Cully said. 'That man has been like a father to me all these years. He made me. Shit, I'd trust him over anybody, even you.'

'OK,' I said. 'Then why didn't you let him know we were leaving? Why did you give him that bullshit about buying antiques in Los Angeles?'

'Because that's the way he taught me to operate,' Cully said. 'Never tell anybody anything he doesn't have to know. He'll be proud of me for that, even though he found out. I did it the right way.' Then he eased up. 'Come on,' he said. 'Get dressed. Tonight I'm going to show you the best time of your life.' For some reason that reminded me of Eli Hemsi.

Like everybody who has seen films about the Orient, I had fantasized about a night in a geisha house: beautiful talented women devoting themselves to my pleasure. When Cully told me that we were going to be entertained by geishas, I expected to be taken to one of those crazy-cornered, gaily ornamented houses I had seen in movies. So I was surprised when the chauffeured car stopped in front of a small restaurant housed in a canopied storefront on one of the main streets of Tokyo. It looked like any

342

Chinese joint in the lower part of Manhattan. But a maître d'
led us through the crowded restaurant to a door that led to a
private dining room.

The room was lavishly furnished in Japanese style. Coloured
lanterns were suspended from the ceiling; a long banquet table,
raised only a foot above the floor, was decorated with exquisitely
coloured dishes, small drinking cups, ivory chopsticks. There
were four Japanese men, all in kimonos. One of them was Mr
Fummiro. He and Cully shook hands, the other men bowed.
Cully introduced me to all of them. I had seen Fummiro
gambling in Vegas but had never met him.

Seven geisha girls came into the room, running with tiny steps.
They were beautifully dressed in heavy brocade kimonos
embroidered with startlingly coloured flowers. Their faces were
heavily made up with a white powder. They sat on cushions
around the banquet table, a girl for each man.

Following Cully's lead, I sat down on one of the cushions
around the banquet table. Serving women brought in huge
platters of fish and vegetables. Each geisha girl fed her assigned
male. They used the ivory chopsticks, picking up bits of fish,
little strands of green vegetables. They wiped our mouths and
faces with countless tiny napkins that were like washcloths. These
were scented and wet.

My geisha girl was very close to me, leaning her body against
mine, and, with a charming smile and entreating gestures, made
me eat and drink. She kept filling my cup with some sort of wine,
the famous sake, I guessed. The wine tasted great, but the food
was too fishy until they brought out platters of heavily marbled
Kobe beef, cut into cubes and drenched in a delicious sauce.

Seeing her close, I knew that my charming geisha had to be
at least forty. Though her body was pressed against mine, I
could feel nothing except the heavy brocade of her kimono; she
was swathed like an Egyptian mummy.

After dinner the girls took turns entertaining us. One played
a musical instrument that was like a flute. By this time I had
drunk so much wine that the unfamiliar music sounded like
bagpipes. Another girl recited what must have been a poem.
The men all applauded. Then my geisha got up. I was rooting
for her. She proceeded to do some astonishing somersaults.

In fact, she scared the hell out of me by somersaulting right
over my head. Then she did the same somersault over Fummiro's
head, but he caught her in midair and tried to give her a kiss or

something like a kiss. I was too drunk to see really well. But she eluded him, tapped him lightly on the cheek in reproach, and they both laughed gaily.

Then the geisha girls organized the men into playing games. I was astonished to see that it was a game involving an orange on a stick, that we had to bite the orange with our hands behind our backs. As we did so, a geisha would try the same thing from the other side of the stick. As the orange bobbed between male and female, the two faces would brush each other with a caress which made the geishas giggle.

Cully, behind me, said in a low voice, 'Jesus, the next thing we'll be playing spin the bottle.' But he smiled hugely at Fummiro, who seemed to be having a great time, shouting at the girls in Japanese and trying to grab them. There were other games involving sticks and balls and juggling acts, and I was so drunk that I was enjoying them as much as Fummiro. At one point I fell down into a pile of cushions and my geisha cradled my head in her lap and wiped my face off with a hot scented napkin.

The next thing I knew I was in the chauffeured car with Cully. We were moving through dark streets, and then the car stopped in front of a mansion in the suburbs. Cully led through the gate and the door opened magically. And then I saw we were in a real Oriental house. The room was bare except for sleeping mats. The walls were really sliding doors of thin wood.

I fell down on one of the mats. I just wanted to sleep. Cully knelt down beside me. 'We're spending the night here,' he whispered. 'I'll wake you up in the morning. Stay here, go to sleep. You'll be taken care of.' Behind him I could see Fummiro's smiling face. I registered that Fummiro was no longer drunk, and that set off some alarm bell in my mind. I tried to struggle up off the mat, but Cully pushed me down. And then I heard Fummiro's voice say, 'Your friend needs some company.' I sank back down on the mat. I was too tired. I didn't give a damn. I fell asleep.

I don't know how long I slept. I was awakened by the slight hiss of sliding doors. In the dim light of the shaded lanterns I saw two young Japanese girls in light blue and yellow kimonos come through the open wall. They carried a small redwood tub filled with steaming water. They undressed me and washed me from head to foot, kneading my body with their fingers, massaging every muscle. While they were doing this, I got an erection

344

and they giggled and one of them gave it a little pat. Then they picked up the redwood tub and disappeared.

I was awake enough to wonder where the hell Cully was but not sober enough to get up and look for him. It was just as well. The wall fell apart as the doors slid back again. This time there was a single girl, a new one, and just by looking at her, I could tell what her function would be.

She was dressed in a long flowing green kimono that hid her body. But her face was beautiful and highlighted exotically with make-up. Her rich jet black hair was piled high on her head and was topped with a brilliant comb that seemed made out of precious stones. She came to me, and before she knelt, I could see that her feet were bare, small and beautifully formed. The toenails were painted dark red.

The lights seemed to become dimmer, and suddenly she was naked. Her body was a pure milky white, the breasts small but full. The nipples were startlingly light pink, as if they had been roughed. She bent over, took the comb out of her hair and shook her head. Long black tresses poured down endlessly over my body, covering it, and then she started kissing and licking my body, her head giving little determined shakes, the silky thick black hair whipping over my thighs. I lay back. Her mouth was warm, her tongue rough. When I tried to move, she pressed me back. When she was finished, she lay down beside me and put my head against her breast. At some time during the night I woke up and made love to her. She locked her legs behind mine and thrust fiercely as if it were a battle between our two sexual organs. It was a fierce fuck, and when we climaxed, she gave a thin scream and we fell off the mat. Then we fell asleep in each other's arms.

The wall sliding back woke me up again. The room was filled with early-morning light. The girl was gone. But through the open wall, in the adjoining room, I saw Cully sitting on the huge brassbound suitcase. Though he was far away, I could see him smiling. 'OK, Merlyn, rise and shine,' he said. 'We're flying to Hong Kong this morning.'

The suitcase was so heavy that I had to carry it out to the car, Cully couldn't manage it. There was no chauffeur, Cully drove. When we got to the airport, he just left the car parked outside the terminal. I carried the suitcase inside, Cully walking ahead to clear a path and lead me to the baggage check-in desk. I was still groggy, and the huge case kept hitting me in the shins. At the check-in the stub was put on my ticket. I figured it didn't make any difference, so I didn't say anything when Cully didn't notice.

We walked through the gate onto the field to the plane. But we didn't board. Cully waited until a loaded baggage truck came around the terminal building. We could see our huge brassbound case sitting on top. We watched while the labourers loaded it into the belly of the plane. Then we boarded.

It was over four hours' ride to Hong Kong. Cully was nervous and I beat him for another four thousand in gin. While we were playing, I asked him some questions.

'You told me we were leaving tomorrow,' I said.

'Yeah, that's what I thought,' Cully said. 'But Fummiro got the money ready sooner than I figured.'

I knew he was full of shit. 'I loved that geisha party,' I said.

Cully grunted. He pretended to study his cards, but I knew his mind wasn't on the game. 'Fucking high school cunt teasing party,' he said. 'That geisha stuff is bullshit, I'll take Vegas.'

'I don't know,' I said. 'I thought it was charming. But I have to admit that little treat I got afterward was better.'

Cully forgot about his cards. 'What treat?' he said.

I told him about the girls in the mansion. Cully grinned. 'That was Fummiro. You lucky son of a bitch. And I was out running around all night.' He paused for a moment. 'So you finally broke. I'll bet that's the first time you've been unfaithful to that broad you got in LA.'

'Yeah,' I said. 'But what the hell, anything over three thousand miles away doesn't count.'

When we landed in Hong Kong, Cully said, 'You go on to the baggage area and wait for the case. I'll stick by the plane until they unload. Then I'll follow the luggage truck. That way no sneak thief can pinch it.'

I walked quickly through the terminal to the baggage carousel. The terminal was thronged, but the faces were different from those in Japan though still mostly Oriental. The carousel started to turn and I watched intently for the brassbound case to come down the chute. After ten minutes I wondered why Cully had not appeared. I glanced around, thankful that none of the people were wearing gauze masks; those things had spooked me. But I didn't see anybody who looked dangerous.

Then the brassbound suitcase shot out of the chute. I grabbed it as it went by. It was still heavy. I checked it to make sure it had not been knifed open. As I did so, I noticed a tiny square name tag attached to the handle. It bore the legend 'John Merlyn', and under the name my home address and passport number. I finally knew why Cully asked me to come to Japan. If anybody went to jail, it would be me.

I sat on the case and about three minutes later Cully appeared. He beamed with satisfaction when he saw me. 'Great,' he said. 'I have a cab waiting. Let's get to the bank.' And this time he picked up the case and without any trouble carried it out of the terminal.

The cab went down winding side streets thronged with people. I didn't say anything. I owed Cully a big favour and now I'd evened him out. I felt hurt that he had deceived me and exposed me to such risk, but Gronevelt would have been proud of him. And out of the same tradition I decided not to tell Cully what I knew. He must have anticipated I would find out. He'd have a story ready.

The cab stopped in front of a ramshackle building on a main street. The window had gold lettering which read 'Futaba International Bank'. On both sides of the door were two uniformed men with submachine guns.

'Tough town, this Hong Kong,' Cully said, nodding at the guards. He carried the case into the bank himself.

Inside, Cully went down the hall and knocked on a door, and then we went in. A small Eurasian with a beard beamed at Cully and shook his hand. Cully introduced me, but the name was a strange combination of syllables. Then the Eurasian led us farther down the hall into a huge room with a long conference table. Cully threw the case on the table and unlocked it. I have to admit the sight was impressive. It was filled with crisp Japanese currency, black print on grey-blue paper.

The Eurasian picked up a phone and barked out some orders in, I guess, Chinese. A few minutes later the room was filled with bank clerks. Fifteen of them, all in those black shiny suits. They pounced on the suitcase. It took all of them over three hours to count and tabulate the money, recount it and check it again. Then the Eurasian took us back into his office and made out a sheaf of papers, which he signed, stamped with official seals and then handed over to Cully. Cully looked the papers over and put them in his pocket. The packet of documents was the 'little' receipt.

347

Finally we were standing in the sunlit street outside the bank. Cully was tremendously excited. 'We've done it,' he said. 'We're home free.'

I shook my head. 'How could you take such a risk?' I said. 'It's a crazy way to handle so much money.'

Cully smiled at me. 'What the hell kind of business do you think it is running a Vegas casino? It's all risk. I've got a risky job. And on this I had a big percentage going with me.'

When we got into a cab, Cully instructed the driver to take us to the airport. 'Jesus,' I said, 'we go halfway across the world and I don't even get to eat a meal in Hong Kong?'

'Let's not press our luck,' Cully said. 'Somebody may think we still have the money. Let's just get the hell home.'

On the long plane ride back to the States, Cully got very lucky and won back seven of the ten grand he owed me. He would have won it all back if I hadn't quit. 'Come on,' he said. 'Give me a chance to get even. Be fair.'

I looked at him straight in the eye. 'No,' I said, 'I want to outsmart you just once on this trip.'

That shook him up a little and he let me sleep the rest of the way back to Los Angeles. I kept him company while he was waiting for his flight to Vegas. While I was sleeping, he had been thinking things over and he must have figured I saw the name plate on the case.

'Listen,' he said. 'You have to believe me. If you had gotten into trouble on this trip, me and Gronevelt and Fummiro would have gotten you out. But I appreciate what you did. I couldn't have made the trip without you, I didn't have the nerve.'

I laughed. 'You owe me three grand from the gin,' I said. 'Just put it in the Xanadu cage and I'll use it for a baccarat stake.'

'Sure thing,' Cully said. 'Listen,' he said. 'Is that the only way you can cheat on your broads and feel safe, with three thousand miles between them? The world isn't big enough to cheat more than two more times.'

We both laughed and shook hands before he got on the plane. He was still my buddy, old Countdown Cully, I just couldn't trust him all the way. I had always known what he was and accepted his friendship. How could I be angry when he was true to his character?

I walked through the LA terminal of Western Airlines and

stopped by the phones. I had to call Janelle and tell her I was in town. I wondered if I should tell her I had been in Japan, but I decided not to. I would act in the Gronevelt tradition. And then I remembered something else. I didn't have any presents from the Orient for Valerie and the kids.

36

IN a way it's interesting being crazy about somebody who's no longer crazy about you. You go sort of blind and deaf. Or choose to. It was nearly a year before I heard the almost inaudible tick of Janelle dealing seconds, and yet I had had plenty of warnings, plenty of hints.

On one of my trips back to Angeles my plane got in a half hour early. Janelle always met me, but she wasn't there and I walked through the terminal and waited outside. In the back of my head, way back, I was thinking I would catch her at something. I didn't know what. Maybe a guy she had picked up for a drink while waiting for the plane. Maybe dropping off another boyfriend catching a plane out of Los Angeles, anything. I was not your trusting lover.

And I did catch her, but not in the way I thought. I saw her come out of the parking lot and cross the wide double streets to the terminal. She was walking very slowly, very reluctantly. She wore a long grey skirt and a white blouse, and her long blond hair was pinned up around her head. At that moment I had almost a sense of pity for her. She looked so reluctant, as if she were a child going to a party her parents had made her go to. On the other side of the continent I had been an hour early for my plane. I had rushed through the terminal to meet her. I was dying to see her, but she, obviously, was not dying to see me. As I was thinking this, she lifted her head and saw me and her

349

face became radiant and then she was hugging and kissing me and I forgot what I had seen.

During this visit she was rehearsing during the day for a play that was to open in a few weeks. Since I was working at the studio during the day, this was fine. We saw each other at night. She would call me at the studio to tell me what time she would be through rehearsing. When I asked her for a number where I could call her, she told me there was no phone in the theatre.

Then one evening, when her rehearsal ran late, I went to the theatre to pick her up. As we were about to leave, a girl came out of the backstage office and said to her, 'Janelle, Mr Evarts is calling you,' and she led the way to the phone.

I waited in the corridor. I knew Evarts was the guy who had written the play. I knew also that she had deliberately not given me the theatre number for some reason, and I realized what that reason must be. She didn't want Evarts to know about us.

When Janelle came out of the office, her face was rosy and flushed with pleasure, but then she took one look at me and said, 'That's the first time he called. I didn't even know they could get me on the phone in the theatre.'

I heard that tick of the second card being dealt. I still had so much pleasure with her company, with her body, in just looking at her face. I still loved the expression that went across her eyes and mouth. I loved her eyes. They could get such a hurt look and yet be so gay. I thought her mouth the most beautiful in the world. Hell, I was really still a kid. It didn't matter that I knew she was lying like hell with that beautiful mouth. But I knew she hated deceiving me. She really hated to lie and did it badly. In a funny kind of way she told you she was lying. Even that was a fake-out.

And it didn't matter. It didn't matter. I suffered, sure, but it was still a good bargain. Yet as time went on, I enjoyed her less and she made me suffer more.

I was sure she and Alice were lovers. One week, when Alice was out of town on a movie production job, I went to Janelle's and Alice's apartment to spend the night. Alice called Janelle long distance to chat with her. Janelle was very short with her, almost angry. A half hour later, when we were making love, the phone rang again. Janelle reached over, took the phone off the hook and threw the receiver under the bed.

One of the things I liked about her was that she hated to be interrupted while making love. Sometimes, at the hotel, she wouldn't let me answer the phone or even answer the door if a waiter was bringing in food or drinks when we were on our way to bed.

A week later in my hotel on a Sunday morning I called Janelle at her apartment. I knew she usually slept late, so I didn't call until eleven o'clock. I got a busy signal. I waited a half hour and called again. I got a busy signal. Then I called every ten minutes for an hour and kept getting a busy signal, and suddenly I got a flash of Janelle and Alice in bed, the phone off its hook. When I finally did get through, it was Alice who answered the phone, her voice soft and happy. I was sure they were lovers.

Another day we were planning a trip to Santa Barbara when she got a rush call to go to a producer's office to read for a part. She said it would take only one-half hour, so I went to the studio with her. The producer was an old friend of hers, and when he came into the office, he made a tender, affectionate gesture, brushing his fingers along her face, and she smiled at him. I read the gesture immediately. It was the tenderness of a former lover, now a dear friend.

When we were on our way to Santa Barbara, I asked Janelle if she had ever been to bed with the producer. She turned to me and said, 'Yes.' And I didn't ask her any more questions.

One night we had a date for dinner and I went to her apartment. She was getting dressed. Alice opened the door for me. I always liked her and in a funny kind of way I didn't mind that she was Janelle's lover. I still wasn't really sure. Alice always kissed me on the lips, a very sweet kiss, she always seemed to enjoy my company. We got along fine. But you could sense the lack of femininity in her. She was very thin, wore tight shirts that showed that she had surprisingly full breasts but was very businesslike. She gave me a drink and put on an Edith Piaf record and we waited until Janelle came out of the bathroom.

Janelle kissed me and said, 'Merlyn, I'm sorry, I tried to call you at the hotel. I have to rehearse tonight. The director's going to come by and pick me up.'

I was stunned. Again I heard the tick of the second card. She was smiling at me radiantly, but there was a little quiver to her mouth which made me think she was lying. She was searching my face intently with her eyes. She wanted me to believe her and she saw that I didn't. She said, 'He's coming here to pick me up. I'll try and get through by eleven.'

'That's OK,' I said. Over her shoulder I could see Alice

looking down in her glass, not watching us, pointedly trying not to hear what we were saying.

So I waited around, and sure enough, the director came up. He was a young guy but already almost bald, and he was very businesslike and efficient. He didn't have time for a drink. He said patiently to Janelle, 'We're rehearsing at my place. I want you absolutely perfect for this dress rehearsal tomorrow. Evarts and I have changed some lines and some business.'

He turned to me. 'I'm sorry I spoiled your evening, but that's show business.' He parodied the cliché.

He seemed like a nice guy. I gave him and Janelle a cold smile. 'It's OK,' I said. 'Take as long as you like.'

At this Janelle became a little panicky. She said to the director, 'Do you think we can get through by ten?'

And the director said, 'If we really work hard, maybe.'

Janelle said, 'Why don't you wait here with Alice and I'll get back by ten and we can still go to dinner? Is that all right?'

I said, 'Sure.'

So I waited with Alice after they left and we talked to each other. She said she had redecorated the apartment and she took me by the hand and led me through the rooms. It was really charming. The kitchen was fixed up with special shutters, the cupboards were decorated with some sort of inlaid patterns. Copper pots and pans were hanging on the ceiling.

'It's lovely,' I said. 'I can't imagine Janelle doing all this.'

Alice laughed. 'No,' she said. 'I'm the homebody.'

Then she led me through the three bedrooms. One was obviously a child's bedroom.

'That's for Janelle's son when he comes to visit us.'

Then she led me to the master bedroom, which had a huge bed. She had really changed it. It was utterly feminine with dolls against the walls, big pillows on a sofa and a television at the foot of the bed.

And then I said, 'Whose bedroom is this?'

Alice said, 'Mine.'

We went to the third bedroom, which was a shambles. It was obviously used as a small storeroom for the apartment. All kinds of odds and ends of furniture scattered all over the room. The bed was small with a quilt on it.

'And whose bedroom is this?' I said almost mockingly, a hairy Goldilocks.

'Janelle's,' Alice said. As she said this, she let go of my hand and turned her head away.

352

I knew she was lying and that she and Janelle shared the huge bedroom. We went back into the sitting room and we waited.

At ten thirty the phone rang. It was Janelle. 'Oh, God!' she said. Her voice was as dramatic as if she had a fatal illness. 'We're not finished. We won't be finished for another hour. Do you want to wait?'

I laughed. 'Sure,' I said. 'I'll wait.'

'I'll call you again,' Janelle said. 'As soon as I know we're through. Is that OK?'

'Sure,' I said.

I waited with Alice until twelve o'clock. She wanted to make me something to eat, but I wasn't hungry. By this time I was enjoying myself. There is nothing so funny as to be made an utter fool of.

At midnight the phone rang again and I knew what she would say and she said it. They weren't through yet. They didn't know what time they would be through.

I was very cheerful with her. I knew that she would be tired. That I wouldn't see her that night and I would call her the next day from home.

'Darling, you're sweet, you're so sweet. I'm really sorry,' Janelle said. 'Call me tomorrow afternoon.'

I said good-night to Alice and she kissed me at the door and it was a sisterly kiss and she said, 'You're going to call Janelle tomorrow, aren't you?'

I said, 'Sure. I'll call her from home.'

The next morning I caught the early plane to New York, and at the terminal in Kennedy Airport I called Janelle. She was delighted to hear from me. 'I was afraid you wouldn't call.'

I said, 'I promised I'd call.'

She said, 'We worked until three this morning and the dress rehearsal isn't until nine o'clock tonight. I could come over to the hotel for a couple of hours if want to see me.'

I said, 'Sure I want to see you. But I'm in New York. I told you I'd call you from home.'

There was a long pause on the other side of the phone.

'I see,' she said.

'OK,' I said. 'I'll call you when I'm coming to Los Angeles again. OK?'

There was another long pause on the phone and she said, 'You've been incredibly good for me, but I can't let you hurt me any more.'

And then she hung up the phone.

But on my next trip to California we made up and started all over again. She wanted to be completely honest with me; there were to be no more misunderstandings. She swore she hadn't been to bed with Evarts and the director. That she was always completely honest with me. That she would never lie to me again. And to prove it, she told me about Alice and her. It was an interesting story, but it didn't prove anything, not to me anyway. Still, it was nice to know the truth for sure.

37

JANELLE lived with Alice De Santis for two months before she realized that Alice was in love with her. It took that long because during the day they both worked so hard, Janelle constantly hustling around to interviews arranged by her agent, Alice working long hours as costume designer on a big-budget film.

They had separate bedrooms. But late at night Alice sometimes came into Janelle's room and sat on her bed to gossip. Alice would prepare something to eat and a hot chocolate drink to help them sleep. Usually they talked about their work. Janelle told stories about the subtle and not so subtle passes made at her through the day and Alice never pointed out that Janelle encouraged these passes with her Southern belle charm.

Alice was a striking-looking, tall woman, very businesslike and hard to the outside world. But she was very soft and gentle with Janelle. She would give Janelle a sisterly kiss before they went to bed in their separate rooms. Janelle admired her for her intelligence, her competent efficiency in her field of costume design.

Alice finished work on her picture at the same time that Janelle's son, Richard, came up to spend part of his summer vacation with Janelle. Usually, when her son came to visit,

Janelle would devote all her time to taking him around Los Angeles, to shows, to a skating rink, to Disneyland. Sometimes she would rent a small apartment on the beach for a week. She always enjoyed her son's visit and was always happy for the month he was with her. This one summer, as luck would have it, she got a small part in a TV series which would keep her busy most of the time but would also pay her living for a year. She started to write a long letter to her ex-husband to explain why Richard could not visit her this summer, and then she put her head down on the table and began to weep. It seemed to her as if now she were truly giving up her child.

It was Alice who saved her. She told Janelle to let Richard come. Alice would take him around. She would bring him to visit Janelle on the set to watch her work and whisk him away before he got on the director's nerves. Alice would take care of him during the day. Then Janelle would be his buddy at night. Janelle felt enormously grateful to Alice.

And when Richard came for his month, the three of them had a great time together. After work Janelle would come back to the apartment and Alice would have a hot dinner waiting and Richard all scrubbed up for a night on the town. They would all three go to the movies and then have a late snack. It was so comfortable and easy. Janelle realized that she and her former husband had never had such a good time with Richard as she and Alice and Richard were having. It was almost a perfect marriage. Alice never quarrelled or reproached her. Richard never got sulky or disobedient. He lived in what perhaps was a dream of children. A life with two adoring mothers and no father. He loved Alice because she spoiled him in some things and was strict with him only rarely. She took him for tennis lessons during the day and they played together. She taught him scrabble and how to dance. Alice, in fact, was the perfect father. She was athletic and coordinated, yet with none of a father's harshness, nothing of male domination. Richard responded extremely well to her. He had never been so loving. He helped Alice serve Janelle her dinner after work and then watched both women pretty themselves up to go out on the town with him. He loved dressing up too in white slacks and dark blue coat and white frilly shirt and no tie. He loved California.

When the day came for him to go home, Alice and Janelle both brought him to the midnight plane, and then, finally alone again, Janelle and Alice held hands, breathing the sigh of relief a married couple might breathe on the departure of a houseguest. Janelle felt so enormously touched that she gave Alice a tight hug and kiss. Alice turned her head to receive the kiss on her soft, delicately thin mouth. For the fraction of a second she held Janelle's mouth on hers.

Back in the apartment they had their cocoa together as if nothing had happened. They went to their bedrooms. But Janelle was restless. She knocked on Alice's bedroom door and went in. She was surprised to find Alice undressed in her lingerie. Though thin, Alice had a full bosom restrained by a very tight bra. They had, of course, seen each other in various stages of undress. But now Alice took off her bra to let her breasts free and then looked at Janelle with a slight smile.

At the sight of the nippled breasts Janelle felt a surge of sexual lust. She could feel herself blushing. It had not occurred to her that she could be attracted to another woman. Especially after Mrs Wartberg. So when Alice slid under the covers, Janelle sat casually on the edge of her bed, and they talked about the good time they had had with Richard, just the three of them. Suddenly Alice burst into tears.

Janelle patted her dark hair and said, 'Alice, what is it?' in a very concerned voice. Yet at the moment both knew they were acting a play that would enable them to do what they both wanted to do.

Alice said, sobbing, 'I don't have anyone to love. I don't have anyone to love me.'

There was just one moment when Janelle someplace in her mind kept an ironic distance. This was a scene she had played with male lovers. But her warm gratitude to Alice for the past month, the moment of lust that had been sparked by her heavy breasts were far more promising than the rewards of irony. And she too loved to play scenes. She pulled the covers down from Alice and touched her breasts and curiously watched the nipples rise. Then she bent her golden head and covered a nipple with her mouth. The effect on her was extraordinary.

She felt an enormous liquid peace flow through her body as she sucked on the nipple of Alice's breast. She felt almost like a child. The breast was so warm, it tasted so richly sweet to her mouth. She slipped her body next to Alice now, but she refused to give up the nipple, though Alice's hands began a steadily increasing pressure on her neck to force her down lower. Finally Alice let her stay on the breast. Janelle was murmuring as she sucked, the murmurs of an erotic child, and Alice caressed the golden head, only stopping for a moment to put out the light beside her bed so that they could be in darkness. Finally, a long time later, with a soft sigh of satisfied pleasure Janelle stopped sucking on Alice's breast and let her head fall between the other woman's legs. A long time later she fell into an exhausted sleep. When she woke up, she found that she had been undressed and was now naked in the bed beside Alice. They were sleeping in each other's arms with complete trust, like two innocent infants, and with the same peace.

So started what was to Janelle the most satisfying sexual partnership she had experienced up to then. Not that she was in love, she was not. Alice was in love with her. That was partly the reason it was so satisfying. Also, quite simply she loved sucking a full breast, it was a blazing new discovery. And she was completely uninhibited with Alice, and her complete lord and master. Which was great. She didn't have to play her Southern belle role.

The curious part of the relationship was that Janelle, sweet and soft and feminine, was the butch, the sexual aggressor. Alice, who looked a little dykey in a very sweet way, was really the woman of the pair. It was Alice who turned their bedroom (they now shared the same bed) into a frilly woman's chamber with dolls hanging on walls, specially made shutters on the windows and all other kinds of knick-knacks. Janelle's bedroom, which they kept up for the sake of appearance, was untidy and messy as a child's.

Part of the thrill of the relationship for Janelle was that she could act the role of a man. Not only sexually but in everyday life, the small details of routine day-to-day living. Around the house she was sloppy in a masculine way. A slob, in fact, while Alice always took care to look attractive to Janelle. Janelle would even do the lustful groping of the male, grabbing Alice by the crotch as she went by in the kitchen, squeezing her breasts. Janelle loved acting the role of the man. She would force Alice to make love. At those times she felt more lust than she could ever feel with a man. Then, although they still both had dates with men, inevitable in their professions where social and business obligations intermingled, it was only Janelle who still enjoyed spending an evening with a male. It was only Janelle who still occasionally stayed out all night. To come back the next morning to find Alice literally sick with jealousy. In fact, so ill that Janelle became frightened and considered moving out. Alice never stayed away all night. And when she was out late, Janelle never worried about whether she was shacking up with a guy. She didn't care. To her mind one thing had nothing to do with another.

But gradually it came to be understood that Janelle was a free agent. That she could do what she pleased. That she was not accountable. Partly because Janelle was so beautiful that it was difficult to avoid attentions and phone calls from all the men she came into contact with: actors, assistant directors, agents, producers, directors. But gradually, during the year they were living together, Janelle lost interest in having sex with men. It became unsatisfying. Not so much physically but because the power relationship was different. She could sense, or imagined she sensed, how they felt they had something on her after they had gotten her to bed. They became too sure of themselves, too sleek with satisfaction. They expected too many attentions. Attentions she did not feel like giving. Also, she found in Alice something she had never felt in any man. An absolute trust. She never felt that Alice gossiped about her or held her cheap. Or that Alice would betray her with another woman or man. Or that Alice would cheat her out of material possessions or break a promise. Many of the men she met were lavish with promises that they never kept. She was truly happy with Alice, who took care to keep her happy in every way.

One day Alice said, 'You know, we could have Richard live with us permanently.'

'Oh, God, I wish I could,' Janelle said. 'We just haven't got the time to take care of him.'

'Sure we do,' Alice said. 'Look, we rarely work at the same time. He'll be in school. On vacations he can go to camp. If there's a pinch, we can hire a woman. I think you'd be much happier if you had Richard with you.'

Janelle was tempted. She realized that their ménage would become more permanent with Richard living with them. But that didn't seem a bad idea. She was getting enough movie work now to live well. They could even get a larger apartment and really fix it up. 'OK,' she said. 'I'll write Richard and see how he feels about it.'

She never did. She knew her ex-husband would reject her. And also she did not want Alice to become too important to her.

38

WHEN I knew for sure that Janelle went both ways, that Alice was also her lover, I was relieved. What the hell. Two women making love together was like two women knitting together. I told that to Janelle to make her angry. Then too, her arrangement was a bailout for me. I was in the position of a guy with a married mistress whose husband was understanding and female, a great combination.

But nothing is simple. Gradually I came to realize that Janelle loved Alice at least as much as she did me. What was worse, I came to realize that Alice loved Janelle better than I did; in a way that was less selfish and much less damaging to Janelle. Because I knew by this time that I wasn't doing Janelle much good emotionally. Never mind that it was a hopeless trap. That no guy would ever solve her problems. But I was using her as an instrument of my pleasure. OK again. But I expected her to accept a strictly subordinate place in my life. After all, I had my wife and kids and my writing. Yet I expected her to place me in a primary position.

Everything is a bargain to some degree. And I was getting a better bargain than she was. It was that simple.

But here's where the gravy came in, having a bisexual girlfriend. Janelle became sick on one of my visits. She had to go to the hospital to get a cyst removed from her ovary. What with that and some complications she was in the hospital for ten days. Sure, I sent flowers, tons and tons of flowers, the usual bullshit that women love and so let men get away with murder. Sure, I went to see her every night for about an hour. But Alice ran all her errands, stayed with her all day. Sometimes Alice was there when I came, and she always left the room a little while so Janelle and I could be alone. Maybe she knew that Janelle would want me to hold her bare breasts when I was talking to her. Not sexy but because that was comforting to her. Jesus, how much of sex is just comforting, like a hot bath, a great dinner, good wine. And if only you could come at sex just that way without love and other complications.

Anyway, just this one time Alice stayed in the room with us. I was always struck by how sweet a face Alice had. In fact, the two women looked like sisters, two very sweet-looking women, soft and feminine. Alice had a small, almost thin mouth, which rarely looked generous, but hers did. I liked her enormously. And why the hell shouldn't I? She was doing all the dirty work I should have been doing. But I was a busy guy. I was married. I had to leave for New York the next day. Maybe if Alice weren't there, I would have done all the things she had done, but I don't think so.

I had sneaked in a bottle of champagne to celebrate our last night together. But I didn't mind sharing it with Alice. Janelle had three glasses stashed. Alice opened the bottle. She was very capable.

Janelle had on a pretty frilled lace nightgown, and as always, she looked somehow dramatic lying there on the bed. I knew that she had deliberately not used make-up for my visit so as to look the part. Wan, pale, another Camille. Except that she really was in great shape and bursting with vitality. Her eyes were dancing with pleasure as she sipped the champagne. She had trapped in this room the two people she loved best. They were not allowed to be mean to her in any way, or hurt her feelings in any way, not even stop her from being mean to them. And maybe it was this that made her reach out and take my hand in hers as Alice sat there watching.

Ever since I had known about them, I had been careful not to act like a lover in front of Alice. And Alice never betrayed her sexual relationship with Janelle. Watching them, you would swear that they were two sisters or two comrades. They were absolutely casual with one another. Their relationship was indicated only by Janelle, who sometimes bossed Alice around like a domineering husband.

Now Alice moved her chair back so that it tilted her against the far wall, away from Janelle's bed, away from us. As if she were giving us the official status of lovers. For some reason this gesture of hers affected me painfully, it was so generous.

I guess I envied them both. They were so comfortable with each other that they could afford to indulge me, my privileged position as an official lover. Janelle played with the fingers on my hand. And now I realized it was not perversity on her part but a genuine desire to make me happy, so I smiled at her. In the next hour we would finish the champagne and I would leave and catch my plane to New York and they would be alone and Janelle would make it up to Alice. And Alice knew that. As she knew that Janelle must have this moment with me. I resisted the impulse to pull my hand away. That would be ungenerous, and the male mystique has it that men are basically more generous than women. But I knew that my generosity was forced. I couldn't wait to leave.

Finally I could kiss Janelle good-bye. I promised to call her the next day. We hugged each other as Alice discreetly left the room. But Alice was waiting outside for me and kept me company down to the car. She gave me another of her soft kisses on the mouth.

'Don't worry,' she said. 'I'll spend the night with her.' Janelle had told me that after her operation Alice spent the whole night curled up on the armchair in her room, so I was not surprised.

I just said, 'Take care of yourself, thanks,' and got into my car and drove to the airport.

It was dark before the plane started its journey east. I could never sleep on a plane.

And so I could think of Alice and Janelle comfortable with each other in the hospital bedroom, and I was glad Janelle was not alone. And I was glad that early in the dawn I would be having breakfast with my family.

39

ONE of the things I never admitted to Janelle was that my jealousy was not merely romantic, but pragmatic. I searched the literature of romantic novels, but in no novel could I find the admission that one of the reasons a married man wants his mistress to be faithful is that he fears catching the clap or worse and then transmitting it to his wife. I guess one of the reasons this couldn't be admitted to the mistress at least is that the married man usually lied and said he was no longer sleeping with his wife. And since he was already lying to his wife and since if he did infect her, if he was human at all, he'd have to tell both. He was caught in the double horn of guilt.

So one night I told Janelle about that and she looked at me grimly and said, 'How about if you caught it from your wife and gave it to me? Or don't you think that's possible?'

We were playing our usual game of fighting but not really fighting, really a duel of wits in which humour and truth were allowed and even some cruelty but no brutality.

'Sure,' I said. 'But the odds are less. My wife is a pretty strict Catholic. She's virtuous.' I held up my hand to stop Janelle's protest. 'And she's older and not as beautiful as you are and has less opportunity.'

Janelle relaxed a bit. Any compliment to her beauty could soften her up.

Then I said, grinning a little, 'But you're right. If my wife gave it to me and I gave it to you, I wouldn't feel guilty. That would be OK. That would be a kind of justice since you and I are both criminals together.'

Janelle couldn't resist any longer. She was almost jumping up and down. 'I can't believe you said something like that. I just can't believe it. I may be a criminal,' she said, 'but you're just a coward.'

Another night in the early-morning hours, when as usual we couldn't sleep because we were so excited by each other after we had made love a couple of times and drunk a bottle of wine, she was finally so persistent that I told her about when I was a kid in the asylum.

As a child I used books as magic. In the dormitory late at night, separate and alone, a greater loneliness than I have ever felt since, I could spirit myself away and escape by reading and then weave my own fantasies. The books I loved best at that early age of ten, eleven or twelve were the romantic legends of Roland, Charlemagne, the American West, but especially of King Arthur and his Round Table and his brave knights Lancelot and Galahad. But most of all, I loved Merlin because I thought myself like him. And then I would weave my fantasies, my brother, Artie, was King Arthur and that was right too, and that was because Artie had all the nobility and fairness of King Arthur, the honesty and true purpose, the forgiving lovingness which I did not have. As a child I fantasized myself as cunning and far-seeing and was firmly convinced that I would rule my own life by some sort of magic. And so I came to love King Arthur's magician, Merlin, who had lived through the past, could foresee the future, who was immortal and all-wise.

It was then I developed the trick of actually transferring myself from the present into the future. I used it all my life. As a child in the asylum I would make myself into a young man with clever bookish friends. I could make myself live in a luxurious apartment and on the sofa of that apartment make love to a passionate, beautiful woman.

During the war on tedious guard or patrol duty I would project myself into the future when I would be on leave to Paris, eating great food and bedding down with luscious whores. Under shellfire I could magically disappear and find myself resting in the woods by a gentle brook, reading a favourite book.

It worked, it really worked. I magically disappeared. And I would remember in later actual time, when I was really doing those great things, I remembered these terrible times and it would seem as if I had escaped them altogether, that I had never suffered. That they were only dreams.

I remember my shock and astonishment when Merlin tells King Arthur to rule without his help because he, Merlin, will be imprisoned in a cave by a young enchantress to whom he has taught all his secrets. Like King Arthur, I asked why. Why would Merlin teach a young girl all his magic simply so he could become her prisoner and why was he so cheerful about sleeping in a cave for a thousand years, knowing the tragic ending of his king? I couldn't understand it. And yet, as I gew older, I felt that I too might do the same thing. Every great hero, I had learned, must have a weakness, and that would be mine.

I had read many different versions of the King Arthur legend, and in one I had seen a picture of Merlin as a man with a long grey beard wearing a conical duncelike cap spangled with stars and signs of the zodiac. In the shop class of the asylum school I made myself such a hat and wore it around the grounds. I loved that hat. Until one day one of the boys stole it and I never saw it again and I never made another one. I had used that hat to spin magic spells around myself, of the hero that I would become; the adventures I would have, the good deeds I would perform and the happiness I would find. But the hat really wasn't necessary. The fantasies wove themselves anyway. My life in that asylum seems a dream. I never was there. I was really Merlin as a child of ten. I was a magician, and nothing could ever harm me.

Janelle was looking at me with a little smile. 'You really think you're Merlin, don't you?' she said.

'A little bit,' I said.

She smiled again and didn't say anything. We drank a little wine, and then she said suddenly, 'You know, sometimes I'm a little kinky and I'm afraid, really, to be that way with you. Do you know what's a lot of fun? One of us ties the other up and then makes love to whoever is tied up. How about it? Let me tie you up and then I'll make love to you and you'll be helpless. It's really a great kick.'

I was surprised because we had tried to be kinky before and failed. One thing I knew: Nobody would ever tie me up. So I told her, 'OK, I'll tie you up, but you're not tying me up.'

'That's not fair,' Janelle said. 'That's not fair play.'

'I don't give a shit,' I said. 'Nobody's tying me up. How do I know when you have me tied up you won't light matches under my feet or stick a pin in my eye? You'll be sorry afterward, but that won't help me.'

'No, you dope. It would be a symbolic bond. I'll just get a

364

scarf and tie you up. You can break loose anytime you want. It can be like a thread. You're a writer, you know what "symbolic" means.'

'No,' I said.

She leaned back on the bed, smiling at me very coolly, 'And you think you're Merlin,' she said. 'You thought I'd be sympathetic about poor you in the orphanage imagining yourself as Merlin. You're the toughest son of a bitch I ever met and I just proved it to you. You'd never let any woman put you under a spell or put you in a cave or tie a scarf around your arms. You're no Merlin, Merlyn.'

I really hadn't seen that coming, but I had an answer for her, an answer I couldn't give. That a less skilful enchantress had been before her. I was married, wasn't I?

The next day I had a meeting with Doran and he told me that negotiations for the new script would take awhile. The new director, Simon Bellfort, was fighting for a bigger percentage. Doran said tentatively, 'Would you consider giving up a couple of your points to him?'

'I don't even want to work on the picture,' I told Doran. 'That guy Simon is a hack, his buddy Richetti is a fucking born thief. At least Kellino is a great actor to excuse his being an asshole. And that fucking prick Wagon is the prize creep of them all. Just get me off the picture.'

Doran said smoothly, 'Your percentage of the picture depends on your getting screenplay credit. That's in the contract. If you let those guys go on without you, they'll work it so you won't get the credit. You'll have to go to arbitration before the Writers Guild. The studio proposes the credits, and if they don't give you partial credit, you gotta fight it.'

'Let them try,' I said. 'They can't change it that much.'

Doran said soothingly, 'I have an idea. Eddie Lancer is a good friend of yours. I'll ask to have him assigned to work with you on the script. He's a savvy guy and he can run interference for you against all those other characters. OK? Trust me this once.'

'OK,' I said. I was tired of the whole business.

Before he left, Doran said, 'Why are you pissed off at those guys?'

'Because not one of them gave a shit about Malomar,' I said. 'They're glad he's dead.' But it wasn't really true. I hated them because they tried to tell me what to write.

365

I got back to New York in time to see the Academy Awards presented on television. Valerie and I always watched them every year. And this year I was watching particularly because Janelle had a short, a half hour film, she had made with her friends that had been nominated.

My wife brought out coffee and cookies, and we settled down to watching. She smiled at me and said, 'Do you think someday you'll be there picking up an Oscar?'

'No,' I said. 'My picture will be lousy.'

As usual, in the Oscar presentations they got all the small stuff out of the way first, and sure enough, Janelle's film won the prize as the Best Short Subject and there was her face on the screen. Her face was rosy and pink with happiness and she was sensible enough to make it short and she was guilty enough to make it gracious. She just simply said, 'I want to thank the women who made this picture with me, especially Alice De Santis.'

And it brought me back to the day when I knew that Alice loved Janelle more than I ever could.

Janelle had rented a beach house in Malibu for a month, and on weekends I would leave my hotel and spend my Saturday and Sunday with her at the house. Friday night we walked on the beach, and then we sat on the porch, the tiny porch under the Malibu moon and watched the tiny birds, Janelle told me they were sandpipers. They scampered out of the reach of the water whenever the waves came up.

We made love in the bedroom overlooking the Pacific Ocean. The next day, Saturday, when we were having lunch instead of breakfast, Alice came out to the house. She had breakfast with us, and then she took a rectangular tiny piece of film out of her purse and gave it to Janelle. The piece of film was no more than an inch wide and two inches long.

Janelle asked, 'What's this?'

'It's the director's credit on the film,' Alice said. 'I cut it out.'

'Why did you do that?' Janelle said.

'Because I thought it would make you happy,' Alice said.

I was watching both of them. I had seen the film. It had been a lovely little piece of work. Janelle and Alice had made it with three other women as a feminist venture. Janelle had screen credit as star. Alice had a credit as director, and the other two women had credits appropriate to the work they had done on the film.

'We need a director's credit. We just can't have a picture without a director's credit,' Janelle said.

366

Just for the hell of it I put my two cents in. 'I thought Alice directed the film,' I said.

Janelle looked at me angrily. 'She was in charge of directing,' she said. 'But I made a lot of the director suggestions and I felt I should get some credit for that.'

'Jesus,' I said. 'You're the star of the film. Alice has to get some credit for the work she did.'

'Of course she does,' Janelle said indignantly. 'I told her that. I didn't tell her to cut out her credit on the negative. She just did it.'

I turned to Alice and said, 'How do you really feel about it?'

Alice seemed very composed. 'Janelle did a lot of work on the directing,' she said. 'And I really don't care for the credit. Janelle can have it. I really don't care.'

I could see that Janelle was very angry. She hated being put in such a false position, but I sensed that she wasn't going to let Alice have full credit for directing the film.

'Damn you,' Janelle said to me. 'Don't look at me like that. I got the money to have this film made and I got all the people together and we all helped write the story and it couldn't have been made without me.'

'All right,' I said. 'Then take credit as the producer. Why is the director's credit so important?'

Then Alice spoke up. 'We're going to be showing this film in competition for the Academy and Filmex, and on films like this, people feel the only thing that's important is the directorship. The director gets most of the credit for the picture. I think Janelle's right.' She turned to Janelle. 'How do you want the director's credit to read?'

Janelle said, 'Have both of us being given credit and you put your name first. Is that OK?'

Alice said, 'Sure, anything you want.'

After having lunch with us, Alice said she had to leave even though Janelle begged her to stay. I watched them kiss each other good-bye and then I walked Alice out to her car.

Before she drove away, I asked her, 'Do you really not mind?'

Her face perfectly composed, beautiful in its serenity, she said, 'No, I really don't mind. Janelle was hysterical after the first showing when everybody came up to me to congratulate me. She's just that way and making her happy is more important to me than getting all that bullshit. You understand that, don't you?'

I smiled at her and kissed her cheek good-bye. 'No,' I said. 'I don't understand stuff like that.' I went back into the house and Janelle was nowhere in sight. I figured she must have gone for a walk down the beach and she didn't want me with her, and sure enough, an hour later I spotted her coming up the sand walking by the water. And when she came into the house, she went up to the bedroom, and when I found her up there, I saw that she was in bed with the covers over her and she was crying.

I sat down on the bed and didn't say anything. She reached out to hold my hand. She was still crying.

'You think I'm such a bitch, don't you?' she said.

'No,' I said.

'And you think Alice is so marvellous, don't you?'

'I like her,' I said. I knew I had to be very careful. She was afraid that I would think Alice was a better person than she was.

'Did you tell her to cut out that piece of negative?' I said.

'No,' Janelle said. 'She just did that on her own.'

'OK,' I said. 'Then just accept it for what it is and don't worry about who behaved better and who seems like a better person. She wanted to do that for you. Just accept it. You know you want it.'

At this she started to cry again. In fact, she was hysterical, so I made her some soup and fed her one of her blue ten-milligram Valiums and she slept from that afternoon till Sunday morning.

That afternoon I read; then I watched the beach and the water until dawn broke.

Janelle finally woke up. It was about ten o'clock, a beautiful day in Malibu. I knew immediately that she wasn't comfortable with me, that she didn't want me around for the rest of the day. That she wanted to call Alice and have Alice come out and spend the rest of the day. So I told her I had gotten a call and had to go to the studio and couldn't spend the rest of the day with her. She made the usual Southern belle protestations, but I could see the light in her eyes. She wanted to call Alice and show her love for her.

Janelle walked me out to the car. She was wearing one of those big floppy hats to protect her skin from the sun. It was really a floppy hat. Most women would have looked ugly in it. But with her perfect face and complexion she was quite beautiful. She had on her specially tailored, secondhand, specially weathered jeans that fitted on the body like skin. And I remembered that one night I had said to her when she was naked in bed that she had a real great woman's ass, that it takes generations to breed an ass like that. I said it to make her angry because she was a feminist, but to my surprise she was delighted. And I remembered that she was partly a snob. That she was proud of the aristocratic lineage of her Southern family.

She kissed me good-bye and her face was all rosy and pink. She wasn't a bit desolated that I was leaving. I knew that she and Alice would have a happy day together and that I would have a miserable day in town at my hotel. But I figured, what the hell? Alice deserved it and I really didn't. Janelle had once said that she, Janelle, was a practical solution to my emotional needs but I was not a practical solution to hers.

The television kept flickering. There was a special tribute in memory of Malomar. Valerie said something to me about it. Was he a nice person? and I answered yes. We finished watching the awards, and then she said to me, 'Did you know any of the people that were there?'

'Some of them,' I said.

'Which ones?' Valerie asked me.

I mentioned Eddie Lancer who had won an Oscar for his contribution to a film script, but I didn't mention Janelle. I wondered for just a moment if Valerie had set a trap for me to see if I would mention Janelle and then I said I knew the blond girl who won a prize at the beginning of the programme.

Valerie looked at me and then turned away.

40

A WEEK later Doran called me to go out to California for more conferences. He said he had sold Eddie Lancer to Tri-Culture. So I went out and hung around and went to meetings and picked up with Janelle again. I was a little restless now. I didn't love California that much any more.

One night Janelle said to me, 'You always tell how great your brother, Artie, is. Why is he so great?'

'Well,' I said, 'I guess he was my father as well as my brother.'

I could see she was fascinated by the two of us growing up, as orphans. That it appealed to her dramatic sense. I could see her spinning all kinds of movies, fairy tales in her head, about how life had been. Two young boys. Charming. One of your real Walt Disney fantasies.

'So, you really want to hear another story about orphans?' I said. 'Do you want a happy story or a true story? Do you want a lie or do you want the truth?'

Janelle pretended to think it over. 'Try me with the truth,' she said. 'If I don't like it, you can tell me the lie.'

So I told her how all the visitors to the asylum wanted to adopt Artie but never wanted to adopt me. That's how I started off the story.

And Janelle said mockingly, 'Poor you.' But when she said it, though her face smiled, she let her hand fall along the side of my body and rest there.

It was on a Sunday when I was seven and Artie was nine that we were made to dress up in what was called our adoption uniforms. Light blue jackets, white starched shirt, dark blue tie and white flannel trousers with white shoes. We were brushed and combed and brought to the head matron's reception room, where a young married couple waited to inspect us. The procedure was that we were introduced and shook hands and showed our best manners and sat around talking and became acquainted. Then we would all take a walk through the grounds of the asylum, past the huge garden, past the football field and the school buildings. The thing I remember most clearly is that the woman of the couple was to me very beautiful. That even as a seven-year-old boy I fell in love with her. It was obvious that her husband was also in love with her but wasn't too crazy about the whole idea. It also became obvious during that day that the woman was crazy about Artie, but not about me. And I really couldn't blame her. Even at eight, Artie looked handsome in almost a grown-up way. Also, the features in all of the planes of his face were perfectly cut, and though people said to me we looked alike and always knew we were brothers, I knew that I was a smudged version of him as if he were the first out of the mould. The impression was clear. As a second impression I had picked up little pieces of wax on the mould, lips thicker, nose bigger. Artie had the delicacy of a girl, the bones in my face and my body were thicker and heavier. But I had never been jealous of my brother until that day.

That night we were told that the couple would return the next Sunday to make their decision on whether to adopt both of us or one of us. We were also told that they were very rich and how important it was for at least one of us to be taken.

I remember the matron gave us a heart-to-heart talk. It was one of those heart-to-heart talks adults give to children warning them against the evil emotions such as jealousy, envy, spitefulness and urging us on to a generosity of spirit that only saints could achieve, much less children. As children we listened without saying a word. Nodding our heads and saying, 'Yes, ma'am.' But not really knowing what she was talking about. But even at the age of seven I knew what was going to happen. My brother next Sunday would go away with the rich, beautiful lady and leave me alone in the asylum.

Even as a child Artie was not vain. But the week that followed was the only week in our lives that we were estranged. I hated him that week. On Monday after classes, when we had our touch football game, I didn't pick him to be on my team. In sports I had all the power. For the sixteen years we were in the asylum I was the best athlete of my age and a natural leader. So I was always one of the captains who picked their teams, and I always picked Artie to be on my team as my first choice. That Monday was the only time in sixteen years that I didn't pick him. When we played the game, though he was two years older than I was, I tried to hit him as hard as I could when he had the ball. I can still remember thirty years later the look of astonishment and hurt on his face that day. At evening meals I didn't sit next to him at the dinner table. At night I didn't talk to him in the dormitory. On one of those days during the week I remember clearly that after the football game was over and he was walking away across the field I had the football in my hand and I very coolly threw a beautiful twenty-yard spiral pass and hit him in the back of the head and knocked him to the ground. I had just thrown it. I really didn't think I could hit him. For a seven-year-old boy it was a remarkable feat. And even now I wonder at the strength of the malice that made my seven-year-old arm so true. I remember Artie's getting off the ground and my yelling out, 'Hey, I didn't mean it.' But he just turned and walked away.

371

He never retaliated. It made me more furious. No matter how much I snubbed him or humiliated him he just looked at me questioningly. Neither of us understood what was happening. But I knew one thing that would really bother him. Artie was always a careful saver of money. We picked up pennies and nickels by doing odd jobs around the asylum, and Artie had a glass jar filled with these pennies and nickels that he kept hidden in his clothes locker. On Friday afternoon I stole the glass jar, giving up my daily football game, and ran out into a wooded area of the grounds and buried it. I didn't even count the money. I could see the copper and silver coins filled the jar almost to the brim. Artie didn't miss the jar until the next morning and he looked at me unbelievingly, but he didn't say anything. Now he avoided me.

The following day was Sunday and we were to report to the matron to be dressed in our adoption suits. I got up early Sunday morning before breakfast and ran away to hide in the wooded area behind the asylum. I knew what would happen that day. That Artie would be dressed in his suit, that the beautiful woman I loved would take him away with her and that I would never see him again. But at least I would have his money. In the thickest part of the woods I lay down and went to sleep and I slept the whole day through. It was almost dark before I awoke and then I went back. I was brought to the matron's office and she gave me twenty licks with a wooden ruler across the legs. It didn't bother me a bit.

I went back to the dormitory, and I was astonished to find Artie sitting in his bed waiting for me. I couldn't believe that he was still there. In fact, if I remember, I had tears in my eyes when Artie punched me in the face and said, 'Where's my money?' And then he was all over me, punching me and kicking me and screaming for his money. I tried to defend myself without hurting him, but finally I picked him up and threw him off me. We sat there staring at each other.

'I haven't got your money,' I said.

'You stole it,' Artie said. 'I know you stole it.'

'I didn't,' I said. 'I haven't got it.'

We stared at each other. We didn't speak again that evening. But when we woke up the next morning, we were friends again. Everything was as it was before. Artie never asked me again about the money. And I never told him where I had buried it.

I never knew what happened that Sunday until years later when Artie told me that when he had found out I had run away, he had refused to put on his adoption suit, that he had screamed and cursed and tried to hit the matron, that he had been beaten. When the young couple that wanted to adopt him insisted on seeing him, he had spit on the woman and called her all the dirty names a nine-year-old boy could think of. It had been a terrible scene and he took another beating from the matron.

When I finished the story, Janelle got up from the bed and went to get herself another glass of wine. She came back into the bed, leaning up against me, and said, 'I want to meet your brother, Artie.'

'You never will,' I said. 'Girls I brought around fell in love with him. In fact, the only reason I married my wife was that she was the only girl who didn't.'

Janelle said, 'Did you ever find the glass jar with the money?'

'No,' I said. 'I never wanted to. I wanted it to be there for some kid who came after me, some kid might dig in that wood and it would be a piece of magic for him. I didn't need it any more.'

Janelle drank her wine and then said jealously, as she was jealous of all my emotions, 'You love him, don't you?'

And I really couldn't answer that. I couldn't think of that word of 'love' as a word that I would use for my brother or any man. And besides, Janelle used the word 'love' too much. So I didn't answer.

On another night Janelle argued with me about women having the right to fuck as freely as men. I pretended to agree with her. I was feeling coolly malicious from suppressed jealousy.

All I said was: 'Sure they do. The only trouble is that biologically women can't handle it.'

At this, Janelle became furious. 'That's all bullshit,' she said. 'We can fuck just as easily as you do. We don't give a shit. In fact, it's you men who make all the fuss about sex being so important and serious. You're so jealous and so possessive: we're your property.'

It was just the trap I hoped she would fall into. 'No, I didn't mean that,' I said. 'But did you know that a man has a twenty to fifty percent chance of catching gonorrhea from a woman, but a woman has a fifty to eighty percent chance of catching gonorrhea from a man?'

She looked astounded for a moment and I loved that look of childish astonishment on her face. Like most people, she didn't know a damn thing about VD or how it worked. As for myself, as soon as I had started cheating on my wife, I had read up on the whole subject. My big nightmare was catching VD, gonorrhea or syphilis, and infecting Valerie, which is one of the reasons that it distressed me when Janelle told me about her love affairs.

'You're just making it up to scare me,' Janelle said. 'I know you when you sound so sure of yourself and so professorial; you're just making stories up.'

'No,' I said. 'It's true. A male has a thin, clear discharge from within one to ten days, but women most of the time never even know they have gonorrhea. Fifty to eighty percent of women have no symptoms for weeks or months or they have a green or yellow discharge. Also, women get a mushroom odour from their genitals.'

Janelle collapsed on the bed, laughing, and threw her bare legs up in the air. 'Now I know you're full of shit.'

'No, it's true,' I said. 'No kidding. But you're OK, I can smell you from here.' Hoping the joke would hide my malice. 'You know usually the only way you know you have it, is if your male partner tells you.'

Janelle straightened up primly. 'Thanks a lot,' she said. 'Are you getting ready to tell me you have it and, therefore, I must have it?'

'No,' I said. 'I'm straight, but if I do get it, I know it's either from you or my wife.'

Janelle gave me a sarcastic look. 'And your wife is above suspicion, right?'

'That's right,' I said.

'Well, for your information,' Janelle said, 'I go to my gynaecologist every month and get a complete checkup.'

'That's full of shit,' I said. 'The only way that you can tell is to take a culture. And most gynaecologists do not. They take it in a thin glass with light brown jelly from your cervix. The test is very tricky and it's not always a positive test.'

She was fascinated now, so I threw her a zinger. 'And if you think you can beat the rap by just going down on a guy, the percentages are much greater for a woman getting a venereal disease from going down on a man than a man has from going down on a woman.'

Janelle sprang up from the bed. She was giggling, but she yelled, 'Unfair! Unfair!'

We both laughed.

'And gonorrhea is nothing,' I said. 'Syphilis is the real *bad* part. If you go down on a guy, you can get a nice chancre on your mouth or your lips or even your tonsils. It would hurt your acting career. What you have to look out for on a chancre is it's dull red and breaks down into a dull red sore that does not bleed easily. Now, here's what's tricky about it. The symptoms can vanish in one to five weeks, but the disease is still in your body and you can infect somebody after this point. You may develop a second lesion or the palms and soles of your feet may have red bumps.' I picked up one of her feet and said, 'Nope, you haven't got them.'

She was fascinated now, and she hadn't caught on either to why I was lecturing her.

'What about men? What do you bastards get out of all this?'

'Well,' I said, 'we get swelling of the lymph glands in the groin, and that's why sometimes you tell a guy he's got two pairs of balls, or sometimes you lose your hair. That's why in the old days the slang for syphilis was "haircut". But still, you're not in too bad a shape. Penicillin can wipe it all out. Again, as I said, the only trouble is men know they got it, but women don't and that's why women are not biologically equipped to be promiscuous.'

Janelle looked a little stunned. 'Do you find this fascinating? You son of a bitch.' She was beginning to catch on.

I continued very blandly. 'But it's not as terrible as it sounds. Even if you don't find out that you have syphilis or, as it happens with most women, you have no symptoms of any kind unless some guy tells you out of the goodness of his heart. In one year you won't be infectious. You won't infect anyone.' I smiled at her. 'Unless you're a pregnant woman and then your child is born with syphilis.'

I could see her shrink away from the thought. 'Now after that one year, two-thirds of those infected will live with no ill effects. They are home free. They are OK.'

I smiled at her.

Janelle said suspiciously, 'And the other one-third?'

'They're in a lot of trouble,' I said. 'It injures the heart, it injures the blood vessels. It can lie low for ten to twenty years, and then it can cause insanity, it can cause paralysis, make you a paralytic. It can also affect your eyes, lungs and liver. So you see, my dear, you're shit out of luck.'

Janelle said, 'You're just telling me this to keep me from going out with other men. You're just trying to scare me just like my mother did when I was fifteen by telling me I'd be pregnant.'

'Sure,' I said. 'But I'm backing it up with science. I have no moral objection. You can fuck whoever you want. You don't belong to me.'

'You're such a smart-ass,' Janelle said. 'Maybe they'll come up with a pill just like the birth control pill.'

I made my voice sound very sincere. 'Sure,' I said. 'They have that already. If you take a tablet of five hundred milligrams of penicillin one hour before you have contact, it knocks out the syphilis completely. But sometimes it doesn't work and it just reaches the symptoms and then ten or twenty years later you can be really screwed. If you take it too early or too late, these spirochetes multiply. Do you know what spirochetes are? They're like cork-screws and they fill up your blood and get into the tissues and there's not enough blood in your tissues to fight it off. There is something about the drug that keeps the cell from increasing and blocking off the infection, and then the disease becomes resistant to penicillin in your body. In fact, the penicillin helps them grow. But there is another thing you can use. There is a female gel, Proganasy, that's used as a contraceptive and they found that it destroys VD bacteria as well, so you can kill two birds with one stone. Come to think of it, my friend Osano uses those penicillin pills whenever he thinks he's going to get lucky with a girl.'

Janelle laughed scornfully. 'That's all right for men. You men will fuck anything, but women never know who or when they are going to fuck until an hour or two hours beforehand.'

'Well,' I said very cheerfully, 'let me give you some advice. Never fuck anybody between the ages of fifteen and twenty-five. They have about ten times more VD than any other age bracket. Another thing is before you go to bed with a guy, give him a short arm.

Janelle said, 'That sounds disgusting. What is that?'

'Well,' I said, 'you strip down his penis, you know, like you're masturbating him, and if there's a yellow fluid coming out like a drippage, you know he's infected. That's what prostitutes do.'

When I said that, I knew I had gone too far. She gave me a cold look, so I went on hastily. 'Another thing is herpes virus. It isn't really a venereal disease and is usually transmitted by uncircumcised men. It can give women cervical cancer. So you see what the score is. You can get cancer from screwing, syphilis from screwing and never even know you're getting them and never even know it and that's why women can't fuck as freely as men.'

Janelle clapped her hands, 'Bravo, Professor. I think I'll just fuck women.'

'That's not a bad idea,' I said.

It was easy for me to say. I wasn't jealous of her women lovers.

41

ON my next trip back a month later I called Janelle, and we decided to have dinner and go to the movies together. There was something a little cold in her voice, so I was wary, which prepared me for the shock of seeing her when I picked her up at her apartment.

Alice opened the door and I kissed her and I asked Alice how Janelle was and Alice rolled her eyes up in her head, which meant I could expect Janelle to be a little crazy. Well, it wasn't crazy, but it was a little funny. When Janelle came out of the bedroom, she was dressed as I had never seen her before.

She had on a white fedora with a red ribbon in it. The brim snapped over her dark brown gold-flecked eyes. She was wearing a perfectly tailored man's suit of white silk, or what looked like silk. The trouser legs were strictly tailored straight as any man's. She had on a white silk shirt and the most beautiful red-and-blue striped tie, and to top it off, she was carrying a delicately slender cream-coloured Gucci cane, which she proceeded to stab me in the stomach with. It was a direct challenge, I knew, what she was doing; she was coming out of the closet and without words she was telling the world of her bisexuality.

She smiled, 'How do you like it?'

I smiled and said, 'Great.' The most dapper dyke I ever met. 'Where do you want to eat?'

She leaned on her cane and watched me very coolly. 'I think,' she said, 'we should eat at Scandia and that for once in our relationship you might take me to a nightclub.'

We had never eaten at the fancy places. We had never gone to a nightclub. But I said OK. I understood, I think, what she was doing. She was forcing me to acknowledge to the world that I loved her despite her bisexuality, testing me to see if I could bear the dyke jokes and snickers. Since I had already accepted the fact myself, I didn't care what anybody else thought.

We had a great evening. Everybody stared at us in the restaurant, and I must admit that Janelle looked absolutely smashing. In fact, she looked like a blonder and fairer version of Marlene Dietrich, Southern belle style, of course. Because, no matter what she did, that overwhelming femininity came off her. But I knew that if I told her that, she would hate it. She was out to punish me.

I really enjoyed her playing the dyke role simple because I knew how feminine she was in bed. So it was a sort of double joke on whoever was watching us. I also enjoyed it because Janelle thought she was making me angry and was watching my every move and was disappointed and then pleased that I obviously didn't mind.

I drew the line at going to a nightclub, but we went and had drinks at the Polo Lounge, where for her satisfaction I submitted our relationship to the stares of her friends and mine. I saw Doran at one table and Jeff Wagon at another, and they both grinned at me. Janelle waved to them gaily and then turned to me and said, 'Isn't it wonderful to go somewhere for a drink and see all your old dear friends?'

I grinned back at her and I said, 'Great.'

I got her home before midnight and she tapped me on the shoulder with her cane and she said, 'You did very well.'

And I said, 'Thank you.'

She said, 'Will you call me?'

And I said, 'Yes.' It had been a nice night anyway. I had enjoyed the double takes of the maître d', the doorman, even the guys who did the valet parking, and at least now Janelle was out of the closet.

There came a time soon after this when I loved Janelle as a person. That is, it wasn't that I just wanted to fuck her brains out; or look into her dark brown eyes and faint; or eat up her pink mouth. And all the rest of it, the staying up all night telling her stories, Jesus, telling her my whole life, and her telling me all her life. In short, there came a time when I realized it was not her sole function to make me happy, to make me delight in her. I saw that it was my job to make her a little happier than she was and not to get pissed off when she didn't make me happy.

I don't mean I became one of those guys who are in love with a girl because it makes them unhappy. I never understood that really. I always believed in getting my share of any bargain, in life, in literature, in marriage, in love, even as a father.

And I don't mean I learned to make her happy by giving her a gift, that was my pleasure. Or to cheer her when she was down, which was just clearing obstacles out of the way so that she could get on with the job of making me happy.

Now what was curious was that after she had 'betrayed' me, after we started to hate each other a little, after we had the goods on each other, I came to love her as a person.

She was really such a good guy. She used to say like a child sometimes, 'I'm a good person,' and she really was. She was really so straight in all the important things. Sure she fucked other guys and women too, but what the hell, nobody's perfect. She still loved the same books I did, the same movies, the same people. When she lied to me, it was to keep from hurting me. And when she told me the truth, it was partly to hurt me (she had a nice vengeful streak and I even loved that too), but also because she was terrified I'd learn the truth in a way that would hurt me more.

And of course, as time went on, I had to understand that she led a hurtful life in many ways. A complicated life. As who indeed does not.

So finally all the falseness and illusion had gone out of our relationship. We were true friends and I loved her as a person. I admired her courage, her indestructability with all the

379

disappointments of her professional life, all the treacheries of her personal life. I understood it all. I was for her all the way.

Then why the hell didn't we have those deliriously good times we had before? Why wasn't the sex as good as it had been, though still better than anyone else? Why weren't we as ecstatic with each other as we used to be?

Magic-magic, black or white. Sorcery, spells, witches and alchemy. Could it really be true that spinning stars decide our destiny and moon blood makes lives wax and wane? Could it be true that the innumerable galaxies decide our fate day by day on earth? Is it quite simply true that we cannot be happy without false illusions?

There comes a point in every love affair when, so it seems, the woman gets pissed off at her lover's being too happy. Sure she knows it's her making him happy. Sure she knows that it's her pleasure, even her job. But finally she comes to the conclusion that in some way, the son of a bitch is getting away with murder. Especially with the man married and the woman not. For then the relationship is an answer to his problem but does not solve hers.

And there comes a time when one of the partners needs a fight before making love. Janelle had come to that stage. I usually managed to sidetrack her, but sometimes I felt like fighting too. Usually when she was pissed off that I stayed married and didn't make any promises for a permanent commitment.

We were in her house in Malibu after the movies. It was late. From our bedroom we could look over the ocean, which wore a long streak of moonlight like a lock of blond hair.

'Let's go to bed,' I said. I was dying to make love to her. I was always dying to make love to her.

'Oh, Christ,' she said, 'you always want to fuck.'

'No,' I said. 'I want to make love to you.' I had become that sentimental.

She looked at me coldly, but her liquid brown eyes were flashing with anger. 'You and your fucking innocence,' she said. 'You're like a leper without his bell.'

'Graham Greene,' I said.

'Oh, fuck you,' she said, but she laughed.

And what had led to all this was that I never lied. And she wanted me to lie. She wanted me to give her all the bullshit married men give to girls they screw. Like 'My wife and I are getting a divorce.' Like 'My wife and I haven't screwed in years.' Like 'My wife and I don't share the same bedroom.' Like 'My wife and I have an understanding.' Like 'My wife and I are unhappy together.' Since none of this was true for me, I wouldn't say it. I loved my wife, we shared the same bedroom, we had sex, we were happy. I had the best of two worlds and I wasn't going to give it up. So much the worse for me.

Once Janelle laughed she was OK for a while. So now she went and drew a tub full of hot water. We always took a bath together before we went to bed. She would wash me and I would wash her and we'd fool around a little and then jump out and dry each other, with big towels. Then we'd wind ourselves around each other, naked under the covers.

But now she lit a cigarette before getting into bed. That was a danger signal. She wanted to fight. A bottle of energy pills had spilled out of her purse and that had pissed me off, so I was a little ready too. I was no longer in so loving a mood. Seeing that bottle of energy pills had set off a whole train of fantasies. Now that I knew she had a woman lover, now that I knew she slept with other men when I was away back with my family in New York, I no longer loved her as much, and the energy pills made me think that she needed them to make love to me because she was fucking other people. So now I didn't feel like it. She sensed this.

'I didn't know you read Graham Greene,' I said. 'That crack about the leper without his bell, that's very pretty. You saved that one up just for me.'

She squinted her brown eyes over the cigarette smoke. The blond hair was loose down over her delicately beautiful face. 'It's true, you know,' she said. 'You can go home and screw your wife and that's OK. But because I have other lovers, you think I'm just a cunt. You don't even love me any more.'

'I still love you,' I said.

'You don't love me as much,' she said.

'I love you enough to want to make love to you and not just fuck you,' I said.

'You're really sly,' she said. 'You're innocent sly. You just admitted you love me less as if I tricked you into it. But you wanted me to know that. But why? Why can't women have other lovers and still love other men? You always tell me you still love your wife and you just love me more. That it's different. Why can't it be different for me? Why can't it be different for all women? Why can't we have the same sexual freedom and men still love us?'

'Because you know for sure whether it's your kid and men don't,' I said. I was kidding, I think.

She threw back the covers dramatically and sprang up so that she was standing in bed. 'I don't believe you said that,' she said incredulously. 'I can't believe that you said such an incredibly male chauvinistic thing.'

'I was kidding,' I said. 'Really. But you know, you're not realistic. You want me to adore you, to be really in love with you, to treat you like a virginal queen. As they did in the old days. But you reject those values that blind surrendering love is built on. Chastity, that the woman belonged solely to one man, that he was responsible for her destiny. You want us to love you like the Holy Grail, but you want to live like a liberated woman. You won't accept that if your values change, so must mine. I can't love you as you want me to. As I used to.'

She started to cry. 'I know,' she said. 'God, we loved each other so much. You know I used to fuck you when I had blinding headaches, I didn't care, I just took Percodan. And I loved it. I loved it. And now sex isn't as good, is it, now that we're honest?'

'No, it isn't,' I said.

That made her angry again. She started to yell and her voice sounded like a duck quacking.

It was going to be a long night. I sighed and reached over to the table for a cigarette. It's very hard to light a cigarette when a beautiful girl is standing so that her cunt is right over your mouth. But I managed it and the tableau was so funny that she collapsed back on to the bed, laughing.

'You're right,' I said. 'But you know there are some practical arguments for women being faithful. You know, I told you that women most of the time don't know that they have a venereal disease. And they get it more easily. Remember, the more different guys you screw, the more chance you have of getting cervical cancer.'

Janelle laughed. 'You liaaarr,' she drawled out.

'No kidding,' I said. 'All the old taboos have a practical basis.'

'You bastards,' Janelle said. 'Men are lucky bastards.'

'That's the way it is,' I said smugly. 'And when you start yelling, you sound just like Donald Duck.'

I got hit with a pillow and had the excuse to grab and hug her and we wound up making love.

382

Afterward, when we were smoking a cigarette together, she said, 'But I'm right, you know. Men are not fair. Women have every right to have as many sexual partners as they want. Now be serious. Isn't that true?'

'Yes,' I said just as seriously as she and more. I meant it. Intellectually I knew she was right.

She snuggled up to me. 'That's why I love you,' she said. 'You really do understand. Even at your male chauvinistic pig worst. When the revolution comes, I'm going to save your life. I'm going to say you were a good male, just misguided.'

'Thanks a lot,' I said.

She put out the light and then her cigarette. Very thoughtfully she said, 'You really don't love me less because I sleep with others, do you?'

'No,' I said.

'You know I love you really and truly,' she said.

'Yeah,' I said.

'And you don't think I'm a cunt for doing that, do you?' Janelle said.

'Nope,' I said. 'Let's go to sleep.' I reached out to hold her. She moved away a little.

'Why don't you leave your wife and marry me? Tell me the truth.'

'Because I have it both ways,' I said.

'You bastard.' She poked me in the balls with her finger.

It hurt. 'Jesus,' I said. 'Just because I'm madly in love with you, just because I like to talk to you better than anybody, just because I like fucking you better than anybody, what gives you the balls to think I'd leave my wife for you?'

She didn't know whether I was serious or not. She decided I was kidding. It was a dangerous assumption to make.

'Very seriously,' she said. 'Honestly I just want to know. Why do you still stay married to your wife? Give me just one good reason.'

I rolled up into a protective ball before I answered. 'Because she's not a cunt,' I said.

One morning I drove Janelle to the Paramount lot, where she had a day's work shooting a tiny part in one of its big pictures.

We were early, so we took a walk around what was to me an amazingly lifelike replica of a small town. It even had a false horizon, a sheet of metal rising to the sky that fooled me momentarily. The fake fronts were so real that as we walked past them,

I couldn't resist opening the door of a bookstore, almost expecting to see the familiar tables and shelves covered with bright-jacketed books for sale. When I opened the door, there was nothing but grass and sand beyond the doorsill.

Janelle laughed as we kept walking. There was a window filled with medicine bottles and drugs of the nineteenth century. We opened that door and again saw the grass and sand beyond. As we kept walking, I kept opening doors and Janelle didn't laugh any more. She only smiled. And finally we came to a restaurant with a canopy leading to the street and beneath the canopy a man in work clothes sweeping. And for some reason the man sweeping really faked me out. I thought that we had left the sets and come into the Paramount commissary area. I saw a menu pasted in the window and I asked the workman if the restaurant was open yet. He had an old actor's rubbery face. He squinted at me. Gave a huge grin then almost closed his eyes and winked.

'Are you serious?' he said.

I went to the restaurant door and opened it, and I was really astonished. Really surprised to see again the sand and grass beyond. I closed the door and looked at the workman's face. It was almost maniacal with glee as if he had arranged this trip for me. As if he were some sort of God and I had asked him 'Is life serious?' and that's why he had answered me, 'Are you serious?'

I walked Janelle to the sound stage where she was shooting and she said to me, 'They're so obviously fake. How could they fool you?'

'They didn't fool me,' I said.

'But you so obviously expected them to be real,' Janelle said. 'I watched your face as you opened the doors. And I know that the restaurant fooled you.'

She gave my arm a playful tug.

'You really shouldn't be let out alone,' she said. 'You're so dumb.'

And I had to agree. But it wasn't so much that I believed. It wasn't that really. What bothered me was that I had wanted to believe that there was something beyond those doors. That I could not accept the obvious fact that behind those painted sets was nothing. That I really thought I was a magician. When I opened those doors, real rooms would appear and real people. Even the restaurant. Just before I opened the door, I saw in my

384

mind red tablecloths and dark wine bottles and people standing silently waiting to be seated. I was really surprised when there was nothing there.

I realized it had been some sort of aberration that had made me open those doors, and yet I was glad I had done so. I didn't mind Janelle laughing at me and I didn't mind working with that crazy actor. God, I had just wanted to be sure, and if I had not opened those doors, I would have always wondered.

42

OSANO came to LA for a movie deal and called me to have dinner. I brought Janelle along because she was dying to meet him. When dinner was over and we were having our coffee, Janelle tried to draw me out about my wife. I shrugged her off.

'You never talk about that, do you?' she said.

I didn't answer. She kept on. She was a little flushed with wine and a little uncomfortable that I had brought Osano with me. She became angry. 'You never talk about your wife because you think that's dishonourable.'

I still didn't say anything.

'You still have a good opinion of yourself, don't you?' Janelle said. She was now very coldly furious.

Osano was smiling a little, and just to smooth things over he played the famous brilliant writer role, caricaturing it ever so slightly. He said, 'He never talks about being an orphan too. All adults are orphans really. We all lose our parents when we grow into adulthood.'

Janelle was instantly interested. She had told me she admired Osano's mind and his books. She said, 'I think that's brilliant. And it's true.'

'It's full of shit,' I said. 'If you're both going to use language to communicate, use words for their meaning. An orphan is a child who grows up without parents and many times without any blood relationships in the world. An adult is not an orphan. He's a fucking prick who's got no use for his mother and father because they are a pain in the ass and he doesn't need them any more.'

There was an awkward silence, and then Osano said, 'You're right, but also you don't want to share your special status with everybody.'

'Yeah, maybe,' I said. Then I turned to Janelle. 'You and your girlfriends call each other "sister". Sisters mean female children born of the same parents who have usually shared the same traumatic experiences of childhood. That's what a sister is, good, bad or indifferent. When you call a girlfriend "sister", you're both full of shit.'

Osano said, 'I'm getting divorced again. More alimony. One thing, I'll never marry again. I've run out of alimony money.'

I laughed with him. 'Don't say that. You're the institution of marriage's last hope.'

Janelle lifted her head and said, 'No, Merlyn. You are.'

We all laughed at that, and then I said I didn't want to go to a movie. I was too tired.

'Oh, hell,' Janelle said. 'Let's go for a drink at Pips and play some backgammon. We can teach Osano.'

'Why don't you two go?' I said coolly. 'I'll go back to the hotel and get some sleep.'

Osano was watching me with a sad smile on his face. He didn't say anything. Janelle was staring at me as if daring me to say it again. I made my voice as cold and loveless as possible. And yet understanding. Very deliberately I said, 'Look, really I don't mind. No kidding. You two are my best friends, but I really feel like just going to sleep. Osano, be a gentleman and take my place.' I said this very straight-faced.

Osano guessed right away I was jealous of him. 'Whatever you say, Merlyn,' he said. And he didn't give a shit about what I felt. He thought I was acting like a jerk. And I knew he would take Janelle to Pips and take her home and screw her and not give me another thought. As far as he was concerned, it was none of my business.

But Janelle shook her head. 'Don't be silly. I'll go home in my car and you two can do what you want.'

I could see what she was thinking. Two male chauvinistic pigs

386

trying to divvy her up. But she also knew that if she went with Osano, it would give me the excuse never to see her again. And I guess I knew what I was doing. I was looking for a reason really to hate her, and if she went with Osano, I could do it and be rid of her.

Finally Janelle went back to the hotel with me. But I could feel her coldness, though our bodies were warm against each other. A little later she moved away, and as I fell asleep, I could hear the rustle of the springs as she left our bed. I murmured drowsily, 'Janelle, Janelle.'

43

JANELLE

I'M a *good* person. I don't care what anybody thinks, I'm a good person. All my life the men I really loved always put me down, and they put me down for what they said they loved in me. But they never accepted the fact I could be interested in other human beings, not just them. That's what screws everything up. They fall in love with me at first and then they want me to become something else. Even the great love of my life, that son of a bitch, Merlyn. He was worse than any of them. But he was the best too. He understood me. He was the best man I ever met and I really loved him and he really loved me. And he tried as hard as he could. And I tried as hard as I could. But we could never beat that masculine thing. If I even liked another man, he got sick. I could see that sick look on his face. Sure I couldn't stand it if he even got into an interesting conversation with another woman. So what? But he was smarter than I was. He covered up. When I was around, he never paid any attention to other women even though they did to him. I wasn't that smart or maybe I felt it was too phoney. And what he did was phoney. But it worked. It made me love him more. And my being honest made him love me less.

I loved him because he was so smart in almost everything. Except women. He was really dumb about women. And he was dumb about me. Maybe not dumb, just that he could live only with illusions. He said that to me once and he said that I should be a better actress, that I should give him a better illusion that I loved him. I really loved him, but he said that wasn't as important as the illusion that I loved him. And I understood that and I tried. But the more I loved him the less I could do it. I wanted him to love the true me. Maybe nobody can love the true me or the true you or the true it. That's the truth—nobody can love truth. And yet I can't live without trying to be true to what I really am. Sure I lie, but only when it's important, and later, when I think the time is right, I always admit I told a lie. And that screws it up.

I always tell everybody how my father ran away when I was a little girl. And when I get drunk, I tell strangers how I tried to commit suicide when I was only fifteen, but I never tell them why. The true why. I let them think it was because my father went away, and maybe it was. I admit a lot of things about myself. That if a man I like buys me a real boozy dinner and makes me like him, I'll go to bed with him even if I'm in love with somebody else. Why is that so horrible? Men do that all the time. It's OK for them. But the man I loved the most in the whole world thought I was just a cunt when I told him that. He couldn't understand that it wasn't important. That I just wanted to get fucked. Every man does the same thing.

I never deceived a man about important things. About material things maybe I mean. I never pulled the cheap tricks some of my best friends pull on their men. I never accused a guy of being responsible when I got pregnant just to make him help me. I never tricked men like that. I never told a man I loved him when I didn't, not at the beginning anyway. Sometimes after, when I stopped loving him and he still loved me and I couldn't bear to hurt him, I'd say it. But I couldn't be that loving afterward and they'd catch on and things would cool off and we wouldn't see each other again. And I never really hated a man once I loved him no matter how hateful he was to me afterward. Men are so spiteful to women they no longer love, most men anyway, or to me anyway. Maybe because they still love me and I never love them afterward or love them a little, which doesn't mean anything. There's a big difference between loving somebody a little and loving somebody a lot.

Why do men always doubt that you love them? Why do men always doubt you are true to them? Why do men always leave you? Oh, Christ, why is it so painful? I can't love them any more. It hurts me so and they are such pricks. Such bastards. They hurt you as carelessly as children, but you can forgive children, you don't mind. Even though they both make you cry. But not any more, not men, not children.

Lovers are so cruel, more loving, more cruel. Not the Casanovas, Don Juans, the 'cunt men' as men always call them. Not those creeps. I mean the men who truly love you. Oh, you really love and they say they do and I know it's true. And I know how they will hurt me worse than any other man in the world. I want to say, 'Don't say you love me.' I want to say, 'I don't love you.'

Once when Merlyn said he loved me, I wanted to cry because I truly loved him and I knew that he would be so cruel later when we both really knew each other, when all the illusions were gone, and when I loved him most, he would love me so much less.

I want to live in a world where men will never love women as they love them now. I want to live in a world where I will never love a man as I love him now. I want to live in a world where love never changes.

Oh, God, let me live in dreams; when I die, send me to a paradise of lies, undiscoverable and self-forgiven, and a lover will love me for ever or not at all. Give me deceivers so sweet they will never cause me pain with true love, and let me deceive them with all my soul. Let us be deceivers never discovered, always forgiven. So that we can believe in each other. Let us be separated by wars and pestilence, death, madness but not by the passing of time. Deliver me from goodness, let me not regress into innocence. Let me be free.

I told him once that I had fucked my hairdresser and you should have seen the look on his face. The cool contempt. That's how men are. They fuck their secretaries, that's OK. But they put down a woman who fucks her hairdresser. And yet it's more understandable, what we do. A hairdresser does something personal. He has to use his hands on us and some of them have great hands. And they know women. I fucked my hairdresser only once. He was always telling me how good he was in bed and one day I was horny and I said OK and he came up that night and he fucked me just that once. While he was fucking me, I saw him watching me turn on. It was a power thing with him. He did all his little tricks with his tongue and his hands and special words, and I have to say it was a good fuck. But it was such a coldhearted fuck. When I came, I expected him to hold up a mirror to see how he did the back of my head. When he asked me if I liked it, I said it was terrific. He said we had to do it again sometime and I said sure. But he never asked me again even though I would have said no. So I guess I wasn't too great either.

Now what the hell is the harm in that? Why do men when they hear a story like that just put a woman down as a cunt? They would do it in a shot, every son of a bitch. It didn't mean a thing. It didn't make me any less a person. Sure, I fucked a creep. How many men, the best of them, fuck creepy women and not just once either?

I have to fight against regressing into innocence. When a man loves me, I want to be faithful to him and never fuck anybody else for the rest of my life. I want to do everything for him, but I know now that it never lasts with him or me. They start putting you down, they start making you love them less. In a million different ways.

The love of my life, the son of a bitch, I really loved him and he really loved me, I'll give him that. But I hated the way he loved me. I was his sanctuary, I was where he ran when the world was too much for him. He always said he felt safe with me alone in our hotel rooms, our different suites like different landscapes. Different walls, strange beds, prehistoric sofas, rugs with different coloured bloods, but always our naked bodies the same. But that's not even true and this is funny. Once I surprised him and it was really funny. I had the big tit operation. I always wanted bigger tits—nice and round and standing up—and I finally did it. And he loved them. I told him I did it especially for him and it was partly true. But I did it so I would be less shy when I read for a part that required some nudity. Producers sometimes look at your tits. And I guess I did it for Alice too. But I told him I did it just for him and the bastard had better appreciate them. And so he did. And so he did. I always loved the way he loved me. That was always the best part of it. He really loved me—my flesh—and always told me it was special flesh, and finally I believed he couldn't possibly make love to

390

anyone else but me. I regressed into that innocence.

But it was never true. It is, finally, never true. Nothing is. Even my reasons. Like another reason. I love women's tits and why is that unnatural? I love to suck another woman's tits and why does that disgust men? They find it so comforting—don't they think women do? We were all babies once together. Infants.

Is that why women cry so much? That they can never be that again? Infants? Men can be. That's true, that's really true. Men can be infants again. Women can't. Fathers can be infants again. Mothers can't.

He always said that he felt safe. And I knew what he meant. When we were alone together, I could see the strain go out of his face. His eyes became softer. And when we were lying down together warm and naked, soft skin touching, and I put my arms around him and truly loved him, I could hear him sigh like a cat purring. And I knew that for that short time he was truly happy. And that I could do that was truly magical. And that I was the only human being in the world who could make him feel like that made me feel so worthwhile. That I really meant something. I wasn't just a cunt to fuck. I wasn't just somebody to talk to and be intelligent with. I was truly a witch, a love witch, a good witch, and it was terrific. At that moment we both could die happy, literally, truly die happy. We could face death and not be afraid. But only for that short time. Nothing lasts. Nothing ever will. And so we deliberately shorten it, make the end come faster, I can see that now. One day he just said, 'I don't feel safe any more,' and I never loved him again.

I'm no Molly Bloom. That son of a bitch Joyce. While she was saying yes, yes, yes, her husband was saying no, no, no. I won't fuck any man who says no. Never, not any more.

Merlyn was sleeping. Janelle got up out of bed and pulled an armchair up to the window. She lit a cigarette and stared out. As she was smoking, she heard Merlyn thrash around the bed in a restless dreaming sleep. He was muttering something, but she didn't care. Fuck him. And every other man.

MERLYN

Janelle had on boxing gloves, dull red with white laces. She stood facing me, in the classic boxing stance, left extended, right hand cocked for the knockout punch. She wore white satin trunks. Her breasts were bare. On her feet were black sneakers, slip-ons, no laces. Her beautiful face was grim. The delicately cut, sensuous mouth was pressed tight, her white chin tucked against her shoulder. She looked menacing. But I was fascinated by her bare breast, creamy white and round nipples red, taut with an adrenaline that came not from love but the desire for combat.

I smiled at her. She didn't smile back. Her left flicked out and caught me on the mouth and I said, 'Ah, Janelle.' She hit me with two more hard lefts. They hurt like hell, and I could feel blood filling the gap beneath my tongue. She danced away from me. I put my hands out and they too had red gloves on them. I slid forward on sneakered feet and hitched up my trunks. At that moment Janelle darted in on me and hit me with a solid right hand. I actually saw green and blue stars as if I were in a comic strip. She danced away again, her breasts bobbing, the dancing red nipples mesmerizing.

I stalked her into a corner. She crouched down, her red-gloved tiny hands protecting her head. I started to throw a left hook into her delicately rounded belly, but the navel I had licked so many times repelled my hand. We went into a clinch and I said, 'Ah, Janelle, cut it out. I love you, honey.' She danced away and hit me again. It was like a cat ripping my eyebrow with its claw and blood started dripping down. I was blinded and I heard myself saying, 'Oh, Christ.'

Brushing away the blood, I saw her standing in the middle of the ring, waiting for me. Her blond hair was pulled tightly back into a bun and the rhinestone clip that held it glittered like a hypnotic charm. She hit me with two more lightning jabs, the tiny red gloves flicking in and out like tongues. But now she left an opening and I could hit the finely boned face. My hands wouldn't move. I knew that the only thing that could save me was a clinch. She tried to dance around me. I grabbed her around the waist as she tried to slip away and spun her around. Defenceless now except that the trunks did not go all the way around her body and I could see her back and her beautiful buttocks, so rounded and full, that I had always pressed against in our bed together. I felt a sharp pain in my heart and wondered what the hell she was fighting me for. I grabbed her around the waist and whispered in her ear, tiny filaments of gold hair remembered on my tongue. 'Lie on your stomach,' I said. She spun quickly. She hit me with a straight right I never saw

392

coming and then I was tumbling in slow motion, upended in the air and floating down on the canvas. Stunned, I managed to get to one knee and I could hear her counting to ten in her lovely warm voice that she used to make me come. I stayed on one knee and stared up at her.

She was smiling and then I could hear her saying, 'Ten, ten, ten, ten,' frantically, urgently, and then a gleeful smile broke over her face and she raised both hands in the air and jumped for joy. I heard the ghostly roar of millions of women screaming in ecstatic glee; another woman, heavyset, was embracing Janelle. This woman wore a heavy turtleneck sweater with 'CHAMP' stencilled across two enormous breasts. Neither of them paid any attention to me. And because I was feeling so sick, I started to cry.

Then Janelle came over to me and helped me. 'It was a fair fight,' she kept saying. 'I beat you fair and square,' and through my tears I said, 'No, no, you didn't.'

And then I woke up and reached out for her. But she was not in bed beside me. I got up and, naked, went into the living room of the suite. In the darkness I could see her cigarette. She was sitting in a chair, watching the foggy dawn come up over the city.

I went over and reached down and traced my hands over her face. There was no blood, her features were unbroken and she reached one velvety hand up to touch mine as it covered her naked breast.

'I don't care what you say,' I said. 'I love you whatever the hell that means.'

She didn't answer me.

After a few minutes she got up and led me back to the bed. We made love and then fell asleep in each other's arms. Half asleep, I murmured, 'Jesus, you nearly killed me.'

She laughed.

44

SOMETHING was waking me out of a deep sleep. Through the cracks of the shutters of the hotel room I could see the rose light of early California dawn, and then I heard the phone ringing. I just lay there for a few seconds. I saw Janelle's blond head snuggled almost under the covers. She was sleeping far apart from me. As the phone kept on ringing, I got a panicky feeling. It must be early in the morning here in Los Angeles, so the call had to be from New York and it had to be from my wife. Valerie never called me except in an emergency, something had happened to one of my kids. There was also the feeling of guilt that I would be receiving this call with Janelle in bed beside me. I hoped she wouldn't wake up as I picked up the phone.

The voice on the other end said, 'Is that you, Merlyn?'

And it was a woman's voice. But I couldn't recognize it. It wasn't Valerie.

I said, 'Yes, who is it?'

It was Artie's wife, Pam. There was a tremor in her voice. 'Artie had a heart attack this morning.'

And when she said it, I felt a lessening of anxiety. It wasn't one of my kids. Artie had had a heart attack before and for some reason in my mind I thought of it as something not really serious.

I said, 'Oh, shit. I'll get on a plane and come back right away. I'll be back today. Is he in the hospital?'

There was a pause at the other end of the phone, and then I heard her voice finally break.

She said, 'Merlyn, he didn't make it.'

I really didn't understand what she was saying. I really didn't. I still wasn't surprised or shocked, and then I said, 'You mean he's dead?'

And she said, 'Yes.'

I kept my voice very controlled. I said, 'There's a nine o'clock plane and I'll be on it and I'll be in New York at five and I'll come right to your house. Do you want me to call Valerie?'

And she said, 'Yes, please.'

I didn't say I was sorry, I didn't say anything. I just said, 'Everything will be all right. I'll be there tonight. Do you want me to call your parents?'

And she said, 'Yes, please.'

And I said, 'Are you all right?'

And she said, 'Yes, I'm all right. Please come back.'

And then she hung up the phone.

Janelle was sitting up in bed and staring at me. I picked up the phone and got long distance and got Valerie. I told her what had happened. I told her to meet me at the plane and she wanted to talk about it, but I told her I had to pack and get on the plane. That I didn't have any time and I would talk to her when she met me. And then I got the operator again and I called Pam's parents. Luckily I got the father and explained to him what had happened. He said he and his wife would catch the next plane to New York and he would call Artie's wife.

I hung up the phone and Janelle was staring at me, studying me very curiously. From the phone conversations she knew, but she didn't say anything. I started hitting the bed with my fist and kept saying, 'No, *no, no, no.*' I didn't know I was shouting it. And then I started to cry, my body flooded with an unbearable pain. I could feel myself losing consciousness. I took one of the bottles of whisky that was on the dresser in the room and drank. I couldn't remember how much I drank, and after that all I could remember was Janelle's dressing me and taking me down through the lobby of the hotel and putting me on a plane. I was like a zombie. It was only much later, when I had come back to Los Angeles, that she told me she had to throw me in the bath to sober me up and bring me back to consciousness and then she had dressed me, she had made the reservations and accompanied me on to the plane and told the stewardess and chief flight attendant to look out for me. I don't even remember the plane ride, but suddenly I was in New York and Valerie was waiting for me and by that time I was OK.

We drove right to Artie's house. I took charge of everything and made all the arrangements. Artie and his wife had agreed that he would be buried as a Catholic with a Catholic ceremony and I went to the local church and arranged for services. I did everything I could do and I was OK. I didn't want him lying above ground alone in the mortuary, so I made sure the services would be next day and he would be buried right afterwards. The wake would be this night. And as I went through the rituals of death, I knew I could never be the same again. That my life would change and the world around me; my magic fled.

Why did my brother's death affect me so? He was quite simple, quite ordinary, I guess. But he was truly virtuous. And I cannot think of anyone else that I have met in my life that I can say this of.

Sometimes he told me of battles on his job against its corruption and administrative pressures to soften reports on additives his tests showed were dangerous. He always refused to be pressured. But his stories were never a pain in the ass in the way of some people who always tell you how they refuse to be corrupted. Because he told them without indignation, with complete coolness. He was not unpleasantly surprised that rich men with money would insist on poisoning their fellowmen for profit. Again he was never pleasantly surprised that he could resist such corruption; he made it very clear that he felt no obligation to do battle for the right.

And he had no delusions of grandeur about how much good his fighting did. They could go around him. I remembered the stories he told me about how other agency chemists made official tests and gave favourable reports. But my brother never did. He always laughed when he told me these stories. He knew the world was corrupt. He knew his own virtue was not valuable. He did not prize it.

He just simply refused to give it up. As a man would refuse to give up an eye, a leg; if he had been Adam, he would have refused to give up a rib. Or so it seemed. And he was that way in everything. I knew that he had never been unfaithful to his wife, though he was really a handsome man and the sight of a very pretty girl made him smile with pleasure; and he rarely smiled. He loved intelligence in a man or a woman, yet never was seduced by that either, as many people are. He never accepted money or favours. He never asked for mercy to his feelings or his fate. And yet he would never judge others, outwardly at least. He rarely spoke, always listened, because that was his pleasure. He demanded the barest minimum of life.

And Christ, what breaks my heart now is that I remember he was virtuous even as a kid. He never cheated in a ball game, never stole from a store, was never insincere with a girl. He never bragged or lied. I envied his purity then and I envy it now.

And he was dead. A tragic, defeated life, so it seemed, and I envied him his life. For the very first time I understood the comfort people get from religion, those people who believe in a just God. That it would comfort me to believe now that my brother could not be refused his just reward. But I knew that was all shit. I was alive. Oh, that I should be alive and rich and famous, enjoying all the pleasures of the flesh on this earth, that I should be victorious and not anywhere near the man he was, and he so ignominiously put to death.

Ashes, Ashes, Ashes. I wept as I had never wept for my lost father or my lost mother, for lost loves and all other defeats. And so at least I had that much decency, to feel anguish at his death.

Tell me, anyone, why all this should be? I cannot bear to look at my brother's dead face. Why was I not lying in that casket, devils dragging me to hell? My brother's face had never looked so strong, so composed, so at rest, but it was grey as if powdered over with the dust of granite. And then his five children came, dressed in neat funerality, and knelt before his coffin to say their final prayers. I could feel my heart break, tears came against my will. I left the chapel.

But anguish is no' important enough to last. In the fresh air I knew that I was alive. That I would dine well the next day, that in time I would have a loving woman again, that I would write a story and walk along the beach. Only those we most love can cause our death, and only of them we must beware. Our enemies can never harm us. And at the core of my brother's virtue was that he feared neither his enemies nor those he loved. So much the worst for him. Virtue is its own reward and fools are they who die.

But then weeks later I heard other stories. How early in his marriage, when his wife became ill, he had gone to her parents weeping and begged for money to get his wife well. How, when the final heart attack came and his wife tried to give him mouth-to-mouth resuscitation, he waved her wearily away the moment before he died. But what had that final gesture really meant? That life had become too much for him, his virtue too heavy to bear? I remembered Jordan again, was he too virtuous a man?

Eulogies for suicides condemn the world and blame it for their deaths. But could it be that those who put themselves to death believed there was no fault anywhere, some organisms must die? And they saw this more clearly than their bereaved lovers and friends?

But all this was too dangerous. I extinguished my grief and my reason and put my sins forward as my shield. I would sin, beware and live forever.

BOOK SEVEN

45

A WEEK later I called Janelle to thank her for getting me on the plane. I got her answering machine voice disguised in a French accent, asking me to leave a message.

When I spoke, her real voice was there, breaking in.

'Who are you ducking?' I said.

Janelle was laughing. 'If you knew how your voice sounded,' she said. 'So sour. . .'

I laughed too.

'I was ducking your friend Osano,' she said. 'He keeps calling me.'

I felt a sick feeling in my stomach. I wasn't surprised. But I liked Osano so much and he knew how I felt about Janelle. I hated the idea that he would do that to me. And then I didn't really give a shit. It was no longer important.

'Maybe he was just trying to find out where I was,' I said.

'No,' Janelle said. 'After I put you on the plane, I called him and told him what happened. He was worried about you, but I told him you were OK. Are you?'

'Yes,' I said.

She didn't ask me any questions about what had happened when I got home. I loved that about her. Her knowing I wouldn't want to talk about it. And I knew she would never tell Osano about what happened that morning when I got the news about Artie, how I fell apart.

I tried to act cool. 'Why are you ducking him? You enjoyed his company at dinner when we were together. I'd think you'd jump at the chance of meeting him again.'

There was a pause at the other end, and then I heard a tone in her voice that showed she was angry. It became very calm.

The words very precise. As if she were pulling back a bow to send her words like arrows.

'That's true,' she said, 'and the first time he called I was delighted and we went out to dinner together. He was great fun.'

Not believing the answer I would get, I asked out of some remaining jealousy, 'Did you go to bed with him?'

Again there was the pause. I could almost hear the bow's twang as she sent off the arrow.

'Yes,' she said.

Neither of us said anything. I felt really lousy, but we had our rules. We could never reproach each other any more, just take our revenge.

Very shittily but automatically I said, 'So how was it?'

Her voice was very bright, very cheery as if she were talking about a movie. 'It was fun. You know he makes such a big deal out of going down on you that it builds up your ego.'

'Well,' I said casually, 'I hope he's better at it than I am.'

Again there was the long pause. And then the bow snapped and the voice was hurt and rebellious. 'You have no right to be angry,' she said. 'You have no goddamn right to be angry about what I do with other people. We settled that before.'

'You're right,' I said. 'I'm not angry.' And I wasn't. I was more than that. At that moment I gave her up as someone I loved. How many times had I told Osano how much I loved Janelle? And Janelle knew how I cared about Osano. They had both betrayed me. There was no other word for it. The funny thing was that I wasn't angry with Osano. Just with her.

'You are angry,' she said, as if I were being unreasonable.

'No, really I'm not,' I said. She was paying me off for my being with my wife. She was paying me off for a million things, but if I hadn't asked her that specific question about going to bed, she wouldn't have told me. She wouldn't have been that cruel. But she wouldn't lie to me any more. She had told me that once, and now she was backing it up. What she did was none of my business.

'I'm glad you called,' she said. 'I've missed you. And don't be mad about Osano. I won't see him again.'

'Why not?' I said. 'Why shouldn't you?'

'Oh, shit,' she said. 'He was fun, but he couldn't keep it up. Oh, shit, I promised myself I wouldn't tell you that.' She laughed.

Now, being a normal jealous lover, I was delighted to hear

that my dearest friend was partially impotent. But I just said carelessly, 'Maybe it was you. He's had a lot of devoted females in New York.'

Her voice was gay and bright. 'God,' she said, 'I worked hard enough. I could have brought a corpse back to life.' She laughed cheerfully.

So now, as she meant me to, I had a vision of her ministering to an invalid Osano, kissing and sucking at his body, her blond hair flying. I felt very sick.

I sighed. 'You hit too hard,' I said. 'I quit. Listen, I want to thank you again for taking care of me. I can't believe you got me in that tub.'

'That's my gym class,' Janelle said. 'I'm very strong, you know.' Then her voice changed. 'I'm awfully sorry about Artie. I wish I could have gone back with you and taken care of you.'

'Me too,' I said. But the truth was that I was glad that she couldn't. And I was ashamed that she had seen me break down. I felt in a curious way that she could never feel the same way about me again.

Her voice came very quietly over the phone. 'I love you,' she said.

I didn't answer.

'Do you still love me?' she said.

Now it was my turn. 'You know I'm not allowed to say things like that.'

She didn't answer.

'You're the one that told me that a married man should never tell a girl he loves her unless he's ready to leave his wife. In fact, he's not allowed to tell her that unless he's left his wife.'

Finally Janelle's voice came over the phone. It was all choked with angered breaths.

'Fuck you,' she said, and I could hear the phone slamming down.

I would have called her back, but then she would let that phoney French-accented voice answer. 'Mademoiselle Lambert isn't at home. Could you please leave your name?' So I thought, Fuck you, too. And I felt great. But I knew we weren't through yet.

46

WHEN Janelle told me about her screwing Osano, she couldn't know how I felt. That I had seen Osano make a pass at every woman he met unless she was absolutely ugly. That she had fallen for his sweeping approach, that she had been so easy for him, made her seem less in my eyes. She had been a pushover, like so many women. And I felt that Osano felt some contempt for me. That I had been so madly in love with a girl he had been able to push over in just one evening.

So I wasn't heartbroken, just depressed. An ego thing, I guess. I thought of telling Janelle all this, and then I saw that that would be just a cheap shot. To make her feel trampy. And then too I knew she would fight back. Why the hell shouldn't she be a pushover? Weren't men pushovers for girls who fucked everybody? Why should she take into account that Osano's motives were not pure? He was charming, he was intelligent, he was talented, he was attractive and he wanted to fuck her. Why shouldn't she fuck him? And where was it any of my business? My poor male ego had its nose out of joint, that's all. Of course, I could tell her Osano's secret, but that would be a cheap, irrelevant revenge.

Still, I was depressed. Fair or not, I liked her less.

On the next trip West, I didn't call Janelle. We were in the final stages of complete alienation, which is classic in affairs of this kind. Again, as I always did in anything I was involved with, I had read the literature and I was a leading expert on the ebb and flow of the human love affair. We were in the stage of saying good-bye to each other but coming back together once in a while to ward off the blow of final separation. And so I didn't call her because it was really all over, or I wanted it to be.

Meanwhile, Eddie Lancer and Doran Rudd had talked me into going back to the picture. It was a painful experience. Simon Bellfort was just a tired old hack doing the best he could and scared shitless of Jeff Wagon. His assistant, 'Slime City' Richetti, was really a gopher for Simon but tried to give us some of his own ideas on what should be in the script. Finally one day after a particular asshole idea I turned to Simon and Wagon and said, 'Get that guy out of here.'

There was an awkward silence. I'd made up my mind. I was going to walk out and they must have sensed it, because finally Jeff Wagon said quietly, 'Frank, why don't you wait for Simon in my office?' Richetti left the room.

There was an awkward silence and I said, 'I'm sorry, I didn't mean to be rude. But are we serious about this fucking script or not?'

'Right,' Wagon said. 'Let's get on with it.'

On the fourth day, after working at the studio, I decided to see a movie. I had the hotel call me a taxi and had the taxi drive me to Westwood. As usual, there was a long line waiting to get in and I took my place in it. I had brought a paperback book along with me to read while waiting in line. After the movie I planned to go to a restaurant nearby and call a taxi to take me back to the hotel.

The line was at a standstill, all young kids talking about movies in a knowledgeable way. The girls were pretty and the young men with their beards and long hair prettier in a Christ-like way.

I sat down on the curb of the sidewalk to read and nobody paid any attention to me. Here in Hollywood this was not eccentric behaviour. I was intent on my book when I became conscious of a car horn honking insistently and I looked up. There was a beautiful Phantom Rolls-Royce stopped in front of me, and I saw Janelle's bright rosy face in the driver's seat.

'Merlyn,' Janelle said, 'Merlyn, what are you doing here?'

I got up casually and said, 'Hi, Janelle.' I could see the guy in the Rolls-Royce passenger seat. He was young, handsome and beautifully dressed in a grey suit and grey silk tie. He had beautifully cut hair, and he didn't seem to mind stopping so that Janelle could talk to me.

Janelle introduced us. She mentioned that he was the owner of the car. I admired the car and he said how much he admired my book and how eagerly he was waiting for the picture. Janelle said something about his working at a studio in some executive position. She wanted me to know that she wasn't just going out with a rich guy in a Rolls-Royce, that he was part of the movie business.

Janelle said, 'How did you get down here? Don't tell me you're finally driving.'

'No,' I said. 'I took a taxi.'

Janelle said, 'How come you're waiting in line?'

I looked by her and said I didn't have beautiful friends with me with their Academy cards to get me in.

She knew I was kidding. Whenever we had to go to a movie, she would always use her Academy card to get ahead. 'You wouldn't use the card even if you had it,' she said.

She turned to her friend and said, 'That's the kind of dope he is.' But there was a little bit of pride in her voice. She really loved me for not doing things like that, even though she did.

I could see that Janelle was stricken, pitied me having to take a taxi to go to the movies alone, forced to wait in line like any peasant. She was building a romantic scenario. I was her desolate, broken husband, looking in through the window and seeing his former wife and happy children with a new husband. There were tears in her gold-flecked brown eyes.

I knew I had the upper hand. This handsome guy in the Rolls-Royce didn't know that he was going to lose out. But then I got to work on him. I got him in a conversation about his work and he started chatting away. I pretended to be very interested and he went on and on with the usual Hollywood bullshit and I could see Janelle getting very nervous and irritated. She knew he was a dummy, but she didn't want me to know he was a dummy. And then I started admiring his Rolls-Royce and the guy really became animated. In five minutes I knew more about a Rolls-Royce than I wanted to know. I kept admiring the car and then I used Doran's old joke that Janelle knew and I repeated it word for word. First I made the guy tell me how much it cost and then I said, 'For that kind of money this car should give head.' She hated that joke.

The guy started to laugh and laugh, and he said, 'That's the funniest thing I ever heard.'

Janelle's face was flushed. She looked at me and then I saw the line moving and I had to get into my place. I told the guy it was very nice meeting him and told Janelle that it was great to see her again.

405

Two and a half hours later I walked out of the movie and I saw Janelle's familiar Mercedes parked in front of the theatre. I got in.

'Hi, Janelle,' I said. 'How did you get rid of him?'

She said, 'You son of a bitch.'

And I laughed and I reached over and she gave me a kiss and we drove to my hotel and spent the night.

She was very loving that night. She asked me once, 'Did you know I would come back to get you?'

And I said, 'Yes.'

And she said, 'You bastard.'

It was a wonderful night, but in the morning it was as if nothing had happened. We said good-bye.

She asked me how long I would be in town. I said I had three days more and then I would be back in New York.

She said, 'Will you call me?'

I said I didn't think I would have time.

She said, 'Not to meet me, just call me.'

I said, 'I will.'

I did, but she wasn't in. I got her French-accented voice on the machine. I left a message and then I went back to New York.

The last time I ever saw Janelle was really an accident. I was in my Beverly Hills Hotel suite and I had an hour to kill before going out to dinner with some friends and I couldn't resist the impulse to call her. She agreed to meet me for a drink at the La Dolce Vita bar, which was only about five minutes away from the hotel. I went right over there and in a few minutes she came in. We sat at the bar and had a drink and talked casually as if we were just acquaintances. She swung around on the barstool to get her cigarette lit by the bartender, and as she did so, her foot hit my leg slightly, not even enough to dirty the trousers, and she said, 'Oh, I'm sorry.'

And for some reason that broke my heart, and when she lifted her eyes after lighting her cigarette, I said, 'Don't do that.'

And I could see the tears in her eyes.

It was in the literature on breaking up, the last tender moments of sentiment, the last flutters of a dying pulse, the last flush of a rosy cheek before death. I didn't think of it then.

We held hands, left the bar and went to my hotel suite. I called my friends to cancel my appointment. Janelle and I had dinner

406

in the suite. I lay back on the sofa, and she took her favourite position with legs tucked underneath her and her upper body leaning on mine so that we were always in touch with each other. In that way she could look down at my face and look into my eyes and see if I lied to her. She still thought that she could read somebody's face. But also from my position, looking up, I could see the lovely line that her neck made between her chin and neck and the perfect triangulation of her face.

We just held each other and for a while, and then, looking deep into my eyes, she said, 'Do you still love me?'

'No,' I said, 'but I find it painful to be without you.'

She didn't say anything for a while, and then she repeated with a peculiar emphasis, 'I'm serious, really I am serious. Do you still love me?'

And I said seriously, 'Sure,' and it was true, but I said it in that way to tell her that even though I loved her, it didn't make any difference, that we could never be the same again and that I would never be at her mercy again, and I saw that she recognized that immediately.

'Why do you say it like that?' she said. 'You still don't forgive me for the quarrels we had?'

'I forgive you for everything,' I said, 'except for going to bed with Osano.'

'But that didn't mean anything,' she said. 'I just went to bed with him and then it was all over. It really didn't mean anything.'

'I don't care,' I said, 'I'll never forgive you for that.'

She thought that over and went to get another glass of wine, and after she had drunk a bit, we went to bed. The magic of her flesh still had its power. And I wondered if out of the silly romanticism of love poems and love stories there could be a basis of scientific fact, that maybe it could be true, that in the tiny cells of our body of many millions and of many disparate cells a person met with a person of the opposite sex who had those very same cells and those cells responded to each other. That it had nothing to do with power or class or intelligence, that it had nothing to do with virtue or sin, that it was quite simply a scientific response of similar cells and how easy it would be then to understand that bed magic.

We were in bed naked, making love, when suddenly Janelle sat up and withdrew from me.

'I have to go home,' she said.

And it wasn't one of her deliberate acts of punishment. I could see that she could no longer bear to be here. Her body seemed to shrivel up, her breasts became flatter, her face gaunt with tension as if she had suffered some frightful blow, and she looked me directly in the eyes without any attempt of apology or excuses, without any attempt to reassure me for my hurt ego. She said again as simply as before, 'I have to go home.'

I didn't dare touch her to reassure her. I started to dress and I said, 'It's OK. I understand. I'll go downstairs with you to get your car.'

'No,' she said. She was dressed now. 'You don't have to.'

And I could see she couldn't bear to be with me, that she wanted me out of her sight. I let her out of the suite. We didn't attempt to kiss each other good-bye. She tried to smile at me before she turned away but could not.

I closed and locked the door and I went to bed. Despite the fact that I had been interrupted in mid-course, I found that I had no sexual excitement left. The repulsion she had for me had killed any sexual desire, but my ego wasn't hurt. I really felt I understood what had happened, and I was as relieved as she was. I fell asleep almost immediately without dreams. In fact, it was the best sleep I had had in years.

47

CULLY, making his final plans to depose Gronevelt, could not think of himself as a traitor. Gronevelt would be taken care of, receive a huge sum of money for his interest in the hotel, be allowed to keep his living quarters suite. Everything would be as it had been before except that Gronevelt would no longer have any real power. Certainly Gronevelt would have 'The Pencil'. He still had many friends who would come to the Xanadu to gamble. But since Gronevelt 'Hosted' them, that would be a profitable courtesy.

Cully thought he would never have done this had Gronevelt not had his stroke. Since that stroke the Xanadu Hotel had slid downhill. Gronevelt had simply not been strong enough to act quickly and make the right decisions when necessary.

But still Cully felt some guilt. He remembered the years he had spent with Gronevelt. Gronevelt had been like a father to him. Gronevelt had helped him ascend to power. He had spent many happy days with Gronevelt listening to his stories, making the rounds of the casino. It had been a happy time. He had even given Gronevelt first shot at Carole, beautiful 'Charlie Brown'. And for a moment he wondered where Charlie Brown was now, why she had run off with Osano, and then he remembered how he had met her.

Cully had always loved to accompany Gronevelt on his casino rounds, which Gronevelt would usually make around midnight, after dinner with friends or after a private dinner with a girl in his suite. Then Gronevelt would come down to the casino and tour his empire. Searching for signs of betrayal, spotting traitors or outside hustlers all trying to destroy his god, percentage.

Cully would walk beside him, noting how Gronevelt seemed to become stronger, more upright, the colour in his cheeks better as if he took strength through the casino's carpeted floor.

One night in the dice pit Gronevelt heard a player ask one of the dice croupiers what time it was. The dice croupier looked at his wristwatch and said, 'I don't know, it stopped.'

Gronevelt was immediately alert, staring at the croupier. The man had on a wristwatch with a black face, very large, very macho with chronometers in it, and Gronevelt said to the croupier, 'Let me see your watch.'

The croupier looked startled for a moment and then thrust out his arm. Gronevelt held the croupier's hand in his, looking at the watch, and then with the quick fingers of the born card mechanic he worked the wristwatch off the man's arm. He smiled at the croupier. 'I'll hold this for you up in my office,' he said. 'In an hour you can come up for it or you can be out of this casino. If you come up for it, I'll give you an apology. Five hundred bucks' worth.' Then Gronevelt turned away, still holding the watch.

Up in Gronevelt's suite Gronevelt had shown Cully how the watch worked. That it was hollow and there was a slot in its top

409

through which a chip could be slipped. Gronevelt easily took the watch apart with some little tools in his desk, and when it was open, there was a single solitary gold-flecked hundred-dollar black chip.

Gronevelt said musingly, 'I wonder if he just used this watch himself or whether he rented it out to other shift workers. It's not a bad idea, but it's small potatoes. What could he take out on the shift? Three hundred, four hundred dollars.' Gronevelt shook his head. 'Everybody should be like him. I'd never have to worry.'

Cully went back down to the casino. The pit boss told him that the croupier had resigned and already left the hotel.

That was the night that Cully met Charlie Brown. He saw her at the roulette wheel. A beautiful, slender blonde girl with a face so innocent and young that he wondered if she was legally of age to gamble. He saw that she dressed well, sexily but without any real flair. So he guessed that she was not from New York or Los Angeles, but from one of the Midwest cities.

Cully kept an eye on her as she played roulette. And then, when she wandered over to one of the blackjack tables, he followed her. He went into the pit behind the dealer. He saw she didn't know how to play the percentages in blackjack, so he chatted with her, telling her when to hit and when to stick. She started making money, her pile of chips growing higher. She gave Cully plenty of encouragement when he asked if she was alone in town. She said no, she was with a girlfriend.

Cully gave her his card. It read, 'Vice-president, Xanadu Hotel'. 'If you want anything,' he said, 'just call me. Would you like to go to our show tonight and have dinner as my guest?'

The girl said that would be marvellous. 'Could it be for me and my girlfriend?'

Cully said, 'OK.' He wrote something on the card before he gave it to her. He said, 'Just show that to the maître d' before the dinner show. If you need anything else, give me a call.' Then he walked away.

Sure enough, after the dinner show he heard himself being paged. He picked up the call and he heard the girl's voice.

'This is Carole,' the girl said.

Cully said, 'I'd know your voice anywhere, Carole, you were the girl at the blackjack table.'

'Yes,' she said. 'I just wanted to call and thank you. We had a marvellous time.'

410

'I'm glad,' Cully said. 'And whenever you come into town, please call me and I'll be happy to do anything I can for you. In fact, if you can't get reservations for a room, call me and I'll fix it for you.'

'Thank you,' Carole said. Her voice sounded a little disappointed.

'Wait a minute,' Cully said. 'When are you leaving Vegas?'

'Tomorrow morning,' Carole said.

'Why don't you let me buy you and your girlfriend a farewell drink?' Cully said. 'It would be my pleasure.'

'That would be wonderful,' the girl said.

'OK,' Cully said. 'I'll meet you by the baccarat table.'

Carole's friend was another pretty girl with dark hair and pretty breasts, dressed a little more conservatively than her friend. Cully didn't push it. He bought them drinks at the casino lounge, found out that they came from Salt Lake City and, though they were not yet working at any job, they hoped to be models.

'Maybe I can help you,' Cully said. 'I have friends in the business in Los Angeles and maybe we can get you two girls a start. Why don't you call me in the middle of next week and I'm sure I'll have something for you two either here or in Los Angeles?' And that's how they left it for that night.

The next week, when Carole called him, he gave her the phone number of a modelling agency in Los Angeles where he had a friend, and told her she would almost surely get some kind of a job. She said she was coming into Vegas the following weekend, and Cully said, 'Why don't you stay at our hotel? I'll comp you. It won't cost you a penny.' Carole said she would be delighted.

That weekend everything fell into place. When Carole checked in, the desk called his office. He made sure there were flowers and fruit in her room, and then he called her and asked if she would like to have dinner with him. She was delighted. After dinner he took her to one of the shows on the Strip and to some of the other casinos to gamble. He explained to her he could not gamble at the Xanadu because his name was on the licence. He gave her a hundred dollars to play blackjack and roulette. She squealed with delight. He kept a sharp eye on her and she didn't try to slip any chips into her handbag, which meant she was a straight girl. He made sure that she would be impressed with the greetings he got from the maître d' at the hotel and pit bosses at the casinos. By the time the night was through Carole had to know that he was a very important man in Vegas. When they got back to the Xanadu, he said to her, 'Would you like to see what a vice-president's suite looks like?'

She gave him an innocent grin and said, 'Sure.' And when they got up to the suite, she made the proper nods of exclamations of delight and then flopped down on the sofa in an exaggerated sprawled show of tiredness. 'Wow,' she said. 'Vegas is sure different from Salt Lake City.'

'You ever think of living here?' Cully said. 'A girl as beautiful as you could have a great time. I'd introduce you to all the best people.'

'Would you?' Carole said.

'Sure,' Cully said. 'Everybody would love to know a beautiful girl like you.'

'Uh-uh,' she said. 'I'm not beautiful.'

'Sure you are,' Cully said. 'You know you are.'

By this time he was sitting beside her on the sofa. He placed one hand on her stomach, bent over and kissed her on the mouth. She tasted very sweet, and as he kissed her, he made his hand go into her skirt. There was no resistance. She kissed him back, and Cully, thinking of his expensive sofa covering, said, 'Let's go into the bedroom.'

'OK,' she said. And holding hands, they went into the bedroom. Cully undressed her. She had one of the most beautiful bodies he had ever seen. Milk white. A golden blonde bush to match her hair, and her breasts sprang out as soon as she took her clothes off. And she wasn't shy. When Cully undressed, she ran her hands over his belly and his crotch and leaned her face against his stomach. He touched her head downward and with that encouragement she did what she wanted to do. He let her for a moment and then took her into the bed.

They made love, and when it was over, she buried her face in his neck with her arms around him and sighed contentedly. They rested and Cully thought about it and evaluated her charms. Well, she was great-looking and not a bad fuck and not a bad cock-sucker, but she wasn't that great. He had a lot to teach her and now his mind was working. She really was one of the most beautiful girls he had ever seen, and the innocence of her face was an extra charm set off by the lushness of her slim body. In clothes she looked slender. Without clothes she was a delightful surprise. She was classically voluptuous, Cully thought. The best body he had ever seen and, though no virgin, still inexperienced, still uncynical, still very sweet. And Cully had a flash of inspira-

412

tion. He would use this girl as a weapon. As one of his tools for power. There were hundreds of good-looking girls in Vegas. But they were either too dumb or too hard or they didn't have the right mentors. He would make her into something special. Not a hooker. He would never be a pimp. He would never take a penny from her. He would make her the dream woman of every gambler that came to Vegas. But first, of course, he would have to fall in love with her and make her fall in love with him. And after that was out of the way, they could get down to business.

Carole never went back to Salt Lake City. She became Cully's mistress and hung out in his suite though she lived in an apartment house next to the hotel. Cully made her take tennis lessons, dancing lessons. He got one of Xanadu's classiest show girls to teach her how to use makeup and dress properly. He arranged modelling jobs in Los Angeles and pretended to be jealous of her. He'd question her about how she spent nights in Los Angeles when she stayed overnight and question her relationship with the photographers at the agency.

Carole would smother him with kisses and say, 'Honey, I couldn't make love with anybody but you now.'

And as far as he could tell, she was sincere. He could have checked on her, but it wasn't important. He let the love affair go on for three months, and then one night, when she was in his suite, he said to her, 'Gronevelt is really feeling low tonight. He's had some bad news. I tried to get him to come out for a drink with us, but he's up in his suite all by himself.' Carole had met Gronevelt in her comings and goings in the hotel and one night had had dinner with him and Cully. Gronevelt had been charming with her in his courtly way. Carole liked him.

'Oh, how sad,' Carole said.

Cully smiled. 'I know whenever he sees you, it cheers him up. You're so beautiful,' he said. 'With that great face of yours. You know all men like him love that innocent face like yours.' And it was true. Her eyes were spaced wide in a face sprinkled with tiny freckles. She looked like a piece of candy. Her blonde hair, tawny yellow, was tousled like a child's.

'You look just like that kid in the comic strip,' Cully said. 'Charlie Brown.' And that became her name in Vegas. She was delighted.

Charlie Brown said, 'Older men always liked me. Some of my father's friends would make passes at me.'

413

Cully said, 'Sure they did. How do you feel about that?'

'Oh, I never got mad,' she said. 'I was sort of flattered and I never told my father. They were really nice. They always brought me presents and they never really did anything bad.'

'I've got an idea,' Cully said. 'Why don't I call Gronevelt and you go up there and keep him company? I have some things to do down in the casino. Do your best to cheer him up.' He smiled at her, and she looked at him gravely.

'Okay,' she said.

Cully gave her a fatherly kiss. 'You know what I mean, don't you?' he said.

'I know what you mean.' And for a moment Cully, looking at that angelic face, felt a tiny arrow of guilt.

But then she gave him a brilliant smile. 'I don't mind,' she said. 'I really don't, and I like him. But are you sure he wants me to?'

And then Cully was reassured. 'Honey,' he said, 'don't worry. You just go up and I'll give him a call. He'll be expecting you, and you just be your natural self. He'll absolutely love you. Believe me.' And as he said that, he reached for the phone.

He called Gronevelt's suite and heard Gronevelt's amused voice say, 'If you're sure she wants to come up, by all means. She's a lovely girl.'

And Cully hung up the phone and said, 'Come on, honey. I'll take you up there.'

They went to Gronevelt's suite. Cully introduced her as Charlie Brown and could see Gronevelt was delighted with the name. Cully made them all drinks and they sat around and talked. Then Cully excused himself, said that he had to go down to the casino and left them together.

He didn't see Charlie Brown that night at all and knew she had spent it with Gronevelt. The next day, when he saw Gronevelt, he said, 'Was she OK?'

And Gronevelt said, 'She was fine. Lovely, lovely girl. Sweet girl. I tried to give her some money, but she wouldn't take it.'

'Well,' Cully said, 'you know she's a young girl. She's a little new at this. But was she OK with you?'

Gronevelt said, 'Fine.'

'Should I make sure that you could see her whenever you want to?'

'Oh, no,' Gronevelt said. 'She's a little too young for me, I'm a little uncomfortable with girls that young, especially when they

414

don't take money. In fact, why don't you buy her a present for me in the jewelry shop?'

When Cully got back to his office, he called Charlie Brown's apartment. 'Did you have a good time?' Cully said.

'Oh, he was just great,' Charlie Brown said. 'He was such a gentleman.'

Cully began to be a little worried. 'What do you mean he was such a gentleman? Didn't you do anything?'

'Oh, sure we did,' Charlie Brown said. 'He was great. You wouldn't think someone that old could be so great. I'll cheer him up anytime he wants.'

Cully made a date with her to have dinner that night, and when he hung up the phone, he leaned back his chair and tried to think it out. He had hoped Gronevelt would fall in love and he could use her as a weapon against Gronevelt. But somehow Gronevelt had sensed all this. There was no way to get to Gronevelt through women. He had had too many of them. He had seen too many of them corrupted. He did not know the meaning of virtue and so could not fall in love. He could not fall in love with lust because it was too easy. 'You don't have a percentage going with you against women,' Gronevelt said. 'You should never give away your edge.'

And so Cully thought, well, maybe not with Gronevelt, but there were plenty of other wheels in town that Charlie could wreck. At first he had thought that it was her lack of technical facility. After all, she was a young girl and not an expert. But in the past few months he had taught her a few things and she was much better than when he had first had her. OK. He couldn't get Gronevelt, which would have been ideal for all of them, and now he would have to use her in a more general way. So in the months that followed Cully 'turned her out'. He fixed her up with weekend dates with the biggest high rollers that came to Vegas, and he taught her never to take money from them and not always to go to bed with them. He explained his reasoning to her. 'You're looking for the big shot only. Someone who's going to fall in love with you and going to lay plenty of money on you and going to buy you plenty of presents. But they won't do that if they think they can lay a couple of hundred on you just for screwing you. You're going to have to play it like a soft, soft hustler. In fact, it could be a good idea sometimes not to screw them the first night. Just like the old days. But if you do, just make believe it's because they overpowered you.'

415

He was not surprised that Charlie agreed to do everything that he told her. He had on the first night detected the masochism so often found in beautiful women. He was familiar with that. The lack of self-worth, the desire to please someone that they thought really cared about them. It was, of course, a pimp's trick, and Cully was no pimp, but he was doing this for her good.

Charlie Brown had another virtue. She could eat more than any person he had ever met. The first time she had let herself go Cully had been amazed. She had eaten a steak with a baked potato, a lobster with French fried potatoes, cake, ice cream, then helped polish off Cully's plate. He would show off her eating qualities, and some of the men, some of the high rollers, were infatuated by this quality in her. They would love to take her to dinner and watch her eat enormous quantities of food, which never seemed to distress her or make her less hungry and never added an inch of fat to her frame.

Charlie acquired a car, some horses to ride; she bought the town house in which she was renting an apartment and she gave her money to Cully to bank for her. Cully opened up a special guardian account. He had his own tax adviser do her taxes. He put her on the casino payroll of the hotel so that she could show a source of income. He never took a penny from her. But in a few years she fucked every powerful casino manager in Vegas, plus some of the hotel owners. She fucked high rollers from Texas, New York and California, and Cully was thinking of springing her on Fummiro. But when he suggested that to Gronevelt, Gronevelt, without giving any reason, said, 'No, not Fummiro.'

Cully asked him why, and Gronevelt said to him, 'There's something a little flaky about that girl. Don't risk her with the real top rollers.' And Cully accepted that judgment.

But Cully's biggest coup with Charlie Brown was fixing her up with Judge Brianca, the federal judge in Las Vegas. Cully arranged the rendezvous. Charlie would wait in one of the hotel's rooms, the judge would come in the back entrance of Cully's suite and the judge would enter Charlie's room. Faithfully, Judge Brianca came every week. And when Cully started asking him for favours, they both knew what the score would be.

He duplicated this setup with a member of the Gaming Commission, and it was Charlie's special qualities that made it all work. Her loving innocence, her great body. She was great fun. Judge Brianca took her on his vacation trips fishing. Some of the bankers took her on business trips to screw them when they weren't busy. When they were busy, she went shopping, and when they were horny, she fucked them. She didn't need to be courted with tender words, and she would take money only for shopping. She had the quality of making them believe that she was in love with them, that she found them wonderful to be with and to make love with, and this without making any demands. All they had to do was call her up or call Cully.

The only trouble with Charlie was that she was a slob at home. By this time her friend Sarah had moved from Salt Lake City to her apartment and Cully had 'turned her out' too after a period of instruction. Sometimes when he went over to their apartment, he was disgusted by the way they kept it, and one morning he was so enraged after looking around the kitchen he kicked them both out of bed, made them wash and clean up the black pots in the sink and hang up new curtains. They did it grouchily, but when he took them both out to dinner, they were so affectionate that all three of them wound up together in his suite that night.

Charlie Brown was the Vegas dream girl, and then, finally, when Cully most needed her, she vanished with Osano. Cully never understood that. When she came back, she seemed to be the same, but Cully knew that if ever Osano called for her, she would leave Vegas.

For a long time Cully was Gronevelt's loyal and devoted right-hand man. Then he started thinking of replacing Gronevelt.

The seed of betrayal had been sown in Cully's mind when he had been made to buy ten points in the Xanadu Hotel and its casino.

Summoned to a meeting in Gronevelt's suite, he had met Johnny Santadio. Santadio was a man of about forty, soberly but elegantly dressed in the English style. His bearing was erect, soldierly. Santadio had spent four years at West Point. His father, one of the great Mafia leaders in New York, used political connections to secure his son, Johnny, an appointment to the military academy.

Father and son were patriots. Until the father had been forced to go into hiding to avoid a congressional subpoena. The FBI had flushed him out by holding his son, Johnny, as a hostage and sending out word that the son would be harassed until the father gave himself up. The elder Santadio had done so and had appeared before a congressional committee, but then Johnny Santadio resigned from West Point.

Johnny Santadio had never been indicted or convicted of any

crime. He had never even been arrested. But merely by being his father's son, he had been denied a licence to own points in the Xanadu Hotel by the Nevada Gaming Commission.

Cully was impressed by Johnny Santadio. He was quiet, well spoken and could even have passed for an Ivy League graduate from an old Yankee family. He did not even look Italian. There were just the three of them in the room, and Gronevelt opened the conversation by saying to Cully, 'How would you like to own some points in the hotel?'

'Sure,' Cully said. 'I'll give you my marker.'

Johnny Santadio smiled. It was a gentle, almost sweet smile. 'From what Gronevelt has told me about you,' Santadio said, 'you have such a good character that I'll put up the money for your points.'

Cully understood at once. He would own the points as a front for Santadio. 'That's OK with me,' Cully said.

Santadio said, 'Are you clean enough to get a licence from the Gaming Commission?'

'Sure,' Cully said. 'Unless they've got a law against screwing broads.'

This time Santadio did not smile. He just waited until Cully had finished speaking, and then he said, 'I will loan you money for the points. You'll sign a note for the amount that I put up. The note will read that you pay six percent interest and you will pay. But you have my word that you won't lose anything by paying that interest. Do you understand that?'

Cully said, 'Sure.'

Gronevelt said, 'This is an absolutely legal operation we're doing here, Cully, I want to make that clear. But it's important that nobody know that Mr Santadio holds your note. The Gaming Commission just on its own can veto your being on our licence for that.'

'I understand,' Cully said. 'But what if something happens to me? What if I get hit by a car or I go down in a plane? Have you thought that out? How does Santadio get his points?'

Gronevelt smiled and patted his back and said, 'Haven't I been just like a father to you?'

'You really have,' Cully said sincerely. And he meant it. And the sincerity was in his voice and he could see that Santadio approved of it.

'Well then,' Gronevelt said, 'you make out your will and you leave me the points in your will. If something should happen to you, Santadio knows I'll get the points or his money back to him. Is that OK with you, Johnny?'

Johnny Santadio nodded. Then he said casually to Cully, 'Do you know of any way that I could get on the licence? Can the Gaming Commission pass me despite my father?'

Cully realized that Gronevelt must have told Santadio that he had one of the gaming commissioners in his pocket. 'It would be tough,' Cully said, 'and it would take time and it would cost money.'

'How much time?' Santadio said.

'A couple of years,' Cully said. 'You do mean that you want to be directly on the licence?'

'That's right,' Santadio said.

'Will the Gaming Commission find anything on you when they investigate you?' Cully asked.

'Nothing, except that I'm my father's son,' Santadio said. 'And a lot of rumours and reports in the FBI files and New York police files. Just raw material. No proof of anything.'

Cully said, 'That's enough for the Gaming Commission to turn you down.'

'I know,' Santadio said. 'That's why I need your help.'

'I'll give it a try,' Cully said.

'That's fine,' Gronevelt said. 'Cully, you can go to my lawyer to have your will made out so that I'll get a copy, and Mr Santadio and I will take care of all the other details.'

Santadio had shaken Cully's hand and Cully left them.

It was a year after that Gronevelt suffered his stroke, and while Gronevelt was in the hospital, Santadio came to Vegas and met with Cully. Cully assured Santadio that Gronevelt would recover and that he was still working on the Gaming Commission.

And then Santadio said, 'You know the ten percent you have is not my only interest in this casino. I have other friends of mine who own a piece of the Xanadu. We're very concerned about whether Gronevelt can run the hotel after this stroke. Now, I want you to take this the right way. I have enormous respect for Gronevelt. If he can run the hotel, fine. But if he can't, if the place starts going down, I'll want you to let me know.'

At that moment Cully had to make his decision to be faithful to Gronevelt to the end or to find his own future. He operated purely on instinct. 'Yes, I will,' he said to Santadio. 'Not only for your interest and mine, but also for Mr Gronevelt.'

Santadio smiled. 'Gronevelt is a great man,' he said. 'Anything we can do for him I would want to do. That's understood. But it's no good for any of us if the hotel goes down the drain.'

'Right,' Cully said. 'I'll let you know.'

When Gronevelt came out of the hospital, he seemed to be completely recovered and Cully reported directly to him. But after six months he could see that Gronevelt really did not have the strength to run the hotel and the casino, and he reported this to Johnny Santadio.

Santadio flew in and had a conference with Gronevelt and asked Gronevelt if he had considered selling his interest in the hotel and relinquishing control.

Gronevelt, much frailer now, sat quietly in his chair and looked at Cully and Santadio. 'I see your point,' he said to Santadio. 'But I think with a little time I can do the job. Let me say this to you. If in another six months things don't get better, I'll do as you suggest, and of course, you get first crack at my interest. Is that good enough for you, Johnny?'

'Sure,' Santadio said. 'You know that I trust you more than any man I know and have more confidence in your ability. If you say you can do it in six months, I believe you, and when you say that you'll quit in six months if you can't do it, I believe you. I leave it all in your hands.'

And so the meeting ended. But that night, when Cully took Santadio to get his plane back to New York, Santadio said, 'Keep a close eye on things. Let me know what's happening. If he gets really bad, we can't wait.'

It was than that Cully had to pause in his betrayal because in the next six months Gronevelt did improve, did get a greater grasp. But the reports that Cully gave to Santadio did not indicate this. The final recommendation to Santadio was that Gronevelt should be removed.

It was only a month later that Santadio's nephew, a pit boss in one of the hotels on the Strip, was indicted for tax evasion and fraud by a federal grand jury and Johnny Santadio flew to Vegas to have a conference with Gronevelt. Ostensibly the meeting was to help the nephew, but Santadio started on another tack.

He said to Gronevelt, 'You have about three months to go. Have you come to any decision about selling me your interest?'

Gronevelt looked at Cully, who saw his face was a little sad, a little tired. And then Gronevelt turned to Santadio and said, 'What do you think?'

Santadio said, 'I'm more concerned about your health and the hotel. I really think that maybe the business is too much for you now.'

Gronevelt sighed. 'You may be right,' he said. 'Let me think it over. I have to go see my doctor next week, and the report he gives me will probably make it tough for me no matter what I want. But what about your nephew?' he said to Santadio. 'Is there anything we can do to help?'

For the first time since Cully had known him Santadio looked angry. 'So stupid. So stupid and unnecessary. I don't give a damn if he goes to jail, but if he gets convicted, it's another black mark on my name. Everybody will think I was behind him or had something to do with it. I came out here to help, but I really haven't got any ideas.'

Gronevelt was sympathetic. 'It's not all that hopeless,' he said. 'Cully here has a lock on the federal judge who will try the case. How about it, Cully? Do you still have Judge Brianca in your pocket?'

Cully thought it over. What the advantages would be. This would be a tough one to spring with the judge. The judge would have to go out on a limb, but Cully, if he had to, would make him. It would be dangerous, but the rewards might be worth it. If he could do this for Santadio, then Santadio would surely let him run the hotel after Gronevelt sold out. It would cement his position. He would be ruler of the Xanadu.

Cully looked at Santadio very intently, he made his voice very serious, very sincere. 'It would be tough,' he said. 'It will cost money, but if you really must have it, Mr Santadio, I promise you your nephew won't go to jail.'

'You mean he'll be acquitted?' Santadio said.

'No, I can't promise that,' Cully said. 'Maybe it won't go that far. But I promise you if he is convicted, he will only get a suspended sentence, and the odds are good the judge will handle the trial and charge the jury so that maybe your nephew can get off.'

'That would be great,' Santadio said. He shook his hand warmly. 'You do this for me and you can ask me for anything you want.'

And then suddenly Gronevelt was in between them, placing

421

his hand like a benediction on both of theirs locked together.

'That's great,' Gronevelt said. 'We have solved all the problems. Now let's go out and have a good dinner and celebrate.'

It was a week later that Gronevelt called Cully into his office. 'I got my doctor's report,' Gronevelt said. 'He advised me to retire. But before I go, I want to try something. I've told my bank to put a million dollars into my checking account and I'm going to to take my shot at the other tables in town. I'd like you to hang out with me either till I go broke or double the million.'

Cully was incredulous. 'You're going to go against the percentage?' he said.

'I'd like to give it one more shot,' Gronevelt said. 'I was a great gambler when I was a kid. If anybody can beat the percentage, I can. If I can't beat the percentage, nobody can. We'll have a great time, and I can afford the million bucks.'

Cully was astonished. Gronevelt's belief in the percentage had been unshakable in all the years he had known him. Cully remembered one period in the history of the Xanadu Hotel when three months straight the Xanadu dice tables had lost money every night. The players were getting rich. Cully was sure there was a sham going on. He had fired all of the dice pit personnel. Gronevelt had had all the dice analyzed by scientific laboratories. Nothing helped. Cully and the casino manager were sure somebody had come up with a new scientific device to control the roll of the dice. There could be no other explanation. Only Gronevelt held fast.

'Don't worry,' he said. 'The percentage will work.'

And sure enough, after three months the dice had swung just as wildly the other way. The dice pit had winning tables every night for over three months. At the end of the year it had all evened out. Gronevelt had had a congratulatory drink with Cully and said, 'You can lose faith in everything, religion and God, women and love, good and evil, war and peace. You name it. But the percentage will always stand fast.'

And during the next week, when Gronevelt gambled, Cully always kept that in mind. Gronevelt gambled better than any man he had ever seen. At the crap table he made all the bets that cut down the percentage of the house. He seemed to divine the ebb and flow of luck. When the dice ran cold, he switched sides. When the dice got hot, he pressed every bet to the limit.

422

At baccarat he could smell out when the shoe would turn Banker and when the shoe would turn Player and ride the waves. At blackjack he dropped his bets to five dollars when the dealer hit a lucky streak and brought it up to the limit when the dealer was cold.

In the middle of the week Gronevelt was five hundred thousand dollars ahead. By the end of the week he was six hundred thousand dollars ahead. He kept going, Cully by his side. They would eat dinner together and gamble only until midnight. Gronevelt said you had to be in good shape to gamble. You couldn't push, you had to get a good night's sleep. You had to watch your diet and you should only get laid once every three or four nights.

By the middle of the second week Gronevelt, despite all his skill, was sliding downhill. The percentages were grinding him into dust. And at the end of two weeks he had lost his million dollars. When he bet his last stack of chips and lost, Gronevelt turned to Cully and smiled. He seemed to be delighted, which struck Cully as ominous. 'It's the only way to live,' Gronevelt said. 'You have to live going with the percentage. Otherwise life is not worthwhile. Always remember that,' he told Cully. 'Everything you do in life use percentage as your god.'

48

ON my last trip to California to do the final rewrite on Tri-Culture's film I ran into Osano at the Beverly Hills Hotel lounge. I was so shocked by his physical appearance that at first I didn't notice he had Charlie Brown with him. Osano must have put on about thirty pounds, and he had a huge gut that bulged out of an old tennis jacket. His face was bloated, it was speckled with tiny white fat dots. The green eyes that had once been so brilliant had faded into pale colourlessness that looked grey, and as he walked toward me, I could see that the curious lurch in his gait had become worse.

We had drinks in the Polo Lounge. As usual, Charlie drew the eyes of all the men in the room. This was not only because of her beauty and her innocent face. There were plenty of those in Beverly Hills, but there was something in her dress, something in the way she walked and glanced around the room that signalled an easy availability.

Osano said, 'I look terrible, don't I?'

'I've seen you worse,' I said.

'Hell, I've seen myself worse,' Osano said. 'You, you lucky bastard, can eat anything you want and you never put on an ounce.'

'But I'm not as good as Charlie,' I said. And I smiled at her and she smiled back.

Osano said, 'We're catching the afternoon plane. Eddie Lancer thought he could fix me up with a script job, but it fell through, so I might as well get the hell out of here. I think I'll go to a fat farm, get in shape and finish my novel.'

'How's the novel coming?' I asked.

'Great,' Osano said. 'I got over two thousand pages, just five hundred more to go.'

I didn't know what to say to him. By this time he had acquired a reputation for not delivering with magazine publishers, even on his nonfiction books. His novel was his last hope.

'You should just concentrate on the five hundred pages,' I said, 'and get the goddamn book finished. That will solve all your troubles.'

'Yeah, you're right,' Osano said. 'But I can't rush it. Even my publisher wouldn't want me to do that. This is the Nobel Prize for me, kid, when this is finished.'

I looked at Charlie Brown to see if she was impressed, and it struck me that she didn't even know what the Nobel Prize was.

'You're lucky to have such a publisher,' I told Osano. 'They've been waiting ten years for that book.'

Osano laughed. 'Yeah, the classiest publishers in America. They've given me over a hundred grand and they haven't seen a page. Real class, not like these fucking movie people.'

'I'll be leaving for New York in a week,' I said. 'I'll call you for dinner there. What's your new phone number?'

Osano said, 'It's the same one.'

I said, 'I've called there and nobody ever answered.'

'Yeah,' Osano said. 'I've been down in Mexico working on my book, eating those beans and tacos. That's why I got so goddamn heavy. Charlie Brown here, she didn't put on an ounce and she ate ten times as much as I did.' He patted Charlie Brown on the shoulder, squeezing her flesh. 'Charlie Brown,' he said, 'if you die before me, I'm going to have them dissect your body and find out what you got that keeps you skinny.'

She smiled back at him. 'That reminds me, I'm hungry,' she said.

So just to cheer things up I ordered lunch for us. I had a plain salad and Osano had an omelette and Charlie Brown ordered a hamburger with French fried potatoes, a steak with vegetables, a salad and a three-scoop ice-cream desert on top of apple pie. Osano and myself enjoyed the people watching Charlie eat. They couldn't believe it. A couple of men in the next booth made audible comments, hoping to draw us into a conversation so they would have an excuse to talk to Charlie. But Osano and Charlie ignored them.

I paid the bill, and when I left, I promised to call Osano when I got to New York.

Osano said, 'That would be great. I've agreed to talk in front of that Women's Lib convention next month, and I'll need some moral support from you, Merlyn. How about if we have dinner that night and then go on to the convention?'

I was a little doubtful. I wasn't really interested in any kind of convention, and I was a little worried about Osano's getting into trouble and I'd have to bail him out again. But I said OK, that I would.

Neither one of us had mentioned Janelle. I couldn't resist saying to Osano, 'Have you seen Janelle in town?'

'No,' Osano said, 'have you?'

'I haven't seen her for a long time,' I said.

Osano stared at me. The eyes for just one second became their usual sneaky pale green. He smiled a little sadly. 'You should never let a girl like that go,' he said. 'You just get one of them in a lifetime. Just like you get one big book in your lifetime.'

I shrugged and we shook hands again. I kissed Charlie on the cheek and then I left.

That afternoon I had a story conference at Tri-Culture Studios. It was with Jeff Wagon, Eddie Lancer, and the director, Simon Bellfort. I had always thought the Hollywood legends of a writer being rude to his director and producer in a story conference were shitty no matter how funny. But for the first time, at this story conference, I could see why such things had happened. In effect, Jeff Wagon and his director were ordering us to write their story, not my novel. I let Eddie Lancer do most of the arguing, and finally Eddie, exasperated, said to Jeff Wagon, 'Look, I'm not saying I'm smarter than you, I'm just saying I'm luckier. I've written four hit pictures in a row. Why not ride with my judgment?'

To me this seemed like a superbly clever argument, but I could see Jeff Wagon and the director had puzzled looks on their faces. They didn't know what Eddie was talking about, and I could see there was no way to change their minds.

Finally Eddie Lancer said, 'I'm sorry, but if that's the way you guys want to go, I have to leave this picture.'

'OK,' Jeff said. 'How about you, Merlyn?'

'I don't see any point in my writing it your way,' I said. 'I don't think I'd do a good job with it.'

'That's fair enough,' Jeff Wagon said. 'I'm sorry. Now is there any writer you know that could work on this picture with us and could have some consultations with you guys since you already have done most of the work? It would be very helpful.'

The thought flashed through my mind that I could get Osano this job. I knew he needed the money desperately and I knew that if I said I would work with Osano he would get the assignment. But then I thought of Osano in a story conference like this taking directions from men like Jeff Wagon and the director. Osano was still one of the great men in American literature, and I thought these guys would humiliate him and then fire him. So I didn't speak up.

It was only when trying to go to sleep that I realized maybe I had denied Osano the job to punish him for sleeping with Janelle.

The next morning I got a call from Eddie Lancer. He told me that he had had a meeting with his agent and his agent said that Tri-Culture Studios and Jeff Wagon were offering him a fifty-thousand-dollar extra fee to stay on the picture, and what did I think?

I told Eddie that it was perfectly OK with me, whatever he did, but that I wasn't going back on. Eddie tried to persuade me. 'I'll tell them I won't go back unless they take you back and pay you twenty-five thousand dollars,' Eddie Lancer said. 'I'm sure they'll go for it.'

Again I thought of helping Osano, and again I just couldn't do it. Eddie was going on. 'My agent told me if I didn't go back on this picture, the studio would put more writers on and then try to get the new writers the credit on the picture. Now, if we don't get script credit, we lose our Writers Guild contract and TV gross points when the picture is sold to television. Also, we both have some net points which we will probably never see. But it's just an off chance the picture may be a big hit, and then we'll be kicking our asses in. It could wind up to be a sizeable chunk of dough, Merlyn, but I won't go back on it if you think we should stick together and try to save our story.'

'I don't give a shit about the percentage,' I said, 'or the credits, and as far as the story goes, what the fuck kind of story is it? It's schlock, it's not my book any more. But you go ahead. I really don't care. I mean that.'

'OK,' Eddie said, 'and while I'm on, I'll try to protect your credit as much as I can. I'll call you when I'm in New York and we'll have dinner.'

'Great,' I said. 'Good luck with Jeff Wagon.'

'Yeah,' Eddie said, 'I'll need it.'

I spent the rest of the day moving out of my office at Tri-Culture Studios and doing some shopping. I didn't want to go back on the same plane as Osano and Charlie Brown. I thought of calling Janelle, but I didn't.

A month later, Jeff Wagon called me in New York. He told me that Simon Bellfort thought that Frank Richetti should get a writing credit with Lancer and me.

'Is Eddie Lancer still with the the picture?' I asked him.

'Yes,' Jeff Wagon said.

'OK,' I said. 'Good luck.'

'Thank you,' Wagon said. 'And we'll keep you posted on what happens. We'll all see each other at the Academy Awards dinner.' And he hung up.

I had to laugh. They were turning the picture into a piece of schlock and Wagon had the nerve to talk about Academy Awards. That Oregon beauty should have taken a bigger piece out of his balls. I felt a sense of betrayal that Eddie Lancer had remained on the picture. It was true what Wagon had once said. Eddie Lancer was a natural-born screenwriter, but he was also a natural-born novelist and I knew he would never write a novel again.

Another funny thing was that though I had fought with everybody and the script was getting worse and worse and I had intended to leave, I still felt hurt. And I guess, too, in the back of my head I still hoped that if I went to California again to work on the script, I might see Janelle. We hadn't seen or spoken to each other for months. The last time I had called her up just to say hello and we had chatted for a while and at the end she had said, 'I'm glad you called me,' and then she waited for an answer.

I paused and said, 'Me too.' At that she started to laugh and mimicked me.

She said, 'Me too, me too,' and then she said, 'Oh, it doesn't matter,' and laughed gaily. She said, 'Call me when you come out again.'

And I said, 'I will.' But I knew that I would not.

A month after Wagon called, I got a call from Eddie Lancer. He was furious. 'Merlyn,' he said, 'they're changing the script to screw you out of your credit. That guy Frank Richetti is writing all new dialogue, just paraphrasing your words. They're changing incidents just enough so that it will seem different from your scenes and I heard them talking, Wagon and Bellfort and Richetti, about how they're going to screw you out of your credit and your percentage. Those bastards don't even pay any attention to me.'

'Don't worry,' I told him. 'I wrote the novel and I wrote the original screenplay and I checked it with the Writers' Guild, and there's no way I can get screwed out of at least a partial credit and that saves my percentage.'

'I don't know,' Eddie Lancer said. 'I'm just warning you about what they're going to do. I hope you'll protect yourself.'

'Thanks,' I told him. 'What about you? How are you coming on the picture?'

He said, 'That fucking Frank Richetti is a fucking illiterate, and I don't know who's the bigger hack, Wagon or Bellfort. This may become one of the worst pictures ever made. Poor Malomar must be spinning in his grave.'

'Yeah, poor Malomar,' I said. 'He was always telling me how great Hollywood was, how sincere and artistic the people there could be. I wish he were alive now.'

'Yeah,' Eddie Lancer said. 'Listen, next time you come to California call me and we'll have dinner.'

'I don't think I'll be coming to California again,' I said. 'If you come to New York, call me.'

'OK, I will,' Lancer said.

A year later the picture came out. I got credit for the book but no credit as the screenwriter. Screenwriting credit was given to Eddie Lancer and Simon Bellfort. I asked for an arbitration at the Writers' Guild, but I lost. Richetti and Bellfort had done a good job changing the script, and so I lost my percentage. But it didn't matter. The picture was a disaster, and the worst of it was Doran Rudd told me that in the industry the novel was blamed for the failure of the film. I was no longer a saleable product in Hollywood, and that was the only thing about the whole business that cheered me up.

One of the most scathing reviews of the film was by Clara Ford. She murdered it from A to Z. Even Kellino's performance. So Kellino hadn't done his job too well with Clara Ford. But Houlinan took a last shot at me. He placed a story on one of the wire services headlined MERLYN NOVEL FAILS AS MOVIE. When I read that, I just shook my head with admiration.

49

SHORTLY after the picture came out I was at Carnegie Hall attending the Women's National Liberation Conference with Osano and Charlie Brown. It featured Osano as the only male speaker.

Earlier we all had dinner at Pearl's, where Charlie Brown astonished the waiters by eating a Peking duck, a plate of crabs stuffed with pork, oysters in black bean sauce, a huge fish and then polished off what Osano and me had left on our plates without even smearing her lipstick.

When we got out of the cab in front of Carnegie Hall, I tried to talk Osano into going on ahead and letting me follow with Charlie Brown on my arm so that the women would think she was with me. She looked so much like the legendary harlot she would enrage the left-wingers of the convention. But Osano, as usual, was stubborn. He wanted them all to know that Charlie Brown was his woman. So when we walked down the aisle to the front, I walked behind them. As I did so, I studied the women in the hall. The only thing odd about them was that they were all women and I realized that many times in the Army, in the orphan asylum, at ball games I was used to seeing either all men or mostly men. 'Seeing all women this time was a shock, as if I were in an alien country.

Osano was being greeted by a group of women and led up to the platform. Charlie Brown and I sat down in the first row. I was wishing we were in the back, so I could get the hell out fast. I was so worried I hardly heard the opening speeches, and then suddenly Osano was being led to the lectern and being introduced. Osano stood for a moment waiting for the applause which did not come.

Many of the women there had been offended by his male chauvinistic essays in the male magazines years ago. Some were offended because he was one of their generation's most important writers and they were jealous of his achievement. And then there were some of his admirers who applauded very faintly just in case Osano's speech met with disfavour from the convention.

Osano stood at the lectern, a vast hulk of a man. He waited a long moment; then he leaned against the lectern arrogantly and said slowly, enunciating every word, 'I'll fight you or fuck you.'

The hall reverberated with boos, catcalls and hisses. Osano tried to go on. I knew he had used that phrase just to catch their attention. His speech would be in favour of Women's Liberation, but he never got a chance to make it. The boos and hisses got louder and louder, and every time Osano tried to speak they started again until Osano made an elaborate bow and marched down off the stage. We followed him up the aisle and out the doors of Carnegie Hall. The boos and hisses turned to cheers and applause, to tell Osano that he was doing what they wanted him to do. Leave them.

Osano didn't want me to go home with him that night. He wanted to be alone with Charlie Brown. But the next morning I got a call from him. He wanted me to do him a favour.

'Listen,' Osano said. 'I'm going down to Duke University in North Carolina to their rice diet clinic. It's supposed to be the best fat farm in the United States and they also get you healthy. I have to lose weight and the doctor seems to think that maybe my arteries are clogged and that's what the rice diet cures. There's only one thing wrong. Charlie wants to come down with me. Can you imagine that poor girl eating rice for two months? So I told her she can't come. But I have to bring my car down and I'd like you to drive it for me. We could both bring it down and hang around together for a few days and maybe have some laughs.'

I thought it over for a minute and then I said, 'Sure.' We made a date for the following week. I told Valerie I would be gone for only three or four days. That I would drive Osano's car down with him, just spend a few days with Osano until he got set, then fly back.

'But why can't he drive his car himself?' Valerie said.

'He really doesn't look good,' I said. 'I don't think he's in shape to make that kind of drive. It's at least eight hours.'

That seemed to satisfy Valerie, but there was still one thing that was bothering me. Why didn't Osano want to use Charlie as his driver? He could have shipped her out as soon as they got down there, so the excuse he gave me about not wanting her to eat rice was a phoney one. Then I thought maybe he was tired of Charlie and this was his way of getting rid of her. I didn't worry too much about her. She had plenty of friends who would take care of her.

So I drove Osano down to the Duke University clinic in his four-year-old Cadillac, and Osano was in great form. He even looked a little better physically. 'I love this part of the country,' Osano said when we were in the Southern states. 'I love the way they run the Jesus Christ business down here, it's almost like every small town has its Jesus Christ store, they have Mom-and-Pop Jesus Christ stores and they make a good living and a lot of friends. One of the greatest rackets in the world. When I think about my life, I think only if I had been a religious leader instead of a writer. What a better time I would have had.'

I didn't say anything. I just listened. We both knew that Osano could not have been anything but a writer and that he was just following a private flight of fantasy.

'Yeah,' Osano said. 'I would have got together a great hill-billy band and I would have called them Shit Kickers for Jesus. I love the way they're humble in their religion and so fierce and

431

proud in their everyday life. They're like monkeys in a training den. They haven't correlated the action to its consequence, but I guess you could say that about all religions. How about those fucking Hebes in Israel? They won't let the buses and trains run on holy days and here they are fighting the Arabs. And then those fucking Ginzos in Italy with their fucking Pope. I sure wish I was running the Vatican. I'd put a logo, "Every priest a thief". That would be our motto. That would be our goal. The trouble with the Catholic Church is that there are a few honest priests left and they fuck everything up.'

He went on about religion for the next fifty miles. Then he switched to literature, then he took on the politicians and finally, near the end of our journey, he talked about Women's Liberation.

'You know,' he said, 'the funny thing is that I'm really all for them. I've always thought women got a shitty deal, even when I was the one handing it out to them, and yet those cunts, they didn't even let me finish my speech. That's the trouble with women. They have absolutely no sense of humour. Didn't they know I was making a joke, that I would turn it around for them afterward?'

I said to him, 'Why don't you publish the speech and that way they will know? *Esquire* magazine would take it, wouldn't they?'

'Sure,' Osano said. 'Maybe when I'm staying down the fat farm I'll work it over so it will look good in print.'

I wound up spending a full week with Osano at the Duke University clinic. In that week I saw more fat people, and I'm talking about your two-hundred-fifty- to three-hundred-fifty-pounders, than I have ever seen in my whole life together. Since that week I have never trusted a girl who wore a cape because every fat girl who is over two hundred pounds thinks she can hide it by draping some sort of Mexican blanket over her or a French gendarme's cloak. What it really made them look like was this huge, threatening mass coming down the street, some hideously engorged Superman or Zorro.

The Duke Medical Centre was by no means a cosmetic-oriented reducing operation. It was a serious endeavour to repair the damage done to the human body by long periods of over-weight. Every new client was put through days of all kinds of blood tests and X-rays. So I stayed with Osano and made sure he went to restaurants that served the rice diet.

For the first time I realized how lucky I was. That no matter how much I ate I never put on a pound. The first week was something I'll never forget. I saw three three-hundred-pound girls bouncing on a trampoline. Then a guy who was over five hundred pounds being taken down to the railroad station and getting weighed on the freight-weighing machine. There was something genuinely sad about that huge form shambling into the dusk, like some elephant wandering toward the graveyard where he knew he had to die.

Osano had a suite of rooms at the Holiday Inn close by the Duke Medical Centre building. Many of the patients stayed there and got together for walks or card games or just sat together trying to start an affair. There was a lot of gossip. A two-hundred-fifty-pound boy had taken his three-hundred-fifty-pound girl to New Orleans for a shack-up date for the weekend. Unfortunately the restaurants in New Orleans were so great they spent the two days eating and came back ten pounds heavier. What struck me as funny is that the gaining of the ten pounds was treated as a greater sin than their supposed immorality.

Then one time Osano and I, at four o'clock in the morning, were startled by the screams of a man in mortal agony. Stretched out on the lawn outside our bedroom windows was one of the male patients who had finally gotten himself down to two hundred pounds. He was obviously dying or sounded like it. People were rushing to him and a clinic doctor was already there. He was taken away in an ambulance. The next day we found out what had happened. The patient had emptied all the chocolate bar machines in the hotel. They counted the wrappers on the lawn, there were a hundred and sixteen. Nobody seemed to think this was peculiar, and the guy recovered and continued on the programme.

'You're going to have a great time here,' I told Osano. 'Plenty of material.'

'Naw,' Osano said. 'You can write a tragedy about skinny people, but you can never write a tragedy about fat people. Remember how popular TB was? You could cry over Camille, but how could you cry over a bag encased in three hundred pounds of fat? It's tragic, but it wouldn't look right. There's only so much that art can do.'

The next day was the final day of Osano's tests and I planned to fly back that night. Osano had behaved very well. He had stayed strictly on the rice diet and he was feeling good because I

433

had kept him company. When Osano went over to the Medical Centre for the results of his tests, I packed my bags while waiting for him to come back to the hotel.

Osano didn't show until four hours later. His face was alive with excitement. His green eyes were dancing and had their old sparkle and colour.

'Everything came out OK?' I said.

'You bet your ass,' Osano said.

For just a second I didn't trust him. He looked too good, too happy.

'Everything is perfect, couldn't be better. You can fly home tonight and I have to say you are a real buddy. No one would do what you did, eating that rice day after day, and worse still, watching those three-hundred-pound broads go by shaking their asses. Whatever sins you have committed against me I forgive you.' And for a moment his eyes were kind, very serious. There was a gentle expression on his face. 'I forgive you,' he said. 'Remember that, you're such a guilty fuck I want you to know that.'

And then for one of the few times since we knew each other he gave me a hug. I knew he hated to be touched except by women and I knew he hated being sentimental. I was surprised, but I didn't wonder about what he meant by forgiving me because Osano was so sharp. He was really so much smarter than anyone else I had ever known that in some way he knew the reason why I had not gotten him the job on the Tri-Culture-Jeff Wagon script. He had forgiven me and that was fine, that was like Osano. He was really a great man. The only trouble was I had not yet forgiven myself.

I left Duke University that night and flew to New York. A week later I got a call from Charlie Brown. It was the first time I had ever spoken to her over the phone. She had a soft, sweet voice, innocent, childlike, and she said, 'Merlyn, you have to help me.'

And I said, 'What's wrong?'

And she said, 'Osano is dying, he's in the hospital. Please, please come.'

50

CHARLIE had already taken Osano to St Vincent's Hospital, so we agreed to meet there. When I got there, Osano was in a private room and Charlie was with him, sitting on the bed where Osano could put his hand in her lap. Charlie let her hand rest on Osano's stomach, which was bare of covers or top shirt. In fact, Osano's hospital nightgown lay in shreds on the floor. That act must have put him in good humour because he was sitting up cheerfully in bed. And to me he really didn't look that bad. In fact, he seemed to have lost some weight.

I checked the hospital room quickly with my eyes. There were no intravenous settings, no special nurses on duty, and I had seen walking down the corridor that it was not in any way an intensive care unit. I was surprised at the amount of relief I felt, that Charlie must have made a mistake and that Osano wasn't dying after all.

Osano said coolly, 'Hi, Merlyn. You must be a real magician. How did you find out I was here? It's supposed to be a secret.'

I didn't want any fooling around or any kind of bullshit, so I said straight out, 'Charlie Brown told me.' Maybe she wasn't supposed to tell me, but I didn't feel like lying.

Charlie just smiled at Osano's frown.

Osano said to her. 'I told you it was just me and you, or just me. However you liked it. Nobody else.'

Charlie said almost absently, 'I know you wanted Merlyn.'

Osano sighed. 'OK,' he said. 'You've been here all day, Charlie. Why don't you go to the movies or get laid or have a chocolate ice-cream soda or ten Chinese dishes? Anyway, take the night off and I'll see you in the morning.'

'All right,' Charlie said. She got up from the bed. She stood very close to Osano and he, with a movement not really lecherous, but as if he were reminding himself of what it felt like, put his hand under her dress and caressed her inner thighs and then she leaned her head over the bed to kiss him.

And on Osano's face as his hand caressed that warm flesh beneath the dress came a look of peace and contentment as if reassured in some holy belief.

When Charlie left the room, Osano sighed and said, 'Merlyn, believe me. I wrote a lot of bullshit in my books, my articles and my lectures. I'll tell you the only real truth. Cunt is where it all begins and where it all ends. Cunt is the only thing worth living for. Everything else is a fake, a fraud and just shit.'

I sat down next to the bed. 'What about power?' I said. 'You always liked power and money pretty good.'

'You forgot art,' Osano said.

'OK,' I said. 'Let's put art in there. How about money, power and art?'

'They're OK,' Osano said. 'I won't knock them. They'll do, But they're not really necessary. They're just frosting on the cake.'

And then I was right back to my first meeting with Osano and I thought I knew the truth about him then, when he didn't know it. And now he's telling it to me and I wonder if it's true because Osano had loved them all. And what he was really saying was that art and money and fame and power were not what he regretted leaving.

'You're looking better than when I saw you last,' I told Osano. 'How come you're in the hospital? Charlie Brown says it's really trouble this time. But you don't look it.'

'No shit?' Osano said. He was pleased. 'That's great. But you know I got the bad news down the fat farm when they took all those tests. I'll give it to you short and sweet. I fucked up when I took those dosages of penicillin pills every time I got laid, so I got syphilis and the pills masked it, but the dosage wasn't strong enough to wipe it out. Or maybe those fucking spirochetes figured out a way to bypass the medicine. It must have happened about fifteen years ago. Meantime, those old spirochetes ate away at my brain, my bones and my heart. Now they tell me I got six months or a year before going cuckoo with paresis, unless my heart goes out first.'

I was stunned. I really couldn't believe it. Osano looked so cheerful. His sneaky green eyes were so brilliant. 'There's nothing that can be done?' I asked him.

436

'Nothing,' Osano said. 'But it's not so terrible. I'll rest up here for a couple of weeks and they'll shoot me up a lot and then I'll have at least a couple of months on the town and that's where you come in.'

I didn't know what to say. I really didn't know whether to believe him. He looked better than I had seen him look in a long time. 'OK,' I said.

'Here's my idea,' Osano said. 'You visit me in the hospital once in a while and help take me home. I don't want to take the chance of becoming senile, so when I think the time is right, I check out. The day I decide to do that I want you to come down to my apartment and keep me company. You and Charlie Brown. And then you can take care of all the fuss afterward.'

Osano was staring at me intently. 'You don't have to do it,' Osano said.

I believed him now. 'Sure, I'll do it,' I said. 'I owe you a favour. Will you have the stuff you need?'

'I'll get it,' Osano said. 'Don't worry about that.'

I had some conferences with Osano's doctors, and they told me he wouldn't leave the hospital for a long time. Maybe never. I felt a sense of relief.

I didn't tell Valerie about anything that had happened or even that Osano was dying. Two days later I went to visit Osano at the hospital. He'd asked me if I would bring him in a Chinese dinner the next time I came. So I had brown paper bags full of food when I went down the corridor and heard yelling and screaming coming from Osano's room. I wasn't surprised. I put the cartons down on the floor outside another patient's private bedroom and ran down the corridor.

In the room was a doctor, two nurses and a nursing supervisor. They were all screaming at Osano. Charlie stood watching in a corner of the room. Her beautiful face freckles startling against the pallor of her skin, tears in her eyes. Osano was sitting on the side of the bed, completely naked and yelling back at the doctor, 'Get me my clothes! I'm getting the fuck out of here.'

And the doctor was almost yelling at him, 'I won't be responsible if you leave this hospital. I will not be responsible.'

Osano said to him, laughing, 'You dumb shit, you were never responsible. Just get me my clothes.'

The nursing supervisor, a formidable-looking woman, said angrily, 'I don't give a damn how famous you are, you don't use our hospital as a whorehouse!'

Osano glared at her, 'Fuck you,' he said. 'Get the fuck out of

437

this room.' And stark naked, he got up off the bed, and then I could see how really sick he was. He took a lurching step and his body fell sideways. The nurse immediately went to help him, quiet now, moved to pity, but Osano struggled erect. Finally he saw me standing at the doorway and he said very quietly, 'Merlyn, get me out of here.' I was struck by their indignation. Surely they had caught patients fucking before. Then I studied Charlie Brown. She had on a short tight skirt with obviously nothing underneath. She looked like a child harlot. And Osano's gross rotting body. Their outrage unconsciously was aesthetic, not moral.

The others now noticed me too. And I said to the doctor, 'I'll check him out and I'll take the responsibility.'

The doctor started to protest, almost pleading, then turned to the supervisor and said, 'Get him his clothes.' He gave Osano a needle and said, 'That will make you more comfortable for the trip.'

And it was that simple. I paid the bill and checked Osano out. I called up a limousine service and we got Osano home. Charlie and I put him to bed and he slept for a while and then he called me into the bedroom and told me what had happened in the hospital. That he had made Charlie undress and get into bed with him because he had felt so bad that he thought he was dying.

Osano turned his head away a bit. 'You know,' he said, 'the most terrible thing in modern life is that we all die alone in bed. In the hospital with all our family around us, nobody offers to get in bed with somebody dying. If you're at home, your wife won't offer to get in bed when you're dying.'

Osano turned his head to me and gave me that sweet smile he sometimes had. 'So that's my dream. I want Charlie in bed with me when I die, at the very moment, and then I'll feel that I've gotten an edge, that it wasn't a bad life and certainly not a bad end. And symbolic as hell, right? Proper for a novelist and his critics.'

'When can you know that final moment?' I said.

'I think it's about time,' Osano said. 'I really don't think I should wait any more.'

Now I was really shocked and horrified. 'Why don't you wait a day?' I said. 'You'll feel better tomorrow. You still have some more time. Six months is not bad.'

Osano said, 'Do you have any qualms about what I'm going to do? The usual moral prejudices?'

I shook my head. 'Just what's the rush?'

Osano looked at me thoughtfully. 'No,' he said, 'that fall when I tried to get out of bed gave me the message. Listen, I've named you as my literary executor, your decisions are final. There's no money left, just copyrights and those go to my ex-wives, I guess, and my kids. My books still sell pretty well, so I don't have to worry about them. I tried to do something for Charlie Brown, but she won't let me and I think maybe she's right.'

I said something I would not ordinarily say. 'The whore with the heart of gold,' I said. 'Just like in the literature,' I said.

Osano closed his eyes. 'You know, one of the things I liked best about you, Merlyn, is that you never said the word "whore", and maybe I've said it, but I never thought it.'

'OK,' I said. 'Do you want to make some phone calls or do you want to see some people? Or do you want to have a drink?'

'No,' Osano said. 'I've had enough of all that bullshit. I've got seven wives, nine kids, I got two thousand friends and millions of admirers. None of them can help and I don't want to see a fucking one of them.' He grinned at me. 'And mind you, I've led a happy life.' He shook his head. 'The people you love most do you in.'

I sat down beside the bed and we talked for hours about different books that we had read. He told me about all the women he had made love to, and for a few minutes Osano tried to remember fifteen years ago, the girl who infected him. But he couldn't track it down. 'One thing,' he said, 'they were all beauties. They were all worth it. Ah, hell, what difference does it make? It's all an accident.'

Osano held out a hand and I shook it and pressed it and Osano said, 'Tell Charlie to come in here and you wait outside.' Before I left, he called after me, 'Hey, listen. An artist's life is not a fulfilling life. Put that on my fucking tombstone.'

I waited a long time in the living room. Sometimes I could hear noises and once I thought I heard weeping and then I didn't hear anything. I went into the kitchen and made some coffee and set two cups on the kitchen table. Then I went into the living room and waited some more. Then not a scream, not a call for help, not even grief-stricken I heard Charlie's voice, very sweet and clear, call my name.

I went into the bedroom. On the night table was the gold Tiffany box he used to keep his penicillin pills in. It was open and empty. The lights were on, and Osano was lying on his back, eyes staring at the ceiling. Even in death his green eyes seemed to glitter. Nestled beneath his arm, pressed against his chest, was Charlie's golden head. She had drawn the covers up to cover their nakedness.

'You'll have to get dressed,' I said to her.

She rose up on one elbow and leaned over to kiss Osano on his mouth. And then she stood staring down at him for a long time.

'You'll have to get dressed and leave,' I said. 'There's going to be a lot of fuss and I think it's one thing Osano wanted me to do. To keep you out of any fuss.'

And then I went to the living room. I waited. I could hear the shower going, and then, fifteen minutes later, she came into the room.

'Don't worry about anything,' I said. 'I'll take care of everything.' She came over to me and put herself into my arms. It was the first time I had ever felt her body and I could partly understand why Osano had loved her for so long. She smelled beautifully fresh and clean.

'You were the only one he wanted to see,' Charlie said. 'You and me. Will you call me after the funeral?'

I said yes, I would, and then she went out and left me alone with Osano.

I waited until morning, and then I called the police and told them that I had found Osano dead. And that he had obviously committed suicide. I had considered for a minute hiding the suicide, hiding the pillbox. But Osano wouldn't care even if I could get the press and authorities to cooperate. I told them how important a man Osano was so that an ambulance would get there right away. Then I called Osano's lawyers and gave them the responsibility of informing all the wives and all the children. I called Osano's publishers because I knew they would want to give out a press release and publish an ad in the *New York Times*, in memoriam. For some reason I wanted Osano to have that kind of respect.

The police and district attorney had a lot of questions to ask as if I were a murder suspect. But that blew over right away. It seemed that Osano had sent a suicide note to his publisher telling him that he would not be able to deliver his novel owing to the fact that he was planning on killing himself.

There was a great funeral out in the Hamptons. Osano was buried in the presence of his seven wives, nine children, literary critics from the *New York Times*, *New York Review of Books*, *Commentary*, *Harper's* magazine and the *New Yorker*. A bus load

440

of people came direct from Elaine's in New York. Friends of Osano and knowing that he would approve, they had a keg of beer and a portable bar on the bus. They arrived drunk for the funeral. Osano would have been delighted.

In the following weeks hundreds of thousands of words were written about Osano as the first great Italian literary figure in our cultural history. That would have given Osano a pain in the ass. He never thought of himself as Italian/American. But one thing would have pleased him. All the critics said that if he had lived to publish his novel in progress he would have surely won the Nobel Prize.

A week after Osano's funeral I got a telephone call from his publisher with a request that I come to lunch the following week. And I agreed.

Arcania Publishing House was considered one of the classy, most literary publishing houses in the country. On its backlist were a half dozen Nobel Prize winners and dozens of Pulitzer and NBA winners. They were famous for being more interested in literature than best-sellers. And the editor-in-chief, Henry Stiles, could have passed for an Oxford don. But he got down to business as briskly as any Babbitt.

'Mr Merlyn,' he said, 'I admire your novels very much. I hope some day we can add you to our list.'

'I've gone over Osano's stuff,' I said, 'as his executor.'

'Good,' Mr Stiles said. 'You may or may not know, since this is the financial end of Mr Osano's life, that we advanced him a hundred thousand dollars for his novel in progress. So we do have first claim to that book. I just wanted to make sure you understood that.'

'Sure,' I said. 'And I know it was Osano's wish that you publish it. You did a great job publishing his books.'

There was a grateful smile on Mr Stiles's face. He leaned back. 'Then there's no problem?' he said. 'I assume you've gone through his notes and papers and you found the manuscript.'

I said, 'Well, that's the problem. There is no manuscript; there is no novel, only five hundred pages of notes.'

Stiles had a stunned, horrified look on his face and behind that exterior I know what he thought: Fucking writers, hundred-thousand-dollar advance, all those years and all he has is notes! But then he pulled himself together. 'You mean there's not one page of manuscript?' he said.

'No,' I said. I was lying, but he would never know. There were six pages.

'Well,' Mr Stiles said, 'it's not something we usually do, but it has been done by other publishing houses. We know that you helped Mr Osano with some of his articles, under his by-lines, that you imitated his style very well. It would have to be secret, but why couldn't you write Mr Osano's book in a six-month period and publish it under Mr Osano's name? We could make a great deal of money. You realize that couldn't show in any contract between us, we could sign a separate very generous contract for your future books.'

Now he had surprised me. The most respectable publishing house in America doing something that only Hollywood would do, or a Vegas hotel? Why the fuck was I surprised?

'No,' I told Mr Stiles. 'As his literary executor I have the power and authority to keep the book from being published from those notes. If you would like to publish the notes themselves, I'll give you permission.'

'Well, think it over,' Mr Stiles said. 'We'll talk about it again. Meanwhile, it's been a pleasure to meet you.' He shook his head sadly. 'Osano was a genius. What a pity.'

I never told Mr Stiles that Osano had written some pages of his novel, the first six. With them was a note addressed to me.

MERLYN:
Here are the six pages of my book. I give them to you. Let's see what you can make of them. Forget the notes, they're bullshit.

OSANO

I had read the pages and decided to keep them for myself. When I got home, I read them over again very slowly, word by word.

'Listen to me. I will tell you the truth about a man's life. I will tell you the truth about his love for women. That he never hates them. Already you think I'm on the wrong track. Stay with me. Really—I'm a master of magic.

'Do you believe a man can truly love a woman and constantly betray her? Never mind physically, but betray her in his mind, in the very "poetry of his soul". Well, it's not easy, but men do it all the time.

'Do you want to know how women can love you, feed you that love

442

*deliberately to poison your body and mind simply to destroy you? And out
of passionate love choose not to love you any more? And at the same time
dizzy you with an idiot's ecstasy? Impossible? That's the easy part.*

'*But don't run away. This is not a love story.*

'*I will make you feel the painful beauty of a child, the animal horniness
of the adolescent male, the yearning suicidal moodiness of the young
female. And then (here's the hard part) show you how time turns man and
woman around full circle, exchanged in body and soul.*

'*And then of course, there is TRUE LOVE. Don't go away! It exists
or I will make it exist. I'm not a master of magic for nothing. Is it worth
what it costs? And how about sexual fidelity? Does it work? Is it love?
Is it even human, that perverse passion to be with only one special person?
And if it doesn't work, do you still get a bonus for trying? Can it work
both ways? Of course not, that's easy. And yet—*

'*Life is a comical business, and there is nothing funnier than love
travelling through time. But a true master of magic can make his audience
laugh and cry at the same time. Death is another story. I will never make
a joke about death. It is beyond my powers. Parallel to death, love is a
tiresome, childish business, though men believe more in love than death.*

'*I am always alert for death. He doesn't fool me. I spot him right
away. He loves to come in his country-bumpkin disguise; a comical
wart that suddenly grows and grows; the dark, hairy mole that sends its
roots to the very bone; or hiding behind a pretty little fever blush. Then
suddenly that grinning skull appears to take the victim by surprise. But
never me. I'm waiting for him. I take my precautions. Women are
another story. They have a powerful secret. They don't take love seriously
and never have.*

'*But again, don't go away. Again, this is not a love story. Forget
about love. I will show you all the stretches of power. First the life of
a poor struggling writer. Sensitive. Talented. Maybe even some genius.
I will show you the artist getting the shit kicked out of him for the sake of
his art. And why he so richly deserves it. Then I will show him as a
cunning criminal and having the time of his life. Ah, what joy the true
artist feels when he finally becomes a crook. It's out in the open now, his
essential nature. No more kidding around about his honour. The son of a
bitch is a hustler. A conniver. An enemy of society right out in the clear
instead of hiding behind his whore's cunt of art. What a relief. What
pleasure. Such sly delight. And then how he becomes an honest man again.
It's an awful strain being a crook.*

'*But it helps you to accept society and forgive your fellowman. Once
that's done no person should be a crook unless he really needs the money.*

'*Then on to one of the most amazing success stories in the history of literature. The intimate lives of the giants of our culture. One crazy bastard especially. The classy world. So now we have the poor struggling genius world, the crooked world, and the classy literary world. All this laced with plenty of sex, some complicated ideas you won't be hit over the head with and may even find interesting. And finally on to a full-blast ending in Hollywood with our hero gobbling up all its rewards, money, fame, beautiful women. And . . . don't go away—don't go away—how it all turns to ashes.*

'That's not enough? You've heard it all before? But remember I'm a master of magic. I can bring all these people truly alive. I can show you what they truly think and feel. You'll weep for them, all of them, I promise you that. Or maybe just laugh. Anyway, we're going to have a lot of fun. And learn something about life. Which is really no help.

'Ah, I know what you're thinking. That conning bastard trying to make us turn the page. But wait, it's only a tale I want to tell. What's the harm? Even if I take it seriously, you don't have to. Just have a good time.

'I want to tell you a story, I have no other vanity. I don't desire success or fame or money. But that's easy, most men, most women don't, not really. Even better, I don't want love. When I was young, some women told me they loved me for my long eyelashes. I accepted. Later it was for my wit. Then for my power and money. Then for my talent. Then for my mind—deep. OK, I can handle all of it. The only woman who scares me is the one who loves me for myself alone. I have plans for her. I have poisons and daggers and dark graves in caves to hide her head. She can't be allowed to live. Especially if she is sexually faithful and never lies and always puts me ahead of everything and everyone.

'There will be a lot about love in this book, but it's not a love book. It's a war book. The old war between men who are true friends. The great "new" war between men and women. Sure it's an old story, but it's out in the open now. The Women's Liberation warriors think they have something new, but it's just their armies coming out of their guerrilla hills. Sweet women ambushed men always: at their cradles, in the kitchen, the bedroom. And at the graves of their children, the best place not to hear a plea for mercy.

'Ah well, you think I have a grievance against women. But I never hated them. And they'll come out better people than men, you'll see. But the truth is that only women have been able to make me unhappy, and they have done so from the cradle on. But most men can say that. And there's nothing to be done.

'What a target I've given here. I know—I know—how irresistible it seems. But be careful. I'm a tricky storyteller; not just one of your

444

vulnerable sensitive artists. I've taken my precautions. I've still got a few surprises left.

'But enough. Let me get to work. Let me begin and let me end.'

And that was Osano's great novel, the book that would cinch the Nobel Prize, restore his greatness. I wish he had written it.

That he was a great con artist, as those pages showed, was irrelevant. Or maybe part of his genius. He wanted to share his inner worlds with the outside world, that was all. And now as his final joke he had given me his last pages. A joke because we were such different writers. He so generous. And I, I realized now, so ungenerous.

I was never crazy about his work. And I don't know whether I really loved him as a man. But I loved him as a *writer*. And so I decided, maybe for luck, maybe for strength, maybe just for the con, to use his pages as my own. I should have changed one line. Death has always surprised me.

51

I HAVE no history. That is the thing Janelle never understood. That I started with myself. That I had no grandparents or parents, uncles and aunts, friends of the family or cousins. That I had no childhood memories of a special house, or a special kitchen. That I had no city or town or village. That I began my history with myself and my brother, Arthur. And that when I extended myself with Valerie and the kids and her family and lived with her in a house in the city, when I became a parent and a husband, they became my reality and my salvation. But I don't have to worry about Janelle any more. I haven't seen her for over two years and it's three years since Osano died.

I can't bear to remember about Artie, and when I even think

of his name, I find tears coming from my eyes, but he is the only person I have ever wept for.

For the last two years I have sat in a working study in my home, reading, writing and being the perfect father and husband. Sometimes I go to dinner with friends, but I like to think that finally I have become serious, dedicated. That I will now live the life of a scholar. That my adventures are over. In short, I am praying that life holds no more surprises. Safely in this room, surrounded by my books of magic, Austen, Dickens, Dostoevsky, Joyce, Hemingway, Dreiser and finally, Osano, I feel the exhaustion of an animal who has escaped many times before reaching it's heaven.

Beneath me in the house below, the house that is now my history, I knew my wife was busy in the kitchen preparing Sunday dinner. My children were watching TV and playing cards in the den, and because I knew they were there, sadness was bearable in this room.

I read all Osano's books again and he was a great writer at the beginning. I tried to analyze his failure in later life, his inability to finish his great novel. He started off amazed by the wonderment of the world around him and the people in it. He ended writing about the wonderment of himself. His concern, you could see, was to make a legend of his own life. He wrote to the world rather to himself. In every line he screamed for attention to Osano rather than to his art. He wanted everyone to know how clever, how brilliant he was. He even made sure that the characters he created would not get credit for his brilliance. He was like a ventriloquist getting jealous of the laughs his dummy earned. And it was a shame. Yet I think of him as a great man. His terrifying humanity, his terrifying love of life, how brilliant he was and what fun to be with.

How could I say that he was a failed artist when his achievements, flawed though they were, seemed much greater than mine? I remembered going through his papers, as his literary executor, and the astonishment growing upon me when I could find no trace of his novel in progress. I could not believe he was such a fake, that he had been pretending to write it all those years and had just been fucking around with notes. Now I realized that he had been burned out. And that part of the joke had not been malicious or cunning, but simply a joke that delighted him. And the money.

He had written some of the most beautiful prose, created some of the most powerful ideas, of his generation, but he had delighted in being a scoundrel. I read all his notes, over five hundred pages of them on long yellow sheets. They were brilliant notes. But notes are nothing.

Knowing this made me think about myself. That I had written mortal books. But more unfortunate than Osano, I had tried to live without illusions and without risk. That I had none of his love for life and his faith in it. I thought about Osano's saying that life was always trying to do you in. And maybe that's why he lived so wildly, struggled so hard against the blows and the humiliations.

Long ago Jordan had pulled the trigger of the gun against his head. Osano had lived life fully, and ended that life when there was no other choice. And I, I tried to escape wearing a magical conical hat. I thought about another thing Osano had said: 'Life is always getting in the way.' And I knew what he meant. The world to a writer is like one of those pale ghosts who with age become paler and paler, and maybe that's the reason Osano gave up writing.

The snow was falling heavily outside the windows of my workroom. The whiteness covered the grey, bare limbs of the trees, the mouldy brown and green of the winter lawn. If I were sentimental and so inclined, it would be easy to conjure up the faces of Osano and Artie drifting smilingly through those swirling snowflakes. But this I refused to do. I was neither so sentimental nor so self-indulgent nor so self-pitying. I could live without them. Their deaths would not diminish me, as they had perhaps hoped it would do.

No, I was safe here in my workroom. Warm as toast. Safe from the raging wind that hurled the snowflakes against my window. I would not leave this room, this winter.

Outside, the roads were icy, my car could skid and death could mangle me. Viral poisonous colds could infect my spine and blood. Oh, there were countless dangers besides death. And I was not unaware of the spies death could infiltrate into the house and even into my own brain. I set up defences against them.

I had charts posted around the walls of my room. Charts for my work, my salvation, my armour. I had researched a novel on the Roman Empire to retreat into the past. I had researched a novel in the twenty-fifth century if I wanted to hide in the future.

Hundreds of books stacked up to read, to surround my brain.

I pulled a big soft chair up to windows so that I could watch the falling snow in comfort. The buzzer from the kitchen rang. Supper was ready. My family would be waiting for me, my wife and children. What the hell was going on with them after all this time? I watched the snow, a blizzard now. The outside world was completely white. The buzzer rang again, insistently. If I were alive, I would get up and go down into the cheerful dining room and have a happy dinner. I watched the snow. Again the buzzer rang.

I checked the work chart. I had written the first chapter on the novel of the Roman Empire and ten pages of notes for the novel on the twenty-fifth century. At that minute I decided I would write about the future.

Again the buzzer rang, long and incessantly. I locked the doors of my workroom and descended into the house and into the dining room, and entering it, I gave a sigh of relief.

They were all there. The children nearly grown and ready to leave. Valerie pretty in a housedress and apron and her lovely brown hair pulled severely back. She was flushed, perhaps from the heat of the kitchen, perhaps because after dinner she would be going out to meet her lover? Was that possible? I had no way of knowing. Even so, wasn't life worth guarding?

I sat down at the head of the table. I joked with the kids. I ate. I smiled at Valerie and praised the food. After dinner I would go back up into my room and work and be alive.

Osano, Malomar, Artie, Jordan, I miss you. But you won't do me in. All of my loved ones around this table might some day, I had to worry about that.

During dinner I got a call from Cully to meet him at the airport the next day. He was coming to New York on business. It was the first time in over a year that I had heard from Cully, and from his voice I knew he was in trouble.

I was early for Cully's plane, so I bought some magazines and read them, then I had coffee and a sandwich. When I heard the announcement that his plane was landing, I went down to the baggage area where I always waited for him. As usual in New York it took about twenty minutes for the baggage to come down a chute. By that time most of the passengers were milling around the carousel into which the chute emptied, but I still didn't see Cully. I kept looking for him. The crowd began to thin, and after a while there were only a few suitcases left on the carousel.

I called the house and asked Valerie if there had been any calls from Cully and she said no. Then I called TWA flight information and asked if Cully Cross had been on the plane. They told me that he had made a reservation but had never shown up. I called the Xanadu Hotel in Vegas and got Cully's secretary. She said yes, that as far as she knew, Cully had flown to New York. She knew he was not in Vegas and would not be due back for a few days. I wasn't worried. I figured something had come up. Cully was always flying off to all parts of the United States and the world on hotel business. Some last-minute emergency had made him change course and I was sure he would get in touch with me. But far back in my mind there was the nagging consciousness that he had never hung me up before, that he had always told me of a change in plans and that in his own way he was too considerate to let me go to the airport and wait for hours when he was not coming. And yet it took me almost a week of not hearing from him and not being able to find out where he was before I called Gronevelt.

Gronevelt was glad to hear from me. His voice sounded very strong, very healthy. I told him the story and asked him where Cully might be and I told him that in any case I thought I should notify him. 'It's not something I can talk about over the phone,' Gronevelt said. 'But why don't you come out for a few days and be my guest here at the hotel and I'll put your mind to rest?'

52

WHEN Cully received a summons to Gronevelt's executive suite, he put in a call to Merlyn.

Cully knew what Gronevelt wanted to see him about and he knew he had to start thinking about an escape hatch. On the phone he told Merlyn he would be taking the next morning's plane to New York and asked Merlyn to meet him. He told Merlyn that it was important, that he needed his help.

When Cully finally went into Gronevelt's suite, he tried to 'read' Gronevelt, but all he could see was how much the man had changed in the ten years he had worked for him. The stroke Gronevelt had suffered had left tiny red veins in the whites of his eyes, through his cheeks and even in his forehead. The cold blue eyes seemed frosted. He seemed not so tall, and he was much frailer. Despite all this, Cully was still afraid of him.

As usual, Gronevelt had Cully make them both drinks, the usual Scotch. Then Gronevelt said, 'Johnny Santadio is flying in tomorrow. He wants to know just one thing. Is the Gaming Commission going to approve his licence as an owner of this hotel or are they not?'

'You know the answer,' Cully said.

'I think I know it,' Gronevelt said. 'I know what you told Johnny, that it was a sure thing. That it was all locked up. That's all I know.'

Cully said, 'He's not going to get it. I couldn't fix it.'

Gronevelt nodded. 'It was a very tough proposition from the word "go", what with Johnny's background. What about his hundred grand?'

'I have it for him in the cage,' Cully said. 'He can pick it up whenever he wants it.'

'Good,' Gronevelt said. 'Good. He'll be pleased about that.'

They both leaned back and sipped their drinks. Both preparing for the real battle, the real question. Then Gronevelt said slowly, 'You and I both know why Johnny's making a special trip here to Vegas. You promised him you could fix it so that Judge Brianca would give his nephew a suspended sentence on that fraud and income tax rap. Yesterday his nephew got sentenced to five years. I hope you have an answer for that one.'

'I haven't got an answer,' Cully said. 'I paid Judge Brianca the forty grand that Mr Santadio gave me. That's all I could do. This is the first time Judge Brianca ever disappointed me. Maybe I can get the money back from him. I don't know. I've been trying to get in touch with him, but I guess he's ducking me.'

Gronevelt said, 'You know that Johnny has a lot to say about what goes on in this hotel, and if he says it's important that I let you go, I have to let you go. Cully, you know that I'm not in my old power position ever since I had that stroke. I had to give away pieces of the hotel. I'm really just an errand boy now, a front. I can't help you.'

450

Cully laughed. 'Hell, I'm not even worried about getting fired. I'm just worried about getting killed.'

'Oh,' Gronevelt said, 'no, no. It's not that serious.' He smiled at Cully as a father might smile at his son. 'Did you really think it was that serious?'

For the first time Cully relaxed and took a big swig of Scotch. He felt enormously relieved. 'I'll settle for that deal right now,' Cully said, 'just getting fired.'

Gronevelt slapped him on the shoulder. 'Don't settle so fast,' he said. 'Johnny knows the great work you've done for this hotel in the last two years since my stroke. You've done a marvellous job. You've added millions of dollars to the revenue coming in here. Now that's important. Not only to me but to guys like Johnny. So you've made a couple of mistakes. Now, I have to admit they are very pissed off, especially about the nephew going to jail and especially because you told them not to worry. That you had the full fix on Judge Brianca. They couldn't understand how you could say such a thing and then not come through for them.'

Cully shook his head. 'I really can't figure it,' he said. 'I've had Brianca in my pocket for the last five years, especially when I had that little blonde Charlie working him over.'

Gronevelt laughed. 'Yeah, I remember her. Pretty girl. Good heart.'

'Yeah,' Cully said. 'The judge was crazy for her. He used to take her on his boat down to Mexico fishing for a week at a time. He said she was always great company. Great little girl.'

What Cully didn't tell Gronevelt was how Charlie used to tell him stories about the judge. How she used to go into the judge's chambers and, while he was still in his robes, go down on him before he went out to conduct a trial. She also told him how on the boat fishing she had made the sixty-year-old judge go down on her and how the judge had immediately rushed into the stateroom, grabbed a bottle of whiskey and gargled to get all the germs out. It was the first time the old judge had ever done this to a woman. But, Charlie Brown said, after that he was like a kid eating ice cream. Cully smiled a little bit, remembering, and then he was aware of Gronevelt going on.

'I think I have a way for you to square yourself,' Gronevelt said. 'I have to admit Santadio is hot. He's steaming, but I can cool him off. All you have to do is come through for him with a big coup, right now, and I think I have it. There's another three million waiting in Japan. Johnny's share of that is a million bucks. If you can bring that out, as you did once before, I think for a million dollars Johnny Santadio will forgive you. But just remember this: It's more dangerous now.'

Cully was surprised and then very alert. The first question he asked was: 'Will Mr Santadio know I'm going?' And if Gronevelt had said yes, then Cully would have turned down the deal. But Gronevelt, looking him right in the eye, said, 'It's my idea, and my suggestion to you is that you tell nobody, not anyone, that you are going. Take the afternoon flight to LA, hook up to the Japanese flight and you'll be in Japan before Johnny Santadio gets here and then I'll just tell him that you're out of town. While you're en route, I'll make all the arrangements for the money to be delivered to you. Don't worry about strangers because we are going through our old friend Fummiro.'

It was the mention of Fummiro's name that dissolved all of Cully's suspicions. 'OK,' he said. 'I'll do it. The only thing is I was going to New York to see Merlyn and he's meeting me at the plane, so I'll have to call him.'

'No,' Gronevelt said. 'You just never know who may be listening on the phone or who he may tell. Let me take care of it. I'll let him know not to meet you at the plane. Don't even cancel your reservation. That will throw people off the track. I'll tell Johnny you went to New York. You'll have a great cover. OK?'

'OK,' Cully said.

Gronevelt shook his hand and clapped him on the shoulder. 'Get in and out as fast as you can,' Gronevelt said. 'If you make it back here, I promise you that you will be squared away with Johnny Santadio. You'll have nothing to worry about.'

On the night before Cully left for Japan he called up two girls he knew. Soft hookers both. One was the wife of a pit boss in a hotel down the Strip. Her name was Crystin Lesso.

'Crystin,' he said, 'do you feel in the mood to get thrashed?'

'Sure,' Crystin said. 'How much will you knock off my markers?'

Cully usually doubled the price for a thrashing, which would mean two hundred dollars. What the hell, he thought, I'm going to Japan, who knows what will happen?

'I'll knock five hundred off,' Cully said.

There was a little gasp at the other end of the wire.

'Jesus,' Crystin said. 'This must be some thrashing. Who do I have to go in the ring with, a gorilla?'

'Don't worry,' Cully said. 'You always have a good time, don't you?'

Crystin said, 'When?'

'Let's make it early,' Cully said. 'I have to catch a plane tomorrow morning. OK with you?'

'Sure,' Crystin said. 'I assume you're not giving me dinner?'

'No,' Cully said. 'I have too many things to do. I won't have time.'

After hanging up the phone, Cully opened the desk drawer and took out a little packet of white slips. They were Crystin's markers, totalling three thousand dollars.

Cully pondered on the mysteries of women. Crystin was a good-looking girl of about twenty-eight. But a really degenerate gambler. Two years ago she had gone down the drain for over twenty grand. She had called Cully for an appointment at his office, and when she came in, she had given him a proposition that she would work off the twenty grand as a soft hustler. But she would take dates only directly from Cully with the utmost secrecy because of her husband.

Cully had tried to talk her out of it. 'If your husband knows, he'll kill you,' Cully said.

'If he finds out about my twenty-grand markers, he'll kill me,' Crystin said. 'So what's the difference? And besides, you know I can't stop gambling and I figure that over and above the fee I can get some of these guys to give me a stake or at least put down a bet for me.'

So Cully had agreed. In addition, he had given her a job as a secretary for the food and beverages officer of the Xanadu Hotel. He was attracted to her and at least once a week they went to bed together afternoons in his hotel suite. After a while he introduced her to thrashing and she had loved it.

Cully took out one of the five-hundred-dollar markers and tore it up. Then on a sudden impulse he tore up all Crystin's markers and threw them in his wastebasket. When he came back from Japan, he would have to cover for it with some paperwork, but he would think about that later. Crystin was a good kid. If something happened to him, he wanted her to be in the clear.

He passed the time cleaning up details on his desk and then went down to his suite. He ordered up some chilled champagne and made a call to Charlie Brown.

Then he took a shower and got into his pyjamas. They were very fancy pyjamas. White silk, edged with red, with his initials on the jacket pocket.

Charlie Brown came first and he gave her some champagne

and then Crystin came. They sat around talking and he made them drink the whole bottle before he led them into the bedroom.

The two girls were a little shy of each other, though they had met before around town. Cully told them to undress and he stripped off his pyjamas.

The three of them got into bed together naked and he talked to them awhile. Kidding them, making jokes, kissing them occasionally and playing with their breasts. And then with an arm around their necks he pressed their faces close together. They knew what was expected of them. The two women kissed each other tentatively on the lips.

Cully lifted the more slender Charlie Brown, slid underneath her so that the two women were next to each other. He felt the quick surge of sexual excitement.

'Come on,' he said. 'You'll love it. You know you'll love it.'

He ran his hand between Charlie Brown's legs and let it rest there. At the same time he leaned over and kissed Crystin on the mouth and then he pressed the two women together.

It took a little time for them to get started. They were very tentative, a little shy. It was always like this. Gradually Cully edged away from them until he was seated at the foot of the bed.

He felt a sudden tranquillity as he watched the two women make love to each other. To him, with all his cynicism about women and love, it was the most beautiful thing he could ever hope to see. They both had lush bodies and lovely faces, and they were both truly passionate as they could never be with him. He could watch it forever.

As they went on, Cully rose from the bed and sat in one of the chairs. The two women were becoming more and more passionate. He watched their bodies flow around and up and down each other until there was a final climaxing of violent thrashing and the two women lay in each other's arms quiet and still.

Cully went over to the bed and kissed them each gently. Then he lay down between them and he said, 'Don't do anything. Let's just sleep a little.'

He dozed off, and when he awoke, the two women were in his living room, dressed and chatting together.

He took five one-hundred-dollar bills, five Honeybees, out of his wallet and gave them to Charlie Brown.

She kissed him good-night and left him alone with Crystin.

454

He sat down on the sofa and put his arm around Crystin. He gave her a gentle kiss.

'I tore up your markers,' he said. 'You don't have to worry about them anymore, and I'm telling the cage to give you five hundred dollars' worth of chips so you can do a little gambling tonight.'

Crystin laughed and said, 'Cully, I can't believe it. You've finally become a mark.'

'Everybody's a mark,' Cully said. 'But what the hell. You've been a good sport these last two years. I want to get you off the hook.'

Crystin gave him a hug and rested against his shoulder and then she said quietly, 'Cully, why do you call it thrashing? You know, when you put me together with a girl?'

Cully laughed. 'I just like the idea of the word. It just describes it someway.'

'You don't put me down for that, do you?' Crystin said.

'No,' Cully said. 'To me it's the most beautiful thing I've ever seen.'

When Crystin left, Cully couldn't sleep. Finally he went down into the casino. He spotted Crystin at the blackjack table. She had a stack of black one-hundred-dollar chips in front of her.

She waved him toward her. She gave him a delighted smile. 'Cully, this is my lucky night,' she said. 'I'm ahead twelve grand.'

She picked up a stack of chips and placed them in his hand. 'This is for you,' she said. 'I want you to have them.'

Cully counted the chips. There were ten of them. A thousand dollars.

He laughed and said, 'OK. I'll hold them for you, someday you'll need gambling money.' And he left her and went up to his office and threw the chips into one of his desk drawers. He thought again of calling Merlyn but decided against it.

He looked around the office. There was nothing left for him to do, but he felt as if he were forgetting something. As if he had counted down the shoe in which some important cards were missing. But it was too late now. In a few hours he would be in Los Angeles and boarding a plane for Tokyo.

In Tokyo Cully took a taxi to Fummiro's office. The Tokyo streets were crowded, many of the people wearing white surgical gauze masks as a guard against the germ-laden air. Even the construction workers with their shiny red coats and white helmets wore the surgical masks. For some reason the sight of them gave Cully a queasy feeling. But he realized that this was because he was nervous about the whole trip.

Fummiro greeted him with a hearty handshake and a wide smile.

'So good to see you, Mr Cross,' Fummiro said. 'We'll make sure you have a good trip, a good time in our country. Just let my assistant know what you require.'

They were in Fummiro's modern American-style office and could speak safely.

Cully said, 'I have my suitcase at the hotel and I just want to know when I should bring it to your office.'

'Monday,' Fummiro said. 'On the weekend, nothing can be done. But there is a party at my house tomorrow night at which I am sure you will enjoy yourself.'

'Thank you very much,' Cully said. 'But I just want to rest. I'm not feeling too good and it's been a long trip.'

'Ah, yes. I understand,' Fummiro said. 'I have a good idea. There is a country inn in Yogawara. It's only an hour's drive from here. I will send you in my limousine. It's the most beautiful spot in Japan. Quiet and restful. You have masseuse girls and I will arrange for other girls to meet you there. The food is superb. Japanese food, of course. It is where all the great men of Japan bring their mistresses for a little holiday and it's discreet. You can relax there without any worries and you can come back Monday completely refreshed and I will have the money for you.'

Cully thought it over. He would be in no danger until he got the money, and the idea of relaxing in the country inn appealed to him.

'That sounds great,' he said to Fummiro. 'When can you have the limousine pick me up?'

'The Friday night traffic is terrible,' Fummiro said. 'Go tomorrow morning. Have a good rest tonight and on the weekend and I will see you on Monday.'

As a special mark of honour Fummiro walked him out of the office to the elevator.

It was longer than an hour by limousine to Yogawara. But when he got there, Cully was delighted that he had made the trip. It was a beautiful country inn, Japanese style.

His suite of rooms was magnificent. The servants floated through the halls like ghosts, nearly invisible. And there was no sign of any other guests.

In one of his rooms there was a huge redwood tub. The bathroom itself was equipped with all different makes of razors and shaving lotions and women's cosmetics. Anything anyone could need.

Two tiny young girls, barely nubile, filled his tub and washed him clean before he got into the fragrant hot water. The tub was so huge that he could almost swim in it. And so deep that the water almost rose above his head. He felt the tiredness and tension go out of his bones, and then finally the two young girls lifted him out of the tub and led him to a mat in the other room. And stretched out, he let them massage him, finger by finger, toe by toe, limb by limb, what seemed each single strand of hair on his head. It was the greatest massage he'd ever had.

They gave him a *futaba*, a little hard square pillow on which to rest his head. And he immediately fell asleep. He slept until late afternoon, and then he took a walk through the countryside.

The inn was on a hillside overlooking a valley, and beyond the valley he could see the ocean, blue, wide, crystal clear. He walked around a beautiful pond sprinkled with flowers which seemed to match the intricate parasols of the mats and hammocks on the porch of the inn. All the bright colours delighted him, and the clear, pure air refreshed his brain. He was no longer worried or tense. Nothing would happen. He would get the money from Fummiro, who was an old friend. When he got to Hong Kong and deposited the money, he would be clear with Santadio and could safely return to Las Vegas. It would all work out. The Xanadu Hotel would be his, and he would take care of Gronevelt as a son would a father in his old age.

For a moment he wished he could spend the rest of his life in this beautiful countryside. So still and clear. So tranquil as if he were living five hundred years ago. He had never wished to be a samurai, but now he thought how innocent their warfare had been.

Darkness was beginning to fall, and tiny drops of rain pitted the surface of the pond. He went back to his rooms in the inn.

He loved the Japanese style of living. No furniture. Just mats. The sliding wood-frame paper doors that cut off rooms and turned a living room into a sleeping room. It seemed to him so reasonable and so clever.

Far away he could hear a tiny bell ringing with silvery claps and a few minutes after that the paper doors slid apart and two young girls came in, carrying a huge oval platter almost five feet

457

long, it could be the top of a table. The platter was filled with every kind of fish the sea could provide.

There was the black squid and the yellow-tailed fish, pearly oysters, grey-black crabs, speckled chunks of fish showing vivid pink flesh underneath. It was a rainbow of colour, and there was more food there than any five men could eat. The women set the platter on a low table and arranged cushions for him to sit on. Then they sat down on either side and fed him morsels of fish.

Another girl came in carrying a tray of sake wine and glasses. She poured the wine and put the glass to his mouth so that he could drink.

It was all delicious. When he finished, Cully stood looking through the window at the valley of pines and the sea beyond. Behind him he could hear the women take away the dinner and the paper wooden doors closing. He was alone in the room, staring at the sea.

Again he went over everything in his mind, counting down the shoe of circumstance and chance. Monday morning he would get the money from Fummiro and he would board the plane to Hong Kong and in Hong Kong he would have to get to the bank. He tried to think of where the danger would lie, if there were a danger. He thought of Gronevelt. That Gronevelt might betray him, or Santadio, or even Fummiro. Why had Judge Brianca betrayed him? Could Gronevelt have engineered that? And then he remembered one night having dinner with Fummiro and Gronevelt. They had been just a little uneasy with him. Was there something there? An unknown card in the shoe? But Gronevelt was an old sick man and Santadio's long arm did not reach into the Far East. And Fummiro was an old friend.

But there was always bad luck. In any case it would be his final risk. And at least now he would have another day of peace here in Yogawara.

He heard the paper wooden doors slide behind him opening up. It was the two tiny girls leading him back to the redwood tub.

Again they washed him. Again they plunged him into the vast fragment waters of the tub.

He soaked, and again they raised him out and laid him on the mat and put the *futaba* pillow beneath his head. Again they massaged him finger by finger. And now, completely rested, he felt the surge of sexual desire. He reached out for one of the young girls, but very prettily she denied him with her face and her hands. Then she pantomimed she would send another girl up. That it was not their function.

And then Cully held up two fingers to tell them he wanted two girls. They both giggled at that, and he wondered if Japanese girls thrashed each other.

He watched them disappear and close the frame doors behind them. His head sank on the small square pillow. His body lustfully relaxed. He dozed into a light sleep. Far away he heard the sliding of the paper doors. Ah, he thought, they're coming. And curious to see what they looked like, whether they were pretty, how they were dressed, he raised his head and to his astonishment he saw two men with surgeon's gauze masks over their faces coming toward him.

At first he thought the girls had misunderstood him. That comically inept, he had asked for a heavier massage. And then the gauze masks struck him with terror. The realization flashed through his mind that these masks were never worn in the country. And then his mind jumped to the truth, but he screamed out, 'I haven't got the money. I haven't got the money!' He tried to rise from the mat, and the two men were upon him.

It was not painful or horrible. He seemed to sink again beneath the sea, the fragrant waters of the redwood tub. His eyes glazed over. And then he was quiet on the mat, the *futaba* pillow beneath his head.

The two men wrapped his body in towels and silently carried it out of the room.

Far across the ocean, Gronevelt in his suite worked the controls to pump pure oxygen into his casino.

BOOK EIGHT

53

I GOT to Vegas late at night and Gronevelt asked me to have dinner in his suite. We had some drinks and the waiters brought up a table with the dinner we had ordered. I noticed that Gronevelt's dish had very small portions. He looked older and faded. Cully had told me about his stroke, but I could see no evidence of it other than perhaps he moved more slowly and took more time to answer me when he spoke.

I glanced at the control panel behind his desk which Gronevelt used to pump pure oxygen into the casino. Gronevelt said, 'Cully told you about that? He wasn't supposed to.'

'Some things are too good not to tell,' I said, 'and besides, Cully knew I wouldn't spread it around.'

Gronevelt smiled. 'Believe it or not, I use it as an act of kindness. It gives all those losers a little hope and a last shot before they go to bed. I hate to think of losers trying to go to sleep. I don't mind winners,' Gronevelt said. 'I can live with luck, it's skill I can't abide. Look, they can never beat the percentage and I have the percentage. That's true in life as well as gambling. The percentage will grind you into dust.'

Gronevelt was rambling, thinking of his own approaching death. 'You have to get rich in the dark,' he said, 'you have to live with percentages. Forget about luck, that's a very treacherous magic.' I nodded my head in agreement. After we had finished eating and were having brandy, Gronevelt said, 'I don't want you to worry about Cully, so I'll tell you what happened to him. Remember that trip you made with him to Tokyo and Hong Kong to bring out that money? Well, for reasons of his own Cully decided to take another crack at it. I warned him against it. I told him the percentages were bad, that he had been lucky that first trip. But for reasons of his own which I can't tell you, but which were important and valid, at least to him, he decided to go.'

'You had to give the OK,' I said.

'Yes,' Gronevelt said. 'It was to my benefit that he go there.'

'So what happened to him?' I asked Gronevelt.

'We don't know,' Gronevelt said. 'He picked up the money in his fancy suitcases, and then he just disappeared. Fummiro thinks he's in Brazil or Costa Rica living like a king. But you and I know Cully better. He couldn't live in any place but Vegas.'

'So what do you guess happened?' I asked Gronevelt again.

Gronevelt smiled at me. 'Do you know Yeats's poem? It begins, I think, "Many a soldier and sailor lies, far from customary skies," and that's what happened to Cully. I think of him maybe in one of those beautiful ponds behind a geisha house in Japan lying on the bottom. And how he would have hated it. He wanted to die in Vegas.'

'Have you done anything about it?' I said. 'Have you notified the police or the Japanese authorities?'

'No,' Gronevelt said. 'That's not possible and I don't think that you should.'

'Whatever you say is good enough for me,' I said. 'Maybe Cully will show up some day. Maybe he'll walk into the casino with your money as if nothing ever happened.'

'That can't be,' Gronevelt said. 'Please don't think like that. I would hate it that I left you with any hope. Just accept it. Think of him as another gambler that the percentage ground to dust.' He paused and then said softly. 'He made a mistake counting down the shoe.' He smiled.

I knew my answer now. What Gronevelt was telling me really was that Cully had been sent on an errand that Gronevelt had engineered and that it was Gronevelt who had decided its final end. And looking at the man now, I knew that he had done so not out of any malicious cruelty, not out of any desire for revenge, but for what were to him good and sound reasons. That for him it was simply a part of his business.

And so we shook hands and Gronevelt said, 'Stay as long as you like. It's all comped.'

'Thanks,' I said. 'But I think I'll leave tomorrow.'

'Will you gamble tonight?' Gronevelt said.

'I think so,' I said. 'Just a little bit.'

'Well, I hope you get lucky,' Gronevelt said.

Before I left the room, Gronevelt walked me to the door and pressed a stack of black hundred-dollar chips in my hand. 'These were in Cully's desk,' Gronevelt said. 'I'm sure he'd like you to have them for one last shot at the table. Maybe it's lucky money.' He paused for a moment. 'I'm sorry about Cully, I miss him.'

'So do I,' I said. And I left.

54

GRONEVELT had given me a suite, the living room decorated in rich browns, the colours overcoordinated in the usual Vegas style. I didn't feel like gambling and I was too tired to go to a movie. I counted the black chips, my inheritance from Cully. There were ten of them, an even thousand dollars. I thought how happy Cully would be if I stuck the chips in my suitcase and left Vegas without losing them. I thought that I might do that.

I was not surprised at what had happened to Cully. It was almost in the seed of his character that he would go finally against the percentage. In his heart, born hustler though he was, Cully was a gambler. Believing in his countdown, he could never be a match for Gronevelt. Gronevelt with his 'iron maiden' percentages crushing everything to death.

I tried to sleep but had no luck. It was too late to call Valerie, at least 1 A.M. in New York. I took up the Vegas newspaper I had bought at the airport, and leafing through it, I saw a movie ad for Janelle's last picture. It was the second female lead, a supporting role, but she had been so great in it that she had won an Academy Award nomination. It had opened in New York just a month ago and I had meant to see it, so I decided to go now. Even though I had never seen or spoken to Janelle since that night she left me in the hotel room.

It was a good movie. I watched Janelle on the screen and saw

464

her do all the things she had done with me. On that huge screen her face expressed all the tenderness, all the affection, all the sensual craving that she had shown in our bed together. And as I watched, I wondered, what was the reality? How had she really felt in bed with me, how had she really felt up there on the screen? In one part of the film where she was crushed by the rejection by her lover, she had the same shattered look on her face that broke my heart when she thought I had been cruel to her. I was amazed by how strictly her performance followed our most intense and secret passions. Had she been acting with me, preparing for this role, or did her performance spring from the pain we had shared together? But I almost fell in love with her again just watching her on the screen, and I was glad that everything had turned out well for her. That she was becoming so successful, that she was getting everything she wanted, or thought she wanted, from life. And this is the end of the story, I thought. Here I am, the poor unhappy lover at a distance, watching the success of his beloved one, and everybody would feel sorry for me, I would be the hero because I was so sensitive and now I could suffer and live alone, the solitary writer making books, while she sparkled in the glittering world of cinema. And that's how I would like to leave it. I had promised Janelle that if I wrote about her, I would never show her as someone defeated or someone to be pitied. One night we had gone to see *Love Story* and she had been enraged.

'You fucking writers, you always make the girl die in the end,' she said. 'Do you know why? Because it's the easiest way to get rid of them. You're tired of them and you don't want to be the villain. So you just kill her and then you cry and you're the fucking hero. You're such fucking hypocrites. You always want to ditch women.' She turned to me, her eyes huge, golden brown going black with anger. 'Don't you ever kill me off, you son of a bitch.'

'I promise,' I said. 'But what about your always telling me you'll never live to forty? That you're going to burn out.'

She often pulled that shit on me. She always loved painting herself as dramatically as possible.

'That's none of your business,' she said. 'We won't even be speaking to each other by then.'

I left the theatre and started the long walk back to the Xanadu. It was a long walk. I started at the bottom of the Strip and passed hotel after hotel, passed through their waterfalls of neon light and kept walking toward the dark desert mountains that stood guard at the top of the Strip. And I thought about Janelle. I had promised her that if I wrote about us, I would never show her as someone defeated, someone to be pitied, even someone to be grieved. She had asked for that promise, and I had given it, all in fun.

But the truth is different. She refused to stay in the shadows of my mind as Artie and Osano and Malomar decently did. My magic no longer worked.

Because by the time I had seen her on the screen, so alive and full of passion I fell in love with her again, she was already dead.

Janelle, preparing for the New Year's Eve party, worked very slowly on her make-up. She tilted her magnified make-up mirror and worked on her eye shadow. The top corner of the mirror reflected the apartment behind her. It was really a mess, clothes strewn about, shoes not put away, some dirty plates and cups on the coffee table, the bed not made. She would have to meet Joel at the door and not let him in. The man with the Rolls-Royce, Merlyn had always called him. She slept with Joel occasionally, but not too often, and she knew that she would have to sleep with him tonight. After all, it was New Year's Eve. So she had already bathed carefully, scented herself, used a vaginal deodorant. She was prepared. She thought about Merlyn and wondered whether he would call her. He hadn't called her for two years, but he just might today or tomorrow. She knew he wouldn't call her at night. She thought for a minute of calling him, but he would panic, the coward. He was so scared of spoiling his family life. That whole bullshit structure he had built up over the years that he used as a crutch. But she didn't really miss him. She knew that he looked back upon himself with contempt for being in love and that she looked back with a radiant joy that it had happened. It didn't matter to her that they had wounded each other so terribly. She had forgiven him a long time ago. But she knew he had not. She knew that he had foolishly thought he had lost something of himself, and she knew that was not true for either of them.

She stopped putting on her make-up. She was tired and she had a headache. She also felt very depressed, but she always did on New Year's Eve. It was another year gone by, another year that she was older, and she dreaded old age. She thought about calling Alice, who was spending the holidays with her mother and father in San Francisco. Alice would be horrified at the mess in the apartment, but Janelle knew she would clean it up without reproaching her. She smiled thinking of what Merlyn said, that she used her women lovers with a brutal exploitation that only the most chauvinistic husbands would dare. She realized now that it was partly true. From a drawer she took the ruby earrings Merlyn had given to her as a first gift and put them on. They looked beautiful on her. She loved them.

Then the doorbell rang and she went and opened it. She let Joel come in. She didn't give a shit whether he saw the mess in the apartment or not. Her headache was worse, so she went into the bathroom and took some Percodan before they went out. Joel was as kind and charming as usual. He opened the door of the car for her and went around the other side. Janelle thought about Merlyn. He always forgot to do that and the times he remembered he looked embarrassed. Until, finally, she told him to forget about it, relinquishing her own Southern belle ways.

It was the usual New Year's Eve party in a great crowded house. The parking lot was filled with red-jacketed valets taking over the Mercedes, the Rolls-Royces, the Bentleys, the Porsches. Janelle knew many of the people there. And there was a good deal of flirting and propositioning, which she courted gaily by making jokes about her New Year's resolution to remain pure for at least one month.

As midnight approached, she was really depressed and Joel noticed it. He took her into one of the bedrooms and gave her some cocaine. She immediately felt better and high. She got through the stroke of midnight, the kissing of all her friends, the gropings, and then suddenly she felt her headache come on again. It was the worst headache she had ever had, and she knew she had to get home. She found Joel and told him she was ill. He took a look at her face and could see that she was.

'It's just a headache,' Janelle said. 'I'll be OK. Just get me home.'

Joel drove her home and wanted to come in with her. She knew he wanted to stay hoping that the headache would go away and at least he could spend a nice day tomorrow in bed with her. But she really felt ill. She kissed him and said, 'Please don't come in. I'm really sorry to disappoint you, but I really feel sick. I feel terribly sick.'

She was relieved that Joel believed her. He asked, 'Do you want me to call a doctor for you?'

And she said, 'No, I'll just take some pills and I'll be OK.'

She watched until he was safely out the door of her apartment.

She went immediately to the bathroom to take more Percodan, wet a towel and wrapped it around her head like a turban. She was on her way to the bedroom, going through the doorway, when she felt a terrible crashing blow on the back of her neck. She almost fell. For a moment she thought someone concealed in the room had hit her, and then she thought she had hit her head against something protruding from the wall. But then another crushing blow brought her to her knees. She knew then that something terrible was happening to her. She managed to crawl to the phone beside the bed and just barely made out the red sticker on which was printed the paramedic number. Alice had pasted it there when her son had been visiting them, just in case. She dialled the number and a woman's voice answered.

Janelle said, 'I'm sick. I don't know what's happening, but I'm sick.' And she gave her name and address and let the phone drop. She managed to pull herself up on the bed, and surprisingly enough she suddenly felt better. She was almost ashamed that she had called, there was nothing really wrong with her. Then another terrible blow seemed to strike her whole body. Her vision diminished and narrowed down to a single focus. Again she was astonished and couldn't believe what was happening to her. She could barely see beyond the stretches of the room. She remembered Joel had given her some cocaine and she still had it in her handbag and she staggered to the living room to get rid of it, but in the middle of the living room her body was struck another terrible blow. Her sphincter loosened, and though the haze of a near unconsciousness, she realized she had voided herself. With a great effort she took off her panties and wiped up the floor and threw them under the sofa and then she felt for the earrings she was wearing, she didn't want anyone to steal the earrings. It took her what seemed a long time to get them out, and then she staggered into the kitchen and pushed them far back on the roof of the cabinet where it was all dusty and where no one would ever look.

Still conscious when the paramedics arrived, she was dimly aware of being examined and of one of the medics looking in her handbag and finding her cocaine. They thought she had overdosed. One of the paramedics was questioning her. 'How much drugs did you take tonight?'

And she said, defiantly, 'None.'

468

And the medic said, 'Come on, we're trying to save your life.'

And it was that line that really saved Janelle. She went into a certain role that she played. She used a phrase that she always used to scorn what others valued. She said, '*Oh, please.*' The *Oh, please* in a contemptuous note to show that saving her life was the least of her worries and, in fact, something not even to be considered.

She was conscious of the ride in the ambulance to the hospital and she was conscious of being put in the bed in the white hospital room, but by now this was not happening to her. It was happening to someone she had created and it was not true. She could step away from this whenever she wished. She was safe now. At that moment she felt another terrible blow and lost consciousness.

On the day after New Year's I got the phone call from Alice. I was mildly surprised to hear her voice; in fact, I didn't recognize it until she told me her name. The first thing that flashed through my mind was that Janelle needed help in some way.

'Merlyn, I thought you'd want to know,' Alice said. 'It's been a long time, but I thought I should tell you what happened.'

She paused, her voice uncertain. I didn't say anything, so she went on. 'I have some bad news about Janelle. She's in the hospital. She had a cerebral haemorrhage.'

I didn't really grasp what she was saying, or my mind refused the facts. It registered as an illness only. 'How is she?' I asked. 'Was it very bad?'

Again there was that pause, then Alice said, 'She's living on machines. The tests show no brain activity.'

I was very calm, but I still didn't really grasp it. I said, 'Are you telling me that she's going to die? Is that what you're telling me?'

'No, I'm not telling you that,' Alice said. 'Maybe she'll recover, maybe they can keep her alive. Her family's coming out and they'll make all the decisions. Do you want to come out? You can stay at my place.'

'No,' I said. 'I can't.' And I really couldn't. 'Will you call me tomorrow and tell me what happens? I'll come out if I can help, but not for anything else.'

There was a long silence, and then Alice said, her voice breaking, 'Merlyn, I sat beside her, she looks so beautiful, as if

469

nothing happened to her. I held her hand and it was warm. She looks as if she were just sleeping. But the doctors say that there's nothing left of her brain. Merlyn, could they be wrong? Could she get better?'

And at that moment I felt certain it was all a mistake, that Janelle would recover. Cully had said once that a man could sell himself anything in his own head and that's what I did. 'Alice, the doctors are wrong sometimes, maybe she'll get better. Don't give up hope.'

'All right,' Alice said. She was crying now. 'Oh, Merlyn, it's so terrible. She lies there on the bed asleep like some fairy princess and I keep thinking some magic can happen, that she'll be all right. I can't think of living without her. And I can't leave her like that. She would hate to live like that. If they don't pull the plug, I will. I won't let her live like that.'

Ah, what a chance it was for me to be a hero. A fairy princess dead in an enchantment and Merlyn the Magician knowing how to wake her. But I didn't even offer to help pull the plug. 'Wait and see what happens,' I said. 'Call me, OK?'

'OK,' Alice said. 'I just thought you'd want to know. I thought you might want to come out.'

'I really haven't seen her or spoken to her for a long time,' I said. And I remember Janelle asking. 'Would you deny me?' and my saying laughingly, 'With all my heart.'

Alice said, 'She loved you more than any other man.'

But she didn't say 'more than anybody', I thought. She left out women. I said, 'Maybe she'll be OK. Will you call me again?'

'Yes,' Alice said. Her voice was calmer now. She had begun to grasp my rejection and she was bewildered by it. 'I'll call you as soon as something happens.' Then she hung up.

And I laughed. I don't know why I laughed, but I just laughed. I couldn't believe it, it must be one of Janelle's tricks. It was too outrageously dramatic, something I knew she had fantasized about and so had arranged this little charade. And one thing I knew, I would never look upon her empty face, her beauty vacated by the brain behind it. I would never, never look at it because I would be turned to stone. I didn't feel any grief or sense any loss. I was too wary for that. I was too cunning. I walked around the rest of the day, shaking my head. Once again I laughed and later I caught myself with my face twisting in a kind of smirk, like someone with a guilty secret wish come true, or of someone who is finally trapped forever.

Alice called me late the next day. 'She's all right now,' Alice said.

And for a minute I thought she meant it, that Janelle had recovered, that it had all been a mistake. And then Alice said, 'We pulled the plug. We took her off the machines and she's dead.'

Neither of us said anything for a long time, and then she asked, 'Are you going to come out for the funeral? We're going to have a memorial service in the theatre. All her friends are coming. It's going to be a party with champagne and all her friends giving speeches about her. Will you come?'

'No,' I said. 'I'll come in a couple of weeks to see you if you don't mind. But I can't come now.'

There was another long pause as if she were trying to control her anger, and then she said, 'Janelle once told me to trust you, so I do. Whenever you want to come out, I'll see you.'

And then she hung up.

The Xanadu Hotel loomed before me, its million-dollar marquee of bright lights drowned the lonely hills beyond. I walked past it, dreaming of those happy days and months and years I had spent seeing Janelle. Since Janelle's death I had thought of her nearly every day. Some mornings I'd wake up thinking about her, imagining how she looked, how she could be so affectionate and so furious at the same time.

Those first few minutes awake I always believed she was alive. I'd imagine scenes between us when we met again. It took me five or ten minutes to remember she was dead. With Osano and Artie this had never happened. In fact, I rarely thought of them now. Did I care for her more? But then if I felt that way about Janelle, why my nervous laugh when Alice told me the news over the phone? Why, during the day I heard of her death, did I laugh to myself three or four times? And I realize now perhaps it was because I was enraged with her for dying. In time, if she had lived, I would have forgotten her. By her trickery she would haunt me all my life.

When I saw Alice a few weeks after Janelle's death, I learned that the cerebral haemorrhage came from a congenital defect which Janelle may have known about.

I remembered how angry I was when she was late or the few times she forgot the day on which we were supposed to meet. I was so sure they were Freudian slips, her unconscious wish to reject me. But Alice told me that this had happened often with Janelle. And had gotten worse shortly before her death. It was certainly linked to the bulging aneurysm, the fatal leakage into her brain. And then I remembered that last night with her when she had asked me if I loved her and I had answered her so insolently. And I thought if she could only ask me now, how different I would be. That she could be and say and do whatever she wished. That I would accept anything she wanted to be. That just the thought that I could see her, that she was someplace I could go to, that I could hear her voice or hear her laugh would be the things that could make me happy. 'Ah, then,' I could hear her ask, pleased but angry too, 'but is it the most important thing to you?' She wanted to be the most important thing to me and to everyone she knew and, if possible, to everyone in the world. She had an enormous hunger for affection. I thought of bitter remarks for her to make to me as she lay in bed, her brain shattered as I looked down upon her with grief. She would say, 'Isn't that the way you wanted me? Isn't that the way men want women? I would think this would be ideal for you.' But then I realized she never would have been so cruel or even so vulgar, and then I realized another odd thing. My memories of her were never about our lovemaking.

I know I dream of her many times at night, but I never remember those dreams. I just wake up thinking about her as if she were still alive.

I was on the very top of the Strip, in the shadow of the Nevada mountains, looking down into the huge, glittering neon nest that was the heart of Vegas. I would gamble tonight and in the early morning I'd catch a plane for New York. Tomorrow night I would sleep with my family in my own house and work on my books in my solitary room. I would be safe.

I entered the doors of the Xanadu casino. I was chilled by the frozen air. Two spade hookers went gliding by arm in arm, their heavy curly wigs glistening, one dark chocolate, the other sweetly brown. Then white hookers in boots and short shorts offering pearly white thighs, but the skin of their faces ghostly, showing skeleton bones thinned by chandeliered light and years of cocaine. Down the gauntlet of green felt blackjack tables a long row of dealers raised their hands and washed them in the air.

I went through the casino toward the baccarat pit. And as I approached the grey-railed enclosure, the crowd in front of me

472

broke to spread around the dice pit and I saw the baccarat pit clear.

Four Saints in black tie waited for me. The croupier running the game held up his right hand to halt the Banker with the shoe. He gave me a quick glance and smiled his recognition. Then with his hand still up he intoned, 'A card for the Player.' The laddermen, two pale Jehovahs, leaned forward.

I turned away to watch the casino. I felt a rush of oxygenated air and I wondered if the senile, crippled Gronevelt in his solitary rooms above had pushed his magic buttons to keep all these people awake. And what if he had pushed the button for Cully and all the others to die?

Standing absolutely still in the centre of the casino, I looked for a lucky table on which to begin.

55

'I SUFFER, but still I don't live. I am an X in an indeterminate equation. I am a sort of phantom in life who has lost all beginning and end.'

I read that in the asylum when I was fifteen or sixteen years old, and I think Dostoevsky wrote it to show the unending despair of mankind and perhaps to instill terror in everyone's heart and persuade them to a belief in God. But long ago, as a child when I read it, it was a beam of light. It comforted me, being a phantom didn't frighten me. I thought that X and its indeterminate equation were a magic shield. And now having remained so prudently alive, having passed through all the dangers and all the suffering, I could no longer use my old trick of projecting myself forward into time. My own life was no longer that painful and the future could not rescue me. I was surrounded by count-less tables of chance and I was under no illusion. I knew now the single fact that no matter how carefully I planned, no matter how cunning I was, lies or good deeds done, I couldn't really win.

Finally I accepted the fact that I was not a magician any more. But what the hell. I was still alive and that's more than I could say for my brother, Artie, or Janelle or Osano. And Cully and Malomar and poor Jordan. I understood Jordan now. It was very simple. Life was too much for him. But not for me. Only fools die.

Was I a monster then that I didn't grieve, that I wished so much to stay alive? That I could sacrifice my only brother, my only beginning, and then Osano and Janelle and Cully and never even grieve for them and only weep for one? That I could be comforted with the world I had built for myself?

How we laugh at primitive man for his worry and terror of all the charlatan tricks of nature, and how we ourselves are so terrified of the terrors and guilts that roar in our own heads. What we think of as our sensitivity is only the higher evolution of terror in a poor dumb beast. We suffer for nothing. Our own death wish is our only real tragedy.

Merlin, Merlin. Surely a thousand years have passed and you must finally be awake in your cave, putting on your star-covered conical hat to walk through a strange new world. And poor bastard, with your cunning magic, did it do you any good to sleep that thousand years, your enchantress in her grave, both our Arthurs turned to dust?

Or do you have one last magic spell that can work? A terrible long shot, but what's that to a gambler? I still have a stack of black chips and an itch for terror.

I suffer, but I still live. It's true that I may be a sort of phantom in life, but I know my beginning and I know my end. It is true that I am an X in an indeterminate equation, the X that will terrify mankind as it voyages through a million galaxies. But no matter. That X is the rock upon which I stand.

BOOK 1

1

In Rome, on the Good Friday before Easter, seven terrorists made their final preparations to assassinate the Pope of the Roman Catholic Church. This band of four men and three women believed they were liberators of mankind. They called themselves the 'Christs of Violence'.

The leader of this particular band was an Italian youth well seasoned in the technique of terror. For this particular operation he had assumed the code name 'Romeo'; it pleased his youthful sense of irony, and its sentimentality sweetened his intellectual love of mankind.

On the late afternoon of Good Friday, Romeo rested in a 'safe' house provided by the International One Hundred. Lying on rumpled bedsheets stained with cigarette ash and night sweat he read a paperback edition of *The Brothers Karamazov*. His leg muscles cramped with tension, perhaps fear, it didn't matter. It would pass as it always did. But this mission was so different, so complex, involved so much danger of the body and the spirit. On this mission he would be truly a Christ of Violence, that name so Jesuitical it always moved him to laughter.

Romeo had been born Armando Giangi, to rich, high society parents who subjected him to a drowsy, luxurious, religious upbringing, a combination that so offended his ascetic nature that at the age of sixteen he renounced worldly goods and the Catholic Church. So now, at twenty-three, what greater rebellion could there be for him than the killing of the Pope? And yet there was still, for Romeo, a super-stitious dread. As a child he had received Holy Confirmation from a red-hatted cardinal. Romeo remembered always that ominous red hat painted in the very fires of hell.

So, confirmed by God in every ritual, Romeo prepared himself to commit a crime so terrible that hundreds of millions would curse his name, for his true name would become known. He would be captured. That was part of the plan. And then what happened depended on Yabril. But in time he, Romeo, would be acclaimed a hero who helped change this cruel social order. What was infamy in one century grew saintly in the next. And vice versa, he thought with a smile. The very first Pope to take the name of Innocent, centuries ago, had published a Papal Bull authorizing torture, and had been hailed for propagating the true Faith, rescuing heretic souls.

It also appealed to Romeo's youthful irony that the Church would canonize the Pope he was planning to kill. He would create a new saint. And how he hated them. All these Popes. Pope Innocent IV, Pope Pius, Pope Benedict, oh they sanctified too much, these amassers of wealth, these suppressors of the true faith of human freedom, these pompous wizards who smothered the wretched of the earth with their magic of ignorance, their hot insults to credulity.

He, Romeo, one of the 'First Hundred' of the Christs of Violence, would help erase that crude magic. The First Hundred, vulgarly called terrorists, were spread over Japan, Germany, Italy, Spain and even the tulipy Dutch. It was worth noting that there were none of the First Hundred in America. That democracy, that birthplace of freedom, had only intellectual revolutionaries who fainted at the sight of blood. Who exploded their bombs in empty buildings after warning people to leave; who thought public fornication on the steps of houses of state an act of idealistic rebellion. How contemptible they were. It was not surprising that America had never given one man to the Revolutionary Hundred.

Romeo put a halt to his day-dreaming. What the hell, he

4

didn't know if there were a hundred. There might be fifty or sixty, it was just a symbolic number. But such symbols rallied the masses and seduced the media. The only fact he really knew was that he, Romeo, was one of the First Hundred, and so was his friend and fellow conspirator, Yabril.

One of the many churches of Rome chimed its bells. It was nearly six in the evening of this Good Friday. In another hour Yabril would arrive to review all the mechanics of the complicated operation. The killing of the Pope would be the opening move of a brilliantly conceived chess game; a series of daring acts that delighted Romeo's romantic soul.

Yabril was the only man who had ever awed Romeo, physically and mentally. Yabril knew the treacheries of governments, the hypocrisies of legal authority, the dangerous optimism of idealists, the surprising deceptions in loyalty of even the most dedicated terrorists. But most of all Yabril was a genius of revolutionary warfare. He was contemptuous of the small mercies and infantile pity that affect most men. Yabril had but one aim, to free the future.

And Yabril was more merciless than Romeo could ever be. Romeo had murdered innocent people, betrayed his parents and his friends, assassinated a judge who had once protected him. Romeo understood that political killing might be a kind of insanity, he was willing to pay that price. But when Yabril said to him, 'If you cannot throw a bomb into a kindergarten, then you are not a true revolutionary,' Romeo told him, 'That I could never do.'

But he could kill a Pope.

Yet in the dark Roman nights, horrible little monsters, only the fetuses of dreams, covered Romeo's body with sweat distilled from ice.

Romeo sighed, rolled off his filthy bed to shower and shave before Yabril arrived. He knew that Yabril would judge his cleanliness a good sign, morale high for the coming mission. Yabril, like many sensualists, believed in a certain amount of spit and polish. Romeo, a true ascetic, could live in shit.

On the Roman streets, on his walk to visit Romeo, Yabril took the usual precautions. But in fact everything really depended on internal security, the loyalty of the fighting cadres, the integrity of the First Hundred. But not they, not even Romeo knew the full extent of the mission.

Yabril was an Arab who easily passed for a Sicilian, as indeed many could. He had the thin dark face but the lower part, the chin and jaw, were surprisingly heavier, coarser, as if with an extra layer of bone. In his leisure time he grew a silky fur of a beard to hide the coarseness. But when he was part of an operation, he shaved himself clean. As the Angel of Death he showed his true face to the enemy.

Yabril's eyes were a pale tan, his hair had only isolated lines of gray and that heaviness of the jaw was repeated in the thickness of his chest and shoulders. His legs were long for the shortness of his body and masked the physical power he could generate. But nothing could hide the alert intelligence of his eyes.

Yabril detested the whole idea of the First Hundred. He thought it a fashionable public relations gimmick, despised its formal renunciation of the material world. These university-trained revolutionaries, like Romeo, were too romantic in their idealism, too contemptuous of compromise. Yabril understood that a little corruption in the rising bread of revolution was necessary.

Yabril had long ago given up all moral vanity. He had the clear conscience of those who believe and know that they are devoted with all their souls to the betterment of mankind. But he never reproached himself for his acts of self-interest. There had been his personal contracts with oil sheiks to kill political rivals. Odd jobs of murder for those new African heads of state, who, educated at Oxford, had learned to

6

delegate; then the random acts of terror for sundry respectable political chiefs. All those men in the world, who control everything except the power of life and death.

These acts were never known to the First Hundred, and certainly never confided to Romeo. Yabril received funds from the Dutch, English and American oil companies, money from Russian Communist fronts, and even long ago in his career, payment from the American CIA for a very special secret execution. But all that was in the early days.

Now, he lived well, he was not ascetic, after all he had been poor, though not born so. He was fond of good wine and gourmet food, preferred luxury hotels, enjoyed gambling, and often succumbed to the ecstasy of a woman's flesh. Always paying for that ecstasy with money, gifts and exerting his personal charm. He had a dread of romantic love.

Despite these 'revolutionary' weaknesses, Yabril was famous in his circles for the power of his will. He had absolutely no fear of death, not so extraordinary, but more uniquely he had no fear of pain. And it was, perhaps, because of this that he could be so ruthless.

Yabril had proved himself over the years. He was absolutely unbreakable under any kind of physical or psychological persuasion. He had survived imprisonment in Greece, France, Russia and two months of interrogation by Israeli Security whose expertness inspired his admiration. He had defeated them, perhaps because his body had the trick of losing feeling under duress. At last everyone understood. Yabril was granite under pain.

When he was the captor, he often charmed his victims. That he recognized a certain insanity in himself was part of his charm and part of the fear he inspired. Or perhaps that there was no malice in his cruelties. Yet all in all he savored life, he was a light-hearted terrorist. Even now he thoroughly enjoyed the fragrant streets of Rome, the twilight of Good

7

Friday filled with the chimes of countless holy bells, though he was preparing the most dangerous operation of his life.

Everything was in place. Romeo's cadre was in place. Yabril's own cadre would arrive in Rome the next day. The two cadres would be in separate safe houses, their only link the two leaders. Yabril knew that this was a great moment. This coming Easter Sunday and the days after would be a brilliant creation.

He, Yabril, would direct nations down roads they abhorred to tread. He would throw off all his shadowy masters, they would be his pawns and he would sacrifice them all, even poor Romeo. Only death could defeat his plans, or failure of nerve. Or to be truthful, one of a hundred errors in timing. But the operation was so complicated, so ingenious, it gave him pleasure. Yabril stopped in the street to enjoy the spires of cathedrals, the happy faces of the citizens of Rome, his melodramatic speculation of the future.

But like all men who think they can change the course of history by their own will, their own intelligence, their own strength, Yabril did not give due weight to the accidents and coincidences of history, nor to the possibility that there could be men more terrible than himself. Men bred in the strict structure of society, wearing the mask of benign law givers, could be far more ruthless and cruel.

Watching the devout and joyful pilgrims in the streets of Rome, believers in an omnipotent God, he was filled with a sense of his own invincibility. Proudly he would go beyond their God's forgiveness, for at the uttermost reach of evil, good must necessarily begin.

Yabril was now in one of the poorer districts of Rome where people could more easily be intimidated and bribed. He came to Romeo's safe house as darkness fell. The ancient four-storey apartment building had a large courtyard half encircled by a stone wall, all the apartments controlled by the underground revolutionary movement. Yabril was admitted by one of the three females in Romeo's cadre. She

8

was a thin woman in jeans and a blue denim shirt that was unbuttoned almost down to her waist. She wore no bra, there was no roundness of breasts visible. She had been on one of Yabril's operations before. He did not like her but he admired her ferocity. They had quarreled once and she had not backed down.

The woman's name was Annee. She wore her jet black hair in a Prince Valiant cut that did not flatter her strong blunt face, but drew notice to her blazing eyes that measured everyone with a sort of fury, even Romeo and Yabril. She had not yet been fully briefed on the mission but the appearance of Yabril told her it was of the utmost importance. She smiled briefly, without speaking, then closed the door after Yabril stepped inside.

Yabril noted with disgust how filthy the interior of the house had become. There were dirty dishes and glasses and remnants of food scattered over the living room, the floor littered with newspapers. Romeo's cadre was composed of four men and three women, all Italian. The women refused to clean up, it was contrary to their revolutionary belief to do domestic chores on an operation unless the men did their share. The men, all university students, still young, had the same belief in the rights of women, but they were the conditioned darlings of Italian mothers, and also knew that a back-up cadre would clean the house of all incriminating marks after they left. The unspoken compromise was that the squalor would be ignored. A compromise that irritated only Yabril.

He said to Annee, 'What pigs you are.'

Annee measured him with a cool contempt. 'I'm not a housekeeper,' she said.

And Yabril recognized her quality immediately. She was not afraid of him or any man or woman. She was a true believer. She was quite willing to burn at the stake. Alarm bells went off in his mind.

Romeo, so handsome, so vital that Annee lowered her

eyes, came racing down the stairs from the apartment above and embraced Yabril with real affection, then led him out into the courtyard where they sat on a small stone bench. The night air was filled with the scent of spring flowers, and with that scent there was a faint hum, the sound of countless thousands of pilgrims shouting and talking in the streets of Lenten Rome. Above it all the ascending and descending tolls of hundreds of church bells acclaimed the approaching Easter Sunday.

Romeo lit a cigarette and said, 'Our time has finally come, Yabril. No matter what happens, our names will be known to mankind for ever.'

Yabril laughed at the stilted romanticism, felt a little contempt for this desire for personal glory. 'Infamous,' he said. 'We compete with a long history of terror.' Yabril was thinking of their embrace. An embrace of professional love on his part, but shot through with remembered terror like parricides standing over a father they had murdered together.

There were dim electric lights along the courtyard walls but their faces were in darkness. Romeo said, 'They will know everything in time. But will they give us credit for our motives? Or will they paint us as lunatics? What the hell, the poets of the future will understand us.'

Yabril said, 'We can't worry about that now.' It embarrassed him when Romeo became theatrical, it made him question the man's efficiency though it had been proved many times. Romeo, despite delicate good looks, his fuzziness of concept, was a truly dangerous man. Romeo was too fearless, Yabril perhaps too cunning.

Just a year before, they had walked the streets of Beirut together. Bravely in their path was a brown paper sack, seemingly empty, greased with the food it had contained. Yabril walked around it. Romeo kicked and sailed the sack into the gutter. Different instincts. Yabril believed that everything on this earth was dangerous. Romeo had a certain innocent trust.

There were other differences. Yabril was ugly with his small marbled tan eyes, Romeo was almost beautiful. Yabril was proud of his ugliness, Romeo was ashamed of his beauty. Yabril had always understood that when an innocent man commits absolutely to political change it must lead to murder. Romeo had come to that belief late, and reluctantly. His conversion had been an intellectual one.

Romeo had won sexual victories with the accident of physical beauty and his family money protected him from economic humiliations. Romeo was intelligent enough to know his good fortune was not morally correct, and so the very 'goodness' of his life disgusted him. He drowned himself in literature and his studies, which confirmed his belief. It was inevitable that his radical professors convinced him that he should help make the world a better place.

He did not want to be like his father, an Italian who spent more time in barber shops than courtesans at their hairdresser's. Did not want to spend his life in the pursuit of beautiful women. Above all he would never spend money reeking with the sweat of the poor. The poor must be made free and happy and then he too could taste happiness. And so he reached out, for a Second Communion, to the books of Karl Marx.

Yabril's conversion was more visceral. As a child in Palestine he had lived in a Garden of Eden. He had been a happy boy, extremely intelligent, devotedly obedient to his parents. Especially to his father who spent an hour each day reading to him from the Koran.

The family lived in large villas with many servants, on extended grounds which were magically green in that desert land. But one day, when Yabril was five years old, he was cast out of this Paradise. His beloved parents vanished, the villa and gardens dissolved into a cloud of purple smoke.

11

And suddenly he was living in a small dirty village on the bottom of a mountain, an orphan living on the charity of blood kin. His only treasure was his father's Koran printed on vellum, with illuminated figures of gold, startling calligraphy of a rich blue. And he always remembered his father reading it aloud, exactly from the text, according to Muslim custom. Those orders of God given to the Prophet Mohammed, words that could never be discussed or argued. As a grown man Yabril had remarked to a Jewish friend, 'The Koran is not a Torah', and they both laughed.

The truth exile from the Garden of Eden had been revealed to him almost at once but he did not fully understand it until a few years later. His father had been a secret supporter of Palestine liberation from the state of Israel, a leader of the underground. His father had been betrayed, gunned down in a police raid, and his mother had committed suicide when the villa and grounds were blown up by the Israelis.

It was most natural for Yabril to become a terrorist. His blood kin and his teachers in the local school taught him to hate all Jews but did not fully succeed. He did hate his God for banishing him from his childhood Paradise. When he was eighteen he sold his father's Koran for an enormous sum of money and enrolled in the University of Beirut. There he spent most of his fortune on women and, finally, after two years, became a member of the Palestinian underground. And over the years he became a deadly weapon in that cause. But his people's freedom was not his final aim. In some way his work was a search for inner peace.

Now, together in the courtyard of the safe house, it took Romeo and Yabril a little over two hours to go over every detail of their mission. Romeo smoked cigarettes constantly. He was nervous about one thing. 'Are you sure they will give me up?' he asked.

Yabril said softly, 'How can they not with the hostage I

will be holding? Believe me, you will be safer in their hands than I will be in Sherhaben.'

They gave each other a final embrace in the darkness, not knowing that after Easter Sunday they would never see each other again.

After Yabril left, Romeo smoked a final cigarette in the darkness of the courtyard. Beyond the stone walls he could see the peaks of the great cathedrals of Rome. Then he went inside. It was time to brief his cadre.

The woman, Annee, served as the cadre's armorer and she unlocked a huge trunk to give out the weapons and ammunition. One of the men spread a dirty bedsheet on the floor of the living room and Annee put gun oil and rags on to it. They would clean and oil their weapons as they listened to the briefing. For hours they listened and asked questions, they rehearsed their movements. Annee distributed the operational clothing and they made jokes about that. Finally they all sat down to a meal together that Romeo and the men had prepared. They toasted the success of their mission with new spring wine and then some of them played cards for an hour before they retired to their rooms. There was no need for a guard, they had locked themselves in securely and they had their weapons beside their beds. Still they all had trouble falling asleep.

It was after midnight when the armament woman, Annee, knocked on Romeo's door. Romeo was reading. He let her in and she quickly threw his copy of *The Brothers Karamazov* on the floor. She said almost contemptuously, 'You're reading that shit again?' Romeo shrugged and smiled and said, 'He amuses me, his characters strike me as Italians trying hard to be serious.'

They undressed quickly and lay down on the soiled sheets, both on their backs. Their bodies were tense not with the excitement of sex but with a mysterious terror. Romeo stared straight up at the ceiling and the woman Annee closed her eyes. She was on his left and used her right hand to slowly and gently masturbate him. Their shoulders barely touched, the rest of their bodies were apart. When she felt Romeo erect she continued the strokes with her right hand and at the same time masturbated herself with her left hand. It was a continuous slow rhythm during which Romeo once reached out tentatively to touch her small breast but she made a grimace like a child, her eyes tightly shut. Now her pulling became tighter and stronger, the stroking frantic and unrhythmical and Romeo came to orgasm. As the semen flowed over Annee's hand she too came to orgasm, her eyes flew open and her slight body seemed to hurl itself into the air, lifting and turning to Romeo as if to kiss him, but she ducked her head and buried it in his chest for a moment until her body shuddered to a stop. Then, very matter of factly, she sat up and wiped her hand on the soiled sheet of the bed. She took Romeo's cigarettes and lighter from the marble night table and started to smoke. 'I feel better,' she said.

Romeo went into the bathroom and wet a towel. He came back and washed her hands and then wiped himself. Then he gave her the towel and she rubbed it between her legs.

They had done this on another mission and Romeo understood that this was the only kind of affection she could permit. She was so fierce in her independence, for whatever reason, that she could not bear that a man she did not love would penetrate her. And as for fellatio and cunnilingus, which he had suggested, they were also another form of surrender. What she had done was the only way she could satisfy her need without betraying her ideals of independence.

Romeo watched her face. It was not so stern now, the eyes not so fierce. She was so young, he thought, how did she become so deadly in so short a time? 'Do you want to sleep with me tonight, just for company?' he said.

Annee stubbed out the cigarette. 'Oh no,' she said. 'Why

14

would I want to do that? We've both got what we need.' She started to dress.

Romeo said jokingly, 'At least you could say something tender before you leave.'

She stood in the doorway for a moment and then turned. For a moment he thought she would return to the bed. She was smiling, and for the first time he saw her as a young girl he could love. But then she seemed to stand up on tiptoe, and said, 'Romeo, Romeo! wherefore art thou Romeo?' She thumbed her nose at him and disappeared behind the door she closed.

At Brigham Young University in Provo, Utah, two students, David Jatney and Cryder Cole, prepared their kits for the traditional once-a-term assassination hunt. This game had again come back into favor with the election of Francis Xavier Kennedy to the Presidency of the United States. By the rules of the game a student team had twenty-four hours to commit the assassination, that is, fire their toy pistols at a cardboard effigy of the President of the United States from no more than five paces away. To prevent this there was a Law and Order fraternity defense team of more than a hundred students. The 'Money Prize Bet' was used to pay for the Victory Banquet at the conclusion of the hunt.

The college faculty and administration, influenced by the Mormon Church, disapproved of these games but they had become popular on campuses all over the United States, one of the vexations of a free society. Poor taste, an appetite for the grossness in life, was part of the very high spirits of the young. And it was an outlet for the resentment of authority, a protest by those who had not yet achieved anything against those who had already become successful. It was a symbolic protest, and certainly preferable to political demonstrations, random violence and sit-ins. The hunting game was a safety valve for rioting hormones.

The two hunters, David Jatney and Cryder Cole, strolled

the campus arm in arm. Jatney was the planner and Cole the actor so it was Cole who did the talking as they made their way towards the fraternity brothers guarding the effigy of the President. The cardboard figure of Francis Kennedy was a recognizable likeness but extravagantly colored to show him wearing a blue suit, a green tie, red socks and no shoes. Where the shoes should have been was the Roman numeral IV.

The Law and Order gang threatened Jatney and Cole with their toy pistols and the two hunters veered off. Cole shouted a cheerful insult but Jatney was grim-faced. He took his mission very seriously. Jatney was reviewing his master plan and already feeling a savage satisfaction over its assured success. This walk in view of the enemy was to establish that they were wearing ski gear, to establish a visual identity and so prepare for a later surprise. Also to plant the idea that they were leaving the campus for the weekend.

Part of the hunting game required the itinerary of the Presidential effigy be published. The effigy would be at the victory banquet that was scheduled for that evening before midnight. Jatney and Cole planned to make their strike before the midnight deadline.

Everything worked out as planned. Jatney and Cole reunited at six p.m. in the designated restaurant. The proprietor had no knowledge of their plans. They were just two young students who had been working for him for the past two weeks. They were very good waiters, especially Cole, and the proprietor was delighted with them.

At nine that evening when the Law and Order guards, a hundred strong, entered with their Presidential effigy, guards were posted at all the entries to the restaurant. The effigy was placed in the center of the circle of tables. The proprietor was rubbing his hand at this influx of business. It was only when he went into the kitchen and saw his two young waiters hiding their toy pistols in the soup tureens that he caught on. 'Oh for Christ's sake,' he said, 'that means you

16

two guys are quitting tonight.' Cole grinned at him but David Jatney gave him a menacing scowl and they marched into the dining room, soup tureens lifted high to shield their faces.

The guards were already drinking victory toasts when Jatney and Cole placed the tureens on the center table, whipped off the covers and lifted out the toy pistols. They held their weapons against the garishly colored effigy and fired the little pops of the mechanism. Cole fired one shot and burst out laughing. Jatney fired three shots very deliberately then threw his pistol on the floor. He did not move, he did not smile until the guards mobbed him with congratulatory curses and all of them sat down to dinner. Jatney gave the effigy a kick so that it slid down to the floor where it could not be seen.

This had been one of the more simple hunts. In other colleges across the country the game was more serious. Elaborate security structures were set up, effigies squirted synthetic blood. In the more liberal colleges the effigy was sometimes black.

But in Washington DC, the Attorney General of the United States, Christian Klee, had his own file of all these playful assassins. And it was the photograph and memo on Jatney that caught his interest. He made a note to assign a case team to the life of David Jatney.

On this same Good Friday before Easter, two far more serious-minded young men with far more idealistic beliefs than Jatney and Cole, far more concerned about the future of their world, drove from the Massachusetts Institute of Technology to New York, and deposited a small suitcase in a baggage locker of the Port Authority Building. They picked their way fastidiously through the drunken homeless bums, the sharp-eyed pimps, the incipient whores who thronged the halls of the building. The two were prodigies, at age twenty professors of physics, part of an advanced program at the University. The suitcase held a tiny atom bomb they had constructed using stolen lab materials and the necessary plutonium oxide. It had taken them two years to steal these materials from their programs, bit by bit, falsifying their reports and experiments so that it would not be noticed.

Their names were Adam Gresse and Henry Tibbot and they had been classified as geniuses since they were twelve. Their parents had brought them up to be aware of their responsibilities to humankind. They had no vices except knowledge. The brilliance of their intelligence made them disdain those appetites that were lice on the hide of humanity, such as alcohol, gambling, women, gluttony and drugs.

But they succumbed to the powerful drug of clear thinking. They had a social conscience and saw all the evil in the world. They knew that the making of atomic weapons was wrong, that the fate of humanity hung in the balance, and they decided to do what they could to avert an eternal disaster. So after a year of boyish talk they decided to scare the government. They would show how easy it was for a crazed individual to inflict grave punishment on mankind. They built the tiny atom bomb, only half a kiloton in power, would plant it, and then warn the authorities of its existence. They thought themselves and their deed unique, Godlike. They did not know that this precise situation had been predicted by the psychological reports of a prestigious 'think tank', funded by the government, as one of the possibilities of the atomic age of mankind.

While they were still in New York, Adam Gresse and Henry Tibbot mailed their warning letter to the *New York Times* explaining their motivations and asking that the letter be published before being sent to the authorities. The composing of the letter had been a long process, not only because it had to be worded so precisely to show no malice but because they used scissored printed words and letters lifted out of old newspapers which they pasted on to blank sheets of paper.

The bomb would not go off till the following Thursday. By that time the letter would be in the hands of the authorities and the bomb surely found. It would be a warning to the rulers of the world.

Oliver Ollifant was one hundred years old and his mind was as clear as a bell. Unfortunately for him.

It was a mind so clear, yet so subtle, that, while breaking a great many moral laws, it had washed his conscience clean. A mind so cunning that Oliver Ollifant had never fallen into the almost inevitable traps of everyday life; he had never married, never run for political office and never had a friend he trusted absolutely.

On a huge, secluded, heavily guarded estate only ten miles from the White House, Oliver Ollifant, the richest man in the America and possibly the most powerful private citizen, awaited the arrival of his godson, the Attorney General of the United States, Christian Klee.

Oliver Ollifant's charm equaled his brilliance, his power rested on both. Even at the advanced age of one hundred his advice was still sought by great men who relied on his analytic powers to such an extent that he had been nick-named the 'Oracle'.

As advisor to presidents the Oracle had predicted economic crises. Wall Street crashes, the fall of the dollar, the flight of foreign capital, the fantasies of oil prices. He had predicted the political moves of the Soviet Union, the unexpected embraces of rivals in the Democratic and Republican parties. But above all he amassed ten billion dollars. It was natural that advice from such a rich man be valued, even when wrong. The Oracle was nearly always right.

Now on this Good Friday the Oracle was worried about one thing. The birthday party to celebrate his one hundred years on this earth. A party to be held on Easter Sunday in the Rose Garden of the White House, the host none other than the President of the United States, Francis Xavier Kennedy.

It was a permissible vanity for the Oracle to take great pleasure in this spectacular affair. The world would again remember him for one brief moment. It would be, he thought sadly, his last appearance on the stage.

And in Rome on that Good Friday, Theresa Catherine Kennedy, daughter of the President of the United States, prepared to end her European exile and return to live with her father in the White House.

Her Secret Service security detail had already made all the travel arrangements. Obeying her instructions they had booked passage on the Easter Sunday flight from Rome to New York.

Theresa Kennedy was twenty-three years old and was studying in Europe, first at the Sorbonne in Paris and then in Rome where she had just ended a serious affair with a radical Italian student, to their mutual relief.

She loved her father but hated his being President because she was too loyal to publicly voice her own views. She was a believer in socialism, in the brotherhood of man, the sisterhood of women. She was a feminist in the American style; economic independence was the foundation of freedom and so she had no guilt about the trust funds that guaranteed her freedom.

With a curious but very human morality she rejected the idea of privilege and rarely visited her father in the White House. And perhaps she unconsciously judged her father for her mother's death, that he had struggled for political power while her mother was dying. Later she had wanted to lose herself in Europe but by law she had to be protected by the Secret Service as a member of the immediate Presidential family. She had tried to 'sign off' on that security protection

20

but her father had begged her not to. Francis Kennedy told her he could not bear it if something were to happen to her.

A detail of twenty men, spread over three shifts a day guarded Theresa Kennedy. When she went to a restaurant, if she went to a movie with her boyfriend, they were there. They rented apartments in the same building, used a command van in the street. She was never alone. And she had to tell her schedule to the chief of the security detail, every single day.

Her guards were two-headed monsters, half-servant, half-master. With advanced electronic equipment they could hear the love-making when she brought a male friend back to her apartment. And they were frightening, they moved like wolves, with silent glides, their heads tilted alertly to catch a scent on the wind, but really straining to listen to their ear-plug radios.

Theresa Kennedy had refused a 'net' security, that is, a close, live-in, drive-in, security. She drove her own car, refused to let the security team take an adjoining apartment, refused to walk with guards alongside her. She had insisted that the security be a 'perimeter' security, that they could erect a wall around her as if she were a large garden. In this way she could lead a personal life. This led to some embarrassing moments. One day she went shopping and needed change for a telephone call. She had seen one of her security detail pretending to shop nearby. She had gone up to him and said, 'Could you give me a quarter?' The man had looked at her with shocked bewilderment and she realized suddenly that she had made a mistake, that he was not her security guard. She had burst out laughing and apologized. The man was amused and delighted as he gave her the quarter. 'Anything for a Kennedy,' he said jokingly.

Like so many of the young, Theresa Kennedy believed, on no particular evidence, that people were 'good'; as she believed herself to be good. She marched for freedom, spoke out for the right and against the wrong. She tried never to commit petty mean acts of everyday life. As a child she gave her piggy bank to the American Indians.

In her position as daughter of the President of the United States it was awkward for her when she spoke out for abortion, lent her name to radical and left-wing organizations. She endured the abuse of the media and the insults of political opponents. Innocently, she was scrupulously fair in her love affairs, she believed in absolute frankness, she abhorred deceit.

She should have learned some valuable lessons. In Paris a group of tramps living under one of the bridges tried to rape her when she roamed the city in search of local color. In Rome two beggars tried to snatch her purse as she was giving them money and in both cases she had to be rescued by her patient, vigilant Secret Service detail. But this made no impression on her general faith, that man was good. Every human being had the immortal seed of goodness in his soul, no one was beyond redemption. She had, of course, as a feminist learned of the tyranny of men over women, but did not really comprehend the brutal force men used when dealing with their world. She had no sense of how one human being could betray another human being in the most false and cruel ways.

The chief of her security detail, a man too old to guard the more important people in government, was horrified by her innocence and tried to educate her. He told her horror stories about men in general, stories taken from his long experience in the service, more frank than he would ordinarily be since this was his last assignment before retiring.

'You're too young to understand this world,' he said. 'And in your position you have to be very careful. You think because you do good for someone they will do good to you.' He was telling her this particular story because just the day before she had picked up a male hitchhiker, who assumed that this was an invitation. The security chief had acted immediately, the two security cars forced Theresa's car to

22

the edge of the road just as the hitchhiker put his hand in Theresa's lap.

'Let me tell you a story,' the chief said. 'I once worked for the smartest and nicest man in the government service. In clandestine operations. Just once he got outsmarted, caught in a trap and this bad guy had him at his mercy. Could just blow him away. And this guy was a real bad guy. But for some reason he let my boss off the hook and said, "Remember, you owe me one."

'Well, we spent six months tracking this guy down and we nailed him. And my boss blew him away, never gave him a chance to surrender or turn double. And you know why? He told me himself. This bad guy once had the power of God and therefore was too dangerous to be allowed to live. And my boss didn't have a feeling of gratitude, he said the guy's mercy was just a whim and you can't count on whims the next time around.' The chief did not tell Theresa Kennedy his boss had been a man named Christian Klee.

All these events converged on one man. The President of the United States, Francis Xavier Kennedy.

President Francis Xavier Kennedy and his election were a miracle of American politics. He had been elected to the Presidency on the magic of his name and his extraordinary physical and intellectual gifts, despite the fact that he had only served one term in the Senate before his election to the Presidency.

He was the 'nephew' of John F. Kennedy, the President who had been assassinated in 1963, but was outside the organized Kennedy clan still active in American politics. He was in reality, a cousin, and the only one of the far-flung family who had inherited the charisma of his two famous 'uncles', John and Robert Kennedy.

Francis Kennedy had been a boy genius in the law, a Professor at Harvard at the age of twenty-four. Later he had organized his own law firm which crusaded for broad liberal

23

reforms in the government and the private business sector. His law firm did not make a great deal of money, which was not important to him since he had inherited considerable wealth but it did not bring him a great deal of national fame. He crusaded for the rights of minorities, the welfare of the economically disabled, he defended the helpless.

All these good deeds would have availed him nothing politically except for his other gifts. He was extraordinarily handsome with the satiny blue eyes of his two dead uncles, pale white skin, and jet black hair. He had a wit that was cutting, yet full of such good humor that it destroyed his opponents without a hint of petty malice. He was never pompous and never overbearing. He was well read in the sciences and in the literary arts and above all he cherished humanitarian values.

But most importantly he was extraordinarily effective on television. On that screen he was mesmerizing. That and the Kennedy name carried him to the Presidency. Four of his closest friends orchestrated his election. Christian Klee, Arthur Wix, Eugene Dazzy and Oddblood Gray. They were appointed his personal Senior Staff.

When he was nominated as the Democratic candidate for the Presidency, Francis Kennedy did an extraordinary thing. Instead of putting his inherited wealth in blind trusts, he donated it to charity. His wife and daughter had trusts that would take care of their needs. He himself was talented enough to earn a rich living by his own efforts. It was no great sacrifice, he claimed, as indeed did some of his opponents. But he wanted to set some sort of example. It was one of his strongest beliefs that no individual citizen should accrue extraordinary wealth. Not that he was a communist, every man should be allowed to provide for wife and children and family, but why should one man have billions of dollars? His action and words aroused the admiration of millions and the hatred of thousands.

Great things were expected, but unfortunately the Democratic Congress elected with Kennedy failed to pass his ambitious social programs. On television Francis Kennedy had promised that every family would be well housed, he had announced extraordinary plans for education, guaranteed equal medical care for every citizen, that a rich America would construct an economic safety net that would catch unfortunates who tumbled to the bottom of society. On television, with his magnetic voice, his handsome physical presence, these promises were electrifying. And when elected, he tried to fulfil them. Congress defeated him.

On this Good Friday he met his Senior Staff of top advisors and his Vice President to give them news that he knew would make them unhappy.

He met with them in the Yellow Oval Room of the White House, his favorite room, larger and more comfortable than the more famous Oval Office. The Yellow Oval Room was more a living room and they could be comfortable while being served an English tea.

They were all waiting for him and they rose when his Secret Service bodyguards ushered him into the room. Kennedy motioned his staff to sit down while telling his bodyguards to wait outside the room. Two things irritated him in this little scene. The first was that he had to personally order the Secret Service men out of the room according to the protocols, and the second was that the Vice President had to stand in respect for the Presidency. What annoyed him about this was that the Vice President was a woman; political courtesy overruled social courtesy. This was compounded by the fact that Vice President Helen DuPray was ten years older than him, was still quite a beautiful woman, and had extraordinary political and social intelligence. Which was, of course, why he had picked her as his running mate, despite the opposition of the heavyweights in the Democratic Party.

'Damn it, Helen,' Francis Kennedy said. 'Stop standing up

when I come into a room. Now I have to pour tea for everybody to show my humility.'

'I wanted to express my gratitude,' Helen DuPray said. 'When the Vice President gets summoned to your staff meeting it's usually to get orders on how to wash the dishes.' They both laughed. The staff did not.

Francis Kennedy waited until everyone had been served their tea and then said, 'I have decided not to run for a second term. Which is why you are invited to this meeting, Helen,' he said to the Vice President. 'I want you to prepare to make your run for the Presidency. You will have my full support. Whatever it's worth.'

They were all struck dumb then Helen DuPray smiled at him. All the men in the room noted that she had a lovely smile and also noted that this smile was one of her great political weapons. She said, 'Francis, I think a decision not to run requires a full length review by your staff without my presence. But before I leave let me say this. At this particular point of time I know how discouraged you are by Congress. But I won't be able to do any better, assuming I could be elected. I think you should be more patient. Your second term could be more effective.'

President Kennedy said impatiently, 'Helen, you know as well as I do that a President of the United States has more clout in his first term than in his second.'

'True in most cases,' Helen DuPray said. 'But maybe we could get a different House of Representatives for your second term. And let me speak of my own self interest. As Vice President for only one term I am in a weaker position than if I served for two terms. Also your support would be more valuable as a two-term President and not a President who's been chased out of office by his own Democratic Congress.'

As she picked up her memorandum file and prepared to leave, Francis Kennedy said, 'You don't have to go.'

Helen DuPray gave everybody the same sweet smile. 'I'm

sure your staff can speak far more freely if I'm not present,' she said and she left the Yellow Oval Room.

The four men around Kennedy were silent as she left. When the door was safely closed there was a small flurry of movement as they fluffed their folders of memoranda sheets and reached for tea and sandwiches. The President's Chief of Staff said casually, 'Helen may be the smartest person in this administration.' This was Eugene Dazzy but he was known to have a weakness for beautiful women.

Francis Kennedy smiled at him. 'And what do you think, Euge?' he said. 'Do you think I should be more patient and run again?'

All the men shifted uneasily in their seats. Helen DuPray, smart as she was, did not know Francis Kennedy as well as they did. All four men had a far closer personal relationship with the President. They had been with him since the beginning of his political career and even before. They knew that his easy and bantering statement, his announcement that he would support DuPray masked an almost irreversible decision. They also knew that it meant the end of their power. They got along well with the Vice President but they had no illusions about what she would do if she became President. She would have her own hand-picked staff.

Kennedy's Chief of Staff, Eugene Dazzy was a large affable man whose great art was to avoid making enemies of people whose important wishes and special requests the President denied. Dazzy bowed his balding head over his notes, his tubby upper body straining the wall of his well tailored jacket. He spoke in a casual voice.

'Why not run?' Dazzy said. 'You'll have a nice goof off job. Congress will tell you what to do and refuse to do what you want done. Everything will stay the same. Except in foreign policy, there you can have some fun. You might even do some good. Sure, the world is falling apart and the other countries sort of shit on us, even the small fry – helped as

27

we know by big American companies with their inter-national affiliates. Our army is fifty per cent under quota, we've educated our kids so well they're too smart to be patriotic. Of course we have our technology but then who buys our goods? Our balance of payments is hopeless. Japan outsells us, Israel has a more effective army. You can only go up. I say go get re-elected and relax and have a good time for four years. What the hell, it's not a bad job and you can use the money.' Dazzy smiled and waved a hand to show that he was at least half kidding.

The four men of the staff watched Kennedy closely, despite their seemingly casual attitudes. None of them felt Dazzy was being disrespectful; the playfulness of his remarks was an attitude that Kennedy had encouraged over the past three years.

Arthur Wix, the National Security Advisor, a burly man with a big city face, that is, ethnic, born of a Jewish father and Italian mother, could be savagely witty, but a little in awe of the Presidential office and Kennedy. He did not indulge himself now. Also as the National Security Advisor, he felt that his responsibilities obliged him to be more serious in tone than the others. He spoke in a quiet persuasive tone that still had a New York buzz. 'Euge,' he said, motioning to Dazzy, 'may think he's kidding, but you can make a valuable contribution in our country's foreign policy. We have far more leverage than Europe or Asia believes. I think it's imperative you run for another term. After all in foreign policy, the President of the United States has the power of a king.'

Again the other men of the staff watched Kennedy for his reaction but he simply turned to the man who was closest to him, even closer than Dazzy.

'What do you feel about this, Chris?' Kennedy said.

Christian Klee was Attorney General of the United States. And in an extraordinary move by Kennedy, he was also appointed the head of the FBI and the Chief of the Secret

Service that guarded the Presidency. Essentially he controlled the whole internal security system of the United States. Kennedy had paid a heavy political price for this. He had traded Congress the appointment of two justices of the Supreme Court, three Cabinet posts and the ambassadorship to Britain.

'Francis, you have to make up your mind about two things,' Christian Klee said. 'First, do you really want to run again for President? You can win just with your voice and smile on TV. Certainly your administration hasn't done shit for this country. So. Do you really want it? The second question is: do you still want to do something for this country? Do you want to fight all its enemies, internal and external? Do you really want to set this country on its true course? Because I think this country is dying, I think it's a dinosaur that will be wiped out. Or do you just want to enjoy a four-year vacation and use the White House as your private country club?' Christian paused for a moment and said with a smile, 'Three questions.'

Christian Klee and Francis Kennedy had first met in college. Christian had been one of the important young men at Harvard, Kennedy had only had his own inner circle of admirers, but Christian became one of them.

Now President Kennedy looked at Christian Klee. He said dryly, 'The answer to all three of your questions is no.' Then he turned to his chief political advisor and liaison with Congress. This was Oddblood Gray, the youngest man on his staff, only ten years out of college.

Oddblood Gray had come out of the black left-wing movement, via Harvard and a Rhodes Scholarship. His youthful idealism had been perhaps corrupted by his instinctive political genius. He knew how government worked, where leverage could be applied, when to use the brute force of patronage, when to skip in place, when to surrender gracefully. Kennedy had ignored his warning against trying to push his new programs through Congress. Gray had foretold the massive defeats.

Kennedy said to him, 'Otto, give us the word.'

'Quit,' Oddblood Gray said. 'While you're only just losing.' Kennedy smiled and the other men laughed. Oddblood Gray went on. 'Congress shits on you, the press kicks your ass. The lobbyists and big business have strangled your programs. The working people are disappointed in you, the intellectuals feel you've betrayed them. The right wing and left wing in this country agree on one thing. That you're a dishrag. You're driving this damn big Cadillac of a country and the steering wheel doesn't work. And to boot, every damn maniac in this country gets another four years to knock you off. The hat trick. Let's all of us get out of this damn White House.'

'Do you think I could be re-elected?' Kennedy asked, smiling.

Oddblood Gray faked a look of astonishment. 'Of course,' he said. 'This country always re-elects useless Presidents. Even your worst enemies want you re-elected.'

Kennedy smiled. They were trying to goad him into running again by appealing to his pride. None of them wanted to leave this center of power, this Washington, this White House. It was better to be this clawless lion than not to be a lion at all.

Then Oddblood Gray spoke again. 'We might do some good if we work differently. If you really put your heart into it.'

Eugene Dazzy said, 'You're really the only hope, Francis. The rich are too rich, the poor are too poor. This country is becoming a feeding ground for the big industries, for Wall Street. They're running wild, with no thought for the future. It may be decades down the road but trouble, big trouble is on the way. There's a chance for you to reverse the whole thing in the next four years.'

They all waited for his answer and with different

emotions. It was unusual for political advisors to have such strong personal attachments to their President but all these men held him in some kind of awe.

Francis Kennedy had an overpowering charisma. It was not only that he was imposing in body, indeed had a kind of physical beauty that echoed his two famous uncles, but that he had intellectual brilliance that was rare, even exotic in a politician. He had been a successful lawyer, a writer on the sciences, had a knowledge of physics and an impeccable taste in literature. He even understood economic theory without the help of financial ghosts. And he had a sympathy for the ordinary man that was unusual in a man who had been born to wealth and had never suffered any kind of economic stress.

Eugene Dazzy broke the silence. 'You have to think about it more, Francis. Helen is right.' But it was clear to all of them that Kennedy had made up his mind. He would not run again. This was the end of the road for all of them.

Kennedy shrugged. 'After the Easter vacation, I'll make a formal announcement. Eugene, start your staff doing the paperwork. My advice to you guys is to start looking for jobs with the big law firms and the defense industries.'

They took this as a dismissal and left, except for Christian Klee.

Christian said casually, 'Will Theresa be home for the holidays?'

Francis Kennedy shrugged. 'She's in Rome with a new boyfriend. She'll be flying in on Easter Sunday. She makes a point of ignoring religious holidays.'

Christian said, 'I'm glad she's getting the hell out. I really can't protect her in Europe. And she thinks she can shoot her mouth off there and it won't be reported here.' He paused a moment. 'If you do run again, you'll have to keep your daughter out of sight or disown her.'

Kennedy laughed. 'It doesn't matter, Christian, I won't run again. Make other plans.'

'OK,' Christian said. 'Now about the birthday party for the Oracle. He's really looking forward to it.'

'Don't worry,' Kennedy said. 'I'll give him the full treatment. My God, a hundred years old and he still looks forward to his birthday party.'

'He was and is a great man,' Christian said.

Kennedy gave him a sharp look. 'You were always fonder of him than I ever was. He had his faults, he made his mistakes.'

'Sure,' Christian said. 'But I never saw a man control his life better. He changed my life with his advice, his guidance.' Christian paused for a moment. 'I'm having dinner with him tonight so I'll just tell him the party is definitely on.'

Kennedy smiled dryly. 'You can safely tell him that,' he said.

At the end of the day Kennedy signed some papers in the Oval Office, then sat at his desk and gazed through the windows. He could see the tops of the gates that surrounded the White House grounds, black iron tipped with white electrified thorns. As always he felt uneasy by his proximity to the streets and to the public, though he knew that the seeming vulnerability to attack was an illusion. He was extraordinarily protected. There were seven perimeters guarding the White House. For two miles away every building had a Security team on the roofs and in apartments. All the streets leading to the White House were commanded by concealed rapid fire and heavy weapons. The tourists who came mornings to visit the ground floor of the White House in their many hundreds were heavily infiltrated with Secret Service agents who circulated constantly, and took part in the small talk, their eyes alert. Every inch of the White House that these tourists were permitted to visit behind the walling off ropes was covered by TV monitors and special audio equipment that could pick up secret whispers. Armed guards manned special computer desks that could serve as barricades at every turn in the corridors. And during these visits by the public Kennedy would always be up in the new specially built fourth floor that served as his living quarters. Living quarters guarded by specially reinforced floors and walls and ceilings.

Now in the famous Oval Office that he rarely used except to sign official documents in special ceremonies, Francis Kennedy relaxed to enjoy one of the few minutes he was completely alone. He took a long thin Cuban cigar from the humidor on his desk, felt the oiliness of the leafy wrapper on his fingers. He cut the end, lit it carefully, took the first rich puff and looked out through the bullet-proof windows.

He could see himself as a child walking across the vast green lawn, the faraway white-painted guard post, then running to greet his Uncle Jack and Uncle Robert. How he had loved them. Uncle Jack so full of charm, so childlike, and yet so powerful, to give hope that a child could wield power over the world. And Uncle Robert, so serious and earnest and yet so gentle and playful. And here Francis Kennedy thought, no, we called him Uncle Bobby, not Robert, or did we sometimes? He could not remember.

But he did remember one day more than forty years ago when he had run to meet both his uncles on that very same lawn and how they had each taken one of his arms and swung him so that his feet never touched the ground as they walked him with them into the White House.

And now he stood in their place. The power that had awed him as a child was now his. It was a pity that memory could evoke so much pain and so much beauty, and so much disappointment. What they had died for, he was giving up.

On this Good Friday Francis Xavier Kennedy did not know that all this could be changed by two insignificant revolutionaries in Rome.

2

On Easter Sunday morning, Romeo and his cadre of four men and three women, in full operational gear, disembarked from their van. They billowed into the Roman streets outside St Peter's Square, mingling with the crowds attired in Easter finery; the women glorious in the pastel colors of spring, operatic in worshipping hats, the men handsome in silky creamy suits, yellow palm crosses stitched into their lapels. The children were even more dazzling, little girls with gloves and frilly frocks, the boys in navy blue suits of Confirmation with red ties bisecting snowy shirts. Scattered throughout were priests smiling approving benedictions to the faithful.

But Romeo was a more sober pilgrim, a serious witness to the Resurrection that this Easter morning celebrated. He was dressed in a dead black suit, a white shirt heavily starched, and a pure white tie almost invisible against it. His shoes were black but rubber-soled. And now he buttoned the camelhair coat to conceal the rifle that hung in its special sling. He had practised with this rifle for the past three months until his accuracy was deadly.

The four men in his cadre were dressed as monks of the Capuchin order; long flowing robes of dingy brown, girdled by fat cloth belts. Their heads were tonsured but covered with skull caps. Concealed inside the loose robes were grenades and handguns.

The three women, one of them Annee, were dressed as nuns and they too had weapons beneath their loose-fitting clothing. Annee and the other two nuns walked ahead, people made way for them, and Romeo followed easily in their black and white wake. After Romeo came the four monks of the cadre, observing everything, ready to interdict if Romeo was stopped by Papal police.

And so Romeo's band made their way to St Peter's Square, invisible in the huge crowd that was assembling. Finally like dark corks bobbing on an ocean of flowery silk, they came to rest on the far side of the square, their backs protected by marble columns and stone walls. Romeo stood a little apart. He was watching for a signal from the other side of the square, where Yabril and his cadre were busy attaching holy figurines to the walls.

Yabril and his cadre of three men and three women were in casual attire with loose-fitting jackets. The men carried concealed handguns and the women were working with the religious figurines. These figurines, small statues of Christ, were loaded with explosives designed to go off by radio signal. The backs had adhesive glue so strong that they could not be detached by any of the curious in the crowd. Also the figurines were beautifully designed and made of an expensive looking white-painted terracotta formed around a wired skeleton. They appeared to be part of the Easter decorations and as such inviolate.

When this was done, Yabril led his cadre through the crowd and out of St Peter's Square to his own waiting van. He sent one of his men in the cadre to Romeo to give him the radio signal device for the setting off of the figurines. Then Yabril and his cadre got into their van and started the drive to Rome airport. Pope Innocent would not appear on the balcony until three hours later. They were on schedule.

In the van, closed off from the Easter world of Rome, Yabril thought about how this whole exercise had begun . . .

On a mission together a few years ago, Romeo had mentioned that the Pope had the heaviest security guard of any ruler in Europe. Yabril had laughed and said, 'Who would want to kill a pope? Like killing a snake that has no poison. A useless old figurehead and with a dozen useless old men ready to replace him. Bridegrooms of Christ, a set of a dozen red-capped dummies. What would change in the world with the death of a pope? I can see kidnapping him, he's the richest man in the world. But killing him would be like killing a lizard sleeping in the sun.'

Romeo had argued his case and intrigued Yabril. The Pope was revered by hundreds of millions of Catholics all over the world. And certainly the Pope was a symbol of capitalism; the bourgeois Western Christian States propped him up. The Pope was one of the great stones of authority in the edifice of that society. And so it followed that if the Pope were assassinated it would be a shocking psychological blow to the enemy world. And killing the representative of that God on earth in which they did not believe. The royalty of Russia and France had been murdered because they too ruled from divine right, and those murders had advanced humanity. God was the fraud of the rich, the swindler of the poor, the Pope an earthly wielder of that evil power. But still it was only half an·idea. Yabril expanded the concept. Now the operation had a grandeur that awed Romeo and filled Yabril with self-admiration.

Romeo for all his talk and sacrifices was not what Yabril considered a true revolutionary. Yabril had studied the history of Italian terrorists. They were very good at assassinating heads of state, they had studied at the feet of the Russians who had killed their Czar finally after many attempts, indeed they had borrowed from the Russians that name Yabril detested, 'the Christs of Violence'.

Yabril had met Romeo's parents once. The father, a useless man, a parasite on humanity. Complete with chauffeur, valet, and a great big lamb-like dog that he used as bait to snare women on the boulevards. But a man with beautiful manners. It was impossible not to like him if you were not his son.

And the mother, another beauty of the capitalistic system, voracious for money and jewels, a devout Catholic. Beautifully dressed, maids in tow, she walked to mass every morning. That penance accomplished, she devoted the rest of her day to pleasure. Like her husband she was self-indulgent, unfaithful, and devoted to their only son, Romeo.

So now, this happy family finally would be punished. The father a Knight of Malta, the mother a daily communicant with Christ and their son the murderer of the Pope. What a betrayal, Yabril thought. Poor Romeo, you will spend a bad week when I betray you.

Except for the final twist that Yabril had added, Romeo knew the whole plan. 'Just like chess,' Romeo said. 'Check to the king, check to the king, and the checkmate. Beautiful.'

Yabril looked at his watch, it would be another fifteen minutes. The van was going at moderate speed along the highway to the airport.

It was time to begin. He collected all the weapons and grenades from his cadre and put them in a suitcase. When the van stopped in front of the airport terminal Yabril got out first. The van went on to discharge the rest of the cadre at another entrance. Yabril walked through the terminal slowly, carrying the suitcase, his eyes searching for undercover security police. Just short of the checkpoint, he walked into a gift and flower shop. A 'Closed' sign in bright red and green letters hung on a peg inside the door. This was a signal that it was safe to enter and also kept the shop clear of customers.

The woman in the shop was a dyed blonde with heavy make-up, quite ordinary looks, but with a warm inviting voice and a lush body shown to advantage in a plain woollen dress belted severely at the waist.

'I'm sorry,' she said to Yabril, 'but you can see by the sign

37

that we are closed. It is Easter Sunday after all.' But her voice was friendly, not rejecting. She smiled warmly.

Yabril gave her the code sentence, designed merely for recognition. 'Christ is risen but I must still travel on business.' She reached out and took the suitcase from his hand.

'Is the plane on time?' Yabril asked.

'Yes,' the woman said. 'You have an hour. Are there any changes?'

'No,' Yabril said. 'But remember, everything depends on you.' Then he went out. He had never seen the woman before and would never see her again and she knew only about this phase of the operation. He checked the schedules on the departure board. Yes, the plane would leave on time.

The woman was one of the few female members of the First Hundred. She had been planted in the shop three years ago as owner and during that time she had carefully and seductively built up relationships with airline terminal personnel and security guards. Her practice of bypassing the scanners at the checkpoints to deliver parcels to people on planes was cleverly established. She had done it not too often but just often enough. In the third year she began an affair with one of the armed guards who could wave her through the unscanned entry. Her lover was on guard duty this day, she had promised him lunch and a siesta in the back room of her shop. And so he had volunteered for the Easter Sunday duty.

The lunch was already laid out on the table in the back room when she emptied the suitcase to pack the weapons in gaily wrapped Gucci gift boxes. She put the boxes into mauve-colored paper shopping bags and waited until twenty minutes before departure time. Then cradling the bag in her arms because it was so heavy and she was afraid the paper might break, she ran awkwardly toward the unscanned entry corridor. Her lover on guard duty waved her through gallantly. She gave him a brilliantly affectionate and apologizing smile. As she boarded the plane the stewardess recognized her and said with a laugh, 'Again, Livia.' The woman walked through to the tourist section until she saw Yabril seated with three men and three women of his cadre beside him. One of the women raised her arms to accept the heavy package.

The woman known as Livia dropped the bag into those waiting arms and then turned and ran out of the plane. She went back to the shop and finished preparing lunch in the back room.

This security guard, Faenzi, was one of those magnificent specimens of Italian manhood who seem deliberately created to delight womanhood. That he was handsome was the least of his virtues. More importantly he was one of those sweet-tempered men who are extraordinarily satisfied with the range of their talents and the scope of their ambition. The woman, Livia, had spotted him almost immediately on his first day of duty as a security guard in the airport.

Faenzi wore his airport uniform as grandly as a Napoleonic Field Marshal, his mustache was as neat and pretty as the tilted nose of a soubrette. You could see he believed that he had a significant job, an important duty to the state. He viewed passing women fondly and benevolently, they were under his protection. Livia immediately marked him as her own. At first he had treated her with an exquisitely filial courtliness, but she had soon put an end to that with a torrent of flattery, a few charming gifts that hinted at hidden wealth, and then evening snacks in her boutique at night. Now he loved her or was at least as devoted to her as a dog to an indulgent master. She was a source of treats.

And Livia enjoyed him. He was a wonderful and cheerful lover without a serious thought in his head. She much preferred him in bed to those gloomy young revolutionaries consumed with guilt, belabored by conscience, that she bedded because they were her political comrades.

39

He became her pet and she fondly called him Zonzi. When he entered the shop and locked the door, she went to him with the utmost affection and desire; she had a bad conscience. Poor Zonzi, the Italian Anti-Terrorist Branch would track everything down, and note her disappearance from the scene. Zonzi had undoubtedly boasted of his conquest, after all she was an older and experienced woman, her honor need not be protected. Their connections would be uncovered. Poor Zonzi, this lunch would be his last hour of happiness.

Quickly and expertly on her side, enthusiastically and joyfully on his, they made love. Livia pondered the irony that here was an act that she thoroughly enjoyed and yet served her purposes as a revolutionary woman. Zonzi would be punished for his pride and his presumption, his condescending love for an older woman, she would achieve a tactical and strategic victory. And yet poor Zonzi. How beautiful he was naked, the olive skin, the large doelike eyes and jet black hair, the pretty mustache, the penis and balls firm as bronze. 'Ah, Zonzi, Zonzi,' she whispered into his thighs, 'always remember that I love you.' Which was not true but might repair his broken ego as he served his time in prison.

She fed him a marvelous meal, they drank a superior bottle of wine and then they made love again. Zonzi dressed, kissed her goodbye, and glowed with the belief that he deserved such good fortune. After he left she took a long look around the shop. She gathered all her belongings together with some extra clothes and used Yabril's suitcase to carry them. That had been part of the instructions. There should be no trace of Yabril. Her last task was to erase all the obvious fingerprints she might have left in the shop but that was just a token task. She would probably not get all of them. Then, carrying the suitcase, she went out, locked up the shop, and walked out of the terminal. Outside in the brilliant sunshine, a woman of her own cadre was waiting with a car. She got into it, gave the driver a brief kiss of greeting and said almost regretfully, 'Thank God that's the end of that.' The other woman said, 'It wasn't so bad. We made money on the shop.'

Yabril and his cadre were in the tourist cabin because Theresa Kennedy, daughter of the President of the United States, was travelling First Class with her six-man Secret Service security detail. Yabril did not want the handover of the gift-wrapped weapons to be seen by them. He also knew that Theresa Kennedy would not get on the plane until just before take off, that the security guards would not be on the plane beforehand, because they never knew when Theresa Kennedy would change her mind and, Yabril thought, because they had become lazy and careless.

The plane, a jumbo jet, was sparsely occupied. Not many people in Italy choose to travel on Easter Sunday and Yabril wondered why the President's daughter was doing so. After all she was a Roman Catholic, though lapsed into the new religion of the liberal left, that most despicable political division. But the sparsity of passengers suited his plans, a hundred hostages, easier to control.

An hour later, the plane in the air, Yabril slumped down in his seat as the women began tearing the Gucci paper off the packages. The three men of the cadre used their bodies as shields, leaning over the seats and talking to the women. There were no passengers seated near them, they had a small circle of privacy. The women handed Yabril the grenades wrapped in gift paper and he adorned his body with them quickly. The three men accepted the small handguns and hid them inside their jackets. Yabril also accepted a small handgun and the three women armed themselves.

When all was ready, Yabril intercepted a stewardess going down the aisle. She saw the grenades and the gun even before Yabril whispered his commands and took her by the hand. The look of shock, then amazement, then fear was

41

familiar to him. He held her clammy hand and smiled. Two of his men positioned themselves to command the tourist section. Yabril still held the stewardess by the hand as they entered First Class. The Secret Service bodyguards saw him immediately, recognized the grenades and saw the guns. Yabril smiled at them. 'Remain seated, gentlemen,' he said. The President's daughter slowly turned her head and gazed into Yabril's eyes. Her face became taut but not frightened. She was brave, Yabril thought, and handsome. It was really a pity. He waited until the three women of the cadre took their positions in the First Class cabin and then had the stewardess open the door leading to the pilot's cockpit. Yabril felt he was entering the brain of a huge whale, and making the rest of the body helpless.

When Theresa Kennedy first saw Yabril her body suddenly shook with a nausea of unconscious recognition. He was the demon she had been warned against. There was a ferocity on his slim dark face. Its brutal, massive lower jaw gave it the quality of a face in a nightmare. The grenades strung over his jacket and in his hand looked like squat green toads. Then she saw the three women dressed in dark trousers and white jackets with the large steel-colored guns in their hands. After the first animal fear, Theresa Kennedy's second reaction was that of a guilty child. Shit, she had gotten her father into trouble, she would never ever be able to get rid of her Secret Service security detail. She watched Yabril go to the door of the pilot cabin holding the stewardess by the hand. She turned her head to look at the chief of her security detail, but he was watching the armed women very intently.

At that moment one of Yabril's men came into the First Class cabin holding a grenade in his hand. One of the cadre women made another stewardess pick up the intercom. The voice came over the phone. It only quavered slightly. 'All passengers fasten your seat belts. The plane has been commandeered by a revolutionary group. Please remain calm and await further instructions. Do not stand up. Do not touch your hand luggage. Do not leave your seats for any reason. Please remain calm. Remain calm.'

In the cockpit the pilot saw the stewardess enter and said to her excitedly, 'Hey, the radio just said somebody shot at the Pope.' Then he saw Yabril enter behind the stewardess and his mouth opened into a silent 'O' of surprise, words frozen there. Just like in a cartoon, Yabril thought, as he raised the hand which held the grenade. But the pilot had said 'shot at the Pope'. Did that mean Romeo had missed? Had the mission already failed? In any case Yabril had no alternative. He gave his orders to the pilot to change their course to the Arab state of Sherhaben.

On the sea of humanity in St Peter's Square, Romeo and his cadre floated to a corner backed by a stone wall and formed their own murderous island. Annee in her nun's habit stood directly in front of Romeo, gun ready beneath her habit. She was responsible for protecting him, giving him time for his shot. The other members of the cadre, in their religious disguises, formed a circle, a perimeter to give him space. They had three hours to wait before the Pope appeared.

Romeo leaned back against the stone wall, shuttered his eyes against the Easter morning sun and quickly ran his mind over the rehearsed moves of the operation. When the Pope appeared he would tap the shoulder of the cadre man on his left. That man would then set off the radio signal device that would explode the holy figurines on the opposite wall of the square. In that moment of the explosions he would have his rifle out and fire. The time had to be exact so that his shot would be a reverberation of the other explosions. Then he would drop the rifle, his monks and nuns would form a circle around him and they would flee with the others. The figurines were also smoke bombs and St Peter's Square would be enveloped with dense clouds. There would be enormous confusion and there would be panic. With all this he should be able to make his escape. Those spectators near him in the crowd might be dangerous, they would be aware, but the motions of the multitude in flight would soon separate them. Those who were foolhardy enough to persist would be gunned down.

Romeo could feel the cold sweat on his chest. The vast multitude waving flowers aloft became a sea of white and purple, pink and red. He wondered at their joy, their belief in the resurrection, their ecstasy of hope against death. He wiped his hands against the outside of his coat, felt the weight of his rifle in its sling. He could feel his legs begin to ache and go numb. He sent his mind outside his body to pass the long hours he would have to wait for the Pope to appear on his balcony.

Lost scenes from his childhood formed again. Tutored for confirmation by a romantic priest, he knew that a red-hatted senior cardinal always certified the death of a pope by tapping him on the forehead with a silver mallet. Was that still really done? It would be a very bloody mallet this time. But how big would such a mallet be? Toy-sized? Heavy and big enough to drive a nail? But of course it would be a precious relic from the Renaissance, crusty with jewels, a work of art. No matter, there would be very little of the Pope's head left to tap, the rifle under his coat held explosive bullets. And Romeo was sure he would not miss. He believed in his left-handedness, to be *sinistra* was to be successful, in sports, love, and certainly by every superstition, in murder.

As he waited, Romeo wondered that he had no sense of sacrilege, after all he had been brought up a strict Catholic in a city whose every street and building reminded one of the beginnings of Christianity. Even now he could see the domed roofs on holy buildings like marble disks against the sky, hear deep, consoling yet intimidating bells of churches. In this great hallowed square he could see the statues of martyrs, smell the very air choked with the countless spring flowers offered by true believers in Christ.

44

The overpowering fragrance of the multitudinous flowers washed over him and he was reminded of his mother and father and the heavy scents they always wore to mask the odor of their plush and pampered Mediterranean flesh.

And then the vast crowd in their Easter finery began shouting, 'Papa, Papa, Papa.' Standing in the lemon light of early spring, stone angels above their heads, the crowd chanted incessantly for the blessing of their Pope. Finally two red-robed cardinals appeared and stretched out their arms in benediction. Then Pope Innocent was on the balcony.

He was a very old man dressed in a cloak of glittering white; on it a cross of gold, the woolly pallium embroidered with crosses. On his head was a white skullcap and on his feet the traditional low, open red shoes, gold crosses embroidered on their fronts. On one of the hands raised to greet the crowd was the pontifical fisherman's ring of St Peter.

The multitude sent their flowers up into the sky, the voices roared, a great motor of ecstasy, the balcony shimmered in the sun as if to fall with the descending flowers.

At that moment Romeo felt the dread these symbols had always inspired in his youth, the red-hatted cardinal of his first confirmation pockmarked like the Devil, and then he felt an elation that lifted his whole being into bliss, ultimate pride. Romeo tapped his cadre man's shoulder to send the radio signal.

The Pope raised his white-sleeved arms to answer the cries of 'Papa, Papa', to bless them all, to praise the Eastertide, the resurrection of Christ, to salute the stone angels that rode around the walls. Romeo slid his rifle out from beneath his coat, two monks of his cadre in front of him knelt to give him a clear shot. Annee placed herself so that he could lay his rifle across her shoulder. The cadre man behind him flashed the radio signal that set off the mined figurines on the other side of the square.

45

The explosions rocked the foundations of the square, a cloud of pink floated in the air, the fragrance of the flowers turned rotten with the stench of burnt flesh. And at that moment Romeo, rifle sighted, pulled the trigger. The explosions on the other side of the square changed the welcoming roar of the crowd to the shrieking of countless gulls.

On the balcony the body of the Pope seemed to rise up off the ground, the white skullcap flew into the air above it, swirled in violent whirlwinds of compressed air and then drifted down into the crowd, a bloody rag. A frightening wail of horror, of terror and animal rage filled the square as the body of the Pope slumped over the balcony rail. His cross of gold dangled free, the pallium drenched red.

Clouds of dust rolled over the square. Marble fragments of shattered angels and saints fell. There was a terrible silence, the crowd frozen by the sight of the murdered Pope. They could see his head blown apart. Then the panic began. The people fled from the square, trampling the Swiss Guards who were trying to seal off the exits. The gaudy Renaissance uniforms were buried by the mass of terror-stricken worshippers.

Romeo let his rifle drop to the ground. Surrounded by his cadre of armed monks and nuns, he let himself be swept out of the square into the streets of Rome. He seemed to have lost his vision, he staggered blindly, and Annee grasped him by the arm and thrust him into the waiting van. Romeo held his hands over his ears to shut out the screams; he was shaking with shock, and then a sense of exaltation and wonder, as if the murder had been a dream.

On the jumbo jet plane scheduled from Rome to New York, Yabril and his cadre were in full control, the First Class section cleared of all passengers except Theresa Kennedy.

Theresa Kennedy was now more interested than frightened. She was fascinated that the hijackers so easily cowed her Secret Service detail by simply showing detonation

46

devices all over their bodies, any bullet fired would send the plane flying into bits through the skies. She noted that the three men and three women terrorists were very slender with faces screwed up in the tension of great athletes, various expressions of emotion changing their features. A male hijacker gave one of her Secret Service agents a violent push out of the First Class cabin and kept pushing him down the open aisle of the tourist section. One of the female hijackers kept her distance, her gun ready. When a Secret Service agent showed some reluctance to leave Theresa Kennedy's side, the woman raised her gun and pressed the barrel to his head. And her eyes showed plainly she was about to shoot. The eyes squinted, facial lines creased, her teeth showed from the extreme compression of the muscles around her mouth which parted the lips slightly to relieve pressure. At that moment Theresa Kennedy pushed her guard away and put her own body in front of the woman hijacker, who smiled with relief and waved her into the seat.

Theresa Kennedy watched Yabril rule the operation. He seemed almost distant as if he were a director watching his actors perform, not seeming to give orders but only hints, suggestions. She noted that he used his cadre as a noose to cut off the tourist body of the plane from its head. With a slight reassuring smile he motioned that she should keep to her seat. It was the action of a man looking after someone who had been put in his special care. Then he went into the pilot's cabin. One of the male hijackers guarded the entry into First Class from the tourist cabin. Two women hijackers stood back to back in the section with her, guns at the ready. There was a stewardess manning the intercom phone that relayed messages to the passengers under the direction of the male hijacker. They all looked too small to cause such terror.

In the cockpit Yabril gave the pilot permission to radio that his plane was hijacked and relay the new flight plan to Sherhaben. The American authorities would think their only problem would be to negotiate the usual Arab terrorist demands. Yabril stayed in the cabin to listen to the radio traffic.

As the plane flew through the air there was nothing to do but wait. Yabril dreamed of Palestine, as it was when he was a child, his home a green oasis in the desert, his father and mother angels of light, the beautiful Koran as it rested on his father's desk, always ready to renew faith. And how it had all finished in dead gray rolls of smoke, fire and the brimstone of bombs falling from the air. And the Israelis came and it seemed as if his whole childhood had been spent in some great prison camp of ramshackle huts, a vast settlement united in only one thing, their hatred of the Jews. Those very same Jews that the Koran praised.

He remembered even at the University, how some of the teachers spoke of a botched job as 'Arab work'. Yabril himself had used the phrase to a gunmaker who had given him defective weapons. Ah, but they would not call this day's business 'Arab work'.

He had always hated the Jews, no not the Jews, the Israelis. He remembered when he was a child of four, maybe five, not later, the soldiers of Israel had raided the settlement camp in which he went to school. They had received false information, 'Arab work', that the settlement was hiding terrorists. All the inhabitants had been ordered out of their houses and into the streets with their hands up. Including the children in the long yellow-painted tin hut that was the school and lay just a little outside the settlement. Yabril with other small boys and girls his age had clustered together wailing, their little arms and tiny hands high in the air, screaming their surrender, screaming in terror. And Yabril had always remembered one of the young Israeli soldiers, the new breed of Jew, blond as a Nazi, looking at the children with a sort of horror, and then the fair skin of that alien Semite's face was streaming with tears. The Israeli lowered his gun and shouted at the children to stop, to put down their hands. They had nothing to fear, he said, little children had nothing to fear. The Israeli soldier spoke almost. perfect Arabic and when the children still stood with their arms held high, the soldier strode among them trying to pull down their arms, weeping all the while. Yabril had never forgotten the soldier, had resolved, later in life, never to be like him, never to let pity destroy him.

Now below the plane he could see the deserts of Arabia. Soon the flight would come to an end and he would be in the Sultanate of Sherhaben.

Sherhaben was one of the smallest countries in the world but had such a richness of oil that its camel riding Sultan begot hundreds of children and grandchildren who drove Mercedes and were educated in the finest universities abroad. The original Sultan owned huge industrial companies in Germany and the United States and had died the single most wealthy person in the world. Only one of these grand-children had endured the murderous intrigues of half-brothers and became the present Sultan – Maurobi.

The Sultan Maurobi was a militant and fanatically devout Muslim and the citizens of Sherhaben, now rich, were equally devout. No woman could go without a veil, no money could be loaned for interest, there was not a drop of liquor in that thirsty desert land except at the foreign embassies.

Long ago Yabril had helped the Sultan establish and consolidate power by assassinating four of the Sultan's more dangerous half-brothers. The Sultan, because of these debts of gratitude, and because of his own hatred of the great powers, had agreed to help Yabril in this operation.

The plane carrying Yabril and his hostages landed and rolled slowly toward the small glass-encircled terminal, pale yellow in the desert sun. Beyond the airfield was an endless stretch of sand studded with oil rigs. When the plane came to a stop Yabril could see that the airfield was surrounded by at least a thousand of Sultan Maurobi's troops.

Now the most intricate and satisfying part of the operation

would begin, and the most dangerous. He would have to be careful until Romeo was finally in place. And he would be gambling on the Sultan's reaction to his secret and final checkmate. No, this was not Arab work.

Because of the European time difference, Francis Kennedy received the first report of the shooting of the Pope at six a.m. Easter Sunday. It was given to him by Press Secretary Matthew Gladyce who had the White House watch for the holiday. Eugene Dazzy and Christian Klee had already been informed and were in the White House.

Francis Kennedy came down the stairs from his living quarters and entered the Oval Office to find Dazzy and Christian waiting for him. They both looked very grim. Far away on the streets of Washington there were long screams of sirens. Kennedy sat down behind his desk. He looked at Eugene Dazzy who, as Chief of Staff, would do the briefing. But to Kennedy's surprise it was Christian who spoke first.

He said, 'Francis, the Pope is dead. But we've received news just as bad. The plane Theresa is on has been hijacked and is now on its way to Sherhaben.'

Francis Kennedy felt the wave of nausea hit him. Then he heard Eugene Dazzy say, 'The hijackers have everything under control, there are no incidents on the plane. As soon as it lands we'll negotiate, we'll call in all our favours, it will come out OK. I don't think they even knew Theresa was on the plane.'

Christian said, 'Arthur Wix and Otto Gray are on their way in. So are CIA, Defense, and the Vice President. They will all be waiting for you in the Cabinet Room within the half hour.'

'OK,' Kennedy said. He forced himself to smile at the two men. 'Is there any connection?' he said.

He saw that Christian was not surprised but that Dazzy didn't get it. 'Between the Pope and the hijacking,' Kennedy said. When neither of them answered, he said, 'Wait for me

in the Cabinet Room. I want a few moments by myself.'
They left.

Francis Kennedy was almost invulnerable to assassins but
he had always known he could never fully protect his
daughter. She was too independent, she would not permit
him to restrict her life. And it had not seemed a serious
danger. He could not recall that the daughter of the head of
a nation had ever been attacked. It was a bad political and
public relations move for any terrorist or revolutionary
organization.

After her father's inauguration Theresa went her own
way, lending her name to radical and feminist political
groups. Stating her own position in life as distinct from her
father. He had never tried to persuade her to act differently,
to present to the public an image false to herself. It was
enough that he loved her. And whenever she visited the
White House for a brief stay, they had a good time together
arguing politics, dissecting the uses of power.

The conservative, Republican press, the disreputable tab-
loids, had taken their shot, hoping to damage the Presidency.
Theresa was photographed marching with feminists, dem-
onstrating against nuclear weapons and once even marching
for a home state for Palestinians. Which would now inspire
ironic columns in the paper.

Oddly enough the American public responded to Theresa
Kennedy with affection, even when it became known she
was living with a radical Italian in Rome. There were
pictures of them strolling the ancient streets of stone, kissing
and holding hands, pictures of the balcony of the flat they
shared. The young Italian lover was handsome, Theresa
Kennedy was pretty in her blondness and her pale milky
Irish skin, the Kennedy satiny blue eyes. And her almost
lanky Kennedy frame draped in casual Italian clothes made
her so appealing that the text beneath the photographs was
drained of poison.

A news photo of her shielding her young Italian lover

from Italian police clubs brought back atavistic feelings in older Americans, memories of that long-ago terrible day in Dallas.

She was a witty heroine. During the campaign she had been cornered by TV reporters and asked, 'So you agree with your father politically?' If she answered 'yes' she would appear a hypocrite or a child commanded by a power-hungry father. If she answered 'no' the headlines would indicate that she did not support her father in his race for the Presidency. But she showed the Kennedy political genius. 'Sure, he's my Dad,' she said, hugging her father, 'and I know he's a good guy. But if he does something I don't like I'll yell at him just like you reporters do.' It came off great on the tube. Her father loved her for it. And now she was in mortal danger.

Pacing the Oval Office, Francis Kennedy knew that he would give the hijackers anything they demanded. That was the message he would send no matter what his advisors said. The hell with world political balance or any of the other arguments. This was one time he would use all his power, no matter what the cost. Suddenly he felt a little faint and leaned against the desk in fearful anguish. But then to his surprise he knew that what he was feeling was rage against his daughter.

If only she had remained close to him, if only she had been more of a loving daughter and lived with him at the White House, if only she had been less radical, none of this would be happening. And why did she have to have a foreign lover, a student radical who perhaps had given the hijacker crucial information? And then he laughed at himself. He was feeling the exasperation of a parent who wanted his child to be as little trouble as possible. He loved her, and he would save her. At least this was something he could fight against, not like the terrible, long and painful death of his wife.

Now, Eugene Dazzy appeared and told him it was time. They were waiting for him in the Cabinet Room.

*

When Kennedy entered, everyone rose from their chairs. He quickly motioned for them to be seated, but they surged around him to offer their sympathy. Kennedy made way to the head of the long oval table and sat in the chair near the fireplace.

Two pure white light chandeliers bleached the rich brown of the table, glistened the black of the leather chairs, six to each side of the table, and more chairs along the back of the far wall. And there were other sconces of white light that burned from the walls. Next to the two windows that opened to the Rose Garden were two flags, the striped flag of the United States and the flag of the President, a field of deep blue filled with pale stars.

Kennedy's staff took the seats next to him, resting their information logs and memoranda sheets on the oval table. Further down were the Cabinet Secretaries and the head of the CIA. And at the other end of the table, the Chairman of the Joint Chiefs of Staff, an Army General in full uniform, a gaudy color cut-out in the funeral-dressed crowd. The Vice President, Helen DuPray sat at the far side of the table, away from Kennedy, the only woman in the room. She wore a fashionable dark blue suit with a pure white silk blouse. Her handsome face was stern. The smell of the Rose Garden filled the room, seeping through the heavy curtains and drapes that covered glass paneled doors. Underneath those drapes the aquamarine rug reflected green light into the room.

It was the CIA Chief, Theodore Tappey, who gave the briefing. Tappey had once been head of the FBI, was not flamboyant or politically ambitious. And had never exceeded the CIA charter with risky, illegal, or empire building schemes. He had a great deal of credit with Kennedy's personal staff, especially Christian Klee.

'In the few hours we had, we've come up with some hard information,' Theodore Tappey said. 'The killing of the Pope was carried out by an all-Italian cadre. The hijacking of

Theresa's plane was done by a mixed team led by an Arab who goes by the name of Yabril. The fact that both incidents happened on the same day and originated in the same city seems to be coincidence. Which of course we must always mistrust.'

Francis Kennedy said softly, 'At this moment the killing of the Pope is not primary. Our main concern is to handle the hijacking problem. Have they made any demands yet?'

Tappey said quickly and firmly, 'No. That's an odd circumstance in itself.'

Kennedy said, 'Get your contacts on negotiation and report to me personally at every step.' He turned to the Secretary of State and asked, 'What countries will help us?'

The Secretary said, 'Everyone, the other Arab states are horrified, they despise the idea of your daughter being held hostage. It offends their sense of honor and also they think of their own customs of blood feud. They believe they cannot achieve any good from this. France has a good relationship with the Sultan. They offered to send in observers for us. Britain and Israel can't help, they are not trusted. But until the hijackers make their demands we're sort of in limbo.'

Francis Kennedy turned to Christian. 'Chris how do you figure it, they're not making demands?'

Christian said, 'It may be too early. Or they have another card to play.'

The Cabinet room was eerie in silence, in the blackness of the many high heavy chairs the white sconces of light on the walls turned the skin of the people in the room into a very light gray. Kennedy waited for them to speak, all of them, and he closed down his mind when they spoke of options, the threat of sanctions, the threat of a naval blockade, the freezing of Sherhaben assets in the United States. The expectation that the hijackers would extend the negotiation interminably to milk the TV time and news reports all over the world.

After a time Francis Kennedy turned to Oddblood Gray and said abruptly, 'Schedule a meeting with the Congressional leaders and the relevant Committee Chairmen for me and my staff.' Then he turned to Arthur Wix. 'Get your National Security working on plans if this thing turns into something wider.' Kennedy stood up to leave. He addressed them all. 'Gentlemen,' he said, 'I must tell you I don't believe in coincidence. I don't believe the Pope of the Roman Catholic Church can be murdered on the same day, in the same city, that the daughter of the President of the United States is kidnapped.'

It was a long Easter Sunday. The White House was filling up with staff personnel of the different action committees set up by the CIA, the Army and Navy, and the State Department. They all agreed the most baffling fact was that the terrorists had not yet made their demands for the release of the hostages.

Outside, the streets were congested with traffic. Newspaper and TV reporters were flocking into Washington. Government staff workers had been called to their desks despite the holiday. And Christian Klee had ordered a thousand extra men from the Secret Service and the FBI to provide additional protection for the White House.

The telephone traffic in the White House increased in volume. There was bedlam, people rushing to and fro from the White House to the Executive Office Building. Eugene Dazzy tried to bring everything under control.

The rest of that Sunday in the White House consisted of Kennedy receiving reports from the Situation Room, long solemn conferences on what options were open, telephone conversations between heads of foreign countries and the Cabinet members of the United States.

Late Sunday night the President's staff had dinner with him and prepared for the next day. They monitored the TV news reports, which were continuous.

Finally, Kennedy decided to go to bed. A Secret Service man led the way as Kennedy went up the small stairway that led to the living quarters on the fourth floor of the White House. Another Secret Service man trailed behind. They both knew that the President hated to take the elevators in the White House.

The top of the stairs opened into a lounge which held a communications desk and two more Secret Service men. When he passed through that lounge Kennedy was in his personal living quarters with only his personal servants: a maid, a butler and a valet whose duty it was to keep track of the extensive Presidential wardrobe.

What Kennedy did not know was that even these personal servants were members of the Secret Service. Christian Klee had invented this set-up. It was part of his overall plan to keep the President free from all personal harm, part of the intricate shield Christian had woven around Francis Kennedy.

When Christian had put this wrinkle into the security system he had briefed the special platoon of Secret Service men and women. 'You're going to be the best goddamn personal servants in the world and you can go straight from here and get a job in Buckingham Palace. Remember, your first duty is to take any bullets thrown at the President. But it will be as much your duty to make the personal life of the President comfortable.'

The chief of the special platoon was the manservant on duty this night. Ostensibly he was a black naval steward named Jefferson with the rank of Chief Petty Officer. Actually he had top rank in the Secret Service and was exceptionally well trained in hand-to-hand combat. He was a natural athlete and had been a college All American in football. And his IQ was 160. He also had a sense of humor which made him take an especial delight in becoming the perfect servant.

Now he helped Kennedy take off his jacket and hung it up

carefully. He handed Kennedy a silk dressing-gown but had learned that the President did not like to be helped putting it on. When Kennedy went to the small bar in the living room of the suite, Jefferson was there before him mixing a vodka with tonic and ice. Then Jefferson said, 'Mr President, your bath is drawn.'

Kennedy looked at him with a little smile on his face. Jefferson was a little too good to be true. Kennedy said, 'Please turn off all the phones. You can wake me personally if I'm needed.'

He soaked in the hot bath for nearly a half-hour. The tub had jet streams which pounded his back and thighs and soothed the weariness out of his muscles. The bathwater had a pleasant masculine scent and the ledge around the tub was filled with an assortment of soaps, liniments and magazines. There was even a plastic basket that held a pile of memos.

When Kennedy came out of the bath he put on a white terry cloth robe that had a monogram in red, white and blue lettering that said, 'THE BOSS'. This was a gift from Jefferson himself who thought it part of the character he was playing to give such a present. Francis Kennedy rubbed his white almost hairless body with the robe to get himself dry and thought he had to get south and get a sun tan. He had always been dissatisfied with the paleness of his skin and his lack of body hair.

In the bedroom, Jefferson had pulled the curtains closed and switched on the reading light. He had also turned down the bed covers. There was a small marble-topped table with specially attached wheels near the bed and a comfortable armchair nearby. The table was dressed with a beautifully embroidered pale rose cloth and on the cloth was a dark blue pitcher which held the hot chocolate. Chocolate had already been poured into a cup of lighter cerulean blue. There was an intricately painted dish which held six varieties of biscuit. The silver accompanying them was so polished it looked like heavy ivory. Comfortingly there was a pure white crock of pale saltless butter and four colored crocks of different jams, green for apple, blue spotted white for raspberry, yellow for marmalade and red for strawberry.

Francis Kennedy said, 'That looks great,' and Jefferson left the room. For some reason these little attentions comforted Kennedy more than they should, he felt. He sat in the armchair and drank the chocolate, ate a biscuit but could not finish it. He rolled the table away and got into bed. He started to read from a pile of memos but he was too tired. He turned off the light and tried to sleep.

But through the muffling of the drapes he could very faintly hear a tiny residue of the immense noise that was building up outside the White House. The media of the whole world was assembling to keep a twenty-four-hour-a-day watch. Hundreds of communications vehicles, the TV cameras and crews, the setting up of a Marine Battalion as extra security.

Francis Kennedy felt that deep sense of foreboding that had only come to him once before in his life. He let himself think directly about his daughter Theresa. She was sleeping on that plane, surrounded by murderous men. And it was not bad luck. Fate had given him many warnings. His two uncles had been killed when he was a boy. And then just over three years ago his wife, Catherine, had died of cancer.

The first great defeat in Francis Kennedy's life was when Catherine Kennedy discovered the lump in her breast six months before her husband won the nomination for President. After the diagnosis of cancer, Francis Kennedy offered to withdraw from the political process, but she forbade him. She wanted to live in the White House she said. She would get well, she said, and her husband never doubted her. At first they worried about her losing her breast and Francis Kennedy consulted cancer experts all over the world about a lumpectomy which could remove the cancer and leave the breast. He and Catherine finally wound up going to one of the greatest cancer specialists available in the United States. The doctor looked at Catherine's medical file and encouraged removal of the breast. He said, and Francis Kennedy forever remembered the words, 'It is a very aggressive strain of cancer.'

She was on chemotherapy when he won the Democratic nomination for the Presidency in July, and her doctors sent her home. She was in remission. She put on weight, her skeleton hid again behind a wall of flesh.

She rested a great deal, she could not leave the house, but she was always on her feet to greet him when he came home. Theresa went back to school, Francis Kennedy went on the political trail, campaigning for the Presidency. But he arranged his schedule so that he could fly home every few days to be with her. Each time he returned she seemed to be stronger and these days were sweet, they never loved each other more. He brought her gifts, she knitted him mufflers and gloves and one time she gave the day off to the nurses and servants so that she and her husband could be alone in the house, to eat the simple supper she prepared. She was getting well.

It was the happiest moment in his life, nothing could be measured against it. Francis Kennedy wept tears of pure joy, relieved of anguish, of dread. The next morning they went for a walk in the green hills around their house, her arm around his waist. When they returned he cooked her breakfast and she ate heartily, more than he had ever remembered her eating. She had always been vain about her appearance, anxious about how she fitted into her new dresses, her bathing suits, the extra fold of flesh beneath her chin. But now she tried to put on weight. He felt each bone in her body when they walked entwined.

Her remission gave Francis Kennedy the energy to rise to the peak of his powers as he continued his campaign for the Presidency. He swept everything before him; he was witty, he was charming, he was sincere, he established a rapport with the voters and the polls showed him far ahead. He bested his opponents in debate, destroyed them with his strategies, skillfully escaped the media traps, won over his enemies, cemented his allies. Everything was malleable, to be shaped to his fortunate destiny. His body generated enormous energy, his mind worked with a precision that was extraordinary.

And then on one of his trips home he was plunged into the netherworld. Catherine was ill again, she was not there to greet him. And all his gifts and strength were powerless.

Catherine had been the perfect wife for him. Not that she had been an extraordinary woman but she had been one of those women who seemed to be almost genetically gifted in the art of love. She had what seemed to be a natural sweetness of disposition and character that was extraordinary. He had never heard her say a mean word about anyone, she forgave other people's faults, never felt herself slighted or done an injury. She never harbored resentments.

She was in all ways pleasing. She had a willowy body and her face had a tranquil beauty that inspired affection in nearly everyone. She had a weakness of course, she loved beautiful clothes and was a little vain. But she could be teased about that. She was witty without being insulting or mordant and she was never depressed. She was well educated and had made her living as a journalist before she married. She had other skills, too: she was a skilled if amateur pianist, she painted as a hobby. She had brought up her daughter well and they loved each other; she was understanding of her husband and never jealous of his achievements. She was one of those rare accidents, a contented and happy human being. She was, therefore, most precious in his life.

The day came when the doctor met Francis Kennedy in the corridor of the hospital and quite brutally and frankly told him that his wife must die. That there was no appeal to a higher court, there could be no retrial, no mitigating circumstances. She was condemned more fiercely than any murderer.

The doctor explained. There were holes in the bones of Catherine Kennedy's body, her skeleton would collapse. There were tumors in her brain, tiny now but that would inevitably expand. And her blood ruthlessly manufactured poisons to put her to death.

Francis Kennedy could not tell his wife this. He could not tell her because he could not believe it. He mustered all his resources, contacted all his powerful friends, even consulted the Oracle. There was one hope. At different research centers in different medical centers all around the United States there were programs with new and dangerous drugs, experimental programs available only to those who had been decreed doomed. Since these new drugs were dangerously toxic, they were used only on volunteers. And there were so many doomed people that there were a hundred volunteers for each spot in the programs.

So Francis Kennedy committed what he would have ordinarily thought an immoral act. He used all his power to get his wife into these research programs, he pulled every string so that his wife could receive these lethal but life-preserving poisons into her body. And he succeeded. He felt a new confidence. A few people had been cured in these research centers. Why not his wife? Why could he not save her? He had triumphed all his life, he would triumph now.

And then began a reign of darkness. At first it was a research program in Houston. He entered her into a hospital there. Stayed with her for the treatment which weakened her so that she was helplessly bedridden. She made him leave her there so that he could continue campaigning for the Presidency. He flew from Houston to Los Angeles to make his campaign speeches, confident, witty, cheerful. Then late at night he flew to Houston to spend a few hours with his wife. Then he flew to his next campaign stop to play the part of lawgiver.

61

The treatment in Houston failed. In Boston they cut the tumor from her brain and the operation was a success though the tumor tested malignant. Malignant, too, the new tumors in her lungs. The holes in her bones on X-ray were larger and even more gracefully sculpted. In another Boston hospital new drugs and protocols worked a miracle. The new tumor in her brain stopped growing, the tumors in her remaining breast shrivelled. Every night Francis Kennedy flew from his campaign cities to spend a few hours with her, to read to her, to joke with her. Sometimes Theresa Kennedy flew from her school in Los Angeles to visit her mother. Father and daughter dined together and then visited the patient in her hospital room to sit in the darkness with her. Theresa told funny stories of her adventures in school, Francis Kennedy related his adventures on the campaign trail. Catherine Kennedy would laugh.

Of course Francis Kennedy again offered to drop out of the campaign to be with his wife. Of course Theresa Kennedy wanted to leave school to be with her mother constantly. But Catherine Kennedy told them she would not, could not bear for them to do so. She might be ill for a long time. They must continue their lives. Only that could give her hope, only that could give her the strength to bear her torture. On this she could not be moved. She threatened to check out of the hospital and return home if they did not continue as if things were normal.

Francis Kennedy on long trips through the night to her bedside could only marvel at her tenacity. Catherine Kennedy, her body filled with chemical poison fighting the poisons of her body, clung fiercely to her belief that she would be well and that the two people she loved most in the world would not be dragged down with her.

Finally the nightmare seemed to end. Again she was in remission. Francis Kennedy could take her home. They had been all over the United States, she had been in seven different hospitals with their protocols of experimental treatments, and the great flood of chemicals seemed to have worked, and Francis Kennedy felt an exultation that he had succeeded once again. He took his wife home to Los Angeles and then one night he, Catherine and Theresa went out to dinner before he resumed the campaign trail. It was a lovely summer night, the soft balmy California air caressed their skins. There was one strange moment. A waiter had spilled just a tiny drop of sauce from a dish on the sleeve of Catherine Kennedy's new dress. She burst into tears and when the waiter left she asked weeping, 'Why did he have to do that to me?' This was so uncharacteristic of her – in former times she would have laughed such an incident away – that Francis Kennedy felt a strange foreboding. She had gone through the torture of all those operations, the removal of her breast, the excision from her brain, the pain of those growing tumors and had never wept or complained. And now obviously this stain seemed to sink into her heart beneath. She was inconsolable.

The next day Francis Kennedy had to fly to New York to campaign. In the morning Catherine made him his breakfast. She was radiant and her beauty seemed even greater, the lovely bones of her face sculpted only by skin. All the newspapers had polls that showed Francis Kennedy was in the lead, that he would win the Presidency. Catherine Kennedy read them aloud. 'Oh, Francis,' she said, 'we'll live in the White House and I'll have my own staff. And Theresa can bring her friends to stay for weekends and on vacations. Think how happy we'll be. And I won't get sick again. I promise. You'll do great things, Francis, I know you will.' She put her arms around him and wept with happiness and love. 'I'll help,' Catherine said. 'We'll walk through all those lovely rooms together and I'll help you make your plans. You'll be the greatest President. I'm going to be all right, darling, and I'll have so much to do. We'll be so happy. We'll be so good. We're so lucky. Aren't we lucky?'

*

63

She died in autumn, October light became her shroud. Francis Kennedy stood amongst fading green hills and wept. Silver trees veiled the horizon and in dumb agony he closed his eyes with his own hands to shut out the world. And in that moment without light, he felt the spine of his mind break.

And some priceless cell of energy fled. It was the first time in his life that his extraordinary intelligence was worth nothing. His wealth meant nothing. His political power, his position in the world meant nothing. He could not save his wife from death. And therefore it all became nothing.

He took his hands away from his eyes and with a supreme effort of his will fought against the nothingness. He reassembled what was left of the world, summoned power to fight against grief. There was less than a month to go before the election and he made the final effort.

He entered the White House without his wife, with only his daughter Theresa, Theresa who had tried to be happy but who had wept all that first night because her mother could not be with them.

And now, three years after his wife's death, Francis Kennedy, President of the United States, one of the most powerful men on earth, was alone in his bed, fearful for his daughter's life, and unable to command sleep. The lament of the powerful, that they could never find such sweet sanctuary.

Sleep forbidden, he tried to stave off the terror that kept him from sleep. He told himself the hijackers would not dare to harm Theresa, that his daughter would come safely home. In this he was not powerless, he did not have to rely on the weak, fallible gods of medicine, he did not have to fight those terrible invincible cancerous cells. No. He could save his daughter's life. He could bend the power of his country, spend its authority. It all rested in his hands and thank God he had no political scruples. His daughter was the only thing

64

he had left on this earth that he really loved. He would save her.

But then anxiety, a wave of such fear it seemed to stop his heart, made him put on the light above his head. He rose and sat in the armchair. He pulled the marble table close and sipped the residue of cold chocolate from his cup.

He believed the plane had been hijacked because his daughter was on it. The hijacking was possible because of the vulnerability of established authority to a few determined, ruthless and possibly high-minded terrorists. And it had been inspired by the fact that he, Francis Kennedy, President of the United States was the prominent symbol of that established authority. So by his desire to be President of the United States, he, Francis Kennedy, was responsible for placing his daughter in danger.

Again he heard the doctor's words. 'It is a very aggressive strain of cancer.' But now he understood. Everything was more dangerous than it appeared. This was a night to plan, to defend, he had the power to turn fate aside. Sleep would never come to the chambers of his brain so sown with mines.

What had been his wish? To work out the destiny of the Kennedy name? But he had been only a cousin. He remembered Great-Uncle Joseph Kennedy, legendary womanizer, a maker of gold, a mind so sharp for the instant, but so blind to the future. He remembered Old Joe fondly, though he would have been Francis Kennedy's opposite right wall politically if he were alive today. But Great-Uncle Joe had given Francis Kennedy gold pieces for his toddler birthdays and set up a trust fund for him though he was just a poor relation. What a selfish life the man had led, screwing Hollywood stars, lifting his sons high. Never mind that he had been a political dinosaur. And what a tragic end. A lucky life until the last chapter. Then the murders of his sons, so young, so high and the old man defeated. A final stroke exploding his brain.

Making your son President, could a father have such joy?

And had the old king-maker sacrificed his sons for nothing? Had the gods punished him not so much for his pride but for his pleasure? Or was it all accident? His sons Jack and Robert, so rich, so handsome, so gifted, killed by those powerless nobodies who wrote themselves into history with the murder of their betters. No, there could be no purpose, it was all accident. So many little things could turn fate aside, tiny precautions reverse tragedy into little grazings of destiny.

So now, Francis Kennedy thought, he would leave nothing to fate. He would bring home his daughter safe with his own sense of terror. He would give the hijackers everything, and surely that must satisfy them, though the United States would be humiliated in the eyes of the world. A small price to pay for Theresa.

And yet – and yet there was the odd feeling of doom. Why the binding of the Pope's killer and the hijacking of the President's daughter? Why the delay before stating their demands? What other strings were there in the labyrinth to be played out? And all this from a man he had never heard of, a mysterious Arab named Yabril, and an Italian youth, named in scornful irony, Romeo.

In the darkness he was terrified at how it all might end. He felt the familiar, always contained rage, the dread. He remembered the terrible day when as a child playing on the White House lawn with his little cousins, he had heard the first whisper that his Uncle John was dead, and from the interior of the White House the long terrible scream of a woman in agony.

Then mercifully, the chambers of his brain unlocked, his memories fled. He fell asleep in his armchair.

3

The member of the President's staff with the most influence on Kennedy was the Attorney General. Christian Klee had been born into a wealthy family stretching back into the first days of the Republic. His trust funds were now worth over a hundred million dollars, due to the guidance and advice of his godfather, the Oracle, Oliver Ollifant. He had never wanted for anything and there had come a time when he wanted nothing. He had too much intelligence, too much energy to become another of the idle rich who invest in movies, chase women, abuse drugs and booze or descend into a religious viciousness. Two men, the Oracle and Francis Xavier Kennedy led him finally into politics.

Christian first met Kennedy at Harvard, not as fellow undergraduates but as teacher and student. Kennedy had been the youngest professor to teach law at Harvard. In his twenties, he had been a prodigy. Christian still remembered that opening lecture. Kennedy had begun with the words, 'Everybody knows or has heard of the majesty of the law. It is the power of the state to control the existing political organization that permits civilization to exist. That is true. Without the rule of law, we are all lost. But remember this, the law is also full of shit.'

Then he had smiled at his student audience. 'I can get around any law you may write. The law can be twisted out of shape to serve a wicked civilization. The rich can escape the law and sometimes even the poor get lucky. Some lawyers treat the law like pimps treat their women. Judges sell the law, courts betray it. All true. But remember this, we have nothing better that works. There is no other way we can make a social contract with our fellow human beings.'

When Christian Klee graduated from Harvard Law School he had not the faintest idea of what to do with his life. Nothing interested him. He was worth over a hundred million dollars, but he had no interest in money, nor did he have a real interest in the law. He had the usual romanticism of a young man. He liked women, had brief affairs but could not summon up that feeling of true belief in love that leads to a passionate attachment. He desperately was looking for something to commit his life to. He was interested in the arts, but had no creative drive, no talent for painting, music, writing. He was paralyzed by his security in society. He was not so much unhappy as bewildered.

He had, of course, tried drugs for a brief period – it was after all as integral a part of American culture as it had once been of the Chinese Empire. And for the first time he discovered a startling thing about himself. He could not bear the loss of control that drugs caused. He did not mind being unhappy as long as he had control of his mind and body. Loss of that control was the ultimate in despair. And the drugs did not even make him feel the ecstasy that other people felt. So at the age of twenty-two, with everything in the world at his feet, he could not feel that anything was worth doing. He did not even feel, what every young man felt, a desire to improve the world he lived in.

He consulted his godfather, the Oracle, then a 'young' man of seventy-five, who still had an inordinate appetite for life, who kept three mistresses busy, who had a finger in every business pie and who conferred with the President of the United States at least once a week. The Oracle had the secret of life.

The Oracle said, 'Pick out the most useless thing for you to do and do it for the next few years. Something that you would never consider doing, that you have no desire to do.

But something that will improve you at least physically and mentally. Learn a part of the world that you think you will never make part of your life. Don't squander your time. Learn. That's how I got into politics originally. And this would surprise my friends, I really had no interest in money. Do something you hate. In three or four years more things will be possible and what is possible becomes more attractive.'

The next day Christian applied for an appointment to West Point and spent the next four years becoming an officer in the United States Army. The Oracle had been astounded, then delighted. 'The very thing,' he said. 'You will never be a soldier. And you will develop a taste for denial.'

Christian, after four years at West Point remained another four years in the Army training in Special Assault Brigades and becoming proficient in armed and unarmed combat. The feeling that his body could perform any task he demanded of it gave him a sense of immortality.

At the age of thirty he resigned his commision and took a post in the operations divisions of the CIA. He became an officer in clandestine operations and spent the next four years in the European theater. From there he went to the Middle East for six years and rose high in the operational division of the Agency until a bomb took off his foot. This was another challenge. He learned to use and manage a prosthetic device, an artificial foot, so that he did not even limp. But that ended his career in the field and he returned home to enter a prestigious law firm.

Then for the first time he fell in love and married a girl he thought was the answer to all his youthful dreams. She was intelligent, she was witty, she was very good-looking and very passionate. For the next five years he was happy in marriage, happy in the fatherhood of two young children and found satisfaction in the political maze through which the Oracle was guiding him. He was, finally, he thought, a man who had found his place in life. Then misfortune. His wife fell in love with another man and sued for divorce.

Christian Klee had been dumbstruck, then furious. He was happy, how could his wife not be? And what had changed her? He had been loving and courteous to her every wish. Of course he had been busy in his work, to build a career. But he was rich and she lacked for nothing. In his rage he was determined to resist her every demand, to fight for custody of the children, deny her the house she wanted so badly, restrict all monetary rewards that come to a divorced woman. Above all he was astounded that she planned to live their house with her new husband. True, it was a palatial mansion but what about the sacred memories they had shared in that house? And he had been a faithful husband.

He had gone again to the Oracle and poured out his grief and pain. To his surprise the Oracle was completely unsympathetic. 'You were faithful so that makes you think your wife should be faithful? How does that follow, if you no longer interest her? Infidelity is the precaution of a prudent man who knows that his wife can unilaterally deprive him of his house and children without moral cause. You accepted that deal when you married, now you must abide by it.' Then the Oracle had laughed in his face. 'Your wife was quite right to leave you,' he said. 'She saw through you though I must say you gave quite a performance. She knew you were never truly happy. But believe me it's the best thing. You are now a man ready to assume his real station in life. You've got everything out of the way, a wife and children would only be a hindrance. You are essentially a man who has to live alone to do great things. I know because I was that way. Wives can be dangerous to men with real ambition, children are the very breeding grounds for tragedy. Use your common sense, use your training as a lawyer. Give her everything she wants, it will make only a small dent in your fortune. Your children are very young, they will forget you. Think of it this way. Now you are free. Your life will be directed by yourself.'

And so it had been.

So late on Easter Sunday night Attorney General Christian Klee left the White House to visit Oliver Ollifant, to ask his advice and also to inform him that his one hundredth birthday party had been postponed by President Kennedy.

The Oracle lived on a fenced estate that was expensively guarded, its security system had bagged five enterprising burglars in the last year. His large staff of servants, well paid and well pensioned, included a barber, a valet, a cook, and maids. For there were still many important men who came to the Oracle for advice, and had to be fed elaborate dinners and sometimes provided with a bedroom.

Christian looked forward to his visit with the Oracle. He enjoyed the old man's company, the stories he told of terrible wars on the battlefields of money, the strategies of men dealing with fathers, mothers, wives and lovers. How to defend against the government, its strength so prodigious, its justice so blind, its laws so treacherous, its free elections so corrupting. Not thet the Oracle was a professional cynic, merely clear-sighted. And he insisted that one could lead a happy successful life, yet observe the ethical values on which true civilization endures. The Oracle could be dazzling.

The Oracle received Christian in his second-storey suite of rooms which consisted of a narrow bedroom, an enormous bathroom tiled blue which held a jacuzzi and a shower with a marble bench and handholds sculptured into its walls. There was also a den with an impressive fireplace, a library and a cozy sitting room with brightly colored sofa and armchairs.

The Oracle was in this sitting room resting in a specially built motorized wheelchair. Beside him was a table. Facing him was an armchair and a table set for an English tea.

Christian took his place in the armchair opposite the

Oracle and helped himself to tea and one of the little sandwiches. As always Christian was delighted by the appearance of the Oracle, the intensity of the man's gaze so remarkable in one who had lived for one hundred years. And it seemed logical to Christian that the Oracle had evolved from a homely sixty-five-year-old to a striking ancientness. The skin was shell-like as was his bald pate which showed liver spots dark as nicotine. Leopardskin hands protruded from his exquisitely cut suit; extreme age had not vanquished his sartorial vanity. The neck encircled loosely by the silk tie was scaly and ridged, the back broad, curved like glass. The front of the body fell away to a tiny chest, his waist you could encircle with your fingers, his legs no more than strands in a spider's web. But the facial features were not yet crenelated by approaching death.

For the first few minutes they smiled at each other, drinking tea; Christian poured the Oracle his cup.

The Oracle spoke first. 'You've come to cancel my birthday party, I assume. I've been watching the TV with my secretaries. I told them the party would be postponed.' His voice had the low growl of a worn larynx.

'Yes,' Christian said. 'But only for a month. Think you can hold out that long?' He was smiling.

'I sure do,' the Oracle said. 'That shit is on every TV station. Take my advice, my boy, buy stock in the TV companies. They will make a fortune out of this tragedy and all the forthcoming tragedies. They are the crocodiles of our society.' He paused for a moment and said more softly, 'How is your beloved President taking all this?'

'I admire that man more than ever,' Christian said. 'I have never seen someone in his position more composed over a dreadful tragedy. He is much stronger now than after his wife died.'

The Oracle said dryly, 'When the worst that can happen to you actually happens and you bear it, then you are the strongest of men in the world. Which, actually, may not be a very good thing.'

He paused for a moment to sip his tea, his colorless lips closed into a pale white line like a scratch on the seamed nicotine-colored skin of his face. Then he said, 'If you feel it's not breaking your oath of office or your loyalty to the President, why don't you tell me what action is being taken.'

Christian knew that this was what the old man lived for. To be inside the skin of power. 'Francis is very concerned that the hijackers have not yet made any demands. It's been ten hours,' Christian said. 'He thinks that's sinister.'

'So it is,' the Oracle said.

They were both silent for a long time. The Oracle's eyes had lost their vibrancy, seemed extinguished by the pouches of dying skin beneath them.

Christian said, 'I'm really worried about Francis. He can't take much more. Right now he'll give up everything to get his daughter back. But if something happens to her . . . He might blow up the whole of Sherhaben.'

The Oracle said, 'They won't let him do it. There will be a very dangerous confrontation. You know, I remember Francis Kennedy as a little boy when he used to play with his cousins on the White House grounds. Even then I was struck at how he dominated the other children.'

The Oracle paused and Christian poured him some hot tea though the cup was still more than half full. He knew the old man could not taste anything unless it was very hot or very cold.

'Who won't let him do it?' Christian asked.

'The Cabinet, the Congress, even some members of the President's staff,' the Oracle said. 'Maybe even the joint Chiefs of Staff. All of them will get together.'

Christian said, 'If the President tells me to stop them, I'll stop them.'

The Oracle's eyes were suddenly very bright and visible. He said musingly, 'You've become a very dangerous man in these past years, Christian. But not terribly original. All through history there have been men, some considered "great", who have had to choose between God and country. And some very religious men have chosen country over God, believing they would go to everlasting hell, thinking it noble. But Christian, we have come to a time when we must decide whether to give our lives to our country or to help mankind continue to exist. We live in a nuclear age. That is the new and interesting question, a question never before posed to individual men. Think in those terms. If you side with your President do you endanger mankind? It's not so simple as rejecting God.'

'It doesn't matter,' Christian said, 'I know Francis is better than Congress, the Socrates Club and the terrorists.'

The Oracle said, 'I've always wondered about your overwhelming loyalty to Francis Kennedy. There are some vulgar gossips who say it's a very faggy business. On your part. Not his. Which is odd since you have women and he does not, not since the death of his wife. But why do the people around Kennedy hold him in a peculiar veneration, though he's recognized as a political dunderhead? All those reformist and regulatory laws he tried to shove down that dinosaur Congress. I thought that you were smarter than that, but I presume you were overruled. Still your inordinate affection for Kennedy is a mystery to me.'

'He's the man I always wished I could be,' Christian said. 'It's as simple as that.'

'Then you and I would not be such longtime friends,' the Oracle said. 'I never cared for Francis Kennedy.'

'He's just better than anybody else,' Christian said. 'I've known him for over twenty years and he's the only politician who has been honest with the public, he doesn't lie to them. And he is religious, not really I think out of true faith, but as a form of humility.'

The Oracle said dryly, 'The man you describe could never

74

be elected President of the United States.' He seemed to puff out his insect body, his shiny-skinned hands tapped the controls of his wheelchair. The Oracle leaned back. In the dark suit, the ivory shirt and simple blue streak of his tie, the glazed face looked like a piece of mahogany wood. He said, 'His charm escapes me, but we never got on. Now I must warn you. Every man in his lifetime makes many mistakes. That is human, and unavoidable. The trick is never to make the mistake that destroys you. Beware of your friend Kennedy who is so good, remember that evil often springs from the desire to do good. The next few days will be terribly dangerous. Be careful.'

'Character doesn't change,' Christian said confidently.

The Oracle fluttered his arms like bird wings. 'Yes, it does,' he said. 'Pain changes character. Sorrow changes character. Love and money certainly. And time erodes character. Let me tell you a little story. When I was a man of fifty, I had a mistress thirty years younger than myself. She had a brother who was ten years older then her, about thirty. I was her mentor, as I was with all my young women. I had their interests at heart. Her brother was a Wall Street hotshot and a careless man, which later got him into big trouble. Now I was never jealous, she went out with young men. But on her twenty-first birthday, her brother gave her a party and as a joke hired a male stripper to perform before her and her friends. It was all above board, they made no secret of it. But I was always conscious of my homeliness, my lack of physical appeal to women. And so I was affronted, and that was unworthy of me. We all remained friends and she went on to marriage and a career. I went on to younger mistressess. Ten years later her brother gets into financial trouble as many of those Wall Street types do. Inside tips, finagling with money entrusted to him. Very serious trouble that landed him a couple of years in prison and of course the end of his career.

'By this time I was sixty years old, still friends with both of them. They never asked for my help, they really didn't know the extent of what I could do. I could have saved him but I never lifted a finger. I let him go down the drain. And ten years later it came to me that I didn't help him because of that foolish little trick of his, letting his sister see the body of a man so much younger than myself. And it wasn't sexual jealousy, it was the affront to my power, or the power I thought I had. I've thought of that often. It is one of the few things in my life that shames me. I would never have been guilty of such an act at thirty or at seventy. Why at sixty? Character does change. That is man's triumph and his tragedy.'

Christian switched to the brandy that the Oracle had provided. It was delicious and very expensive. The Oracle always served the best. Christian enjoyed it though he would never buy it; born rich he never felt he deserved to treat himself so well. He said, 'I've known you all my life, over forty-five years, and you haven't changed. You are going to be a hundred next week. And you're still the great man I always thought you were.'

The Oracle shook his head. 'You know me only in my old age, from sixty to a hundred. That means nothing. The venom is gone then and the strength to enforce it. It's no trick to be virtuous in old age, as that humbug Tolstoy knew.' He paused and sighed. 'Now how about this great birthday party of mine? Your friend Kennedy never really liked me and I knew you pushed the idea of the White House Rose Garden and a big media event. Is he using this crisis situation to get out of it?'

Christian said, 'No, no, he values your life's work, he wants to do it. Oliver, you were and are a great man. Just hang on. Hell, what's a few months after a hundred years?' He paused. 'But if you prefer, since you don't like Francis, we can forget about his big plans for your birthday party, mass coverage by the media, your name and picture in all the papers and on TV. I can always throw you a little private party right away and get the whole thing over with.' He smiled at the Oracle to show that he was joking. Sometimes the old man took him too literally.

'Thank you, but no,' the Oracle said. 'I want to have something to live for. Namely, a birthday party given by the President of the United States. But let me tell you, your Kennedy is shrewd. He knows my name still means something. The publicity will enhance his image. Your Francis Xavier Kennedy is as crafty as was his Uncle Jack. Now Bobby would have shown me the back of his hand.'

Christian said. 'None of your contemporaries are left. But your protégés are some of the great men and women in the country, and they look forward to doing you this honor. Including the President. He doesn't forget that you helped him on his way. He's even inviting your buddies in the Socrates Club and he hates them. It will be your best birthday party.'

'And my last,' the Oracle said. 'I'm hanging on by my fucking fingernails.'

Christian laughed. The Oracle had never used bad language until he was ninety, so now he used it as innocently as a child.

'That's settled,' the Oracle said. 'Now let me tell you something about great men, Kennedy and myself included. They finally consume themselves and the people around them. Not that I concede your Kennedy is a great man. After all what has he done so noteworthy except become President of the United States? And that is an illusionist's trick. Do you know, by the way, that in show business the magician is considered to be completely without artistic talent?' Here the Oracle cocked his head, he astonishingly resembled an owl.

'I will concede that Kennedy is not your typical politician,' the Oracle said. 'He is an idealist, he is far more intelligent and he has morals, though I wonder whether sexual rigidity is healthy. But, all these virtues are a handicap to political greatness. A man without a vice? A sailing ship without a sail!'

Christian asked. 'You disapprove of his actions. What course would you take?'

'That is not relevant,' the Oracle said. 'His whole three years, he's got his dick half in, half out, and that's always trouble.' Now the Oracle's eyes became cloudy. 'I hope it doesn't interfere with my birthday party too long. What a life I had, eh? Who had a better life than me? Poor at birth so that I could appreciate the wealth I earned later. A homely man who learned to captivate and enjoy beautiful women. A good brain, a learned compassion so much better than genetic. Enormous energy, enough to power me past old age. A good constitution, I've never been sick really in my life, and long! And that's the trouble, maybe a little too long. I can't bear to look at myself in the mirror now but as I said, I was never handsome.' He paused for a time and then said abruptly to Christian, 'Leave government service. Disassociate yourself from everything that is happening now.'

'I can't do that,' Christian said. 'It's too late.' He studied the old man's head, freckled with the chromosomes of death, and marveled at the brain still so alive. Christian stared into those aged eyes, shrouded like a never-ending misty sea. Would he ever be so old with his body shriveling like some dead insect?

And the Oracle, watching him, thought, how transparent they all are, as guileless as little children to parents. It was obvious to the Oracle that his advice had been given too late, that Christian would commit a treachery to himself, and was in some way exhilarated by it.

Christian finished his brandy and rose to leave. He tucked the blankets around the old man and rang for the nurses to come into the room. Then he whispered into the Oracle's glazed skin ear, 'Tell me the truth about Helen DuPray, she was one of your protégées before she got married. I know you arranged for her first entry into politics. Did you ever screw her, or were you too old?'

The Oracle shook his head. 'I was never too old until after ninety. And let me tell you that when your cock leaves you, that is real loneliness. But to answer your question. She didn't fancy me, I was no beauty. I must say I was disappointed, she was very beautiful and very intelligent, my favorite combination. I could never love intelligent homely women, they were too much like myself. I could love beautiful, dumb women but when they were intelligent then I was in heaven. Helen DuPray, ah, I knew she would go far, she was very strong, a strong will. Yes I tried but never succeeded, a rare failure I must say. But we always remained good friends. That was a talent she had, to refuse a man sexually and yet be an intimate friend. Very rare. That was when I knew she was a seriously ambitious woman.'

Christian touched his hand, it felt like a scar. 'I'll phone or drop in to see you every day,' he said. 'I'll keep you up to date.'

The Oracle was very busy after Christian left. He had to pass on the information Klee had given him to the Socrates Club, whose members were important figures in the structure of America. He did not consider this a betrayal of Christian whom he dearly loved. Love was always secondary.

And he had to take action, his country was sailing dangerous waters. It was his duty to help guide it to safety. And what else could a man his age do to make life worth living. And to tell the truth he had always despised the Kennedy legend. Here was a chance to destroy it for ever.

Finally the Oracle let the nurse fuss over him and prepare his bed. He remembered Helen DuPray with affection, and now without disappointment. She had been very young, early twenties, her beauty enhanced by a tremendous vitality. He had often lectured her on power, its acquisition and uses,

79

and more importantly to abstain from its use. And she had listened with the patience that is necessary to acquire power.

He told her that one of the great mysteries of mankind was how people acted against their own self-interests. Points of pride ruined their lives. Envy and self-delusion led them down paths that led to nothingness. Why was it so important for people to maintain self-images? There were those who would never truckle, never flatter, never lie, never back down, never betray, never deceive. There were those who lived in envy and jealousy of the happier fate of others.

It had all been a special sort of pleading and she had seen through it. She rejected him and went on without his help, to achieve her own dream of power.

One of the problems of having a mind as clear as a bell when you are a hundred years old, is that you can see the hatching of unconscious villainy in yourself, and ferret it out in past history. He had been mortified when Helen DuPray had refused to make love with him. He knew she had other lovers, she was not prissy. But at seventy he, amazingly, had still been vain.

He had gone to the rejuvenation center in Switzerland, submitted to surgical erasing of wrinkles, the sanding of his skin, the injection of animal fetus pulp into his own veins. But nothing could be done for the shrinking of his skeleton, the freezing of his joints, the very turning of his blood into water.

Though it no longer did him any good, the Oracle believed he understood men and women in love. Even past his sixtieth year young mistresses adored him. The whole secret was never to impose any rules on their behavior, never to be jealous, never hurt their feelings. They took young men as their true loves and treated the Oracle with careless cruelty, it didn't matter. He showered them with expensive gifts, paintings, jewelry in the best of taste. He let them call on his power to get unearned favors from society, and the use of his money in generous but not lavish amounts. But he was a prudent man and would always have three or four mistresses at one time. For they had their own lives to lead. They would fall in love and neglect him, they would take trips, they would be working hard at their careers. He could not make too many demands on their time. But when he needed female company (not only for sex but for the sweet music of their voices, the innocent deviousness of their wiles), one of the four would be available. And of course to be seen at important functions in his company gave them entrée into circles it would be difficult for them to penetrate on their own. That was one of his assets of power.

He made no secrets, they all knew about each other. He believed that in their hearts women disliked monogamous men.

How cruel that he remembered bad things he had done more often than good. His money had built medical centers, churches, rest homes for the elderly, he had done many good things. But his memories of himself were not good. Fortunately he thought about love often. In an interesting and peculiar way, it had been the most commercial thing in his life. And he had owned Wall Street firms, banks, airlines.

Anointed with money he had been invited to share in world-shaking events, been advisor to the powerful. He had helped shape the very world people lived in. A fascinating, important, valuable life. And yet the managing of his countless mistresses was far more valid in his hundred-year-old brain. Ah those intelligent headstrong beauties, how delightful they had been, and how they had vindicated his judgment, most of them. Now they were judges, heads of magazines, powers in Wall Street, TV news queens. How cunning they had been in their love affairs with him and how he had outwitted them. But without cheating them of their due. He had no guilts, only regrets. If one of them had truly loved him, he would have raised her to the skies. But then his mind reminded him that he had not deserved to be

81

so loved. They had recognized his love, it was a hollow drum that made his body thump.

It was at the age of eighty that his skeleton began to contract inside its envelope of flesh. Physical desire receded and a vast ocean of youthful and lost images drowned his brain. And it was at this time he found it necessary to employ young women to lie innocently in his bed just so that he could look at them. Oh that perversity so scorned in literature, so mocked by the young who must grow old. And yet what a peace it gave his crumbling body to see the beauty he could no longer devour. How pure it was. The rolling mound of breast, satiny white skin crowned with its tiny red rose. The mysterious thighs, their rounded flesh giving off a golden glow, the surprising triangle of hair, a choice of colors, and then on the other side the heartbreak of buttocks divided into two exquisite haunches. So much beauty, to his bodily senses dead and lost, but sparking the flickering billions of cells in his brain. And their faces, the mysterious shells of ears spiraling into some inner sea, the hollowed eyes with their banked fires of blue and gray and brown and green looking out from their private eternal cells, the planes of their faces descending into unshielded lips, so open to pleasure and to wounds. He would look upon them before he went to sleep. He would reach out and touch the warm flesh; the satin of thigh and buttock, touch the burning lips, and oh so rarely smooth the crinkled vulva hair to feel the throbbing pulse beneath. There was so much comfort there that he would fall asleep and the pulse softened the terror of his dreams. In his dreams he hated the very young and would devour them. He dreamed of the bodies of young men piled high in trenches, sailors by the thousands floating fathoms deep beneath the sea, vast skies clouded by the space-suited bodies of celestial explorers spinning endlessly into black holes of the universe.

Awake he dreamed. But awake he recognized his dreams

as a form of senile madness, his disgust of his own body. He hated his skin that gleamed like scar tissue, the brown spots on his hands and bald pate, those deadly freckles of death, his failing sight, the feebleness of his limbs, the spinning heart, the evilness tumoring his brain clear as a bell.

Oh, what a pity that fairy godmothers came to the cradle of newborn infants to bestow their three magical wishes! Those infants had no need, old men like himself should receive such gifts. Especially those with minds clear as a bell.

BOOK II

4

Romeo's escape from Italy had been meticulously planned. From St Peter's Square the van took his cadre to a safe house where he changed clothes, was furnished with an almost foolproof passport, picked up an already packed suitcase and was taken by underground routes over the border into Southern France. There in the city of Nice he boarded the flight to Paris that continued on to New York. Though he had gone without sleep for the past thirty hours, Romeo remained alert. This was all tricky detail, the easy portion of an operation that sometimes went wrong because of some crazy fluke or hitch in planning.

The dinner and wine on Air France planes was always good and Romeo gradually relaxed. He gazed down at endless pale green oceans and horizons of white and blue sky. He took two strong sleeping pills. But still some nerve of fear in his body kept him awake. He thought of passing through United States Customs, would something go wrong there? But even if he was caught at that time and place, it would not make any difference to Yabril's scheme. A treacherous survival instinct kept him awake. Romeo had no illusions about the suffering he would have to endure. He had agreed to commit an immolating act of sacrifice for the sins of his family, his class and his country but now that mysterious nerve of fear tautened his body.

Finally the pills worked and he fell asleep. In his dreams he fired the shot and ran out of St Peter's Square, and now still running, he came awake. The plane was landing at

Kennedy Airport in New York. The stewardess handed him his jacket, and he reached for his carry-on case from the overhead bin. When he passed through Customs, he acted his part perfectly, and carried his bag outside to the central plaza of the airport terminal.

He spotted his contacts immediately. The girl wore a green ski cap with white stripes. The young man pulled out a red billed cap and put it on his head so that the blue stencil reading 'Yankees' was visible. Romeo himself wore no signal markers, he had wanted to keep his options open. He bent down and fiddled with his bags, opening one and rummaging through it as he studied the two contacts. He could observe nothing that was suspicious. Not that it really mattered.

The girl was skinny and blonde and too angular for Romeo's taste, but her face had a feminine sternness that some serious-minded girls have and he liked that in a woman. He wondered how she would be in bed and hoped he would remain free long enough to seduce her. It shouldn't be too difficult. He had always been attractive to women. In that way he was a better man than Yabril. She would guess that he was connected to the killing of the Pope, and to a serious-minded revolutionary girl, sharing his bed might be the fulfillment of a romantic dream. He noticed that she did not lean toward or touch the man who was with her.

That young man had such a warm, open face, he radiated such American kindliness, that Romeo immediately disliked him. Americans are such worthless shits, they had too comfortable a life. Imagine, in over two hundred years they had never come close to having a revolutionary party. And this in a country that had come into existence through revolution. The young man sent to greet him was typical of such softness. Romeo picked up his bags and walked directly to them.

'Excuse me,' Romeo said smiling, his English heavily accented. 'Could you tell me where the bus leaves for Long Island?'

The girl turned her face toward him. She was much prettier up close. He saw a tiny scar on her chin and that aroused his desire. She said, 'Do you want the North Shore or the South Shore?'

'East Hampton,' Romeo said.

The young girl smiled, it was a warm smile, even a smile of admiration. The young man took one of Romeo's bags and said, 'Follow us.'

They led the way out of the terminal. Romeo followed. The noise of traffic, the density of people, almost stunned him. A car was waiting with a driver who wore another red billed baseball cap. The two young men sat in the front, the girl got into the back seat with Romeo. As the car rolled into traffic, the girl extended her hand and said, 'My name is Dorothea. Please don't worry.' The two young men up front also murmured their names. Then the girl said, 'You will be very comfortable and very safe.' And in that moment Romeo felt the agony of a Judas.

That night the young American couple took great pains to cook Romeo a good dinner. He had a comfortable room overlooking the ocean, and although the bed was lumpy it made little difference since Romeo knew he would sleep in it one night, if he slept at all. The house was expensively furnished but it had no real taste, it was modern, beach America. The three of them spent a quiet evening talking in a mixture of Italian and English.

The girl Dorothea was a surprise. She was extremely intelligent as well as pretty. She also turned out not to be flirtatious, which destroyed Romeo's hopes of spending his last night of freedom playing sexual fun games. The young man, Richard, was quite serious. It was evident that they had guessed he was involved in the murder of the Pope, but they did not ask specific questions. They simply treated him with the frightening respect that people show to someone slowly dying of a terminal illness. Romeo was impressed by them. They had such lithe bodies when they moved. They

89

talked intelligently, they had compassion for the unfortunate and they radiated confidence in their beliefs and their abilities.

Spending that quiet evening with the two young people, so sincere in their beliefs, so innocent in the necessities of true revolution, Romeo felt a little sick of his whole life. Was it necessary that these two be betrayed along with himself? He would be released eventually, he believed in Yabril's plan, he thought it so simple, so elegant. And he had volunteered to place himself in the noose. But this young man and woman were also true believers, people on their side. And they would be in handcuffs, they would know the sufferings of revolutionaries. For a moment he thought of warning them. But it was necessary that the world know that there were Americans involved in the plot, these two were sacrificial lambs. And then he was angry with himself, he was too softhearted. True he could never throw a bomb into a kindergarten, like Yabril, but surely he could sacrifice a few adults. He had killed a pope, after all.

And what real harm would come to them? They would serve a few years in prison. America was so soft from top to bottom that they might even go free. America was a land of lawyers who were fearsome as the knights of the Round Table. They could get anybody off.

And so he tried to go to sleep. But all the terrors of the past few days came over the ocean air blowing through the open window. Again he raised his rifle, again he saw the Pope fall, again he was rushing through the Square, and heard the celebrating pilgrims screaming in horror.

Early the next morning, Monday morning, twenty-four hours after he had killed the Pope, Romeo decided he would walk along the American ocean and get his last whiff of freedom. The house was silent as he came down the stairs but he found Dorothea and Richard sleeping on the two couches in the living room, as if they were standing guard. The poison of his treachery drove him out of the door into the salt breeze of the beach. On sight, he hated this foreign beach, the barbaric gray shrubs, the tall wild yellow weeds, the flashing sunlight off silver-red soda cans. Even the sunshine was watery, early spring colder in this strange land. But he was glad to be out in the open while treachery was being done. A helicopter sailed overhead and then out of sight, there were two boats motionless in the water with not a sign of life aboard. The sun rose the color of a blood orange then yellowed into gold as it rose higher in the sky. He walked for a long time, rounded a corner of the bay, and lost sight of his house. For some reason this panicked him or perhaps it was the sight of a vast forest of thin high mottled gray weeds that came almost to water's edge. He turned back.

It was then he heard the sirens of police cars. Far down the beach he saw the flashing lights and he walked rapidly toward them. He felt no fear, no doubt in Yabril, though he could still flee. He felt contempt for this American society that could not even organize his capture properly, how stupid they were. But then the helicopter reappeared in the sky, the two ships that had seemed so still and deserted were racing in to shore. He felt the fear and panic. Now that there was no chance of escape he wanted to run and run and run. But he steeled himself and walked toward the house surrounded with men and guns. The helicopter hovered over its roof. There were more men coming up the beach and down the beach. Romeo prepared his charade of guilt and fright, he started to run out into the ocean but men rose out of the water in masks. Romeo turned and ran back toward the house and then he saw Richard and Dorothea.

They were chained, in handcuffs, ropes of iron rooted their bodies to the earth. And they were weeping. Romeo knew how they felt, so he had stood once long ago. They were weeping in shame, in humiliation, stripped of their sense of power, bewilderingly defeated. And filled with the unutterably nightmarish terror of being completely helpless. Their fate no longer in the laps of the whimsical perhaps merciful gods but in the hands of their implacable fellow man.

Romeo gave them both a smile of helpless pity. He knew he would be free in a matter of days, he knew he had betrayed these true believers in his own faith, but after all, it had been a tactical decision, not an evil or malicious one. Then he was swarmed over by armed men and linked in steel and heavy iron.

Far across the world, that world whose roof of sky was riddled with spying satellites, its ozone patrolled by voodoo radar, across the seas filled with American warships sweeping toward Sherhaben, across continents spaced with missile silos and stationary armies rooted to the earth to act as lightning rods for death, Yabril had breakfast in the palace with the Sultan of Sherhaben.

The Sultan of Sherhaben was a believer in Arab Freedom, in the Palestinian right to a homeland. He regarded the United States as the bulwark of Israel, Israel could not stand without American support. Therefore America was the ultimate enemy. And Yabril's plot to destabilize America's authority had appealed to his subtle mind. The humiliation of a great power by Sherhaben, militarily so helpless, delighted him.

The Sultan had absolute power in Sherhaben. He had vast wealth, every pleasure in life was his for the asking. Quite simply this had all become unsatisfying. The Sultan had no perculiar vices to spice up his life. He observed Muslim law, he lived a virtuous life. The standard of living in Sherhaben, with its vast revenues of oil, was one of the highest in the world, because the Sultan built new schools, new hospitals. Indeed his dream was to make Sherhaben the Switzerland of the Arab world. His only eccentricity was his mania for cleanliness, on his person and in his state.

92

The Sultan had taken part in this conspiracy because he missed the sense of adventure, the gambling for high stakes, the striving for high ideals. So this action of Yabril's had appealed to him. And there was little personal risk to himself and to his country, since he had a magic shield, billions of barrels of oil safely locked beneath his desert land.

Another strong motive was his love and sense of gratitude to Yabril. When the Sultan had been a minor prince, there had been a fierce struggle for power in Sherhaben, especially after the oil fields proved so vast. The American oil companies supported the Sultan's opponents who would naturally favor the American cause. The Sultan, educated abroad, understood the true value of the oil fields, and fought for their value. Civil war broke out. It had been the then very young Yabril who helped the Sultan achieve power by killing off the Sultan's opponents. For the Sultan, though a man of personal virtue, recognized that political struggle had its own rules.

After his assumption of power, the Sultan gave Yabril sanctuary when needed. Indeed Yabril had spent more time in Sherhaben in the last ten years than in any other place. He established a separate identity with a home and servants and a wife and children. He was also, in that identity, employed as a special government minor official. This identity was never penetrated by any foreign intelligence service. During the next ten years he and the Sultan became close. They were both students of the Koran, educated by foreign teachers and they were united in their hatred of Israel. And here they made an especial distinction, they did not hate the Jews as Jews, they hated the official state of the Jews.

The Sultan of Sherhaben had a secret dream, one so bizarre he did not dare to share it with anyone, not even Yabril. That one day Israel would be destroyed and the Jews dispersed again all over the world. And then he, the Sultan, would lure Jewish scientists and scholars to Sherhaben. He would establish a great university that would collect the Jewish brain. For had not history proved that this race owned the genes to greatness of the mind? Einstein and other Jewish scientists had given the world the atom bomb. What other mysteries of God and nature could they not solve? And were they not fellow Semites? Time erodes hatred, Jew and Arab could live in peace together and make Sherhaben great. Oh, he would lure them with riches and sweet civility, he would respect all their stubborn whims of culture, he would create them a paradise of the brain. Who knew what would happen? Sherhaben could be another Athens. The thought made the Sultan smile at his own foolishness, but still what was the harm in a dream?

But now Yabril was perhaps a nightmare. The Sultan had summoned him to the palace, spirited him from the plane, to make sure that Yabril's ferocity would be controlled. Yabril had a history of adding his own little twists to his operations.

The Sultan insisted that Yabril be bathed and shaved and enjoy a beautiful dancing girl of the palace. Then they sat in the glassed air-conditioned terraced room, Yabril refreshed and in the Sultan's minor debt.

The Sultan felt he could speak frankly. 'I must congratulate you,' he said to Yabril. 'Your timing has been perfect, and I must say lucky. Allah watches over you without a doubt.' Here he smiled affectionately at Yabril. Then he went on. 'I have received advance notice that the United States will meet any demands you make. Be content. You have humiliated the greatest country in the world. You have killed the world's greatest religious leader. You will achieve the release of your killer of the Pope and that will be like pissing in their face. But go no further. Give thought to what happens afterwards. You will be the most hunted man in the history of this century.'

Yabril knew what was coming, the probing for more

information on how to handle the negotiations. For a moment he wondered of the Sultan would try to take over the operation. 'I will be safe here in Sherhaben,' Yabril said. 'As always.'

The Sultan shook his head. 'You know as well as I do, that they will concentrate on Sherhaben after this is over. You will have to find another refuge.'

Yabril laughed. 'I will be a begger in Jerusalem. But you should worry about yourself. They will know you have been a part of it.'

'Not probable,' the Sultan said. 'And I sit on the greatest and cheapest ocean of oil in the world. Also the Americans have fifty billion dollars invested here, the cost of the oil city of Dak and even more. Then I have the Russian Army who will resist any American attempt to control the Gulf. No, I think I will be forgiven much more quickly than you and your Romeo. Now, Yabril, my friend, I know you well, you have gone far enough this time, really a magnificent performance. Please, do not ruin everything with one of your little flourishes at the end of the game.' He paused for a moment. 'When do I present your demands?'

Yabril said softly, 'Romeo is in place. Give the ultimatum this afternoon. They must agree by eleven Tuesday morning, Washington time. I will not negotiate.'

The Sultan said, 'Be very careful, Yabril. Give them more time.'

They embraced before Yabril was taken back to the plane, which was now held by the three men of his cadre and four other men who had come aboard in Sherhaben. The hostages were all in the tourist section of the plane, including the crew. The plane was sitting isolated in midfield, the crowds of spectators, the TV people with their camera equipment vehicles from all over the world pushed back five hundred yards from the aircraft, where the Sultan's army had established a picket line.

Yabril was smuggled back on to the plane as a member of

the crew of a provisioning truck that was bringing food supplies and water for the hostages.

In Washington DC it was very early Monday morning. The last thing that Yabril had said to the Sultan of Sherhaben was, 'Now we will see what this Kennedy is made of.'

5

It is often dangerous to all concerned when a man rejects the pleasures of this world and devotes his life to helping his fellow man. The President of the United States, Francis Xavier Kennedy, was such a man.

Francis Xavier Kennedy first showed specialness after entry into Havard University. There it became evident that people were attracted to him. It helped that he was a good athlete. Physical grace, unlike intellectual force, is one of the very few traits that is universally admired. It helped that he was a brilliant student, it helped, especially with the unworldly, that he was virtuous.

The friendships he made and the followers he won, were due to his charisma, his generosity of spirit. He was never critical in a personal fashion but he was never the professional good guy. He argued politics vigorously but with humor. Though he was somewhat grave in temperament, the part of him that was Irish sparked a high-spiritedness that was irresistible. Above all he was a good listener who made a real effort to understand completely what someone was trying to say, and then took great care to make an appropriate answer. He had a cheerful wit that he used mainly to prick general hypocrisies.

But above all this he had a natural honesty and sincerity. The young with their keen, if somewhat unfair nose for hypocrisy, could find none in him. True he was a practising Catholic but never discussed his religion. He said simply that it was a matter of faith. This was his only unreasonableness.

97

No man can hide his villainy over a period of time, Iago is a conceit. No man can hide his faults but faults are easily forgiven or explained. True virtue, especially to the young, can be so dazzling that it blinds common sense. It was not remarked that Francis Kennedy was subject to depression when he was defeated in some endeavor. After all, what could be more natural? It was not remarked that he could be extraordinarily single-minded, not ruthless exactly, but perhaps reckless.

Francis Kennedy, from the very beginning of his political career, posed a simplistic question that was to be his motif. How was it, he said, that after every war that consumed trillions of dollars in goods, there was a period of economic prosperity? He compared it to a bank being looted of its billions and then becoming more profitable.

What if those trillions of dollars were spent building homes for the people, what if those billions and trillions were spent on medical care, on education? What if this money was spent to help the people? What a glorious country this would be and indeed a far better world.

When he was elected to the Presidency, his administration, he said, would declare an internal war, on all the miseries of people who could not afford lobbyists and other pressure groups.

All this in ordinary circumstances would have been far too radical for the voting populace of America if it were not for Kennedy's magical presence on the TV screen. He was handsomer than his two famous uncles and a far better actor. He also had a better brain than his two uncles and was far superior in education, a true scholar. He could back up his rhetoric with figures, eonomic rules. He could present the skeleton of plans that had been prepared by eminent men in the different fields with dazzling elegance. And a somewhat caustic wit.

'With a good education,' Francis Kennedy said, 'any burglar, stick-up man, any mugger, will know enough to steal without hurting anyone. They'll know how to steal like the people on Wall Street, learn how to evade their taxes, like respectable people in our society. We may create more white-collar crime but at least nobody will get hurt.'

Francis Xavier Kennedy had won his election to the Presidency by a landslide on the Democratic ticket, and with a Democratic Congress.

But from the very first, the Presidency and the Legislative branch were enemies. Kennedy lost the extreme right wing in Congress because he was for abortion. He lost the extreme left wing because he supported the death penalty for certain crimes. He claimed he was consistent. He often pointed out that the left who were for abortion were usually against the death penalty. And the right who were against abortion as a form of murder usually were avidly in favor of the death penalty.

Kennedy also made enemies of Congress because he proposed severe restrictions on the huge corporations of America, the oil industry, the grain industry, the medical industry, and also proposed the TV stations, newspapers and magazines should not be held by one company. This last was attacked as an attempt to destroy the freedom of the press. The First Amendment was brandished in all its holiness.

Now in the last year of his Presidency, on the Monday after Easter, at seven in the morning, the members of President Francis Kennedy's staff, his cabinet and Vice President Helen DuPray assembled in the Cabinet Room of the White House. And on this Monday morning they were fearful of what action he would take.

In the Cabinet Room, the CIA Chief, Theodore Tappey, waited for a signal from Kennedy and then opened the session. 'Let me say first that Theresa is OK,' he said. 'No one has been injured. As yet no specific demands have been made. But demands will be made by evening and we have been warned that they must be met immediately, without negotiation. But that's standard. The hijacker leader, Yabril, is a name famous in terrorist circles and indeed known in our files. He is a maverick and usually does his own operations with help from some of the organized terror groups, like the mythical First Hundred.'

Klee cut in. 'Why mythical, Theo?'

Theodore Tappey said, 'It's not like Ali Baba and the forty thieves. Just liaison actions between terrorists of different countries.'

Francis Kennedy said curtly, 'Go on.'

Theodore Tappey consulted his notes. 'There is no doubt that the Sultan of Sherhaben is co-operating with Yabril. His army is protecting the airfield to prevent any rescue attempt. Meanwhile the Sultan pretends to be our friend and volunteers his services as a negotiator. What his purpose is in this no one can guess, but it is to our interest. The Sultan is reasonable and vulnerable to pressure. Yabril is a wild card.'

The CIA Chief hesitated, then at a nod from Kennedy, went on reluctantly. 'Yabril is trying to brainwash your daughter, Mr President. They have had several long conversations. He seems to think she's a potential revolutionary and that it would be a great coup if she gave out some sort of sympathetic statement. She doesn't seem afraid of him.'

The others in the room remained silent. They knew better than to ask Tappey how he had gotten such information.

The hall outside the Cabinet Room hummed with voices, they could hear the excited shouts of the TV camera crews waiting on the White House lawn. Then one of Eugene Dazzy's assistants was let into the room and handed Dazzy a handwritten memo. Kennedy's Chief of Staff read it at a glance.

'This has all been confirmed?' he asked the aide.

'Yes, sir,' the aide said.

Dazzy stared directly at Francis Kennedy. 'Mr President,' he said. 'I have the most extraordinary news. The assassin of the Pope has been captured here in the United States. The prisoner confirms that he is the assassin of the Pope, that his code name is Romeo. He refuses to give his real name. It has been checked with the Italian Security people and the prisoner gives details that confirm his guilt.'

Arthur Wix exploded, as if an uninvited guest had arrived at some intimate party, 'What the hell is he doing here? I don't believe it.'

Eugene Dazzy patiently explained the verification. Italian Security had already captured some of Romeo's cadre and they had confessed and identified Romeo as their leader. The Chief of the Italian Security, Franco Sebbediccio, was famous for his ability to get confessions. But he could not learn why Romeo had fled to America and how he had been so easily captured.

Francis Kennedy went to the french doors overlooking the Rose Garden. He watched the military detachments patrolling the White House grounds and adjoining Washington streets. He felt a familiar sense of dread. Nothing in his life was an accident, life was a deadly conspiracy, not only between fellow humans but between faith and death. In one instant of paranoid divination he comprehended the whole plan that Yabril had created with such pride and cunning. Now for the first time he truly feared for his daughter's safety.

Francis Kennedy turned back from the window and returned to the conference table. He surveyed the room filled with the highest ranking people in the country, the most clever, the most intelligent, the schemers, the planners. None of them knew. He said, almost jokingly, 'What do you guys want to bet, that today we get a set of demands from the hijacker? And one of the demands will be that we release this killer of the Pope.'

The others stared at Kennedy in amazement. Otto Gray said, 'Mr President, that's an awful big stretch. That is an outrageous demand, it would be non-negotiable.'

Theodore Tappey said carefully, 'Intelligence shows no

101

connection between the two acts. Indeed it would be inconceivable for any terrorist group to launch two such important operations in the same city on the same day.' He paused for a moment and turned to Christian Klee. 'Mr Attorney General,' he asked, 'just how did you capture this man?' and then added with distaste, 'Romeo.'

Christian Klee said, 'An informer we've been using for years. We thought it impossible but my deputy, Peter Cloot, followed through with a full-scale operation, which seems to have succeeded. I must say I'm surprised. It just doesn't make any sense.'

Francis Kennedy said quietly, 'Let's adjourn this meeting until the hijackers make their demands. But here are my preliminary instructions. We will give them what they want. The Secretary of State and the Attorney General will stall off the Italians when they request Romeo's extradition. Wix, you and Defense and State get ready to lean on Israel if the demands include release of Arab prisoners they have. And Otto, prepare Congress and any of our friends there for what our opponents will call our complete capitulation.'

Kennedy spoke directly to his Chief of Staff. 'Euge, tell the Press Secretary that I will have no contact personally with the media until this crisis is over. And that every press release has to be cleared by me, not through you.'

Eugene Dazzy said, 'Yes, sir.'

Francis Kennedy now addressed the room full of people almost sternly. 'There will be no comments directly from you to the media. And I hope no leaks. That is all, gentlemen. Please remain on call.'

Yabril's demands came through the White House Communications Center late Monday afternoon, relayed through the seemingly helpful Sultan of Sherhaben. The first demand was ransom of fifty million dollars for the aircraft. The second, the freeing of six hundred Arab prisoners in Israeli jails. The third was for the release of the newly captured assassin of the Pope, Romeo, and his transport to Sherhaben. Also, that if the demands were not met in twenty-four hours, one hostage would be shot.

The President, his staff, his Cabinet, his special advisors met immediately to discuss Yabril's demands. Francis Kennedy put himself in the minds of the terrorists, he had always had this gift of empathy. Their primary aim was to humiliate the United States, to destroy its mantle of power in the eyes of the world, even in the eyes of friendly nations. And Kennedy thought it a master psychological stroke. Who could ever take America seriously again, after its nose was rubbed in dirt by a few armed men and a small oil Sultanate? But Kennedy knew he must allow this to happen to bring his daughter safely home. Yet in his empathy he divined that the scenario was not complete, that there were more surprises to come. But he did not speak. He let the others in the Cabinet Room continue their briefings.

The Secretary of State gave his Departmental Staff's recommendations. That they ship the Pope's assassin back to Rome and let the Italian authorities deal with the situation. The hijackers would have to route their demand for Romeo's release to the Italian government. They all noticed that Francis Kennedy turned his head away at this suggestion.

The threat by the hijackers that they would execute one of the hostages if the demands were not met in twenty-four hours was discounted by all the advisors. Time could be stretched, the threat was an accustomed ploy.

One of the Congressional leaders present suggested that President Kennedy remove himself from all the decisions in this affair because his daughter was involved and he might not be able, emotionally, to make the most effective decisions.

The Congressman who made this suggestion was a Republican veteran with twenty years of service in the House. His name was Alfred Jintz and in three years of Kennedy's

103

administration he had been one of the most effective blockers of social welfare laws proposed by the White House. Like most Congressmen who got through the first few terms and did what was necessary for big business firms, Jintz was automatically re-elected term after term.

Kennedy did not hide his distaste for the suggestion and the Congressman. In his three years as President, Francis Kennedy had acquired a disdain for the legislative branch of the government. Both branches, the House and the Senate, had become self-perpetuating. In the House, even though Congressmen had to run every two years, the power of their positions, especially as heads of Committees, effectively gave them lifelong tenure. Once a Congressman made it clear that he was a believer in the virtue and importance of big business, millions of dollars poured into his campaign, millions to buy lifeblood TV time to be re-elected. And in the 435-member House there was not one working man. As for the Senate with its six-year terms, it would be a very stupid or a very idealistic Senator who did not get re-elected for two or three terms. Kennedy thought this traitorous to democracy.

At this moment Francis Kennedy felt a cold rage, at Jintz, at all the members of the House and Senate.

When Alfred Jintz made his suggestion that Kennedy remove himself from the negotiations, he did so with the utmost courtesy and tact. The New York Senator, Thomas Lambertino, stated that the Senate also thought the President should remove himself.

Kennedy stood up again. He addressed the room in general. 'I thank you for your help and your suggestions. My staff and I will meet later on and you will all be notified of the decisions made. I especially thank Congressman Jintz and Senator Lambertino for their suggestion. I will consider it. But for now I must tell you that all instructions and orders will come from me personally. Nothing in this matter will be delegated. That will be all gentlemen. Please remain on call.'

Vice President Helen DuPray observed everything silently. She knew that this was not the time to oppose the President, even privately.

Francis Kennedy had dinner with his personal staff in the large northwest dining room on the second floor of the White House. The antique table was set for Otto Gray, Arthur Wix, Eugene Dazzy and Christian Klee. Kennedy's place was at one end of the table and set so that he had more space than the others. Kennedy remained standing while the others sat down. He smiled at them grimly. 'Forget all the bullshit you heard today. Dazzy, you tell the Sultan that we will comply with all the hijacker's demands before the expiration of the twenty-four-hour limit. We do not return the Pope's killer to Italy, we send him to Sherhaben. And Wix, you lean hard on Israel. They turn those prisoners loose or they will never see an American gun as long as I'm in office. Tell the Secretary of State, no diplomatic talk, just lay it on the line.'

He sat finally and allowed the stewards to serve him. Then he spoke again. 'I want all of you here to know, that no matter what I have to say at all these meetings, there is only one priority; to get Theresa home safely. No giving them any excuse to commit another crime.'

Arthur Wix kept his hand in his lap as if he planned to refuse his dinner. He said, 'You're leaving yourself very vulnerable. There should be some bargaining, it's mandatory in all hostage cases. You have to go through some of the motions before you do what you want to do, then we can whitewash it.'

'I know that,' Kennedy said. 'I just don't want to take the chance. And besides I only have another year in office and you know I won't run again. So what the hell can they do to me? Otto, you sweet-talk the Congressional leaders. Don't waste time on Jintz. That son of a bitch has been against me on everything for the past three years.'

They all started eating quietly, all thinking that Kennedy was putting the Administration into a difficult position.

As they were drinking their coffee the White House duty officer was ushered into the room. He handed a message slip to Christian Klee. Christian read it and then said to Kennedy, 'Francis, I have to get back to my office. This message has the highest classification, it can't be done by phone. As soon as I get briefed, I'll come back to you. Obviously it's something that must have your immediate attention.'

Francis Kennedy said harshly to him, 'Then why the hell didn't they come and brief us both?'

Christian smiled at him. 'I don't know, but there must be a reason. Maybe they didn't want to bother you with it until I give the OK.' He was lying. His system was set up so that the President could never be briefed before Christian himself had been briefed. What Christian did know was that this message was the first he had ever received from his office that bore the ultra secrecy code. It had to be devastating news.

Francis Kennedy waved him away with an impatient gesture. He knew that there was something not quite right about Christian's answer, that he was being deceived in some way, but he was always careful not to be critical of the people working for him or even of his friends. Kennedy knew that the power of his office gave his words and actions too much weight, he could not indulge his minor irritations.

Shortly after being elected President, he had one of his usual friendly political disagreements with his daughter Theresa. He had delighted in parrying her arguments with his superior skill and then delivering a lightening slash of his own at her radical friends. He had been surprised when she burst into tears and fled. It was then he realized that because of the public weight of his office he could not indulge in natural verbal swordplay with close friends and relatives. He even had to be careful with Christian. In the old days he would have told Christian he was full of shit and demanded the truth.

It was Oddblood Gray who broke into his thoughts. He said, 'Mr President, why don't you try to get some sleep? We'll hold the watch and wake you if anything needs your attention.'

Kennedy saw the look of concern on their faces. During dinner they had done all they could to reassure him about the safety of his daughter, that she was in no real danger. And they had been more formal with him than usual, as people are with each other going through periods of danger or tragedy.

Kennedy said, 'I'll do that, Otto, and thank you all.'

He left them.

When Christian Klee left the White House, he went directly to FBI Headquarters. By protocol, two security vehicles preceded him and another tailed closely behind. In his office he found his Deputy Director waiting for him, the man who actually did the administrative job of running the FBI.

Peter Cloot was a man that Christian understood but could not bring himself to really like. Cloot was part of the trade-off Kennedy had negotiated with Congress when Christian Klee was made Attorney General, FBI Director and head of the Secret Service. Cloot was the man Congress designated to keep an eye on Klee. Cloot was very spare, his body a flat slate of muscles. He had a tiny mustache which did nothing to soften the bony face. As deputy commanding the FBI Cloot had his faults. He was too unbending in the discharge of responsibilities, too fierce in the discharge of his duties, and believed too much in internal security. He lobbied for stricter laws, Draconian punishment for drug dealers and spies. When he could, he dodged the civil liberties sections of the law. But he always exercised good judgment. And certainly he had never spooked before. He had never sent such a message in the last three years he had worked with Christian in running the FBI.

Over three years ago when Christian had interviewed Peter Cloot for the job of Deputy Director of the FBI (Congress had given him three candidates), it was obvious that Cloot did not give a damn if he got the job or not. He had been extraordinarily frank.

'I'm a reactionary to the left and a terror to the right,' Cloot said. 'When a man commits what is called a criminal act, I feel it is a sin. Law enforcement is my theology. A man who commits a criminal act exercises the power of God over another human being. Then it becomes the decision of the victim whether to accept this other god in his life. When the victim and society accepts the criminal act in any way, we destroy our society's will to survive.' He went on. 'Society and even the individual has no right to forgive or ameliorate punishment. Why impose the tyranny of the criminal over a law-abiding populace that adheres to the social contract. In terrible cases of murder and armed robbery and rapes, the criminal proclaims his godhead.'

Christian said smilingly, 'Put them all in jail?'

Peter Cloot said grimly, 'We haven't got enough jails.'

Christian had given him the latest computerized statistical report on crime in America. Cloot studied it for a few minutes.

Cloot said, 'Nothing's changed.' And he began to rage. At first Christian thought him a nut. Cloot said many things . . .

'If only people knew the statistics on crime,' he said. 'If people only knew the crimes that never got into statistics. Burglars, with prior records, rarely go to prison. That home which the government shall not invade, that precious freedom, that sacred social contract, that sacred home, is invaded routinely by armed fellow citizens intent on theft, murder and rape.' Cloot recited that beloved bit of English law, 'The rain may enter, the wind may enter, but the king may not enter.'

'What a piece of bullshit that is,' Cloot said. He went on. 'California alone, by itself, had six times as many murders than the whole of England last year. In America murderers do less than five years in prison. Providing that by some miracle you could convict them.'

Cloot droned on in a grating voice that bored Christian . . .

The Supreme Court in its magestic innocence of everyday life, the lower courts in their venality, the army of greedy lawyers ready for battle as samurai, protected criminals so evil they came out of Grimms' fairy tales.

And the social scientists, the psychiatrists, the pundits of ethics wrapped up all these criminals in the mantle of environment and the general population who supplied jurors too cowardly to convict.

'The people of America are terrorized by a few million lunatics,' Cloot said. 'Afraid to walk the streets at night. Guarding their homes with private security that costs thirty billion dollars a year.'

Cloot rambled on that the whites feared the blacks, the blacks feared the whites, the rich feared the poor. Senior citizens carried guns in their shopping bags because they feared the young. Women in fear of rapists aspired to Black Belts and millions of them carried guns.

'Our fucking Bill of Rights,' Cloot said. 'We have the highest rates of crime in the civilized world.'

But Cloot especially hated one aspect. He said, 'Do you know that ninety-eight per cent of crimes go unpunished? Nietzsche said a long time ago, "A society when it becomes soft and tender takes side with those who harm it." The religious outfits with all their mercy shit forgive criminals. They have no right to forgive criminals, those bastards. The worst thing I ever saw was this mother on TV whose daughter was raped and killed in an awful way, saying "I forgive them". What fucking right did she have to forgive them?'

And then to Christian's slightly snobbish surprise, Cloot attacked literature. 'Orwell had it all wrong in *1984*,' he said. 'The individual is the beast, and Huxley in *Brave New World*, he made it out as a bad thing. But I wouldn't mind living in a Brave New World, it's better than this. It's the individual who is the tyrant, not the government.' And he went on.

Cloot hated lawyers in particular though he himself had a law degree. He thought the Supreme Court a joke. He thought that criminals had all the best of it in American society, and he was not above using all the evasions in his power to thwart any restrictions on his agency. He was careful not to do anything illegal, plant evidence or distort it too obviously but he was not above burying evidence he did not want used.

Christian was undecided about Cloot until their final interview. He had given Peter Cloot the huge statistical report to study and make notes on.

Cloot tapped the computer pages. 'Old stuff,' he said. 'Is this what you want to talk about?'

Christian said earnestly and a little ingenuously, 'I am really astonished by the figures. The population of this country is being terrorized. Maybe that's too strong a word. But was this never addressed by the former President during your term of office?'

Cloot puffed on his cigar. 'We tried. But Congress would never pass the legislation we needed. The newspapers and other media scream bloody murder about the Bill of Rights, the sacred Constitution. And the Civil Liberties outfits are always on our ass. To say nothing of the black lobbies to whom law and order are dirty words. And special groups and unorganized liberals. And those women, special types, who love criminals behind bars and petition to get them loose. So it was a no win situation for Congress.'

Christian pushed over a huge ashtray of red glass and

Cloot tapped his cigar ash into it. Christian picked up his copy of the report and asked, 'Was it this bad before?'

'Worse,' Cloot said. Smoke circled his head like a halo and he smiled sardonically through it. He was digesting the excellent lunch, enjoying his cigar, and so was in the proper state of physical relaxation to pontificate. 'Let me give you a little insight, buy it or not. The really amazing thing is that I've discussed this situation with the really powerful men in this country, the ones with all the money. I gave a speech to the Socrates Club. I thought that they would be concerned. But what a surprise. They had the clout to move Congress. they wouldn't do it. And you could never in a million years guess the reason. I couldn't.' He paused as if he expected Christian to guess.

His face grimaced in what could be a smile or an expression of contempt. 'The rich and powerful in this country can protect themselves. They don't rely on the police or government agencies. They surround themselves with expensive security systems. They have private bodyguards. They are sealed off from the criminal community. And the prudent ones don't get mixed up with the wild drug elements. They can sleep peacefully at night behind their electric walls.'

Cloot paused for a moment. Christian moved restlessly and took a sip of brandy as Cloot swallowed half his glass. Then Cloot went on.

'This is a private consultation so I can speak frankly. You are not allowed in politics to say that blacks commit far more crimes than is proportionate to their population. Sure we both know all the reasons, economic and cultural, and there's a long scandalous history in this country of repressing the black population. But there it is.'

Cloot picked up his cigar. 'By the way, whites are the more dangerous criminals. I never knew a black to be a serial killer, I never knew a black who stole as much money

111

as a Wall Street conniver. And never a black political assassin.'

Christian said, 'You're trying as hard as you can not to get to the point.'

Cloot laughed. 'OK,' he said. 'The point is this. Let's say we pass laws to crush crime, we are then punishing the black criminals more than anyone else. And where are those ungifted, uneducated, unpowered people going to go? What other resource do they have against our society? If they have no outlet in crime they will turn to political action. They will become active radicals. And they will shift the political balance of this country. We may not have a capitalist democracy.'

Christian said, 'Do you believe that crap?'

Cloot sighed. 'Jesus, who knows? But the people who run this country believe it. They figure, let the jackals feast on the helpless. What can they steal, a few billion dollars? A small price to pay. Thousands get raped, burglarized, murdered, mugged, it doesn't matter, it happens to unimportant people. Better that minor damage than a real political upheaval.'

Christian said, 'You're going too far.'

'That may be,' Cloot said.

'And when it goes too far,' Christian said, 'you'll have all kinds of vigilante groups, fascism in an American form.'

'But that's the kind of political action that can be controlled,' Cloot said. 'That will actually help the people who run our society.'

They were both silent, then Cloot went on.

'You show me that fucking computer report,' Peter Cloot said. 'Am I supposed to faint? When I was a young DA I saw those statistics in blood. We had a beeper twenty-four hours a day and in the middle of the night I'd get called on to the street. Husbands who took an axe to their wives and then served only five years in prison. Young doped-up punks murdering old ladies for their social security check, ninety bucks. And then the murderers get off because their civil

112

rights were not observed. Burglars, stick-up artists, bank robbers, it was like winning a gold medal. What a fucking joke. And newspapers quoting 1984 and that fucking George Orwell. Listen I saw the parents of murdered girls weeping, their lives ruined for ever, and the killer getting a slap on the wrist because they had a high-powered lawyer, dumb jurors and some faggy church mogul going to bat for him. And what would they get, these killers, if you convicted them at all? Three years, five years. The criminal system in this country is a complete joke. The people who run this country, the rich, the church, the politicians, my fellow lawyers, they *like* things this way. No radical political movements, fat fees, very nice bribes. So what if a few hundred thousand ordinary people got murdered, who cares that millions get mugged, beaten and raped?' Cloot stopped himself and wiped his clammy face with the table napkin then said in a bewildered voice, 'It never made any sense.'

Then he smiled at Christian and picked up the computer report. 'I'd like to keep this,' he said. 'Not to wipe my ass with it as I should. Just to frame it and put up on the wall of my den where it will be safe. I know it will be safe because I have a fifty-thousand-dollar security system around my house.'

But Cloot had proved to be a superbly efficient Deputy in running the FBI, and tonight, grim-faced, he greeted Christian with a handful of memos and a three-page letter which he handed to him separately.

It was a letter composed with type cut from newspapers. Christian read. Another one of those crazy warnings that a home-made atom bomb would explode in New York City. Christian said, 'For this you pull me out of the President's office?'

Peter Cloot said, 'I waited until we went through all the checking procedures. It qualifies as a possible.'

'Oh Christ,' Christian said. 'Not now.' He read the letter

again but much more carefully. The different types of print disoriented him. The letter looked like a bizarre avant-garde painting. He sat down at his desk and read it slowly word for word. The letter was addressed to the *New York Times*. First he read the paragraphs that were isolated by heavy green marker to identify the hard information. The marked parts of the letter read:

'We have planted a nuclear weapon with minimum potential one half kiloton, and maximum of 2 kiloton, in the New York City area. This letter is written to your newspaper so that you may print it and warn the inhabitants of the city to vacate and escape harm.

'The device is set to trigger off seven days from the date above. So you know how necessary it is to publish this letter immediately.'

Klee looked at the date. The explosion would be Thursday. He read on:

'We have taken this action to prove to the people of the United States that the government must unite with the rest of the world on an equal partnership basis to control nuclear energy or our planet can be lost.

'There is no other way we can be bought off by money or by any other condition. By publishing this letter and forcing the evacuation of New York City you will save thousands of lives.

'To prove that this is not a crackpot letter, have the envelope and paper examined by government laboratories. They will find residues of plutonium oxide.

'Print this letter immediately.'

The rest of the letter was a lecture on political morality and an impassioned demand that the United States cease making nuclear weapons.

114

Christian said to Peter Cloot, 'Have you had it examined?'

'Yes,' Peter Cloot said, 'it does have residue. The individual letters are cut from newspapers and magazines to form the message but they give a clue. The writer or writers were smart enough to use papers from all over the country. But there is just a slight over normal edge for Boston newspapers. I sent an extra fifty men to help the bureau chief up there.'

Christian sighed. 'We have a long night ahead of us. Let's keep this very low key. And seal it off from the media. Command post will be my office and all papers to me. The President has enough headaches, let's just make this thing disappear. It's a piece of bullshit like all those other crank letters.'

'OK,' Peter Cloot said. 'But you know, someday one of them *will* be real.'

It was a long night. The reports kept flowing in. The Nuclear Energy and Research Agency chief was informed so that his Agency Search teams could be alerted. These teams were specially recruited personnel with sophisticated detecting equipment that could search out hidden nuclear bombs.

Christian had supper brought in for him and Cloot and read the reports. The *New York Times* of course had not published the letter, they had routinely turned it over to the FBI. Christian called the publisher of the *Times* and asked him to blackout the item until the investigation was completed. This was also a matter of routine. Newspapers had received thousands of similar letters over the years. But because of this very casualness the letter had gotten to them Monday instead of Saturday.

Sometime before midnight Peter Cloot returned to his own office to manage his staff which was receiving hundreds of calls from the agents in the field, most of them from Boston. Christian kept reading the reports as they were brought in. More than anything else he didn't want this to add to the President's burdens. For a few moments he thought about the possibility that this might be another twist to the hijacker's plot, but even they would not dare to play for such high stakes. This had to be some aberration that the society had thrown up. There had been atomic scares before, crazies who had claimed they planted home-made atom bombs and demanded ransom of ten to a hundred million dollars. One letter had even asked for a portfolio of Wall Street stocks, shares of IBM, General Motors, Sears, Texaco and some of the gene technology companies. When the letter had been submitted to the Energy Department for a psycho profile the report had come back that the letter posed no bomb threat but that the terrorist was very savvy about the stock market. Which had led to the arrest of a minor Wall Street broker who had embezzled his clients' funds and was looking for a way out.

This had to be another of those crackpot things, Christian thought, but meanwhile it was causing trouble. Hundreds of millions of dollars would be spent. Luckily on this issue the media would suppress the letter. There were some things that those cold-hearted bastards didn't dare fuck around with. They knew that there were classified items in the atom bomb control laws that could be invoked, that could even make a hole in the sacred freedom of the Bill of Rights erected around them. He spent the next hours praying that this would all go away. That he would not have to go to the President in the morning and lay this load of crap on him.

6

In the Sultanate of Sherhaben, Yabril stood in the doorway of the hijacked aircraft preparing for the next act he would have to play. Then his absolute concentration lessened and he let himself check the surrounding desert. The Sultan had arranged for missiles to be in place, radar had been set up. An armored division of troops had established a perimeter so that the TV vans could come no nearer to the plane than one hundred yards, and beyond them there was a huge crowd. And Yabril thought that tomorrow he would have to give the order that the TV vans and the crowds would be allowed to come closer, much closer. There would be no danger of assault, the aircraft was lavishly booby-trapped, Yabril knew he could blow everything into fragments of metal and flesh so completely that the bones would have to be sifted out of the desert sands.

Finally he turned from the aircraft doorway and sat down next to Theresa Kennedy. They were alone in the First Class cabin. There were terrorist guards to keep the passenger hostages in the tourist section, there were guards in the cockpit with the crew.

Yabril did his best to put Theresa Kennedy at ease. He told her that the passengers, her fellow hostages, were being well looked after. Naturally, they were not all that comfortable, neither was she or himself. He said with a wry face, 'You know it is to my own best interests that no harm comes to you.'

Theresa Kennedy believed him. Despite everything, she

found that dark, intense face sympathetic, and though she knew he was dangerous she could not really dislike him. In her innocence she believed her high station made her invulnerable.

Yabril said almost pleadingly, 'You can help us, you can help your fellow hostages. Our cause is just, you once said so yourself a few years ago. But the American Jewish establishment was too strong. They shut you up.'

Theresa Kennedy shook her head. 'I'm sure you have your justifications, everybody always has. But the innocent people on this plane have never done you or your cause any harm. They are just people like you people. They should not suffer for the sins of your enemies.'

It gave Yabril a peculiar pleasure that she was courageous and intelligent. Her face so pleasant and pretty in the American fashion also pleased him, as if she were some kind of American doll.

Again he was struck by the fact that she was not afraid of him, was not fearful of what would happen to her. Again the blindness of the highborn to fate, the hubris of the rich and powerful. And of course it was in her family history.

'Miss Kennedy,' he said in a courteous voice that cajoled her to merely listen, 'it is well known to us that you are not the usual spoiled American woman, that your sympathies go out to the poor and oppressed of the world. You have doubts even about Israel's right to expel people from their own land to found a warring state of their own. Perhaps you would make a videotape saying this and be heard all over the world.'

Theresa Kennedy studied Yabril's face. His tan eyes were liquid and warm, the smile made his dark thin face almost boyish. She had been brought up to trust the world, to trust other human beings and to trust her intelligence and her own beliefs. She could see this man sincerely believed in what he was doing. In a curious way he inspired respect.

She was polite in her refusal. 'What you say may be true.

118

But I would never do anything to hurt my father.' She paused for a moment, then said, 'And I don't think your methods are intelligent. I don't think murder and terror change anything.'

With this remark Yabril felt a powerful surge of contempt. But he replied gently, 'Israel was established by terror and American money. Did they teach you that in your American college? We learned from Israel but without their hypocrisy. Our Arab oil sheiks were never as generous with money to us as your Jewish philanthropists were to Israel.'

Theresa Kennedy said, 'I believe in the state of Israel, I also believe the Palestinian people should have a homeland. I don't have any power with my father, we argue all the time. But nothing justifies what you're doing now.'

Yabril became impatient. 'You must realize that you are my treasure,' he said. 'I have made my demands. A hostage will be shot every hour after my deadline. And you will be the first.'

To Yabril's surprise, there was still no fear on her face. Was she stupid? Could such an obviously sheltered woman be so courageous? He was interested in finding out. So far she had been well treated. She had been isolated in the First Class cabin and treated with the utmost respect by her guards. She looked very angry, but calmed herself by sipping the tea he had served her.

Now she looked up at him. He noticed how severely her pale blonde hair framed the delicate features. Her eyes were bruised with fatigue, the lips without make-up, a pale pink.

Theresa Kennedy said in a flat even voice, 'Two of my great-uncles were killed by people like you. My family grew up with death. And my father worried about me when he became President. He warned me that the world had men like you, but I refused to believe him. Now I'm curious. Why do you act like such a villain? Do you think you can frighten the whole world by killing a young girl?'

Yabril thought, maybe not, but I killed a pope. She didn't

know that, not yet. For a moment he was tempted to tell her. The whole grand design. The undermining of authority which all men fear, the power of great nations and great churches. And how man's fear of power could be eroded by solitary acts of terror.

But he reached out a hand to touch her reassuringly. 'You will come to no harm from me,' he said. 'They will negotiate. Life is negotiation. You and I as we speak, we negotiate. Every terrible act, every word of insult, every word of praise is negotiation. Don't take what I've said too seriously.'

She laughed.

He was pleased she found him witty. She reminded him of Romeo, she had the same instinctive enthusiasm for the little pleasures of life, even just a play on words. Once Yabril had said to Romeo, 'God is the ultimate terrorist,' and Romeo had clapped his hands in delight.

And now Yabril's heart sickened, he felt a wave of dizziness. He was ashamed of his wanting to charm Theresa Kennedy. He had believed he had come to a time in his life when he was beyond such weakness. If only he could persuade her to make the videotape he would not have to kill her.

7

On the Tuesday morning after the Easter Sunday hijacking and the murder of the Pope, President Francis Kennedy entered the White House screening room to watch a CIA film smuggled from Sherhaben.

The White House screening room was a disgraceful affair, with ratty dingy green armchairs for the favored few and metal folding chairs for anyone under Cabinet level. The audience was CIA personnel, the Secretary of State, Secretary of Defense, their respective staffs, and the members of the White House Senior Staff.

All rose when the President entered. Kennedy took a green armchair, the CIA Director, Theodore Tappey, stood up alongside the screen to give comments.

The film started. It showed a supply truck pulling up to the back of the hijacked plane. The workers unloading wore brimmed hats against the sun, they were clad in brown twill trousers and short-sleeved brown cotton shirts. The film showed the workers leaving the plane and then froze on one of the workers. Under the floppy hat the features of Yabril could be seen, the dark angled face with brilliant eyes, the slight smile on his lips. Yabril got into the supply truck with the other workers.

The film stopped and Tappey spoke. 'That truck went to the compound of the Sultan of Sherhaben. Our information is that they had an elaborate banquet complete with dancing girls. Afterwards Yabril returned to the plane in the same fashion. Certainly the Sultan of Sherhaben is a fellow conspirator in these acts of terrorism.'

The voice of the Secretary of State boomed in the darkness. 'Certain only to us. Secret intelligence is always suspect. And even if we could prove it, we couldn't make it public. It would upset all political balances in the Persian Gulf. We would be forced to take retaliatory action, and that would be against our best interest.'

Otto Gray muttered, 'Jesus Christ.'

Christian Klee laughed outright.

All of the President's staff hated the Secretary of State whose agenda was primarily the placating of foreign governments.

Eugene Dazzy, who could write in the dark, a sure mark of administrative genius, he always told everyone, made notes on a pad.

Kennedy said dryly, '*We* know it. That's good enough. Thank you, Theodore. Please go on.'

The CIA Chief said, 'Our information boils down to this – you'll get the memos in detail later – This seems to be an operation cadre financed by the international terrorist group called the "First Hundred", or sometimes the "Christs of Violence". To repeat what I said in the previous meeting, it really is a liaison between revolutionary groups in different countries, supplying safe houses and material. And it is limited mostly to Germany, Italy, France and Japan, and very vaguely in Ireland and England. But according to our information even the First Hundred never really knew what was going on here. They thought the operation ended with the killing of the Pope. So what we come down to is that only this man Yabril, with the Sultan of Sherhaben, controls this conspiracy.'

The film started to roll again. It showed the airplane isolated on the tarmac, it showed the ring of soldiers and anti-aircraft guns that protected the approaches to the plane. It showed the crowds that were kept over a hundred yards away.

The CIA Director's voice sounded over the film. 'This film

and other sources indicate there can be no rescue mission. Unless we decide to just overpower the whole state of Sherhaben. And of course Russia will never allow that, nor perhaps will the other Arab states. Also, over fifty billion dollars of American money has gone to build up their city of Dak, which is another sort of hostage they hold. We are not going to blow away fifty billion dollars of our citizen investor money. Plus the fact that the missile sites are manned mostly by American mercenaries but at this point we come to something much more curious.'

On the screen appeared a wobbly shot of the hijacked plane's interior. The camera was obviously hand-held and moved down the aisle of the tourist section to show the mass of frightened passengers trapped into their seats. Then the camera moved back up into the First Class cabin and held on a passenger sitting there. Then Yabril moved into the picture. He wore cotton slacks of whitish brown and a tan short-sleeved shirt the color of the desert outside the plane. The film cut to Yabril sitting next to that lone passenger revealed now as Theresa Kennedy. Yabril and Theresa seemed to be talking in an animated and friendly way.

Theresa Kennedy had a small, amused smile on her face and this made her father, watching the screen, almost turn his head away. It was a smile he remembered from his own childhood, the smile of people entrenched in the central halls of power, who never dream they can be touched by the malicious evil of their fellow man. Francis Kennedy had seen that smile often on the faces of his dead uncles.

Kennedy asked the CIA director, 'How recent is that film and how did you get it?'

Theodore Tappey said, 'It is twelve hours old. We bought it at great cost, obviously from someone close to the terrorists. I can give you the details in private after this meeting, Mr President.'

Kennedy made a dismissive motion. He was not interested in details.

123

Theodore Tappey went on. 'Further information. None of the passengers have been mistreated. Also, curiously enough, the female members of the hijacking cadre have been replaced, certainly with the connivance of the Sultan. I regard this development as a little sinister.'

'In what way?' Kennedy asked sharply.

Tappey said, 'The terrorists on the plane are male. There are more of them, at least ten. They are heavily armed. It may be they are determined to slaughter their hostages if an attack is made. They may think that female guards would not be able to carry through such a slaughter. Our latest Intelligence evaluation forbids a rescue operation by force.'

Christian Klee said sharply, 'They may be using different personnel simply because this is a different phase of the operation. Or Yabril might just feel more comfortable with men, he's Arab, after all.'

Tappey smiled at him. He said, 'Chris, you know as well as I do that this replacement is an aberration. I think it's happened only once before. From your own experience in clandestine operations you know damn well this rules out a direct attack to rescue the hostages.'

Christian remained silent.

They watched the little bit of film remaining. Yabril and Theresa talking animatedly, seeming to grow more and more friendly. Then finally Yabril was actually patting her shoulder. It was obvious that he was reassuring her, giving her some good news, because Theresa laughed delightedly. Then Yabril made her an almost courtly bow, a gesture that she was under his protection and that she would come to no harm.

Francis Kennedy said, 'I'm afraid of that guy. Let's get Theresa out of there.'

Eugene Dazzy sat in his office going over all his options to help President Kennedy. First he called his mistress to tell her he would not be able to see her until the crisis was over.

Then he called his wife to check their social schedule and cancel everything. After much thought he called Bert Audick who over the last three years had been one of the most bitter enemies of the Kennedy administration.

'You've got to help us, Bert,' he said. 'I'll owe you a big one.'

Audick said, 'Listen, Eugene, in this we are all Americans together.'

Bert Audick had always been an oil man. Conceived in oil, raised in oil, matured in oil. Born wealthy, he increased that wealth a hundredfold. His privately held company was worth twenty billion dollars and he owned fifty-one per cent of it. Now at seventy he knew more about oil than any man in America. He knew every spot on the globe where it was buried beneath the earth.

In his Houston corporate headquarters, computer screens made a huge map of the world that showed the countless tankers at sea, their ports of origin and destinations. Who owned it, what price it had been bought for, how many tons it carried. He could slip any country a billion barrels of oil as easily as a man about town slips a fifty-dollar bill to a *maître d'*.

He had made part of his great fortune in the oil scare of the 1970s, when the OPEC cartel seemed to have the world by the throat. But it was Bert Audick who applied the squeeze. He had made billions of dollars out of a shortage he knew was just a sham.

But he had not done so out of pure greed. He loved oil and was outraged that this life-giving force could be bought so cheaply. He helped rig the price of oil with the romantic ardor of a youth rioting against the injustices of society. And then he had given a great part of his booty away to worthy charities.

He had built non-profit hospitals, free nursing homes for the elderly, art museums. He had established thousands of college scholarships for the under-privileged without regard to race or creed. He had of course taken care of his relatives and friends, made distant cousins rich. He loved his country and his fellow Americans, and never contributed money for anything outside the United States. Except of course for the necessary bribes to foreign officials.

He did not love the political rulers of his country or its crushing machinery of government. They were too often his enemies with their regulatory laws, their anti-trust suits, their interference in his private affairs. Bert Audick was fiercely loyal to his country but it was his business, his democratic right, to squeeze his fellow citizens, make them pay for the oil he worshipped.

Audick believed in holding his oil in the ground as long as possible. He often thought lovingly of those billions and billions of dollars that lay in great puddles beneath the desert sands of Sherhaben and other places on earth, safe as they could be. He would keep that vast golden lake as long as possible. He would buy other people's oil, buy other oil companies. He would drill the oceans, buy into England's North Sea, get a piece of Venezuela. And then there was Alaska. Only he knew the size of the great fortune that lay beneath the ice.

Bert Audick had already swallowed two of the giant American oil companies, gulping them like a frog swallowing flies, so his enemies said. For he did look like a frog, the wide mouth in a great jowly face, eyes slightly popping. And yet he was an impressive man, tall with large bulk, massive head with a jaw as boxy as his oil rigs. But in his business dealings he was as lithe as a ballet dancer. He had a sophisticated intelligence apparatus that gave him a far more accurate estimate of the oil reserves of the Soviet Union than the CIA. Information he did not share with the United States government, as why should he, since he paid an enormous amount of cash to get it, and its value to him was its exclusivity.

And he truly believed, as did many Americans, indeed he proclaimed it as a lynchpin of a democratic society, that a free citizen in a free country has the right to put his personal interests ahead of the aims of elected government officials. For if every citizen promoted his own welfare how could the country not prosper?

On Dazzy's recommendation, Francis Kennedy agreed to see this man. Audick was one of the most influential men in the United States. Not with the public, to them he was a shadowy figure presented in the newspapers and *Fortune* magazine as a cartoonish Czar of Oil. But he had enormous influence with the elected representatives in the Congress and the House. He also had many friends and associates in the few thousand men who controlled the most important industries of the Unites States – the Socrates Club. The men in this club controlled the printed media, the TV media, ran companies that controlled the buying and shipping of grain, the Wall Street giants, the colossi of electronics and automobiles, the Templars of Money who ran the banks. And, most importantly, Audick was a personal friend of the Sultan of Sherhaben.

Bert Audick was escorted into the Cabinet Room where Francis Kennedy was meeting with his staff and the appropriate Cabinet members. Everybody understood that he had come not only to help the President but to caution him. It was Audick's oil company that had fifty billion dollars invested in the oilfields of Sherhaben and the principal city of Dak. He had a magical voice, friendly, persuasive and so sure of what he was saying that it seemed as if a cathedral bell tolled at the end of every sentence. He could have been a superb politician except that in all his life he had never been able to lie to the people of his country on political issues, and his beliefs were so far right that he could not be elected in the most conservative districts of the country.

He started off by expressing his deepest sympathy for

Kennedy with such sincerity that there could be no doubt that the rescuing of Theresa Kennedy was the main reason he had offered his service.

'Mr President,' he said to Kennedy, 'I have been in touch with all the people I know in the Arab countries. They disavow this terrible affair, and they will help us in any way they can. I am a personal friend of the Sultan of Sherhaben and I will bring all my influence to bear on him. I've been informed that there is certain evidence that the Sultan is part of the hijacking conspiracy and the murder of the Pope. I assure you that no matter what the evidence, the Sultan is on our side.'

This alerted Francis Kennedy. How did Audick know about the evidence against the Sultan? Only the Cabinet members and his own staff held this information and it had been given the highest security classification. Could it be that Audick was the Sultan's free ticket to absolution after this affair was over? That there would be a scenario where the Sultan and Audick would be the saviors of his daughter?

Then Audick went on. 'Mr President, I understand that you are prepared to meet the hijackers' demands. I think that is wise. True, it will be a blow to American prestige and authority. That can be repaired later. But let me give you my personal assurance on the matter that I know is closest to your heart. No harm will come to your daughter.' The cathedral bell in his voice tolled with assurance.

It was the certainty of this speech that made Kennedy doubt him. For Kennedy knew from his own experience in political warfare, that complete confidence is the most suspect quality in any kind of leader.

'Do you think we should give them the man who killed the Pope?' Kennedy asked. It didn't matter, he had given orders to grant Yabril everything, but he wanted to hear this man keep talking.

Audick misread the question. 'Mr President, I know you are a Catholic. But remember that this is mostly a Protestant country. Simply as a foreign policy matter we need not make the killing of a Catholic pope the most important of our concerns. It is necessary for the future of our country that we preserve our lifelines of oil. We need Sherhaben. We must act carefully, with intelligence, not passion. Again here is my personal assurance. Your daughter is safe.'

He was beyond a doubt sincere, and impressive. Kennedy thanked him and walked him to the door. When he was gone Kennedy turned to Dazzy and asked, 'What the hell did he really say?'

'He just wants to make points with you,' Dazzy said. 'And maybe he doesn't want you to get any ideas of using that fifty billion dollar oil city of Dak as a bargaining chip.' He paused for a moment and then said, 'I think he can help.'

Kennedy seemed lost in thought.

Christian took advantage of this and said, 'Francis, I have to see you alone.'

Kennedy excused himself from the meeting and took Christian to the Oval Office. Though Kennedy hated using the small room the other rooms of the White House were filled with advisors and staff planners awaiting final instructions.

Christian liked the Oval Office. The light coming from the three long bullet-proof windows, the two flags, one cheerful red white and blue flag of the country on the right of the small desk, on the left the Presidential flag more somber and dark blue. Kennedy waved to Christian to sit down. Christian wondered how the man could look so composed. Though they had been such close friends for so many years, he could detect no sign of emotion.

Kennedy said, 'A whole hour of useless discussion. I've already made clear we're going to give them everything they want. Still they go on.'

'We have more trouble,' Christian said. 'Right here at home. I hate to bother you but it's necessary.'

He briefed Kennedy on the atom bomb letter. 'It's probably all bullshit,' Christian said. 'There's one chance in a million there is such a bomb. But if there is it could destroy ten city blocks and kill thousands of people. Plus radioactive fallout would make the area uninhabitable for who knows how long. So we have to treat that one chance in a million seriously.'

Francis Kennedy sighed. 'I hope to hell you're not going to tell me this is tied up with the hijacker?'

'Who knows,' Christian said.

'Then keep this contained, clean it up without a fuss,' Kennedy said. 'Slap the Atomic Secrecy classification on it.' Kennedy flipped on the speaker to Eugene Dazzy's office. 'Euge,' he said, 'get me copies of the classified Atomic Secrecy Act. Also get me all the medical files on brain research. And set up a meeting with Dr Annaccone. Make the meeting after this hostage crisis is over.'

Kennedy switched off the intercom. He stood up and glanced through the windows of the Oval Office. He absently ran his hand over the furled cloth of the American flag. For a long time he stood there thinking.

Christian wondered at the man's ability to separate this from everything else that was happening. He said, 'I think this is a domestic problem, some kind of psychological fallout that has been predicted in think tank studies for years. We're closing in on some subjects.'

Again Kennedy stood by the window for a long time. Then he spoke softly. 'Chris, seal this off from every other compartment of government. This is just between you and me. Not even Dazzy or other members of my personal staff. It's just too much to add on to everything else.'

'I understand,' Christian said.

Eugene Dazzy walked into the office. 'Guess what,' he said. 'The Italian Security Chief, Sebbediccio, was delighted when he heard that we're going to turn that Pope-killer loose to that guy in Sherhaben. He says now he can track him down and kill the bastard.'

The city of Washington overflowed with the influx of media people and their equipment from all over the world. There was a hum in the air as in a crowded stadium and the streets were filled with people who gathered in vast crowds in front of the White House as if to share the suffering of the President. The skies were filled with transport aircraft, specially chartered overseas airliners. Government advisors and their staff were flying to foreign countries to confer about the crisis. Special envoys were flying in. An extra division of Army troops was brought into the area to patrol the city and guard the White House approaches. The huge crowds seemed to be prepared to maintain an all night vigil as if to reassure Francis Xavier Kennedy that he was not alone in his trouble. The noise of that crowd enveloped the White House and its grounds.

On television most of the regular programming had been preempted to report on the hostage crisis and to speculate on the fate of Theresa Kennedy. The word had leaked out that the President was willing to free the killer of the Pope to obtain the release of the hostages and his daughter. Political experts recruited by the TV networks were divided about the wisdom of such a move but they all agreed that President Kennedy had acted too hastily, that the opening demands were certainly open to negotiation as in the many other hostage crises over the past years. They more or less agreed that the President had panicked because of the danger to his daughter.

Some channels had religious groups praying for Theresa Kennedy's safety and pleading to their audiences to suppress any feelings of hatred for fellow human beings no matter how evil. There were a few channels, mercifully with small audiences, that had satirists portraying Francis Kennedy and the United States as a spineless wimp caving in to threats.

And then there was the eminent left-wing lawyer, Whitney Cheever III. He made his position clear, the terrorists were freedom fighters, that was understood and they had only done what any revolutionary would do in the fight against the worldwide tyranny of the United States. But Cheever's main point was that Kennedy was paying a huge ransom from the coffers of the United States government to ransom his daughter. Did anyone think, Cheever asked his audience, that if the hostages were no relation, or if they were black, the President would be so pliable? As for the killer of the Pope being released, Cheever did not condone assassination, but that killing was a problem for the Italian government, certainly not the United States with its separation of state and church. But then Cheever concluded by approving the deal Kennedy had made to release the hostages. It could lead to a new period of negotiation and understanding with the revolutionary forces in the world today. And it showed that the authority of the State could not so cavalierly trample the rights of individuals in the dust.

All these programs were recorded by the monitoring government agencies, the film of Cheever's speech was put in a special file for the attention of the Attorney General, Christian Klee.

And while all of this was going on the crowds outside the White House grew larger and larger through the night. The streets of Washington were clogged with vehicles and pedestrians all converging on the symbolic heart of their country. Many of them brought food and drink for the long vigil. They would wait through the night with their President, Francis Xavier Kennedy.

When Francis Kennedy went to bed Tuesday night, he was almost certain that the hostages would be released the next day. The stage set, Yabril would win. Romeo was being prepared for his trip to Sherhaben and freedom. On Kennedy's night table were stacked the papers prepared by the

CIA, the National Security Council, the Secretary of State, the Secretary of Defense and the covering memos from his own staff. When his butler, Jefferson brought him hot chocolate and biscuits, he settled down to read these reports.

They all said the same thing. His complete capitulation was an enormous loss of prestige for the United States. It would be obvious that the most powerful country on earth had been defeated and humiliated by a handful of determined men.

He barely noticed when Jefferson came into the room and wheeled out the table, asking him if he wanted more hot chocolate, saying, 'Good night, Mr President.'

He read on and read between the lines. He brought together the seemingly divergent viewpoints of the different agencies. He tried to put himself in the role of a rival world power reading these reports.

They would see that America was a country on its last decadent leg, an obese, arthritic giant getting its nose tweaked by malevolent urchins. Within the country itself there was an internal blood draining of the giant. The rich were getting much richer, the poor sank into the ground. The middle class fought desperately for their balance in the good life.

The world held the giant money-making America in contempt, waited for it to fall off its own fatty wealth. Perhaps not in a decade, not in two, perhaps not in three, but suddenly it would be a giant carcass eaten away by all these cancers.

Francis Kennedy recognized that this latest crisis, the killing of the Pope, the hijacking of the plane, the kidnapping of his daughter, the humiliating demands to which he had yielded, was a deliberate, planned blow at the moral authority of the United States.

But then there was also the internal attack, the planting of the atom bomb, if there was one. The cancer from within. The psychological profiles had predicted that such a thing could happen and precautions had been taken. But not enough. And it had to be internal, it was too dangerous a ploy for terrorists, too rough a tickling of the obese giant. It was a wild card that the terrorists, no matter how bold, would never dare to play. It could open a Pandora's box of repression. And they knew that if governments, especially the United States, suspended the laws of civil liberties, any terrorist organization could easily be destroyed.

Francis Kennedy studied the reports that summarized known terrorist groups and the nations that lent them support. He was surprised to see that China gave the terrorist Arab groups more financial support than did Russia. But then that was understandable. The Russian-Arab axis was caught in a trap. The Russians had to support the Arabs against Israel because Israel was the American presence in the Far East. The Arab feudal regimes had to worry that Russia wanted to make their state apparatus disappear into communism. But there were specific organizations that at this moment did not seem to be linked with Yabril's operation; it was too bizarre and without a definite advantage for the cost involved, the negative aspect. The Russians had never advocated free enterprise in terrorism. But there were the splinter Arab groups, the Arab Front, the Saiqua, the PLFP-G and the host of others designated with just initials. Then there were the Red Brigades, the Japanese Red Brigade, the Italian Red Brigade, the German Red Brigade which had swallowed up all the German splinter groups in a murderous internecine warfare. And there was the famous 'First Hundred' that the CIA claimed did not exist but was simply a loose international linkage. Yabril and Romeo were classified as part of that group also known as the Christs of Violence. This infamous First Hundred was regarded with horror by even China and Russia.

But what was curious was that not even the First Hundred seemed to be controlling Yabril. Yabril had planned and executed this operation on his own. True he had drawn cadre and material from the Red Brigades, but he had done this by using Romeo. Romeo had certainly been his right-hand man, but nothing else showed, except the final and surprising link with the Sultan of Sherhaben.

Finally it was all too much for Kennedy. In the morning, on the Wednesday, the negotiations would be completed, the hostages would be safe. Now there was nothing he could do but wait. All this took longer than the twenty-four-hour deadline, but it was all agreed. The terrorists would surely be patient.

Before he fell asleep he thought of his daughter Theresa and her bright confident smile as she spoke to Yabril, the reincarnated smile of his own dead uncles. The he fell into tortured dreams, and groaned aloud, called for help. When Jefferson came running to the bedroom, he stared at the agonized, sleep-masked face of the President, waited a moment, then woke him out of his nightmare. He brought in another cup of hot chocolate and gave Kennedy the sleeping pill the doctor had ordered.

As Francis Kennedy slept, Yabril rose. Yabril loved the early morning hours of the desert, the coolness fleeing the sun's eternal fire, the sky turning to incandescent red. He always thought in these moments of the Mohammedan Lucifer, called Azazel.

The angel Azazel, standing before God, refused to worship the creation of man, and God hurled Azazel from Paradise to ignite these desert sands into hellfire. Oh, to be Azazel, Yabril thought. When he had been young and romantic, he had used Azazel as his first operational name.

This morning the sun flaming with heat made him dizzy. Though he stood in the shaded door of the air-conditioned aircraft, a terrible surf of scalding air sent his body reeling backwards. He felt nausea and wondered if it was because of what he had to do. Now he would commit the final irrevocable act, the last move in his chess game of terror that he had not told Romeo, the Sultan of Sherhaben, nor the supporting cadres of the Red Brigades. A final sacrilege.

Far away by the air terminal he saw the perimeter of the Sultan's troops that kept the thousands of newspaper, magazine and TV reporters at bay. He had the attention of the entire world, he held the daughter of the President of the United States. He had a bigger audience than any ruler, any Pope, any prophet. With his hands he could mask the globe. Yabril turned away from the open door to face the plane's interior.

Four men of his new cadre were eating breakfast in the First Class cabin. Twenty-four hours had passed since he gave the ultimatum. Time was up. He made them hurry, then sent them on their errands. One went with Yabril's handwritten order to the Chief of Security on the perimeter, ordering TV crews to be allowed close to the plane. Another of the cadre was given the stack of printed leaflets proclaiming that since Yabril's demands had not been met within the twenty-four hour deadline, one of the hostages would be executed.

Two men of the cadre were ordered to bring the President's daughter back from the isolated front row of the tourist cabin into the First Class cabin and Yabril's presence.

When Theresa Kennedy came into the First Class cabin and saw Yabril waiting her face relaxed into a relieved smile. Yabril wondered how she could look so lovely after spending these days on the plane. It was the skin, he thought, she had no oil in her skin to collect dirt. He smiled back at her and said in a kindly half-joking way, 'You look beautiful but a little untidy. Freshen yourself, put on some make-up, comb your hair. The TV cameras are waiting for us. The whole world will be watching and I don't want them to think I've been treating you badly.'

He let her into the aircraft toilet and waited. She took almost twenty minutes. He could hear flushing and he imagined her sitting there like a little girl and he felt a needle-like pain lance his heart and he prayed, Azazel, Azazel be with me now. And then he heard the great thunderous roar of the crowd standing in the blazing desert sun; they had read the leaflets. He heard the vast threshing of the TV mobile units as they came closer.

Theresa Kennedy appeared. Yabril saw a look of sadness in her face. Also stubbornness. She had decided she would not speak, would not let him force her to make his videotape. She was well scrubbed, pretty, with faith in her strength. But she had lost some of her heart's innocence. Now she smiled at Yabril and said, 'I won't speak.'

Yabril took her by the hand. 'I just want them to see you,' he said. He led her to the open door of the aircraft, they stood on the ledge. The red air of the desert sun fired their bodies. Six mobile TV tractors seemed to guard the plane like prehistoric monsters, almost blocking the huge crowd beyond the perimeter. 'Just smile at them,' Yabril said, 'I want your father to see you are safe.'

At that moment he smoothed the back of her head, feeling the silky hair, pulling it to leave the nape of her neck clear, the white ivory skin so frighteningly pale, the only blemish a small black mole that stole down to her shoulder.

She flinched at his touch and turned to see what he was doing. His grip tightened and he forced her head to turn front so that the TV cameras could see the beauty of her face. The desert sun framed her in gold, his body was her shadow.

One hand raised and pressed against the roof door to give him balance, he pressed the front of his body into her back so that they teetered on the very edge, a tender touching. He drew the pistol with his right hand and held it to the exposed skin of her neck. And then before she could understand the touch of metal, he pulled the trigger and let her body fall from his.

She seemed to float upward into the air, into the sun, into the halo of her own blood. Then her body tumbled so that her legs pointed to the sky and then turned again before she hit the cement runway, lying there, smashed beyond any mortality, with her ruined head cratered by the burning sun. At first the only sound was the whirring of TV cameras and mobile trucks, the grinding of sands, then rolling over the desert came the wail of thousands of people, an endless scream of terror.

The primal sound, without the expected jubilance, surprised Yabril. He stepped back from the door to the interior of the aircraft. He saw his cadre men looking at him with horror, with loathing, with almost animal terror. He said to them, 'Allah be praised,' but they did not answer him. He waited for a long moment then told them curtly, 'Now the world will know how serious we are. Now they will give us what we ask.' But his mind noted that the roar of the crowd had not had the ecstasy he expected. The reaction of his own men seemed ominous. The execution of the daughter of the President of the United States, that extinction of some exempt symbol of authority violated a taboo he had not taken into account. But so be it.

He thought for one moment of Theresa Kennedy, her sweet face, the violet smell of her white neck, he thought of her body caught in the red halo of dust. And he thought, let her be with Azazel, flung from the golden frame of heaven down into the desert sands for ever and for ever. His mind held one last picture of her body, her loose-fitting white slacks bunched around her calves, showing her sandalled painted feet. Fire from the sun rolled through the aircraft and he was drenched in sweat. And he thought, I am Azazel.

Before dawn on Wednesday morning, deep in nightmare, filled with the anguished roar of a huge crowd, President Kennedy found himself being shaken by Jefferson. And oddly, though he was now awake, he could still hear the massive roll of thunderous voices that penetrated the walls of the White House.

There was something different about Jefferson, he did not look like a maker of hot chocolate, a brusher of clothes, the deferential servant. He looked more like a man who had tensed his body and face to receive a dreadful blow. He was saying over and over, 'Mr President, wake up, wake up.'

But Kennedy was awake and he said, 'What the hell is that noise?'

The whole bedroom was awash with light from the overhead chandelier and an ensemble of men stood behind Jefferson. He recognized the naval officer who was the White House physician, the warrant officer entrusted with the nuclear football, and there was Eugene Dazzy, Arthur Wix and Christian Klee. He felt Jefferson almost lifting him out of the bed to stand him on his feet, then in a quick motion slipping him into a bathrobe. For some reason his knees sagged and Jefferson held him up.

All the men seemed stricken, the features of their faces disturbed, ghostly white, eyes unusually wide open, no lids. Kennedy stood facing them with astonishment and then with an overwhelming dread. For a moment he lost all sense of vision, all sense of hearing, the dread poisoned every sense in his being. The naval officer opened his black bag and took out a needle already prepared and Kennedy said, 'No.' He looked at the other men one by one but they did not speak. He said tentatively, 'It's OK, Chris, I knew he would do it. He killed Theresa, didn't he?' And then waited for Christian to say no, that it was something else, that it was some natural catastrophe, the blowing up of a nuclear installation, the death of a great head of state, the sinking of a battleship in the Persian Gulf, a devastating earthquake, flood, fire, pestilence. Anything else. But Christian, his face so pale, said, 'Yes.'

And it seemed to Kennedy that some long illness, some lurking fever crested over. He felt his body bow and then was aware that Christian was beside him, as if to shield him from the rest of the people in the room because his face was streaming with tears and he was gasping to get his breath. Then all the people in the room seemed to come close, the doctor plunged the needle into his arm, Jefferson and Christian were lowering his body into the bed.

They waited for Francis Kennedy to recover from shock. Finally he gave them instructions. To commence all the necessary staff sections, to set up liaisons with congressional leaders and to clear the crowds from the streets of the city and from around the White House. And to bar all media. And that he would meet with them at seven a.m.

Just before daybreak, Francis Kennedy made everyone leave. Then Jefferson brought in a tray of hot chocolate and biscuits. 'I'll be right outside the door,' Jefferson said. 'I'll check with you every half-hour if that is OK, Mr President.' Kennedy nodded and Jefferson left.

Kennedy extinguished all the lights. The room was gray with approaching daybreak. He forced himself to think clearly. His grief was a calculated attack by an enemy and he tried to repulse that grief. He looked at the long oval windows, remembering as he always did that they were special glass, he could look out but nobody could see in, and they were bullet-proof. Also the vista he faced, the White House grounds, the buildings beyond, were occupied by Secret Service personnel, the park with special beams and dog patrols. He himself was always safe, Christian had kept his promise. But there had been no way to keep Theresa safe.

It was over, she was dead. And now after the initial wave of grief he wondered at his calmness. Was it because she had insisted on living her own life after her mother died? Refused to share his life in the White House because she was far to the left of both parties and so his political opponent? Was it a lack of love for his daughter?

He absolved himself. He loved Theresa and she was dead. It was just that he had been preparing himself for that death in the last days. His unconscious and cunning paranoia, rooted in the Kennedy history, had sent him warning signals.

There was the co-ordination of the killing of the Pope and the hijacking of the plane that held the daughter of the leader of the most powerful nation on earth. There was the delay in the demands until the assassin had been in place and captured in the United States. Then the deliberate arrogance of the demand for the release of the assassin of the Pope.

By a supreme effort of will Francis Kennedy banished all personal feeling from his mind. He tried to follow a logical line. It was really all so simple.

On the surface a pope and a young girl had lost their lives. Essentially not terribly important in the world scale. Religious leaders can be canonized, young girls mourned with sweet regret. But there was something else. The people the world over would have a contempt for the United States and its leaders. Other attacks would be launched in ways not foreseen. Authority spat upon cannot keep order. Authority taunted and defeated cannot presume to hold together the fabric of its particular civilization. How could he defend?

The door of the bedroom opened and light flooded in from the hall. But the bedroom now aglow with the rising sun blotted it out. Jefferson, in fresh shirt and jacket, wheeled the breakfast table through and prepared it for Kennedy. He gave Kennedy a searching look, as if enquiring whether to stay, then finally went out.

Kennedy felt tears on his face and knew suddenly that they were the tears of impotence. Again he realized that his grief was gone and wondered. Then he felt consciously overwhelming his brain the waves of blood carrying terrible rage, a rage he had never known and which all his life he had disdained in others. He tried to resist it.

He thought now of how his staff had tried to comfort him.

Christian had shown his personal affection shared over

long years, Christian had embraced him, helped him to his bed. Oddblood Gray, usually so cool and impersonal, had gripped him by the shoulders and just whispered, 'I'm sorry, I'm goddamn sorry.'

Arthur Wix and Eugene Dazzy had been more reserved. They had touched him briefly and murmured something he could not hear. And Kennedy had noted the fact that Eugene Dazzy as his Chief of Staff had been one of the first to leave the bedroom to get things organized in the rest of the White House. Wix had left with Dazzy. As head of the National Security Council he had urgent work and perhaps he was afraid of hearing some wild order of retaliation from a man overwrought by a father's grief.

In the short time before Jefferson came back with the breakfast, Francis Kennedy knew his life would be completely different, perhaps out of his control. He tried to exclude anger from his reasoning process.

He remembered strategy sessions in which such events were discussed. Arthur Wix had been the most emphatic on strong action. He brought up the former President, Jimmy Carter.

'When Iran held those hostages, Carter should have taken strong action, no matter what the cost,' Wix said. 'When he ran for re-election the public spurned him because they could not forgive him the months of humiliation they had to bear, that they, the strongest nation on earth, had to eat shit a small country shoveled over them.'

Otto Gray said, 'Carter knew that, he was a very decent man. He put getting the hostages back alive ahead of his re-election.'

Wix said scornfully, 'Sure Carter was decent, but so what? That wasn't his job. The American public didn't care if the hostages got out alive. Not at the price we paid.'

Dazzy said, 'It came out OK. Not one of those hostages was killed. They all got back to their families.'

'You're missing the point,' Wix said. 'Carter lost the

142

election. When all he had to do was make a military attack and kill a bunch of Iranians even if the hostages got killed in the process. Then he would have been re-elected in a landslide.'

Eugene Dazzy said thoughtfully, 'You know, it could have gone the other way. Carter holding off and the hostages still getting killed. Then Carter, despite his good conscience would have been driven out of office.'

'Tarred and feathered,' Wix said, in his voice his habitual disdain for anyone ineffectual. 'His balls cut off.'

Francis Kennedy did not remember what he had said in that discussion. But now his mind went back almost forty years. He was a seven-year-old boy playing on the lawn and around the porticoes of the White House, running in flowers and grass and then on rich marble, playing with the children of his Uncle John and Uncle Bobby. And the two uncles so tall and slim and fair had played with them a few minutes before ascending into their waiting helicopter like gods. As a child he had always liked his Uncle John best because he had known all his secrets. He had once seen his Uncle John kiss a woman, then lead her into his bedroom. And he had seen them come out an hour later. He had never forgotten the look on Uncle John's face, such a happy look as if he had received some unforgettable gift. They had never noticed the little boy hidden behind one of the tables in the hallway. At that time of innocence the Secret Service were not so close to the President.

And there were other scenes out of his childhood, vivid tableaux of power. His two uncles being treated like royalty by men and women much older than themselves. The music starting when his Uncle John stepped out on the lawn, all faces turning toward him, the cessation of speech until he spoke. His two uncles sharing their power and their grace in wearing it. How confidently they waited for the helicopters to drop out of the sky, how safe they seemed surrounded by strong men who shielded them from hurt, how they were whisked up to the heavens, how grandly they descended from aloft . . .

Their smiles gave light, their godhead flashed knowledge and command from their eyes, the magnetism radiated from their bodies. And with all this they took the time to play with the little boys and girls who were their sons and daughters, their nieces and nephews, playing with the utmost seriousness, gods who visited tiny mortals in their keeping. And then. And then . . .

President John Fitzgerald Kennedy, born rich, married to a woman who was beautiful, leader of the most powerful nation on earth, had been destroyed by such an insignificant little man with only a cheap thin tube of iron. A little man without any resources, with barely the money to buy a rifle. And so, a little boy, Francis Xavier Kennedy, had been banished from the fairyland of power and happiness that he thought would last for ever.

Francis Kennedy, forty years later, remembered that terrible day. He had been playing with the other children and then had gone apart to sit absorbed in the Rose Garden tearing pink silky flowers into ribbons. And then suddenly a swarm of women weeping hysterically swept them into the White House. Into the Red Room, he remembered, filled with people weeping, until his mother had appeared and taken him away. And he had never seen his little friends again, had never played on that lawn again, or dodged around the portico pillars or the brown-gold marble floors.

But he had watched on television, with his weeping mother, the funeral of Uncle John, the gun carriage, the riderless horse, the millions of grief-stricken people and had seen his little playmate as one of the actors on the worldwide stage. And his Uncle Bobby and his Aunt Jackie. His mother at some point took him into her arms and said, 'Don't look, don't look,' and he was blinded by her long hair and sticky tears.

And then his Uncle Bobby was killed a few years later,

and his mother had taken him to a hunting lodge in the Sierra mountains that had no television. It was not until he was an adult that he saw the tapes of that murder. And again it was an insignificant man with a cheap tube of iron who destroyed what was left of his mother's world.

Now, the shaft of yellow light from the open door cut through his memories and he saw that Jefferson had wheeled in a fresh table. Francis Kennedy said quietly, 'Take that away and give me an hour. Don't interrupt me before then.' He had rarely spoken so abruptly or sternly and Jefferson gave him an appraising look. Then he said, 'Yes, Mr President,' and wheeled the table back out and closed the door.

The sun was strong enough to light the bedroom, yet not to give it heat. But the throb of Washington entered the room. The television trucks were filling streets outside the gates and countless car motors hummed like a giant swarm of insects. Planes flew constantly overhead, all military – air space had been closed to civilian traffic.

President Francis Kennedy tried to fight the overwhelming rage, the bitter nauseating bile in his mouth. What was supposed to be the greatest triumph of his life had proved to be his greatest misfortune. He had been elected to the Presidency and his wife had died before he assumed the office. His great programs for a utopian America had been smashed to bits by Congress and he had not been strong enough to muster his will, his strength, his intelligence to overcome that defeat. And now his daughter had paid the price for his ambition and his dreams. Nauseating saliva made him gag as it ran over his tongue and lips. His body seemed to fill with a poison that weakened him in every limb and only rage could make him well, and at that moment something happened in his brain, an electric charge fighting the sickness of his body cells. So much energy flowed through his body that he flung his arms outward, fists clenched to the now sun-filled windows.

He had power, he would use that power. He could make his enemies tremble, he could make their saliva bitter in their mouths. He could sweep away all the small insignificant men with their cheap tubes of iron, all those who had brought such tragedy into his life and to his family.

He felt now like a man who, long sick and feeble, is finally cured of a serious illness, wakes one morning and has regained his strength. He felt an exhilaration, almost a peace he had not felt since before his wife died. He sat on the bed and tried to control his feelings, to restore caution and a rational train of thought. More calmly he reviewed all his options and all their dangers and then finally he knew what he must do and what dangers he must forestall. He felt one last thrust of pain that his daughter no longer existed. Then he opened the door and called out for Jefferson.

BOOK III

8

Just four hours after the killing of his daughter, Francis Kennedy met with his staff. They breakfasted in the family dining room of the White House with its small fireplace and yellow-white walls and rugs. This was a preliminary to the larger meeting which would include the Vice President, the Cabinet and the representatives of the Senate and Congress.

Eugene Dazzy as Chief of the President's staff had prepared a memo of staff recommendations made in the hours since the killing of Theresa Kennedy. Otto Gray had briefed by phone the leaders of Congress, Wix had briefed members of the National Security Council and the Chief of the Central Intelligence Agency and the Chief of the Joint Chiefs of Staff. Christian Klee had consulted with no one. The situation was beyond any legal theory.

While Kennedy read Dazzy's memo, the other men ate breakfast. Wix had milk and toast. Oddblood Gray tried to eat some eggs and bacon and a small steak but gave up after a mouthful of each. Dazzy and Klee made no pretense of eating, they watched Kennedy reading the memo.

Kennedy put the six pages on top of Dazzy's briefcase. None of the recommendations even approached what he planned to do. But he had to be careful.

'Thank you,' he said. 'It covers all options you could have foreseen. But I have something else in mind.' He smiled at them to show he was in command of his feelings, not knowing how ghastly the smile appeared on his bloodless face.

Eugene Dazzy said, 'Mr President, could you please initial the memo to show it's been read.' Kennedy noted the formality of the language and knew it came from the awkwardness of the terrible event of the morning. Kennedy wrote 'NO' in large letters on the memo and signed it in full.

Then he surveyed each one of them in turn before he spoke. He wanted to show them how calm he was, that he was not acting in angry grief, that he was rational, that what he was going to say was logic unmarred by personal emotions. He spoke very slowly.

'I wanted to tell you what I'm going to tell everyone else at the meeting later. This is not a consultation. This is a plea for your support. I want us all to be together on this. Anybody who feels strongly that they can't go along, I want them to resign right now before we go into that meeting.'

Very quickly Kennedy gave his analysis of the situation and what he was going to do. He could see that they were stunned, even Christian. Not by the analysis but the solution he proposed. And they were stunned too by the curtness he showed. He was rarely ceremonious in their staff meetings. His invitation of their resignations was completely out of character. He made it very clear to them. They would go along without any discussion or resign.

This demand by President Francis Kennedy to the four men of his Senior Staff was in the nature of an insult to a close family. The President's Senior Staff was personally picked by the President. They were responsible solely to him. He could appoint them, he could fire them. The President was like a Cyclops with one brain and four arms. The Senior Staff were his four arms. It went without saying that they would approve Francis Kennedy's decision. But it was an insult that they were forbidden to analyze and discuss it. After all, they were not the Cabinet members who were approved by Congress. The Presdent's staff must sink with the President.

Official distinctions aside, the Senior Staff was always

much closer to the President than anyone in the Cabinet or Congress. In fact the staff had evolved to weaken the different Secretaries in the Cabinet. And in Kennedy's case, all four of these men were his closest personal friends. And since the death of his wife, his only personal family. Francis Kennedy knew that he had insulted them and he watched their reactions closely.

Christian Klee, he saw, didn't give a damn. Christian was his dearest and closest friend of the four. The one who had always held him in some sort of reverence. Which always surprised Kennedy because he knew that Christian valued physical bravery and knew that Kennedy had a fear of assassination. It was Christian who had begged Francis to run for the Presidency and guaranteed his personal safety if he was appointed Attorney General and head of the FBI and Secret Service. And Christian believed in Kennedy's political theories more as a patriot than as a left-wing idealist. Kennedy knew that Christian was with him.

Arthur Wix was the man whose reaction he feared most. Wix believed in analyzing every situation in depth. Francis Kennedy had met Wix ten years before when he had first run for the Senate. Wix was an Eastern Seaboard liberal, a professor of ethics and political science at Columbia University. He was also a very rich man who had contempt for money. Their relationship had grown into a friendship based on their intellectual gifts. Kennedy thought Arthur Wix the most intelligent man he had ever met. Wix thought Kennedy the most moral man in politics. This was not, could not be, the basis of a warm friendship, but did form the basis for a trusting relationship. Kennedy could see that Wix had to make an effort to restrain a protest against his ultimatum. But restrain he did, he would agree out of trust.

The third man, his Chief of Staff, Eugene Dazzy, Kennedy was sure of because of the political realities involved. Eugene Dazzy had been the head of a huge computer firm ten years before when Francis Kennedy first entered politics. He had

151

been a cruncher, a man who could eat up rival companies, but he had come originally from a poor family, and he retained his sense of justice more out of a practical sense than a romantic idealism. He had come to a belief that concentrated money held too much power in America and that in the long run this would destroy the true democracy. And so when Francis Kennedy entered politics under the banner of a true social democracy, Eugene Dazzy organized the financial support that helped Kennedy ascend to the Presidency.

During that time a curious friendship had evolved. Dazzy was an eccentric. A big wheel businessman who cared nothing for outward appearances. A huge rumpled man who dressed in cheap suits and ties, he also always wore a Walkman on his head to listen to music while in his office. He loved music and he loved young women but his marriage had lasted thirty years. His wife often claimed he wore the Walkman radio cassette player to discourage conversation, not to listen to music. She never mentioned his women.

But what had astonished and fascinated Francis Kennedy most was that Eugene Dazzy was such a paradox. A rare combination of hard-headed businessman and a devoted student of literature with a passionate love of poetry, especially Yeats. Dazzy had been chosen as staff because he was a master of the 'half yes' and still had the sensitivity to give a flat 'no' without making an implacable enemy. But he was the President's shield against the Cabinet and the Congress. The Secretary of State and the Speaker of the House had to satisfy Dazzy before they could get to see the President.

But what brought Kennedy and Dazzy close in a more personal way was the exercise to pardon criminals. Dazzy would screen the Presidential Pardoning Committee for outlandish cases where a citizen had been mangled by the judicial system or the bureaucracy and would persuade the President to use his power to pardon. 'Look at it this way,'

Eugene Dazzy told Francis Kennedy, 'the President of the United States has the power to pardon anyone. The Congress and the Courts can't interfere. Think how that burns their ass. You have to use that power as much as you can, just for that reason.'

Francis Kennedy had not studied and practised the law without being subjected to the best of cons. So in the beginning he had watched Dazzy closely on the pardoning business. But each case Dazzy brought to his attention had its own particular poetic merit. And they rarely disagreed. And these special regal mercies to their fellow man created a special bond between them.

And so Kennedy could see that Dazzy would agree, would not insist on a discussion. Which left only Oddblood Gray.

Oddblood Gray's association with Francis Kennedy was longer than that of Wix and Dazzy. Gray had been a firebrand on the left of the black political movement when they first met. A tall imposing man, he had been a brilliant scholar and a first-rate orator in his college days. Kennedy had spotted under the firebrand, a man with a natural courtesy and diplomacy, a man who could persuade without threats. And then, in a potentially violent situation in New York, Kennedy had won Oddblood's admiration and trust. Kennedy had used his extraordinary legal skills, his intelligence and charm, his complete lack of racial bias to defuse the situation, to serve the agreement and win the admiration of both sides.

Afterwards Oddblood Gray had asked him, 'How the hell did you do that?'

Kennedy had grinned and said, 'Easy. I convinced them there was nothing in it for me.'

After that, Oddblood Gray had drifted from the left of the movement to the right. Which lessened his power in the movement but brought him to the center of national power. He had supported Kennedy in his political career, urged him to run for the Presidency. Kennedy appointed Oddblood

153

Gray to his staff as liaison to the Congress, head man to get the President's bills pushed through.

Now Oddblood Gray yielded his judgment to his trust.

But superseding all this, even the admiration all four of these men held for Kennedy, for his moral character, his intelligence, his charm, his unending string of achievements, was their respect for his gallantry when he met with his first defeat, the death of his wife, Catherine. That he persevered in his campaign for the Presidency, that he still pursued his aims for political and social reform. And their affection for him deepened when he searched for some personal stability by designating the four of them as his personal family.

Each night at least one of them ate dinner with Kennedy in the White House. There were many times when they all dined together as friends. Enthusiastically making plans for the betterment of their country, discussing the details of particular bills to Congress, and outlining strategies to deal with foreign countries. They were often as excited as when they were young college students as they plotted against the oligarchy of the rich, and still they suffered over the anarchy of the poor. After dinner they all went home to dream of a new and better America that they would create together.

But they had been defeated by the Congress and the Socrates Club. Not only President Francis Xavier Kennedy, but all of them.

And so now when Kennedy looked around the breakfast table, they all nodded their assent and then prepared to go to the general meeting in the Cabinet Room. It was eleven a.m. Wednesday morning in Washington.

In the Cabinet Room the most politically significant people in the government had gathered to decide what the country should do. There was the Vice President Helen DuPray, there were the members of the Cabinet, the head of the CIA, the Chief of the Joint Chiefs of Staff, not usually present at such meetings but instructed to be so by Eugene Dazzy following the President's request. When Kennedy entered the room they all rose.

Kennedy motioned to them to sit down.

Only the Secretary of State remained standing. He said, 'Mr President, all of us here wish to express our heartbreak at your loss. We offer our personal condolences, our love. We assure you of our utmost loyalty and devotion in your personal crisis and this crisis in our nation. We are here to give you more than our professional counsel. We are here to give you our indiviaul devotion.' There were tears in the eyes of the Secretary of State. And he was a man noted for his coolness and reserve.

Kennedy bowed his head for a moment. He was the only man in the room who seemed to show no emotion except for the paleness of his face. He looked at them all for a long moment, as if acknowledging every person in the room, their feelings of affection and his gratefulness. Knowing that he was about to shatter this good feeling. He said, 'I want to thank all of you, I am grateful and I am counting on you. But now I beg all of you to put my personal misfortune out of the context of this meeting. We are here to decide what is best for our country. This is our duty and sacred obligation. The decisions I have made are strictly non-personal.' He paused for a moment to let the shock and recognition sink in that he alone would control.

Helen DuPray thought, 'Oh Christ, he's going to do it.'

Kennedy went on. 'This meeting will deal with our options. I doubt that any of your options will be taken but I must give you your opportunity to argue them. But first let me present my scenario. Let me say that I have the support of my personal staff.' He paused again to project all his personal magnetism. He stood up and said, 'One: The analysis. All the recent tragic events have been the dynamic of one boldly conceived and ruthlessly executed masterplan. The murder of the Pope on Easter Sunday, the hijacking of

155

the plane on the same day, the deliberate logistical impossibility of the demands for the release of the hostages, and though I agreed to meet all those demands, finally the unnecessary murder of my daughter early this morning. And even the capture of the assassin of the Pope here in our country, an event far beyond the realm of any chance of destiny, that too was part of the overall plan so that they could demand the release of the assassin. The evidence supporting this analysis is overwhelming.'

He could see the looks of disbelief on their faces. He paused and then went on.

'But what could be the purpose of such a terrifying and complicated scenario? There is in the world today a contempt for authority, the authority of the state, but specifically a contempt for the moral authority of the United States. It goes far beyond the usual historical contempt for authority exhibited by the young, which is often a good thing. The purpose of this terrorist plan is to discredit the United States as an authority figure. Not only in the lives of billions of common people but in the eyes of the governments of the world. We must at some time answer these challenges and that time is now.

'For the record. Russia has no part in this plot. The Arab states have no part. Except for Sherhaben. Certainly the terrorist worldwide underground know as the "First Hundred" gave logistical and personnel support. But the evidence points to only one man in control. And it seems that he does not accept being controlled except perhaps by the Sultan of Sherhaben.'

Again he paused. He was surprised at his own calm. He went on.

'We now know for certain that the Sultan is an accomplice. His troops are stationed to guard the aircraft from outside attacks, not to help us with the hostages. The Sultan claims to act in our interest, but in reality is involved in these acts. However, to give him his due, there is evidence

156

that he did not know that Yabril would murder my daughter.'

Kennedy paused but it was not a pause that inviteed interruption. He glanced around the table to again impress them with his calmness. Then he said, 'Second: The prognosis. This is not the usual hostage situation. This is a clever plot to humiliate the United States to the utmost. To make the United States beg for the return of the hostages after suffering a series of humiliations that make us seem impotent. It is a situation that will be wrung dry for weeks with media coverage all over the world. And with no guarantee that all the remaining hostages will be returned safely. Under those circumstances I cannot imagine anything but chaos afterwards. Our own people will lose faith in us and our country.'

Again Kennedy paused, he saw that he was making an impression now. That the men in this room understood that he had a point. He went on.

'Remedies: I've studied the memo on options we have. I think they are the usual lame recourses of the past. Economic sanctions, armed rescue missions, political arm-twisting, concessions given in secret while maintaining that we never negotiate with terrorists. The concern that the Soviet Union will refuse to permit us to make a large-scale military assault in the Persian Gulf. All these imply that we must submit and accept our profound humiliation in the eyes of the world. And in my opinion more of the hostages may well be lost.'

The Secretary of State interrupted. 'My department has just received a definite promise from the Sultan of Sherhaben to release all the hostages when the terrorists' demands have been met. He is outraged by Yabril's action and claims he is ready to launch an assault on the plane. He has secured Yabril's promise to release fifty of the hostages now to show good faith.'

Kennedy stared at him for a moment. The cerulean eyes seemed veined with tiny black dots. Then his voice, cold with taut courtesy, and so controlled that the words rang metallically, said, 'Mr Secretary, when I am done, everyone here will be given time to speak. Until that time please do not interrupt. Their offer will be suppressed, it will not be made known to the media.'

The Secretary of State was obviously surprised. The President had never spoken so coolly to him before, had never so blatantly shown his power. The Secretary of State bowed his head to study his copy of the memo, only his cheeks reddened slightly. Kennedy went on.

'Solution: I hereby instruct the Chief of Staff to direct and plan an air strike on the oilfields of Sherhaben and their industrial oil city of Dak. The mission of the airstrike will be the destruction of all oil equipment, drilling rigs, pipelines, etc. The city will be destroyed. Four hours before the bombing leaflets will be dropped on the city warning the inhabitants to evacuate. The air strike will take place exactly thirty-six hours from now. That is on Thursday, eleven p.m. Washington time.'

There was dead silence in the room that held more than thirty people who wielded all the arms of power in America. Kennedy went on.

'The Secretary of State will contact the necessary countries for overflight approval. He will make it plain to them that any refusal will be a cessation of all economic and military accommodations with this country. That the results of a refusal will be dire.'

The Secretary of State seemed to levitate from his seat to protest, then restrained himself. There was a murmur through the room of suprise or shock.

Kennedy held up his hands, the gesture almost angry, but he was smiling at them, a smile that seemed to be one of reassurance. He seemed to become less commanding, almost casual, smiling at the Secretary of State and speaking directly to him. 'The Secretary of State will send to me, at once, the Ambassador from the Sultan of Sherhaben. I will tell the

Ambassador this: the Sultan must deliver up the hostages by tomorrow afternoon. He will deliver up the terrorist, Yabril, in a way that he will not be able to take his own life. If the Sultan refuses, the entire country of Sherhaben itself will cease to exist.' Kennedy paused for a moment, the room was absolutely still. 'This meeting has the highest security classification. There will be no leaks. If there are, the most extreme action under the law will be taken. Now you all can speak.'

He could see the audience was stunned by his words, that his staff had looked down refusing to meet the eyes of the others in the room.

Kennedy sat down, sprawling in his black leather chair, his legs out from under the table and visible to the side. He stared out into the Rose Garden as the meeting continued.

He heard the Secretary of State say, 'Mr President, again I must argue your decision. This will be a disaster for the United States. We will become a pariah among nations by using our force to crush a small nation.' And the voice went on and on but he could not hear the words.

Then he heard the voice of the Secretary of the Interior, a voice almost flat and yet commanding attention. 'Mr President, when we destroy Dak, we destroy fifty billion American dollars, that's American oil company money, money the middle class of American spent to buy stock in the oil companies. Also, we curtail our import of oil. The price of gasoline will double for the consumers of this country.'

There was the confused babble of other arguments. Why did the city of Dak have to be destroyed before any satisfaction was given? There were many avenues still be be explored. The great danger was in acting too hastily. Kennedy looked at his watch. This had been going on for over an hour. He stood up.

'I thank each of you for your advice,' he said. 'Certainly the Sultan of Sherhaben could save the city of Dak by meeting my demands immediately. But he won't. The city of Dak must be destroyed or our threats will be ignored. The

159

alternative is for us to govern a country that any man with courage and small weapons can humiliate. Then we might as well scrap our Navy and Army and save the money. I see our course very clearly and I will follow it.

'Now as to the fifty billion dollar loss to American stockholders. Bert Audick heads the consortium that owns that property. He has already made his fifty billion dollars and more. We will do our best to help him, of course. I will permit Mr Audick an opportunity to save his investment in another way. I am sending a plane to Sherhaben to pick up the hostages and a military plane to transport the terrorists to this country to stand trial. The Secretary of State will invite Mr Audick to go to Sherhaben on one of those planes. His job will be to help persuade the Sultan to accept my terms. To persuade him that the only way to save the city of Dak, the country of Sherhaben and the American oil in that country is to accede to my demands. That's the deal.'

The Secretary of Defense said, 'If the Sultan does not agree that means we lose two more planes, Audick, and the hostages.'

Kennedy said, 'Most likely. Let's see if Audick has the balls. But he's smart. He will know as I do, that the Sultan must agree. I'm so sure that I am also sending the National Security Advisor, Mr Wix.'

The CIA Chief said, 'Mr President, you must know that the anti-aircraft guns around Dak are manned by Americans on civilian contract to the Sherhaben government and the American oil companies. Specially trained Americans who man missile sites. They may put up a fight.'

Kennedy smiled. 'Audick will order them to evacuate. Of course, as Americans, if they fight us they will be traitors, and the Americans who pay them will also be prosecuted as traitors.'

He paused to let that sink in. Audick would be prosecuted. He turned to Christian. 'Chris, you can start working on the legal end.'

Among those present were two members of the legislative branch. The Senate Majority Leader, Thomas Lambertino, and the Speaker of the House, Alfred Jintz. It was the Senator who spoke first. He said, 'I think this too drastic a course of action to be taken without a full discussion in both houses of the Congress.'

Kennedy said to him courteously, 'With all due respect, there is no time. And it is within my power as the Chief Executive to take this action. Without question the legislative branch can review it later and take action as they see fit. But I sincerely hope that Congress will support me and this nation in its extremity.'

Senator Lambertino said almost sorrowfully, 'This is dire, the consequences severe. I implore you, Mr President not to act so quickly.'

For the first time Francis Kennedy became less than courteous. 'I haven't won a battle in the Congress in all the three years of my administration,' he said. 'We can argue all the complicated options until the hostages are dead and the United States is ridiculed in every nation and every little village in the world. I hold by my analysis and my solution, my decision is within my power as Chief Executive. When the crisis is over I will go before the people and give them a full report. Until then, I remind you all again, this discussion is of the highest classification. Now I know you all have work to do. Report your progress to my Chief of Staff.'

It was Alfred Jintz, the Speaker of the House, who answered. 'Mr President,' he said, 'I had hoped not to say this. But Congress now insists that you remove yourself from these negotiations. Therefore, I must give notice that this very day the Congress and the Senate will do everything to prevent your course of action on the grounds that your personal tragedy makes you incompetent.'

Kennedy stood over them. His face with its beautifully planed lines was frozen into a mask. His satiny blue eyes were as blind as a statue. 'You do so at your peril,' he said, 'and America's.' He left the room.

All the others rose and remained standing until the door closed behind him and his two Secret Service bodyguards.

In the Cabinet room, there was a flurry of movement, a babble of voices. Oddblood Gray huddled with Senator Lambertino and Congressman Jintz. But their faces were grim, their voices cold. The Congressmen said, 'We can't allow this to happen. I think the President's staff has been delinquent in not dissuading him from this course of action.'

Oddblood Gray said, 'He convinced me he was not acting out of personal anger. That it was the most effective solution to the problem. It is dire of course, but so are the times. We can't let the situation be drawn out. That can be catastrophic.'

Senator Lambertino said, 'This is the first time that I have ever known Francis Kennedy to act in so high-handed a fashion. He was always a courteous President to the legislative branch. He could at least have pretended that we were party to the decision process.'

Oddblood Gray said, 'He's under a great deal of stress. It would be helpful if the Congress did not add to that stress.' Fat chance, he thought as he said it.

Congressman Jintz said worriedly, 'Stress may be the issue here.' Oddblood Gray thought, Oh shit, hastily said a cordial farewell and ran back to his office to make the hundreds of calls to members of the Congress.

The National Security Advisor, Arthur Wix, was trying to sound out the Secretary of Defense. And making sure that there would be an immediate meeting with the Joint Chiefs of Staff. But the Secretary of Defense seemed to be stunned by events and mumbled his answers, agreeing but not volunteering anything.

Eugene Dazzy had noted Oddblood Gray's difficulties with the legislators. There was going to be big trouble. He looked around for Christian Klee. But Klee had vanished, which surprised Dazzy, it was not like him to disappear at a crucial moment like this.

Dazzy turned to Helen DuPray. 'What do you think?' he asked her.

She looked at him coolly. She was a very beautiful woman, Dazzy thought. He must invite her to dinner. Then she said, 'I think you and the rest of the President's staff have let him down. His response to this crisis is far too drastic.'

Dazzy was angry. 'His position has logic and even if we disagreed we have to support him.' He did not tell her of Kennedy's ultimatum to the staff.

Helen DuPray said, 'It's how Francis presented it. Obviously, Congress will try to take the negotiations out of his hands. They will try to suspend him from office.'

'Over the graves of his staff,' Dazzy said.

Helen DuPray said to him quietly, 'Please be careful. Our country is in great danger.'

In his office Dazzy got his personal secretaries working, his aides briefed other staff on what was to be done. It would be his job to co-ordinate everything for the President. When the direct telephone line from the President's office rang, he answered it so quickly that papers flew out of his hand and on to the floor. He said, 'Yes, Mr President.' And he heard the calm voice of Francis Kennedy say the words he knew he would say, that he had been dreading to hear.

Kennedy said, 'Euge?' in that questioning, friendly way, 'I'd like to have my personal staff meet me in the Yellow Oval Room. Arrange to show the film of the television news coverage of my daughter's death.'

Eugene Dazzy said, 'Sir, maybe it would be better if you witnessed that by yourself, without anyone present.'

'No,' the President said. 'I want all of us to see it together.'

'Yes, sir,' Eugene Dazzy said. He did not mention that the personal staff had already viewed the film of Theresa Kennedy's murder.

9

On this Wednesday afternoon Peter Cloot was certainly the only official in Washington who paid almost no attention to the news that the President's daughter had been murdered. His energies were focused on the nuclear bomb threat.

As Deputy Chief of the FBI he had almost full responsibility for that agency. Christian Klee was the titular head but only to hold the reins of power, to bring it more firmly under the direction of the Attorney General's office which Christian Klee also held. That combination of offices had always bothered Peter Cloot. It also bothered him that the Secret Service had also been placed under Klee. That was too much concentration of power for Cloot's taste. He also knew that there was a separate elite branch ostensibly in the FBI Table of Organization that Klee administered directly and that this Special Security branch was composed of Christian Klee's former colleagues in the CIA. That affronted him.

But this nuclear threat was Peter Cloot's baby. He would run this show. And luckily there were specific directives to guide him and he had attended the think-tank seminars that directly addressed the problem of internal nuclear threats. If anyone was an expert on this particular situation it was Cloot. And there was no shortage of manpower. During Klee's tenure the number of FBI personnel had increased threefold.

When he had first seen the threatening letter with its accompanying diagrams Cloot had taken the immediate action as outlined in the standing directives. He had also felt a thrill of fear. Up to this time there had been hundreds of such threats, only a few of them plausible, but none so convincing as this. All these threats had been kept secret again according to directives.

Immediately, Cloot forwarded the letter to the Department of Energy Command Post in Maryland, using the special communications facilities for this purpose only. He also alerted the Department of Energy Search Teams based in Las Vegas called NEST. NEST was already flying their pod containing tools and detection equipment to New York. Other planes would be flying specially trained personnel into the city, where they would use disguised vans loaded with sophisticated equipment to explore the streets of New York. Helicopters would be used, men on foot carrying Geiger counter briefcases would cover the city. But all this was not Cloot's headache. All he would have to do was supply armed FBI guards to protect the NEST searchers. Cloot's job was to find the villains.

The Maryland Department of Energy people had studied the letter and sent him a psychological profile of the writer. Those guys were really amazing, Cloot thought, he didn't know how they did it. Of course one of the obvious clues was that the letter did not ask for money. Also it did define a definite political position. As soon as he got the profile Cloot sent a thousand men checking.

The profile had said that the letter writer was probably very young and highly educated. That he was probably a student of physics in a highly rated university. And on this information alone Cloot in a matter of hours had two very good suspects and after that it was amazingly easy. He had worked all through the night, directing his field office teams. When he was informed of the murder of Theresa Kennedy he had resolutely put it out of his mind except for the flash that all this stuff might be linked together in some way. But his job tonight was to find the author of the nuclear bomb threat. Thank God the bastard was an idealist. It made him easier to track down. There were a million greedy son-of-a-bitches who would do something like this for money and it would have been tough to find them.

While he waited for the information to come in he put the files of all previous nuclear threats though his computer. There had never been a nuclear weapon found, and those blackmailers who had been caught while trying to collect their bribe money had confessed that there had never been one. They had, some of them, been men with a smattering of science. Others had picked up convincing information from a left-wing magazine that had printed an article describing how to make a nuclear weapon. The magazine had been leaned on not to publish that article but it had gone to the Supreme Court which had ruled that suppression would be a violation of free speech. Even thinking of that now made Peter Cloot tremble with rage. The fucking country was going to destroy itself. One thing he noted with interest. None of the over two hundred cases had involved a woman or black or even a foreign terrorist. They were all fucking true blue greedy American men.

When he had finished with the computer files he thought a minute about his boss, Christian Klee. He really didn't like the way Klee was running things. Klee thought the whole job of the FBI was to guard the President of the United States. Klee didn't use only the Secret Service Division but had special squads in every FBI office in the country whose main job was to sniff out possible dangers to the office of the President. Klee diverted a great deal of manpower from other operations of the FBI to do this.

Cloot was leery of Christian Klee's power, his Special Division of ex-CIA men. What the hell did they do? Peter Cloot didn't know and he had every right to know. That division reported directly to Klee and that was a very bad thing in a government agency so sensitive to public opinion as the FBI. So far nothing had happened. Peter Cloot spent

166

a great deal of time covering his ass, making sure that he could not be caught in the fireworks when that Special Division pulled some shit that would bring the Congress down on their heads with their special investigation committees.

At one in the morning Cloot's assistant deputy came in to report that two suspects were under surveillance, proof was in hand that confirmed the psychological profile, there was other circumstantial evidence. Only the order to make the arrest was needed.

Cloot said to his deputy, 'I have to brief Klee first. Stay here while I call him.'

Cloot knew that Klee would be in the President's Chief of Staff office or that the omnipotent White House telephone operators would track him down if he was not. He got Klee on his first try.

'We have that special case all wrapped up,' Cloot told him. 'But I think I should brief you before we bring them in, can you come over?'

Klee's voice was strained. 'No, I cannot. I have to be with the President now, surely you understand that.'

'Shall I just go ahead and fill you in later?' Cloot asked.

There was a long pause at the other end. Then Klee said, 'I think we have time for you to come over here. If I'm not available, just wait. But you have to rush.'

'I'm on my way,' Peter Cloot said.

It had not been necessary to either of them to suggest doing the briefing over the phone. That was out of the question. Anybody could pick messages out of the infinite trailways of airspace.

Peter Cloot got to the White House and was escorted into a small briefing room. Christian Klee was waiting for him, his prosthesis was off and he was massaging his stump through his stocking.

'I only have a few minutes,' Klee said. 'Big meeting with the President.'

'Jesus, I'm sorry about that,' Cloot said. 'How is he taking it?'

Klee shook his head, 'You can't ever tell with Francis. He seems OK.' He shook his head in a sort of bewilderment then said briskly, 'OK, let's have it.' He looked at Cloot with a sort of distaste. The man's physical appearance always irritated him.

Cloot never looked tired and he was one of those men whose shirt and suit never got wrinkled. He always wore ties of knitted wool with square knots, usually of a light gray color and sometimes a sort of bloody black.

'We spotted them,' Cloot said. 'Two young kids, twenty years old in MIT nuclear labs. Geniuses, IQs in the 160s, come from wealthy families, left wing, marched with the nuclear protesters. They have access to classified memoranda. They fit the think-tank profile. They are sitting in their lab up in Boston, working on some government and university project. A couple of months ago they came to New York and a buddy got them laid and they loved it. He was sure it was their first time. A deadly combination, idealism and the raging hormones of youth. Right now I have them sealed off.'

'Do you have any firm evidence?' Christian asked. 'Anything concrete?'

'We're not trying them or even indicting them,' Cloot said. 'This is preventive arrest as authorized under the atom bomb laws. Once we have them, they'll confess and tell us where the damn thing is if there is one. I don't think there is. I think that part is bullshit. But they certainly wrote the letter. They fit the profile. Also the date of the letter, the day they registered at the Hilton in New York. That's the clincher.'

Christian had often marveled at the resources of all the government agencies with their computers and high-grade electronic gear. It was amazing that they could eavesdrop on anyone anywhere no matter what precautions were taken. That computers could scan hotel registers all over the city in

168

less than an hour. And other complicated serious things. At ghastly expense, of course.

'OK, we'll grab them,' Christian said. 'But I'm not sure you can make them confess. They're smart kids.'

Cloot stared into Christian's eyes. 'OK, Chris, they don't confess, we're a civilized country. We just let the bomb explode and kill thousands of people.' He smiled for a moment almost maliciously. 'Or you go to the President and make him sign a Medical Interrogation order. Section IX of the Atomic Weapons Control Act.'

Which was what Cloot had been coming to all the time.

Christian had been avoiding the same thought all night. He had always been shocked that the country like the United States could have such a secret law. The press could easily have uncovered it but again there was that covenant between the owners of the media and the governors of the country. So the law was not really known to the public, as was true of many laws governing nuclear science.

Christian knew Section IX very well. As a lawyer he had marveled at it. It was that savagery in the law that had always repelled him.

Section IX essentially gave the President the right to order a chemical brain scan that had been developed to make anyone tell the truth, a lie detector right in the brain. The law had been especially designed to extract information about the planting of a nuclear device, it fitted this case perfectly. There would be no torture, the victim would suffer no physical pain. Simply the neurons of the brain would be measured so that he would invariably tell the truth when asked questions. It would be humane, the only catch being that nobody really knew what happened to the brain after the operation. Experiments indicated that in rare cases there would be some loss of memory, some slight loss of functioning. He would not be retarded, that would be unconscionable, but as the old joke had it, there went the music lessons. The only catch was that there was a ten per cent chance that there would be complete memory loss. Complete long-term amnesia. The subject's entire past would be erased.

Christian said, 'Just a long shot, but could this be linking up with the hijacking and the Pope? Even that guy being captured on Long Island looks like a trick. Could this all be a part of it, a smoke screen, a booby trap?'

Cloot studied him for a long time as if debating his answer. But when the answer came it showed no doubt. 'Not a chance,' Cloot said. 'This is one of those famous coincidences of history.'

'That always lead to tragedy,' Christian said wryly.

Cloot went on. 'These two kids are just crazy in their own genius style. They are political. They are obsessed by nuclear danger to the whole world. They are not interested in current political quarrels. They don't give a shit about the Arabs and Israel or the poor and rich in America. Or the Democrats and Republicans. They just want the globe to rotate faster on its axis. You know.' He smiled contemptuously. 'They all think they're God. Nothing can touch them.'

But Christian's mind was at rest on one thing. If Cloot did not suspect a link between this crazy atom bomb stuff and the hijackers, there could be none. Cloot suspected everyone of everything. But then another thought occurred. There was political shrapnel flying all around with these two problems. Don't move too fast, he thought. Francis was in terrible danger now. Kennedy would have to be protected. Maybe they could play one off against the other.

He said to Cloot, 'Listen, Peter, I want this to be the most secret of operations. Seal it off from everybody else. I want those two kids grabbed and put into the hospital detention facility we have here in Washington. Just you and me and the agents we use from Special Division. Shove the agents' noses into the Atomic Security Act, absolute secrecy. Nobody sees them, nobody talks to them except me. I'll do the interrogation personally.'

Cloot gave him a funny look. He didn't like the operation

being turned over to Klee's Special Division. 'The medical team will want to see a Presidential order before they shoot chemicals into those kids' brains.'

Christian said, 'I'll ask the President.'

Peter Cloot said casually, 'Time is crucial on this thing, and you said nobody interrogates except you. Does that include me? What if you're tied up with the President?'

Christian Klee smiled and said, 'Don't worry, I'll be there. Nobody but me, Peter. Now give me the details.' He had other things on his mind. Shortly he would meet with the chiefs of his FBI Special Division and order them to mount an electronic and computer surveillance on the most important members of the Congress and the Socrates Club.

The Department of Energy's command post in Maryland, officially known as the Emergency Action Co-ordination Team, sat on think-tank profiles of possible nuclear bomb terrorists. It had profiles of psychotics and how they might pick up enough knowledge to present a plausible threat. It had profiles on idealists who might try to explode a nuclear weapon. It had profiles on fortune hunters who would demand money, agents of foreign terrorist organizations who might bring themselves to commit such a terrible act. They had profiles that fitted almost exactly the case of Adam Gresse and Henry Tibbot. This made it an easy task for Peter Cloot and his three thousand agents.

Adam Gresse and Henry Tibbot were certified as scientific whiz-kids at the age of twelve, and were furnished with the finest education that a wealthy and a supportive federal government can provide. They were instructed in the humanities, in art, in law, and the immortal struggle of the upstarts in history, Antigone, Baudelaire, Sacco and Vanzetti, Martin Luther King. They were as perfectly educated as civilization could make them.

But they were young and their raging hormones warred with their sensibilities. The vulgarities of life, political and intellectual, produced in them what could only be called a contempt for an existing world that must be made better.

They admitted even to themselves that the excitement of stealing their materials from the official programs, the gratification of solving the technical problems, the excitement of finally constructing a viable and explodable two-kiloton nuclear bomb, gave them such a feeling of power that it cemented their final decision to use it. But they never intended it to explode.

They would plant the bomb. They would send a letter to the *New York Times* that declared their intent. That this was a warning that if nations continued to manufacture nuclear weapons to further their own narrow interests, then every individual had the right to also develop nuclear weapons to stop the dictators of the world from burning the entire universe into cinders. They had no knowledge of the elaborate and secret measures that had been taken by government agencies to thwart just such threats. They also had no knowledge of how the real world worked. They could not conceive of that underworld of everyday life where seemingly inconsequential carelessness has dire consequences. It was beyond their comprehension that a mail clerk in the *New York Times* would get the sack of incoming letters two days late and so hold up their warning letter. Nor did they realize that that letter would immediately be handed over to the FBI.

And so they had planted their tiny atomic bomb, a bomb they had constructed with much labor and ingenuity. They were perhaps so proud of their labors they could not resist using it for such a high cause.

Adam Gresse and Henry Tibbot kept watching the newspapers, but their letter did not appear on the front page of the *New York Times*. There were no news items. They had not been given the opportunity to lead the authorities to the bomb after their demand was met. They were being ignored. This frightened them and yet angered them too. Now the bomb would explode and cause thousands of deaths. But possibly that would be for the best. How else could the world be alerted to the dangers of the use of atomic power? How else could the necessary action be taken for the men in authority to install the proper safeguards? They had calculated that the bomb would destroy at least four to six square blocks of New York City. They regretted that, it would cost a certain amount of human lives. But it would be a small price for mankind to pay to see the error of its ways. Impregnable safeguards must be established, the making of nuclear bombs must be banned by all the nations of the world.

On Wednesday Gresse and Tibbot worked in the laboratory until after everyone in the Institute had gone home and then they argued whether they should make a phone call to alert the authorities. At the beginning it had never been their intention to actually let the bomb go off. They had wanted to see their letter of warning published in the *New York Times* and then they would go back to New York to disarm the bomb. But now it seemed a war of wills. Were they to be treated as children, sneered at, when they could accomplish so much for humanity? Or would they be listened to? In all conscience they could not go on with their scientific work if it was to be misused by the political establishment.

They had chosen New York City to be punished because on their visits there they had been so horrified by the feeling of evil that seemed to them to pervade the streets. The threatening beggars, the insolent drivers of wheeled vehicles, the rudeness of clerks in stores, the countless burglaries, street muggings and murders. They had been particularly revolted by Times Square, that area so crowded with people that it seemed to them like a huge sink of cockroaches. In Times Square, the pimps, the dope pushers, the whores seemed so menacing that Gresse and Tibbot had retreated with fright to their hotel room uptown. And so with fully justifiable anger they had decided to plant the bomb in Times

173

Square itself. They would have been horrified and hurt if it was pointed out to them that most of the faces they had seen in Times Square were black.

Adam Gresse and Henry Tibbot were as shocked as the rest of the nation when the television screen showed the murder of Theresa Kennedy. But they were also a little annoyed that this diverted attention from their own operation, more important to the fate of humanity.

But they had become nervous. Adam had heard peculiar clickings on his telephone, he had noticed that his car seemed to be followed, he had felt an electric disturbance when certain men passed him in the street. He told Tibbot about these things.

Henry Tibbot was very tall and very lean. He seemed to be made of wires joined together with scraps of flesh and transparent skin. He had a better scientific mind than Adam and stronger nerves. 'You're reacting like all criminals act,' he told Adam. 'It's normal. Every time there's a knock on the door I think it's the Feds.'

'And if it is one time?' Adam Gresse asked.

'Keep your mouth shut until the lawyer comes,' Henry Tibbot said. 'That is the most important thing. We would get twenty-five years just for writing the letter. So if the bomb explodes it will just be a few more years.'

'Do you think they can trace us?' Adam asked.

'Not a chance,' Henry Tibbot said. 'We've gotten rid of anything that could be evidence. Christ, are we smarter than them or not?'

This reassured Adam but he wavered a bit. 'Maybe we should make a call and tell them where it is,' he said.

'No,' Henry Tibbot said. 'They are on the alert now. They will be ready to zero in on our call. That will be the only way to catch us. Just remember, if things go wrong, just keep your mouth shut. Now let's go to work.'

Adam Gresse and Henry Tibbot were working late in the lab this night really because they wanted to be together.

They wanted to talk about what they had done, what recourse they had. They were young men of intense will, they had been brought up to have the courage of their convictions, to detest an authority that refused to be swayed with a reasonable argument. Though they conjured up mathematical formulae that might change the destiny of mankind they had no idea of the complicated relationships of civilization. Glorious achievers, they had not yet grown into humanity.

As they were preparing to leave, the phone rang. It was Henry Tibbot's father. He said to Henry. 'Son, listen carefully. You are about to be arrested by the FBI. Say nothing to them until they let you see your lawyer. Say nothing. I know . . .'

At that moment the door of the room opened and men swarmed in.

10

The rich in America, without a doubt are more socially conscious than the rich in any other country of the world. This is true, of course, especially of the extremely rich, those who own and run huge corporations, exercise their economic strength in politics, propagandize all the forms of culture. And this was especially true of members of the Socrates Club.

The Socratic Country Golf and Tennis Club of Southern California had been formed and founded nearly seventy years before by real estate, media, cinematic and agricultural tycoons, as a politically liberal organization devoted to recreation. It was an exclusive resort, you had to be very rich to join. Technically, you could be black or white, Jewish or Catholic, man or woman, artist or magnate. In reality there were very few blacks and no women.

The Socrates Country Club finally evolved into a club for the very enlightened, very responsible rich. Prudently, it had an ex-Deputy Director of CIA Operations as head of Security Systems, and its electronic fences were the highest in America.

Four times a year, the club was used as a retreat for fifty to a hundred men who in effect owned nearly everything in America. They came for a week and in that week, service was reduced to a minimum. They made their own beds, served their own drinks and sometimes even cooked their own food in the evening on outside barbecues. There were of course some waiters, cooks and some maids, and there were the inevitable aides to those important men; after all, the world of American business and politics could not come to a stop while they recharged their spiritual batteries.

During this week-long stay these men would gather into small groups and spend their time in private discussions. They would have seminars headed by distinguished professors from the most famous universities on questions of ethics, philosophy, the responsibility of the fortunate elite to the less fortunate in society. They would be given lectures by famous scientists on the benefits and dangers of nuclear weapons, brain research, the exploration of space, on economics.

They also played tennis, swam in the pool, had backgammon and bridge tournaments and discussed far into the night on virtue and villainy, on women and love, on marriage and adventure. And these were responsible men, the most responsible men in American society. But they were trying to do two things, they were trying to become better human beings while recovering their adolescence, and they were trying to unite in bringing about a better society as they perceived a better society to be.

After a week together they returned to their normal lives, refreshed with new hope, a desire to help mankind, and a sharper perception of how all their activities could be meshed to preserve the structure of their society, and perhaps with closer personal relationships that could help them do business.

This present week had started on the Monday after Easter Sunday. Because of the crisis in national affairs with the killing of the Pope and the hijacking of the plane carrying the President's daughter and her murderer, the attendance had dropped to less than twenty.

George Greenwell was the oldest of these men. At eighty, he could still play tennis doubles, but out of a carefully bred courtesy did not inflict himself on the younger men who would be forced to play a forgiving style. Yet, he was still a tiger in long sessions of backgammon.

Greenwell considered the national crisis none of his business unless it involved grain in some way. For his company was privately owned and controlled most of the wheat in America. His shining hour had been thirty years ago when the United States had embargoed grain to Russia as a political ploy, to muscle Russia in the Cold War.

George Greenwell was a patriot but not a fool. He knew that Russia could not yield to such pressure. He also knew that the Washington-imposed embargo would ruin American farmers. So he had defied the President of the United States and shipped the forbidden grain by diverting it to other foreign companies who relayed it to Russia. He had brought down the wrath of the American executive branch on his head. Laws had been presented to Congress to curtail the power of his family-held company, to make it public, to put it under some sort of regulatory control. But the Greenwell money contributed to Congressmen and Senators soon put a stop to that nonsense.

Greenwell loved the Socrates Country Club because it was luxurious but not so luxurious as to invite the envy of the less fortunate. Also, because it was not known to the media, for its members owned most of the TV stations, newspapers and magazines. And also it made him feel young, enabled him to participate socially in the lives of younger men who were equal in power.

He had made a good deal of extra money during that grain embargo, buying wheat and corn from embattled American farmers and selling it dear to a desperate Russia. But he had made sure that the extra money benefited the people of the United States. What he had done had been a matter of principle. The principle being that his intelligence was greater than that of government functionaries. The extra money, hundreds of millions of dollars, had been funneled into museums, educational foundations, cultural programs on TV, especially music, which was Greenwell's passion.

Greenwell prided himself on being civilized, based on his being sent to the best schools, where he was taught the social behavior of the responsible rich and a civilized feeling of affection for his fellow man. That he was strict in the dealings of his business was his form of art, the mathematics of millions of tons of grain sounded in his brain as clearly and sweetly as chamber music.

One of his few moments of ignoble rage had occurred when a very young professor of music in a university chair established by one of his foundations, published an essay that elevated jazz and rock and roll music above Brahms and Schubert and dared to call classical music 'Funeral'. George Greenwell had vowed to have the professor removed from his chair but his inbred courtesy prevailed. Then, the young professor had published another essay in which the unfortunate phrase was 'Who gives a shit for Beethoven?' And that was the end of that. The young professor never really knew what happened but a year later he was giving piano lessons in San Francisco.

The Socrates Country Club had one extravagance, an elaborate communications system. On the morning that President Francis Xavier Kennedy announced to the secret meeting of advisors the ultimatum he would give the Sultan of Sherhaben, all twenty men in the Socrates Country Club had the information within the hour. Only Greenwell knew that this information had been supplied by Oliver Ollifant, the Oracle.

It was a matter of doctrine that these yearly retreats of great men were in no way used to plan or conspire, they were merely a way to communicate general aims, to inform a general interest, to clear away confusion as to the general operation of a complicated society. In that spirit George Greenwell on Tuesday invited three other great men to one of the cheerful pavilions just outside the tennis courts to have lunch.

The youngest of these men, Lawrence Salentine, owned a major TV network and some cable companies, newspapers in three major cities, five magazines and one of the biggest movie studios. He owned, through subsidiaries, a major book publishing house. He also owned twelve local TV stations in major cities. That was in the United States alone. He was also a powerful presence in the media of foreign countries. Salentine was a lean and handsome man with a full head of silvery hair, a crown of curls in the style of Roman emperors, but now much in fashion with intellectuals and people in the arts and in Hollywood. He was impressive in appearance and in intelligence and one of the men most powerful in the politics of America. There was not a Congressman or Senator or a member of the Cabinet who did not return his calls. He had not however been able to become friendly with President Kennedy who seemed to take personally the hostile attitude the media had shown the new social programs prepared by the Kennedy administration.

The second man was Louis Inch who owned more important real estate in the great cities of America then any other company or individual. As a very young man – he was now only forty – he had grasped the true importance of building straight up into the air to an impossible degree. He had bought rights over many existing buildings and then built the enormous skyscrapers that increased the value of buildings tenfold. He more than anyone else had changed the very light of the cities, had made endless dark canyons between commercial buildings that proved to be more needed than anyone supposed. He had made rents so impossibly high in New York, Chicago and Los Angeles for ordinary families that only the rich or very well off could live comfortable in these cities. He had cajoled and bribed municipal officials to give him tax abatements; to do away with rent controls to such a degree that he boasted that his rental charge per square foot would someday equal Tokyo.

His political influence, despite his ambitions, was less than anyone in the pavilion. He had a personal wealth of over five billion dollars but his wealth had the inertness of land. His real strength was more sinister. His aims were the amassing of wealth and power without real responsibility to the civilization he lived in. He had extensively bribed public officials and construction unions. He owned casino hotels in Atlantic City and Las Vegas, shutting out the mobster overlords in these cities. But in doing so he had, in the curious way of the democratic process, acquired the support of the secondary figures in criminal empires. All the service departments of his numerous hotels had contracts with firms that supplied tableware, laundry services, service help, liquor and food. He was a link through subordinates to this criminal underworld. He was of course not so foolish as to make that link more than a microscopic thread. The name of Louis Inch had never been touched by any hint of scandal. This was due not only to his sense of prudence, but the absence of any personal charisma.

For all these reasons he was actually despised on a personal level by nearly all the members of the Socrates Country Club. But he was tolerated because by his particular brand of magic, one of his own companies owned land surrounding the Club and there was always the underlying fear that he might put up cheap housing for fifty thousand families and drown the Club area with Hispanics and blacks.

The third man, Martin Mutford, was dressed in slacks, pure white shirt open at the collar, and a blue blazer. He was a man of sixty and he was perhaps the most powerful of the four because he had control of money in so many different areas. As a young man he had been one of the Oracle's protégés and had learned his lessons well. In fact he would tell admiring stories about the Oracle to the delight of the audiences in the Socrates Country Club.

181

Martin Mutford had based his career on investment banking and because of the influence of the Oracle, or so he claimed, he had gotten off to a shaky start. As a young man he had been sexually vigorous, as he put it. Much to his surprise the husbands of some of the young wives he seduced came looking for him not for revenge but for a bank loan. They had little smiles on their faces and were very good-humored. By instinct he granted the personal loans which he knew they would never pay back. At the time he did not know that loan officials at banks took gifts and bribes to give unsafe loans to small businesses. The paperwork was easy to get around, the people who ran banks wanted to loan money, that was their business, that was their profit and so their regulations were purposely written to make it easy for loan officers. Of course there had to be a parade of paperwork, memo of interviews, etc. But Martin Mutford cost the bank a few hundred thousand dollars before he was transferred to another branch and another city by what he thought was fortunate circumstance but what he later realized was simply a tolerant shrug of his superiors.

The errors of youth behind him, forgiven, forgotten, valuable lessons learned, Mutford rose in his world.

Thirty years later he sat in the pavilion of the Socrates Country Club and was the most powerful financial figure in the United States. He was chairman of a great bank, he owned substantial stock in the TV networks, he and his friends had control of the giant automobile industry, and had linked up with the air travel industry. He had used money as a spider web to snare a large share of electronics. Even in those areas he did not control were the thin filaments hanging that showed he had at least tried. He also sat above Wall Street investment firms who put together deals to buy out conglomerates to add to another huge conglomerate. When these battles were at their most fierce Martin Mutford could send out a wave of money as drenching as the sea to settle the issue. Like the other three he 'owned' certain members of the Congress and the Senate.

The four men sat at the round table in the pavilion outside the tennis courts. California flowers and New England-like greenery surrounded them. George Greenwell said, 'What do you fellows think of the President's decision?'

Martin Mutford said, 'It's a damn shame what they did to his daughter. But destroying fifty billion dollars of property is way out of proportion.'

A waiter, a Hispanic wearing white slacks and a white silky-looking short-sleeved shirt with the club logo, took their drink orders.

Lawrence Salentine said thoughtfully, 'The American people will think of Kennedy as a real hero if he pulls it off. He will be re-elected in a landslide.'

George Greenwell said, 'But it is far too drastic a response, we all know that. Foreign relations will be injured for years to come.'

Martin Mutford said, 'The country is running wonderfully well. The legislative branch finally has the executive branch under some sort of control. Will the country benefit in a swing of power the opposite way?'

Louis Inch said, 'What the hell can Kennedy do even if he gets re-elected? The Congress controls and we have a big say with them. There are not more than fifty members of the House who are elected without our money. And in the Senate, there's not a man among them that is not a million-aire. We don't have to worry about the President.'

George Greenwell had been looking beyond the tennis courts to the marvelous Pacific Ocean so quiet yet majestic. The ocean which at this moment was cradling billions of dollars worth of ships carrying his grain all over the world. It gave him a slightly guilty feeling that he could starve or feed the world.

He started to speak but then the waiter came with their drinks. Greenwell was prudent at his age and had asked for mineral water. He sipped at his glass and after the waiter left he spoke in careful modulated tones. He was always exquisitely courteous, the courtesy that comes to a man who has regretfully made brutal decisions in his life. 'We must never forget,' he said, 'that the office of the President of the United States can be a very great danger to the democratic process.'

Salentine said, 'That's nonsense. The other officials in the government prevent him from making a personal decision. The military, benighted as they are, would not permit it unless it was reasonable, you know that George.'

George Greenwell said, 'That's true, of course. In normal times. But look at Lincoln, he actually suspended habeas corpus and civil liberties during the Civil War, look at Franklin Roosevelt, he got us into World War II. Look at the personal powers of the President. He has the power to absolutely pardon any crime. That is the power of a king. Do you know what can be done with such a power? What allegiance that can create? He has almost infinite powers if there is not a strong Congress to check him. Luckily we have such a Congress. But we must look ahead, we must make sure that the executive arm remains subordinate to the duly elected representatives of the people.'

Salentine said, 'With TV and other media Kennedy wouldn't last a day if he tried anything dictatorial. He simply hadn't got that option. The strongest belief in America today is the creed of individual freedom.' He paused for a moment and said, 'As you know well, George. You defied that infamous embargo.'

Greenwell said, 'You're missing the point. A bold president can surmout those obstacles. And Kennedy is being very bold in this crisis.

Louis Inch said impatiently, 'Are you arguing we should present a united front against Kennedy's ultimatum to Sherhaben? Personally, I think it's great that he's being tough. Force works, pressure works, on governments as well as people.'

Early in his career Louis Inch had used pressure tactics on tenants in housing developments under rent control when he wanted to empty the buildings. He had withheld heat, water and prohibited maintenance, he had made the lives of thousands of people uncomfortable. He had 'tipped' certain sections of suburbia, flooding them with blacks to drive out white residents, he had bribed city and state governments, he made rich the Federal regulators. He knew what he was talking about. Success was built on applying pressure.

George Greenwell said, 'Again, you're missing the point. In an hour we have a screen conference call with Bert Audick. Please forgive me that I promised this without consulting you, I thought it too urgent to wait, events are moving so quickly. But it's Bert Audick whose fifty billion dollars will be destroyed, he is terribly concerned. And it is important to look into the future. If the President can do this to Audick, he can do it to us.'

'Kennedy is unsound,' Martin Mutford said thoughtfully.

Salentine said, 'I think we should have some sort of consensus before the conference call with Audick.'

'He's really perverted with his oil preservation,' Inch said. Inch had always felt oil in some way conflicted with the interests of real estate.

'We owe it to Bert to give him our fullest consideration,' Greenwell said.

The four men were gathered in the communications center of the Socrates Country Club when the image of Bert Audick flashed on the TV screen. He greeted them with a smile, but the face on the screen was an unnatural red which could be the color tuning or some sort of rage. Audick's voice was calm.

'I'm going to Sherhaben,' he said. 'It may be a last look at my fifty billion bucks.'

The men in the room could speak to the image as if he

were present at the club. They could see their own images on their monitor, the image that Audick could see in his office. They had to guard their faces as well as their voices.

'You're actually going?' Louis Inch said.

'Yes,' Audick said. 'The Sultan is a friend of mine and this is a very touchy situation. I can do a lot of good for our country if I'm there personally.'

Lawrence Salentine said, 'According to the correspondents on my media payroll, Congress and the Senate are trying to veto the President's decision. Is that possible?'

The image of Audick smiled at them. 'Not only possible but almost certain. I've talked to Cabinet members. They are proposing that the President be removed temporarily from office by reason of his personal vendetta which shows a temporary imbalance of the mind. Under an Amendment of the Constitution that is legal. We need only get the signatures of the Cabinet and the Vice President on a petition that Congress will ratify. Even if the impeachment is for only thirty days, we can halt the destruction of Dak. And I guarantee that the hostages will be released while I am in Sherhaben. But I think all of you should offer support to Congress to remove the President. You owe that to American democracy, as I owe it to my stockholders. We all know damn well that if anybody but his daughter had been killed, he would never have chosen this course of action.'

George Greenwell said, 'Bert, the four of us have talked this over and we have agreed to support you and the Congress, that's our duty. We will make the necessary phone calls, our efforts will be co-ordinated. But Lawrence Salentine has a few pertinent observations he'd like to present.'

Audick's face on the screen showed anger and disgust. He said, 'Larry, this is no time for your media to sit on the fence, believe me. If Kennedy can cost me fifty billion dollars there may come a time when all your TV stations could be without a Federal licence and then you can go fuck yourself. I won't lift a finger to help you.'

George Greenwell winced at the vulgarity and directness of the response. Louis Inch and Martin Mutford smiled. Lawrence Salentine showed no emotion. He answered in a calm soothing voice.

'Bert,' he said. 'I'm with you all the way, never doubt that. I think a man who arbitrarily decides to destroy fifty billion dollars to reinforce a threat, is undoubtedly unbalanced and not fit to head the government of the United States. I'm with you, I assure you. The television media will be breaking into their scheduled programs with bulletins that President Kennedy is being psychiatrically evaluated, that the trauma of his daughter's death may have temporarily disordered his reason. That should prepare the groundwork for Congress. But this touches an area where I have a little more expertise than most. The President's decision will be embraced by the American people, the natural mob reaction to all acts of national power plays. If the President succeeds in his action and he gets the hostages back, he will command untold allegiance and votes. Kennedy has intelligence and energy, if he gets one foot in the door he can sweep Congress away.' Salentine paused for a moment, trying to choose his words very carefully. 'But if his threats fail, hostages killed, problem not solved, then Kennedy is finished as a political power.'

On the console the image of Bert Audick flinched. He said in a very quiet serious tone, 'That is not an alternative. If it goes that far, then the hostages must be saved, our country must win. Besides the fifty billion dollars will already be lost. No true American wants the Kennedy mission to fail. They may not want a mission with such drastic action, but once started we must see that it succeeds.'

'I agree,' Salentine said, though he did not. 'I absolutely agree. I have another point. Once the President sees the danger of Congress, the first thing he will want to do is address the nation on television. Whatever Kennedy's faults, he is a magician on the tube. Once he presents his case on that TV screen the Congress will be in a great deal of trouble

187

in this country. What if Congress does depose Kennedy for thirty days? Then there is the possibility that the President is right in his diagnosis, that the kidnappers make this a long drawn out affair with Kennedy on the sidelines, out of all the heat.' Again Salentine paused trying to be careful. He said, 'Then Kennedy becomes an even greater hero. Our best scenario is to just let him alone, win or lose. That way there is no long-term danger to the political structure of this country. That may be best.'

'I lose fifty billion dollars that way, right?' Bert Audick said. The face on the huge TV screen was reddening with anger. There had never been anything wrong with the color control.

Mutford said, 'It is a considerable sum of money, but it's not the end of the world.'

Bert Audick's face on the screen was an astonishing bloody red. Salentine thought again that it might be the controls, no man could stay alive and turn such vivid hues, the fucking oil maniac wasn't an autumn forest. But then Audick's voice reverberated through the room.

'Fuck you, Martin, fuck you. And it's more than fifty billion. What about the loss of revenue while we rebuild Dak? Will your banks loan me the money then without interest? You've got more cash up your asshole than the US Treasury, but would you give me the fifty billion? Like shit you would.'

George Greenwell said hastily, 'Bert, Bert, we are with you. Salentine was just pointing out a few options you may not have thought of under the pressure of events. In any event we could not stop Congress's action even if we tried. Congress will not permit the Executive to dominate on such an issue. Now we all have work to do, so I suggest this conference come to an end.'

Salentine smiled and said, 'Bert, those bulletins about the President's mental condition will be on television in three hours. The other networks will follow our lead. Call me and tell me what you think, you may have some ideas. And one other thing, if Congress votes to depose the President before he requests time on TV, the networks can refuse him the time on the basis that he has been certified as mentally incompetent and no longer President.

'You do that,' Audick said, his face now a natural color. And the conference call ended with courteous goodbyes.

Lawrence Salentine said, 'Gentlemen, I suggest we all fly to Washington in my plane. I think we should all pay a visit to our old friend Oliver Ollifant.'

Martin Mutford smiled. 'The Oracle, my old mentor. He'll give us some answers.'

Within the hour they were all on their way to Washington.

Summoned to meet with President Kennedy, the Ambassador of Sherhaben, Sharif Waleeb, was shown secret CIA video tapes of Yabril having dinner with the Sultan in the Sultan's palace. The Sherhaben Ambassador was genuinely shocked. How could his Sultan be involved in such a dangerous endeavour? Sherhaben was a tiny country, a gentle country, peace loving, as was wise for a militarily weak power.

The meeting was in the Oval office with Bert Audick present. The President was accompanied by two staff members, Arnold Wix, the National Security Advisor, and Eugene Dazzy, the Chief of Staff.

After he was formally presented, the Sherhaben Ambassador said to Kennedy, 'My dear Mr President, you must believe I had no knowledge of this. You have my personal, my most abject, my most heartfelt apologies.' He was close to tears. 'But I must say one thing I truly believe. The Sultan could never have agreed to harm your poor daughter.'

Francis Kennedy said gravely, 'I hope that is true because then he will agree to my proposal.'

The Ambassador listened with an apprehension that was more personal than political. He had been educated at an American university, and he was an admirer of the American way of life. He loved American food, American alcoholic drinks, American women and their rebelliousness to the male yoke. He loved American music and films. He had donated money to all the necessary politicos and made bureaucrats in the American State Department rich. He was an expert on oil and a friend of Bert Audick.

Now he despaired for his personal misfortune, but he was not really worried about Sherhaben and its Sultan. The worst that could happen would be economic sanctions. The American CIA would mount covert operations to displace the Sultan, but this might be to his advantage.

So he was profoundly shocked by Kennedy's carefully articulated speech to him. 'You must listen closely,' Francis Kennedy said. 'In three hours you will be on a plane to Sherhaben to bring my message to your Sultan personally. Mr Bert Audick, whom you know, and my National Security Advisor, Arnold Wix, will accompany you. And the message is this. In twenty-four hours your city of Dak will be destroyed.'

The Ambassador, horrified, his throat constricted, could not speak.

Kennedy continued, 'The hostages must be released and the terrorist Yabril must be turned over to us. Alive. If the Sultan does not do this, the state of Sherhaben itself will cease to exist.'

The Ambassador looked so stricken that Kennedy thought he might have trouble comprehending. Kennedy paused for a moment and then he went on reassuringly. 'All this will be in the documents I will send with you to present to your Sultan.'

Ambassador Waleeb said dazedly, 'Mr President, forgive me, you said something about destroying Dak?'

Kennedy said, 'That is correct. Your Sultan will not believe my threats until he sees the city of Dak in ruins. Let me repeat: the hostages must be released, Yabril must be surrendered and secured so that he cannot take his own life. There will be no more negotiations.'

The Ambassador said incredulously, 'You cannot threaten to destroy a free country, tiny as it is. And if you destroy Dak you destroy fifty billions of dollars of American investment.'

'That may be true,' Kennedy said. 'We will see. Make sure your Sultan understands that I am immovable in this matter, that is your function. You, Mr Audick and Mr Wix will go in one of my personal planes. Two other aircraft will accompany you. One to bring back the hostages and the body of my daughter. The other to bring back Yabril.'

The Ambassador could not speak, he could scarcely think. This was surely a nightmare. The President had gone mad.

When he was alone with Bert Audick, Audick said to him grimly, 'That bastard meant what he said but we have a card to play. I'll talk to you on the plane.'

In the Oval Office Eugene Dazzy took notes.

Francis Kennedy said, 'Have you arranged for all the documents to be delivered to the Ambassador's office and to the plane?'

Dazzy said, 'We dressed it up a little. Wiping out Dak is bad enough but we can't say in print we will destroy the whole country of Sherhaben. But your message is clear. Why send Wix?'

Kennedy smiled and said, 'The Sultan will know that when I send him my National Security Advisor I'm very serious. And Arthur will repeat my verbal message.'

'Do you think it will work?' Dazzy said.

'He'll wait for Dak to go down,' Kennedy said. 'Then it sure as hell will work unless he's crazy.' He paused for a moment and then said, 'Tell Christian I want to have dinner with him before we see that film tonight.'

11

To impeach the President of the United States in twenty-four hours seemed almost impossible. But four hours after Kennedy's ultimatum to Sherhaben, Congress and the Socrates Club had this victory well within their grasp.

After Christian Klee had left the meeting, the computer surveillance section of his FBI Special Division gave him a complete report on the activities of the leaders of Congress and the members of the Socrates Club. Three thousand calls were listed. Charts and records of all the meetings held were also part of the report. The evidence was clear and overwhelming. Within the next twenty-four hours, the House and Senate of the United States would try to impeach the President.

Christian, trembling with rage, put the reports in his briefcase and rushed over to the White House. But before he left, he told Peter Cloot to move ten thousand agents from their normal duty posts and send them to Washington.

At this same time late Wednesday Senator Thomas Lambertino, the strong man of the Senate, with his aide Elizabeth Stone and Congressman Alfred Jintz, the Democratic Speaker of the House, were meeting in Lambertino's office. Patsy Troyca, chief aide to Congressman Jintz, was there to cover up, as he often said, the asshole of his boss who was an idiot *manqué*. About Patsy Troyca's cunning there was no doubt, not only in his own mind, but on Capitol Hill.

In that warren of rabbity legislators, Patsy Troyca was also a champion womanizer and genteel promoter of avuncular relationships between the sexes. Troyca had already noted that the Senator's chief aide, Elizabeth Stone, was a beauty but he had to find out how devoted she was. And right now he had to concentrate on the business at hand.

Troyca read aloud the pertinent sentences of the Twenty-fifth Amendment to the United States Constitution, editing out odd sentences and words. He read slowly and carefully in a beautifully controlled tenor voice.

'Whenever the Vice President and majority of either of the principal officers of the executive departments,' Troyca said – then in an aside to Jintz, he whispered, 'that's the Cabinet.' Then his voice grew more emphatic – 'or of *such other body as Congress may by law provide*, transmit to the Senate and House of Representatives their written declaration that the President is unable to discharge the powers and duties of his office, the Vice President shall immediately assume the powers and dutes of the office as Acting President.'

'Bullshit,' Congressman Jintz yelled. 'It can't be that easy to impeach a President.'

'It's not,' said Senator Lambertino in a soothing voice. 'Read on, Patsy.'

Patsy Troyca thought bitterly that it was typical that his boss did not know the Constitution, holy as it was. He gave up. Fuck the Constitution, Jintz would never understand. He would have to put it in plain language. He said, 'Essentially, the Vice President and the Cabinet must sign a declaration of incompetence to impeach Kennedy. Then the Vice President becomes President. One second later Kennedy enters his counter-declaration and says he's OK. He's President again. Then Congress decides. During that delay Kennedy can do what he wants.'

Congressman Jintz said, 'And there goes Dak.'

Senator Lambertino said, 'Most of the Cabinet members will sign the declaration. We'll have to wait for the Vice President, we can't proceed without her signature. Congress will have to meet no later than ten p.m. Thursday to decide the issue in time to prevent the destruction of Dak. And to win we must have a two-thirds vote of each the House and Senate. Now can the House do the job? I guarantee the Senate.'

'Sure,' Congressman Jintz said. 'I got a call from the Socrates Country Club, they are going to lean on every member of the house,'

Patsy Troyca said respectfully, 'The Constitution says, "Any other body the Congress may by law provide." Why not bypass all that Cabinet and Vice Presidential signing and make Congress that body? Then they can decide forthwith.'

Congressman Jintz said patiently, 'Patsy, it won't work. It can't look like a vendetta. The voting public would be on his side and we'd have to pay for it later. Remember Kennedy is popular with the people, a demagogue has that advantage over responsible legislators.'

Senator Lambertino said, 'We should have no trouble following procedure. The President's ultimatum to Sherhaben is far too extreme and shows a mind temporarily unbalanced by his personal tragedy. For which I have the utmost sympathy and sorrow. As indeed do we all.'

Congressman Jintz said, 'My people in the House come up for re-election every two years. Kennedy could knock a bunch of them out if he's declared competent after the thirty-day period. We have to *keep* him out.'

Senator Lambertino nodded. He knew that the Senatorial six-year term always grated on House members. 'That's true,' he said, 'but remember it will be established that he has serious psychological problems and that can be used to keep him out of office simply by the Democratic party refusing him the nomination.'

Patsy Troyca had noted one thing. Elizabeth Stone, the chief aide to the Senator, had not uttered a word during the meeting. But she had a brain for a boss, she didn't have to protect Lambertino from his own stupidity.

So Troyca said, 'If I may summarize, if the Vice President

and the majority of the Cabinet vote to impeach the President, they will sign the declaration this afternoon. The President's personal staff will still refuse to sign. It would be a great help if they did, but they won't. According to the Constitutional procedure the one essential signature is that of the Vice President. A Vice President, by tradition, endorses all of the President's policies. Are we absolutely positive she will sign? Or that she won't delay? Time is of the essence.'

Jintz laughed and said, 'What Vice President doesn't want to be President? She's been hoping for the last three years that he has a heart attack.'

For the first time Elizabeth Stone spoke. 'The Vice President does not think in that fashion. She is absolutely loyal to the President,' she said coolly. 'It is true that she is almost certain to sign the declaration. But for all the right reasons.'

Congressman Jintz looked at her with patient resignation and made a pacifying gesture. Lambertino frowned. Troyca kept his face impassive, but inwardly he was delighted.

Patsy Troyca said, 'I still say bypass everybody. Let Congress go right to the bottom line.'

Congressman Jintz rose from his comfortable armchair. 'Don't wory, Patsy, the Vice President can't seem to be too much in a hurry to push Kennedy out. She will sign. She just doesn't want to look like a usurper.' Usurper was a word often used in the House of Representatives in reference to President Kennedy.

Senator Lambertino regarded Troyca with distaste. He disliked a certain familiarity in the man's manner, the questioning of the plans of his betters. 'This action to impeach the President is certainly legal if unprecedented,' he said. 'The Twenty-fifth Amendment to the Constitution doesn't specify medical evidence. But his decision to destroy Dak is evidence.'

Patsy Troyca couldn't resist. 'Once you do this there will certainly be a precedent. A two-thirds vote of Congress can impeach any President. In theory anyway.' He noted with satisfaction that he had won Elizabeth Stone's attention at least. So he went on. 'We'd be another banana republic only in reverse, the legislature being the dictator.'

Senator Lambertino said curtly, 'By definition that cannot be true. The legislature is elected by the people directly, it cannot dictate as one man can.'

Patsy Troyca thought with contempt, not unless the Socrates Country Club gets on your ass. Then he realized what had made the Senator angry. The Senator thought of himself as Presidential timber and didn't like someone saying that the Congress could get rid of the President whenever it liked.

Jintz said, 'Let's wind this up, we all have a hell of a lot of work to do. This is really a move to a more genuine democracy.'

Patsy Troyca was still not used to the direct simplicity of great men like the Senator and the Speaker, how with such sincerity they struck to the very heart of their own self-interest. He saw a certain look on the face of Elizabeth Stone and realized she was thinking exactly what he was thinking. Oh, he was going to take his shot at her no matter what the cost. But he said with his patented sincerity, humbly, 'Is it at all possible that the President may declare that Congress is overruling an executive order that they disagree with and then defy the vote of the Congress? May he not go to the nation on television tonight before the Congress meets? And won't it seem plausible to the public that since Kennedy's staff refuses to sign the declaration, Kennedy is OK? There could be a great deal of trouble. Especially if the hostages are killed after Kennedy has been impeached. There could be tremendous repercussions on the Congress.'

Neither the Senator nor the Congressman seemed impressed by this analysis. Jintz patted him on the shoulder and said, 'Patsy, we've got it all covered, you just make sure the paperwork gets done.'

At that moment the phone rang and Elizabeth Stone

picked it up. She listened for a moment and then said, 'Senator, it's the Vice President.'

Before making her decision, Vice President Helen DuPray decided to take her daily run.

The first woman Vice President of the United States, she was fifty-five years of age and by any standard an extraordinarily intelligent woman. She was still beautiful, possibly because when in her twenties, then a pregnant wife and Assistant District Attorney, she became a health food nut. She had also become a runner in her teens before she was married. An early lover had taken her on his runs, five miles a day and not jogging. He had quoted Latin, 'In corpore sanus mente sanus,' and translated for her, 'If one is healthy in body, one is healthy in mind.' For his condescension in translating and his taking literally the truth of the quotation (how many healthy minds have been brought to dust by a too healthy body?) she had 'discharged' him as a lover.

But just as important were her dietary disciplines, which dissolved the poisons in her system and generated a high energy level with the extra bonus of a magnificent figure. Her political opponents would joke that she had no taste buds but this was not true. She could enjoy a rosy peach, a mellow pear, the tangy taste of fresh vegetables, and in her dark days of the soul which no one escapes she could eat a gallon jar of chocolate cookies.

She had become a health food nut by chance. In her early days as a District Attorney she had prosecuted a diet book author for making fraudulent and injurious claims. To prepare for the case she had researched the subject, read everything in the field of nutrition, on the premise that to detect the false you must know what is true. She had convicted the author, made him pay an enormous fine but always felt she owed him a debt.

And even as Vice President of the United States Helen DuPray ate sparingly and always ran at least five miles a

197

day. On weekends, she did ten miles. Now, on what could be the most important day of her life, the declaration to impeach the President waiting for her signature, she decided to take a mind-clearing run.

Her Secret Service guard had to pay the price. Originally the chief of her security detail thought her morning run would be no problem. After all, his men were good physical specimens. But Vice President DuPray not only took her runs early in the morning through woods where guards could not follow, but her once-a-week ten-mile run left her security men straggling far to her rear. The Chief was amazed that this woman, in her fifties, could run so fast. And so long.

The Vice President did not want her run disturbed, it was after all a sacred thing in her life. It had replaced 'fun', meaning it had replaced the enjoyment of food, liquor and sex, the warmth and tenderness that had gone out of her life when her husband had died six years before.

She had lengthened her runs and put aside all thoughts of remarrying; she was too far up the political ladder to risk allying herself to a man who might be a booby trap, with secret skeletons in his closet to drag her down. Her two daughters and an active social life were enough and she had many friends, male and female.

She had won the support of the feminist groups of the country not with the usual empty political blandishments but with a cold intelligence and a steadfast integrity. She had mounted an unrelenting attack on the anti-abortionists and had crucified in debate those male chauvinists who without personal risk tried to legislate what women might do with their bodies. She had won that fight and in the process climbed high up the political ladder. From a lifetime of living she disdained the theories that men and women should be more alike, she celebrated their differences. The difference was valuable in a moral sense, as a variation in music is valuable, as a variation in gods is valuable. Oh, yes there was a difference. She had learned from her political life, from her years as a district attorney, that women were better than men in the most important things in life. And she had the statistics to prove it. Men committed far more murders, robbed more banks, perjured themselves more, betrayed their friends and loved ones more. As public officials they were far more corrupt, as believers in God they were far more cruel, as lovers they were far more selfish, in all fields they exercised power far more ruthlessly. Men were far more likely to destroy the world with war because they feared death so much more than women. But all this aside, she had no quarrel with men.

Helen DuPray started running from her chauffeured car parked in the woods of the Washington suburb. Running from the fateful document waiting on her desk. The Secret Service men spread out, one ahead, another behind, two on the flanks all at least twenty paces from her. There had been a time when she had delighted in making them sweat to keep up. After all they were fully clothed while she was in running gear, and they were loaded with guns, ammo, communications equipment. They had a rough time until the chief of security detail, losing patience, recruited champion runners from small colleges, and that had chastened Helen DuPray a bit.

The higher Helen DuPray rose on the political ladder, the earlier in the morning she got up to run. Her greatest pleasure was when one of her daughters ran with her. It also made for great photos in the media. Everything counted.

Vice President Helen DuPray had overcome many handicaps to achieve such high office. Obviously, the first was being a woman, and then, not so obviously, being beautiful. Beauty because of its external power often aroused hostility in both sexes. She overcame this hostility with her intelligence, her modesty and an ingrained sense of morality. She also had her fair share of cunning. It was commonplace in American politics that the electorate preferred handsome males and ugly females as candidates for office. So Helen

DuPray had transformed a seductive beauty into the stern handsomeness of a Joan of Arc. She wore her silver blond hair close cropped, she kept her body lean and boyish, she suppressed her breasts with tailored suits. For armor she wore a necklace of pearls and on her fingers only her gold wedding ring. A scarf, a frilly blouse, sometimes gloves, were her badges of womanhood. She projected an image of stern femininity until she smiled or laughed and then her sexuality flashed out brilliant as lightning. She was feminine without being flirtatious, she was strong without a hint of masculinity. She was in short the very model for the first woman President of the United States. Which she must become if she signed the declaration on her desk.

Now she was in the final stage of her run, emerging from the woods and on to a road where another car was waiting. Her detail of Secret Service men closed in like a collapsing diamond and she was on her way to the Vice President's mansion. After showering she dressed in her 'working' clothes, a severely cut skirt and jacket, and left for her office. The declaration was waiting for her.

It was strange, she thought. She had fought all her life to escape the trap of a single funneled life. She had been a brilliant lawyer while having two children, she had pursued a political career while happily and faithfully married. She had been a partner in a powerful law firm, then a Congresswoman, then a Senator and all the time a devoted and caring mother. She had managed her life impeccably only to wind up another kind of housewife, namely the Vice President of the United States.

As Vice President she had to tidy up after her political husband, the President, and perform his menial tasks. She received leaders of small nations, served on powerless committees with high-sounding titles, accepted condescending briefings, gave advice that was accepted with courtesy but not given truly respectful consideration. She had to parrot the opinions and support the policies of her political husband.

She admired President Francis Xavier Kennedy and was grateful that he had selected her to be on the ticket with him as Vice President, but she differed with him on many things. She was sometimes amused that as a married woman she had escaped being trapped as an unequal partner, yet now in the highest political office ever achieved by an American woman, political laws made her subservient to a political husband.

But today she could become a political widow and she certainly could not complain about her insurance policy, the Presidency of the United States of America. After all, this had become an unhappy 'marriage'. Francis Kennedy had moved too quickly, too aggressively. Helen DuPray had begun fantasizing about his death, as many unhappy wives do.

But by signing this declaration she could become a political divorcée and get all the loot. She could take his place. For a lesser woman this would have been a miraculous delight.

She knew it was impossible to control the pragmatic exercises of the brain, so she did not really feel guilty about her fantasies, but she might feel guilty about a reality she had helped become true. When rumors floated that Kennedy would not run for a second term, she had alerted her political network. Kennedy had then given his blessing. This was all changed.

Now she had to clear her mind. The declaration, the petition, had already been signed by most of the Cabinet, the Secretary of State, the Secretary of Defense, Treasury and others. CIA was missing, that clever, unscrupulous bastard, Tappey. And of course, Christian Klee, a man she detested. But she had to make up her mind according to her judgment and her conscience. She had to act for the public good, not out of her own ambition.

201

Could she sign, commit an act of personal betrayal and keep her self-respect? But what was personal was extraneous. Consider only the facts.

Like Christian Klee and many others she had noted the change in Kennedy after his wife died just before his election to the Presidency. The loss of energy, the loss of political skills. Helen DuPray knew, as everyone knew, that to make the Presidency work you could only lead by building a consensus with the legislative branch. You had to court and cajole and maybe give a few kicks. You had to outflank, infiltrate and seduce the bureaucracy. You had to have the Cabinet under your thumb and your personal senior staff had to be a band of Attila the Huns and a gaggle of Solomons. You had to haggle, you had to reward and you had to throw a few thunderbolts. In some way you had to make everyone say, 'Yes, for the good of the country and the good of me.'

Not doing these things had been Kennedy's faults as President, also that he was too far ahead of his time. His staff should have known better. A man as intelligent as Kennedy should have known better. And yet she sensed in Kennedy's ill-fated moves a kind of moral desperation, an all-out gamble on good against evil.

But after his defeats he had retreated into his office like a sullen child and like a child put out the word that he would not run for re-election. And she believed, and hoped she was not regressing into an outmoded female sentimentality, that the death of Kennedy's wife was the root for the failure of his administration. But then did extraordinary men like Kennedy fall apart because of some personal tragedy? The answer to that was yes. Or maybe the power load of the Presidency had been too much for him. She herself had been born to politics but she had always thought that Kennedy himself had not the temperament. He was more scholar, scientist, teacher. He had too much idealism, he was in the best sense of the word, naive. That is, he was trusting.

But a central fact. The Congress, both houses, had waged brutal war against the executive branch, and won the war. Well it would not happen to her.

Now, she picked up the declaration from her desk, and analyzed it. The case presented was that Francis Xavier Kennedy was no longer capable of exercising the duties of President because of a temporary mental breakdown. Caused by the murder of his daughter. Which now affected his judgement, so that his decision to destroy the city of Dak and threaten to destroy a sovereign nation, became an irrational act, far out of proportion to the case, a dangerous precedent that must turn world opinion against the United States.

But then there was Kennedy's argument which he had presented at the staff and Cabinet conference.

This was an international conspiracy in which the Pope of the Catholic Church had been assassinated and the daughter of the President of the United States murdered. A number of hostages were still being held and the conspiracy could spin out the situation for weeks or even months. And the United States would have to set the killer of the Pope free. What an enormous loss of authority to the most powerful nation on earth, the leader of democracy and, of course, democratic capitalism.

So who was to say that the Draconian answer proposed by the President was not the correct answer? Certainly, if Kennedy was not bluffing, his measures would succeed. The Sultan of Sherhaben must go to his knees. What were the real values here?

Point: Damage – Kennedy had made his decision without proper discussion with his Cabinet, his staff, the leaders of Congress. That was very grave. That indicated danger. A gang leader ordering a vendetta.

But: He had known they would all be against him. He was convinced he was right. Time was short. This was the decisiveness of Francis Kennedy in the years before he became President.

Point: He had acted within the powers of the Chief Executive. His decision was legal. The declaration to impeach Kennedy had not been signed by any member of his personal staff, those people close to him. Therefore the charge of unfitness and mental instability was a matter of opinion which rested on the decision he had made. Therefore, this declaration to impeach was an illegal attempt to circumvent the power resting in the Executive branch of the government. The Congress disagreed with the Presidential decision and so, therefore, was attempting to reverse his decision by removing him. Clearly in violation of the Constitution.

Those were the moral and legal issues. Now she had to decide what was in her own best interests. That was not unreasonable in a politician.

She knew the mechanics. The Cabinet had signed, so now if she signed this declaration she would be the President of the United States. Then Kennedy would sign his declaration and she would be Vice President again. Then Congress would meet and in a two-thirds vote impeach Kennedy and she would be the President for at least thirty days, until the crisis was over.

The plus factor: She would be the first woman President of the United States for a few moments at the very least. Maybe for the rest of Kennedy's term which would end the following January. But no illusions. She would never get the nomination after the term ran out.

She would achieve the Presidency by what some would see as an act of betrayal. And she a woman. It was enough that the literature of civilization had always portrayed women as causing the downfall of great men, that there was the ever-present myth that men could never trust women. It would be regarded as 'unfaithful': that great sin of womankind which men never forgave. And she would be betraying the great national myth of the Kennedys. She would be another Mordred.

And it struck her. She smiled as she realized that she was in a 'no lose' situation. Just by refusing to sign the declaration.

Congress would not be denied.

Congress, possibly acting illegally without her signature, would impeach Kennedy and the Constitution decreed that she would succeed to the Presidency. But she would have proved her 'faithfulness' and if and when Francis Kennedy was restored after thirty days, she would still have his support. She would still have the Kennedy power group behind her nomination. As for the Congress, they were her enemies no matter what she did. So why be their political Jezebel? Their Delilah?

It became clearer and clearer to her. If she signed the declaration the voting public would never forgive her and the politicians would hold her in contempt. And then when and if she became President, they would most likely try to perform the same castrative act on her. They would, she thought, probably blame it on her menstrual flow, the cruel male expression would be the inspiration for comics all over the country.

She made her decision. She would *not* sign the declaration. That would show she was not greedily ambitious, that she was loyal.

She started writing the statement she would give to her administrative aide to prepare. In it she simply wrote that she could not sign, with a clear conscience, a document that would elevate her to such high power. That she would remain neutral in this struggle. But even this could be dangerous. She crumpled up the paper. She would just refuse to sign, Congress would carry it forward from there. She placed a call to Senator Lambertino. After that she would call other legislators and explain her position. But nothing in writing.

*

Vice President Helen DuPray's refusal to sign was a shocking blow to Congressman Jintz and Senator Lambertino. Only a female could be so contrary, blind to political necessity, so dull of wit not to grab this chance to be President of the United States. But they would have to do without her. They went over their options, the deed must be done. Patsy Troyca had been on the right track, all the preliminary steps must be eliminated. The Congress must designate itself the body to decide from the very beginning. But Lambertino and Jintz were still trying for some way to make Congress seem impartial. They never noticed that in that moment Patsy Troyca fell in love with Elizabeth Stone.

'Never fuck a woman over thirty,' had always been Patsy Troyca's creed. But for the first time he was thinking the exception might be the aide to Senator Lambertino. She was tall and willowy with wide gray eyes and a face that was sweet in repose. She was obviously intelligent yet knew how to keep her mouth shut. But what made him fall in love was that when they learned Vice President Helen DuPray was refusing to sign the declaration, she gave Patsy a smile that acknowledged him as a prophet, only he had proposed the correct solution.

For Troyca there were many good reasons for his stance. One, women didn't really like to fuck as much as men, they were more at risk in many different ways. But before thirty, they had more juice and less brains. Over thirty their eyes got squinty, they got too crafty, they started to think that men had it too good, were getting the better of nature and society's bargain. You never knew whether you were getting a casual piece of ass or signing some sort of promissory note. But Elizabeth Stone looked demurely horny in that slender virginal way some women have, and besides she had more power than him. He would not have to worry that she was hustling. It didn't matter that she must be close to forty.

Planning strategy with Congressman Jintz, Senator Lambertino noted that Troyca had an interest in his female aide.

That didn't bother him. Lambertino was one of the personally virtuous men in the Congress. He was sexually clean, with a wife of thirty years and four grown children. He was financially clean, wealthy in his own right. He was as politically clean as any political man in America can be but in addition he genuinely had the interest of the people and country at heart. True he was ambitious, but that was the very essence of political life. His virtue did not make him innocent of the machinations of the world. The refusal of the Vice President to sign the declaration had astonished Congressman Jintz but the Senator was not so easily surprised. He had always thought the Vice President a very clever woman. Lambertino wished her well, especially since he believed that no woman had the enduring political connections, or money patrons, to win the Presidency. She would be a very vulnerable opponent in a fight for the coming nomination.

'We have to move fast,' Senator Lambertino said. 'The Congress must designate a body or itself to declare the President unfit.'

'How about ten Senators on a blue ribbon panel?' Congressman Jintz said with a sly grin.

Senator Lambertino said, with a burst of irritation, 'How about a fifty House of Representatives committee with their heads up their asses.'

Jintz said placatingly, 'I have a helpful surprise for you, Senator. I think I can get one of the President's staff to sign the declaration to impeach him.'

That would do the trick, Troyca thought. But which one could it be? Never Klee, not Dazzy. It had to be either Oddblood Gray or the NSA guy, Wix. He thought, no, Wix was in Sherhaben.

Lambertino said briskly, 'We have a very painful duty today. A historical duty. We better get started.'

Troyca was surprised that Lambertino did not ask for the

name of the Staff member. Then he realized that the Senator did not want to know.

'You have my hand on that,' Jintz said and extended his arm to give that handshake that was famous as an unbreakable pledge.

Albert Jintz had achieved his eminence as a great Speaker of the House by being a man of his word. The newspapers often carried articles to this effect. A Jintz handshake was better than any handcuffing legal document. Though he looked like an alcoholic bank embezzler cartoon, short and round, cherry-red nose, head dripping with white hair like a Christmas tree in a snowstorm, he was considered the most honorable man in Congress, politically. When he promised a chunk of pork from the bottomless barrel of the budget, that pork was delivered. When a fellow Congressman wanted a bill blocked, and Jintz owed him a political debt, that bill was blocked. When a Congressman who wanted a personal bill paid his quid pro quo, it was a done deal. True he often leaked secret matters to the press but that was why so many articles on his impeccable handshake were printed.

And now this afternoon Jintz had to do the scut work of making sure the House would vote for the impeachment of President Kennedy. Make hundreds of phone calls, thousands of promises, to insure that two-thirds vote. It was not that Congress wouldn't do it, but a price had to be paid. And it all had to be done in less than twenty-four hours.

Patsy Troyca moved through his Congressman's suite of offices, his brain marshaling all the phone calls he had to make, all the documents he had to prepare. He knew he was involved in a great moment of history and he also knew that his career could be washed away if there was some terrible reversal. He was amazed that men like Jintz and Lambertino, whom he held in a certain kind of contempt, could be so courageous as to put themselves in the front line of battle.

This was a very dangerous step they were taking. Under a very shady interpretation of the Constitution they were prepared to make the Congress a body that could impeach the President of the United States.

He moved through the spooky green light of a dozen computers being worked by office staff. Thank God for computers. How the hell did things ever get done before? Passing one computer operator he touched her shoulder in a comradely gesture that could not be taken for sexual harassment and said, 'Don't make any dates – we'll be here until morning.'

The *New York Times* magazine section had recently published an article on the sexual mores of Capitol Hill, the building that housed both the Senate and the House and their staffs. The article noted that of the elected hundred Senators and 435 Congressmen and their huge staffs, the population was in the many thousands, of which more than half were females.

The article had suggested that there was a great deal of sexual activity among these free citizens. The article had said that due to long hours and the tension of working under political deadlines the staff had little social life and had to perforce seek a little recreation on the job. It was noted that Congressional offices and Senator suites were furnished with couches. The article explained that in government bureaus there were special medical clinics and doctors whose duties were the discreet treatment of venereal infection. The records were of course confidential, but the writer claimed he had been given a peek and the percentage of infection was higher than the national average. The writer attributed this not so much to promiscuity as to the incestuous social environment. The writer then wondered if all this fornication was affecting the quality of law-making on Capitol Hill which he referred to as the 'Rabbit Warren'.

Patsy Troyca had taken the article personally. He averaged a sixteen-hour working day six days a week and was on call

Sundays. Was he not entitled to a normal sex life like any other citizen? Damn it, he didn't have time to go to parties, to romance women, to commit himself to a relationship. It all had to happen here, in the countless suites and corridors, in the smoky green light of computers and military ringing of telephones. You had to fit it into a few minutes of banter, a meaningful smile, the involved strategies of work. That fucking *Times* writer went to all the publisher parties, took out people for long lunches, chatted leisurely with journalist colleagues, could go to hookers without a newspaper reporting the seamy details.

Troyca went into his private office, then into the bathroom, and gave a sigh of relief as he sat on the toilet, pen in hand. He scribbled notes on all the things he had to do. He washed his hands, juggling pad and pen, Congressional logo etched in gold computer lines; and feeling much better (the tension of impeaching a President had knotted his stomach) went to the small mobile liquor cart, took ice from the tiny refrigerator to fix himself a gin and tonic. He thought about Elizabeth Stone. He was sure there was nothing between her and her Senator boss. And she was smart, smarter then him, she had kept her mouth shut.

The door of his office opened and the girl he had patted on the shoulder came into the office. She had an armful of computer printout sheets and Patsy Troyca sat at his desk to go over them. She stood beside him. He could feel the heat of her body, a heat generated by the long hours she had put in on the computer that day.

Patsy Troyca had interviewed this girl when she had applied for the job. He often said that if only the girls who worked in the office kept looking as good as on their interview day, he could put them all in *Playboy*. And if they remained as demure and sweet he would marry them. The girl's name was Janet Wyngale and she was really beautiful. The first day he saw her, a line from Dante had flashed through Patsy Troyca's mind, 'Here is the goddess that will subjugate me.' Of course he would not allow such a misfortune to happen. But she was that beautiful, that first day. She was never as beautiful again. Her hair was still blonde, but not gold, her eyes were still that amazing blue but she wore glasses and was a little ugly without the first perfect make-up. Nor were her lips as cherry-red. Her body was not as voluptuous as the first day, which was natural since she was a hard worker and dressed comfortably now to increase her efficiency. He had, all in all, made a good decision, she was not yet squinty-eyed.

Janet Wyngale, what a great name. She was leaning over his shoulder to point out things on the computer sheets. He was conscious she switched her feet so that she was standing more beside him than behind him. Her golden hair brushed his cheek, silky warm and smelling of minced flowers.

'Your perfume is great,' Patsy Troyca said, and he was almost shivering when the heat of her body gusted over him. She didn't move or say anything. But her hair was like a Geiger counter over his cheek picking up the radiating lust in his body. It was a friendly lust, two buddies in a jam together. They would be going over computer sheets all through the night, answering a witch's brew of telephone calls, calling emergency meetings. They would fight side by side.

Holding the computer sheets in his left hand, Patsy Troyca let his right hand touch the back side of her thigh under her skirt. She didn't move. They were both staring intently at the computer sheets. He let his hand stay perfectly still, let it burn on satiny skin that electrified his scrotum. He was not conscious that the computer sheets had fallen to the desk. Her flowered hair drowned his face and he swiveled and both his hands were under her skirt, both his hands like little feet running over that field so satiny under the synthesized nylon of her panties. Underneath to the pubic hair and the wet agonizing sweetness of the flesh beneath. Patsy Troyca levitated from his seat, it seemed to him he was motionless

211

in the air, his body forming a supernatural eagle's nest into which Janet Wyngale, with a fluttering of wings, came to rest on his lap. Miraculously she was sitting right on his cock which had mysteriously emerged and they were face to face kissing; he drowning in blonde minced flowers, groaning with passion and Janet Wyngale kept repeating a passionate endearment which he finally understood. 'Lock the door,' she was saying and Patsy Troyca freed his wet left hand and flipped the electronic button which enclosed them in that perfect brief moment of ecstasy. Both tumbled to the floor in a graceful wing-like dive and she had her long legs wrapped around his neck, and he could see the long milk-white thighs and they climaxed together in perfect unison, Patsy Troyca whispered ecstatically, 'Ah, heaven, heaven.'

Then miraculously they were both standing, rosy-cheeked, their eyes flashing with delight, renewed, jubilant, ready to face the grueling long hours of work together. Gallantly Patsy Troyca passed her the gin and tonic with its joyful tinkling of ice cubes. Graciously and thankfully she wet her parched mouth. Sincerely and gratefully Patsy Troyca said, 'That was wonderful.' Lovingly she patted his neck and kissed him. 'It was great.'

Moments later they were back at the desk studying the computer sheets in earnest, concentrating on the language and the figures. Janet was a wonderful editor. Patsy Troyca felt an enormous gratitude. He murmured with genuine courtesy, 'Janet, I'm really crazy about you. As soon as this crisis is over we got to have a date, OK?'

'Umm,' Janet said. She gave him a warm smile. A friendly smile. 'I love working with you,' she said.

12

Television never had such a glorious week. On Sunday the assassination of the Pope had been repeated scores of times on the networks, on the cable channels, on PBS special reports. On Tuesday the murder of Theresa Kennedy had been even more continuously repeated, her murder floated through the airways of the universe endlessly and endlessly. Messages of sympathy by the millions poured into the White House. In all of the great cities the citizens of America appeared on the streets wearing black armbands. And so when the television stations climaxed late Wednesday with the leaked news of President Francis Kennedy's ultimatum to the Sultan of Sherhaben, great mobs congregated all through the United States in a wild frenzy of jubilation. There was no question they supported the President's decision. Indeed the TV correspondents who interviewed citizens on the street were appalled at the ferocity of the comments. The common cry was 'Nuke the bastards'. Finally orders came from the top TV network news chiefs to stop covering the street scenes and to halt the interviews. The orders originated from Lawrence Salentine who had formed a council with the other owners of the media.

In the White House President Francis Kennedy didn't have time to grieve for his daughter. He was on the hotline to Russia to reassure them there was to be no territorial grabbing in the Far East. He was on the phone to heads of other states to plead for co-operation and to make them understand his own stance was irrevocable. That the President of the United States was not bluffing, the city of Dak would be destroyed, and that if the ultimatum was not obeyed the Sultanate of Sherhaben too would be destroyed.

Arthur Wix and Bert Audick were already on their way to Sherhaben in a fast jet passenger plane not yet available to the civilian aircraft industry. Oddblood Gray was frantically trying to rally Congress behind the President and by the end of the day knew he had failed. Eugene Dazzy calmly dealt with all the memoranda from Cabinet members and the Defense establishment, his Walkman firmly set over his ears to discourage unnecessary conversation from his staff. Christian Klee was appearing and disappearing on mysterious errands.

Senator Thomas Lambertino and Congressman Alfred Jintz held constant meetings through Wednesday with colleagues in the House and Senate on the action to impeach Kennedy. The Socrates Club called in all their markers. True the interpretation of the Constitution was a little murky, that Congress could designate itself as the deciding body, but the situation warranted such a drastic action. Kennedy's ultimatum to Sherhaben was so obviously based on personal emotions and not on reasons of State.

By late Wednesday the coalition was set. Both Houses, with barely two-thirds of the vote assured, would convene on Thursday night, just hours before Kennedy's deadline to destroy the city of Dak.

Lambertino and Jintz kept Oddblood Gray fully informed, hoping he could persuade Francis Kennedy to rescind his ultimatum to Sherhaben. Oddblood Gray told them that the President would not do so. He then briefed Francis Kennedy.

Francis Kennedy said, 'Otto, I think you and Chris and Dazzy should have late dinner with me tonight. Make it about eleven. And don't plan to get home right away.'

The President and his staff ate in the Yellow Room which was Kennedy's favorite though this was a lot of extra work for the kitchen and waiters. As usual the meal was very simple for Kennedy, a small grilled steak, a dish of thinly sliced tomatoes and then coffee with a variety of cream and fruit tarts. Christian and the others were offered the option of fish. None of them ate more than a few bites.

Kennedy seemed to be perfectly at ease, the others were awkward. They all wore black armbands on their jacket sleeves, as did Kennedy. Everyone in the White House including the servants wore the identical black band and it seemed archaic to Christian. He knew that Eugene Dazzy had sent out the memorandum for this to be done.

'Christian,' he said. 'I think it's time we share our problem. But it goes no further. No memorandum.'

'It's serious,' Christian said. And he outlined what had happened in the atomic bomb scare. He informed them that the two young men had refused to talk on the advice of their lawyer.

Oddblood Gray said incredulously, 'There's a nuclear device planted in New York City? I don't believe it. All this shit can't be happening at once.'

Eugene Dazzy said, 'Are you sure they really did plant a nuclear device?'

Christian said, 'I think there is only a ten per cent chance.' He believed that there was more than a ninety per cent chance but he was not willing to tell them that.

'What are you doing about it?' Dazzy said.

'We've got the nuclear search teams out,' Christian said. 'But there's a time element.' He spoke directly to Kennedy. 'I still need your signature to activate the Medical Interrogation Team for the PET test.' He explained the secret law in the Atomic Security Bill.

'No,' Francis Kennedy said.

They were all astonished by the President's refusal.

'We can't take a chance,' Dazzy said. 'Sign the order.'

Kennedy smiled and said, 'The invading of an individual's brain by government officials is a dangerous action.' He paused for a moment and said, 'We can't sacrifice a citizen's individual rights just on suspicion. Especially such potentially valuable citizens as those two young men. Chris when you have more confirmation, ask again.' Then Kennedy said to Oddblood Gray, 'Otto, brief Christian and Dazzy on the Congress.'

Gray said, 'Here is their game plan. They know now that the Vice President will not sign the declaration to impeach you under the Twenty-fifth Amendment. But enough of the Cabinet members have signed so that they can still take action. They will designate Congress as the other body to determine your fitness. They will convene late Thursday and then vote to impeach. Just to cancel you from the negotiations for the release of the hostages. Their argument is that you are under too much stress because of the death of your daughter.

'When you're removed, the Secretary of Defense will countermand your orders to bomb Dak. They are counting on Bert Audick to convince the Sultan to release the hostages during that thirty-day period. The Sultan will almost certainly comply.'

Kennedy turned to Dazzy. 'Put out a directive. No member of this government will contact Sherhaben. That will be regarded as treason.'

Eugene Dazzy said softly, 'With most of your Cabinet against you, there is no possibility your orders will be carried out. At this moment you have no power.'

Kennedy turned to Christian Klee. 'Chris,' he said, 'they need a two-thirds vote to remove me from office, right?'

'Yes,' Christian said. 'But without the Vice President's signature, it's basically illegal.'

Kennedy looked into his eyes. 'Isn't there anything you can do?'

In that moment Christian Klee's mind made another leap. Francis thought he could do something, but what was it? Christian said tentatively, 'We can call on the Supreme

Court and say the Congress is acting against the Constitution. The language is vague in the Twenty-fifth Amendment. Or we can argue that Congress is acting contrary to the spirit of the Amendment by substituting themselves as the instigating party after the Vice President refuses to sign. I can contact the Court so they'll rule right after Congress votes.'

He saw the look of disappointment in Kennedy's eyes and he racked his brain furiously. He was missing something.

Oddblood Gray said worriedly, 'The Congress is going to attack your mental capacity. They keep bringing up the week you disappeared. Just before your inauguration.'

Kennedy said, 'That's nobody's business.'

Christian became aware that the others were waiting for him to speak. They knew he had been with the President that mysterious week. He said, 'What happened in that week won't damage us.'

Francis Kennedy said, 'Euge, prepare the papers for firing the whole Cabinet except for Theodore Tappey. Prepare them as soon as possible and I'll sign right away. Have the Press Secretary give it to the media before Congress meets.'

Eugene Dazzy made notes then asked, 'What about the Chairman of the Joint Chiefs of Staff? Fire him too?'

'No,' Francis Kennedy said. 'Basically he's with us, the others ruled against him. Congress couldn't do this if it weren't for those bastards in the Socrates Club.'

Christian said, 'I've been handling the interrogation of the two young kids. They choose to remain silent. And if their lawyer has it his way, they will be released on bail tomorrow.'

Dazzy said sharply, 'There's a section in the Atomic Security Act that enables you to hold them. It suspends the right of habeas corpus, civil liberties. You must know that, Christian.'

'Number one,' Christian said, 'what's the point of holding them if Francis refuses to sign the medical interrogation order? Their lawyer applies for bail and if we refuse them we still must have the President's signature to suspend habeas corpus in this case. Francis, are you willing to sign an order for a suspension of habeas corpus?'

Kennedy smiled at him. 'No, Congress will use that against me.'

Christian was confident now. Still, for a moment, he felt a little sick and bile rose in his mouth. Then it passed and he knew what Kennedy wanted, he knew what he had to do.

Kennedy sipped his coffee, they had finished their meal, but none of them had taken more than a few bites. Kennedy said, 'Let's discuss the real crisis. Am I still going to be President in forty-eight hours?'

Oddblood Gray said, 'Rescind the order to bomb Dak, turn over the negotiations to a special team, and no action to remove you will be taken by Congress.'

'Who gave you that deal?' Kennedy asked.

'Senator Lambertino and Congressman Jintz,' Otto Gray said. 'Lambertino is a genuine good guy and Jintz is responsible, in a political affair like this. They wouldn't double-cross us.'

'OK, that's another option,' Kennedy said. 'That and going to the Supreme Court. What else?'

Eugene Dazzy said, 'Go on TV tomorrow before Congress convenes and appeal to the nation. The people will be for you and that may give Congress pause.'

'OK,' Kennedy said. 'Euge, clear it with the TV people for me to go on over all the networks. Just fifteen minutes is what we need.'

Eugene Dazzy said softly, 'Francis, it's an awful big step we're taking. The President and the Congress in such a direct confrontation and then calling upon the masses to take action? It could get very messy.'

Oddblood Gray said, 'I think the President is making the right decision. That guy Yabril will string us out for weeks and make this country look like a big lump of shit.'

Christian said, 'There's a rumor that one of the staff in

this room or Arthur Wix is going to sign that declaration to remove the President. Whoever it is should speak now.'

Kennedy said impatiently, 'That rumor is nonsense. If one of you were going to do that you would have resigned beforehand. I know all of you too well, none of you could betray me.'

After dinner they went from the Yellow Room to the little movie theater on the other side of the White House. Francis Kennedy had told Dazzy that he wanted to see all the TV footage of the murder of his daughter.

In the darkness, the nervous voice of Eugene Dazzy said, 'The TV coverage starts now.' For a few seconds the movie screen was streaked with black lines that seemed to scramble from top to bottom.

The screen lit up with brilliant colors, the TV cameras covering the hugh aircraft squatting on the desert sand like some horror bug. Then the cameras zoomed to the figure of Yabril presenting Theresa Kennedy in the doorway. Kennedy saw that his daughter was smiling slightly and then she waved to the camera. It was an odd wave, a wave of reassurance, yet of subjugation. Yabril was beside her, then slightly behind her. And then there was the movement of the right arm, the gun not visible, and the flat report of the shot and then the billowing ghostly pink mist and the body of Theresa Kennedy falling. Kennedy heard the wail of the crowd and recognized it as grief and not triumph. Then the figure of Yabril appeared in the doorway. He held his gun aloft, an oily gleaming tube of black metal. He held it as a gladiator holds a sword but there were no cheers. The film came to an end. Eugene Dazzy had edited it severely.

The lights came on but Francis Kennedy remained still. He was surprised that he felt a weakening of his body. He couldn't move his legs or his torso. But his mind was clear, there was no shock or disorder in his brain. He did not feel the helplessness of tragedy's victim. He would not have to struggle against fate or God. He only had to struggle against his enemies in this world and he would conquer them.

He would not let mortal man defeat him. When his wife had died he had no recourse against the hand of God, the faults of nature. He had bowed his entire being in acceptance. But his daughter's malicious man-made death, oh, that he could punish, and redress. That was within his material world. This time he would not bow his head. Woe to that world, to his enemies, woe to the wicked in this world.

When he was finally able to lift his body from the chair he smiled reassuringly to the men around him. He had accomplished his purpose. He had made his closest and most powerful friends suffer with him. They would not now so easily oppose the actions he must take.

Christian thought about that day in early December, over three years ago, when Francis Kennedy, the President elect of the United States, who would be sworn into office the following January, had waited for him outside the monastery in Vermont. For that was the secret that newspapers and his political opponents often referred to. That Kennedy had disappeared for a week. There had been speculations that he had been under psychiatric care, that he had broken down, that he had a secret love affair. But only two people knew the truth, the Abbot of the monstery and Christian Klee.

It was a week after his election that Christian had driven Francis Kennedy to the Catholic monstery just outside of White River Junction in Vermont. They were greeted by the Abbot who was the only one who knew Kennedy's identity.

The resident monks lived apart from the world, cut off from all media and even the town itself. These monks communicated only with God and the earth on which they grew their livelihood. They had all taken a vow of silence and did not speak except in prayer or yelps of pain when they were ill or injured themselves in some domestic accident.

Only the Abbot had a television set and access to newspapers. The TV news programs were a constant source of amusement to him. He particularly fancied the concept of the 'anchor man' on the night broadcasts and often ironically thought of himself for humility.

When the car drove up, the Abbot was waiting for them at the monastery gate, flanked by two monks in ragged brown robes and sandaled feet. Christian took Kennedy's bag from the trunk and watched the Abbot shake hands with the President elect. The Abbot seemed more like an inn keeper than a holy man. He had a jolly grin to welcome them and when he was introduced to Christian he said jocularly, 'Why don't you stay? A week of silence wouldn't do you any harm. I've seen you on television and you must be tired of talking.'

Christian smiled his thanks but did not reply. He was looking at Francis Kennedy as they shook hands. The handsome face was very composed, the handshake was not emotional, Kennedy was not a demonstrative man. He seemed not to be grieving the death of his wife. He had more the preoccupied look of a man forced to go into hospital for a minor operation.

'Let's hope we can keep this secret,' Christian had said. People don't like these religious retreats. They might think you've gone nuts.'

Francis Kennedy's face twisted into a little smile. A controlled but natural courtesy. 'They won't find out,' he said. 'And I know you'll cover. Pick me up in a week. That should be enough time.'

Christian thought, what would happen to Francis in those days? He felt close to tears. He took hold of Francis by the shoulders and said, 'Do you want me to stay with you?' Kennedy had shaken his head and walked through the gates of the monastery. On that day Christian thought he had seemed OK.

The day after Christmas was so clear and bright, so

cleansed by cold that it seemed as if the whole world was enclosed in glass, the sky a mirror, the earth brown steel. And when Christian drove up to the monastery gate, Francis Kennedy was alone, waiting for him without any luggage, his hands stretched over his head, his body taut and straining upward. He seemed to be exulting in his freedom.

When Christian got out of the car to greet him, Francis Kennedy gave him a quick embrace and a shout of joyous welcome. He seemed to have been rejuvenated by his stay in the monastery. He smiled at Christian and it was one of his rare brilliant smiles that had enchanted multitudes. The smile that reassured the world that happiness could be won, that man was good, that the world would go on forever to better and better things. It was a smile that made you love him because of its delight in his seeing you. Christian had felt such relief at seeing that smile. Francis would be OK. He would be as strong as he had always been. He would be the hope of the world, the strong guardian of his country and fellow man. Now they would do great deeds together.

And then with that same brilliant smile Kennedy took Christian by the arm, looked into his eyes, and said, simply and yet with amusement, as if it didn't really mean anything, as if he were reporting some minor detail of information, 'God didn't help.'

And in the cold scrubbed world of a winter morning. Christian saw that finally something had been broken in Kennedy. That he would never be the same man again. That part of his mind had been chopped away. He would be almost the same but now there was a timy lump of falseness that had never before existed. He saw that Kennedy himself did not know this and that nobody else would know. And that he, Christian, only knew because he was the one who was here at his point of time, to see the brilliant smile and hear the joking words, 'God didn't help.'

Christian said, 'What the hell, you only gave him seven days.'

Kennedy laughed. 'And he's a busy man,' he said.

So they had gotten into the car. They had a wonderful day. Kennedy had never been more witty, had never been in such high spirits. He was full of plans, anxious to get his administration together and make wonderful things happen in the four years to come. He seemed to be a man who had reconciled himself to his misfortune, renewed his energies. And it almost convinced Christian.

Late Tuesday afternoon Christian Klee slipped away from the frenetic White House for a few hours to get all the ducks in a row. He had to see first of all Eugene Dazzy, then a certain Jeralyn Albanese, then the Oracle, and also the great Dr Zed Annaccone.

Dazzy he cornered for a few moments in the Chief of Staff's office and that was easy. His next stop was Dr Annaccone in the building of the National Science Institute and he wanted to make that fast. He had to be in the White House when Kennedy called for a final strategy meeting before Congress voted. He thought grimly he would solve a few of the problems this afternoon, give Francis Kennedy a fighting chance. And then his mind did a curious trick. Somewhere this afternoon he would have to secretly interrogate Adam Gresse and Henry Tibbot but his mind refused to include the two young scientists in his agenda. He would have to do it but he would not think about it, it would not be part of his agenda until he did it.

Dr Zed Annaccone was one of those short thin men with a big chest. His face was extraordinarily alert and the expression on it was not really supercilious, just the confidence of a man who believed he knew more about the important things on this earth than anyone else. Which was quite true.

Dr Annaccone was the Medical Science Advisor to the President of the United States. He was also the Director of the National Brain Research Institute and the administrative head of the Medical Advisory Board of the Atomic Security Commission. Once at a White House dinner party, Klee had heard him say that the brain was such a sophisticated organ that it could produce whatever chemicals the body needed. And Klee simply thought, 'So what?'

The Doctor, reading his mind, patted him on the shoulder and said, 'That fact is more important to civilisation than anything you guys can do here in the White House. And all we need is a billion dollars to prove it. What the hell is that, one aircraft carrier?' Then he had smiled at Klee to show that he meant no offense.

And now he was smiling when Klee walked into his office.

'So,' Dr Annaccone said, 'finally even the lawyers come to me. You realize our philosophies are directly opposed?'

Klee knew that Dr Annaccone was about to make a joke about the legal profession and was slightly irritated. Why did people always have wise-ass remarks about lawyers?

'Truth,' Dr Annaccone said. 'Lawyers always seek to obscure it, we scientists try to reveal it.' He smiled again.

'No, no,' Klee said and smiled to show he had a sense of humor. 'I'm here for information. We have a situation that calls for that special PET study under the Atomic Security Act.'

'You know you have to get the President's signature on that?' Dr Annaccone said. 'Personally I'd do the procedure for many other situations but the civil libertarians would kick my ass.'

'I know,' Christian said. Then he explained the situation of the atom bomb and capture of Gresse and Tibbot. 'Nobody thinks there is really a bomb, but if there is, then the time factor is crucially important. And the President refused to sign the order.'

'Why?' Dr Annaccone asked.

'Because of the possible brain damage that could occur during the procedure,' Klee said.

This seemed to surprise Annaccone. He thought for a moment. 'The possibility of significant brain damage is very small,' he said. 'Maybe ten per cent. The greater danger is the rare incidence of cardiac arrest and the even rarer side effect post procedure of complete and total memory loss. Complete amnesia. But even that shouldn't dissuade him in this case. I've sent the President papers on it, I hope he reads them.'

'He reads everything,' Christian said. 'But I'm afraid it won't change his mind.'

'Too bad we don't have more time,' Dr Annaccone said. 'We are just completing tests that will result in an infallible lie detector based on computer measurement of the chemical changes in the brain. The new test is much like the PET but without the ten per cent damage risk. It will be completely safe. But we can't use that now, there would be too many elements of doubt until further data are compiled to satisfy the legal requirements.'

Christian felt a tinge of excitement. 'A safe, infallible lie detector that would be admitted into court?' he said.

'As to being admitted into a court of law, I don't know,' Dr Annaccone said. 'Scientifically, when our tests have been thoroughly analyzed and compiled by the computers, the new brain lie detector test will be as infallible as DNA and fingerprinting. That's one thing. But to get it enacted into law is another. The Civil Liberties groups will fight it to the death. They're convinced that a man should not be used to testify against himself. And how would people in Congress like the idea that they could be made to take such a test under criminal law?'

Klee said, 'I wouldn't like to take it.'

Annaccone laughed. 'Congress would be signing their own political death warrant. And yet where's the true logic? Our laws were made to prevent confessions obtained by foul means. However, this is science.' He paused for a moment.

'How about business leaders or even errant husbands and wives?'

'That's a little creepy,' Klee admitted.

Dr Annaccone said, 'But what about all those old sayings. Like "The truth shall make you free?" Like, "Truth is the greatest of virtues." Like, "Truth is the very essence of life." That man's struggle to discover truth is his greatest ideal?' Dr Annaccone laughed. 'When our tests are verified, I'll bet my Institute budget will get chopped.'

Christian said, 'That's my area of competence. We dress up the law. We specify that your test can only be used in important criminal cases. We restrict its use to the government. Make it like a strictly controlled narcotic substance or arms manufacturing. So if you can get the test proven scientifically, I can get the legislation.' Then he asked, 'Exactly how the hell does that work anyway?'

'The new PET?' Dr Annaccone said. 'It's very simple. Physically not invasive. No surgeon with a blade in his hand. No obvious scars. Just a small injection of a chemical substance into the brain through the blood vessels. Chemical self-sabotage with psychopharmaceuticals.'

'It's voodoo to me,' Christian said. 'You should be in jail with those two physics guys.'

Dr Annaccone laughed. 'No connection,' he said. 'Those guys work to blow up the world. I work to get at the inner truths. How man really thinks, what he really feels.'

Dr Zed Annaccone had caused President Kennedy more political trouble than any other member of the administration. And he had done it by doing his job too well. His National Science Institute had provided a hailstorm of political fire by harvesting vital organs from dead babies to use as transplants. Dr Annaccone had used funds for genetic engineering experiments on human volunteers. Genetic transplants for people prone to cancer, to Alzheimer's, to all the still mysterious maladies that struck kidneys, livers, eyes. He had proposed a program of genetic experiments that outraged most of the different church establishments, the general public and the political powers. And Dr Annaccone didn't really know why there was such a fuss. He had contempt for his opponents and he showed it.

But even he knew that a brain lie detector test meant legal trouble. 'This will be perhaps the most important discovery in the medical history of our time,' Dr Annaccone said. 'Imagine if we can read the brain. All your lawyers will be out of a job.'

Christian said. 'Do you think it's possible to figure out how the brain works, really?

Dr Annaccone shrugged. 'No,' he said. 'If the brain were that simple, we would be too simple to figure it out.' He gave Christian another grin. 'Catch 22. Our brain will never catch up with the brain. Because of that, no matter what happens, mankind can never be more than a higher form of animal.' He was overjoyed by this fact.

He became abstracted for a moment. 'You know there's a "ghost in the machine," Koestler's phrase. Man has two brains really, the primitive brain and the overlying civilized brain. Have you noticed there is a certain unexplainable malice in human beings. A useless malice?'

Christian said, 'Call the President about the PET. Try to persuade him.'

Dr Annaccone said, 'I will. He is really being too chicken. The procedure won't damage those kids a bit.'

Christian Klee next went to pay a call on Jeralyn Albanese who owned the famous restaurant in Washington DC, naturally named 'Jera'. It had three huge dining rooms separated from each other by a very lush lounge bar. The Republicans gravitated to one dining room, the Democrats to another, and members of the Executive Branch and the White House ate in the third room. The one thing on which all parties agreed was that the food was delicious, the service superb, and the hostess one of the most charming women in the world.

Twenty years ago, Jeralyn, then a woman of thirty, had been employed by a lobbyist for the banking industry. He had introduced her to Martin Mutford, who had not yet earned the nickname 'Private' but was already on the rise. Martin Mutford had been charmed by her wit, her brashness, and her sense of adventure. For five years, they had an affair which did not interfere with their private lives. Jeralyn Albanese continued her career as a lobbyist, a career much more complicated and refined than generally supposed, requiring a great deal of research skill and administrative genius. Oddly enough, one of her most valuable assets was having been a champion college tennis player.

As an assistant to the chief lobbyist or the banking industry, a good part of her week was amassing financial data to convince experts on the Congressional Finance Committees to pass legislation favorable to banking. Then she included hostess conference dinners with Congressmen and Senators. She was astonished by the horniness of these calm, judicial legislators. In private, they were rioting golddust miners, they drank to excess, they sang lustily, they grabbed her ass in a spirit of old time American folksiness. She was amazed and delighted by their lust. It developed naturally that she went to the Bahamas and to Las Vegas with the younger and more personable Congressmen, always under the disguise of conferences, and even once to London to a convention of economic advisors from all over the world. Not to influence the vote on a bill, not to perpetrate a swindle, but if the vote on a bill was borderline, when a girl as pretty as Jeralyn Albanese presented the customary foot-high stack of opinion papers written by eminent economists, you had a very good chance of getting that teetering vote. As Martin Mutford said, 'On the close ones it's very hard for a man to vote against a girl who sucked his cock the night before.'

It was Mutford who had taught her to appreciate the finer things in life. He had taken her to the museums in New York, he had taken her to the Hamptons to mingle with the rich and the artists, the old money and the new money, the famous journalists and the TV anchors, the writers who did serious novels and the important screenplays of big movies. Another pretty face didn't make much of a splash there, but being a good tennis player gave her an edge.

Jeralyn had more men fall in love with her because of her tennis playing than her beauty, the intrinsic grace of her female form more revealed by tennis. And it was a sport that men who were mere 'hackers', as politicians and artists usually were, loved to play with good looking women. In mixed doubles, Jeralyn could establish a sporting rapport with partners, her golden skin and lovely limbs linked to her partner in their struggle for conquest.

But there came a time when Jeralyn had to think of her future. She was not married, and at forty years of age the Congressmen she would have to lobby were in their unappealing sixties and seventies.

Martin Mutford was eager to promote her in the high realms of banking, but after the excitement of Washington, banking seemed dull. American lawmakers were so fascinating with their outrageous mendacity in public affairs, their charming innocence in sexual relationships. It was Martin Mutford who came up with the solution. He, too, did not want to lose Jeralyn in a maze of computer reports. In Washington her beautifully furnished apartment was a refuge from his heavy responsibilities. It was Martin Mutford who came up with the idea that she could own and run a restaurant that would be a political hub.

The funds were supplied by American Sterling Trustees, a lobbyist group that represented banking interests, in the form of a five million dollar loan. Jeralyn had the restaurant built to her specification. It would be an exclusive club, an auxiliary home for the politicos of Washington. Many

Congressmen were separated from their families while Congress was in session and the Jera restaurant was a place where they could spend lonely nights. In addition to the three dining rooms and waiting lounge and bar, there was a room with TV and a reading room that had a copy of all the major magazines published in the United States and England. There was another room for chess or checkers or cards. But the ultimate attraction was the residential building built on top of the restaurant.

It was three storeys high and held twenty apartments. These apartments were rented by the lobbyists who loaned them out to Congressmen and important bureaucrats for secretive liaisons. 'Jera' was known to be the very soul of discretion in these matters. Jeralyn kept the keys.

It amazed Jeralyn that these hardworking men had the time for so much dalliance. They were indefatigable. And it was the older ones with established families, some with grandchildren, who were the most active. Jeralyn loved to see these same Congressmen and Senators on television, so sedate and distinguished looking, lecturing on morals, decrying drugs and loose living and the importance of old-fashioned values. She never felt they were hypocrites really. After all, men who had spent so much of their lives and time and energy for their country deserved extra consideration.

She really didn't like the arrogance, the smarmy self-assured smugness of the younger Congressmen, but she loved the old guys, like the stern-faced wrathful Senator who never smiled in public but cavorted at least twice a week bare-assed with young 'models'. And old Congressman Jintz with his body like a scarred zeppelin and a face so ugly that the whole country believed he was honest. All of them looked absolutely awful in private, shedding their clothes. But they charmed her. Why did men keep wanting to do that?

Rarely did the women members of Congress come to the restaurant and never did they make use of the apartments.

Feminism had not yet advanced so far. To make up for this Jeralyn gave little lunches in the restaurant for some of her girlfriends in the arts, pretty actresses, singers and dancers.

It was none of her business if these young pretty women struck up friendships with the highly placed servants of the people of the United States. But she was surprised when Eugene Dazzy, the huge slobby Chief of Staff to the President of the United States, took up with a promising young dancer and arranged for Jeralyn to slip him a key to one of the apartments above the restaurant. She was even more astonished when the liaison grew to the status of a 'relationship'. Not that Dazzy had that much time at his disposal, the most he spent in the apartment was a few hours after lunch. And Jeralyn was under no illusion as to what the rent-paying lobbyist could get out of it. Dazzy's decisions would not be influenced, but at least he would, on rare occasions, take the lobbyists' calls to the White House so that the lobbyists' clients would be impressed by such access.

Jeralyn gave all this information to Martin Mutford when they gossiped together. It was understood that the information between the two of them was not to be used in any way and certainly not in any form of blackmail. That could be disastrous and destroy the main purpose of the restaurant, which was to further the atmosphere of good fellowship and earned a sympathetic ear for the lobbyists who were footing the bill. Plus the fact that the restaurant was Jeralyn's main source of livelihood and she would not allow it to be jeopardized.

So Jeralyn was very much surprised when Christian Klee dropped in on her when the restaurant was almost empty between lunch and dinner. She received him in her office. She liked Klee though he ate at 'Jera' infrequently and had never tried to make use of the apartments above. But she had no feeling of apprehension, she knew that there was nothing he could reproach her for. If some scandal was

231

brewing, no matter what newspaper reporters were up to, or what one of the young girls would say, she was in the clear.

She murmured some words of commiseration about the terrible times he must be going through, what with the murders and the hijacking, but careful not to sound as if she were fishing for inside information. Klee thanked her.

Then he said, 'Jeralyn, we've known each other a long time and I want to alert you, for your protection. I know what I'm about to say will shock you as much as it does me.'

Oh, shit, Jeralyn thought. Somebody is making trouble for me.

Christian Klee went on. 'A lobbyist for financial interests is a good friend of Eugene Dazzy and he tried to lay some bullshit on him. He urged Dazzy to sign a paper that would do President Kennedy a great deal of harm. He warned Dazzy that his using your apartments could be made public and ruin his career and his marriage.' Klee laughed. 'Jesus, who would ever have thought Eugene was capable of a thing like that. What the hell, I guess we're all human.'

Jeralyn was not fooled by Christian's good humor. She knew she had to be very careful or her whole life might go down the drain. Klee was Attorney General of the United States. And had acquired the reputation of being a very dangerous man. He could give her more trouble than she could handle, even though her ace in the hole was Martin Mutford. She said, 'I didn't have anything to do with all that. Sure, I gave Dazzy the key to one of the apartments upstairs. But hell, that was just a courtesy of the house. There are no records of any kind. Nobody could pin anything on me or Dazzy.'

'Sure, I know that,' Christian said. 'But don't you see, that lobbyist would never dare pull that shit on his own? Somebody higher up told him what to do.'

Jeralyn said uneasily, 'Christian, I swear I never blabbed to anyone. I would never put my restaurant in jeopardy. I'm not that dumb.'

'I know, I know,' Christian said reassuringly. 'But you and Martin have been very good friends for a very long time. You may have told him, just as a piece of gossip.'

Now Jeralyn was really horrified. Suddenly she was between two powerful men who were about to do battle. More than anything else in the world she wanted to step outside the arena. She also knew that the worst thing to do was lie.

'Martin would never try such a dumb thing,' she said. 'Not that kind of stupid blackmail.' By saying this, she admitted she had told Martin and yet she could deny that she had explicitly confessed.

Christian was still reassuring. He saw that she had not guessed the real purpose of his visit. He said, 'Eugene Dazzy told the lobbyist to go fuck himself. Then he told me the story and I said I would take care of it. Now, of course, I know they can't expose Dazzy. For one thing, I'd come down on you and this place so you'd think a tank hit you. I'd make you identify all the people in Congress who used those apartments. There would be one hell of a scandal. Your friend was just hoping Dazzy would lose his nerve. But Eugene figured that one out.'

Jeralyn was still unbelieving. 'Martin would never instigate something so dangerous. He's a banker.' She smiled at Christian who sighed and decided it was time to get tough.

'Listen, Jeralyn,' he said. 'Old "Take Me Private" Martin is not your usual nice stolid conservative banker. He's had a few trouble spots in his life. And he didn't make his billions by playing it safe. He's cut things a bit close before.' He paused for a moment. 'Now he's meddling in something very dangerous for you and for him.'

Jeralyn gave a contemptuous wave of her hand. 'You said yourself you knew I had nothing to do with what the hell ever he is doing.'

'True,' Christian said. 'I know that. But now Martin is a

man I have to watch. And I want you to help me watch him.'

Jeralyn was adamant. 'Like hell,' she said. 'Martin has always treated me decently. He's a real friend.'

Christian said, 'I don't want you to be a spy. I don't want any information about his business dealing or about his personal life. All I'm asking is that if you know anything or find out any moves he's going to make against the President, you give me fair warning.'

'Oh, fuck you,' Jeralyn said. 'Get the hell out of here, I have to get ready for the supper crowd.'

'Sure,' Christian said amiably. 'I'm leaving. But remember this, I *am* the Attorney General of the United States. We're in tough times and it doesn't hurt to have me as a friend. So use your own judgment when the time comes. If you slip me just a little warning, no one will ever know. Use your own good sense.'

He left. He had accomplished his purpose. Jeralyn might tell Martin Mutford about their interview, which was fine, for that would make Mutford more cautious. Or she would not tell Martin and when the time came, she'd snitch. Either way he couldn't lose.

Christian Klee had spent no more than thirty minutes with Jeralyn Albanese. Back in his official car he had the driver put on the siren. He had to get back to the White House as soon as possible, Kennedy would be looking for him. But first he had another stop to make. He had received a message from the Oracle. It was a request that he come to see him at his mansion and the message had been urgently phrased.

As his car snaked through traffic, siren screaming, he stared at the monuments, the buildings of marble with fluted columns, the stately domed buildings of embassies with flags flying, the eternal architecture with which established authority proclaimed its existence and supreme power. How worthless they seemed now, just waiting to be razed by

234

outside barbaric hordes, if not physically, then psychologically.

He reviewed the meeting he'd had with Dazzy. The rumor that one of the White House personal staff would sign the petition to remove Kennedy from the Presidency had set off warning signals. After the meeting, he had followed Eugene Dazzy back to the Office of the Chief of Staff.

Eugene Dazzy was at his desk surrounded by three secretaries taking notes for actions to be taken by his own personal staff. He wore his Walkman over his ears but the sound was turned off. And his usual good-humored face was grim. He looked up and said, 'Chris, this is the worst possible time for you to come snooping around.'

Christian said, 'Eugene, don't bullshit me. Nobody seems curious to know who the rumored traitor on the staff is. That means everybody knows, except me. And I'm the guy who should know.'

Dazzy dismissed his secretaries. They were alone in the office. Dazzy smiled at Christian. 'It never occurred to me you didn't know. You keep track of everything with your FBI and Secret Service, your stealth intelligence and listening devices. Those thousands of agents the Congress doesn't know you have on the payroll. How come you're so ignorant?'

Christian said coldly, 'I know you're fucking some dancer twice a week in those apartments that belong to Jeralyn's restaurant.'

Dazzy sighed. 'That's it. This lobbyist who loans me the apartment came to see me. He asked me to sign the removal of the President document. He wasn't crude about it, there were no direct threats but the implication was clear. Sign it or my little sins would be all over the papers and television.' Dazzy laughed. 'I couldn't believe it. How could they be so dumb?'

Christian said, 'So what answer did you give?'

Dazzy smiled. 'I crossed his name off my "friends" list. I

barred him access. And I told him I would give my old buddy Christian Klee his name as a potential threat to the security of the President. Then I told Francis. He told me to forget the whole thing.'

Christian said, 'Who sent the guy?'

Dazzy said 'The only guy who would dare is a member of the Socrates Club. And that would be our old friend, Martin "Take Me Private" Mutford.'

Christian said, 'He's smarter than that.'

'Sure he is,' Dazzy said grimly. 'Everybody is smarter than that until they get desperate. When the VP refused to sign the impeachment memorandum, they became desperate. Besides, you never know when somebody will cave in.'

Christian still didn't like it. 'But they know you. They know that under all that flab you're a tough guy. I've seen you in action. You ran one of the biggest companies in the United States, you cut IBM a new asshole just five years ago. How could they think you'd cave in?'

Dazzy shrugged. 'Everybody always thinks they're tougher than anybody else.' He paused. 'You do it yourself, though you don't advertise it. I do it. So does Wix and so does Gray. Francis doesn't think it. He just can be. And we have to be careful for Francis. We have to be careful he doesn't get too tough.'

The driver cut off the siren and they were gliding through the gates of the Oracle's estate. Christian noted that there were three limousines waiting in the circular driveway. And it was curious that the drivers were in their seats behind the wheel and not outside smoking cigarettes. Beside each car lounged a tall well-dressed man. Christian nailed them at once. Bodyguards. So the Oracle had important visitors.

Christian was greeted by the butler who led him to a living room furnished for a conference. The Oracle was in his wheelchair waiting. Around the table were five members of the Socrates Club. Christian was surprised to see them. His latest report was that all five had been in California.

The Oracle motored his wheelchair to the head of the table. 'You must forgive me, Christian, for this slight deception,' he said, 'I felt it was important that you meet with my friends at this critical time. They are anxious to talk to you.'

Servants had set the conference table with coffee and sandwiches. There were also drinks being served, the servers summoned by a buzzer the Oracle could reach beneath the table. The five members of the Socrates Club had already refreshed themselves. Martin Mutford had lit up a huge cigar and unbuttoned his collar, loosened his tie. He looked a little grim, but Christian knew that his grimness of face was often a tightening of the muscles to conceal fear.

He said, 'Martin, Eugene Dazzy told me one of your lobbyists gave him some bad advice today. I hope you had nothing to do with that.'

'Dazzy can weed out good from bad,' Mutford said. 'Otherwise he wouldn't be the President's Chief of Staff.'

'Sure he can,' Christian said. 'And he doesn't need advice from me on how to break balls. But I can give him a hand.'

Christian could see that the Oracle and George Greenwell did not know what he was talking about. But Lawrence Salentine and Louis Inch were smiling slightly.

Louis Inch said impatiently, 'That's unimportant, not relevant to our meeting here tonight.'

'What the hell is the purpose?' Christian said.

It was Lawrence Salentine who answered him in a smooth calming voice, he was used to handling confrontations. 'This is a very difficult time,' he said. 'I think even a dangerous time. All the people here favor the deposing of President Kennedy for a period of thirty days. Congress will vote tomorrow night in special session. Vice President DuPray's refusal to sign makes things difficult, but not impossible. It would be very helpful if you as a member of the President's personal staff would sign. That is what we are asking you to do.'

Christian was so astonished he could not answer. The Oracle broke in. 'I agree. It will be better for Kennedy not to handle this particular issue. His action today was completely irrational and springs from a desire for vengeance. It could lead to terrible events. Christian, I implore you to listen to these men.'

Christian Klee said very deliberately, 'There is not one chance in hell.' He spoke directly to the Oracle. 'How could you be party to this? How can you, of all people, be against me?'

The Oracle shook his head. 'I'm not against you,' he said.

Lawrence Salentine said, 'He can't just destroy fifty billion dollars because he suffered a personal tragedy. That's not what democracy is about.'

Christian had regained his composure. He said in a reasonable tone of voice, 'That is not the truth. Francis Kennedy has reasoned this out. He doesn't want the hijackers to string us along for weeks milking TV time on your networks, Mr Salentine, with the United States being held up to ridicule. For Christ's sake, they killed the Pope of the Catholic Church, they murdered the daughter of the President of the United States. You want to negotiate with them now? You want to set the killer of the Pope free? You call yourself patriots? You say you worry about this country? You are a bunch of hypocrites.'

For the first time, George Greenwell spoke. 'What about the other hostages? Are you willing to sacrifice them?'

And Christian shot back without thinking. 'Yes.' He paused and then said, 'I think the President's way is the best possible chance to get them out alive.'

George Greenwell said, 'Bert Audick is in Sherhaben now, as you know. He has assured us that he can persuade the hijackers and the Sultan to release the remaining hostages.'

Christian said contemptuously, 'I heard him assure the

President of the United States that no harm would come to Theresa Kennedy. And now she's dead.'

Lawrence Salentine said, 'Mr Klee, we can argue all these minor points till Domesday. We haven't got the time. We were hoping you would join us and make it easier. What must be done will be done whether you agree to it or not. I assure you of that. But why make this struggle more divisive? Why not serve the President by working with us?'

Christian Klee looked at him coldly. 'Don't bullshit me. Let me tell you this, I know you men carry a lot of weight in this country, weight that is unconstitutional. My office will investigate all of you as soon as this crisis is over.'

George Greenwell gave a sigh. The violent and senseless ire of young men was boring to a man of his experience and age. He said to Christian, 'Mr Klee, we all thank you for coming. And I hope there will be no personal animosity. We are acting to help our country.'

Christian said, 'You are acting to save Audick his fifty billion dollars.' He had a flash of insight. These men did not have a real hope of recruiting him. This was simply intimidation. That he would possibly remain neutral. Then he got their sense of fear. They feared him. That he had the power and more importantly he had the will. And the only one who could have warned them about him was the Oracle.

They were all silent. Then the Oracle said, 'You can go, I know you have to get back. Call me and let me know what's happening. Keep me abreast.'

Christian, hurt by the Oracle's betrayal, said, 'You could have warned me.'

The Oracle shook his head. 'You wouldn't have come. And I couldn't convince my friends that you wouldn't sign. I had to give them their shot.' He paused for a moment. 'I'll see you out,' he said to Christian. And he rolled his wheelchair out of the room. Christian followed him.

Before Christian left the room he turned to the members of the Socrates Club and said, 'Gentlemen, I beg of you,

239

don't let the Congress do this.' He gave off such a grave menace that nobody spoke.

When the Oracle and Klee were alone on the top of the ramp leading to the entrance foyer, the Oracle braced his wheelchair. He lifted his head, so freckled with the brown of aging skin, and said to Christian, 'You are my godson, and you are my heir. All this doesn't change my affection for you. But be warned. I love my country and I perceive your Francis Kennedy as a great danger.'

For the first time Christian Klee felt a bitterness against this old man he had always loved. 'You and your Socrates Club have Francis by the balls,' he said. 'You people are the danger.'

The Oracle was studying him. 'But you don't seem too worried. Christian, I beg of you don't be rash. Don't do something irrevocable. I know you have a great deal of power and more importantly a great deal of cunning. You are gifted, I know. But don't try to overpower history.'

'I don't know what you are talking about,' Christian said. He was in a hurry now. He had his last stop to make before going back to the White House. He had to interrogate Gresse and Tibbot.

The Oracle sighed, 'Remember, no matter what happens I still have my affection. You are the only living person I love. And if it is within my power I will never let anything happen to you. Call me, keep me abreast.'

Christian felt again his old affection for the Oracle. He squeezed his shoulder and said, 'What the hell, it's only a political difference, we've had them before. Don't worry, I'll call you.'

The Oracle gave him a crooked smile. 'And don't forget my birthday party. When this is all over if we are both alive.'

And Christian to his astonishment saw the tears dropping on to that withered, aged, seamed face. He leaned only to kiss that cheek, so parched that it was cool as glass.

*

When Christian Klee got back to the White House, he went directly to Oddblood Gray's office but the secretary told him that Gray was having a conference with Congressman Jintz and Senator Lambertino. The secretary looked frightened. She had heard rumors that Congress was trying to remove President Kennedy from office.

Christian said, 'Buzz him, tell him it's important and let me use your desk and phone. You go to the ladies' room.'

Gray answered the phone, thinking he was talking to his secretary. 'It better be important,' he said.

Christian said, 'Otto, it's Chris. Listen I've just been asked by some guys in the Socrates Club to sign the removal memo. Dazzy was asked to sign, they tried to blackmail him over that affair with the dancer. I know Wix is on his way to Sherhaben so he's not signing the petition. Are you signing?'

Oddblood Gray's voice was very silky. 'It's funny, I've just been asked to sign by the two gentlemen in my office. I already told them I would not. And I told them nobody else on the personal staff would sign. I didn't have to ask you.' There was sarcasm in his voice.

Christian said impatiently, 'I knew you wouldn't sign, Otto. But I had to ask. But look, put out some lightning bolts. Tell those guys that as the Attorney General, I'm launching an investigation into the blackmail threat on Dazzy. Also, that I have a lot of stuff on some of those Congressmen and Senators that won't look too good in the papers and I'll leak it. Especially their business with members of the Socrates Club. This is no time for your English Oxford bullshit.'

Oddblood Gray said smoothly, 'Thanks for the advice, old buddy. But why don't you take care of your stuff and I'll take care of mine. And don't ask other people to wave your sword around, wave it yourself.'

There had always been a subtle antagonism between Oddblood Gray and Christian Klee. Personally they liked

241

and respected each other. Both were physically impressive, Gray had a social bravery. But he had achieved everything on his own. Christian Klee had been born to wealth but had refused to live the life of a rich man. He had been a physically brave officer and then a CIA Field Director directly involved in clandestine operations. They were both respected men in the world. They were both devoted to Francis Kennedy. They were both skilled lawyers.

And yet they were both wary of each other. Oddblood Gray had the utmost faith in the progress of society through law, which was why he was so valuable as the President's liaison man with Congress. And he had always distrusted the consolidation of power Klee had put together. It was too much that in a country like the United States any man should be Director of the FBI, Chief of the Secret Service and also Attorney General. True, Francis Kennedy had explained his reasons for this concentration of power. That it was to help protect the President himself against the threat of assassination. But Gray still didn't like it.

Christian Klee had always been a little impatient with Gray's scrupulous attention to every legality. Gray could afford to be the punctilious statesman. He dealt with politicians and political problems. But Christian Klee felt he had to shovel away the murderous shit of everyday life. The election of Francis Kennedy had brought all the cockroaches from the fabric of America. Only Klee knew the thousands of murder threats the President had received. Only Klee could stamp those cockroaches dead. And he couldn't always observe the finer points of the law to do his job. Or so Klee believed.

Now was a case in point. Klee wanted to use power, Gray the velvet glove.

'OK,' said Christian said. 'I'll do what I have to do.'

'Fine,' Oddblood Gray said. 'Now me and you can go together to see the President. He wants us in the Cabinet Room as soon as I'm through here.'

Oddblood Gray had been deliberately indiscreet while on the phone with Christian Klee. Now he faced Congressman Jintz and Senator Lambertino and gave them a rueful smile. 'I'm sorry you had to hear that,' he said to them. 'Christian doesn't like this impeachment business, but he makes it a personal thing when it's a matter of the country's welfare.'

Senator Lambertino said, 'I advised against approaching Klee. But I thought we had a chance with you, Otto. When the President appointed you as liaison to Congress, I thought it a foolhardy thing to do, what with all our Southern colleagues who are not fully reconstructed. But I must say you have won them over in these past three years. If the President listened to you, his programs would not have gone down in Congress.'

Oddblood Gray kept his face impassive. He said in his silky voice, 'I'm glad you came to me. But I think Congress is making a big mistake with this impeachment proceeding. The Vice President hasn't signed up. Sure you've got nearly all of the Cabinet, but none of the staff. So Congress can override the express vote of the people of this country.'

Oddblood Gray got up and started pacing the room. Usually he never did this when he was negotiating. He knew the impression he made. He was too overpowering physically, and it would seem like an offensive gesture of domination. He was nearly six feet four, his clothes were beautifully tailored and his physique was that of an Olympic athlete. He had just a touch of intimidation.

'You are both men I have admired in Congress,' he said. 'We have always understood each other. You know I advised Kennedy not to go forward with his social programs until he laid a better groundwork. All three of us understand one important thing. There is no greater opening for tragedy than a stupid exercise of power. It is one of the most common mistakes in politics. But that is exactly what Congress is going to do when they impeach the President. If you succeed, you start a very dangerous precedent in our

243

government that could lead to fatal repercussions when some President acquires excess power in the future. He may then make his first aim the emasculation of Congress. And what do you gain here in the short term? You prevent the destruction of Dak and its fifty billion dollar investment by Bert Audick, and the people of this country will despise you, for make no mistake, the people support Kennedy's action. Maybe for the wrong reasons, we all know that the electorate is too easily swayed by obvious emotions, emotions we as governors have to control and redirect. Kennedy right now can order atom bombs dropped on Sherhaben and the people of this country would approve. Stupid? OK. But that's how the masses feel. You know that. So the smart thing is for the Congress to lay back, to see if Kennedy's actions get the hostages back and the hijackers in our prisons. Then everybody's happy. If the policy fails, if the hijackers slaughter the hostages, then you can remove the President and look like heroes.'

Oddblood had tried his best pitch but he knew it was hopeless. From long experience, he had learned that even the wisest of men or women once they wished to do a thing, they would do it. No manner of persuasion could change their minds. They would do what they wanted to do, simply because it was their will.

Congressman Jintz did not disappoint him. 'You are arguing against the will of the Congress, Otto.'

Senator Lambertino said, 'Really, Otto, you're fighting a lost cause. I know your loyalty to the President. I know that if everything had gone well the President would have made you a Cabinet member. And let me tell you, the Senate would have approved. That still can happen, but not under Kennedy.'

Oddblood Gray nodded his thanks. 'I appreciate that, Senator. But I can't comply with your request. I think the President is justified in the action he's taken. I think that action will be effective. I think the hostages will be released and the criminal given into custody.'

Jintz said abruptly and crudely, 'This is all beside the point. We can't let him destroy the city of Dak.'

Senator Lambertino said softly, 'It's not just the money. Such a savage act would hurt our relationships with every country in the world. You see that, Otto.'

Oddblood Gray said, 'I don't have to worry about foreign relations. I just deal with the Congress for the President. And I can see you gentlemen don't agree with me. So let me tell you this. Unless Congress cancels its special session tomorrow, unless it withdraws the motion to impeach, the President will appeal directly to the people of the United States on television. And you know how good the President is on the tube. He will massacre Congress. And then, who knows what will happen? Especially if your plans go wrong and the hostages are killed anyway. Please present this to your fellow members.' He resisted saying, 'And to the Socrates Club.'

They parted company with those protestations of good will and affection that have been political good manners since the murder of Julius Caesar. Then Oddblood Gray went out to pick up Christian Klee for the meeting with the President.

But his last speech had shaken Congressman Jintz. Jintz had accrued a great deal of wealth during his many years in Congress. His wife was a partner or stockholder in cable television companies in his home state, his son's law firm was one of the biggest in the south. He had no material worries. But he loved his life as a Congressman, it brought him pleasures that could not be bought with mere money. The marvellous thing about being a successful politician was that old age could be as happy as your youth. Even as a doddering old man, your brain floating away in a flood of senile cells, everyone still respected you, listened to you, kissed your ass. You had the Congressional committees and subcommittees, you could wallow in the pork barrels. You could still help steer the course of the greatest country in the world. Though your body was old and feeble, young virile men trembled before you. At some time, Jintz knew, his appetite for food and drink and women would fade, but if there was still one last living cell in his brain he could enjoy power. And how can you really fear the nearness of death when your fellow man still obeys you?

And so Jintz was worried. Was it possible by some catastrophe his seat in Congress could be lost? There was no way out. His very life depended on the removal of Francis Kennedy from office. He said to Senator Lambertino, 'We can't let the President go on TV tomorrow.'

13

Matthew Gladyce, the Press Secretary to the President, knew that in the next twenty-four hours he would make the most important decisions of his professional life. It was his job to control the responses of the media to the tragic and world-shocking events of the last three days. It would be his job to inform the people of the United States just exactly what their President was doing to cope with these events, and to justify his actions. Gladyce had to be very careful.

Now on this Thursday morning after Easter, in the middle of the crisis fireball, Matthew Gladyce cut himself off from direct contact with the media. His junior assistants held the meetings in the White House Press Conference Room but were limited to handing out carefully composed press releases and ducking shouted questions.

Matthew did not answer the phones constantly ringing in his office, his secretaries screened all his calls and brushed off insistent reporters, the highest powered TV commentators trying to call in markers he owed them. It was his job to protect the President of the United States.

Matthew Gladyce knew from his long experience as a journalist that there was no ritual more revered in America than the traditional insolence of the print and TV media toward important members of the establishment. Imperious TV anchor stars shouted down affable Cabinet members, knocked chips off the shoulders of the President himself, grilled candidates for high office with the ferocity of prosecuting attorneys. The newspapers printed libelous articles in

247

the name of free speech. At one time he had been a part of all this and even admired it. He had enjoyed the inevitable hatred that every public official has for representatives of the media. But three years as Press Secretary had changed this. Like the rest of the Administration, indeed like all government figures down through history, he had come to distrust and devalue that great institution of democracy called free speech. Like all authority figures he had come to regard it as assault and battery. The media were sanctified criminals who robbed institutions and private citizens of their good name. Just to sell their newspapers and commercials to three hundred million people.

And today he would not give those bastards an inch. He was going to throw his fast ball by them.

He thought back on the last four days and all the questions he had fielded from the media. The President had cut himself off from all direct communication and Matthew Gladyce had carried the ball. On Monday it had been, 'Why haven't the hijackers made any demands? Is the kidnapping of the President's daughter linked to the killing of the Pope?' Those questions eventually answered themselves, thank God. Now it was established. They were linked. The hijackers had made their demands.

Gladyce had issued the press release under the direct supervision of the President himself. These events were a concerted attack on the prestige and worldwide authority of the United States. Then the murder of the President's daughter and the stupid fucking questions. 'How did the President react when he heard of the murder?' Here Gladyce lost his temper. 'What the fuck do you think he felt, you stupid bastard?' he told the anchor person. Then there had been another stupid question, 'Does this bring back memories of when the President's uncles were murdered?' At that moment Gladyce decided he would leave these press conferences to his juniors.

But now he had to take the stage. He would have to

defend the President's ultimatum to the Sultan of Sherhaben. He would cut out the threat to destroy the Sultanate of Sherhaben. He would say that if the hostages were released and Yabril imprisoned, the city of Dak would not be destroyed. In language to leave him an out when Dak was destroyed. But most important of all he would say that the President of the United States would go on televison in the afternoon with a major address to the nation.

He glanced out of the window of his office. The White House was surrounded by TV trucks and media correspondents from all over the world. Well fuck them, Gladyce thought. They would only know what he wanted them to know.

The envoys of the United States arrived in Sherhaben. Their plane set down on a parallel runway far away from the hostage lane commanded by Yabril and still surrounded by Sherhaben troops. Behind those troops were the hordes of TV trucks, media correspondents from all over the world and a vast crowd of onlookers who had travelled from the city of Dak.

The Ambassador of Sherhaben, Sharif Waleeb, had taken pills to sleep through most of the voyage. Bert Audick and Arthur Wix had talked, Audick trying to persuade Wix to modify the President's demands, so that they could get the release of the hostages without any drastic action.

Finally Wix told Audick, 'I have no leeway to negotiate. I have a very strict brief from the President, they've had their fun and now they are going to pay.'

Audick said grimly, 'You're the National Security Advisor, for God's sake, advise.'

Wix said stonily, 'There is nothing to advise. The President has made his decision.'

Upon arrival at the Sultan's palace, Wix and Audick were escorted to their palatial suites by armed guards. Indeed the palace seemed to be overrun with military formations.

Ambassador Waleeb was ushered into the presence of the Sultan where he formally presented the ultimatum documents.

In the ornate official conference room they formally embraced, but since they were in Western clothes they both felt awkward doing so.

The Sultan said, 'The cables and your telephone conversation with me is something I cannot believe. Surely, my dear Waleeb, it must be a bluff. It goes against everything in the American character. They will destroy their world reputation for international morality, and they will go against their own ingrained greed. If they destroy Dak they lose fifty billion. What is this threat of the most dire circumstances?'

Waleeb, a tiny man, dapper as a puppet, was so terrified that the Sultan pressed his hand to give him courage enough to speak.

'Your Highness,' Sharif Waleeb said, 'I beg of you to consider this most carefully. They have film that shows you support Yabril. It is beyond question. As for President Kennedy, he is not bluffing. The city of Dak will be destroyed. And as for the dire consequences which are in his memorandum, and which are known to his Congress and government staff, that is even worse than it appears. He gave me this message to give you personally. A message which he cleverly does not allow to be official. He swears that if you do not comply with his demands to free the hostages and give up Yabril, the state of Sherhaben will cease to exist.'

The Sultan did not believe the threat, anybody could terrify this little man. He said, 'And when Kennedy told you this, how did he appear? Is he a man who utters such wild threats merely to frighten? Would his government even support such an action? He would be gambling his whole political career on this one throw of the dice. Is it not merely a negotiating ploy?'

Waleeb rose from the gold brocaded chair in which he

had been sitting. Suddenly his tiny puppet-like figure became impressive. He had a good voice, the Sultan noted. 'Your Highness,' Waleeb said. 'Kennedy knew exactly what you would say, word for word. Within twenty-four hours after the destruction of Dak, if you do not comply with his demands, all Sherhaben will be destroyed. And that is why Dak cannot be saved. That is the only way he can convince you of his most serious intent. He also said that after Dak is destroyed you will agree to his demands but not before. He was calm, he smiled. He is no longer the man he was. He is Azazel.'

Later, the two envoys of the President of the United States were brought to a beautiful reception room that included air-conditioned terraces and a swimming pool. They were attended by male servants in Arab dress who brought them food and drinks, that were not alcoholic. Surrounded by counselors and bodyguards, the Sultan greeted them.

Ambassador Waleeb made the introductions. Bert Audick, the Sultan knew. They had been closely interlocked on past oil deals. And Audick had been his host the several times he had visited America, a discreet and obliging host. The Sultan greeted Audick warmly.

The second man was the surprise and in the stirring clutch of his heartbeat, the Sultan recognized the presence of danger and began to believe the reality of Kennedy's threat. For the second Tribune, as the Sultan thought of them, was none other than Arthur Wix, the President's National Security Advisor, and a Jew. He was by reputation the most powerful military figure in the United States and the ultimate enemy of the Arab States in their fight against Israel. The Sultan noted that Arthur Wix did not offer his hand, only bowed with cold courtesy.

The next thought in the Sultan's mind was that if the President's threat was real, why would he send such a high official into such danger? What if he took these Tribunes as hostages, would they not perish in any attack on Sherhaben? And indeed would Bert Audick come and risk a possible death? From what he knew of Audick, certainly not. So that meant there was room for negotiation and that the Kennedy threat was a bluff. Or, Kennedy was simply a madman and did not care what happened to his envoys and would carry out his threat anyway. He looked around at his reception room that served as his chamber of State. It was far more luxurious than anything in the White House. The walls were painted gold, the carpets were the most expensive in the world with exquisite patterns that could never be duplicated, the marble the purest and most intricately worked. How could all this be destroyed?

The Sultan said with quiet dignity, 'My Ambassador has given me the message from your President. I find it very hard to believe that the leader of the free world would dare to utter such a threat, much less implement it. And I am at a loss. What influence can I have over this bandit, Yabril? Is your President another Attila the Hun? Does he imagine he rules ancient Rome rather than America?'

It was Audick who spoke first. He said, 'Sultan Maurobi, I came here as your friend, to help you and your country. The President means to do as he threatens. It seems you have no alternative, you must give up this man Yabril.'

The Sultan was quiet for a long moment then turned to Arthur Wix. He said ironically, 'And what are you doing here? Can America spare an important man like yourself if I refuse to comply with your President's demands?'

'The fact you would hold us as hostages if you refused those demands was carefully discussed,' Arthur Wix said. He was absolutely impassive. He did not show the anger and hatred he was feeling for the Sultan. 'As the head of an independent country you are quite justified in your anger and in your counter threat. But that is the very reason I am here. To assure you that the necessary military orders have been given. As the Commander in Chief of American military forces, the President has that power. The city of Dak will shortly be no more. Twenty-four hours after that, if you do not comply, the country of Sherhaben will also be destroyed. All this will be no more,' he gestured around the room, 'and you will be living on the charity of the rulers of your neighboring countries. You will be a Sultan still, but you will be a Sultan of nothing'

The Sultan did not show his rage. He turned to the other American. He said, 'Do you have anything to add?'

Bert Audick said almost slyly, 'There is no question Kennedy means to carry out his threat. But there are other people in our government who disagree. This action may doom his Presidency.' He said almost apologetically to Arthur Wix, 'I think we have to bring this out in open.'

Wix looked at him grimly. He had feared this possibility. Strategically it was always possible that Audick might try to make an end run. The bastard was going to try to undermine the whole deal. Just to save his fucking fifty billion.

Arthur Wix looked venomously at Audick and said to the Sultan, 'There is no room for negotiation.'

Audick gave Wix a defiant glance and then addressed the Sultan again. 'I think it fair, based on our long relationship, to tell you there is one hope. And I feel I must do it now in front of my countryman, rather than in a private audience with you as I could easily do. The Congress of the United States is holding a special session to impeach President Kennedy. If we can announce the news that you are releasing the hostages, I guarantee Dak will not be destroyed.'

The Sultan said, 'And I will not have to give up Yabril?'

'No,' Audick said. 'But you must not insist on the release of the Pope's killer.'

The Sultan, for all his good manners, could not completely disguise the note of glee when he said, 'Mr Wix, is this not a more reasonable solution?'

'My President impeached because a terrorist murdered his

253

daughter? And then the murderer goes free?' Wix said. 'No, it is not.'

Audick said, 'We can always get that guy later.'

Wix gave him a look of such contempt and hatred, that Audick knew this man would be his enemy for life.

The Sultan said, 'In two hours we will all meet with my friend Yabril. We will dine together, and come to an agreement. I will persuade him with sweet words or force. But the hostages will go free as soon as we learn that the city of Dak is safe. Gentlemen, you have my promise as a Muslim and as the ruler of Sherhaben.'

Then the Sultan gave orders for his communications center to notify him of the congressional vote as soon as it was known. He had the American envoys escorted to their rooms to bathe and change their clothing.

The Sultan had ordered Yabril to be smuggled off the plane and brought to the palace. Yabril was made to wait in the huge reception hall and he noted that it was filled with the Sultan's uniformed security guards. There had been other signs that the palace was on an alert status. Yabril sensed immediately that he was in danger but there was nothing to be done.

When Yabril was ushered into the Sultan's reception room he was relieved that the Sultan embraced him. Then the Sultan briefed him on what had happened with the American Tribunes. The Sultan said, 'I promised them you would release the hostages without further negotiations. Now we await the decision of the American Congress.'

Yabril said, 'But that means that my friend, Romeo, has been deserted by me. It is a blow to my reputation.'

The Sultan smiled and said, 'When they try him for murder of the Pope, your cause will gain that much more publicity. And the fact that you go free after that coup and murdering the daughter of the President of the United States, *that* is glory. But what a nasty little surprise you gave me at the end. To kill a young girl in cold blood. That was not to my liking and really not clever.'

'It made a certain point,' Yabril said.

'And now you must be satisfied,' the Sultan said. 'In effect you have unseated the President of the United States. Which was beyond your wildest dreams.'

The Sultan gave a command to one of his retinue. 'Go to the quarters of the American, Mr Audick, and bring him here to us.'

When Bert Audick came into the room he did not offer to shake hands with Yabril or make any gesture of acknowledgment. He simply stared. Yabril bowed his head and smiled. He was familiar with these types, these bloodsuckers of Arabian lifeblood, who made contracts with Sultans and Kings to enrich America and other foreign states.

The Sultan said, 'Mr Audick, please explain to my friend the mechanics of how your Congress will dispose of your President.'

Audick did so. He was convincing, Yabril believed him. But he asked, 'What if something goes wrong and you do not get your two-thirds vote?'

Audick said grimly, 'Then you, me and the Sultan here, are shit out of luck.'

President Francis Xavier Kennedy looked over the papers that Matthew Gladyce presented and then initialed them. He saw the look of satisfaction on Gladyce's face and knew exactly what it meant. That together they were putting one over on the American public. At another time, in other circumstances, he would have destroyed that look of smugness, but Francis Kennedy realized that this was the single most dangerous moment in his political career, and he must use every weapon available.

This evening the Congress would try to impeach him. They would use the vague wording of the Twenty-fifth Amendment to the Constitution to do so. Maybe he could win the battle in the long run, but by then it would be too late. Bert Audick would arrange the release of the hostages, the escape of Yabril in return for the remaining hostages. The death of his daughter would go unavenged, the murderer of the Pope would go free. But Kennedy counted on his appeal to the nation over TV to launch such a wave of protesting telegrams as to make Congress waver. He knew the people would support his action, they were outraged at the murder of the Pope and of his daughter. They felt his heartbreak. And at that moment he felt a fierce communion with the people. They were his allies against the corrupt Congress, the pragmatic and merciless businessmen like Bert Audick.

As all through his life, he felt the tragedies of the unfortunate, the mass of people struggling through life. Early in his career he had sworn to himself that he would never be corrupted by that love of money that seemed to generate all the accomplishments of gifted men. He grew to despise the power of the rich, money used as a sword. But he had always felt, he realized now, that he was some sort of champion who was invulnerable and above the woes of his fellow man. He had always felt a part of the rich though he championed the poor. He had never before grasped the hatred that the underclass must feel. But he felt it now. Now the rich, the powerful, would bring him down, now he must win for his own sake. And now he felt the hatred.

But he refused to indulge himself. His mind must be clear in the coming crisis. Even if he were impeached, he must make sure he would return to power. And then his plans would be far-reaching. The Congress and the rich might win this battle but he saw clearly that they must lose the war. The people of the United States would not suffer humiliation gladly, there would be another election in November. This whole crisis could be in his favor even if lost; his tragedy one of his weapons. But he had to be careful to hide these long-range plans even from his staff.

Kennedy understood he was preparing himself for ultimate power. There was no other course except to submit to defeat and all its anguish and that he could never survive.

On Thursday afternoon, nine hours before the special session of Congress that would impeach the President of the United States from office, Francis Kennedy met with his advisors, his staff and Vice President Helen DuPray.

It was to be their last strategy session before the Congressional vote and they all knew the enemy had the necessary two thirds. Francis Kennedy saw immediately the mood in the room was one of depression and defeat.

He gave them all a cheerful smile and opened the meeting by thanking the CIA Chief, Theodore Tappy, for not having signed the impeachment proposal. Then he turned to the Vice President, Helen DuPray, and laughed, a genuine good-humored laugh.

'Helen,' he said with unaffected delight, 'I wouldn't be in your shoes for anything in the world. Do you realize how many enemies you made when you refused to sign the impeachment papers? You could have been the first woman President of the United States. Congress hates you because without your signature they can't get away with it. Men will hate you for being so magnanimous. Feminists will consider you a traitor. God, how did an old pro like you get in such a fix? By the way, I want to thank you for your loyalty.'

'They are wrong, Mr President,' Helen DuPray said. 'And they are wrong now to pursue it. Is there a chance for any negotiation with Congress?'

'I can't,' Francis Kennedy said. 'And they won't.' Then Kennedy said to Dazzy, 'Have my orders been followed, is the naval air fleet on its way to Dak?'

'Yes, sir,' Dazzy said, then shifted uncomfortably in his chair. 'But the Chiefs of Staff have not given the final go. They will hold back until Congress votes tonight. If the impeachment succeeds, they will send the planes home.' He paused for a moment. 'They haven't disobeyed you. They have followed your orders. They just figure they can countermand everything if you lose tonight.'

Kennedy turned to Helen DuPray. His face was grave. 'If the impeachment succeeds you will be the President,' he said. 'You can order the Chiefs of Staff to proceed with the destruction of the city of Dak. Will you give that order?'

'No,' Helen DuPray said. There was a long uncomfortable silence in the room. Helen DuPray kept her face composed and spoke directly to Kennedy. 'I have proved my loyalty to you,' she said. 'As your Vice President, I supported your decision on Dak, as it was my duty to do. I resisted the demand to sign the impeachment papers. But if I become President, and I hope with all my heart I will not, then I must follow my own conscience and make my own decision.'

Francis Kennedy nodded. He smiled at her and it was a gen+le smile that broke her heart. 'You are perfectly right,' he said gently. 'I asked the question merely as a point of information, not to persuade.' He addressed the others in the room. 'Now the most important thing is to get a bare bones script ready for my television speech. Eugene, have you cleared networks? Have they broadcast bulletins that I will speak tonight?'

Eugene Dazzy said cautiously, 'Lawrence Salentine is here to see you about that. It looks fishy. Shall I have him sent here? He's in my office.'

Francis Kennedy said softly, 'They wouldn't dare. They wouldn't dare to show their muscle so out in the open.' He was thoughtful for a long moment. 'Send him in.'

While they waited they discussed how long the speech would be. 'Not more than a half-hour,' Kennedy said. 'I should get the job done by then.'

And they all knew what he meant. Francis Kennedy on television could overpower any audience except Congress. It was the handsomeness of the face, the startling blue eyes, the controlled energy of his body. It was the magical speaking voice with the melodies in the lyrics of the great Irish poets. It didn't hurt that his thinking, the progress of his logic was always absolutely clear. Congress and the Socrates Club would be the villains of America. And all this backed by the magical myth of his two martyred uncles.

When Lawrence Salentine was ushered in, Kennedy spoke to him directly and without greeting. 'I hope you're not going to say what I think you're going to say.'

Salentine said coolly, 'I have no way of knowing what you're thinking. I've been chosen by the other networks to give you our decision not to give you air time tonight. For us to do so would be to interfere in the impeachment process.'

Kennedy smiled and said to him, 'Mr Salentine, the impeachment, even if successful, will only last for thirty days. And then what?'

It was not Francis Kennedy's style to be threatening. It occurred to Salentine that he and the heads of the other networks had embarked on a very dangerous game. The legal justification of the federal government to issue and review licenses for TV stations had become archaic in practical terms, but a strong President could put new teeth in it. Salentine knew he had to go very carefully.

'Mr President,' he said. 'It is because we feel our responsibility is so important that we must refuse you the air time. You are in the process of impeachment, much to my regret, and to the sorrow of all Americans. It is a very great tragedy, and you have all my sympathy. But the networks agree that letting you speak would not be in the best interests of the nation or our democratic process.' He paused for a moment. 'But after Congress votes, win or lose, we will give you air time.'

Francis Kennedy laughed angrily and said, 'You can go.'

Lawrence Salentine was escorted out by one of the Secret Service guards.

Then Kennedy said to his staff, 'Gentlemen, believe me

259

when I tell you this,' Kennedy's face was unsmiling, the blue of his eyes seemed to have gone from a light to heavier slatier blue, 'They have overplayed their hand. They have violated the spirit of the Constitution.'

For miles around the White House, traffic had become congested with only thin corridors to pass through official vehicles. TV cameras and their back-up trucks commanded the whole area. Congressmen on their way to Capitol Hill were unceremoniously grabbed by TV journalists and questioned on this special meeting of the Congress. Finally, an official bulletin appeared on TV networks that the Congress was convening at eleven p.m. to vote on a motion to remove President Kennedy from office.

In the White House itself, Kennedy and his staff had already done everything they could to ward off the attack. Oddblood Gray had called Senators and Congressmen, pleading with them. Eugene Dazzy had made countless calls to different members of the Socrates Club trying to enlist the support of some segments of big business. Christian Klee had sent legal briefs to the leaders of Congress stressing that without the signature of the Vice President, the removal was illegal. Congress had rejected this.

Just before eleven, Kennedy and his staff met in the Yellow Room to watch the big television screen that was wheeled in. For though the session of Congress would not be broadcast over commercial networks, it was being photographed for later use and a special cable brought it to the White House.

Congressman Jintz and Senator Lambertino had done their work well. Everything had been synchronized perfectly. Patsy Troyca and Elizabeth Stone had worked closely together to iron out administrative details. All the necessary documents had been prepared for the turnover of government.

In the Yellow Room, Francis Kennedy and his personal

staff watched the proceedings on their television. It would take Congress time to go throuh all the formalities of speeches and roll calls to vote. But they knew what the outcome would be. Congress and the Socrates Club had built a steamroller for this occasion. Kennedy said to Oddblood Gray, 'Otto, you did your best.'

At that moment, one of the White House duty officers came in and handed Dazzy a memo sheet. Dazzy looked at it, then studied it. The shock on his face was evident. He handed the memorandum to Kennedy.

On the TV screen, Congress had just voted to impeach Francis Xavier Kennedy from the Presidency.

It was eleven p.m. Thursday, Washington time, but six in the morning in Sherhaben when the Sultan had everyone summoned to the terraced reception room for an early breakfast. The Americans, Bert Audick and Arthur Wix arrived shortly. Yabril was escorted in by the Sultan. A huge table was laden witn countless fruits and beverages, both hot and cold.

Sultan Maurobi was smiling broadly. He did not introduce Yabril to the Americans and there was no pretense of any courtesy.

The Sultan said, 'I am happy to announce, more than that, my heart overflows with joy, that my friend Yabril has agreed to the release of your hostages. There will be no further demands from him and I hope no further demands from your country.'

Arthur Wix, his face beaded with sweat, said, 'I cannot negotiate or change in any way the demands of my President. You must give up this murderer.'

The Sultan smiled and said, 'He is no longer your President. The American Congress has voted to impeach him. I am informed that the orders to bomb the city of Dak have already been canceled. The hostages will be freed, you have your victory. There is nothing else you can ask.'

Yabril stared into Wix's eyes and saw the hatred there.

This was the highest man in the mightiest army on the face of the globe and he, Yabril, had defeated him. Yabril felt a great rush of energy go through his body, he had impeached the President of the United States. For a moment his mind held the image of himself pressing the gun against the silky hair of Theresa Kennedy. He remembered again that sense of loss, of regret when he pulled the trigger, the little burn of anguish as her body tumbled away in the desert air. He bowed his head to Wix and the other men in the room.

The Sultan Maurobi motioned for the servants to bring platters of fruit and drink to his guests. Arthur Wix put down his glass and said, 'Are you sure that your information that the President has been impeached is absolutely correct?'

The Sultan said, 'I will arrange for you to speak directly to your office in the United States.' He paused. 'But first, I have my duty as a host.'

The Sultan commanded they must have one last full meal together, and insisted that the final arrangements for the release of the hostages be made over this meal. Yabril took his place at the right hand of the Sultan, Arthur Wix on the left.

They were resting on the divans along the low table when the Sultan's Prime Minister came hurrying in and begged the Sultan to come into the other room for a few moments. The Sultan was impatient until finally the Prime Minister whispered something into his ear. The Sultan raised his eyebrows in surprise and then he said to his guest, 'Something has happened quite unforeseen. All communication to the United States has been cut off, not just to us, but all over the world. Please continue your breakfast while I confer with my staff.'

But after the Sultan left, the men around the table did not speak. Only Yabril helped himself to the hot smoking dishes and fruits.

Gradually the Americans moved away from the table and gathered on the terrace. The servants brought them cool drinks. Yabril continued to eat.

On the terrace, Bert Audick said to Wix, 'I hope Kennedy hasn't done something foolish. I hope he hasn't tried to buck the constitution.'

Wix said, 'God, first his daughter, now he's lost his country. All because of that little prick in there eating like a fucking beggar.'

Bert Audick said, 'It is terrible, all of it.' Then Audick went in to the dining table inside and said to Yabril, 'Eat well, I hope you have a good place to hide in the years to come. There will be a lot of people looking for you.'

Yabril laughed. He had finished eating and was lighting a cigarette. 'Oh, yes,' he said. 'I will be a beggar in Jerusalem.'

At that moment the Sultan Maurobi came into the room. He was followed by at least fifty armed men who stationed themselves to command the room. Four of them stood behind Yabril. Four others stood behind the Americans on the terrace. There was surprise and shock on the Sultan's face. His skin seemed yellow, his eyes were wide open, the eyelids seemed to fold back. 'Gentlemen,' he said, haltingly, 'my dear sirs, this will be as incredible to you as it is to me. Congress has annulled their vote impeaching Kennedy and he has declared martial law.' He paused and let his hand rest on Yabril's shoulder. 'And gentlemen, at this moment planes from the American Sixth Fleet are destroying my city of Dak.'

Arthur Wix asked almost jubilantly, 'The city of Dak is being bombed?'

'Yes,' the Sultan said. 'A barbaric act but a convincing one.'

They were all looking at Yabril who now had four armed men very closely surrounding him. Yabril lit a cigarette and said thoughtfully, 'Finally I will see America, it has always been my dream.' He looked at the Americans but spoke to the Sultan. 'I think I would have been a great success in America.'

'Without a doubt,' the Sultan said. 'Part of the demand is

that I deliver you alive. I'm afraid I must give the necessary orders so that you do not harm yourself.'

Yabril said, 'America is a civilized country. I will go through a legal process that will be long and drawn out, since I will have the best lawyers. Why should I harm myself? It will be a new experience and who knows what can happen? The world always changes. America is too civilized for torture and besides I have endured torture under the Israelis so nothing will surprise me.' He smiled at Wix.

Arthur Wix said quietly, 'As you once observed, the world changes. You haven't succeeded. You won't be such a hero.'

Yabril laughed delightedly. His arms went up in an exuberant gesture. 'I have succeeded,' he almost shouted. 'I've torn your world off its axis. Do you think your mealy-mouthed idealism will be listened to after your planes have destroyed the city of Dak? When will the world forget my name? And do you think I will step off the stage now when the best is yet to come?'

The Sultan clapped his hands and shouted an order to the soldiers. They grabbed Yabril and put handcuffs on his wrists and rope around his neck. 'Gently, gently,' the Sultan said. When Yabril was secure he touched him gently on the forehead. He said, 'I beg your forgiveness, I have no choice. I have oil to sell and a city to rebuild. I wish you well, old friend. Good luck in America.'

As Congress impeached President Francis Xavier Kennedy, possibly illegally, as the world awaited the resolution of the terrorist crisis, there were many hundreds of thousands of people in New York who didn't give a flying fuck. They had their own lives to lead and their own problems. This Thursday night many of these thousands converged in the Times Square area of New York City, a place that once had been the very heart of the greatest city in the world, where once Great White Way, Broadway itself, ran down from Central Park to Times Square.

These people had varied interests. Horny, yearning, sub-urban, middle-class men haunted the adult pornographic book shops. *Cinéastes* surveyed miles of film of naked men, naked women indulging themselves in the most intimate sexual acts with varied animals in best-friend character roles. Teenaged gangs with lethal but legal screwdrivers in their pockets sallied forth as gallantly as the knights of old to slay the dragons of the well-to-do, and with the irrepressible high good spirits of the young, to have some laughs. Pimps, prostitutes, muggers, murderers, set up shop after dark without even having to pay overheads for the bright neon light of what was left of the Great White Way. Tourist lambs came bleating to see Times Square where the ball fell on New Year's Eve and proclaimed the coming of another joyous New Year. On most of the buildings in the area and the slum streets leading into it were posters with a huge red heart and inside that red heart the inscription 'I LOVE NEW YORK'. Courtesy of Louis Inch.

On that Thursday near midnight, Blade Booker was hanging out in the Times Square Bar and Cinema Club looking for a client. Blade Booker was a young black man noted for his ability to hustle. He could get you coke, he could get you H, he could get you a wide assortment of pills. He could also get you a gun but nothing big. Pistols, revolvers, little .22s but after he got himself one he didn't really get into that any more. He wasn't a pimp, but he was very good with the ladies. He could really talk to their shit, and he was a great listener. Many a night he spent with a girl and listened to her dreams. Even the lowest down hooker who would do things with men that took his breath away, had dreams to tell. Blade Booker listened, he enjoyed listening, it made him feel good when ladies told him their dreams. He loved their shit. Oh, they would hit the numbers, their astrological chart showed that the coming year a man would love them, they would have a baby, or have kids grow up to be doctors, lawyers, college professors, be on TV; their kids could sing or dance or act or do comedy as good as Richard Pryor, maybe even another Eddie Murphy.

Blade Booker was waiting for the Swedish Cinema Palace to empty out after the completion of its X-rated film. Many of the cinema lovers would stop here for a drink and a hamburger and the hopes of seeing some pussy. They would straggle in singly but you could spot them by the abstracted look in their eyes, as if they were pondering an insoluble scientific problem. Also most of them had a melancholy look on their faces. They were lonely people.

There were hookers all over the place but Blade Booker had his very own placed in a strategic corner. Men at the bar could see her at a little table that her huge red purse almost covered. She was a blonde girl from Duluth, Minnesota, big-boned, her blue eyes iced with heroin. Blade Booker had rescued her from a fate worse than death, namely a life on a farm where the cold winter would chill her tits as hard as boulders. But he was always careful with her. She had a reputation and he was one of the few who would work with her.

Her name was Kimberly Ansley and just six years ago she had chopped her pimp up with an axe while he was sleeping. Watch out for girls named Kimberly and Tiffany, Booker always said. She had been arrested and prosecuted, tried and convicted, but convicted only of manslaughter with the defense proving she had numerous bruises and had been 'not responsible' because of her heroin habit. She had been sentenced to a correctional facility, cured, declared sane and released on to the streets of New York. There she had taken up residence in the slums around Greenwich Village, supplied with an apartment in one of the housing projects built by the city which even the poor were fleeing.

Blade Booker and Kimberly were partners. He was half pimp, half roller; he took pride in that distinction. Kimberly would pick up a *cinéaste* in the Times Square Bar, and then lead her customer to a tenement hallway near Ninth Avenue for quick sexual acts. Then Blade would step from the shadows and clunk the man on the head with a New York Police Department blackjack. They would split the money in the man's wallet but Blade got the credit cards and jewelry. Not out of greed but because he didn't trust Kimberly's judgement.

The beauty of this was that the man was usually an errant husband reluctant to report the incident to the police and have to answer questions about just what he was doing in a dark hall of Ninth Avenue when his wife was waiting for him in Merrick, Long Island or Trenton, New Jersey. For safety's sake both Blade and Kim would simply avoid the Times Square Cinema Bar for a week. And Ninth Avenue. They would move to Second Avenue. In a city like New York that was like going to another black star in the galaxy. That was why Blade Booker loved New York. He was invisible, like The Shadow, The Man With a Thousand Faces. And he was like those insects and birds he saw on the TV public broadcasting channels who changed color to blend with the terrain, the insects who could burrow into the earth to escape predators. In short, unlike most citizens, Blade Booker felt safe in New York.

On Thursday night the pickings were lean. But Kimberly was beautiful in this light, her blonde hair glowing like a halo, her white powdered breasts, moonlike, rising none too shyly out of her green low-cut dress. A gentleman with sly good-humored charm only faintly overladen with lust, brought his drink to her table and politely asked her if he could sit down. Blade watched them and wondered at the ironies of the world. Here was this well-dressed man, undoubtedly some kind of hot-shot like a lawyer or professor or, who knows, some low-grade politician like a City Counselor or State Senator, sitting down with an axe-murderer, and for dessert would get a bop on the head. And just because of his cock. That was the trouble. A man walked through life with only half a brain because of his cock. It was really too bad. Maybe before he bopped the guy he would let him stick it into Kimberly and get his nuts off and then bop him. He looked like a nice guy, he was really being a gentleman, lighting Kimberly's cigarette, ordering her a drink, not rushing her, though he was obviously dying to get off.

Blade finished his drink when Kim gave him the signal. He saw Kim start to get up, fussing with her red purse, rummaging in it for God knows what. Blade left the bar and went out into the street. It was a clear night of early spring and the smell of hot dogs and hamburgers and onions frying on the grills of open-air restaurants made him hungry, but he could wait until work was done. He walked up 42nd Street. There were still crowds although it was midnight, and people's faces were colored by the countless neon lights of the rows of cinemas, the open-air restaurants, the giant billboards, the cone-shaped glares of hotel searchlights. He loved the walk from Seventh Avenue to Ninth. He entered the hallway and positioned himself in the well. He could step out when Kim embraced her client. He lit a cigarette and took the blackjack out of its holster beneath the jacket.

He could hear them coming into the hall, the door clicking shut, Kim's purse clattering. And then he heard Kim's voice giving the code word. 'It's just one flight.' He waited for a couple of minutes before he stepped out of the well and hesitated because he saw such a pretty picture. There was Kim on the first step, legs apart, lovely massive white thighs uncovered and the nice man so well dressed, with his dick out and shoving it into her. Kim seemed to rise for a moment into the air and then Blade saw with horror that she was still rising, and the steps were rising with her and then he saw above her head the clear sky as if the whole top of the building had been sheared off. He tried to find a hole, he tried to change his color to match the stones falling into the hole that showed the sky. He*lifted the blackjack to beg, to pray, to give witness, that his life could not be over. All this happened in a fraction of a second.

Cecil Clarkson and Isabel Domaine had come out of a Broadway theater after seeing a charming musical and strolled down to 42nd Street and Times Square. They were both black, as indeed were a majority of the people to be seen on the streets here, but they were in no way similar to Blade Booker. Cecil Clarkson was nineteen years of age and took writing courses at the New School for Social Research. Isabel was eighteen and went to every Broadway and off-Broadway play because she loved the theater, and hoped to be an actress. They were in love as only teenagers can be, absolutely convinced that they were the only two people in the world. And as they walked up from Seventh Avenue to Eight the blinding neon lights bathed them in benevolent light, their beauty created a magic around them which shielded off the wino beggars, the half-crazed drug addicts, the hustlers, the pimps and the would-be muggers. And Cecil was big, obviously a strong young man who looked as if he would kill anybody who even touched Isabel's body.

They stopped at a huge frankfurter and hamburger open air grill and ate alongside the counter, they did not venture inside where the floor was filthy with discarded paper napkins and paper plates. Cecil drank a beer and Isabel a Pepsi with their hot dogs and hamburgers. They watched the surging humanity that filled the sidewalks even at this late hour. They looked with perfect equanimity at the wave of human flotsam, the dregs of the city, rolling past them and it never entered their minds that there was any danger. They felt pity for these people who did not have their promise, their future, their present and everlasting bliss. When the wave receded they went back into the street and started the walk from Seventh to Eight. Above the painted ceiling of neon lights shone a lighter sky twinkling with fainter lights. Isabel felt the spring air on her face and buried her face in

Cecil's shoulder, one hand at his chest, the other caressing his neck. Cecil felt a vaulting tenderness. They were both supremely happy, the young in love as billions and billions of human beings had been before them, living one of the few perfect moments in life. Then suddenly to Cecil's astonishment all the garish red and green lights blotted out and all he could see was the vault of the sky with its faint stars, and then both of them in their perfect bliss dissolved into nothing.

A group of eight tourists visiting New York City for an Easter week vacation, walked down from St Patrick's cathedral and on Fifth Avenue turned up 42nd Street and sauntered up toward where a forest of neon light beckoned. When they reached Times Square they were disappointed. They had seen it on TV when on New Year's Eve hundreds of thousands gathered to appear on television and greet the coming New Year.

It was so dirty, there was a carpet of garbage that covered the streets. The crowd seemed menacing, drunk, drugged, or driven insane by being enclosed by the great towers of steel through which they had to move. The women were garishly dressed, they matched the women in the stills outside the porno cinemas. They seemed to move through different levels of hell, the void of a sky with no stars, the street lamps a puslike spurt of yellow.

The tourists, four married couples from a small town in Ohio, their children grown, had decided to take a trip to New York as a sort of celebration. They had completed a certain duty in their lives, fulfilled a necessary destiny. They had married, they had brought up children, they had been able to make their moderately successful careers. Now there would be a new beginning for them, the start of a new kind of life. The main battle had been won.

The X cinemas didn't interest them, there were plenty in Ohio. What did interest and frighten them about Times

Square was that it was so ugly and the people filling the streets seemed so evil in the neon light stained on the night. The tourists all wore great big red 'I LOVE NEW YORK' buttons that they had purchased on their first day. Now one of the women took off her button and threw it into the gutter.

'Let's get out of here,' she said.

The group turned and walked back toward Sixth Avenue away from the great corridor of neon. They had almost turned the corner when they heard a distant 'boom' and then a faint rustle of wind, and then down the long Avenues from Ninth to Sixth came rushing a tornado of air filled with metal soda cans, garbage baskets and a few cars that seemed to be flying. The group with an animal instinct turned the corner of Sixth Avenue out of the path of that rushing wind, but were swept off their feet by a tumult of air. From far away they heard the crashing of buildings falling to the ground, the screams of thousands of dying people. They stood crouched low in the shelter of the corner, not knowing what had happened.

They had walked just outside the radius of destruction caused by the explosion of the nuclear bomb. They were eight survivors of the greatest calamity that had befallen a peacetime United States.

One of the men struggled to his feet and helped the others. 'Fucking New York,' he said. 'I hope all the cab drivers got killed.'

The police patrol car that moved slowly through traffic between Seventh and Eighth Avenue held two young cops, one Italian and one black. They didn't mind being stuck in traffic, it was the safest place in the precinct. They knew that down the darker side streets they could flush thieves stealing radios out of cars, low-grade pimps and muggers making menacing moves toward the peaceful pedestrians of New York, but they didn't want to get involved in those crimes.

Also, it was now a policy of the New York Police Department to allow petty crimes. There had spread in New York a sort of licence for the underprivileged to prey on the successful law abiding citizens of the city. After all, was it right that there were men and women who could afford fifty thousand dollar cars with radios and music systems worth a thousand dollars, while there were thousands of homeless who didn't have the price of a meal or who could not afford a sterile healthy needle for a fix? Was it right that these well-to-do, mentally fat, placid, oxlike citizens who had the effrontery to walk the streets of New York without a gun or even a lethal screwdriver in their pockets, could enjoy the fabulous sights of the greatest city on earth and not pay a certain price? After all there still was a spark in America of that ancient revolutionary spirit that could not resist such a temptation. And the courts of law, the higher echelons of the police, the editorials of the most respectable newspapers slyly endorsed the republican spirit of thievery, mugging, burglaries, rapes and even murders on the streets of New York. The poor of the city had no other recourse, their lives had been blighted by poverty, by a stultified family life, the very architecture of the city. Indeed one columnist made a case that all these crimes could be laid at the door of Louis Inch, the real estate lord who was restructuring the city of New York with mile-high condos that shielded the sun and starfilled skies with slats of steel.

The two police officers watched Blade Booker leave the Times Square Cinema restaurant, they knew him well. One officer said to the other, 'Should we follow him,' and the other said, 'A waste of time, we could catch him in the act and he'd get off.' They saw the big blonde and her john came out and take the same route up toward Ninth Avenue. 'Poor guy,' one of the cops said. 'He thinks he's going to get laid and he's gonna get rolled.' The other cop said, 'He'll have a lump on his head as big as his hard on.' They both laughed.

Their car still moving slowly by inches, both policemen watched the action on the street. It was midnight, their shift would soon be over and they didn't want to get into anything that would keep them out on the street. They watched the innumerable prostitutes stand in the way of pedestrians, the black drug dealers hawking their wares as bodly as a TV pitchman, the muggers and pickpockets jostling prospective victims and trying to engage tourists in conversation. Sitting in the darkness of the patrol car and gazing out on the streets lit brightly by neon sun they saw all the dregs of New York slouched toward their particular hells.

The two cops were constantly alert, afraid that some maniac would shove a gun through the window and start shooting. They saw two drug hustlers fall into step beside a well-dressed man who tried to hurry away but was restrained by four hands. The driver of the patrol car pressed the gas pedal and drew up alongside. The drug hustlers dropped their hands, the well-dressed man smiled with relief. At that moment both sides of the street caved in and buried 42nd Street from Ninth to Seventh Avenue.

All the neon lights of the Great White Way, fabulous Broadway, blotted out. The darkness was lit by fires, buildings burning, bodies on fire. Flaming cars moving like torches aimless in the night. And there was a great clanging of the bells, the countless shrieking of sirens as fire engines, ambulances and police vehicles moved into the stricken heart of New York.

These were just a few of the ten thousand or so people who were killed and the twenty thousand who were injured when the nuclear bomb planted by Gresse and Tibbot exploded in the Port Authority Building on Ninth Avenue and 42nd Street.

The explosion was a great boom of sound followed by a howling wind and then the screaming of cement and steel torn asunder. The blast did its damage with mathematical precision. The area from Seventh Avenue to the Hudson River, and from 42nd Street to 45th Street was completely flattened. Outside that area, the damage was by comparison minimal. Radiation was lethal only within that area. The most valuable real estate outside of Tokyo was now worthless.

Of the dead more than seventy per cent were black or Hispanic, the other thirty per cent were white and foreign tourists. On Ninth and Tenth Avenue which had become a camping ground for the homeless, in the Port Authority Building itself in which many transients were sleeping, the bodies were charred into small logs.

Beyond the radius of complete destruction, all through the borough of Manhattan, glass windows shattered, cars in the streets were smashed by falling debris. And within an hour after the explosion the bridges of Manhattan were clogged with vehicles fleeing the city to New Jersey and Long Island.

BOOK IV

14

The White House Communications Center received news of the atom bomb explosion in New York City exactly six minutes after midnight and the Duty Officer immediately informed the President.

Francis Kennedy turned to Christian Klee and said, 'Give your order to isolate Congress. Cut all their communications. Now all of you will accompany me to Capitol Hill. Eugene, give the Communications office the order to transmit that martial law is declared.'

Twenty minutes later, he appeared before the assembled House of Representatives and Senate who had just voted to impeach him. They had received the news of the nuclear attack in New York and were in a state of shock.

President Francis Kennedy ascended the rostrum to address the Congress. He was attended by the Vice President, Helen DuPray, Oddblood Gray and Christian Klee. Eugene Dazzy had remained in the White House to handle the enormous amount of work necessary.

Kennedy was very grave. This was no time for anything but the most straightforward dialogue. He spoke to them without a trace of rancor or threat. He said, 'I come to you tonight knowing that whatever differences we have had, we are united in our devotion to our country.

'There has been a hostile nuclear explosion in New York City that has taken thousands of lives. Two suspects have been arrested and are in custody. These two suspects indicate that the terrorist, Yabril, is implicated. We must come to the conclusion that there is a huge conspiracy against the United States that may be the greatest danger that this country has ever faced. I have declared martial law. This decision brings me into conflict with your vote to remove me. Let me say that this sacred legislative body is safe from any attack. You are protected by six divisions of the Secret Service and an Army Special Forces Regiment that has just moved into position.'

At this announcement of their imprisonment, the Senators and Congressmen moved uneasily in their seats. There were murmurs and whispers as Kennedy went on. 'This is no time for the Presidency and the Congress to be in conflict. This is a time for us to unite against the enemy. I therefore ask you to nullify your previous vote to remove me from my office.'

Francis Kennedy paused and smiled at them. These people, most of them, had been his bitter enemies for three years, now he had them at his mercy. He said quietly, 'I know you all will vote with conscience and judgment. I have made my decision in the same spirit. No matter what the outcome here, I must tell you that this country will still be under martial law and I will remain President until this new crisis is resolved. But I beg you to avoid this confrontation until the crisis is over.'

Senator Lambertino was the first to speak after Kennedy. He proposed that the vote be nullified and that both Houses of Congress give its full support to the President of the United States, Francis Xavier Kennedy.

Congressman Jintz rose to second the motion. He declared that events had proven Kennedy to be in the right, that it had been an honest disagreement. He implied that the President and the Congress would go forward hand in hand to preserve America against its enemies. He gave his word on that and sealed it with his famous handshake which Francis Kennedy could not avoid.

The vote was taken. The previous vote to impeach the President was nullified. Unanimously. Then another vote was taken. That the Congress had the fullest faith in Francis Xavier Kennedy and would follow unswervingly any policy he set to solve the crisis.

At noon Thursday morning, less than twelve hours later, President Francis Xavier Kennedy spoke to the nation on all TV and cable networks.

During the early hours of the morning, Christian Klee had Lawrence Salentine brought to his office and talked to him as the Attorney General of the United States under martial law.

'I don't want you to give me any bullshit,' Klee said. 'I'm going to tell you exactly what you and the other TV moguls have to do in the next twenty-four hours. I want you to listen very carefully. For your own sake.'

'In this crisis everybody is behind the President,' Salentine said.

'No bullshit, remember,' Christian said. 'Now here's the program. Dazzy laid it out but I thought it might be better if I, as the Attorney General, presented it to you, in case you find a legal problem.'

Lawrence Salentine said softly, 'No, Mr Attorney General, I don't think there will be a legal problem at this time.'

Christian Klee had an intimate knowledge of men like Salentine. He had listened in on many of the telephone conversations of the Socrates Club through his computer surveillance system. Salentine meant to convey a threat without being overt. Very well, you son of a bitch, Klee thought, you want to get tough later on, I'll be waiting for you.

So when President Kennedy went on the air at noon Eastern Standard time, all the TV media had prepared for an audience by using a spot every thirty minutes, advertising his coming speech.

The people of the United States never forgot that speech. They never forgot his authority and the physical beauty of his presence. The pallor of his face, the satiny blue eyes, the resolute voice. He was overwhelming on the TV screen and to an audience of three hundred million people, bewildered and terrified by the events of the past four days, he brought an absolute reassurance.

Francis Kennedy told them that the crisis was over. He gave a short summary of the events of Easter week. The assassination of the Pope, the hijacking of the plane by Yabril, the murder of Theresa Kennedy, and the demands of Yabril. And then finally the explosion of the atom bomb in New York.

He explained the motives of the terrorists, that all these crimes had been committed to undermine the authority and prestige of the United States. He told his audience of his ultimatum to the Sultan of Sherhaben and his threat; to destroy the Sultanate of Sherhaben if his ultimatum was defied. And that Dak was in ruins.

Suddenly the cameras shifted away from Kennedy in the Oval Office and the audience saw planes descending and landing. One plane was adorned with funeral black markings and when it landed the audience saw an honor guard of Marines surround it. A coffin was wheeled from a bay beneath the plane. A TV reporter anchor voiceover announced quietly, 'The body of Theresa Kennedy has been returned for burial in the United States.'

The cameras caught the other two planes landing. From one plane the released hostages descended. The TV announcer intoned that all the hostages, except Theresa Kennedy, were now in the United States unharmed. But to the surprise of the audience the cameras left this scene very quickly to focus on the third plane.

From this plane first descended Arthur Wix then Bert Audick. Then the camera focused on a man who had his arms shackled behind his back and who moved slowly and awkwardly because of the chains that hobbled his lower

280

body. This man had a shield of guards which the camera pierced to focus on the face of the prisoner, Yabril.

The TV announcer told his audience that this was the leader of the hijackers, the man who murdered Theresa Kennedy and that this man would now stand trial in a United States Court.

Then the TV screen showed a huge photo of Romeo and the voiceover informed the audience that this was the man who had assassinated the Pope. This man was also in custody in the United States.

The TV screen showed photos of Gresse and Tibbot and told the audience their background and that they had been arrested as suspects in the planting of the atom bomb in New York. And that it was believed that there was some link between these two young men and Yabril.

Then the screen faded and President Francis Kennedy appeared before the people of the United States.

He spoke slowly. 'Again, I repeat, the crisis is over. All the men who have committed these crimes are in custody. Now our task is to judge and punish these criminals. It has already been decided that the terrorist Romeo will be extradited to Italy to stand trial for the killing of the Pope. That is a matter of law. But the others will be tried in the courts of the United States. It has been established by interrogation and investigation by our intelligence agencies that there is no further danger from this conspiracy. And so I declare the end of martial law.'

Everything had gone as programmed by Dazzy, Klee and Matthew Gladyce. The villains had been presented as defeated and helpless, and Francis Kennedy as triumphant and sympathetic. There was a final shot of Theresa Kennedy's coffin being wheeled off into the distance surrounded by the honor guard. And then a final shot of a safe America as symbolized by the Stars and Stripes flying over the White House.

Here the broadcast was supposed to end. So it was a

surprise to everyone when Kennedy spoke once again. He said, 'But I must tell you in conclusion that though the external dangers have been conquered, there is an internal danger. Last night Congress violated the Constitution and voted to impeach me as President of the United States because of my ultimatum to Sherhaben. When the atom bomb exploded in New York they had to nullify their vote. I have no powers to discipline the Congress but the popular vote can do so . . .'

Kennedy paused for a long moment. His eyelids closed so tight that he seemed sightless as a statue is sightless. Then the eyes were open again, sky blue sparkling with restrained tears. He resumed his speech, his voice modulated to one of compassion and pity. He told his audience to go to bed as he would tell a tired child to go to bed. 'Trust in me,' he said. 'The danger is past. Tomorrow we plan so that this country will never suffer such trauma again. Bless you all. Sleep well.'

For the Congress and members of the Socrates Country Club the speech spoke very clearly. The President of the United States had declared war upon them.

15

President Francis Kennedy, secure in power and office, his enemies defeated, contemplated his destiny. There was a final step to be taken, the final decision to be made. He had lost his wife and child, his personal life had lost all meaning. What he did have was a life entwined with the people of America. How far did he want to go with that commitment?

He announced that he would run for re-election in November, and organized his campaign. Oddblood Gray was instructed to neutralize the Reverend Foxworth. Christian Klee was ordered to put legal pressure on all the big businesses especially the media companies to keep them from interfering with the election process. Vice President Helen DuPray was mobilizing the women of America. Arthur Wix who was power in Eastern liberal circles and Eugene Dazzy, who monitored the enlightened business leaders of the country, mobilized money. But Francis Kennedy knew that in the last analysis all this was peripheral. Everything would rest on himself, on how far the people of America would be willing to go with him personally.

There was one crucial point, this time the people must elect a Congress solidly behind the President of the United States. Kennedy smiled and thought to himself that he did not have to censor his own brain. What he wanted was a Congress that would do exactly what he wanted them to do.

So now Francis Kennedy had to perceive the innermost feelings of America. It was a nation in shock. The atom bomb explosion in New York was a psychological trauma the country had never before experienced. And that the act had been committed by two of the most gifted and privileged of its citizens was bewildering. That act was the most daring extension of the philosophy of individual freedom on which the United States prided itself. The right of the individual was the most sacred right in American democracy. But Francis Kennedy sensed that the mood of the American people had now changed.

In the smaller cities and rural areas, after the shock and horror wore off there was a grim satisfaction. New York had gotten what it deserved. It was too bad that the bomb had not been bigger and blown up the whole city with its hedonistic rich, its conniving Semites, criminal blacks. There was after all a just God in heaven. He had picked the right place for this great punishment. But through the country there was also fear. That their fate, their lives, their very world and their posterity were in hostage to fellow men who were aberrant. All this Kennedy sensed.

Every Friday night Francis Kennedy made a TV report to the people. These were really thinly disguised campaign speeches but now he had no trouble getting air time.

He announced that in his second term he would be even tougher on crime. He would again fight to give every American the opportunity to buy a new home, cover their healthcare costs, and make certain they were able to get a higher education. He emphasized that this was not socialism. The costs of these programs would simply be paid for by taking a little bite out of the rich corporations of America. He declared he did not advocate socialism, that he just wanted to protect the people of America from its 'royal' rich. And he did this over and over again.

The members of the Socrates Club watched these perform-ances with a great deal of anger, and contempt. They had seen such demagogues before, the tattered political prophets from the south lands, Puritan communists from the heart of the west, all preaching a gospel to steal from the rich. These movements had always been overwhelmed by the good sense of the people of America. But now two things worried the Socrates Club. It was one thing for some politician, even a President, to promise the electorate pie in the sky, but a man like Kennedy was another matter. Francis Kennedy was the most charismatic speaker that television had ever seen. It was not so much that he was so extraordinarily a physical presence, his perfect style, the mingling of the patrician with the common. He was never condescending in his good humor. He had the cheerful frankness of a best friend, the familiarity of a favorite older brother; he made his point with a flashing wit. He enchanted the TV audiences with all of these but most of all he propounded his theories of government with a sharpness and clarity that made the people understand him and his goals.

He used certain catchphrases and little speeches that went straight to the heart.

'We will declare war on the everyday tragedies of human existence,' he said, 'not on other nations.'

He repeated the famous question used in his first campaign. 'How is it that at the end of every great war, when trillions of dollars have been spent and thrown away on death, then there is prosperity in the world? What if those trillions had been spent for the betterment of mankind?'

He joked that for the cost of one nuclear submarine the government could finance a thousand homes for the poor. For the cost of a fleet of Stealth bombers it could finance a million homes. 'We'll just make believe they got lost on maneuvers,' he said. 'Hell, it's happened before, and with valuable lives lost besides. We'll just make believe it happened.' And when critics pointed out that the defense of the United States would suffer, he said that statistical reports from the Defense Department were classified and that nobody would know. These flippant rejoinders enraged the

285

news media far more than they did the Congress and the Socrates Club.

But what the Socrates Club viewed with more immediate alarm was Kennedy's nominations to head regulatory agencies; left-wingers who would follow Kennedy's vision of severely modifying the power of huge corporations. There was his program to limit the ownership of TV stations and newspapers and book publishing companies to separate units. No longer could one corporate umbrella shield all three divisions of the media. If you owned TV, you could only own TV, if you owned books you could only own books, if you owned newspapers you could only own newspapers, if you owned movie studios, you could only own movie studios. On this Francis Kennedy made a powerful address to the nation. He cited Lawrence Salentine as a prime example. Salentine not only owned a major network and some of the bigger cable companies, but also owned a movie studio in California, one of the major book publishing houses and a string of newspapers. Kennedy told his audience that it was against every principle of democracy that one man should control so many methods of communication. It amounted to the same thing as giving a man more than one vote.

The Congress, the Socrates Club, and nearly all the other big business interests united to oppose him. The stage was set for one of the greatest political battles in the history of the United States.

The Socrates Club decided to hold a seminar in California on how to defeat Kennedy in the November election. Lawrence Salentine was very worried. He knew that the Attorney General was preparing serious indictments on the activities of Bert Audick and mounting investigations of Martin Mutford's financial dealings. Greenwell was too clean to be in trouble, Salentine didn't worry about him. But Salentine knew his own media empire was very vulnerable. They had gotten away with murder for so many years that they had gotten careless. His publishing company, books and magazines were OK. Nobody could harm print media, the Constitutional protection was too strong. Except of course that a prick like Klee might get the postal charges raised.

But Salentine really worried about his TV empire. The airwaves, after all, belonged to the government and were doled out by them. The TV stations were only licensed. And it had always been a source of bewilderment to Salentine that the government allowed private enterprise to make so much money out of these airwaves without levying the proper tax. He shuddered at the thought of a strong Federal Communication Commissioner under Kennedy's direction. It could mean the end of the TV and cable companies as now constituted.

And Salentine also worried about Louis Inch. He was constantly annoyed at Inch's stupidity and lack of sensitivity. How could a guy so dumb get so rich? He was like one of those idiots who could mysteriously do mathematical equations. The man had a genius for real estate and a simple idiot's dream which consisted of one thought. Build vertically always, horizontal never.

And the man had no inkling of how much he was hated, even by those closest to him. But especially by the inner city people, by the slum-dwelling blacks and Hispanics and by the working-class whites in the countryside and the small cities. It seemed that all these people could smell his greed, his insensitivity to the human. The man could become a serious liability if things went really wrong. But they needed him in the coming fight against Kennedy. Louis Inch was not afraid to stick his neck out. The man had real courage. He was not afraid of bribing anybody. In a democracy or a dictatorship this was an invaluable asset.

Louis Inch, certainly the most hated man in New York City, volunteered to restore the atom-blighted area in that city.

The eight blocks were to be purified with marble monuments enclosed in a green woodland. He would do it at cost, take no profit and have it up in six months. Thank God the radiation had been minimal.

Everybody knew that Louis Inch got things done much better than any government agency. Of course Louis Inch knew he would still make a geat deal of money through his subsidiary companies in construction, planning commissions and advisory committees. And the publicity would be invaluable.

Louis Inch was one of the richest men in America. His father had been the usual hardnosed big city landlord, failing to keep up the heat in apartment buildings, skimping on services, forcing out tenants so as to build more expensive apartments. Bribery of building inspectors was a skill Louis Inch had learned at his father's knee. Later, armed with a university degree in business management and law, he bribed city councilmen, borough presidents and their staffs, even mayors.

It was Louis Inch who fought the rent control laws in New York, it was Louis Inch who put together the real estate deals that built skyscrapers alongside Central Park. A park that now had an awning of monstrous steel edifices to house Wall Street brokers, professors at powerhouse universities, famous writers, chic artists, the chefs of expensive restaurants.

It was charged by the Reverend Foxworth that Louis Inch was responsible for the horrible slums in the upper West Side and the Bronx, in Harlem, in Coney Island, simply by the amount of reasonable housing he had destroyed in his rebuilding of New York. Also that he was blocking the rehabilitation of the Times Square district, while secretly buying up buildings and blocks. To this Inch retorted that the Reverend Foxworth was representing people who, if you had a bag full of shit, would demand half of it.

Another Inch strategy was his support of city laws that

required landlords to rent housing space to anyone regardless of race, color or creed. He had given speeches supporting those laws, because they helped to drive the small landlord out of the market. A landlord who had only the upstairs and/or the basement of his house to rent, had to take in drunks, schizophrenics, drug hustlers, rapists, stick-up artists. Eventually these small landlords would become discouraged, sell their houses and move to the suburbs.

But Louis Inch was beyond all that now, he was stepping up in class. Millionaires were a dime a dozen, Louis Inch was one of the hundred or so billionaires in America. He owned bus systems, he owned hotels and he owned an airline. He owned one of the great hotel casinos in Atlantic City and he owned apartment buildings in Santa Monica, California. It was the Santa Monica properties that gave him the most trouble.

Louis Inch had joined the Socrates Club because he believed that its powerful members could help solve his Santa Monica real estate problems. Golf was a perfect sport to hatch conspiracies. There were the jokes, the good exercise and the agreements struck. And what could be more innocent? The most rabid investigator from Congressional Committees or the hanging judges of the press could not accuse golfers of criminal intent.

The Socrates Country Club turned out to be better than Inch suspected. He became friendly with the hundred or so men who controlled the country's economic apparatus and political machinery and it was in the Socrates Country Club that Louis Inch became a member of the Money Guild that could buy the entire Congressional delegation of a State in one deal. Of course you couldn't buy them body and soul, you were not talking abstracts here, like the devil and God, good and evil, virtue and sin. No, you were talking politics. You were talking of what was possible. There were times when a Congressman had to oppose you to win re-election. It was true that ninety-eight per cent of the Congressmen were always re-elected, but there was always the two per cent that had to listen to their constituents.

Louis Inch dreamed the impossible dream. No, not to be President of the United States, he knew his landlord imprint could never be erased. His smudging the very face of New York was an architectural murder. There were a million slum dwellers in New York, Chicago, and especially Santa Monica who would fill the streets ready to put his head on a pike. No, his dream was to be the first trillionaire in the modern civilized world. A plebeian trillionaire, his fortune won with the calloused hands of a working man.

Inch lived for the day when he could say to Bert Audick, 'I have a thousand units.' It had always irritated him that Texan oil men talked in units, a 'unit' in Texas was one hundred million dollars. Audick had said about the destruction of the city of Dak, 'God, I lost 500 units there.' And Inch vowed some day to say to Audick, 'Hell, I got about a thousand units tied up in real estate,' and Audick would whistle and say, 'A hundred billion dollars.' And then Inch would say to him, 'Oh, no, a trillion dollars. Up in New York a unit is a billion dollars.' That would settle that Texas bullshit once and for all.

To make that dream come true, Louis Inch came up with the concept of 'air space'. That is, he would buy the air space above existent buildings and build on top of them. Air space could be bought for peanuts, it was a new concept as marsh lands had been when his grandfather bought them knowing that technology would solve the problem of draining the swamps and turn them into profitable building acres. In the same way Louis Inch knew that he could build over the existing buildings of the major cities. The problem was to prevent the people and their legislators from stopping him. That would take time and an enormous investment, but he was confident it could be done. True, cities like Chicago, New York, Dallas, Miami would be gigantic steel and concrete prisons but people didn't have to live there, except for the elite who loved the museums, the cinemas, the theater, the music. There would of course be little boutique neighborhoods for the artists.

And of course the thing was that when Louis Inch finally succeeded, there would no longer be any slums in New York City. There would be simply no affordable rent for the criminal and the working classes. They would come in from the suburbs, on special trains, on special buses, and they would be gone by nightfall. The renters and buyers of the Inch Corporation condos and apartments could go to the theater, the discos, the expensive restaurants and not worry about the dark streets outside. They could stroll along the Avenues, even venture into the side streets, they could walk the parks, in comparative safety. And what would they pay for such a paradise? Fortunes.

Louis Inch had one weakness. He loved his wife Theodora. An opulent blonde with a social conscience and a tender heart. Inch had met her when she was student at NYU and he had given a lecture there on how the owners of real estate affected the culture of geat cities. As many money-oriented men, Louis admired women who considered money worthless itself. He liked Theodora's social conscience, her love for her fellow man and her desire to help them. He liked her good humor and easygoingness. And he was delighted by her no-nonsense healthy sexuality, that an hour or two in bed before supper was an important and constructive part of her day. Late at night she studied before going to sleep, reading, listening to instructional tapes on her headset and making notes on what she would do the next day.

They complemented each other perfectly. Louis Inch was that rarity in American society, a very rich man who was happily married, happy in work, delighted in his wife's ambitions, and so he could devote all of his dreams to becoming a trillionaire. For adventure and risk, he had the infinite air space of the geat cities to purchase.

The happiness of the Inch marriage lasted ten years. And

the first tiny break was caused by the Reverend Baxter Foxworth. Theodora Inch admired him as one of the country's great black leaders in the Martin Luther King tradition.

Theodora Inch became a leader in the society of rich women determined to give their husbands' money back to the poor and so she decided to organize a huge society ball for the homeless. The tickets were ten thousand dollars a couple and the proceeds would go to build a huge shelter for the homeless. The ball would be held in the Plaza Hotel and it would be one of the greatest social events in the history of New York. It would also prove that the Inch family had the welfare of the city at heart.

Theodora Inch asked for the help of the Reverend Baxter Foxworth to make sure the representatives of the black power elite would be at the ball. The Reverend told her with bemused amiability that there were very few black men rich enough to afford the price of a ticket. Theodora Inch assured him that there would be a block of fifty tickets set aside, free of charge. The Reverend accepted.

The newspapers were sown with intriguing items about the event, the participants would all be required to come in costume showing the different ages of the city of New York. They would wear masks of former mayors and famous politicians and robber barons. There would be a thousand people at the ball and indeed more tickets than that had been sold. All the giant corporations understood that they had to buy a block of tickets to keep the good will of the city officials and the Inch real estate empire. Wall Street firms had been especially generous, the stock brokers were tired of coming to work and stepping over drunken bums sleeping on the ornate plazas of the beautiful skyscrapers Louis Inch had built for them.

On the night of the ball everything was in place. The TV mobile units surrounded the Plaza Hotel, the long lines of limousines stretched and stacked up back to 72nd Street to roll up to the Plaza entrance on 59th. And as the limousines hit 60th Street they were greeted by swarms of homeless men and women armed with dirty rags who wiped the limousine windows and then stretched out dirty palms for a tip. And got nothing.

The TV audience did not understand that the very rich rarely carry cash; who has not met a celebrity who must borrow a dollar to tip the washroom attendant? But the TV image to America was poor people being refused by the very rich.

This was the Reverend Foxworth's little joke. The good Reverend had recruited alcoholics and drug addicts, then transported them to the Plaza Hotel in special vans to do their begging. It was his message to the Inch empire that they could not buy off opposition so easily.

Louis Inch the very next day countered this. He ordered one million 'I Love New York' buttons, huge red and white ovals, and distributed them free to everyone in his hotels and corporations.

But his wife was enchanted by this humiliating joke and the next day, meeting with the Reverend Baxter Foxworth to reproach him, she became his secret mistress.

Summoned to the meeting of the Socrates Club in California, Louis Inch began to trip across the United States to confer with great real estate corporations of the big cities. From them he exacted their promise to contribute money to defeat Kennedy. Arriving in Los Angeles a few days later, he decided to make a side trip to Santa Monica before going to the seminar.

Santa Monica is one of the most beautiful towns in America. Mainly because its citizens have successfully resisted the efforts of real estate interests to build sky-scrapers, voted laws to keep rents stable and control construction. A fine apartment on Ocean Avenue, overlooking the

Pacific itself, only cost one sixth of the citizen's income. This was a situation that had driven Inch crazy for twenty years.

Louis Inch thought Santa Monica an outrage, an insult to the American spirit of free enterprise; these units under today's conditions could be rented for ten times the going rate. Louis Inch had bought up many of the apartment buildings. These were charming Spanish-style complexes, wasteful in their use of valuable real estate, with their inner courtyards and gardens, their scandalously low two-storey heights. Oh, this air space above Santa Monica was worth billions, the view of the Pacific Ocean worth more billions. Sometimes Louis Inch had crazy ideas of building vertically on the ocean itself. This made him too dizzy.

He did not of course try to directly bribe the three city counselors he invited to Michael's (the food delicious but again the restaurant a scandalous misuse of valuable real estate) but he told them his plans, he showed how everybody could become multimillionaires if certain laws were changed. He was dismayed when they showed no interest. But that was not the worst part. When Louis Inch got into his limousine, there was a shattering explosion. Glass flew all around the interior of the limo, the back window disintegrated, the windshield suddenly sprouted a large hole and spider webs in the rest of the glass.

When the police arrived they told Inch that a rifle bullet had done the damage. When they asked him if he had any enemies, Louis Inch assured them with all sincerity that he did not.

The Socrates Club's special seminar on 'Demagoguery in Democracy' commenced the next day.

Those present were Bert Audick, now under a RICO indictment; George Greenwell who looked like the old wheat stored in his gigantic Midwest silos; Louis Inch, his handsome pouting face pale from his near death the day before;

Martin 'Take me Private' Mutford wearing an Armani suit that could not hide his going to fat; and Lawrence Salentine.

Bert Audick took the floor first. 'Would somebody explain to me how Kennedy is not a communist?' he said. 'Kennedy wants to socialize medicine and home building. He has me indicted under the RICO laws and I'm not even Italian.' Nobody laughed at his little joke so he went on. 'We can dick around all we want but we have to face one central fact. He is an immense danger to everything we in this room stand for. We have to take drastic action.'

George Greenwell said quietly, 'He can get you indicted but he can't get you convicted, we still have due process in this country. Now I know you have endured great provocation. But if I hear any dangerous talk in this room I walk out. I will listen to nothing treasonous or seditious.'

Bert Audick took offense. 'I love my country better than anyone in this room,' he said. 'That's what gripes me. The indictment says I was acting in a treasonable way. Me! My ancestors were in this country when the fucking Kennedys were eating potatoes in Ireland. I was rich when they were bootleggers in Boston. Those gunners fired at American planes over Dak but not by my orders. Sure I gave the Sultan of Sherhaben a deal, but I was acting in the interest of the United States.'

Lawrence Salentine said dryly, 'We know Kennedy is the problem. We're here to discuss a solution. Which is our right and our duty.'

Martin Mutford said, 'What Kennedy's telling the country is bullshit. Where is the capital mass going to come from to support all these programs? He is talking a modified form of communism. If we can hammer that home in the media, the people will turn away from him. Every man and woman in this country thinks they'll be a millionaire some day and they're already worrying about the tax bite.'

'Then how come all the polls show Francis Kennedy will win in November?' Lawrence Salentine asked irritably. As so many times before he was a little astonished by the obtuseness of powerful men. They seemed to have no awareness of Kennedy's enormous personal charm, his appeal to the mass of people, simply because they themselves were impervious to that charm.

There was a silence and then Martin Mutford spoke. 'I had a look at some of the legislation being prepared to regulate the stock market and banks. If Kennedy gets in, there will be mighty slim pickings. And if he gets his regulatory agency people in, the jails will be filled with very rich people.'

'I'll be there waiting for them,' Audick said, grinning. For some reason he seemed to be in a very good humor despite his indictment. 'I should be a trustee by then, I'll make sure you all have flowers in your cells.'

Louis Inch said impatiently, 'You'll be in one of those country club jails playing with computers that keep track of your oil tankers.'

Bert Audick had never liked Louis Inch. He didn't like a man who piled up human beings from underground to the stars, and charged a million dollars for apartments no bigger than a spittoon. Audick said, 'I'm sure my cell will have more room than one of your fancy apartments. And once I'm in, don't be too fucking sure you can get oil to heat those skyscrapers. And another thing, I'll get a better break gambling in jail than in your Atlantic City casinos.'

George Greenwell as the oldest and most experienced in dealing with the government felt he had to take charge of the conversation. 'I think we should, through our companies and other representatives, pour a great deal of money into the campaign of Kennedy's opponent. Martin, I think you should volunteer to be the campaign manager.'

Martin Mutford said, 'First let's decide what kind of money we are talking about and how it's to be contributed.'

George Greenwell said, 'How about a round sum of five hundred million dollars.'

Bert Audick said, 'Wait a minute, I've just lost fifty billion and you want me to go for another unit?'

Louis Inch said maliciously, 'That's one unit, Bert. Is the oil industry going chicken shit on us? You Texans can't spare a lousy one hundred million?'

Salentine said, 'TV time costs a lot of money. If we are going to saturate the air waves from now until November that's five whole months. That's going to be expensive.'

'And your TV network gets a big chunk of that,' Louis Inch said aggressively. He was proud of his reputation as a fierce negotiator. 'You TV guys put in your share out of one pocket and it appears like magic in your other pockets. I think that should be a factor when we contribute.'

Martin Mutford said, 'Look we are talking peanuts here,' which outraged the others. 'Take Me Private' Mutford was famous for his cavalier treatment of money. To him it was only a telex transporting some sort of spiritual substance from one ethereal body to another. It had no reality. He gave casual girlfriends a brand new Mercedes, a bit of eccentricity he had learned from rich Texans. If he had a mistress for a year he bought her an apartment house to secure her old age. Another mistress had a house in Malibu, another a castle in Italy and an apartment in Rome. He had bought an illegitimate son a piece of a casino in England. It had cost him nothing, merely slips of paper signed. And he always had a place to stay whenever he traveled. The Albanese girl owned her famous restaurant and building the same way. And there were many others. Money meant nothing to 'Private' Mutford.

Audick said aggressively, 'I paid my share with Dak.'

Mutford said, 'Bert, you're not in front of Congressional committees arguing oil depletion allowances.'

'You have no choice,' Louis Inch told Audick. 'If Kennedy gets elected and he gets his Congress, you go to jail.'

George Greenwell was wondering again whether he should disassociate himself officially from these men. After

297

all he was too old for these adventures. His grain empire stood in less danger than the fields of these other men. The oil industry too obviously blackmailed the government to make scandalous profits. His own grain business was low key, people in general did not know that only five or six privately held companies controlled the bread of the world. Greenwell feared that a rash, belligerent man like Bert Audick could get them all in really serious trouble. Yet he enjoyed the life of the Socrates Club, the week-long seminars filled with interesting discussions on the affairs of the world, the sessions of backgammon, the rubbers of bridge. But he had lost that hard desire to get the better of his fellow man.

Inch said, 'Come on, Bert, what the hell is a lousy unit to the oil industry? You guys have been sucking the public tit dry with your oil depletion allowance for the last hundred years.'

Salentine said dryly, 'And what about our friend, "Take Me Private"? He has more money than all of us put together. We can tap into the government treasury, he taps into the GNP. Banking and Wall Street will be the first to get kicked in the ass. They've been so blatant Kennedy could hang them from the lamp posts on Wall Street and citizens would celebrate with a ticker tape parade.'

Inch grinned and said, 'Private, you money guys are outrageous. That last decline in the market you engineered cost ordinary stockholders at least two hundred billion dollars.'

Martin Mutford laughed. 'Stop the bullshit,' he said. 'We are all in this together. And we will all hang together if Kennedy wins. Forget about the money and let's get down to business. Let's figure out how to attack Kennedy in this campaign. How about his failure to act on that atom bomb threat in time to stop the explosion? How about the fact that he has never had a woman in his life since his wife died? How about that maybe he's secretly screwing broads in the White House like his Uncle Jack did? How about a million things? How about his personal staff? We have a lot of work to do.'

This distracted them. Audick said thoughtfully, 'He doesn't have any woman. I've already had that checked out. Maybe he's a fag.'

'So what?' Salentine said. Some of his top stars on his network were gay and he was sensitive on the subject. Audick's language offended him.

But Louis Inch unexpectedly took Audick's point. 'Come on,' he said to Salentine, 'the public doesn't mind if one of your goofy comedians is gay, but the President of the United States?'

'The time will come,' Lawrence Salentine said.

'We can't wait,' Mutford said. 'And besides the President is not gay. He was in some sort of sexual hibernation. And besides word has come to me that he is beginning to be interested in a certain young lady.'

'How young?' Louis Inch asked eagerly.

'Not young enough for our purposes,' Mutford said dryly. 'I think our best shot is to attack him through his staff.' He considered for a moment and then said, 'The Attorney General, Christan Klee, I've had some people check into him. You know he's a somewhat mysterious guy for a public figure. Very rich, much richer than people think, I've taken a sort of unofficial peek at his banking records. Doesn't spend much, he's not keeping women or into drugs, that would have showed up in his cash flow. A brilliant lawyer who doesn't really care that much for law. Not into good works. We know he is devoted to Kennedy and his protection of the President is a marvel of efficiency. But that efficiency hampers Kennedy's campaign because Klee won't let him press the flesh. All in all I'd concentrate on Klee.'

Audick said, 'Klee was CIA, high up in operations. I've heard some weird stories about him.'

'Maybe those stories could be our ammunition,' Mutford said.

'Only stories,' Audick said. 'And you'll never get anything out of the CIA files, not with that guy Tappey running the show.'

George Greenwell said casually, 'I happen to have some information that the President's Chief of Staff, that man Dazzy, has a somewhat messy personal life. His wife and he quarrel and he sees a young girl.'

Oh shit, Mutford thought, I have to get them off this. Jeralyn Albanese had told him all about Christian Klee's full weight.

'That's too minor,' he said. 'What do we gain even if we force Dazzy out? The public will never turn against the President for a staff member screwing a young girl, not unless it's rape or harassment.'

Audick said, 'So we approach the girl and give her a million bucks and have her yell rape.'

Mutford said, 'Yeah but she'd have to holler rape after three years of screwing and having her bills paid. It won't wash.'

It was George Greenwell who made the most valuable contribution. 'We should concentrate on the atom bomb explosion in New York. I think Congressman Jintz and Senator Lambertino should create investigating committees in the House and in the Senate, subpoena all the government officials. Even if they come up with nothing concrete, there will be enough coincidences so that the news media can have a field day. That's where you have to use all your influence,' he said to Salentine. 'That is our best hope. And now I suggest we all get to work.' Then he said to Mutford, 'Set up your campaign committees. I guarantee you'll get my hundred million. It is a very prudent investment.'

When the meeting broke up it was only Bert Audick who considered more radical measures.

Right after this meeting Lawrence Salentine was summoned by President Francis Kennedy. Lawrence Salentine prepared

300

for the meeting by having a conference with his fellow TV network owners. Salentine told them, 'Gentlemen, as I once gave him our bad news, he is going to give me bad news. We are all in a geat deal of trouble.'

And so it had been. Francis Kennedy told Salentine that action would be taken against the networks for unlawfully barring access to the President of the United States to the TV audience on the day Congress voted to impeach him. The charges were already being drawn up by the Attorney General. Francis Kennedy also told Lawrence Salentine that the lax regulatory policies of the past were over. All the TV networks and cable channels were carrying far too many minutes of advertising. That would be cut in half.

When Salentine told the President that Congress would not allow him to do this, Kennedy grinned at him, and said, 'Not this Congress, but we have an election in November. And I'm going to run for re-election. And I'm going to campaign for people in Congress who will support my views.'

Lawrence Salentine went back to his fellow TV station owners and gave them the bad news. 'We have two courses of action,' he said. 'We can start helping the President out by how and when we cover his actions and his policies. Or we can remain free and independent and oppose him when we feel it necessary.' He paused for a moment and said, 'This may be a very perilous time for us. Not just loss of revenue, not just regulatory restrictions, but if Kennedy goes far enough it may be even our losing our licenses.'

This was too much. It was inconceivable that the network licenses could be lost. No more than the homesteaders in early frontier days could lose their land back to the government. The granting of TV station licenses, the free access to the airwaves had always belonged to them. It seemed to them now a natural right. And so the owners made the decision that they would not truckle to the President of the United States, that they would remain free and independent.

And that they would expose President Kennedy for the dangerous menace to American democratic capitalism that he surely was. Lawrence Salentine would relay this decision to the important members of the Socrates Club.

Salentine brooded for days on how to mount a TV campaign against the President on his TV network without making it seem too obvious. After all the American public believed in fair play, they would resent an overwhelming hatchet job. The American public believed in the due process of law though they were the most criminal populace in the world.

He moved carefully. First step, he had to enlist Cassandra Chutt who had the highest-rated national news program. Of course, he couldn't be too direct, anchor people jealously guarded against overt interference. But they had not achieved their eminence without playing ball with top management. And Cassandra Chutt knew how to play ball.

Salentine had nurtured her career over the last twenty years. He had known her when she was on the early morning programs and then when she had switched to evening news. She had always been shameless in her pursuit of advancement. She had been known to collar a Secretary of State and burst into tears, shouting that if he did not give a two-minute interview she would lose her job. She had cajoled and flattered and blackmailed the celebrated into appearing on her prime time interview program and then savaged them with personal and vulgar questions. Lawrence Salentine thought Cassandra Chutt the rudest person he had ever known in the broadcasting business.

Lawrence Salentine invited her to dinner in his apartment. He enjoyed the company of rude people.

When Cassandra arrived the next evening, Salentine was editing a videotape. He brought her to his work room, which had the latest equipment in videos and TV and monitoring and cutting machines, all behatted with small computers.

Cassandra sat on a stool and said, 'Oh shit, Lawrence, do

I have to watch you make your cut of *Gone with the Wind* again?' By answer he brought her a drink from the small bar in a corner of the room.

Lawrence Salentine had a hobby. He would take a videotape of a movie (he had a collection of what he thought were the hundred best movies ever made) and he would recut these tapes to make them better. Even in his most favorite movies there would be a scene or dialogue that he thought not well done or unnecessary and he would cut it out with editing machines. Now arrayed in the bookcase of his living room were a hundred videotapes of the best motion pictures, somewhat shorter, but perfect. There were even some movies that had their unsatisfactory endings chopped off.

While he and Cassandra Chutt ate the dinner served by a butler, they talked about her future programs. This always put Cassandra Chutt in a good mood. She told Salentine of her plans to visit the Arab states and bring them together on one program with Israel. Then a program with three Prime Ministers of Western Europe chatting with her. And then she was exuberant about going to Japan to interview the Emperor. Salentine listened patiently. Cassandra Chutt had delusions of grandeur but every once in a while she came up with a stunning coup.

Finally he interrupted her and said jokingly, 'Why don't you get President Kennedy on your program?'

Cassandra Chutt lost her good humor. 'He'll never give me a break after what we did to him.'

'It didn't turn out so well,' Lawrence Salentine said. 'But if you can't get Kennedy, then why not go to the other side of the fence? Why not get Congressman Jintz and Senator Lambertino to give their side of the story?'

Cassandra Chutt was smiling at him. 'You sneaky bastard,' she said. 'They lost. They are losers and Kennedy is going to slaughter them in the elections. Why should I have losers on my program? Who the hell wants to watch losers on TV?'

Lawrence Salentine said, 'Jintz tells me they have very important information on the atom bomb explosion, that maybe the Administration dragged its heels. That they didn't utilize properly the Nuclear Search Teams who might have located the bomb before it exploded. And they will say that on your program. You'll make headlines all over the world.'

Cassandra Chutt was stunned. Then she started to laugh. 'Oh, Christ,' she said. 'This is terrible but right after you said that, the question, the very next question I thought to ask those two losers was this, "Do you honestly think the President of the United States is responsible for the ten thousand deaths in the explosion of the nuclear bombs in New York?"'

'That's a very good question,' Lawrence Salentine said.

In the month of June, Audick traveled on his private plane to Sherhaben to discuss with the Sultan the rebuilding of Dak. The Sultan entertained him royally. There were dancing girls, fine food, and a consortium of international financiers the Sultan had assembled who would be willing to invest their money in a new Dak. Bert Audick spent a wonderful week of hard work picking their pockets for a hundred million dollar 'unit' here and a 'unit' there, but the real money would have to come from his own oil firm and the Sultan of Sherhaben.

On the final night of his stay he and the Sultan were alone together in the Sultan's palace. At the end of the meal the Sultan banished the servants and bodyguards from the room.

He smiled at Bert Audick and said, 'I think now we should get down to our real business.' He paused for a moment. 'Did you bring what I requested?'

Bert Audick said, 'I want you to understand one thing. I am not acting against my country. I just have to get rid of that Kennedy bastard or I'll wind up in jail. And he's going to track down all the ins and outs of our dealings over the past ten years. So what I am doing is very much in your interest.'

'I understand,' the Sultan said gently. 'And we are far removed from the events that will happen. Have you made sure the documents cannot be traced to you in any way?'

Bert Audick said, 'Of course.' He then handed over the leather briefcase beside him. The Sultan took it and drew out a file which contained photographs and diagrams.

The Sultan looked at them. They were photos of the White House interiors and the diagrams showed the control posts in different parts of the building. 'Are these up to date?' the Sultan asked.

'No,' Bert Audick said. 'After Kennedy took office three years ago, Christian Klee who's head of the FBI and the Secret Service changed a lot of it around. He added another floor to the White House for the Presidential Residence. I know that the fourth floor is like a steel box. Nobody knows what the set-up is. Nothing is ever published and they sure as hell don't let people know. It's all secret except to the President's closest advisors and friends.'

'Then this isn't much help,' the Sultan said.

Audick shrugged. 'I can help with money, we need fast action. Preferably, before Kennedy gets re-elected.'

'The Hundred can always use the money,' the Sultan said. 'I'll see that it gets to them. But you must understand these people act out of their own true faith. They are not hired assassins. So they will have to believe. The money comes from me as an oppressed small country.' He smiled. 'After the destruction of Dak, I believe Sherhaben qualifies.'

Bert Audick said, 'That's another matter I've come to discuss. My company lost fifty billion dollars when Dak was destroyed. I think we should reconstruct the deal we have on your oil. You were pretty rough last time.'

The Sultan laughed but in a friendly way. 'Mr Audick,' he said, 'for over fifty years the American and British oil companies raped the Arab lands of their oil. You gave

305

ignorant nomad sheiks pennies while you made billions. Really it was shameful. And now your countrymen get indignant when we want to charge what the oil is worth. As if we had anything to say about the price of your heavy equipment and your technological skills for which you charge so dearly. But now it is your turn to pay properly, it is your turn even to be exploited if you care to make such a claim. Please don't be offended but I was even thinking of asking you to "sweeten" our deal.'

They smiled at each other in a friendly fashion. They recognized in each other kindred souls, bargaining men who never missed the chance to pursue a negotiation.

'I guess the American consumer will have to pick up the bill for the crazy President they voted into office,' Audick said. 'I sure hate to do it to them.'

'But you will,' the Sultan said. 'You are a businessman after all, not a politician.'

'On my way to being a jailbird,' Audick said with a laugh. 'Unless I get lucky and Kennedy disappears. I don't want you to misunderstand me. I would do anything for my country but I sure as hell won't let the politicians push me around.'

The Sultan smiled in agreement. 'No more than I would let my parliament.' He clapped his hands for servants and then he said to Audick, 'Now I think it is time for us to enjoy ourselves. Enough of this dirty business of rule and power. Let us live life while we still have it.'

Soon they were sitting down to an elaborate dinner. Audick enjoyed Arab food, he was not squeamish like other Americans, the heads and eyeballs of sheep were mother's milk to him.

As they were eating Audick said to the Sultan, 'If you have someone in America, or anyplace else, who needs a job or some other help send me a message. And if you need money for some worthy cause I can arrange for its transfer from an untraceable source on my end. It is very important to me that we do something about Kennedy.'

'I understand completely,' the Sultan said. 'And now, no more talk of business. I have a duty as your host.'

Annee, who had been hiding out with her family in Sicily, was surprised when she was summoned to a meeting with fellow members of the first Hundred.

She met with them in Palermo. They were two young men she had known when they were all university students in Rome. The oldest, now about thirty years of age, she had always liked very much. He was tall, but stooped and he wore gold-rimmed glasses. He had been a brilliant scholar, destined for a distinguished career as a Professor of Etruscan Studies. In personal relationships he was gentle and kind. His political violence sprang from a mind that detested the cruel illogic of a capitalistic society. His name was Giancarlo.

The other member of the Hundred she knew as the firebrand of leftist parties at the University. A loudmouth, and a brilliant orator who enjoyed fanning crowds to violence but was essentially inept in action. This had been changed when he had been picked up by the Anti-Terrorist Special Police and severely interrogated. In other words, Annee thought, they had kicked the shit out of him and put him in the hospital for a month. Sallu, for that was his name, then talked less and acted more. Finally he was recognized as one of the Christs of Violence, one of the First Hundred.

Both of these men, Giancarlo and Sallu, now lived underground to elude the Italian Anti-Terrorist Security Police. And they had arranged this meeting with care. Annee had been summoned to the town of Palermo and instructed to wander and sightsee until she was contacted. And on the second day, she had encountered a woman named Livia in a boutique who had taken her to a meeting in a small restaurant in which they were the only customers. The restaurant had then closed its doors to the public, the proprietors and the single waiter were obviously cadre. Then Giancarlo and Sallu had emerged from the kitchen. Giancarlo was in chef's regalia and his eyes were twinkling with amusement. In his hands was a huge bowl of spaghetti dyed black with the ink of chopped squid. Sallu, behind him, carried the wooden basket of sesame-seeded golden bread and a bottle of wine.

The four of them, Annee, Livia, Giancarlo and Sallu, sat down to lunch. They could not see into the street because protective curtains shielded them from passers-by.

Giancarlo served them portions of spaghetti from the bowl. The waiter brought them salad and a dish of pink ham and a black and white grainy cheese.

'Just because we fight for a better world, we shouldn't starve,' Giancarlo said. He was smiling and seemed completely at ease.

'Nor die of thirst,' Sallu said as he poured the wine. But he was nervous.

The women let themselves be served; as a matter of revolutionary protocol they did not assume the stereotypic feminine role. But they were both amused. They were here to take orders from men.

As they were eating, Giancarlo opened the conference. 'You two have been very clever,' he said. 'It seems you are not under suspicion for the Easter operation. So it has been decided that we can use you for our new task. You are both extremely qualified. You have the experience but more important, you have the will. So you are being called. But I must warn you. This is more dangerous than Easter.'

Livia asked, 'Do we have to volunteer before we hear the details?'

It was Sallu who answered, and abruptly, 'Yes.'

Annee said impatiently, 'You always go through this routine and ask, "Do you volunteer?" Do we come here for this lousy spaghetti? When we come, we volunteer. So go on with it.'

Giancarlo nodded, he was amused by her. 'Of course. Of course,' he said.

Giancarlo took his time. He ate and said contemplatively, 'The spaghetti is not so bad.' They all laughed and right off that laugh he said, 'The operation is directed against the President of the United States. Mr Kennedy is linking our organization with the atom bomb explosion in his country. His government is planning Special Operations Teams to target us on a global basis. I have come from a meeting where our friends from all over the world have decided to co-operate on this operation.'

Livia said, 'In America, that's impossible for us. Where would we get the money, the lines of communication, how can we set up safe houses and recruit personnel? And above all, the necessary intelligence. We have no base in America.'

Sallu said, 'Money is no problem. We are being funded. Personnel will be infiltrated and have only limited knowledge.'

Giancarlo said, 'Livia, you will go first. We have secret support in America. Very powerful people. They will help you set up safe houses and lines of communication. You will have funds available in certain banks. And you, Annee, will go in after as Chief of Operations. So you will have the tricky part.'

Annee felt a thrill of delight. Finally she would be an operational chief. Finally she would be the equal of Romeo and Yabril.

Livia's voice broke into her thoughts. 'What are our chances?' she asked.

Sallu said reassuringly, 'Yours are very good, Livia. If they get on to us, they'll let you ride free so they can scoop up the whole operation. By the time Annee goes operational, you will be back in Italy.'

Giancarlo said to Annee, 'That's true. Annee, you will be at the greater risk.'

'I understand that,' Annee said.

'So do I,' Livia said. 'I meant what are our chances to succeed?'

'Very small,' Giancarlo said. 'But even if we fail, we gain. We state our innocence.'

They spent the rest of the afternoon going over the operational plans, the codes to be used, the plans for development of the special networks.

It was dusk when they were finished and Annee asked the question that had been unasked the whole afternoon. 'Tell me then, is the worst scenario that this could be a suicide mission?'

Sallu bowed his head. Giancarlo's gentle eyes rested on Annee and then he nodded. 'It could be,' he said, 'but that would be your decision, not ours. Romeo and Yabril are still alive, and we hope to free them. And I promise the same if you are captured.'

President Francis Kennedy instructed Oddblood Gray to contact the Reverend Baxter Foxworth, the most influential and charismatic black leader in America. The way it looked, the black vote might prove to be crucial.

The Reverend Foxworth was forty-five years old and movie-star handsome. He was lithe, his skin showed the infusion of the white blood that he so implored his fellow blacks to shed, figuratively. His hair was crinkly and grown out into a huge Afro that rejected his Caucasian appearance. When he was ushered into Oddblood Gray's office he said, 'The White House at last. Someday, Brother, you and me will be sitting in that Oval Office and handing out the shit.' His voice was as sweet as the birds in his native Louisiana.

Oddblood Gray had risen to greet the preacher and shake his hand. The Reverend always irritated him but they were on the same side, allied in the same battle. And Oddblood Gray was too intelligent not to realize that the Reverend's methods, though contrary to his own, were as necessary in the battle they fought.

Gray said to the Reverend, 'Sideass, I got no time for bullshit today. This is off the record, just you and me.'

The Reverend Foxworth never lost his cool with white folk and he considered Oddblood Gray as white as Simon Legree. He didn't take offense at the use of his nickname. If Oddblood Gray had said Reverend Sideass then there would have been big trouble, White House or cotton shack.

The name Sideass had come from the way the Reverend moved when he was one of the great dancers in New Orleans. He had the moves of a cat, feet crossing sideways over the other. In fact it had been his father who had given him the nickname. Oddblood Gray reminded Foxworth of his father. Gray and his father were both powerfully built, both scornful of religion, severely disciplined, and contemptuous of Baxter Foxworth's high-spirited rebelliousness.

Foxworth was an inflammatory issue between black and white political leaders because of his outrageousness. It was his extremeness that barred him from running for political office but he didn't want political office, or so he claimed.

At the beginning of the Francis Kennedy administration Reverend Foxworth believed that something might be done for the poor blacks of America. But that hope was gone. He had supported Kennedy and respected him. And Kennedy had tried, but Congress and the Socrates Club had been too much for him. So now Foxworth was in for the long haul, to lay down a bed of coals for the fire next time.

He fought the cause of each and every black person, right or wrong. It was the Reverend Foxworth who led marches for convicted murderers caught redhanded. It was the Reverend Foxworth who asked for indictments of police officers who shot and killed black criminals. As the Reverend himself said, in public, on television with his own special grin, 'It's all black and white to me.'

All this could be accepted, in fact, was in the fine liberal tradition and even had some logic since the police were always suspects in American society; here and there the

311

random arrow found a sensitive mark. What made Reverend Foxworth the subject of condemning editorials, his alienation from the two major parties, was his sly anti-Semitism. He implied that Jews sweated money out of the ghettos, Jews controlled political power in the great cities. Jews scooped black maids out of their culture to clean houses and wash dishes. It was worse than the old South, the Reverend said. At least in the South they trusted the niggers with their white children. In fact the Reverend always compared the old South favorably to the modern North.

Therefore it was no surprise, not even to the Reverend himself, that he was hated by many whites in America. And he did not blame the people who hated him. After all he was shooting craps and they were fading him, he often said, the analogy deliberately one that would inflame both sides.

The Reverend Baxter Foxworth was rubbing the cancer in American society until the pain produced the cure. At the beginning of Francis Xavier Kennedy's administration he restrained himself. But when he saw all of Kennedy's social measures defeated by Congress, he shouted to the crowds that this Kennedy was like all the other Kennedys, impotent against the big money people in Congress. And he went on a rampage. All the more so because he had supported Kennedy on the urging of Oddblood Gray. So at this particular moment he was not pleased with Oddblood Gray.

'It's nice having one of the Brothers in this nice office in the White House,' Foxworth said to Gray. 'The Brothers expected you to do a lot for us but you haven't done shit. And then I'm nice enough to come at your beckoning and you call me out of my name. What can I do for you this time, Brother?'

Oddblood Gray had sat down again and the Reverend also sat down. Gray looked at the Reverend grimly. 'I told you not to fuck around. And don't call me brother. In the English language a brother means we have the same mother and father. Use English. You're like those old time leftists, those Jewish Communists you hate so much, who used to call everybody comrade. Today we talk serious business.'

The Reverend took this in good part. He said, 'Isn't the word "friend" a little cold? That white-assed Kennedy, isn't he like a brother? Or why would you support all this crazy stuff he's doing? Otto, we've known each other a long time and you can call me Sideass. But if you weren't so big and mean, your name would have been "Tightass".' The Reverend gave his great laugh. He was immensely tickled. Then he said in a conversational voice, 'How come a man as black as you got the name of Gray? You are the only black named Gray I ever heard of. We get called "White", we get called "Blue", we get called "Green", we even get called "Black". So how come you got called Gray?'

Oddblood Gray smiled. For some reason the Reverend cheered him up. It was the man's high spirits, his energy now as he roamed the office chuckling over the special honoring plaques, the White House ashtrays, even going around the desk and taking a couple of pieces of White House stationery as a joke but Oddblood Gray took them out of his hands. He didn't trust the Reverend.

A long time ago they had been close friends but they had split because of their political differences. The Reverend was too rash for Oddblood Gray, too revolutionary; Gray believed in making the black's place in the existing structure. They had argued the point many times and remained friends and sometimes allies. The Reverend himself had put the difference: 'The trouble with you, Otto,' he said, 'is that you have faith and I don't.'

And that had been the case. The Reverend had adorned himself with the holy cloth as a knight in a joust puts on armor. Nobody dared call a man of the church a liar and a thief and fornicator, not on the TV or even in the sleaziest tabloid. America and its media held the established authority of God's churches in the utmost reverence. A kind of voodoo instinct but also because the churches of every religion had

313

enormous financial clout and expensive lobbyists. Special laws exempted church revenue from taxes.

Oddblood Gray knew all this and in public he always treated the Reverend Baxter Foxworth with the utmost respect. But in private because they were such old friends, because he knew that Foxworth had not a speck of religious feeling, he could be familiar. And besides they had done each other many favors over the years, they had a basic understanding. So now they settled down after the sparring.

'Reverend,' Oddblood Gray said, 'I am going to do you a favor and ask you one. You are smart enough to know we are living in very dangerous times.'

The Reverend smiled and said, 'No shit.'

Oddblood Gray said, 'If you keep fucking around, you could be in serious trouble. The National Security is the overriding interest of the government right now and if you start any of your riots and demonstrations even the Supreme Court can't help you. Not right now. In fact the FBI and the National Security and even the CIA are asking questions, paying you close attention. So that's my favor I'm giving you. Lay low.'

The Reverend was serious now. 'I appreciate the favor, Otto,' he said. 'It's that bad, huh?'

'Yes it is,' Oddblood Gray said. 'This country is scared shitless after that atom bomb explosion. The people of this country will back any repressive actions the Government takes. They won't tolerate anything that even hints at rebellion against authority. Forget about the Constitution right now. And don't think that whitey lawyer of yours can pull one of his tricks.'

Foxworth chuckled. 'Old Whitney Cheever Number III. How I love that man. You ever see him on TV? I swear to God he looks more American than the Stars and Stripes. You print his name and face on the currency, a Shylock would take it. And smart. And sincere. He's one of the best lawyers in the country. He loves anybody breaking the law

314

especially when it's for social progress, especially if it's robbing an armored car and shooting three guards to death. He can turn the defendants into Martin Luther King and keep a straight face. That's why I love the man.'

'Don't trust him,' Oddblood Gray said. 'If things get tough he's the first guy that gets picked up.'

'Whitney Cheever III,' Foxworth said incredulously. 'It would be like locking up Abraham Lincoln.'

'Don't trust him,' Oddblood Gray said.

'Oh, I never trusted him,' Foxworth said. 'He's the worst combination there is. He's white, he's red. Now he's black before he is white. But I understand he's red before he's black.'

Oddblood Gray said, 'I want you to quiet down. I want you to co-operate with this administration. Because new thing are going to happen, that you will love. And also to save your ass.'

Foxworth said, 'Don't worry about my ass. I know enough to lay low right now. What's the favor I do you?'

Gray said, 'I'm going to be named to the Cabinet. And guess as what? The new Secretary of Health, Education and Welfare, the HEW. And I'll have a mandate. Everybody in this country, black or white, never goes hungry, never has to lack medical care, always has a home.'

Foxworth whistled and then smiled at Gray. Same old shit. 'Hundreds of thousands of new jobs. Brother, you and I are going to do great things together. We must stay in touch.'

'You bet,' Oddblood Gray said. 'But lay low.'

'I can't lay *that* low,' Foxworth said. 'And, Otto, I know basically you're on our side but why are you chickenshit and you so black? Why are you so cautious when you know things are not right? Why aren't you out on the streets with us and fighting the good fight?' He was earnest now, not mocking.

Oddblood Gray shrugged. 'Because some day I'm going to

have to save your ass. Listen, Reverend, every once in a while I have to listen to Arthur Wix go on about Israel and how we have to prop it up. How there can never be another holocaust. And I want to say to him that if concentration camps and ovens come in this country it won't be the Jews, it will be us blacks. Don't you see? If ever there is a great calamity, if we should lose a war or something else, the blacks will become the scapegoats in this country. You can see it in the movies. You can see it in the literature. Oh it's not overt, they don't come right out with it. They are not as straight as you are when you come out with your anti-whitey stuff. But that's what I'm afraid of all the time.'

The Reverend listened to him intently. Now he pushed himself against the huge desk and stared into Oddblood Gray's eyes. He said angrily, 'Let me tell you this, our brothers don't walk into those camps like the Jews did. We'll burn down the cities, we'll take them with us.'

Oddblood Gray said gently, 'You'll never know what hit you. You have no idea what a government can muster in power, in deceit, in division, in sheer unfeeling cruelty. You have no idea.'

'Sure I do,' the Reverend said. 'Guys like you will be the Judas goats. Like you're practicing for now.'

'Oh, fuck you, Sideass,' Gray said. 'I was talking about a thousand-to-one shot. Now here's the favor you do me. Kennedy runs for re-election. We need you to get him re-elected by the greatest majority vote in the history of the United States. And to get him his very own Congress.'

Whitney Cheever III was a brilliant, ultra WASP lawyer who firmly believed that the form of the United States government was wrong. He believed in Communism, he believed capitalism was now a great evil, that the pursuit of money had become a cancer in the human psyche. But he was a civilized man, that is, he enjoyed the pleasures of life, classical music, French gourmet food, literature, an exquisitely furnished home, sculpture, painting and young girls. He had been raised rich and enjoyed it but had noted, even as a very young boy, the humiliations of his family servants in their forced deferentiality and their fate resting in the hands of his mother and father. So that everything that was a pleasure in his life had the taint of blood and shit.

Whitney Cheever knew there were many kinds of lawyers. There were the fighters who loved to be in court, but these were few. There were the lawyers who believed in the sanctity of the law, who could forgive anything on this earth, except the breaking of the forms of law, and these were few. There were the workaday lawyers who hacked away at the underbrush of civilization, the guarding of estates, the selling of houses, the arbiter of divorce between husband and wife, between business partners, and many other duties. There were the criminal lawyers, prosecution and defense, a little bleary-eyed and exhausted in spirit who did not escape from the slimy pit in which they labored. There were the constitutional lawyers who aspired to a high judgeship and there were the fierce guardians of the great corporate structures of America who were as ferocious as saints. And then there were lawyers who believed that lasting and beneficial change could only be made fighting against the law. Whitney Cheever III proudly counted himself as one of these.

He was a craggy-faced, handsome man with a full mop of unruly gray hair and he wore his huge black eyeglasses on the top of his head when he was not reading. On television this gave a sort of dashing, intellectual look. He was always being attacked for being a Communist and furthering the interests of the Soviet Union under the sheep's clothing of civil libertarian. He never replied to these attacks, treating them as beneath contempt. Altogether he made a favorable impression on even the most conservative viewers. When he was attacked for defending black criminals or any criminal in which there was political subtext, he would say that it was his duty as a lawyer and an American who believed in the Constitution.

Cheever was having dinner in a New York restaurant with the Reverend Baxter Foxworth and listening to the description of the events in Oddblood Gray's office. When the Reverend had finished, Whitney Cheever said, 'Didn't you bring up the brutal suppression of the demonstrations in New York after that atom bomb exploded?'

The Reverend Foxworth studied that all-American crag of a face, the eyeglasses pushed up on his hair. Is this guy for real, he thought, does Otto have the same shit with those people he works for up in Washington? 'No,' Foxworth said, 'he told me to lay low.'

'Well you and I have always co-operated in these things,' Whitney Cheever said. 'I think we should take the initiative. I think we should start an action of police brutality.'

'Mr Cheever,' Foxworth said, he was most of the time formal with this white man, preserving mutual respect, 'it wasn't the police that shot them, it was the National Guard.'

'But the police were also present,' Whitney Cheever said, 'It is their duty not only to protect against crime, it is also their duty to protect civil rights.'

With some exasperation, Foxworth realized the man was serious. Then he realized he was being argued into an untenable position. 'You're not going to do anything,' he said flatly. 'Reason number one. That was not a demonstration or a free assembly. That was looters out there taking advantage of a national disaster. If we try to exploit that situation we do ourselves more harm than good. Sure a couple of them got shot and there are hundreds in jail, so what. They deserve it. We only weaken our cause if we defend them.'

'But there were no whites shot or arrested,' Cheever said. 'Surely that tells us something.'

'What it tells us is that whites don't need the loot,' the

318

Reverend Foxworth said. 'No good, we don't go along if you do anything.'

'Very well,' Cheever said. 'I agree it may not be the time. And also I've decided on something which will keep me busy and which I know you will not want to be associated with in any way.'

'What's that?' Foxworth asked.

Cheever pushed his glasses down and pushed a little bit away from the table. 'I've decided to defend those two immature boys who set off the atom bomb. Pro bono.'

'JESUS CHRIST,' the Reverend Foxworth said.

16

Christian Klee's Special Division of the FBI ran computer surveillance on the Socrates Club, members of Congress, the Reverend Foxworth and on Whitney Cheever. Klee always started his morning going through their reports. He personally operated his desktop computer which held personal dossiers under his own secret codes.

This particular morning he called up the file of David Jatney. Klee had a fondness for his hunches and his hunch was that Jatney could be trouble. He studied the video image of the young man that appeared on his monitor, the sensitive face, the dark recessed eyes. How the face changed from handsomeness in repose to one of frightening intensity when he became emotional. Were the emotions ugly or just the structure of the face? Jatney was under a loose surveillance, it was just a hunch. But when Klee read the written reports on the computer, he felt a sense of satisfaction. The terrible insect buried in the egg of David Jatney was breaking out of its shell.

Two days after David Jatney assassinated the cardboard effigy of Kennedy, he was kicked out of Brigham Young University. Jatney did not go back to his home in Utah, to his strict Mormon parents who owned a string of dry cleaning stores. He knew his fate there, he had suffered it before. His father believed in starting his son at the bottom, handling bundles of sweaty clothes, male trousers, female dresses, male suit jackets that seemed to weigh a ton. All that cloth and cotton soaked with the warmth of human flesh was agonizing to Jatney's touch.

And like many of the young, he had had quite enough of his parents. They were good, hard-working people who enjoyed their friends, the business they had built up, and the comradeship of the Mormon Church. They were to him the two most boring people in the world.

And then too they lived a happy life which irritated David Jatney. His parents had loved him when he was little, but grown he was so difficult that they joked that they had been given the wrong child in the hospital. They had videos of David Jatney at every stage, the small baby crawling on the floor, the tottering around the room on holidays, leaving him at school for the first time, his graduation from grammar school, his receiving a prize for English composition in high school, fishing with his father, hunting with his uncle.

After his fifteenth birthday he refused to let himself be photographed. He was sensitive, horrified by the banalities of his life recorded on video, an insect programmed to live a short existence in an eternity of sameness. He was determined he would never be like his parents, never realizing that this too was another banality.

Physically he was the opposite pole. Where they were tall and blonde, and then massive by middle age, David Jatney was dark-skinned, thin and wiry. His parents joked about it but predicted that with age he would grow to be more like them, which filled him with horror. By his fifteenth year he showed a coldness toward them that was impossible to ignore. Their own affection in no way lessened, but they were relieved when he went off to Brigham Young.

He grew handsome with dark hair that glowed in its blackness. His features were all-American, that is the nose without a bump, the mouth strong but not too generous, the chin protruding but not intimidatingly so. What his photos did not show was the continuing reaction of his features and of his body. In the beginning, if you knew him for only a short time he seemed merely vivacious. A small motor ran his lips, his nose, his eyelids. His hands were busy when he spoke. His voice inflected sharply on an unimportant note. Then at other times he would sink into a lassitude that froze him into a sort of sullenness.

In college, his vivaciousness and intelligence made him attractive to the other students. But he was just a little too bizarre in his reactions and his earnestness; and sometimes brutally insulting, almost always condescending.

The truth was that David Jatney was in an agony of impatience to be famous, to be a hero, to have the world know he was special.

With women he had a shy confidence that won them over initially. They found him interesting and so he had his little love affairs. But they never lasted. He was off-putting, he was distant; after the first few weeks of vivaciousness and good humor he would sink into himself. Even in sex he seemed detached as if he did not want to lose control of his body. His greatest failing in the area of love was that he refused to worship the beloved, even in the courtship phase, and when he did his best to fall deeply in love it had the aura of a valet exerting himself for a generous tip.

He had always been interested in politics and the social order. Like most young men, he had contempt for authority in any form, the study of history revealed that the story of humanity was simply endless warfare between the powerful elite and the helpless multitude. He desired fame to join the powerful.

It was natural that he was voted Chief Hunter in the assassination game played every year at Brigham Young. And it was his clever planning that resulted in victory. He had also supervised the making of the effigy that so resembled Kennedy.

With the shooting of that effigy and the victory banquet afterwards, David Jatney experienced a revulsion for his student life. It was time to make a career. He had always written poetry, kept a diary in which he felt he could show his wit and intelligence. Since he was so sure he would be famous, this keeping of a diary with an eye on posterity was not necessarily immodest. And so he recorded, 'I am leaving college, I have learnt all that they can teach me. Tomorrow I drive to California to see if I can make it in the movie world.'

When David Jatney arrived in Los Angeles, he did not know a single soul. That suited him, he liked the feeling. With no responsibilities, he could concentrate on his thoughts, he could figure out the world. The first night he slept in a small motel room and then found a one-room apartment in Santa Monica that was cheaper than he had expected. He found this through the kindness of a matronly woman who was a waitress in a coffee shop where he took his first breakfast in California.

David Jatney ate frugally, a glass of orange juice, toast and coffee, and the waitress noticed him studying the rental section of the *Los Angeles Times*. She asked him if he was looking for a place to live and he said yes. She wrote down a phone number on a piece of paper and said it was just a one-room apartment but the rent was reasonable because the people in Santa Monica had fought a long battle with the real estate interests and there was a tough rent control law. And Santa Monica was beautiful and he would be only a few minutes away from the Venice beach and its board-walk and it was a lot of fun.

Jatney at first was suspicious. Why would this stranger be interested in his welfare? She looked motherly but she had a sexy air about her. Of course she was very old, she must be forty at least. But she didn't seem to be coming on to him. And she gave him a cheery goodbye when he left. He was to learn that people in California did things like this. The constant sunshine seemed to mellow them. Mellowing. That's what it was. It cost her nothing to do him the service.

Jatney had driven from Utah in the car that his parents

had given him for college. In it was his every worldly possession, except for a guitar that he had once tried to learn and which was back in Utah. Most important was a portable typewriter which he used to write his diary, poetry, short stories and novels. Now that he was in California he would try his first screenplay.

Everything fell into place easily. He got the apartment, a little place with a shower but no bath. It looked like a dollhouse with frilly curtains over its one window and prints of famous paintings on the wall. The apartment was in a row of two-storey houses behind Montana Avenue and he could even park his car in the alley. He had been very lucky.

He spent the next fourteen days hanging around the Venice beach and boardwalk taking rides up to Malibu to see how the rich and famous lived. He leaned against the steel link fence that cut off the Malibu Colony from the public beach and peered through. There was this long row of beach houses that stretched far to the north. Each worth three million dollars and more, and yet they looked like ordinary countrified shacks. They wouldn't cost more than twenty thousand in Utah. But they had the sand, the purple ocean, the brilliant sky, the mountains behind them across the Pacific Coast Highway. Some day he would sit on the balcony of one of those houses and gaze over the Pacific.

At night in his dollhouse he sank into long dreams of what he would do when he too was rich and famous. He would lay awake until the early hours of the morning weaving his fantasies. It was a lonely and curiously happy time.

He called his parents to give them his new address and his father gave him the number of a producer to call at the movie studio, a childhood friend named Dean Hocken. Jatney waited a week. Finally he made the call and got through to Hocken's secretary. She asked him to hold. In a few moments she came back on the phone and told him that Mr Hocken was not in. He knew it was a con, that he was being sloughed off and he felt the surge of anger at his father for being so dumb. But he gave the secretary his phone number when she asked. He was still on his daybed brooding angrily an hour later when the phone rang. It was Dean Hocken's secretary and she asked him if he was free at eleven the next morning to see Mr Hocken in his office. He said he was and she told him that she would leave a pass at the gate so that he could drive on the studio lot.

When he hung up the phone David Jatney was surprised at the gladness welling up in him. A man he had never seen had honored a schoolboy friendship. And then he was ashamed of his own debasing gratitude. Sure the guy was a big wheel, sure his time was valuable, but eleven in the morning? That meant he would not be asked to lunch. It would be one of those quick courtesy interviews so the guy wouldn't feel guilty. So that his relatives back in Utah could point out that he didn't have a big head. A mean politeness basically without value.

But the next day turned out differently than he expected. Dean Hocken's office was in a long low building on the movie lot, and impressive. There was a receptionist in a big waiting room whose walls were covered with posters of bygone movies. Two other offices behind the reception room held two more secretaries, and then a larger, grander office. This office was furnished beautifully with deep armchairs and sofas and rugs, the walls were hung with original paintings, it had a bar with a large refrigerator. In a corner was a working desk topped with leather. On the wall above the desk was a huge photograph of Dean Hocken shaking hands with President Francis Xavier Kennedy. There was a coffee table littered with magazines and bound scripts. The office was empty.

The secretary who had brought him in said, 'Mr Hocken will be with you in ten minutes. Can I get you a drink or some coffee?'

Jatney was polite in his refusal. He could see that the young secretary was giving him an appraising glance so he used his real shitkicker's voice. He knew he made a good impression. Women always liked him at first, it was only when they got to know him better that they didn't like him, he thought. But maybe that was because he didn't like them when he got to know them better.

He had to wait for fifteen minutes before Dean Hocken came into the office from a back door that was almost invisible. David Jatney was for the first time in his life really impressed. This was a man who truly looked successful and powerful, he radiated confidence and friendliness as he grabbed David Jatney's hand.

Dean Hocken was tall and David Jatney cursed his own shortness. Hocken was at least six foot two and he looked amazingly youthful, though he must be the same age as Jatney's father which was fifty-five. He wore casual clothes, but his white shirt was whiter than any Jatney had ever seen. His jacket was some sort of linen and hung beautifully on his frame. The trousers were linen also, sort of off white. Hocken's face seemed without a wrinkle and painted over with bronze ink sprayed from the sun.

Dean Hocken was as gracious as he was youthful. He diplomatically revealed a homesickness for the Utah mountains, the Mormon life, the silence and peace of rural existence, the quiet Tabernacled cities. And he also revealed that he had been suitor to the hand of David Jatney's mother.

'Your mother was my girlfriend,' Dean Hocken said. 'Your father stole her away from me. But it was for the best, those two really loved each other, made each other happy.' And Jatney thought, yes, it was true, his mother and father really loved each other and with their perfect love they had shut him out. In the long winter evenings they sought their warmth in a conjugal bed while he watched his TV. But that had been a long time ago.

He watched Dean Hocken talk and be charming and he saw the age beneath that carefully preserved outward armor of bronzed skin stretched too tight for nature. The man had no flesh beneath his chin, not a sign of the wattles that had grown on his father. He wondered why the man was being so nice to him.

'I've had four wives since I left Utah,' Dean Hocken said, 'and I would have been much happier with your mother.' Jatney watched for the usual signs of satisfaction, the hint that his mother too might have been much happier if she had stuck with the successful Dean Hocken. But he saw none. The man was still a country boy beneath that California polish.

Jatney listened politely and laughed at the jokes. He called Dean Hocken 'Sir' until the man told him to please just call him 'Hock', and then he didn't call him anything. Hocken talked an hour and then looked at his watch and said abruptly, 'It was good seeing somebody from down home, but I guess you didn't come to hear about Utah. What do you do?'

'I'm a writer,' David Jatney said. 'The usual stuff, a novel that I threw away and some screenplays, I'm still learning.' He had never written a novel.

Dean Hocken nodded approval of his modesty. 'You have to earn your dues. Here's what I can do for you right now. I can get you a spot in the reader's department on the studio payroll. You read scripts and write a summary and your opinion. Just a half page on each script you read. That's how I started. You get to meet people and learn the basics. Truth is, nobody pays much attention to the reports, but do your best. It's just a starting point. Now I'll arrange all this and one of my secretaries will get in touch with you in a few days. And soon, we'll have dinner together. Give my best to your mother and father.' And then Hock escorted David Jatney to the door. They were not going to have lunch, Jatney thought, and the promise of dinner would stretch out for ever. But at least he would get a job, he would get one

327

foot in the door, and then when he wrote his screenplays, everything would change.

Jatney spent a month reading scripts which seemed to him utterly worthless. He wrote the short, less than half page of summary, then wrote his opinion on the same page. His opinion was supposed to be only a few sentences but he usually finished using the rest of the space on the page.

At the end of the month the office supervisor came to his desk and said, 'David, we don't have to know how witty you are. Just two sentences of opinion will be fine. And don't be so contemptuous of these people, they didn't piss on your desk, they just try to write movies.'

'But they are terrible,' Jatney said.

The supervisor said, 'Sure they are, do you think we'd let you read the good ones? We have more experienced people for that. And besides this stuff you call dreadful, every one of them has been submitted by an agent. An agent hopes to make money from them. So they have passed a very stringent test. We don't accept scripts over the transom because of lawsuits, we're not like book publishers. So no matter how lousy they are, when agents submit, we have to read them. If we don't read the agent's bad scripts they don't send us the good ones.'

Jatney said, 'I could write better screenplays.'

The supervisor laughed. 'So can we all.' He paused for a moment and then said, 'When you've written one let me read it.'

A month later David Jatney did just that. The supervisor read it in his private office. He was very kind. He said gently, 'David, it doesn't work. That doesn't mean you can't write. But you don't really understand how movies work. It shows in your summaries and critiques but your screenplay shows it too. Listen, I'm trying to be helpful. Really. So starting next week you'll be reading the novels that are published and that have been considered possible for movies.'

David Jatney thanked him politely but felt the familar rage. Again it was the voice of the elder, the supposedly wiser, the ones who had the power.

It was just a few days later that Dean Hocken's secretary called and asked if he was free for dinner that night with Mr Hocken. He was so surprised it took him a moment to say yes. She told him it would be at Michael's restaurant in Santa Monica at eight p.m. She started to give him directions to the restaurant but he told her he lived in Santa Monica and knew where it was, which was not strictly true.

But he had heard of Michael's restaurant. David Jatney read all the newspapers and magazines and he listened to the gossip in the office. Michael's was the restaurant of choice for the movie and music people who lived in the Malibu Colony. When he hung up the phone he asked the manager if he knew exactly where Michael's was located mentioning casually that he was having dinner there that night. He saw that the manager was impressed. He realized that he should have waited until after this dinner before submitting his screenplay. It would have then been read in a different context.

That evening when David Jatney walked into Michael's restaurant he was surprised that only the front part was under a roof, the rest of the restaurant was in a garden made beautiful with flowers and large white umbrellas that formed a secure canopy against rain. The whole area was glowingly lit. It was just beautiful, the balmy open air of April, the flowers gushing their perfume and even a gold moon over-head. What a difference from a Utah winter. It was at this moment that David Jatney decided never to go home again.

He gave his name to the receptionist and was surprised when he was led directly to one of the tables in the garden. He had planned on arriving ahead of Hocken, he knew his role and intended to play it well. He would be absolutely respectful, he would be waiting at the restaurant for good old Hock to arrive and that would be acknowledging his power. He still wondered about Hocken. Was the man genuinely kind or just a Hollywood phony being condescending to the son of a woman who once rejected him and now must, of course, be regretting it?

He saw Dean Hocken at the table he was being led to and with Hocken was a man and a woman. The first thing that registered on David Jatney was that Hocken had deliberately given him a later time so that he would not have to wait, an extraordinary kindness that almost moved him to tears. For in addition to being paranoid and ascribing mysterious evil motives for other people's behavior, David Jatney could also ascribe wildly benevolent reasons.

Hocken got up from the table to give him a down-home hug and then introduced him to the man and woman. Jatney recognized the man at once. His name was Gibson Grange and he was one of the most famous actors in Hollywood. The woman's name was Rosemary Belair, a name that Jatney was surprised he didn't recognize because she was beautiful enough to be a movie star. She had glossy black hair worn long and her face was perfect in its symmetry. Her make-up was professional and she was dressed elegantly in a dinner dress over which was some sort of little jacket.

They were drinking wine, the bottle rested in a silver bucket. Hocken poured Jatney a glass.

The food was delicious, the air balmy, the garden serene, none of the cares of the world could enter here, Jatney felt. The men and women at the tables around them exuded confidence, these were the people who controlled life. Someday he would be like them.

He listened through the dinner, saying very little. He studied the people at his table. Dean Hocken, he decided was legitimate and as nice as he appeared to be. Which did not necessarily mean that he was a good person, Jatney thought. He became conscious that though this was ostensibly a social occasion, Rosemary and Hock were trying to talk Gibson Grange into doing a picture with them.

It seemed that Rosemary Belair was also a producer, in fact the most important female producer in Hollywood.

David Jatney listened and watched, he took no part in the conversation, and when he was immobile his face was handsome as his photographs. The other people at the table registered it but he did not interest them and Jatney was aware of this.

And it suited him right now. Invisible, he could study this powerful world he hoped to conquer. That Hocken had arranged this dinner to give his friend Rosemary a chance to talk Gibson Grange into doing a picture with her. But why? There was a certain easiness between Hocken and Rosemary that could not be there unless they had been through a sexual period. It was the way Hocken soothed Rosemary when she became too excited in her pursuit of Gibson Grange. At one time she said to Gibson, 'I'm a lot more fun to do a picture with than Hock.'

And Hocken laughed and said, 'We had some pretty good times didn't we, Gib?'

And the actor said, 'Nah, we were all business.' He said this without cracking a smile.

Gibson Grange was a 'bankable' star in the movie business. That is, if he agreed to do a movie, that movie was financed immediately by any studio. Which was why Rosemary was so anxiously pursuing him. He also looked exactly right. He was in the old American Gary Cooper style, lanky, with open features: he looked as Lincoln would have looked if Lincoln had been handsome. His smile was friendly and he listened to everyone intently when they spoke. He told a few good-humored anecdotes about himself that were funny. This was especially endearing. Also he dressed in the style that was more homespun than Hollywood, baggy trousers and a ratty yet obviously expensive sweater with an old suit jacket over a plain woolen shirt. And yet he magnetized everyone in the garden. Was it because his face had been seen by so many millions and shown so intimately by the camera? Were there mysterious ozone layers where his face remained for ever? Was it some physical manifestation not yet solved by science? The man was intelligent, Jatney could see that. His eyes as he listened to Rosemary were amused but not condescending and though he seemed to always agree with what she was saying, he never committed himself to anything. He was the man David Jatney dreamed to be.

They lingered over their wine. Hocken ordered dessert, wonderful French pastries, Jatney had never tasted anything so good. Both Gibson Grange and Rosemary Belair refused to touch the desserts, Rosemary with a shudder of horror and Gibson Grange with a slight smile. But it was Rosemary who would surely let herself be tempted in the future. Grange was secure, Jatney thought. Grange would never touch dessert again in his life but Rosemary's fall was inevitable.

At Hocken's urging, David Jatney ate the other desserts, and then they still lingered and talked. Hocken ordered another bottle of wine but only he and Rosemary drank from it and then Jatney noticed another undercurrent in the conversation. Rosemary was putting the make on Gibson Grange.

Rosemary had barely talked to Jatney at all during the evening and now she ignored him so completely that he was forced to chat with Hocken about the old days in Utah. But both of them finally became so entranced by the contest between Rosemary and Gibson that they fell silent.

For as the evening wore on and more wine was drunk Rosemary mounted a full seduction. It was of alarming intensity, an awesome display of sheer will. She presented her virtues. First were the movements of her body and face, somehow the front of her dress had slipped down to show more of her breasts. There were the movements of her legs which crossed and recrossed then hiked the gown higher to show a glint of thigh. Her hands moved about, touching Gibson on his face when she was carried away by what she was saying. She showed her wit, told funny anecdotes, and

332

revealed her sensitivity. Her beautiful face was alive to show each emotion, her affection for the people she worked with, her worries about members of her immediate family, her concern about the success of her friends. She avowed her deep affection for Dean Hocken himself, how good old Hock had helped her in her career, rewarded her with advice and influence. Here good old Hock interrupted to say how much she deserved such help because of her hard work on his pictures and her loyalty to him and as he said this Rosemary gave him a long look of grateful acknowledgement. At this moment Jatney, completely enchanted, said that it must have been a great experience for both of them. But Rosemary, eager to renew her pursuit of Gibson, cut Jatney off in mid-sentence.

Jatney felt a tiny shock at her rudeness but surprisingly no resentment. She was so beautiful, so intent on gaining what she desired, and what she desired was becoming clearer and clearer. She must have Gibson Grange in her bed that night. Her desire had the purity and directness of a child, which made her rudeness almost endearing.

But what Jatney admired above all was the behavior of Gibson Grange. The actor was completely aware of what was happening. He noticed the rudeness to Jatney and tried to make up for it by saying, 'David, you'll get a chance to talk someday,' as if apologizing for the self-centeredness of the famous who have no interest in those who have not yet acquired their fame. But Rosemary cut him off too. And Gibson politely listened to her. But it was more than politeness. He had an innate charm that was part of his being. He regarded Rosemary with genuine interest. His eyes sparkled and never wandered from her eyes. When she touched him with her hands he patted her back. He made no bones about it, he liked her. His mouth too, always parted in a smile that displayed a natural sweetness which softened his craggy face into a humorous mask.

But he was obviously not responding in the proper fashion

for Rosemary. She was pounding on an anvil that gave off no sparks. She drank more wine and then played her final card. She revealed her innermost feelings.

Talking directly to Gibson, ignoring the other two men at the table. Indeed she had maneuvered her body so that it was very close to Gibson isolating them from David Jatney and Hocken.

No one could doubt the passionate sincerity in her voice. There were even tears in her eyes. She was baring her soul to Gibson. 'I want to be a real person,' she said. 'I would like to give up all this shit of make-believe, this business of movies. It doesn't satisfy me. I want to go out to make the world a better place. Like Mother Teresa, or Martin Luther King. I'm not doing anything to help make the world grow. I could be a nurse or a doctor, I could be a social worker. I hate this life, these parties, this always being on a plane for meetings with important people. Making decisions about some damned movie that won't help humanity. I want to do something real.' And then she reached out and clutched Gibson Grange's hand.

It was marvelous for David Jatney to see why Grange had become such a powerful star in the movie business, why he controlled the movies he appeared in. For Gibson Grange somehow had his hand in Rosemary's, somehow he had slid his chair away from her, somehow he had captured the central position in the tableau. Rosemary was still staring at him with an impassioned look on her face waiting for his response. He smiled at her warmly, then tilted his head downward and to the side so that he addressed Jatney and Hocken.

Gibson Grange said with affectionate approval, 'She's slick.'

Dean Hocken burst into laughter, David Jatney could not repress a smile. Rosemary looked stunned but then said in a tone of jesting reproof, 'Gib, you never take anything seriously except your lousy movies.' And to show she was not offended she held out a hand which Gibson Grange gently kissed.

David Jatney wondered at all of them. They were so sophisticated, they were so subtle. He admired Gibson Grange most of all. That he would spurn a woman as beautiful as Rosemary Belair was awe-inspiring, that he would outwit her so easily was godlike.

Jatney had been ignored by Rosemary all evening, but he acknowledged her right to do so. She was the most powerful woman in the most glamorous business in the country. She had access to men far worthier than he. She had every right to be rude. Jatney recognized that she did not do so out of malice. She simply found him non-existent.

They were all astonished that it was nearly midnight, they were the last ones in the restaurant. Hocken stood up and Gibson Grange helped Rosemary put on her jacket again, which she had taken off in the middle of her passionate discourse. When Rosemary stood up she was a little off balance, a little drunk.

'Oh, God,' she said. 'I don't dare drive myself, the police in this town are so awful. Gib, will you take me back to my hotel?'

Gibson smiled at her. 'That's in Beverley Hills. Me and Hock are going out to my house in Malibu. David will give you a ride, won't you, David?'

'Sure,' Dean Hocken said. 'You don't mind do you, David?'

'Of course not,' David Jatney said. But his mind was spinning. How the hell was this coming about? Good old Hock was looking embarrassed. Obviously Gibson Grange had lied, didn't want to take Rosemary home because he didn't want to have to keep fending the woman off. And Hock was embarrassed because he had to go along with the lie or else he would get on the wrong side of a big star, something a movie producer avoided at all costs. Then he saw Gibson give him a little smile and he could read the man's mind. And of course that was it, that was why he was such a great actor. He could make audiences read this mind just wrinkling his eyebrows, tilting his head, a dazzling smile. With just that look, without malice but celestial good humor, he was saying to David Jatney, 'The bitch ignored you all evening, she was rude as hell to you, now I have put her in your debt.' Jatney looked at Hocken and saw that he was now smiling, not embarrassed. In fact he looked pleased as if he too had read the actor's look.

Rosemary said abruptly, 'I'll drive myself.' She did not look at Jatney when she said it.

Dean Hocken said smoothly, 'I can't allow that, Rosemary, you are my guest and I did give you too much wine. If you hate the idea of David driving you then of course I'll take you back to your hotel. Then I'll order a limo to Malibu.'

It was Jatney realized, superbly done. For the first time he detected insincerity in Hocken's voice. Of course Rosemary could not accept Hocken's offer. If she did so she would be offering a grievous insult to the young friend of her mentor. She would be putting both Hocken and Gibson Grange to a great deal of inconvenience. And her primary purpose in getting Gibson to take her home would not be accomplished anyway. She was caught in an impossible situation.

Then Gibson Grange delivered the final blow. He said, 'Hell, I'll ride with you, Hock. I'll just take a nap in the back seat to keep you company to Malibu.'

Rosemary gave David a bright smile. She said, 'I hope it won't be too much trouble for you.'

'No, it won't,' David Jatney said. Hocken clapped him on the shoulder, Gibson Grange gave him a brilliant smile and a wink. And that smile and wink gave Jatney another message. These two men were standing by him as males. A lone powerful female had shamed one of their fellow males and they were punishing her. Also she had come on too strong to Gibson, it was not in a woman's place to do so

336

with a male more than equal in power. They had just administered a patriarchal blow to her ego, to keep her in her place. And it was all done with such marvelous good humor and politeness. And there was another factor. These men remembered when they had been young and powerless as Jatney was now, they had invited him to dinner to show that their success did not leave them faithless to their fellow males, a time-hallowed practice perfected over centuries to forestall any envious revenge. Rosemary had not honored this practice, had not remembered her time of powerlessness and tonight they had reminded her. And yet Jatney was on Rosemary's side, she was too beautiful to be hurt.

They walked out into the parking lot together and then when the other two men roared away in Hocken's Porsche, David Jatney led Rosemary to his old Toyota.

Rosemary said, 'Shit I can't get out at the Beverly Hills Hotel from a car like that.' She looked around and said, 'Now I have to find my car. Look, David, do you mind driving me back in my Mercedes? It's somewhere around here, and I'll have a hotel limo bring you back. That way I won't have to have my car picked up in the morning. Could we do that?' She smiled at him sweetly then reached into her pocketbook and put on spectacles. She pointed to one of the few remaining cars in the lot and said, 'There it is.' Jatney, who had spotted her car as soon as they were outside, was puzzled. Then he realized she must be extremely nearsighted. Maybe it was nearsightedness that made her ignore him at dinner.

She gave him the key to her Mercedes and he unlocked the door on her side and helped her in. He could smell the wine and perfume composted on her body and felt the heat of her bones like burning coal. Then he went to the other side of the car to get in the driver's seat and before he used the key, the door swung open, Rosemary had unlocked it from the inside to open it for him. He was surprised by this, he would have judged it not in her character.

337

It took him a few minutes to figure how the Mercedes worked. But he loved the feel of the seats, the smell of the reddish leather, was it a natural smell or did she spray the car with some sort of special leather perfume? And the car handled beautifully, for the first time he understood the acute pleasure some people took from driving.

The Mercedes seemed to just flow through the dark streets. He enjoyed driving so much that the half hour to the Beverly Hills Hotel seemed to pass in an instant. In all that time Rosemary did not speak to him. She took off her spectacles and put them back into her purse and then sat silent. Once she glanced at his profile as if appraising him. Then she just stared straight ahead. Jatney never once turned to her or spoke. He was enjoying the dream of driving a beautiful woman in a beautiful car, in the heart of the most glamorous town in the world.

When he stopped at the canopied entrance to the Beverly Hills Hotel, he took the keys out of the ignition and handed them to Rosemary. Then he got out and went around to open her door. At the same moment one of the valet parking men came down the red-carpeted runway and Rosemary handed him the keys to her car. Jatney realized he should have left them in the ignition.

Rosemary started up the red-carpeted runway to the entrance of the hotel and Jatney knew she had completely forgotten about him. He was too proud to remind her about offering a limo to take him back. He watched her. Under the green canopy, the balmy air, the golden lights, she seemed like a lost princess. Then she stopped and turned, he could see her face, and she looked so beautiful that David Jatney's heart stopped.

He thought she had remembered him, that she expected him to follow her. But she turned again and tried to go up the three steps that would bring her to the doors. At that moment she tripped, her purse went flying out of her hands and everything in that purse scattered on the ground. By that

338

time Jatney had dashed up the red carpet runway to help her.

The contents of the purse seemed endless, it was magical in the way it continued to spill out its contents. There were solitary lipsticks, a make-up case which burst open and poured mysteries of its own, there was a ring of keys which immediately broke and scattered at least twenty keys around the carpet. There was a bottle of aspirin and prescription vials of different drugs. And a huge pink toothbrush. There was a cigarette lighter and no cigarettes, there was a tube of Binaca and a little plastic bag that held blue panties and some sort of device that looked sinister. There were innumerable coins, some paper money and a soiled white linen handkerchief. There were spectacles, gold-rimmed, spinsterish without the adornment of Rosemary's classically sculptured face.

Rosemary looked at all this with horror then burst into tears. Jatney knelt on the red carpet runway and started to sweep everything into the purse. Rosemary didn't help him. When one of the bellmen came out of the hotel, Jatney had him hold the purse with its mouth open while he shoveled the stuff into it.

Finally he had gotten everything and he took the now full purse from the bellman and gave it to Rosemary. He could see her humiliation and wondered at it. She dried her tears and said to him, 'Come up to my suite for a drink until your limo comes, I haven't had a chance to speak to you all evening.'

Jatney smiled. He was remembering Gibson Grange saying, 'She's slick.' But he was curious about the famous Beverly Hills Hotel and he wanted to stay around Rosemary.

He thought the green-painted walls were weird for a high-class hotel, dingy in fact. But when they entered the huge suite he was impressed. It was beautifully decorated and it had a large terrace, a balcony, in fact. There was also a bar in one corner. Rosemary went to it and mixed herself a drink, then, after asking him what he wanted, mixed him one. He had asked for just a plain scotch, though he rarely drank he was feeling a little nervous. She unlocked the glass sliding doors to the terrace and led him outside. There was a white glass-topped table and four white chairs. 'Sit here while I go to the bathroom,' Rosemary said, 'then we'll have a little chat.' She disappeared back into the suite.

David Jatney sat in one of the chairs and sipped his scotch. Below him were the interior gardens of the Beverly Hills Hotel. He could see the swimming pool and the tennis courts, the walks that led to the bungalows. There were trees and individual lawns, the grass greener under moonlight and the lighting glancing off the pink-painted walls of the hotel gave everything a surrealistic glow.

It was no more than ten minutes later when Rosemary reappeared. She sat in one of the chairs and sipped her drink. Now she was wearing loose white slacks and a white pullover cashmere sweater. She had pushed the sleeves of her sweater up above her elbows. She smiled at him, it was a dazzling smile. She had washed her face clean of make-up and he liked her better this way. Her lips were now not voluptuous, her eyes not so commanding. She looked younger and more vulnerable. Her voice when she spoke seemed easier, softer, less commanding.

'Hock tells me you're a screenwriter,' she said. 'Do you have anything you'd like to show me? You can send it to my office.'

'Not really,' Jatney said. He smiled back at her. He would never let himself be rejected by her.

'But Hock said you had one finished,' Rosemary said. 'I'm always looking for new writers. It's so hard to find something decent.'

'No,' Jatney said. 'I wrote four or five but they were so terrible I tore them up.'

They were silent for a time, it was easy for David Jatney

to be silent, it was more comfortable for him than speech. Finally Rosemary said, 'How old are you?'

David Jatney lied and said, 'Twenty-six.'

Rosemary smiled at him. 'God, I wish I were that young again. You know when I came here I was eighteen, I wanted to be an actress, and I was a half-assed one. You know those one-line parts on TV, the salesgirl the heroine buys something from? Then I met Hock and he made me his executive assistant and taught me everything I know. He helped me set up my first picture and he helped all through the years. I love Hock, I always will. But he's so tough, like tonight. He stuck with Gibson against me.' Rosemary shook her head. 'I always wanted to be as tough as Hock,' she said. 'I modeled myself after him.'

David Jatney said, 'I think he's a very nice gentle guy.'

'But he's fond of you,' Rosemary said. 'Really, he told me so. He said you look so much like your mother and you act just like her. He says you're a really sincere person, not a hustler.' She paused for a moment and then said, 'I can see that too. You can't imagine how humiliated I felt when all that stuff spilled out of my purse. And then I saw you picking everything up and never looking at me. You were really very sweet.' She leaned over and kissed him on the cheek. He could smell a different sweeter fragrance coming from her body now.

Abruptly she stood up and sent back into the suite, he followed her. She closed the glass door of the terrace and locked it and then said, 'I'll call for your limo.' She picked up the phone. But instead of pressing the buttons she held it in her hand and looked at David Jatney. He was standing very still, standing far enough away not to be in her space. She said to him, 'David, I'm going to ask you something that might sound odd. Would you stay with me tonight? I feel lousy and I need company but I want you to promise you won't try to do anything. Could we just sleep together like friends?'

Jatney was stunned. He had never dreamed this beautiful woman would want someone like him. He was dazzled by his good fortune. But then Rosemary said sharply, 'I mean it, I just want someone nice like you to be with me tonight. You have to promise you won't do anything. If you try, I'll be very angry.'

This was so confusing to Jatney that he smiled and as if not understanding, he said, 'I'll sit on the terrace or sleep on the couch here in the living room.'

'No,' Rosemary said. 'I just want somebody to hug me and go to sleep with. I just don't want to be alone. Can you promise?'

David Jatney heard himself say, 'I don't have anything to wear. In bed I mean.'

Rosemary said briskly, 'Just take a shower and sleep naked, it won't bother me.'

There was a foyer from the living room of the suite that led to the bedroom. In this foyer was an extra bathroom in which Rosemary told David Jatney to take his shower. She did not want him to use her bathroom. Jatney showered and brushed his teeth using soap and tissues. There was a bathrobe hanging from the back of the door with blue stitching script that said elegantly 'Beverly Hills Hotel'. He went into the bedroom and found Rosemary was still in her bathroom. He stood there awkwardly not wanting to get into her bed which had already been turned down by the night maid. Finally Rosemary came out of the bathroom wearing a flannel nightgown that was so elegantly cut and printed that she looked like a doll in a toy store. 'Come on, get in,' she said. 'Do you need a Valium or a sleeping pill?' And he knew she had already taken one. She sat at the edge of the bed and then got in and finally Jatney got into the bed but kept his bathrobe on. They were lying side by side when she turned the light out on her night table. They were in darkness. 'Give me a hug,' she said and they embraced for a

342

long moment and then she rolled away to her side of the bed and said briskly, 'Pleasant dreams.'

David Jatney lay on his back staring up at the ceiling. He didn't dare take off the bathrobe, he didn't want her to think that he wanted to be naked in her bed. He wondered if he should tell Hock about this the next time they met but he understood that it would become a joke that he had slept with such a beautiful woman and nothing had happened. And maybe Hock would think he was lying. He wished he had taken the sleeping pill Rosemary had offered him. She was already asleep, she had a tiny snore just barely audible.

Jatney decided to go back to the living room and got out of bed. Rosemary came awake and said sleepily, 'Could you get me a drink of Evian water.' Jatney went into the living room and fixed two Evian waters with a little ice. He drank from his glass and refilled it. Then he went back into the bedroom. By the light in the foyer he could see Rosemary sitting up, the bedsheets tight around her. He offered a glass and she reached out a bare arm for it. In the dark room he touched her upper body before finding her hand to give her the glass, and realized she was naked. As she was drinking he slipped into the bed but he let his bathrobe fall to the floor.

He heard her put the glass on the night table and then he put out his hand and touched her flesh. He felt the bare back and the softness of her buttocks. She rolled over and into his arms and his chest was against her bare breasts. Her arms were around him and the hotness of their bodies made them kick off the covers as they kissed. They kissed for a long time, her tongue in his mouth, and then he couldn't wait any longer and he was on top of her, and her hand as smooth as satin, a permission, guided him into her. They made love almost silently as if they were being spied upon until both their bodies together arched in the flight toward climax and they lay back separate again.

343

Finally she whispered, 'Now go to sleep.' She kissed him gently on the side of the mouth.

He said, 'I want to see you.'

'No,' she whispered.

David Jatney reached over and turned on her table light. Rosemary closed her eyes. She was still beautiful. Even with desire sated, even though she was stripped of all the arts of beauty, the enhancements of coquetry, the artifices of special light, but it was a different beauty.

He had made love out of animal need and proximity, a natural physical expression of his body. She had made love out of a need in her heart, or some spinning need in her brain. And now in the glow of the single light, her naked body was no longer formidable. Her breasts were small with tiny nipples, her body smaller, her legs not so long, her hips not so wide, her thighs a little slender. She opened her eyes, looking directly into his and he said, 'You're so beautiful.' He kissed her breasts and as he did so she reached up and turned out the light. They made love again and then fell asleep.

When Jatney woke and reached out, she was gone. He threw on his clothes and put on his watch. It was seven in the morning. He found her out on the terrace in a red jogging suit against which her black hair seemed to char. A table had been wheeled in by room service and on it were silver coffee pitchers and silver milk jugs and an array of plates with metal covers over them to keep the food warm.

Rosemary smiled at him and said, 'I ordered for you. I was just going to wake you up. I have to get my run in before I start work.'

He sat down at the table and she poured him coffee and uncovered a dish that held eggs and sliced up bits of fruit. Then she drank her orange juice and got up. 'Take your time,' she said. 'Thanks for staying last night.'

David Jatney wanted her to have breakfast with him, he wanted her to show that she really liked him, he wanted to

344

have a chance to talk, to tell her about his life, say something that would make her interested in him. But now she was putting a white headband over her charred hair and lacing up her jogging shoes. She stood up. David Jatney said, not knowing his face was twitching with emotion, 'When will I see you again?' And as soon as he said it he knew he had made a terrible mistake.

Rosemary was on her way to the door but she stopped. 'I'm going to be awfully busy the next few weeks. I have to go to New York. When I come back I'll give you a call.' She didn't ask for his number.

Then another thought seemed to strike her. She picked up the phone and called for a limo to bring Jatney back to Santa Monica. She said to him, 'It will be put on my bill. Do you need any cash to tip the driver?'

Jatney just looked at her for a long moment. She picked up her purse, opened it and said, 'How much will you need for the tip?'

Jatney couldn't help himself. He didn't know his face was twitching with a malice and a hatred that was frightening. He said insultingly, 'You'd know that better than me.' Rosemary snapped her purse shut and went out of the suite.

He never heard from her. He waited for two months and then one day on the movie studio lot he saw her come out of Hocken's office with Gibson Grange and Dean. He waited near Hocken's parking space so that they would have to greet him. Hocken gave him a little hug and said they had to have dinner and asked how the job was going. Gibson Grange shook his hand and gave him a sly but friendly smile, the handsome face radiating its easy good humor. Rosemary looked at him without smiling. And what really hurt was that for a moment it seemed to Jatney that she had forgotten him.

David Jatney had fired his rifle at Louis Inch because of a young woman named Irene Fletcher. Irene was delighted that someone had tried to kill Inch but never knew it was her lover who fired the shot. This despite the fact that every day she beseeched him to tell her his most innermost thoughts.

They had met on Montana Avenue where she was one of the salesgirls in the famous Fioma Bake Shop, which sold the best breads in America. David Jatney went there to buy biscuits and rolls and chatted with Irene when she served him. One day she said to him, 'Would you like to go out with me tonight? We can eat Dutch.'

Jatney smiled at her. She was not one of the typical blonde California girls. She had a pretty round face with a determined look, her figure was just a little buxom and she looked like she might be just a little too old for him. She was about twenty-five or twenty-six, but her gray eyes had a lively sparkle to them and she always sounded intelligent in their conversations, so he said yes. And truth to tell he was lonely.

They started a casual, friendly love affair, Irene Fletcher did not have the time for something more serious, nor the inclination. She had a four-year-old son and lived in her mother's house and also she was very active in local politics and Eastern religions, not at all unusual for a young person in Southern California. For Jatney it was a refreshing experience. Irene often brought her young son, Campbell, to these meetings which sometimes lasted far into the night, and she simply rolled her little boy into an Indian blanket and put him to sleep on the floor as she vigorously argued her points of view on the merits of the candidate for the Santa Monica Council or the latest seer from the Far East. Sometimes Jatney went to sleep on the floor with the young boy.

To Jatney, it was a perfect match, they had nothing in common. Jatney hated religion and despised politics. Irene detested the movies and was only interested in books on exotic religions and left-wing social studies. But they kept each other company, they filled in the holes in their existence.

346

When they had sex they were both a little offhand, but were always friendly. Sometimes Irene succumbed to a tenderness during sex which she immediately made an excuse for afterwards.

It was helpful that Irene loved to talk and David Jatney loved to be silent. They would lie in bed and Irene would talk for hours and David would listen. Sometimes she was interesting and sometimes she was not. It was interesting that there was a continuous guerrilla struggle between the real estate interests and the small home owners and renters in Santa Monica. Jatney could sympathize with this. He loved Santa Monica, he loved the low skyline of two-storey houses and one-storey shops, the Spanish-looking villas, the general air of serenity, the total absence of chilling religious edifices like the Mormon tabernacles in his home state of Utah. He loved the many slitted looks at the ocean, the great Pacific lying unobscured by the cataracts of glass and stone skyscrapers. He thought Irene a heroine for fighting to preserve all this against the ogres of the real estate interests.

She talked about her current Indian gurus and played their mantras and lectures on her tapes. These gurus were far more pleasant and humorous than the stern elders of the Mormon Church he had listened to while growing up and their beliefs seemed more poetic, their miracles purer, more spiritual, more ethereal than the famous Mormon bible of gold and the Angel Moroni. But finally they were just as boring with their rejection of the pleasures of this world, the fame on earth, all of which Jatney so desperately desired.

And Irene would never stop talking, she achieved a kind of self ecstasy when she talked even of the most ordinary things. Unlike Jatney, she found her life, ordinary as it was, too meaningful.

Sometimes when she was carried away and dissected her emotions for a full hour without interruption he would feel that she was a star in the heavens growing larger and brighter and that he himself was falling into a black endless hole that was the universe, falling further in that darkness while she never noticed.

He liked too that she was generous in material things but thrifty with her personal emotions. She would never really come to grief, she would never fall in that universal darkness. Her star would always expand, never lose its light. And he was grateful that this should be so. He did not want her company in the darkness.

One night they went for a walk on the beach just outside Malibu. It seemed weird to David Jatney that here was this great ocean on one side, then a row of houses and then mountains on the other. It didn't seem natural to have mountains almost bordering an ocean. Irene had brought along blankets and a pillow and her little child. They lay on the beach and the little boy, wrapped in blankets, fell asleep.

Irene and David Jatney sat on their blanket and the beauty of the night overcame them. For that little moment they were in love with each other. They watched the ocean blue-black in the moonlight, the little thin birds hopping ahead of the incoming waves. 'David,' Irene said, 'you never have told me anything really about yourself. I want to love you. You won't let me know you.'

David Jatney was only twenty-one years old and this touched him. He laughed a little nervously and then said, 'The first thing you should know about me is that I'm a Ten Mile Mormon.'

'I didn't even know you were a Mormon,' Irene said.

'If you are brought up a Mormon, you are taught that you must not booze or smoke or commit adultery,' David said. 'So when you do it you make sure you are at least ten miles from where anybody knows you.' And then he told her about his childhood. And how he hated the Mormon Church.

'They teach you that it's OK to lie if it helps the church,' David Jatney said. 'And then the hypocritical bastards give you all this shit about the Angel Moroni and some gold bible. And they wear angel pants, which I have to admit my mother and father never believed in, but you could see those fucking angel pants hanging on their clotheslines. The most ridiculous thing you ever saw.'

'What's angel pants?' Irene asked. She was holding his hand to encourage him to keep speaking.

'It's sort of a robe they wear so they won't enjoy screwing,' David Jatney said. 'And they are so ignorant they don't know that Catholics in the sixteenth century had the same kind of garment, a robe that covers your whole body except for a single hole in it so you can screw without supposedly enjoying it. When I was a kid I could see angel pants hanging from the laundry lines. I'll say this for my parents, they didn't buy that shit, but because he was an elder in the church they had to fly the angel pants.' Jatney laughed and then said, 'God, what a religion.'

'It's fascinating but it sounds so primitive,' Irene said.

David Jatney thought and what the hell is so civilized in you believing all those fucking gurus who tell you that cows are sacred, that you are reincarnated, but that this life means nothing, all that voodoo karma bullshit. But she felt his tensing and wanted to keep him talking. She slid her hands inside his shirt and felt his heart beating furiously.

'Did you hate them?' she asked.

'I never hated my parents,' he said. 'They were always good to me.'

'I meant the Mormon Church,' Irene said.

David Jatney said, 'I hated the Church ever since I can remember. I hated it as a little kid. I hated the faces of the elders, I hated the way my mother and father kissed their asses. I hated their hypocrisies. If you disagree with the rulings of the church they could even have you murdered. It's a business religion, they all stick together. That's how my father got rich. But I'll tell you the thing that disgusted me the most. They have special anointments and the top elders get secretly anointed and so they get to go to heaven ahead of other people. Like somebody slipping you to the head of the line while you're waiting for a taxi or a table in a popular restaurant.'

Irene said, 'Most religions are like that except the Indian religions. You just have to watch out for karma.' She paused a moment. 'That is why I try to keep myself pure of greed for money, why I can't fight my fellow human being for the possessions of this earth. I have to keep my spirit pure. We're having special meetings, there is a terrible crisis in Santa Monica right now. If we're not on the alert, the real estate interests will destroy everything we've fought for and this town will be full of skyscrapers. And they'll raise the rents and you and I will be forced out of our apartments.'

She went on and on and David Jatney listened with a feeling of peace. He could lie on his beach for ever, lost in time, lost in beauty, lost in the innocence of this girl who was so unafraid of what would happen to her in this world. She was telling him about a man named Louis Inch who was trying to bribe the city council so that they would change the building and rental laws. She seemed to know a lot about this man Inch, she had researched him. The man could be an elder in the Mormon Church. Finally Irene said, 'If it wasn't so bad for my karma, I'd kill the bastard.'

David Jatney laughed. 'I shot the President once.' And he told her about the assassination game, the Hunt, when he had been a one-day hero at Brigham Young University. 'And the Mormon elders who run the place had me thrown out,' he said.

But Irene was now busy with her small son who had a bad dream and woke up screaming into uncomprehended moonlight. She soothed him and said to Jatney, 'This guy Inch is having dinner with some of the town council tomorrow night. He's taking them to Michael's and you know what that means. He'll try to bribe them. I really would like to shoot the bastard.'

David Jatney said, 'I'm not worried about my karma, I'll shoot him for you.' They both laughed.

The next night David Jatney cleaned the hunting rifle he had brought from Utah and fired the shot that broke the glass in the limousine of Louis Inch. He had not really aimed to hit anyone, in fact the shot came much closer than he had intended. He was just curious to see if he could bring himself to do it.

17

It was Patsy Troyca who tricked Peter Cloot and nailed Christian Klee. Going over testimonies to the Congressional Committees of Inquiry into the atom bomb explosion he noted Klee's testimony that the great international crisis of the hijacking took precedence. But then there were glitches, Troyca noticed that there was a time gap. Christian Klee had disappeared from the White House scene. Where did he go?

They wouldn't find out from Klee, that was certain. But the only thing that could have made Klee disappear during that crisis was something terribly important. What if Klee had gone to interrogate Gresse and Tibbot?

Troyca did not consult with his boss, Congressman Jintz; he called Elizabeth Stone, the administrative aide to Senator Lambertino, and arranged to meet her at an obscure restaurant for dinner. In the months since the atom bomb crisis the two of them had formed a partnership, both in public and private life.

On their first date, initiated by Troyca, they had come to an understanding. Elizabeth Stone beneath her cool, impersonal beauty had a fiery sexual temperament, her mind however was cold steel. The first thing she said was, 'Our bosses are going to be out of their jobs in November. I think you and I should make plans for our future.'

Patsy Troyca was astonished. Elizabeth Stone was famous for being one of those aides who are the loyal right arms to their Congressional chiefs.

'The fight isn't over yet,' he said.

'Of course it is,' Elizabeth Stone said. 'Our bosses tried to impeach the President. Now Kennedy is the biggest hero this country has known since Washington. And he will kick their asses.'

Troyca, was instinctively a more loyal person to his chief. Not out of a sense of honor, but because he was competitive, he didn't want to think of himself as being on a losing side.

'Oh, we can stretch it out,' Elizabeth Stone said. 'We don't want to look like the kind of people who desert a sinking ship. We'll make it look good. But I can get us both a better job.' She smiled at him mischievously and Troyca fell in love with that smile. It was a smile of gleeful temptation, a smile full of guile and yet an admission of that guile, a smile that said that if he wasn't delighted with her, he was a jerk. He smiled back.

Patsy Troyca had, even to his own way of thinking, a sort of greasy, pig-like charm which worked only on certain women, and which always surprised other men and himself. Men respected Troyca because of his cunning, his high level of energy, his ability to execute. But the fact that he could charm women so mysteriously aroused their admiration.

Now he said to Elizabeth Stone, 'If we become partners, does that mean I get to fuck you?'

'Only if you make a commitment,' Elizabeth Stone said.

There were two words Patsy Troyca hated more than any of the others in the English language. One was commitment and the other was relationship.

'You mean like we should have a real relationship, a commitment to each other, like love?' he said. 'Like the house niggers used to make to their masters down in your dear old South?'

She sighed. 'Your macho bullshit could be a problem,' she said. Then she went on. 'I can make a deal for us. I've been a big help to the Vice President in her political career. She owes me. Now you have to see reality. Jintz and Lambertino are going to be slaughtered in the November election. Helen

353

DuPray is reorganizing her staff and I'm going to be one of her top advisors. I have a spot for you as my aide.'

Patsy Troyca said smilingly, 'That's a demotion for me. But if you're as good in the sack as I think you are, I'll consider it.'

Elizabeth Stone said impatiently, 'It won't be a demotion since you won't have a job. And then when I go up the ladder, so do you. You'll wind up with your own staff section to the Vice President.'

She paused for a moment. 'Listen,' she said. 'We were attracted to each other in the Senator's office, not love maybe, but certainly lust at first sight. And I've heard about you screwing your aides. But I understand it. We both work so hard, we don't have time for a real social life or a real love life. And I'm tired of screwing guys just because I'm lonely a couple a times a month. I want a real relationship.'

'You're going too fast,' Patsy Troyca said. 'Now if it was on the staff of the President . . .' He shrugged and grinned to show that he was kidding.

Elizabeth Stone gave him her smile again. It was really a hardboiled sort of grin but Patsy Troyca found it charming. 'The Kennedys have always been unlucky,' she said. 'The Vice President could be the President. But please be serious. Why can't we have a partnership, if that's what you prefer to call it? Neither one of us wants to get married. Neither of us wants children. Why can't we sort of half live with each other, keep our own places of course but sort of live together? We can have companionship and sex and we can work together as a team. We can satisfy our human needs and operate at the higher point of efficiency. If it works, it could be a great arrangement. If it doesn't, we can just call it quits. We have until November.'

They went to bed that night and Elizabeth Stone was a revelation to Patsy Troyca. Like many shy reserved people, man or woman, she was genuinely ardent and tender in bed. And it helped that the act of consummation took place in her townhouse. Patsy Troyca had not known that she was independently wealthy. Like a true WASP, he thought, she had concealed that fact, where he would have flaunted it. Troyca immediately saw that the townhouse would be a perfect place for both of them to live, much better than his just adequate flat. Here with Elizabeth Stone he could set up an office. The townhouse had three servants and he would be relieved of time consuming and worrying details like sending clothes out for cleaning, shopping for food and drink.

And Elizabeth Stone, ardent feminist in politics and her social life, performed like some ancient courtesan in bed. She was a slave to his pleasure. Well it was only the first time they were like that Patsy Troyca thought. Like when they first came to be interviewed for a job, they never looked as good after that. But in the month that followed, she proved him wrong.

They built up an almost perfect relationship. It was wonderful for both of them after their long hours with Jintz and Lambertino to come home, go out for a late supper then sleep together and make love. And in the morning they would go to work together. He thought for the first time in his life about marriage. But he knew instinctively that this was something Elizabeth Stone would not want.

They lived contained lives, a cocoon of work, companionship and love, for they did come to love each other. But the best and most delicious part of their times together was their scheming on how to change the plots of their world. They both agreed that Kennedy would be re-elected to the Presidency in November. Elizabeth Stone was sure that the campaign being mounted against the President by Congress and the Socrates Club was doomed to failure. Patsy Troyca was not so sure. There were many cards to play.

Elizabeth Stone hated Francis Kennedy. It was not a personal hatred, it was that steely opposition to someone she thought of as a tyrant. 'The important thing,' she said, 'is that Kennedy should not be allowed to have his own Congress in the next election. That should be the battleground. It's clear from Kennedy's statements in the campaign that he will change the structure of American democracy. And that would create a very dangerous historical situation.'

'If you are so opposed to him now, how can you accept a position on the Vice President's staff after the election?' Patsy asked her.

'We're not policy makers,' Elizabeth said. 'We're administrators. We can work for anybody.'

So after a month of intimacy, Elizabeth Stone was surprised when Patsy Troyca asked that they meet in a restaurant rather than the comfort of the townhouse they now shared. But he had insisted.

In the restaurant over their first drinks, Elizabeth said, 'Why couldn't we talk at home?'

Patsy Troyca said thoughtfully, 'You know, I've been studying a lot of documents going a long way back. Our Attorney General is a very dangerous man.'

'So?' Elizabeth Stone said.

'He may have your house bugged,' Patsy said.

Elizabeth Stone laughed. 'You are paranoid,' she said.

'Yeah,' Patsy Troyca said. 'Well how about this. Christian Klee had those two kids, Gresse and Tibbot, in custody and didn't interrogate them right away. But there's a time gap. And the kids were tipped off and told to keep their mouths shut until their families supplied lawyers. And what about Yabril? Klee has him stashed, nobody can get to see or talk to him. Klee stonewalls and Kennedy backs him up. I think Klee is capable of anything.'

Elizabeth Stone said thoughtfully, 'You can get Jintz to subpoena Klee to appear before a Congressional committee. I can ask Senator Lambertino to do the same thing. We can smoke Klee out.'

'Kennedy will exercise executive privilege and forbid him

to testify,' Patsy Troyca said. 'We can wipe our asses with those subpoenas.'

Elizabeth Stone was usually amused by his vulgarities, especially in bed, but she was not amused now. 'His exercising executive privilege will damage him,' she said. 'The papers and TV will crucify him.'

'OK, we can do that,' Patsy Troyca said. 'But how about if just you and me go to see Peter Cloot and try to pin him down? We can't make him talk but maybe he will. He's a law and order nut, and maybe psychologically he's horrified at Klee's handling of the atom bomb incident. Maybe he even knows something concrete.'

Two days later they went to see Peter Cloot. He received them in his office and told them he could not give them any information, but when pressed, admitted that he had been surprised at Christian Klee's order that Tibbott and Gresse not be interrogated immediately. He also admitted that since the warning call could not be traced, it was likely placed through a phone electronically protected against tracing. He also admitted that only highly placed government officials had such phones. When asked about the time gap in which Klee had disappeared from the White House, he shrugged.

It was Elizabeth Stone who put the question to him directly. 'Did he interrogate those two young men during the time period?'

Cloot looked them in the eye. 'That whole thing bothers me,' he said. 'I can't believe that Klee would deliberately foster such a situation. Now I tell you this privately, but I will deny it, unless under oath. Klee did come back and interrogate Gresse and Tibbot. Alone for five minutes with all the listening devices turned off. No record was made of that meeting. What was said I don't know.'

Elizabeth Stone and Patsy Troyca tried to hide their excitement. Back in their offices they notified their chiefs and subpoenas were prepared for Peter Cloot to testify before a joint House and Senate Committee.

18

President Francis Kennedy pondered his problems, what countermeasures to take. He was worried about the accusations against Christian Klee. They were fabrications of course and he would have to unravel that story but not now.

Right now he had to decide what to do with Yabril and those two young professors, Adam Gresse and Henry Tibbot. The people of America would cheer if he hung them from the balcony of the White House but such power could not be exercised in a democracy. As President he could pardon them, but not execute them. Meanwhile the finest lawyers in America had been retained to defend these men. Whitney Cheever who had joined the defense of Gresse and Tibbot, pro bono, would be formidable. But Francis Kennedy knew he had reached another crossroad in his mind. He had potent cards he could play, but did he have the will to play them? Could he discard his democratic and ethical principle, so useless in this particular power struggle? Could he become as ruthless as his opponents, the Congress, the Socrates Club, the criminals presently held incommunicado by Christian Klee in the detention hospitals? Oh, he could destroy them all if he had the will. For a moment he felt despair, then he brought back the memories of his helplessness when his wife and daughter died. Again he felt as though his brain was being compressed with hatred and he thought, nothing is meaningful if I am helpless again.

He isolated the most immediate dangers to be addressed.

*

In the beginning of June Congress launched its first attack signaling the end of the short peace after the defeat of Yabril. A joint House and Senate committee was formed to investigate the circumstances of the atom bomb explosion in New York. There had already been rumors planted in the newspapers and the TV that there was some sort of negligence on the part of the Kennedy administration. The suspected planters of the bomb, Gresse and Tibbot, had been captured twenty-four hours before the explosion. Why had they not been interrogated to force them into revealing the location of the bomb? There were also reports that the two young physicists had been warned just before their arrest. Who had warned them? Had there been some sort of conspiracy in the higher reaches of government? Kennedy's worried staff had already isolated this issue as a 'wrecker' in the coming campaign for re-election.

A Congressional committee was also investigating how many people in the Secret Service were being used to protect the President. Congress claimed there were over ten thousand. Did Kennedy really need such a large army in a democracy like America?

At a special meeting with his staff, Kennedy also summoned Vice President Helen DuPray; Dr Zed Annaccone; Theodore Tappey, the CIA chief; and his press secretary, Matthew Gladyce.

Helen DuPray had long ago reasoned out the male definition of honor. Quite simply when men owed a debt to a fellow male or female, they believed paying that debt was a greater debt than the one they owed to the social contract.

Females on the other hand took too literally the social contract, that is the understanding that a human being subordinates his personal motives to the broad needs of his fellow human beings. In that sense, females, as men often insisted, did not have that sense of 'honor'. Helen DuPray, within the limits of political prudence, despised this concept of hypocritical bribery. That she classified it as a male concept did not blind her to its power and its restriction on her own political movement.

On this early May morning before the President's meeting, she decided to go for her five-mile run to clear her head. She knew she was a hero to the Senior Staff since she had refused to sign the petition to remove Kennedy. But she also knew that they thought of it as an act of 'male' honor. She would have to be careful at the coming meeting.

In her secret heart she truly believed that the only solution to the world's ills was the transfer of power from the Patriarch. She had no wild dreams that this could be done in her lifetime. She could only push it a few inches and wait for a new history to begin. Or a new 'herstory', a word ardent feminists loved to use and men hated. She smiled. History, herstory, she didn't give a damn. Her job was to make the world work. She prepared her mind for the meeting with Francis Kennedy. It was, she knew, an important and dangerous occasion.

Dr Zed Annaccone dreaded his meeting with President Kennedy and his staff. It made him slightly ill to talk science and mix it in with political and sociological targets. He would never have accepted being the President's Medical Science Advisor except for the fact that he knew it was the only way to assure the proper funding of his beloved National Brain Research Institute.

It wasn't so bad when he dealt with Francis Kennedy directly. The man was brilliant and had a flair for science though the newspaper stories that claimed the President would have made a great scientist were simply absurd. But he certainly understood the subtle values of research and how it affected all walks of life. He could also use his imagination to see the almost miraculous results of even the most far-fetched of scientific theories. Kennedy was not the problem. It was the staff and the Congress and all the bureaucratic dragons. Plus the CIA and the FBI who kept looking over his shoulder.

Until serving in Washington, Dr Zed Annaccone had not truly realized the awful gap between science and society in general. It was scandalous that the human brain had made such a great jump forward in the sciences and that political and sociological disciplines had remained almost stationary. Science had solved so many mysteries of the body and brain and yet society in general was still muddling along in the Dark Ages.

He found it incredible that mankind still waged internal war, at enormous cost and to no advantage. That individual men and women still killed each other when there were treatments that would dissipate the murderous tendencies in human beings. He found it contemptible when the science of genetic splicing was attacked by politicians and the news media as if the tampering with the spirit of mankind was a corruption of some holy spirit. Especially when it was obvious that the human race as now genetically constituted was doomed.

Dr Zed Annaccone had been briefed on what the meeting would be about. There was still some doubt about whether the exploding of the atom bomb had been part of the terrorist plot to destabilize American influences in the world, whether there was a link between the two young physics professors, Gresse and Tibbot, and the terrorist leader Yabril. He would be asked whether they should use the PET brain scan to question the prisoners and determine the truth.

Which made Dr Zed Annaccone irritable. Why hadn't they asked him to run the PET before the atom bomb exploded? Christian Klee claimed that he had been tied up in the hijacking crisis and that the bomb threat had not seemed that threatening. Typical asshole reasoning. And President Kennedy had refused Klee's request for the PET brain scan out of humanitarian reasons. Yes, if the two young men were innocent and damage was done to their brains during the scan it would be an inhuman act. But Annaccone knew that this was a politician covering his ass. He had thoroughly briefed Kennedy on the procedure and Kennedy had understood. The PET scan was almost completely safe, and it would make the subject answer truthfully. They could have located the bomb and disarmed it. There would have been time.

It was regrettable, surely, so many people killed and injured. But Dr Annaccone felt a sneaking admiration for the two young scientists. He wished he had their balls, for they had made a real point, a lunatic one, true, but a point. That as man in general became more knowledgeable, individuals causing an atomic disaster became more probable. It was also true that the greed of the individual entrepreneur or the megalomania of a political leader could do the same. But these two kids were obviously thinking of sociological controls not scientific ones. They were thinking of repressing science, halting its march forward. The real answer of course was to change the genetic structure of man so that violence would become an impossible act. To put brakes in the genes and in the brain as you put brakes on a locomotive. It was that simple.

While waiting in the Cabinet Room of the White House for the President to arrive, Dr Zed Annaccone dissociated himself from the rest of the people there by reading his stack of memoranda and articles. He always felt himself resistant to the President's staff. Christian Klee kept track of the National Brain Institute and sometimes slapped a Secrecy order on his research. Annaccone didn't like that and used evasionary tactics when he could. He was often surprised that Klee could outwit him in such matters. The other staff members, Eugene Dazzy, Oddblood Gray and Arthur Wix, were primitives with no understanding of science, immersed in those comparatively unimportant matters of sociology and statecraft.

He noted that the Vice President Helen DuPray was present, as was Theodore Tappey, the CIA Chief. He was always surprised that a woman was Vice President of the United States. He felt that science ruled against something like this. In his researches of the brain he always felt he would some day come upon a fundamental difference between the male and female brain and was amused that he did not. Amused because if he found a discrepancy the fur would fly in a delightful way.

Theodore Tappey, he always regarded as Neanderthal. Those futile machinations for a slight degree of advantage in foreign affairs against fellow members of the human race. So futile an endeavor in the long run.

Dr Zed Annaccone took some papers out of his briefcase. There was an interesting article on the hypothetical particle called the tachyon. Not one person in this room had ever heard of the work, he thought. Though his field of expertise was the brain, Dr Annaccone had a vast knowledge of all the sciences.

So now he studied the paper on tachyons. Did tachyons really exist? Physicists had been quarreling about that for the last twenty years. Tachyons, if they existed, would fracture Einstein's theories, tachyons would travel faster than the speed of light which Einstein had said was impossible. Sure there was the apology that tachyons were already moving faster than light from the beginning but what the hell was that? Also the mass of a tachyon is a negative number. Which supposedly was impossible. But the impossible in real life could be possible in the spooky world of mathematics. And then what could happen? Who knew? Who cared? Certainly nobody in this room which held the most powerful men on the planet. An irony in itself. Tachyons might change human life more than anything these men could conceive.

Finally the President made his entrance and the people in the room stood up. Dr Annaccone put away his papers. He might enjoy this meeting if he kept alert and counted the eye blinks in the room. Research showed that eye blinks could reveal whether a person was lying or not. There was going to be a lot of blinking.

Francis Kennedy came to the meeting dressed comfortably in slacks, a white shirt covered by a sleeveless blue cashmere sweater, and with a good humor extraordinary in a man beset by so many difficulties.

Vice President Helen DuPray wondered why it was that being in love made men cheerful and women distressed.

After greeting them he said, 'We have Dr Annaccone with us today so that we can settle the problem of whether the terrorist Yabril was in any way connected with the atom bomb explosion. Also to respond to the charges that have been made in the newspapers and on television that we in the administration could have found the bomb before it exploded. Now to set the record straight, Christian, is there any evidence at all to link Yabril?'

They had already discussed this many times, Christian Klee thought. Francis just wanted to put it on record at this moment and specifically with Dr Annaccone.

'No, there is no hard evidence,' Christian said.

Dr Annaccone had been scribbling mathematical equations on the memo pad in front of him.

Kennedy gave him a friendly grin and said, 'Dr Annaccone, what are your thoughts on this subject? Maybe you can help us. And as a favor to me, stop figuring out the secrets of the universe on that pad of yours. You've discovered enough to get us into trouble.'

Dr Annaccone realized that this was a rebuke in the disguise of a compliment. He said, 'I still don't understand why you didn't sign the order for the PET scan before the nuclear device exploded. You already had the two young men in custody. You had the authority under the Atomic Security Act.'

Christian said quickly, 'We were in the middle of what we thought was a far more important crisis if you remember. I thought it could wait another day. Gresse and Tibbot claimed they were innocent and we had only enough evidence to grab them. We didn't have enough to indict. Then Tibbot's father got tipped off and we had a bunch of very expensive lawyers threatening a lot of trouble. So we figured we'd wait until the other crisis was over and maybe we had a little more evidence.'

Vice President Helen DuPray said, 'Christian, do you have any idea how Tibbot Senior was tipped off?'

Christian said, 'We are going over all the telephone company records in Boston to check the origin of calls received by Tibbot Senior. So far no luck.'

The head of the CIA, Theodore Tappey, said, 'With all your high-tech equipment, you should have found out.'

'Helen, you've got them off on a tangent,' Kennedy said. 'Let's stick to the main point. Dr Annaccone, let me answer your question. Christian is trying to take some heat off me, which is why a President has a staff. But I made the decision not to authorize the brain probe. According to the protocols, there is some danger of damaging the brain and I didn't want to risk it. The two young men denied everything, and there was no evidence that a bomb existed except for the warning letter. What we have here is really a scurrilous attack by the news media supported by the members of Congress. I want to pose a specific question. Do we eliminate any collusion between Yabril and Professors Tibbot and Gresse by having the PET scan done on all of them? Would that solve the problem?'

Dr Annaccone said crisply, 'Yes. But now you have a different circumstance. You are using the Medical Interrogation to gather evidence in a criminal trial, not to discover the whereabouts of a nuclear device. The Security Act does not authorize PET scanning under those circumstances.'

President Kennedy gave him a cold smile. 'Doctor,' he

said, 'You know how much I admire your work in the sciences, but you are not really instructed in the law.' Kennedy seemed to stiffen, to become more erect when he added, 'Listen to me carefully. Now I want Gresse and Tibbot to undergo the brain scan. And, more important, I want Yabril to undergo the brain scan. The question they will all be asked is this. "Was there a conspiracy? And was the atom bomb explosion part of Yabril's plan?" Now if the answer is yes, the implications are enormous. There may still be a conspiracy going on. And it may involve much more than New York City. Other members of the terrorist One Hundred could plant other nuclear devices. Now do you understand?'

Dr Annaccone said, 'Mr President, do you think that is really a possibility?'

Kennedy said, 'We have to erase any doubt. I will rule that these medical interrogations of the brain are justified under the Atomic Security Act.'

Arthur Wix said, 'There will be one hell of an uproar. They'll claim we're performing a lobotomy.'

Eugene Dazzy said dryly, 'Aren't we?'

Dr Annaccone was suddenly as angry as anyone was allowed to be in the presence of the President of the United States. 'It is not a lobotomy,' he said. 'It is a brain scan with chemical intervention. The patient is completely the same after the interrogation is completed.'

'Unless there's a little slip-up,' Dazzy said.

The Press Secretary, Matthew Gladyce, said, 'Mr President, the outcome of the test will dictate what kind of announcement we make. We have to be very careful. If the test proves there was conspiracy linking Yabril, Gresse and Tibbot, we'll be in the clear. If the scan proves there is no collusion, we just make an announcement to that effect without mentioning the probe.'

Francis Kennedy said gently, 'We can't do that, Matthew. There will be a written record that I have signed the order.

Our opponents will surely unearth it in the future and that will be a terrible problem.'

'We don't have to lie about it,' Matthew Gladyce said. 'Just don't mention it.'

Kennedy said curtly, 'Let's go on to other things.'

Eugene Dazzy read from the memo in front of him. 'The Congress wants to haul Christian up in front of one of their investigation committees. Senator Lambertino and Congressman Jintz want to take a crack at him. They are claiming, and they planted it all over in the media, that Attorney General Christian Klee is the key to any funny work that went on.'

'Invoke Executive Privilege,' Kennedy said. 'As President, I order him not to appear before any Congressional Committee.'

Dr Annaccone, bored with the political discussions, said jokingly, 'Christian, why don't you volunteer for our PET scan? You can establish your innocence irrevocably. And endorse the morality of the procedure.'

'Doc,' Christian said, 'I'm not interested in establishing my innocence as you call it. Innocence is the one fucking thing your science will never be able to establish. And I'm not interested in the morality of a brain probe that will determine the veracity of another human being. We are not discussing innocence or morals here. We are discussing the employment of power to further the functioning of society. Another area in which your science is useless. As you've often said to me, don't dabble with something in which you are not expert. So go fuck yourself.'

It was rare at these staff meetings that anyone let their emotions go unrestrained. It was even rarer for vulgar language to be used when Vice President Helen DuPray was attending staff meetings. Not that the Vice President was a prudish woman. Yet the people in the Cabinet room were surprised at Christian Klee's outburst.

Dr Annaccone was taken aback. He had just made a little

joke. He liked Christian Klee, as most people did. The man was urbane and civilized and he seemed more intelligent than most lawyers. Dr Annaccone, though a great scientist, prided himself on his serene understanding of everything in the universe. He now suffered the regrettable petty human vulnerability of having his feelings hurt. So without thinking he said, 'You used to be in the CIA, Mr Klee. The CIA headquarter building has a marble tablet that reads, "Know the truth and the truth shall set you free".'

But Christian had regained his good humor. 'I didn't write it,' he said. 'And I doubt it.'

Dr Annaccone had also recovered. He had started analyzing. Why the furious response to his jocular question? Did the Attorney General, the highest law official in the land, really have something to hide? He'd dearly love to have the man on the scan's test table.

Francis Kennedy had been watching this byplay with a gravely amused eye. Now he said gently, 'Zed, when you have the brain lie detector test perfected, so it can be done without side effects, we may have to bury it. There's not a politician in this country who could live with that.'

Dr Annaccone interrupted. 'All these questions are irrelevant. The process had been discovered. Science has begun its exploration of the human brain. You can never halt that process, Luddites proved that when they tried to halt the Industrial Revolution. You couldn't outlaw the use of gunpowder as the Japanese learned when they banned firearms for hundreds of years and were overwhelmed by the Western world. Once the atom was discovered you could no longer stop the bomb. The brain lie detector test is here to stay, I assure you all.'

Christian Klee said, 'It violates the Constitution.'

President Kennedy said briskly, 'We may have to change the Constitution.'

Matthew Gladyce said, with a look of horror on his face,

'If the news media heard this conversation they could run us right out of town.'

President Kennedy said, 'It's your job to tell the public what we've said in the proper language, and at the proper time. Remember this. The people of America will decide. Under the Constitution. Now I think the answer to all our problems is to mount a counter attack. Christian, press the prosecution of Bert Audick under the RICO laws. His company will be charged as a criminal conspiracy with the country of Sherhaben to defraud the American public by illegally creating oil shortages to raise prices. That's number one.'

He turned to Oddblood Gray. 'Rub the Congressional nose in the news that the new Federal Communications Commissions will deny the licenses of the major network TV stations when they come up for renewal. And the new laws will control those stacked deck deals on Wall Street and by the big banks. We'll give them something to worry about, Otto.'

Helen DuPray knew that she had every right to disagree in the private meetings even though as the Vice President it was mandatory to agree with the President publicly. Yet she hesitated before she said cautiously, 'Don't you think we're making too many enemies at one time? Wouldn't it even be better to wait until we've been elected for a second term? If we do indeed get a Congress more sympathetic to our policies, why fight the present Congress? Why unnecessarily set all the business interests against us when we are not in a position of prime strength?'

'We can't wait,' Kennedy said. 'They are going to attack us no matter what we do. They are going to continue to prevent my re-election, and my Congress, no matter how conciliatory we are. By attacking them we make them reconsider. We can't let them go ahead as if they didn't have a worry in the world.'

They were all silent and then Kennedy rose and said to his

369

staff. 'You can work out the details and draw up the necessary memos.'

It was then that Matthew Gladyce spoke about the Congress-inspired media campaign to attack President Kennedy by highlighting how many men and how much money was spent to guard the President.

Gladyce said, 'The whole thrust of their campaign is to paint you as some kind of Caesar and your Secret Service as some sort of Imperial Palace guard. To the public, ten thousand men and one hundred million dollars to guard just one man, even the President of the United States, seems excessive. It makes a lousy public relations image.'

They were all silent. The memory of Francis Kennedy's two uncles' assassinations made this a particularly touchy issue. Also all of them being so close to Kennedy were aware that the President went in some sort of physical fear. So they were surprised when Francis Kennedy turned to the Attorney General and said, 'In this case I think our critics are right. Christian, I know I gave you the veto on any change in protection but how about if we make an announcement that we will cut the Secret Service White House Division in half. And the budget in half also. Christian, I'd like you not to use your veto on this.'

Christian smiled and said, 'Maybe I went a little over board, Mr President. I won't use my veto that you could always veto.' Everyone laughed. But Matthew Gladyce was a little worried by this seemingly easy victory.

'Mr Attorney General, you can't just say you'll do it and not do it. The Congress will be all over our budget and appropriations figures,' Gladyce said.

'OK,' Christian said. 'But when you give out the press release, make sure you emphasize it is over my strong objections and make it seem like the President is bowing to the pressure of the Congress.'

Kennedy said, 'I thank you all. Dr Annaccone, give me thirty minutes in the Yellow Room, just you and I. Dazzy, the Secret Service will not be in that room, neither will you or anyone else.'

It was almost two hours later that Kennedy buzzed his Chief of Staff and said, 'Dazzy, please escort Dr Annaccone out of the White House.'

Dazzy did so. He noticed that Dr Annaccone, for the first time, seemed frightened. The President must have really socked it to him.

The Director of the White House Military Office, Colonel Henry Canoo (Retired), was the most cheerful and unflappable man in the Administration. He was cheerful because he had what he thought was the best job in the country. He was responsible to no one but the President of the United States and he controlled Presidential secret funds credited to the Pentagon that were not subject to audit except by himself and the President. Also he was strictly an administrator, he decided no questions of policy, did not even have to offer advice. He was the one who arranged for all the airplanes and helicopters and the limos for the President and his staff. He was the one who disbursed funds for the building and maintenance of buildings used by the White House that were classified secret. He ran the administration of the 'Football', the warrant officer and his briefcase that held atom bomb codes for the President. Whenever the President wanted to do something that cost money that he didn't want Congress or the news media to know about, Henry Canoo disbursed money from the Secret Fund, and stamped the fiscal sheets with the highest security classification.

So in the late May afternoon when the Attorney General Christian Klee came into his office, Henry Canoo greeted him warmly. They had done business together before, and early on in his administration the President had given Canoo instructions that the Attorney General could have anything he wanted from the Secret Fund. The first few times Canoo had checked it out with the President but not any longer.

'Christian,' he said jovially, 'are you looking for information or cash?'

'Both,' Christian said. 'First the money. We are going to promise publicly to cut down on the Secret Service Division fifty per cent and to cut the Security budget. I have to go through the motions. It will be a paper transfer, nothing will change. But I don't want Congress to sniff out a financial trail. So your Office of the Military Advisor will tap the Pentagon Budget for the money. Then stamp it with your top security classification.'

'Jesus,' Henry Canoo said. 'That's a lot of money. I can do it, but not for too long.'

'Just until the election in November,' Christian said. 'Then we'll either be out on our ass or in too strong for Congress to make any difference. But right now we have to look good.'

'OK,' Canoo said.

'Now the information,' Christian said. 'Have any of the Congress committees been sniffing around lately?'

'Oh, sure,' Canoo said. 'More than usual. They keep trying to find out how many helicopters the President has, how many limos, how many big aircraft, shit like that. They try to find out what the executive branch is doing. If they knew how many we really have, they'd shit.'

'What Congressman in particular?' Christian asked.

'Jintz,' Canoo said. 'He has that admin assistant, Patsy Troyca, a clever little bastard. He says he just wants to know how many copters we have and I tell him three. He says I hear you have fifteen and I say what the hell would the White House do with fifteen? But he was pretty close, we have sixteen.'

Christian Klee was surprised. 'What the hell do we do with sixteen?'

'Copters always break down,' Canoo said. 'If the President asks for a chopper, am I going to tell him no because they're in the shop? And besides somebody on the staff is always

372

asking for a chopper. You're not so bad, Christian, but Tappey at CIA and Wix sure put in a lot of chopper time. And Dazzy too, for what reason I don't know.'

'And you don't want to know,' Christian said. 'I want reports from you on any Congress snooper who tries to find out what the logistics are in supporting the Presidential mission. It has a bearing on security. Reports to me and top classifications.'

'OK,' Henry Canoo said cheerfully. 'And any time you need some work done on your personal residence we can tap the fund for that too.'

'Thanks,' Christian said, 'I have my own money.'

In the late evening of that day, President Francis Xavier Kennedy sat in the Oval Office and smoked his thin Havana cigar. He reviewed the events of the day. Everything had gone exactly as he had planned. He had showed his hand just enough to win the support of his staff.

Klee had reacted in character, as if he read his President's mind. Canoo had checked with him. Annaccone was more difficult but would come around. Helen DuPray might be a problem if he wasn't careful, but he needed her intelligence and her political base of the women's organizations.

Francis Kennedy was surprised at how well he felt. There was no longer any depression and his energy level was higher than it had ever been since his wife had died. Was it because he had finally found a woman who interested him or was it because he had at last gained control of the huge and complex political machinery of America?

19

In May Francis Kennedy, to his astonishment and even dismay, had fallen in love. This was not the time, and the woman not appropriate. She was on the legal staff of the Vice President.

Kennedy loved her charm, which was natural, her guileless smile, her brown eyes so lively and sparkling with wit. She was cuttingly sharp in argument, sometimes too much the lawyer. She had physical beauty, a lovely voice, and the body of a pocket Venus; long legs to a tiny waist and full bust, though she was not a tall woman. She could be dazzling in full regalia, but dressed so casually that most men were not aware that she was a legitimate beauty.

Lanetta Carr had that kind of naiveté and frankness that bordered sometimes on vulgarity. She had the romantic air of a Southern belle underneath a sharp intelligence that had led her to the study of law. It was as a lawyer that she had come to Washington and finally, after being on the staff of government agencies devoted to application of social programs and woman's rights, she had become a very junior member of the staff of the Vice President.

It was a courtesy extended to all the Vice Presidential staff that they were invited to at least one large Presidential reception in the White House during a four-year term. Lanetta Carr had been one of the four hundred guests to receive an invitation to a reception late in July.

Lanetta Carr was thrilled that she would be able to see Francis Kennedy in the flesh. Now, far down on the receiving line in the White House she saw President Francis Kennedy greeting his guests. To her he was the most beautiful man she had ever seen. The planes of his face had that lovely symmetry that only the Irish seem to breed. He was tall and very thin and had to stoop a little to say a few words to each of the guests. She noticed that he treated everyone with an exquisite courtesy. And then as she waited, he turned his head toward her, not yet seeing her, seemingly caught in some inward movement of isolation, and she saw the look of sadness in those cerulean eyes, his face frozen in some sort of grief. And then in an instant, he was the politician greeting her.

Vice President Helen DuPray was at Kennedy's side and she murmured that Lanetta Carr was one of her assistants. Kennedy instantly became warmer, more friendly, she was one of his more immediate official family. His two hands pressed hers and she felt so drawn to him that she said impulsively, though she had been briefed that it was a subject never to be discussed, 'Mr President, I'm so sorry about your daughter.'

She could see the slight look of disapproval on the face of Helen DuPray. But Kennedy said quietly, 'Thank you.' He released her hand and she moved on. Lanetta joined other Vice Presidential staff at the party. She had just finished drinking a glass of white wine when she was surprised to see the President and Vice President making their way slowly through the crowd, chatting briefly with the people in their way, but obviously making a path to her group.

Her companions immediately fell silent. Vice President Helen DuPray introduced the five members of the staff to the President with intimate friendly comments on the value she attached to their work. For the first time, Lanetta noticed how attractive the Vice President was as a woman, how feminine she could be. How instinctively she was sensitive to all the psychological needs of her staff and their need to be singled out to the President of the United States. How she gave off a sexual aura that had never been visible before. Lanetta divined instantly that this was stimulated not by Kennedy as a male, but as a male who had supreme power. Still she felt a strange twinge of jealousy.

The rest of the group fell into an awed silence showing only grateful smiles at the words of praise. Kennedy made a few polite comments but he was looking at Lanetta directly. So she said the first thing that occurred to her. 'Mr President, in all my years in Washington I've never been in the White House. Could I ask one of your aides to show me through? Just the public rooms of course.'

She did not really know the pretty picture she made, great eyes in a very young face for her years, an extraordinary complexion, the skin a mixture of creamy white and an exquisite pink on her cheeks and ears. President Kennedy smiled, a genuine smile not a political smile. He was delighted with just the sight of her. And her voice beguiled him. It was very soft with just a trace of Southern accent. Suddenly he realized that he had, in the last few years, missed that kind of voice. So he took her by the hand and said, 'I'll show you myself.'

He took her on the ground floor, they went through the Green Room with the white-mantled fireplace and white-bottomed chairs and settees, then the Blue Room with its wall with the blue and gold silk, through the Red Room hung in cerise silk, red and beige carpet on the floor, and then the Yellow Oval Room which he told her was his favorite, the yellow walls, the similarly colored rugs and couches seemed to relax him, he said. And all the time he was asking her questions about herself and observing her.

He noticed that she was more interested in conversation than by the awe-inspiring beauty of the rooms. That she asked intelligent questions about the historic paintings and the various antiques. She did not seem overly impressed by her awesome surroundings. Finally, he showed her the famous Oval Office of the President. 'I hate this room,'

Kennedy said. And she seemed to understand him. The Oval Office was always used for public photographs that were published in all the newspapers. The chats with visiting foreign dignitaries, the signing of important bills and treaties. It gave off an aura of insincerity.

Lanetta, though she did not show it, was thrilled by the tour and by the company of the President. She was aware that this treatment was more than an ordinary courtesy.

On the way back to the huge reception room, he asked her if she would like to come to a small dinner at the White House the following week. She said she would.

In the days that followed before the night of the dinner, Lanetta expected Vice President Helen DuPray to call her in for a chat on how to behave, to inquire about how she had gotten the President to invite her, but the Vice President never did so. In fact, she seemed not even to know about it, though this could not be true.

Lanetta Carr knew, as what woman would not, that Francis Kennedy had an interest in her that was sexual. He sure as hell wasn't thinking of her for Secretary of State.

The small informal dinner in the White House was not a success. No woman could have faulted Francis Kennedy's behavior toward her. He was unfailing in his courteous friendliness, he prompted her into conversation and kept the discussions going, nearly always taking her side when she disagreed with the members of his staff. She was not awed that these men were the most powerful in the country. Eugene Dazzy she liked despite the scandal that had appeared in the media. She wondered how his wife could bear to be with him in public afterwards, but none of the others seemed to be embarrassed. Arthur Wix was reserved but they quarreled in a civilized way when Lanetta said she thought the Defense budget should be cut in half. She found Otto Gray charming. Their wives were subdued.

Christian Klee she disliked. She could not say why.

Perhaps it was the sinister reputation he now had in Washington. But she told herself that she of all people with her training in the law should not hold such prejudice. Charges are not proof, accusations are mere hearsay without the backing of evidence, he was still innocent. What repelled her was his complete absence of interest or response to her as a woman. He seemed constantly vigilant. One of the stewards serving dinner had hovered behind Klee for a moment longer than was necessary and Klee had immediately turned his head, his body beginning to move out of his chair, the ball of his right foot sliding forward. The steward, who had merely paused to unfold a napkin, was obviously startled by Klee's look.

But what made the dinner unpleasant for Lanetta was the constant show of power. There were Secret Service men in every doorway, even in the dining room, posted at the door.

She had been brought up in the South but by no means the redneck South. She had been brought up in a cultured civilized progressive little city which prided itself on its relationship with black people. But even as a little girl she had caught the nuances of a society which believed that the two races should be separated. She had caught that tiny trace of meanness, with which even the most civilized of the privileged proclaimed their superiority to fellow men less well equipped in the human struggle for survival. And she had hated it.

She could not detect the meanness here, but she felt that it must exist when one man had so much more power than any of the others present and she was determined not to succumb to that kind of power. And so she automatically resisted Kennedy's charm without being anything less than bright and friendly.

But Kennedy had caught it. And she was astonished when he said, 'You didn't have a good time, I'm sorry.'

'Oh, I did,' she said. And then in her best and slyest

378

Southern Belle manner gave him his dismissal. 'I'll be bragging about this night to my kids when I'm old and gray.'

The others invited to the dinner party had already taken their leave and two aides were waiting to escort Lanetta to her car. Almost humbly Kennedy said, 'I know all this is awfully offputting. But let's give it one more chance. Why don't I cook dinner for you at your place?'

At first she really didn't get it. That the President of the United States was asking for a date. That he would come to her apartment like any other boyfriend and cook in her kitchen. The image so delighted her that she burst out laughing and Francis Kennedy was laughing too.

'OK,' she said. 'There goes the neighborhood.'

Francis Kennedy smiled gravely. 'Yes,' he said. 'Thank you. I'll call you when I'm sure I have a night free.'

From that night on, Secret Service men blanketed the area of her apartment. Two apartments were rented on her floor and in a building across the street. Christian Klee had her phone bugged. Her history was explored through documents and personal interviews with anyone she had ever worked with and with people in her home town.

Christian Klee personally supervised this exercise, deliberately not planting a bug that would record any sound in Lanetta's apartment. He didn't want his Secret Service agents listening when the President of the United States dropped his trousers.

What he found completely reassured him. Lanetta Carr had been a model of bourgeois behavior until she went to college. In college she had for some reason pursued the study of the law and on passing the bar had taken a position as a public defender in the City of New Orleans. She had defended women, mostly. She had become involved with the feminist movement but he noted with satisfaction that she had had three serious love affairs. The lovers were interviewed and the one thing they said about Lanetta Carr was that she was a stable, serious woman.

At the White House dinner, she had said, with anger and contempt, 'Do you know that under our system the breaching of a contract is not against the law?' Not realizing she was saying this at a table where two men, Kennedy and Klee, were considered amongst the foremost legal minds in the country.

For one moment Klee had been irritated and had said, 'So what.'

Lanetta had turned on him and said, 'The person who suffers under a breach of contract then has to go to law. It costs him a lot of money and then he usually has to settle for less than he is entitled to under his original contract. And if the plaintiff is less powerful and has less money, if he's up against a big corporation who can string the case out for years, then he has to lose something. It's gangsterism pure and simple.' She paused for a moment and then said, 'The very concept is immoral.'

Christian Klee had said, 'Law is not a moral discipline. It's a machinery that makes a society work.'

He remembered that she had turned away from him with a gesture that dismissed his explanation.

Christian Klee believed in overkill when providing security for his President. On the night of Francis Kennedy's date with Lanetta Carr, he already had his men in two apartments and he had a hundred men covering the streets, the roofs of buildings, the hallways of the apartment building itself. But he knew that the procedure had to change, that these 'dates' could not continue. That if the affair lasted, it would have to be conducted in the safety of the White House. But he was glad Francis had finally found some hint of personal happiness. He hoped everything would turn out all right. He didn't worry about how the affair would affect the election results. All the world loved a lover, especially one so handsome and doomstruck as Francis Kennedy.

On the night that the President of the United States was going to cook her dinner, Lanetta dressed with just a little

380

extra care. She wore a floppy sweater, loose slacks, and flat-heeled shoes. Of course she tried to look pretty, the sweater was from Italy, the slacks bought in New York's Bloomingdale's. She made up her eyes very carefully and she wore a favorite bracelet. And she cleaned up her apartment.

Francis Kennedy arrived wearing a sports jacket over a loose white shirt. He wore slacks and shoes she had never seen before, dress shoes with rubber soles and heels, the tops a beautifully soft leather almost blue.

After they chatted for a few minutes Francis Kennedy began to prepare a very simple meal, roasted chicken with oven fried potatoes, and a string bean and tomato salad with raspberry vinaigrette dressing. He laughed when Lanetta offered him an apron, but stood still as a small boy when she placed it over his head and then turned him around so she could tie it around his waist.

Lanetta watched silently as he did everything with complete concentration and she smiled to herself when she realized that he actually cared about how the dinner turned out. As the soft classical music of the Pachelbel Kanon played in the background, Lanetta couldn't help but think about how unlike the other men she had gone out with this man was. Certainly, he had more power than they, but what she responded to more was some deep vulnerability that she perceived in his eyes when he wasn't paying attention.

Lanetta had observed that Francis Kennedy was not really a man to whom food was interesting. She had bought a bottle of decent wine. She was excited, as what woman would not be, but was also a little terrified. She knew he expected something from her, and she was sure she would not be able to respond. And yet how do you refuse a President? She resented the feeling of awe inside her, and feared she would accede to him because of that awe. But she was curious and excited as to what would happen and had enough self-confidence to believe it would all end happily.

It proved to be an amazingly simple evening. He helped

her clear the table in the kitchen of her apartment and then they had coffee in her living room.

Lanetta was proud of her apartment. She had furnished it slowly, with good taste. There were reproductions of famous paintings on the walls and bookcases had been fitted in all around the living room.

All through the evening Francis Kennedy did not make any of the moves of a courting male and Lanetta was not seductive. Kennedy had caught all of her signals in dress and bearing.

But as the evening wore on, they became more and more friendly to each other. He was very skillful in making her talk about herself, her family life in the South, her experiences in Washington. About her work as one of the legal advisors to the Vice President. And what she was impressed by, even more than by his unique good looks, was that he was always in good taste, that his questions were not prying questions, merely leads to let her tell what she wanted to tell him.

There is nothing more enjoyable than having dinner with someone who is eager to listen to the story of your life, your true beliefs, your hopes and your sorrows. So Lanetta had a good time and then suddenly realized that Kennedy had never said anything about himself. She had forgotten her manners.

'I've been going on about myself,' she said, 'when I have an opportunity very few people get. How is it being President of the United States? I'll bet it's awful.' She said the last with such sincerity that Kennedy laughed.

'It was terrible,' Kennedy said, 'but it's getting better.'

'You've had such bad luck,' Lanetta said.

'But my luck is changing,' Kennedy said. 'Politically and personally.' They were both embarrassed by this, by the callowness of the avowal. Kennedy went on to repair the damage. He did so in perhaps the worst possible way.

'I miss my wife, I miss my daughter, maybe you remind me of my daughter. I don't know.'

When they said good night, he leaned over, not able to resist and brushed her lips with his. She did not respond so he said, 'Can we have dinner again?' And she, liking him but not sure, just nodded her head.

She watched from the window and was surprised that her normally quiet street was so busy. When Kennedy left the building he was preceded by two men, another four men came behind him. There were two cars waiting for him, each car surrounded by four men. Kennedy got into one of the cars and it zoomed away. Far down the street a parked car pulled out and preceded Kennedy's. Then other cars in the street started up, followed, and then men who had been on foot turned corners and disappeared. To Lanetta it was an offensive display of power that one human being should be guarded so jealously. She stood at the window struggling with this feeling and then remembered how kind and caring he had been in this evening alone with her.

20

In Washington, Christian Klee turned on his computer. First he called up the file on David Jatney. Nothing happening there. Then he called up the files on the Socrates Club. He had all of them under computer surveillance. There was only one item of real interest – Bert Audick had flown to Sherhaben ostensibly to plan the rebuilding of the city of Dak. Klee was interrupted by a call from Eugene Dazzy.

President Kennedy wanted Christian Klee to come to breakfast in the White House bedroom suite. It was rare that meetings were held in Kennedy's private living quarters.

Jefferson, the President's private butler and Secret Service guard, served the large breakfast and then discreetly withdrew to the pantry room, to appear only when summoned by the buzzer.

Kennedy said casually, 'Did you know Jefferson was a great student, a great athlete? Jefferson never took shit from anybody.' Kennedy paused and said, 'How did he become a butler, Christian?'

Christian knew he had to tell the truth. 'He is also the best agent in the Secret Service. I recruited him myself and especially for this job.'

Kennedy said. 'The same question applies, why the hell would he take a Secret Service job? And as a butler?'

Christian said, 'He has a very high rank in the Secret Service.'

Kennedy said, 'Yeah, but still.'

'I organized a very elaborate screening procedure for these jobs. Jefferson was the best man and in fact he is the White House team leader.'

'Still,' Kennedy said.

'I promised him that before you left the White House I would get him an appointment in Health, Education and Welfare, a job with clout.'

'Ah, that's clever,' Kennedy said, 'but how does his resumé look from butler to clout? How the hell can we do that?'

'His resumé will read executive assistant to me,' Christian said.

Kennedy lifted the coffee mug, its white glaze adorned with stenciled eagles. 'Now don't take this wrong but I've noticed that all my immediate servants in the White House are very good at their jobs. Are they all in the Secret Service? That would be incredible.'

'A special school and a special indoctrination appealing to their professinal pride,' Christian said. 'Not all.'

Kennedy laughed out loud and said, 'Even the chefs?'

'Especially the chefs,' Christian said smiling. 'All chefs are crazy.' Like many men, Christian always used a gag line to give himself time to think. He knew Kennedy's method for preparing to go on dangerous ground, showing good humor plus a piece of knowledge he wasn't supposed to have.

They ate their breakfast, Kennedy playing what he called 'mother', passing plates and pouring. The china, except for Kennedy's special coffee mug, was beautiful, with blue Presidential seals and as fragile as an eggshell. Kennedy finally said almost casually, 'I'd like to spend an hour with Yabril. I expect you to handle it personally.' He saw the anxious look on Christian's face. 'Only for an hour and only for this one time.'

Christian said, 'What's to be gained, Francis? It could be too painful for you to bear. I worry about your health.' And indeed Francis Kennedy did not look well. He was very pale

385

these days and seemed to have lost weight. And there were lines in his face that Christian had never noticed before.

'Oh, I can bear it,' Kennedy said.

'If the meeting leaks there will be a lot of questions,' Christian said.

'Then make sure it doesn't leak,' Kennedy said. 'There will be no written record of the meeting and the White House log won't be entered. Now when?'

'It will take a few days to make the necessary arrangements,' Christian said. 'And Jefferson has to know.'

'Anybody else?' Kennedy asked.

'Maybe six other men from my Special Division,' Christian said. 'They will have to know Yabril is in the White House but not necessarily that you're seeing him. They'll guess but they won't know.'

Kennedy said, 'If it's necessary I can go to where you're holding him.'

'Absolutely not,' Christian said. 'The White House is the best place. It should be in the early hours after midnight. I suggeest one a.m.'

Kennedy said, 'The night after tomorrow, OK.'

'Yes,' Christian said. 'You'll have to sign some papers, which will be vague, but will cover me if something goes haywire.'

Kennedy sighed as if in relief then said briskly, 'He's not a superman. Don't worry. I want to be able to talk to him freely and for him to answer lucidly and of his own free will. I don't want him drugged or coerced in any way. I want to understand how his mind works and maybe I won't hate him so much. I want to find out how people like him truly feel.'

'I must be physically present at this meeting,' Christian said awkwardly. 'I'm responsible.'

'How about you waiting outside the door with Jefferson?' Kennedy asked.

Christian, panicked by the implication of this request,

slammed the fragile blue line coffee cup and said earnestly, 'Please, Francis, I can't do that. Naturally he'll be secured, he will be physically helpless, but I still have to be between the two of you. This is one time I have to use the veto you gave me.' He tried to hide his fear of what Francis might do.

They both smiled. It had been part of their deal when Christian had guaranteed the safety of the President. That Christian as head of the Secret Service could veto any Presidential exposure to the public. 'I've never abused that power,' Christian said.

Kennedy made a grimace. 'But you've exercised it vigorously. OK, you can stay in the room but try to fade into the Colonial woodwork. And Jefferson stays outside the door.'

'I'll set everything up,' Christian said. 'But, Francis, this can't help you.'

Christian Klee prepared Yabril for the meeting with President Kennedy. There had of course been many interrogations but Yabril had smilingly refused to answer any questions. He had been very cool, very confident and was willing to make conversation in a general way; discuss politics, Marxist theory, the Palestinian problem which he called the Israeli problem; but he refused to talk about his background or his terrorist operations. Refused to talk about Romeo, his partner, or about Theresa Kennedy and her murder and his relationship with the Sultan of Sherhaben.

Yabril's prison was a small ten-bed hospital built by the FBI for the holding of dangerous prisoners and valuable informers. This hospital was staffed by Secret Service medical personnel and guarded by Christian's Secret Service Special Division agents. There were five of these detention hospitals in the United States; one in Washington DC area, another in Chicago, one in Los Angeles, one in Nevada and another on Long Island.

These hospitals were sometimes used for secret medical experiments on volunteer prison inmates. But Christian Klee had cleared out the hospital in Washington DC to hold Yabril in isolation. He had also cleared out the hospital in Long Island to hold the two young scientists who had planted the atom bomb.

In the Washington hospital, Yabril had a medical suite fully equipped to abort any suicide attempt by violence or fasting. There were physical restraints and equipment for intravenous feeding.

Every inch of Yabril's body had been X-rayed, including his teeth and he was always restrained by a loose specially made jacket that only permitted him partial use of his arms and legs. He could read and write and walk with little steps, but could not make violent movements. He was also under twenty-four-hour surveillance through a two-way mirror by teams of Secret Service agents from Klee's Special Division.

After Christian left President Kennedy he went to visit Yabril, knowing that he had a problem. With two of the Secret Service agents he entered Yabril's suite. He sat on one of the comfortable sofas and had Yabril brought in from the bedroom. He pushed Yabril gently into one of the armchairs and then had his agents check the restraints.

Yabril said contemptuously, 'You're a very careful man with all your power.'

'I believe in being careful,' Christian told him gravely. 'I'm like those engineers who built bridges and buildings to withstand a hundred times more stress than possible. That's how I run my job.'

'They are not the same thing,' Yabril said. 'You cannot foresee the stress of Fate.'

'I know,' Christian said. 'But it relieves my anxieties and it serves well enough. Now the reason for my visit; I've come to ask you a favor.' At this Yabril laughed, a fine derisive laugh, a genuine mirth.

Christian stared at him and smiled. 'No, seriously, this is a favor it is in your power to grant or refuse. Now listen carefully. You've been treated well, that is my doing and

388

also the laws of this country. I know it's useless to threaten. I know you have your pride but it is a small thing I ask, one that will not compromise you in any way. And in return I promise to do everything I can so that nothing unlucky should happen. I know that you still have hope. You think your comrades of the famous First Hundred will come up with something clever so that we must set you free.'

Yabril's thin dark face lost its saturnine mirthfulness. He said, 'We tried several times to mount an action against your President Kennedy, very complicated and clever operations. They were all suddenly and mysteriously wiped out before we could even get into this country. I personally conducted an investigation into these failures and the destruction of our personnel. And the trail always led to you. And so I know we're in the same line of work. I know that you're not one of those cautious politicians. So just tell me the courtesy you want. Assume I'm intelligent enough to consider it very carefully.'

Christian leaned back on the sofa. Part of his brain noted that since Yabril had found his trail he was far too dangerous ever to be let free under any circumstances. Yabril had been foolish to let out that information. Then Christian concentrated on the business at hand. He said, 'President Kennedy is a very complicated man, he tries to understand events and people. And so he wanted to meet you face to face and ask you questions, engage in a dialogue. As one human being to another. He wants to understand what made you kill his daughter; he wants, perhaps, to absolve himself of his own feelings of guilt. Now all I ask is that you do talk to him, answer his questions. I ask you not to reject him totally. Will you do that?'

Yabril loosely locked in his steel fabric tried to raise his arms in a gesture of rejection. He totally lacked physical fear and yet the idea of meeting the father of the girl he had murdered aroused an agitation that surprised him. After all it had been a political act and a President of the United

389

States should understand that better than anyone. Still, it would be interesting to look into the eyes of the most powerful man in the world and say, 'I killed your daughter. I injured you more grievously than you can ever injure me, you with your thousand ships of war, your tens of thousands of thunderbolt aircraft.'

Yabril said, 'Yes, I will do you this little favor. But you may not thank me in the end.'

Christian Klee got up from the sofa and caressed Yabril's shoulder as Yabril shrugged him away with contempt. 'It doesn't matter,' Christian said. 'And I will be grateful.'

Two days later, an hour after midnight, President Francis Kennedy entered the Yellow Oval Room of the White House to find Yabril already seated in a chair by the fireplace. Christian was standing behind him.

On a small oval table inlaid with a shield of the Stars and Stripes was a silver platter of tiny sandwiches, a silver coffee pot and cups and saucers rimmed with gold. Jefferson poured the coffee into the three cups and then retreated to the door of the room and put his wide shoulders back against it. Kennedy could see that Yabril, who bowed his head to him, was immobilized in the chair. 'You haven't sedated him?' Kennedy said sharply.

'No, Mr President,' Christian said. 'Those are jacket and legging restraints.'

'Can't you make him more comfortable?' Kennedy said.

'No, sir,' Christian said.

Kennedy spoke directly to Yabril. 'I'm sorry but I don't have the last word in these matters. I won't keep you too long. I would just like to ask you a few questions.'

Yabril nodded. The restraints making his arm move in slow motion, he helped himself to one of the sandwiches. They were delicious. And it helped his pride in some way that his enemy could see that he was not completely helpless. Also with these motions he could study Kennedy's face. And

390

he was struck by the fact that this was a man who in other circumstances he would have instinctively respected and trusted to some degree. The face showing suffering but a powerful restraint of that suffering. It also showed a genuine interest in his discomfort, there was no condescension or false compassion, but the interest of one human being to another. And yet with all this there was a grave strength.

Yabril said softly and more politely and perhaps more humbly than he intended, 'Mr Kennedy, before we begin you must first answer me one question. Do you really believe that I am responsible for the atom bomb explosion in your country?'

'No,' Kennedy said. And Christian was relieved that he did not give any further information.

'Thank you,' Yabril said. 'How could anyone think me so stupid? And I would resent it if you tried to use that accusation as a weapon. You may ask me anything you like.'

Kennedy motioned to Jefferson to leave the room and watched him do so. Then he spoke softly to Yabril. Christian lowered his head as if not to hear. He really did not want to hear.

Kennedy said, 'We know you orchestrated the whole series of events. The murder of the Pope, the hoax of letting your accomplice be captured so that you could demand his ransom. The hijacking of the plane. And the killing of my daughter, which was planned from the very beginning. Now we know this for certain but I would like you to tell me if this is true. By the way, I can see the logic of it.'

Yabril looked at Kennedy directly. 'Yes, that is all true. But I'm amazed that you put it all together so quickly. I thought it clever.'

Kennedy said, 'I'm afraid it's nothing to be proud of. It means that basically I have the same kind of mind that you do. Or that there is not much difference in the human mind when it comes to deviousness.'

'Still it was maybe too clever,' Yabril said. 'You broke the

391

rules of the game. But of course it was not chess, the rules were not so strict. You were supposed to be a pawn with only a pawn's moves.'

Kennedy sat down and drank a bit of his coffee, a polite social gesture. Christian could see he was very tense and of course to Yabril the casualness of the President was transparent. Yabril wondered what the man's real intentions were. It was obvious that they were not malicious, there was no intent to use power to frighten or harm.

'I knew from the very beginning,' Kennedy said. 'With the hijacking of the plane, I knew you would kill my daughter. When your accomplice was captured I knew it was part of your plan. I was surprised by nothing. My advisors did not agree until later in your scenario. So what concerns me is that my mind must be something like yours. And yet it comes to this. I can't imagine myself doing such an operation. I want to avoid taking that next step and that is why I wanted to talk to you. To learn and foresee, to guard myself against myself.'

Yabril was impressed by Kennedy's courteous manner, the evenness of his speech, his seeming desire for some kind of truth.

Kennedy went on. 'What was your gain in all this? The Pope will be replaced, my daughter's death will not alter the international power structure. Where was your profit?'

Yabril thought, the old question of capitalism, it comes down to that. Yabril felt Christian's hands rest lightly on his shoulders for a moment. Then he hesitated before he said, 'America is the colossus to which the Israeli state owes its existence. This by definition oppresses my countrymen. And your capitalistic system oppresses the poor people of the world and even your own country. It is necessary to break down the fear of your strength. The Pope is part of that authority, the Catholic Church has terrorized the poor of the world for countless centuries, with hell and even heaven; how disgraceful. And it went on for two thousand years. To

392

bring about the Pope's death was more than a political satisfaction.'

Christian had wandered away from Yabril's chair but was still alert, ready to interpose himself. He opened the door to the Yellow Oval Room to whisper to Jefferson for a moment. Yabril noted all this in silence then went on.

'But all my actions against you failed. I mounted two very elaborate operations to assassinate you and they failed. You may one day ask your Mr Klee the details, they may astonish you. The Attorney General, what a benign title, I must confess it misled me at the beginning. He destroyed my operations with a ruthlessness that compelled my admiration. But then, he had so many men, so much technology. I was helpless. But your own invulnerability ensured your daughter's death, and I know how that must trouble you. I speak frankly since that is your wish.'

Christian came back to stand behind the chair and tried to avoid Kennedy's look. Yabril felt a strange tinge of fear but he went on. 'Consider,' Yabril said and tried to raise his arms to make an emphatic gesture, 'if I hijack a plane, I am a monster. If the Israelis bomb a helpless Arab town and kill hundreds they are striking a blow for freedom; more they are avenging the famous holocaust with which Arabs had nothing to do. But what are our options? We do not have the military power, we do not have the technology. Who is the more heroic? Well in both cases the innocent die. And what about justice? Israel was put in place by foreign powers, my people were thrown out into the desert. We are the new homeless, the new Jews, what an irony. Does the world expect us not to fight? What can we use except terror? What did the Jews use when they fought for the establishment of their state against the British? We learned everything about terror from the Jews of that time. And those terrorists are now heroes, those slaughterers of the innocent. One even became the Prime Minister of Israel and was accepted by the

393

heads of states as if they never smelled the blood on his hands. Am I more terrible?'

Yabril paused for a moment and tried to rise but Christian pushed him down back in his chair. Kennedy made a gesture for him to go on.

Yabril said, 'You ask what I accomplished. In one sense I failed and the proof is that I am here a prisoner. But what a blow I dealt to your authority figure in the world. America is not so great after all. It could have ended better for me, but it's still not a total loss. I exposed to the world how ruthless your supposedly humane democracy really is. You destroyed a great city, you mercilessly subdued a foreign nation to your will. I made you peel off your thunderbolts to frighten the whole world and you alienated part of the world. You are not so beloved, your America. And in your own country you have polarized your political factions. Your personal image has changed and you have become the terrible Mr Hyde to your saintly Dr Jekyll.'

Yabril paused for a moment to control the violent energy of the emotions that had passed over his face. He became more respectful, more grave.

'I come now to what you want to hear and what is painful for me to say. Your daughter's death was necessary. She was a symbol of America because she was the daughter of the most powerful man on earth. Do you know what that does to people who fear authority? It gives them hope, never mind that some may love you, that some may see you as benefactor or friend. People hate their benefactors in the long run. They see you are no more powerful than they are, they need not fear you. Of course it would have been more effective if I had gone free. How would that have been? The Pope dead, your daughter killed and then you are forced to set me free. How impotent you and America would have seemed before the world.'

Yabril leaned back in the chair to lessen the weight of restraint and smiled at Kennedy. 'I only made one mistake. I misjudged you completely. There was nothing in your history that could foretell your actions. You, the great liberal, the ethical modern man. I thought you would release my friend. I thought you would not be able to put the pieces together quickly enough and I never dreamed you would commit such a great crime.'

Kennedy said, 'There were very few casualties when the city of Dak was bombed, we dumped leaflets hours before.'

Yabril said, 'I understand that. It was a perfect terrorist response. I would have done the same myself. But I would never have done what you did to save yourself. Set off an atom bomb in one of your own cities.'

'You are mistaken,' Kennedy said. And Christian was relieved again that he did not offer more information. And he was also relieved to see that Kennedy did not take the accusation seriously. In fact Kennedy went on immediately to something else. He poured himself another cup of coffee and then said, 'Answer me this as honestly as you can. Did the fact that my name is Kennedy have any bearing on your plans?'

Both Christian and Yabril were astonished by this question. Christian for the first time stared Kennedy in the face. Kennedy seemed entirely calm. Yabril pondered this question as if he did not quite understand. Finally he answered.

'To be honest, I did think about that aspect, the martyrdom of your two uncles, the love that most of the world and your country in particular has for that tragic legend. It added to the force of the blow I intended. Yes, your name was a small part of the plan, I must confess.'

There was a long pause, Christian turned his head away and thought, I will never let this man live.

'Tell me,' Kennedy said, 'how can you justify in your own heart the things you have done, your betrayals of human trust? I've read your dossier. How can any human being say to himself, I will better the world by killing innocent men, women and children. I will raise humanity out of its despair

395

by betraying my best friend, all this without any authority given by God or your fellow beings. Compassion aside, how do you even dare to assume such power?'

Yabril waited courteously as if he expected another question. Then he said, 'The acts I committed are not so bizarre as the press and moralists claim. What about your bomber pilots who rain down destruction as if the people below them were mere ants? Those good-hearted boys with every manly virtue. But they were taught to do their duty. I think I am no different. Yet I do not have the resources to drop death from thousands of feet in the air. Or naval guns that obliterate from twenty miles away. I must dirty my hands with blood. I must have moral strength, the mental purity to shed blood directly for the cause I believe in. Well, that is all terribly obvious, an old argument and it seems cowardly to even make it. But you say how do I have courage to assume that authority without being approved by some source? That is more complicated. Let me believe that the suffering I have seen in my world has given me that authority. Let me say that the books I have read, the music I have heard, the example of far greater men than myself, have given me the strength to act on my own principles. It is more difficult for me than you who have the support of hundreds of millions and so commit your terror as a duty to them, as their instrument.'

Here Yabril paused to sip helplessly at his coffee cup. Then he went on with a calm dignity.

'I have devoted my life to revolution against the established order, the authority I despise. I will die believing what I have done is right. And as you know, there is no moral law that exists for ever.'

Finally Yabril was exhausted and leaned back in his chair, arms appearing broken from the restraints. Kennedy had listened without any sign of disapproval. He did not make any counter argument. There was a long silence and finally Kennedy said, 'I can't argue morals, basically I've done what

396

you have done. And as you say it is easier to do when one does not personally bloody one's hands. But again as you say I act from a core of social authority not of my own personal animosity.'

Yabril interrupted him. 'That is not correct. Congress did not approve your actions, neither did your Cabinet Officers. Essentially you acted as I did on your own personal authority. You are my fellow terrorist.'

Kennedy said, 'But the people of my country, the electorate, approve.'

'The mob,' Yabril said. 'They always approve. They refuse to foresee the dangers of such actions. What you did was wrong politically and morally. You acted on a desire for personal vengeance.' Yabril smiled. 'And I thought you would be above such an action. So much for morality.'

Kennedy was silent for a time as if giving careful consideration to his answer. Then he said, 'I hope you're wrong, time will tell. I want to thank you for speaking to me so frankly, especially since I understand you refused to co-operate in former interrogations. You know of course that the best law firm in the United States has been retained for you by the Sultan of Sherhaben and shortly they will be permitted to consult with you on your defense.'

Kennedy smiled and rose to leave the room. He was almost to the door when it swung open. Then as he walked through it he heard Yabril's voice. Yabril had struggled to his feet despite his restraints and fought to keep his balance. He was erect when he said, 'Mr President.'

Kennedy turned to face him.

Yabril lifted his arms slowly, ending them crookedly under the nylon and wire corset. 'Mr President,' he said again, 'you do not deceive me. I know I will never see or talk to my lawyers.'

Christian had interposed his body between the two men and Jefferson was by Kennedy's side.

Kennedy gave Yabril a cold smile. 'You have my personal

397

guarantee that you will see and talk to your lawyers,' he said. And walked out of the room.

At that moment Christian Klee felt an anguish close to nausea. He had always believed he knew Francis Kennedy but now he realized he did not. For in one clear moment he had seen a look of pure hatred on Kennedy's face that was alien to everything in his character.

BOOK V

21

Just before the Democratic Convention in August, the Socrates Club and Congress unleashed a full-scale attack against the Presidency.

The first shot was the exposure of Eugene Dazzy having an affair with a young dancer. The girl was persuaded to go public and give exclusive interviews to the more respected papers. Salentine tipped off a publisher of a literate semipornographic magazine who paid for exclusive rights and explicit photos which showed the opulent physical charms Eugene Dazzy had enjoyed. Enriched by the money and spurred by a newly inspired morality, the dancer made innumerable appearances on Salentine's TV network and on Cassandra Chutt's *Five Star Interview*, revealing how she had been seduced by an older, more powerful man. When Kennedy refused to fire Dazzy, Salentine was overjoyed.

Then Peter Cloot was subpoenaed by the Jintz and Lambertino committees and repeated the information he had given Patsy Troyca and Elizabeth Stone in their private discussion. The committees leaked this testimony to the media and it was spread over the newspapers and TV. Christian Klee issued a denial and again Kennedy supported his staff. Kennedy refused on the grounds of executive privilege to have Christian Klee testify before any Congressional Committee. Again the Socrates Club was delighted. Kennedy was digging his own grave.

Then the Congressional Committees managed to get information on Klee's deal with Canoo and the secret funds that were being used for thousands of Secret Service personnel to guard Kennedy. This was published as proof that the Kennedy administration had lied to the American Congress and the American people. Here Kennedy gave ground and personally ordered that the use of the Office of the Military Advisor funds be cut off and the Secret Service protection reduced. Canoo refused to answer any questions and hid himself behind the shield of the President. Again Kennedy refused to take action. He asserted that he would not give in to an obvious vendetta by the media and Congress. He said he might take action after the election if the facts warranted.

Then there was a big story that Kennedy would propose a Constitutional Convention and would ask that the limitation of the Presidency to only two terms be annulled. That his obvious plan was to be re-elected to a third and fourth and fifth term. This story, though unsubstantiated, was given a great deal of play by the media. Kennedy ignored it. When questioned, he said with a disarming smile, 'I'm worried about getting elected to my second term.'

But Lawrence Salentine was proudest of the special story that was run in the most widely read magazine in the country. This article was about the woman that was reputed to be Kennedy's mistress and the woman whom he expected to marry after the election. It was a completely laudatory article, she was a woman wise beyond her years, though rather young. She was witty. She was beautiful, she dressed elegantly while spending no more than the ordinary professional woman. She was modest, she was shy, yet a good conversationalist and had a knowledge of world affairs. She was well read and had a social conscience, she had no vices, she did not drink to excess, nor did she do drugs. Her sexual history was short, she was not promiscuous for a woman of twenty-eight, not married. And in a short paragraph dropped in the middle of the story was the information, given with the utmost casualness, that she was one-eighth 'Negro'.

Lawrence Salentine regarded that little paragraph as the

one drop of poison that would effectively erase a good fifteen per cent of Kennedy's popularity. This particular item was not true. It was simply one of those small-time rumors or gossip that abounded in small Southern towns. As Klee found when he sent a small army of investigators to her birthplace.

All this had its effect in the last poll before the Democratic Convention, Kennedy's strength dropped to only sixty of the electorate, a loss of twenty points.

The television talk show hostess, Cassandra Chutt, had Peter Cloot on her show, the highest-rated interview program on television. She asked him the ultimate question. 'Do you think that the Attorney General Christian Klee is responsible for the explosion of the atom bomb and the death and injury of over ten thousand people?'

And Peter Cloot answered, 'Yes.'

Then Chutt asked another question. 'Do you think that President Kennedy and Attorney General Klee are responsible to some degree for what is probably the greatest tragedy in American history?'

Here Peter Cloot was more careful. 'President Kennedy was mistaken out of some humanitarian impulse. I happen to be a strong believer in law enforcement. So I have my bias. But, yes, I think he was wrong. Strictly a matter of beliefs and judgment.'

Cassandra Chutt said, 'But you have no doubts about the Attorney General's guilt?'

Peter Cloot faced the camera squarely and sincerely. His voice was filled with anger, righteous pain. 'Attorney General Christian Klee was guilty of a criminal act. He deliberately delayed an important interrogation. I believe he is the man who made the phone call that tipped off the defendants. I believe that Christian Klee wanted that bomb to go off and so precipitated a crisis that would prevent President Kennedy from being impeached by Congress. I believe he committed the most terrible crime in American history, and I believe he should be brought to justice. President Kennedy, by protecting the Attorney General, is an accomplice.'

Then Cassandra Chutt addressed her TV audience of sixty million people and said simply, 'Our guest, Peter Cloot, was formerly Assistant and Executive Director of the FBI under Attorney General Christian Klee. He was forced to resign from that post after testifying to a Senate Committee on this matter he has discussed here with us tonight. The Kennedy administration denied all his charges and to this very day Christian Klee is still the Attorney General of the United States and the Director of the FBI.'

The program had an enormous impact and was picked up by every TV and cable company and quoted extensively in all the newspapers.

At the same time Whitney Cheever III had given a press conference on TV in which he stated that his clients, Gresse and Tibbot, were innocent, that they were the victims of a gigantic conspiracy by the government, that he would prove that a fascistic cabal had engineered the catastrophic crime to save the Presidency of Francis Kennedy.

Christian Klee was worried about many things. There were the charges by Tibbot's father that Klee had made the warning call. There was the Peter Cloot testimony. There was the leakage on the arrangement he had made with Canoo to divert funds to the Secret Service. There was the drop in Kennedy's popularity after these massive attacks. But most of all he was worried about Bert Audick's visit to the Sultan of Sherhaben. That Audick had gone to arrange the detail for the rebuilding of Dak was, to him, just a cover story.

Klee decided to take a vacation but to combine business with pleasure. He would go around the wide world. First to London, then to Rome to check on Romeo in prison and then on to Sherhaben to check on Bert Audick's visit there.

He pulled up the David Jatney file again on the computer screen and checked. Still nothing there.

In London, Christian Klee touched base with his opposite numbers in the English Security establishment. During dinner at the Ritz Hotel, they were exquisitely polite but he sensed a coldness. Cloot's charges had done their work and the English had never liked any of the Kennedys. In any case they had no information to give him.

Klee had a woman friend in England who lived in a small country house just outside of London. It was extremely rural, with roses climbing over everything and even some sheep in a nearby meadow. Christian Klee spent a long weekend there and relaxed.

The woman was the widow of a wealthy newspaper publisher and led a quiet life. She had two house servants but drove her own car. Klee loved the times he spent with her. There was nothing remotely exciting in her life. She read, she tended her garden, managed the estate and always seemed eager to receive him when he visited England. She never made any demands, never asked him questions about his work. She was a perfect hostess and she made love like a gentlewoman, as though it was a necessary courtesy.

He relaxed there for three days and then his idyll was interrupted by a special courier. A message that the terrorist named Romeo, who had been extradited to Italy, had just committed suicide in a Roman prison. Christian immediately called Franco Sebbediccio and caught the next flight for Rome. At the airport, he called his office in Washington and ordered a special suicide watch on Gresse and Tibbot. And on Yabril.

Franco Sebbediccio when a little boy in Sicily had chosen the side of law and order not only because it seemed the stronger side but because he loved the sweet consolation of living under strict rules of authority. The Mafia had been too impressionistic, the world of commerce too dicey and so he had become a policeman and thirty years later he was the head of the Italian Anti-Terrorist Division of all of Italy.

He had now had under his arrest the assassin of the Pope, a young Italian of good family named Armando Giangi, codenamed Romeo. This code name irritated Franco Sebbediccio enormously. Sebbediccio had incarcerated Romeo in the deepest cells of his Roman prison.

Under surveillance was Rita Fallicia whose code name was Annee. She had been easy to track down because she had been a troublemaker since her teens, a firebrand at the University, a pugnacious leader of demonstrations and linked in Security to the abduction of a leading banker of Milan.

The evidence had come flooding in. The 'safe houses' had been cleaned by the terrorist cadres but those poor bastards had no way of knowing the scientific resources of a national police organization. There was a towel with traces of semen that identified Romeo. One of the captured men had given evidence under severe interrogation. But Sebbediccio had not arrested Annee. She was to remain free.

Franco Sebbediccio worried that the trial of these guilty parties would glorify the Pope's murder and that they would become heroes and spend their prison sentences without too much discomfort. Italy did not have a death penalty, they could only receive life imprisonment, which was a joke. With all the reductions for good behavior and the different conditions for amnesties they would be set free at a comparatively young age.

It would have been different if Sebbediccio could have conducted the interrogation of Romeo in a more serious fashion. But because this scoundrel had killed a Pope, his rights had become a cause in the Western world. There were protesters and human rights groups from Scandinavia and England and even a stern letter from a lawyer in America named Whitney Cheever. All these proclaimed that the two murderers must be handled as human beings, not subjected to torture, not ill-treated in any way. And orders had come down from the top, don't disgrace Italian justice with anything that might offend the left-wing parties in Italy. Kid gloves.

Franco Sebbediccio had gone through this before, and it was a disgrace. But the killing of a Pope was something else. And the resurgence of the terrorist groups was again something else. He had to get information and the prisoners had not co-operated. But the final straw was that just a week ago Franco Sebbediccio's Administrative Judge had been assassinated with a message to the effect that this would continue until the killers of the Pope were freed. A ridiculous request but a public relations excuse to kill a judge.

But he, Franco Sebbediccio, would cut through all the nonsense and send a message to the Red Army. Franco Sebbediccio was determined that this Romeo, this Armando Giangi, would commit suicide.

Romeo had spent his months in prison weaving a romantic dream. Alone in his cell he had chosen to fall in love with the American girl, Dorothea. He remembered her waiting for him at the airport, the tender scar on her chin. In his reveries, she seemed so beautiful, so kind. He tried to remember their conversation that last night he spent with her in the Hamptons. Now in his memory, it seemed to him that she had loved him. That her every gesture had dared him to declare his desire so that she could show her love. He remembered how she sat, so gracefully, so invitingly. How her eyes stared at him, great dark pools of blue, her white skin suffused with blushes. And now he cursed his timidity. He had never touched that skin. He remembered the long slim legs and imposed them around his neck. He imagined the kisses he would rain on her, her eyes, the length of her lithesome body.

And then Romeo dreamed of how she stood in the

sunlight, draped in chains, staring at him in reproach and despair. He weaved fantasies of the future. She would only serve a short term in prison. She would be waiting for him. And he would be freed. By amnesty or by the trading of hostages, perhaps by pure Christian mercy. And then he would find her.

There were nights that he despaired and thought of Yabril's treachery. The murder of Theresa Kennedy had never been in the plan and he believed in his heart that he would never have consented to such an act. He felt a disgust for Yabril, for his own beliefs, for his own life. Sometimes he would weep quietly in the darkness. Then he would console himself and lose himself in his fantasies of Dorothea. It was false, he knew. It was a weakness, he knew, but he could not help himself.

Romeo in his bare, smooth cell received Franco Sebbediccio with a sardonic grin. He could see the hatred in this old man's peasant eyes, could sense his bewilderment that a person from a good family who enjoyed a pleasant, luxuriant life, could also become a revolutionary. He was also aware that Sebbediccio was frustrated that the international public watch restrained him from treating his prisoner as brutally as he might wish.

Sebbediccio had himself locked in with the prisoner, the two of them alone with two guards and an observer from the governor's office watching but unable to hear from right outside the door. It was almost as if the burly older man were inviting some sort of attack. But Romeo knew that it was simply that the older man had confidence in the authority of his position. Romeo had a contempt for this kind of man, rooted in law and order, handcuffed by his beliefs and bourgeois moral standards. Therefore he was terribly surprised when Sebbediccio said to him casually, but in a very low voice, 'Giangi, you are going to make life easier for everyone. You are going to commit suicide.'

Romeo laughed. 'No, I'm not, I'll be out of jail before you die of high blood pressure and ulcers. I'll walk the streets of Rome when you're lying in your family cemetary. I'll come and sing to the angels on your tombstone. I'll be whistling when I walk away from your grave.'

Franco Sebbediccio said patiently, 'I just wanted to let you know that you and your cadre are going to commit suicide. Two of my men were killed by your friends to intimidate me and my associates. Your suicides will be my answer.'

Romeo said, 'I can't please you. I'm enjoying life too much. And with all the world watching you don't dare to even give me a good kick in the ass.'

Franco Sebbediccio gave him a benevolent smile. He had an ace in the hole.

Romeo's father, who all his life had done nothing for humanity, had done something for his son. He had shot himself. A Knight of Malta, father of the murderer of the Pope, a man who had lived his whole life for his own selfish pleasure, he had unfathomably decided to don the mantle of guilt.

When Romeo's newly widowed mother asked to visit her son in his prison cell and was refused, the newspapers took up her cause. The telling blow was struck by Romeo's defense lawyer as he was interviewed on television. 'For God's sake he just wants to see his mother.' Which struck a responsive chord, not only in Italy but all over the Western world. Every newspaper gave it a front page headline, verbatim, 'For God's sake, he just wants to see his mother.'

Which was not strictly true, Romeo's mother wanted to see him, he did not want to see her.

With pressure so great, the government was forced to allow Mother Giangi to visit her son. Franco Sebbediccio had opposed this visit, he wanted to keep Romeo in seclusion, to keep him cut off from the outside world. But the governor of the prison overrode him.

The governor had a grand palatial office and summoned

409

Sebbediccio to it. He said, 'My dear sir, I have my instructions, the visit is to be allowed. And not in his cell where the conversation can be monitored but in this office itself. With nobody within earshot, but recorded by cameras in the last five minutes of the hour, after all the media must be allowed to profit.'

Sebbediccio said, 'And for what reason is this allowed?'

The governor gave him the smile he reserved usually for the prisoners and the members of his staff who had become almost like the prisoners themselves. 'For a son to see his widowed mother. What could be more sacred?'

Sebbediccio hated the governor who always had observers outside the door during interrogations. He said harshly, 'A man who murders the Pope? He has to see his mother? Why didn't he talk to his mother before he shot the Pope?'

The governor shrugged. 'Those far above us have decided. Reconcile yourself. Also the defense lawyer insists that this office be swept for bugs so don't think you can plant electronic gear.'

'Ah,' Sebbediccio said. 'And how is the lawyer going to do the debugging?'

'He will hire his own electronic specialists,' the governor said. 'They will do their job in the lawyer's presence immediately before the meeting.'

Sebbediccio said, 'It is essential, it is vital that we hear that conversation between them.'

'Nonsense,' the governor said. 'His mother is your typical rich Roman matron. She knows nothing and he would never confide anything of importance to her. This is just another silly episode in the quite ridiculous drama of our times. Don't take it seriously.'

But Franco Sebbediccio did take it seriously. He considered it another mockery of justice, another scorn of authority. And he hoped Romeo might let something slip when he talked to his mother.

As head of the Anti-Terrorist Division for all Italy Sebbediccio had a great deal of power. The defense lawyer was already on the secret list of left-wing radicals who could be put under surveillance. Which was done, the phone tapped, the mail intercepted and read before it was delivered. And so it was easy to find the electronic company the defense would use to sweep the governor's office. Sebbediccio used a friend to set up an 'accidental' meeting in a restaurant with the owner of the electronics company.

Even without the help of force, Franco Sebbediccio could be persuasive. It was a small electronics corporation, making a living but by no means an overwhelming success. Sebbediccio pointed out that the Anti-Terrorist Division had great need of electronic sweeping equipment and personnel, that it could interpose security vetoes on the companies selected. In short that he, Sebbediccio, could make the company rich.

But there must be trust and profit on both sides. In this particular case why should the electronics company care about the murderers of the Pope, why should it jeopardize its future prosperity over such an inconsequential matter as the recording of a meeting between the mother and son? Why could not the electronics company plant the bug as it was supposedly debugging the governor's office? And who would be the wiser? And Sebbediccio himself would arrange to have the bug removed.

It was done in a very friendly way, but somewhere during the dinner Sebbediccio made it understood that if he was refused, the electronics company would run into a great deal of trouble in the coming years. Without any personal animosity, but how could his government service possibly trust people who protected the murderer of the Pope?

It was all agreed and Sebbediccio let the other man pick up the check. He was certainly not going to pay for it out of his personal funds, and to be reimbursed on his expense voucher might lead to a paper trail years later. Besides, he was going to make the man rich.

411

The meeting between Armando 'Romeo' Giangi and his mother was therefore fully recorded and heard only by Franco Sebbediccio and he was delighted with it. Though he took his time in removing the bug simply out of curiosity at what the snotty governor of the prison was really like but there he got nothing.

Sebbediccio took the precaution of playing the tape in his home while his wife slept. None of his colleagues must know about it. He was not a bad man and he almost wept when Mother Giangi sobbed over her son, implored him to tell the truth that he had not really killed the Pope, that he was shielding a bad companion. Sebbediccio could hear the woman's kisses as she rained them down upon the face of her murderous son and he wondered for a moment does it ever matter what anyone does in reality? But then the kissing and wails stopped and the conversation became very interesting to Franco Sebbediccio.

He heard Romeo's voice attempting to calm the mother down. And then Romeo said, 'I don't understand why your husband killed himself. He didn't care about his country or the world, and forgive me, he didn't even love his family. He lived a completely selfish and egocentric life. Why did he feel it necessary to shoot himself?'

The mother's voice came hissing from the tape. 'Out of vanity,' she said. 'All his life your father was a vain man. Every day to his barber, once a week to his tailor. At the age of forty he took singing lessons. To sing where? And he spent a fortune to become a Knight of Malta and never a man so devoid of the Holy Spirit. On Easter he had a white suit made with the palm cross woven specially into the cloth. Oh, what a grand figure in Roman society. The parties, the balls, his appointment to cultural committees whose meetings he never attended. And the father of a son graduated from the University, he was proud of your brilliance. Oh, how he promenaded on the streets of Rome. I never saw a

412

man so happy and so empty.' There was a pause on the tape. 'After what you did, your father could never appear in Roman society again. That empty life was finished and for that loss he killed himself. But he can rest easy. He looked beautiful in his coffin with his new Easter suit.'

Then came Romeo's voice on the tape saying what delighted Sebbedicco. 'My father never gave me anything in life and by his suicide he stole my option. And death was my only escape.'

Sebbedicco listened to the rest of the tape in which Romeo let his mother persuade him to see a priest and then when the TV cameras and reporters were let into the room he turned it off. He had seen the rest on TV. But he had what he wanted.

When Sebbedicco paid his next visit to Romeo, he was so delighted that when the jailer unlocked the cell he entered doing a little dance step and greeted Giangi with great joviality.

'Giangi,' he said, 'you are becoming even more famous. It is rumored that when we have a new Pope he may ask mercy for you. Show your gratitude, give me some of the information I need.'

Romeo said, 'What an ape you are.'

Sebbedicco bowed and said, 'That's your last word then?'

It was perfect. He had a recording that said Romeo was thinking of killing himself.

A week later the news was released to the world that the murderer of the Pope, Armando 'Romeo' Giangi, had committed suicide by hanging himself in his cell.

Christian Klee arrived in Rome from London to have dinner with Sebbedicco. He noted that Sebbedicco had almost twenty bodyguards, which did not seem to affect his appetite.

Sebbedicco was in high spirits. 'Wasn't it fortunate that our Pope-killer took his own life?' he said to Christian Klee.

413

'What a circus the trial would have been with all our left-wingers marching in support. It's too bad that fellow Yabril wouldn't do you the same favor.'

Christian Klee laughed and said ironically, 'Different systems of government. I see you're well protected.'

Sebbediccio shrugged. 'I think they are after bigger game. I have some information for you. That woman, Annee, that we've let run loose. Somehow we lost her. But we have some information that says she's now in America.'

Christian Klee felt a thrill of excitement. 'Do you know what port of embarkation? What name she is using?'

'No,' Sebbediccio said. 'But we think she is now operational.'

'Why didn't you pick her up?' Christian said.

'I have high hopes for her,' Sebbediccio said. 'She is a very determined young lady and she will go far in the terrorist movement. I want to use a big net when I take her. But you have a problem my friend. We hear rumors that there is an operation in the United States. It can only be against Kennedy. Annee, as fierce as she may be, cannot do it alone. Therefore, there must be other people involved. Knowing your security for the President, they will have to mount an operation that would require a goodly number with material and safe houses. On that I have no information. You had better set to work.'

Christian Klee didn't ask why the Italian Security Chief had not sent this information through regular channels to Washington. He knew Sebbediccio did not want his close surveillance of Annee made part of an official record in the United States, he did not trust the Freedom of Information Act in America. Also, he wanted Christian Klee in his personal debt.

In Sherhaben, Sultan Maurobi received Christian Klee with the utmost friendliness. As if there had never been the crisis of a few months before. The Sultan was affable but on guard

414

and appeared a little puzzled. 'I hope you bring me good news,' he said to Christian Klee. 'After all the regrettable unpleasantness, I am very anxious to repair relations with the United States and, of course, your President Kennedy. In fact, I hope your visit is in regard to this matter.'

Christian Klee smiled. 'I came for that very purpose,' he said. 'You are in a position, I think, to do us a service which might heal the breach.'

'Ah, I am very happy to hear that,' the Sultan said. 'You know, of course, that I was not privy to Yabril's intentions. I had no foreknowledge of what Yabril would do to the President's daughter. Of course, I have expressed this officially, but would you tell the President personally that I have grieved over this for the past months. I was powerless to avert the tragedy.'

Christian Klee believed him. The murder had not been in the original plans. And he thought how all powerful men like Sultan Maurobi and Francis Kennedy were helpless in the face of uncontrollable events, the will of other men.

But now he said to the Sultan, 'Your giving up Yabril has reassured the President on that point.' This they both knew was mere politeness. Klee paused for a moment and then went on. 'But I'm here to ask you to do me a personal service. You know I am responsible for the safety of my President. I have information that there is a plot to assassinate him. That terrorists have already infiltrated into the United States. But it would be helpful if I could get information as to their plans and to their identity and location. With your contacts I thought you might have heard something through your intelligence agencies. That you might give me some scraps of information. Let me emphasize that it will only be between the two of us. You and I. There will be no official connection.'

The Sultan seemed astonished. His intelligent face screwed up into amused disbelief. 'How can you think such a thing?' he asked. 'After all the tragedies, would I get involved in such dangerous activities? I am the ruler of a small rich country that is powerless to remain independent without the friendship of great powers. I can do nothing for you or against you.'

Christian Klee nodded his head in agreement. 'Of course that is true. However Bert Audick came to visit you and I know that had to do with the oil industry. But let me tell you that Mr Audick is in very serious trouble in the United States. He would be a very bad ally for you to have in the coming years.'

'And you would be a very good ally?' the Sultan asked, smiling.

'Yes,' Klee said. 'I am the ally that could save you. If you co-operate with me now.'

'Explain,' the Sultan said. He was obviously angered by the implied threat.

Christian Klee spoke very carefully. 'Bert Audick is under indictment for conspiracy against the United States government because his mercenaries or those of his company fired on our planes bombing your city of Dak. And there are other charges. His oil empire could be destroyed under certain of our laws. He is not a strong ally at this moment.'

The Sultan said slyly, 'Indicted but not convicted. I understand that will be more difficult.'

'That is true,' Christian Klee said. 'But in a few months Francis Kennedy will be re-elected. His popularity will bring in a Congress that will ratify his programs. He will be the most powerful President in the history of the United States. Then Audick is doomed, I can assure you. And the power structure of which he is a part will be destroyed.'

'I still fail to see how I can help you,' the Sultan said. And then more imperiously, 'Or how you can help me. I understand you are in a delicate position yourself in your own country.'

'That may or may not be true,' Christian Klee said. 'As for my position, delicate as you say, that will be resolved when Kennedy is re-elected. I am his closest friend and closest advisor and Kennedy is noted for his loyalty. As to how we can help each other, let me be direct without intending any disrespect. May I do so?'

The Sultan seemed to be impressed and even amused by this courtesy. 'By all means,' he said.

Klee said, 'First, and most importantly, here is how I can help you. I can be your ally. I have the ear of the President of the United States and I have his trust. We live in difficult times.'

The Sultan interrupted smilingly, 'I have always lived in difficult times.'

'And so you can appreciate what I am saying better than most,' Klee retorted sharply.

'And what if your Kennedy does not achieve his aims?' the Sultan said. 'Accidents befall, heaven is not always kind.'

Christian Klee was cold now as he answered. 'What you are saying is, what if the plot to kill Kennedy succeeds? I am here to tell you that it will not. I don't care how clever and daring the assassins may be. And if they try and fail and there is any trace to you, then you will be destroyed. But it doesn't have to come to that. I'm a reasonable man and I understand your position. What I propose is an exchange of information between you and myself on a personal basis. I don't know what Audick proposed to you, but I'm a better bet. If Audick and his crowd wins, you still win. He doesn't know about us. If Kennedy wins, you have me as your ally. I'm your insurance.'

The Sultan nodded and then led him into a sumptuous banquet. During the meal, the Sultan asked Klee innumerable questions about Kennedy. Then finally, almost hesitantly, he asked about Yabril.

Klee looked him directly in the eyes. 'There is no way that Yabril can escape his fate. If his fellow terrorists think they can get him released by holding even the most important of hostages, tell them to forget about it. Kennedy will never let him go.'

The Sultan sighed. 'Your Kennedy has changed,' he said. 'He sounds like a man going berserk.' Klee didn't answer. The Sultan went on, very slowly. 'I think you have convinced me,' he said. 'I think you and I should become allies.'

When Christian Klee returned to the United States, the first person he went to see was the Oracle. The old man received him in his bedroom suite, sitting in his motorized wheelchair, an English tea spread on the table in front of him, a comfortable armchair waiting for Christian opposite.

The Oracle greeted him with a slight wave that he should sit down. Christian served him tea and a tiny bit of cake and a small finger sandwich. Then served himself. The Oracle took a sip of tea, crumbled the bit of cake in his mouth. They sat there for a long moment.

Then the Oracle tried to smile, a slight movement of the lips, the skin so dead it could not move. 'You've got yourself into a fine mess for your fucking friend Kennedy,' he said.

The vulgarism, spoken as if from the mouth of an innocent child, made Christian smile. Again he wondered, was it a mark of senility, a decaying of the brain, that the Oracle who had never used profanity, now was using it so freely? He waited until he had eaten one of the sandwiches and gulped down some hot tea then he answered. 'Which fix?' he said. 'I'm in a lot of them.'

'I'm talking about that atom bomb thing,' the Oracle said. 'The rest of the shit doesn't matter. But they are accusing you of being responsible for the murder of thousands of citizens of this country. They've got the goods on you it seems, but I refuse to believe you to be so stupid. Inhuman, yes, after all you're in politics. Did you really do it?' The old man's face was not judgmental, just curious.

Who else in the world was there to tell? Who else in the

world would understand. 'What I'm astonished about,' Christian Klee said, 'is how quickly they got on to me.'

'The human mind *leaps* to an understanding of evil,' the Oracle said. 'You are surprised because there is a certain innocence in the doer of an evil deed. He thinks the deed so terrible that it is inconceivable to another human being. But that is the first thing they jump at. Evil is no mystery at all, love is the mystery.' He paused for a moment, started to speak again and then relaxed back in his chair, his eyes half closed, dozing.

'You have to understand,' Christian said, 'that letting something happen is so much easier than actually doing something. There was the crisis, Francis Kennedy was going to be impeached by the Congress. And I thought just for a second, if only the atom bomb exploded it would turn things around. It was in that moment that I told Peter Cloot not to interrogate Gresse and Tibbot. That I had the time to do it. The whole thing flashed by in that one second and it was done.'

The Oracle said, 'Give me some more hot tea and another piece of cake.' He put the cake in his mouth, tiny crumbs appearing on his scar-like lips. 'What about Peter Cloot's testimony, that you came back and interrogated them. That you got the information out of them and then didn't act on it?'

Christian sighed. 'They were only kids. I squeezed them dry in five minutes. That's why I couldn't have Cloot at the interrogation. But I didn't want the bomb to explode. It just went so quick.'

The Oracle started to laugh. It was a curious laugh even in so old a man. It was a series of grunted 'heh, heh, heh's'. 'You've got it ass backwards,' the Oracle said. 'You had already made up your mind that you would let the bomb explode. Before you told Cloot not to interrogate them. It didn't go by in a second, you planned it all out.'

Christian Klee was a little startled. What the Oracle said

was true. Then how had he twisted it in his own mind? He said to the Oracle, 'You have to understand how it was. I wasn't sure that it all would happen. If I was sure, I would have prevented it. I was just hanging to some sort of hope that something might solve Kennedy's situation.'

'And all to save your hero, Francis Kennedy,' the Oracle said. 'The man who can do no wrong except when he sets the whole world on fire.' The Oracle had placed a box of thin Havana cigars on the table and Christian took one of them and lit it. 'You were lucky,' the Oracle said. 'Those people that were killed were mostly worthless. The drunken, the homeless, the criminal. And it's not so great a crime. Not in the history of our human race.'

'Francis really gave me the go ahead,' Christian Klee said. And that made the Oracle touch a button on his chair so that the back of it straightened to make his body upright and alert.

'Your saintly President?' the Oracle said. 'He is far too much a victim of his own hypocrisy, like all the Kennedys were. He could never be party to such an act.'

'Maybe I'm just trying to make excuses,' Christian said. 'It was nothing explicit. But remember I know Francis so intimately, we're almost like brothers. I asked him for the order so that the Medical Interrogation team would be able to do the chemical brain probe. That would have settled the whole atom bomb problem immediately. And Francis refused to sign the authorization. Sure he gave his grounds, good civil liberty and humanitarian grounds. That was in his character. But that was in his character before his daughter was killed. Not in his character afterwards. Remember, he had ordered the destruction of Dak by this time. He gave the threat that he would destroy the whole nation of Sherhaben if the hostages were not released. So his character had changed. His new character would have signed the Medical Interrogation order. And then when he refused to sign, he

420

gave me a look, I can't describe it, but it was almost as if he were telling me to let it happen.'

The Oracle was fully alive now. He spoke sharply. 'All that doesn't matter. What matters is that you save your ass. If Kennedy doesn't get re-elected, you may spend years in jail. And even if Kennedy gets re-elected, there may be some danger.'

'Kennedy will win the election,' Christian said. 'And after that, I'll be OK.' He paused for a moment. 'I know him.'

'You know the old Kennedy,' the Oracle said. Then as if he had lost interest he said, 'And how about my birthday party? I'm a hundred years old and nobody gives a shit.'

Christian laughed. 'I do. Don't worry. After the election you'll have a birthday party in the White House Rose Garden. A birthday party for a king.'

The Oracle smiled with pleasure, then said slyly, 'And your Francis Kennedy will be the king. You do know, don't you, that if he is re-elected and carries his Congressional candidates with him, he will in effect be a dictator?'

'That's highly unlikely,' Christian Klee said. 'There has never been a dictator in this country. We have safeguards, too many safeguards I think sometimes.'

'Ah,' the Oracle said. 'This is a young country yet. We have time. And the devil takes many seductive forms.'

They were silent for a long time and then Christian rose to take his leave. They always touched hands when they parted, the Oracle too fragile for a real handshake.

'Be careful,' the Oracle said. 'When a man rises to absolute power, he usually gets rid of those closest to him, those who know his secrets.'

22

Two months before the Presidential election, polls showed Francis Kennedy's margin of victory would not be enough to carry his Congressional candidates into office.

There were problems. The scandal of Eugene Dazzy's mistress, the charges that Attorney General Christian Klee had deliberately permitted the explosion of the atom bomb, the scandal of Canoo and Klee using the funds of the Office of the Military Advisor to beef up the Secret Service.

That the President of the United States was having an affair with a girl twenty years younger than himself and reputedly with a strain of Negro blood did damage and the possibility that they would marry and that she would be First Lady lost Kennedy votes.

And perhaps Francis Kennedy himself went too far. America was not ready for a brand of socialism. It was not ready to reject the corporate structure of America. The people of America did not want to be equal, they wanted to be rich. Nearly all the states had their own lottery with prizes running high up into the millions. More people bought lottery tickets than voted in the national elections.

The power of the Congressmen and Senators already in office was also overwhelming. They had their staffs paid for by the government. They had the vast sums of money contributed by the corporate structure which they used to dominate TV with brilliantly executed ads. By holding government office they could appear on special political programs on TV and in the newspapers, increasing their name-recognition factor.

Lawrence Salentine had organized the overall campaign against Kennedy so brilliantly that he was now the leader of the Socrates Club group. With the delicate precision of a Renaissance poisoner, he had dropped little references of Lanetta Carr's Negro blood on TV and in the prints. And then only in a way that praised. Salentine was counting on the fact that a part of the United States of America which prided itself on its racial tolerance was, underneath, racially biased.

On the third day of September, Christian Klee secretly went to the office of the Vice President. As an extra precaution, he gave special instructions to Helen DuPray's Secret Service detail chief before he announced himself to Helen DuPray's secretary and said his business was urgent.

The Vice President was astonished to see him, it was against all protocol that he should visit her without advance warning or even permission. For a moment, he was afraid she might take offense, but she was too intelligent to do so. She knew immediately that Christian Klee would only breach protocol for the most serious problem. In fact, what she felt was apprehension. What new terrible thing could have happened now after the past months?

Christian Klee sensed this immediately. 'There's nothing to be worried about,' he said. 'It's just that we have a security problem involving the President. As part of our coverage, we have sealed off your office. You will not answer the phone but you can deal with your immediate staff. I will remain with you the entire day, personally.'

Helen DuPray understood immediately that no matter what happened, she was not to take command of the country and that's why Klee was there. 'If the President has a security problem, why are you with me?' she said. But without waiting for an answer from Klee, she said, 'I will have to check this with the President personally.'

423

'He is appearing at a political luncheon in New York,' Christian Klee said.

'I know that,' Helen DuPray said.

Christian Klee looked at his watch. 'The President will be calling you in about one half hour,' he said.

When the call came, Klee watched Helen DuPray's face. She seemed to show no astonishment, only twice she asked questions. Good, Klee thought, she would be OK, he didn't have to worry about her. Then she did something that aroused Christian's admiration; he didn't think she had it in her – Vice Presidents were noted for their timidity. She asked Kennedy if she could speak to Eugene Dazzy, the President's Chief of Staff. When Dazzy came on the phone, she made a simple query about their work schedule for the next week. Then she hung up. She had been checking to see if the person on the phone had really been Kennedy, despite the fact that she recognized his voice. Of the questions she had asked, only Dazzy would recognize the reference. She was making sure that there was no voice impersonation.

She addressed him icily, she knew something was fishy, Klee thought. She said, 'The President has informed me that you will be using my office as a command post, that I will be under your instruction. I find this extraordinary. Perhaps you will give me an explanation.'

'I apologize for all this,' Christian Klee said. 'If I could have some coffee, I'll give you a full briefing. You will know as much as the President about this matter.' Which was true but a little devious. She would not know as much as Klee.

Helen DuPray was studying him very intently. She didn't trust him, Christian knew. But women didn't understand power, they didn't understand the stark efficiency of violence. He gathered up all his energy to convince her of his sincerity. When he was through almost an hour later, she seemed won over. She was a very beautiful woman and intelligent, Christian thought. Too bad that she would never become the President of the United States.

*

On this glorious summer day, President Francis Kennedy was to speak at a political luncheon held in New York City's Sheraton Hotel Convention Center which would be followed by a triumphal motorcade down Fifth Avenue. Then he would make a speech near the atom bomb destruction area. The event had been scheduled three months before and had been well publicized. It was the kind of situation that Christian Klee detested, the President too exposed. There were deranged people, even the police were a danger in Klee's eyes because they were armed and also because as a police force, they were completely demoralized by the uncontrolled crime in the city.

For these reasons Klee didn't trust the police in any of the big cities. He took his own elaborate precautions. Only his operational staff in the Secret Service knew the awesome detail and manpower that was used to protect the President in his rare public appearances.

Special Advance teams had been sent ahead. These teams patrolled and searched the area of the visit twenty-four hours a day. Two days before the visit, another thousand men were sent to become part of the crowds that greeted the President. These men formed a line on both sides of the motorcade and in the front of the motorcade and acted as part of the crowd but actually formed a sort of Maginot line. Another five hundred men manned the rooftops, constantly scanning the windows that overlooked the motorcade and these men were heavily armed. In addition to this there was the President's own special and personal detail which numbered a hundred men. And then, of course, there were the Secret Service men under deep cover who were accredited to newspapers and TV stations, who carried newspaper cameras and manned mobile TV vehicles.

And Christian Klee had other tricks up his sleeve. In the nearly four years of the Kennedy administration there had been five assassination attempts, what the more lurid newspapers commonly referred to as the 'hat trick', a reference to the expression in hockey when a man scores three goals. Meaning the assassinations of three Kennedy's. None of them had even come close. They had been crazies, of course, and were now behind bars in the toughest of Federal prisons. And Klee made sure that if they got out, he would find a reason to put them back in again. It was impossible to jail all the lunatics in the United States who made threats to kill the President of the United States: by mail, by phone, by conspiring, by shouting it in the streets. But Christian Klee had made their lives miserable for them, so that they would be too busy preserving their own safety to worry about grandiose ideas. He put them under mail surveillance, phone surveillance, personal surveillance, computer surveillance, he had their tax returns examined carefully. If they spit on the sidewalk, they were in trouble.

All these precautions, all these arrangements, were in effect this September third when President Francis Xavier Kennedy gave his speech at the political luncheon at the Sheraton Convention Center in New York. Hundreds of Secret Service men were scattered through the audience, and the building was sealed off after his entrance.

On the morning that Christian Klee went to the Vice President's office, he knew that he had the situation under control. The Sultan of Sherhaben had sent him valuable information and Sebbediccio's briefing on Annee had made the job that much easier. He had tremendous resources; unlimited manpower, technical facilities, information the terrorists did not know he had. He had Annee under surveillance, individual, computer and telephonic. He had the two assassination teams blanketed. But he did not want anyone, not even the President or Helen DuPray, to know all this. The only part he did let them know was that he had certain information that on September the third in New York City, an attempt would be made on the life of Francis Kennedy. And, he told them, this was by no means a

426

certainty, that it was only one chance in a hundred that the tip was legitimate, that he was just taking precautions for any eventuality.

The opposite was the case. He knew the attempt on the President's life would be made that day. He knew that he could crush the whole operation before it started but he wanted the attempt made. And then the whole nation would see how the President of the United States always lived in mortal danger. There would be an overwhelming tide of love for Kennedy throughout the nation. It was the kind of event that the media could not downplay, in fact, they would be swept into the very vortex of public emotion. That tide of love would carry over into the elections two months away and Francis Kennedy would sweep everything before him. Not only would he be re-elected by a vast majority, but he would carry his Congressional candidates in with him.

Congressman Jintz would be back on his farm, Senator Lambertino would be back with his law firm in New York, and Bert Audick would be in prison.

Three weeks before, Annee had received her orders. She had traveled under the name of Isabella Cesaro and was met at the airport by a married couple who took her to a luxurious apartment on the Lower East Side. There, the married couple handed over documents which gave her access to funds in the Chemical Bank branch nearby. She had been astonished to see that she had control of over five hundred thousand dollars. She also had a list of encoded phone numbers to call.

The married couple stayed with her for a week guiding her around New York in what was actually a heavy training period. Annee spoke English passably and picked up things very quickly. In that week, two furnished condos were rented and stocked with food and medicines. When all this was done, the married couple said their goodbyes and vanished.

During the next three weeks, Annee remained in place and

used telephones in public places to call the encoded numbers. She moved freely about the city, and like a true radical, she toured the black neighborhoods to marvel at their poverty and squalor with a certain amount of satisfaction. She was actually having a good time moving about in the heart of the enemy. She could not know Christian Klee's FBI was picking up her phone calls in the very air, that every move she made was covered, that the two assassination teams sent from Europe had been spotted immediately when they arrived as crewmen on one of Bert Audick's oil tankers, and that their phone calls to her in the public booths had been intercepted and read by Christian Klee.

On September third, summoned, Lanetta Carr came into the office of Vice President Helen DuPray and was astonished by two things. The first was that the large TV set was tuned into one of the networks with the sound so low that she could barely hear it; the second was that Attorney General Christian Klee was seated opposite the Vice President's desk.

Christian Klee smiled at her pleasantly and said, 'Hello, Lanetta,' and watched her carefully as she put her papers on the Vice President's desk.

Helen DuPray said in a cold voice, 'Mr Attorney General, I think you should tell Miss Carr what you told me.'

'She has no need to know,' Christian said.

'If you don't tell her, I will,' Helen DuPray said.

'That would be a breach of security,' Christian Klee said. 'Acting under the authority of the President, I forbid you to disclose any information.'

'How do you propose to stop me?' Helen DuPray said contemptuously.

There was a long moment of silence.

Then Klee said cautiously, 'Nothing may happen.'

'I don't give a damn,' Helen DuPray said. 'Do you tell her or do I?'

'Nothing may happen,' Klee repeated.

Helen DuPray said briskly to Lanetta, 'Sit down, you won't be able to leave this office after I tell you what's going on.'

Christian Klee sighed and said, 'There's only one chance in a hundred that anything will happen.' And then he briefed Lanetta as thoroughly as he had briefed the Vice President.

On that same September third, the woman terrorist named Annee went shopping on Fifth Avenue. In her three weeks in the United States, she had helped everything move into place. She had made her phone calls, had her meeting with the two assassination teams that had finally made their way to New York and moved into the two apartments prepared for them. These apartments had already been stocked with weapons procured by a special underground logistics team which had no part of the central plan.

Annee thought how strange it was that she would go shopping just four hours before what might be the end of her life.

Patsy Troyca and Elizabeth Stone were working hard together interviewing Peter Cloot on his testimony that Christian Klee could have prevented the explosion of the atom bomb. They were going to leak the story in full detail to blow up the original charges made before the Congressional committee. They were so elated by Peter Cloot's obvious hatred of Christian Klee, his sincere indignation at the monstrousness of Klee's crime and giving them the 'off the record' information about the workings of the FBI, that they decided to celebrate. Elizabeth Stone's townhouse was only a ten-minute ride away. So at lunch-time, they spent a couple of hours in bed.

Once in bed, they forgot all the stress of the day. After an hour, Elizabeth went into the bathroom to take a shower and Patsy Troyca wandered into the living room, still naked, to turn on the TV. He stood in amazement at what he was seeing. He watched for a few moments longer and then ran into the bathroom and pulled Elizabeth Stone out of the shower. She was startled and a little frightened by his brutality as he dragged her naked and dripping wet into the living room.

There, watching the TV screen, she began to weep. Patsy Troyca took her into his arms. 'Look at it this way,' he said, 'our troubles are over.'

The campaign speech in New York on September third was to be one of the most important stops in President Kennedy's bid for re-election. And it had been planned to have a great psychological effect on the nation.

First, there would be a luncheon at the Sheraton Convention Center on 58th Street. There, the President would address the most important and influential men of the city. This luncheon was sponsored oddly enough by Louis Inch, who was a backer of the Democratic party.

The luncheon was to raise funds to build the eight blocks in New York that had been leveled by the atom bomb explosion during the Easter week crisis. An architect, without a fee, had designed a great memorial for the devastated area, the rest of the acreage to be a small park with a tiny lake. The city was to buy and donate the land.

After luncheon, the Kennedy party would lead a motorcade that would begin at 125th Street and go down Seventh and Fifth Avenues to place the first symbolic wreath of marble on the rubbled heap that was what remained of Times Square.

As one of the sponsors of the luncheon, Louis Inch was seated on the dais with President Kennedy and expected to accompany him to his waiting car and so get in newspaper and TV coverage. But to his surprise, he was cut off by Secret Service men who isolated Kennedy in a human net. The President was escorted through a door at the rear of the platform. As the President disappeared, Louis Inch saw that the whole vast room had been sealed off so that all those people who had paid ten thousand dollars each to attend were now imprisoned and unable to leave.

In the streets outside, huge crowds gathered. The Secret Service had cleared the area so that there was a space of at least a hundred feet around the Presidential limousine. There were enough Secret Service men to protect the inner hundred feet with a solid phalanx. Outside that, the crowd was controlled by the police. On the edge of this perimeter were photographers and TV camera crews who immediately surged forward when the advance guard of Secret Service men came out of the hotel. And then, unaccountably, there was a fifteen-minute wait.

The figure of the President finally emerged from the hotel shielded from the TV cameras as he rushed toward his waiting car. At that very moment, the Avenue exploded into a beautifully choreographed but bloody ballet.

Six men burst through the police restraining line mowing down part of the police wall, running toward the President's armored limousine. A second later, as if to tempo, another group of six men burst through the opposite perimeter and raked the fifty Secret Service men around the armored limousine with their automatic weapons.

In the very next second eight cars swung into the open area and Secret Service men in combat gear and bulletproof vests that made them seem like inflated gigantic balloons came tumbling out with shotguns and machine pistols and caught the attackers in the rear. They shot with precision and short bursts. All twelve attackers were lying in the Avenue dead, their guns silenced. The Presidential limousine roared away from the curb, other Secret Service cars following.

At that moment, Annee, with a supreme effort of will, stepped in the path of the Presidential limousine with her two Bloomingdale shopping bags in her hand. The shopping bags were filled with explosive gel, two powerful bombs that detonated as the car hit her. The Presidential car flew up into the air at least ten feet off the ground and came down a mass of flames. The force of the explosion blew everyone inside it to bits. And there was absolutely nothing left of Annee except tiny bits of gaily colored paper from the shopping bags.

The TV cameraman had the wit to swing his camera for a panoramic shot of everything that was visible. The crowd, thousands of people, had flung themselves to the ground when the firing broke out and were still lying prone as if begging some unforgiving God to remit them from an obscene terror. From that prone mass issued small brooks of blood coming from spectators that had been hit by the heavy fire from the assassination teams or killed by the explosion of the powerful bombs.

Many of the crowd suffered from concussions and when it was quiet, rose and staggered in circles. The camera caught all this for television to horrify the nation.

In the office of Vice President Helen DuPray, Christian Klee jumped out of his chair and cried out, 'That wasn't supposed to happen.' Lanetta Carr was staring wide-eyed at the screen.

Helen DuPray watched the TV screen and then said sharply to Christian Klee, 'Who was the poor bastard who took the President's place?'

'One of my Secret Service men,' Christian Klee said. 'They were not supposed to get that close.'

'You told me there was only one chance in a hundred that anything might happen.' DuPray was looking at Klee very coldly. And then she became angrier than Lanetta Carr had ever seen her. 'Why the hell didn't you cancel the whole thing?' she shouted. 'Why didn't you avert this whole tragedy? There are citizens dead out there in the streets who came to see their President. You've wasted the lives of your own men. I promise you, your actions will be questioned by me to the President and to the appropriate Congressional Committee.'

'You don't know what the hell you're talking about,' Christian Klee said. 'Do you know how many tips I get, how many threats against the President are made by mail? If we listened to all of them, the President would be a prisoner in the White House.'

Helen DuPray was studying his face while he spoke. 'Why did you use a double this time?' she said. 'That is an extreme measure. And if it was *that* serious, why did you have the President go there at all?'

'When you are the President, you can ask me those questions,' Christian Klee said curtly.

Lanetta said softly, 'Where is Francis now?'

It was an inappropriate question at this moment and an inappropriate form of address. They both looked at her. Helen DuPray gave a slight shrug and waited for Klee to speak.

Christian Klee stared at her for a moment as if he would not answer. But he noticed the anguish on her face and said quietly, 'He's on his way to Washington. We don't know how extensive this plot is, so we want him here. He is very safe.'

Helen DuPray said in a sardonic voice, 'OK, now she knows he's safe. I assume you've briefed the other members of the staff, they know he's safe, you and I know he's safe, what about the people of America? When will they know he's safe?'

Christian Klee said, 'Dazzy has made all the arrangements. The President will go on television and speak to the nation as soon as he sets foot in the White House.'

'That's rather a long wait,' the Vice President said. 'Why can't you notify the media and reassure people now?'

'Because we don't know what's out there,' Christian Klee told her smoothly. 'And maybe it won't hurt the American public to worry about him a bit.'

In that moment, it seemed to Helen DuPray that she understood everything. She understood that Klee could have cut the whole thing off before it reached the culminating point. She felt an overwhelming contempt for the man and then, remembering the charges that he could have stopped the atom bomb explosion but didn't, she was convinced that that charge was also true.

BOOK VI

BOOK VII.

23

In November, Francis Xavier Kennedy was re-elected to the Presidency of the United States. It was a victory so over-whelming that it carried into office nearly all his handpicked candidates for the House and Senate. Finally the President controlled both houses of Congress.

In that time period before the Inauguration, from November to January, Francis Kennedy set his Administration to work drafting new laws for his captured Congress.

The release of Gresse and Tibbot created such a firestorm of public outrage that Francis Kennedy knew the time was right to rally support for his new laws. In this he was helped by the newspapers and TV who were weaving fantasies to the effect that Gresse and Tibbot were linked with Yabril and the attempted assassination of the President in one giant conspiracy. The *National Enquirer* had run a full front page headline.

Summoned, the Reverend Baxter Foxworth met with Odd-blood Gray at the latter's White House office.

'Otto,' he said, 'you're on the President's staff, you're one of the men closest to him. What's this I hear about the new criminal laws that are being drawn up. And what's this I hear about these concentration camps planned up in Alaska?'

Oddblood Gray said, 'They are not concentration camps. They are prison work camps being built for habitual offenders.'

The Reverend Foxworth laughed. 'Brother,' he said. 'The least you could do was have them built in a warm climate. Most of those criminals are going to be black. They'll freeze their asses off up there. And as time goes on, who knows, you and I might be with them.'

Oddblood Gray sighed. He said softly, 'You've got a point.'

That sobered the Reverend. He was all business now. He said in a flat serious voice, 'Otto, you can see it, can't you? Your fucking Kennedy will be the first American dictator. You're not that dumb. He's laying the groundwork.'

It was not a token meeting in the Oval Office where things were done for publicity purposes. It was lunch with the President, Eugene Dazzy and Oddblood Gray.

The lunch went well. Kennedy thanked the Reverend Foxworth for his help in the election and accepted the Reverend's list of candidates for the housing and social welfare department appointments. Then Reverend Foxworth, who had been extremely courteous and showing the deference due to the office of the President of the United States, said somewhat abruptly, 'I must say to you, Mr President, that I oppose the new laws you propose to control crime in this country.'

Francis Kennedy said curtly, 'Those laws are necessary.'

'And the work camps in Alaska?' the Reverend said.

Kennedy smiled at him. 'That opponents of mine are calling concentration camps?'

'That's right,' the Reverend said.

'The only people that will go to those camps are habitual offenders,' Kennedy said. His voice was quiet, explanatory. 'They will be work camps, there is a lot of work to be done in Alaska and they need population. But it will also be a whole educational system as well. The people who go there will not be in the work camps for life. They will be trained

438

as they work. If they behave well, they will be the Alaskan population of the future.'

Thinking, shit, at least they can't make us pick cotton in Alaska, the Reverend Baxter Foxworth said, 'Mr President, my people will oppose this with all the means we have available.'

Eugene Dazzy knew that this was one of the few times he was observing pure anger in Kennedy's handsome face. There was a long silence. Finally, it seemed that Kennedy had mastered his emotion. He said to the Reverend Foxworth, 'I want you to understand one thing very clearly. This is not a racial issue, this is a criminal justice issue.'

The Reverend was in no way intimidated. 'The majority who go to your Alaska work camps will be black.'

Oddblood Gray and Eugene Dazzy had never seen Kennedy so cold. He said to Foxworth, 'Then let them stop committing criminal acts.'

The Reverend was just as cold. 'Then let your bankers and your real estate guys and your big corporations stop using blacks for cheap labor.'

'I'll give you the reality,' Francis Kennedy said. 'Trust me or trust the Socrates Club.'

'We don't trust anybody,' the Reverend said.

Kennedy seemed not to have heard. 'It's very simple,' he said. 'Black criminals will be weeded out from the black people. Thank me for that. Black people are the chief victims, though, of course, that doesn't make much of a fuss. The primary thing is that black people must not be regarded as a permanent criminal class.'

'And what about the white criminal class?' the Reverend said. 'Do they go to Alaska?' He couldn't believe what he was hearing and from the President of the United States.

The President said softly, 'Yes, they will. Let me make it more simple, Reverend. The white people in this country are afraid of the black criminal class. When we get through, the great majority of middle-class blacks will be integrated with the white middle class.'

Oddblood Gray noted that for the first time, he was seeing his friend Foxworth so astonished he could not even use his rhetoric. So Oddblood said, 'Mr President, I think you should tell the Reverend the other side of the story.'

Francis Kennedy said, 'Crime is not going to run this country any more. More to the point, money is not going to run this country any more. You're worried about criminal blacks going to a work camp in Alaska? Why? The black communities will be better off. Let them go.'

'But the camps will be there,' the Reverend Foxworth said, 'for true revolutionaries. They will be there for anyone who doesn't want to live a middle-class life. They are a threat to individual freedom.'

Kennedy said, 'That is an argument, but it is no longer valid. We can't afford an excess of liberty any more. Take those two young Professors Tibbot and Gresse. They killed thousands of people and they get off. They could not even be convicted of the crime they really committed because of the technical violations of due process, and most of those dead people were black. Those two young men go free, because of our treasured due process of the law.' He paused for a moment. 'That's all going to change,' he said.

The Reverend turned to Oddblood Gray. He said, 'Otto, do you really go along with this?'

Oddblood Gray smiled back at him and said softly, 'When I don't, I'll resign.'

Kennedy said, 'In my personal life and political career, I have always supported your basic cause, Reverend. Isn't that true?'

'Yes, Mr President, but that doesn't mean you're always right,' the Reverend shot back. 'And you can't always control the administrative side down to the lowest level. Those Alaskan work camps will wind up being black concentration camps.'

Kennedy said, 'That's a possibility.' The Reverend was surprised by this answer. Otto Gray was not. He had known Kennedy for a long time, knew that he could see such dangers. And then Gray saw another look of Kennedy's, the one of absolute determination, an overpowering force of will that usually subdued everyone else in his presence.

'I've followed your career,' Kennedy said with a tiny smile. 'What you have done was a necessary prodding of our society. And its always a pleasure to see a man like you operate with a certain wit. And I never doubted your sincerity no matter how much you fucked around.' Odd-blood Gray was surprised by the obscenity. Kennedy went on. 'But these times are dangerous, wit will be less important. So I want you to listen to me very carefully.'

'I'm listening,' Reverend Foxworth said. His face was impassive.

Kennedy bowed his head and then lifted it. 'You must know,' he said, 'that many people of the United States hate the blacks. Out of fear. They love the athletes, they love the artists, they love the blacks who have achieved distinction in various different fields.'

'You astonish me,' the Reverend Foxworth said. He laughed.

Francis Kennedy looked at him speculatively. Then he went on. 'Then who do they hate? They certainly don't hate the truly middle-class black. Maybe hate is too strong a word, maybe dislike is a better word.'

'Either one,' the Reverend said.

'We agree so far then,' Kennedy said. 'So the object of this scorn, this dislike, this hate, is generated by the poor blacks and the criminal blacks.'

The Reverend interrupted him. 'It's not all that simple.'

'I know,' Kennedy said. 'But it will do for a start. Now I'm telling you this. My way is the way it's going to be and you might as well get on the train. Black or white, if you take to crime as a way of life, you go to Alaska.'

'I'll fight it,' Foxworth said.

'Let me give you the alternative scenario,' Kennedy said and his voice had an elegant courtesy. 'We go on as we are. You fight for affirmative actions on the part of government agencies, you fight against acts of racial injustice. As you pointed out, good laws are one thing, enforcing them is another. Do you think the people who run this country now will really want to give up a source of cheap labor? Do you think they really want your people to be a powerful voting influence? Do you think you'll get a better break from the Socrates Club than you will from me?'

The Reverend was looking at Kennedy intently. He took a long time before he answered. 'Mr President,' he said, 'what you're saying is that we sacrifice the next generation of blacks for what you see as a political strategy. I don't believe in that kind of thinking. That's not to say that we can't work together on other issues.'

President Kennedy said, 'Either you are with us or you are the enemy. Think it over carefully.'

The Reverend Foxworth, smiling, said, 'Are you going to talk the same way to the Socrates Club?'

For the first time Kennedy smiled back at him. 'Oh, no,' he said. 'They don't get the option.'

'If I go along,' Foxworth said, 'I want to make sure that white asses freeze with black asses.'

A Federal judge set Henry Tibbot and Adam Gresse free. In what he thought was the greatest day in his life, Whitney Cheever III appeared in court on behalf on his clients. They might go to jail or not, it didn't matter, he would be a winner. The media coverage was enormous and the Kennedy administration was playing into his hands.

The government did not contest that the arrest had been illegal. The government did not contest that there had been no warrants. Cheever exploited every legal loophole.

The fate of his clients was a minor issue, in fact, like all

442

sophisticated clients, they had confessed their guilt to him. But Cheever was outraged by the Atomic Secrecy Act itself. Its provisions were so sweeping that they constituted an abolition of the Bill of Rights itself.

Whitney Cheever was so eloquent he was one of TV's folk heroes for two days. And when the judge sentenced Gresse and Tibbot to three years of community service and freed them, Cheever was for one day the most famous man in America.

But the realization soon dawned on him that he had been suckered. Hate mail poured in by the hundreds of thousands. The two murderers of thousands of people had gone free due to the legal cunning of a left-wing lawyer notorious for his defense of revolutionaries opposed to the legal authority of the United States. The people of America were infuriated.

Cheever was an intelligent man and when the Reverend Foxworth sent him a letter that the black movement would no longer have anything to do with him, he knew he was finished. He believed he was, in his small way, a hero, and believed that in future histories, he would rate a small asterisk as a fighter for true freedom. But now the hatred coming at him through the mails, the telephones, and even in his public political meetings was overwhelming.

Gresse and Tibbot had been, for the time being, spirited out of the country by their relatives, were in hiding some-place in Europe and all the public fury was concentrated on Cheever. But what dismayed him most was coming to the realization that his victory had been engineered by the Kennedy government. And that it had one purpose. To arouse in the public a raging contempt for the due process of law. When he heard about the new reforms that Kennedy proposed for the legal system, the work camps in Alaska, the restrictions on due process, he knew that his battle had been lost with that one victory he had achieved by getting Gresse and Tibbot free. He then had a frightening thought. Was it possible that there would come a time when he would be in real danger? Was it possible that Francis Kennedy had it in him to become the first dictator of the United States of America? It might be a good idea to have a personal meeting with Attorney General Christian Klee.

President Francis Kennedy met with his staff in the Yellow Room. Also present by special invitation were Vice President Helen DuPray and Dr Zed Annaccone. Kennedy knew he had to be very careful, these were the people who knew him best, he must not let them know what he really wanted to accomplish. He said to them, 'Dr Annaccone has something to say that may astound you.'

Francis Kennedy listened abstractedly while Dr Annaccone announced that the PET Scan Verification Test had been perfected so that the ten per cent risk of cardiac arrest and complete memory loss had been reduced to one tenth of one per cent. He smiled faintly when Helen DuPray voiced her outrage at any free citizen being forced by law to take such a test. He had expected that of her. He smiled when Dr Annaccone showed his hurt feelings, too learned a man to be so thin-skinned.

He listened with less amusement when Oddblood Gray, Arthur Wix and Eugene Dazzy agreed with the Vice President. He had known that Christian Klee would not speak.

They were all watching him, waiting for him, trying to see which way he would go. He would have to convince them he was right. He began slowly. 'I know all the difficulties,' he said, 'but I am determined to make this test part of our legal system. Not totally, there is still some amount of danger, small as it is. Though Dr Annaccone has assured me that with further research even that will be reduced to zero. But this is a scientific test that will revolutionize our society. Never mind the difficulties, we will iron them out.'

Oddblood Gray said quietly, 'Even the Congress we own won't pass such a law.'

'We'll make them,' Kennedy said grimly. 'Other countries

444

will use it. Other intelligence agencies will use it. We have to.' He laughed and said to Dr Annaccone, 'I'll have to cut your budget. Your discoveries cause too much trouble, and put all the lawyers out of work. But with this test no innocent man will ever be found guilty.'

Very deliberately he rose and walked to the doors that looked out on to the Rose Garden. Then he said, 'I will show how much I believe in this. Our enemies constantly accuse me of being responsible for the atom bomb going off. They say that I could have stopped it. Euge, I want you to help Dr Annaccone set it up for me. I want to be the first to undergo the PET Verification Test. Immediately. Arrange for witnessing, the legal formalities.'

He smiled at Christian Klee. 'They will ask the question, "Are you in any way responsible for the explosion of the atom bomb?" And I will answer.' He paused for a moment and then said, 'I will take the test, and so will my Attorney General. Right, Chris?'

'Sure,' Christian Klee said, 'but you first.' Both knew that this was what Kennedy had been coming to all along.

At Walter Reed Hospital, the suite reserved for President Kennedy had a special conference room. In it were the President and his personal staff and a panel of three qualified physicians who would monitor and verify the results of the brain scan test. Now they listened to Dr Annaccone as he explained the procedure.

Dr Annaccone prepared his slides and turned on the projector. Then he began his lecture. He said, 'This test is, as some of you already know, an infallible lie detector test, the truth assessed by measuring the levels of activity from certain chemicals in the brain. This has been done by the refinement of positron emission tomography (PET) scans. The procedure was first shown to work in a limited way at Washington University School of Medicine in St Louis. Slides were made of human brains at work.'

A large slide showed on the huge white screen in front of them. Then another, and another. Brilliant colors appeared lighting up the different parts of the brain as patients read, listened or spoke. Or simply just thought about the meaning of a word. Dr Annaccone used blood and glucose to tag them with radioactive labels.

'In essence, under the PET scan,' Dr Annaccone said, 'the brain speaks in living color. A spot in back of the brain lights up during reading. In the middle of the brain against that background of dark blue, you can see an irregular white spot appear with a tiny blotch of pink and a seepage of blue. That appears during speech. In the front of the brain, a similar spot lights up during the thinking process. Over these images we have laid a magnetic resonance image of the brain's anatomy. The whole brain is now a magic lantern.'

Dr Annaccone looked around the room to see if everyone was following him. Then he went on. 'You see that spot in the middle of the brain changing? When a subject lies, there is an increase in the amount of blood flowing through the brain which then projects another image.'

Startlingly, in the center of the white spot there was now a circle of red within a larger yellow irregular field. 'The subject is lying . . .' Dr Annaccone said. 'When we test the President, that red spot within the yellow is what we must look for.' Dr Annaccone nodded to the President. 'Now we will proceed to the examining room,' he said.

Inside the lead-walled room, Francis Kennedy lay on the cold hard table. Behind him, a large long metal cylinder loomed. As Dr Annaccone strapped the plastic mask over Kennedy's forehead and across his chin, Francis Kennedy felt a momentary shiver of fear. He hated anything over his face. His arms were then tied down along his sides. Then Francis Kennedy felt Dr Annaccone slide the table into the cylinder. Inside the cylinder, it was narrower than he expected, blacker. Silent. Now Francis Kennedy was surrounded by a ring of radioactive detection crystals.

Kennedy heard the echo of Dr Annaccone's voice instructing him to look at the white cross directly in front of his eyes. The voice sounded hollow. 'You must keep your eyes on the cross,' the doctor repeated.

In a room five storeys below, in the basement of the hospital, a pneumatic tube held a syringe containing radioactive oxygen, a cyclotron of tagged water.

When the order came from the scanning room above, that tube flew, a lead rocket twisting through hidden tunnels behind the walls of the hospital until it reached its target.

Dr Annaccone opened the pneumatic tube and held the syringe in his hands. He walked over to the foot of the PET scanner and called in to Francis Kennedy. Again the voice was hollow, an echo, when Kennedy heard, 'The injection,' and then felt the doctor reach in to the dark and plunge the needle into his arm.

From the glass-enclosed room at the end of the scanner, the staff could see only the bottom of Kennedy's feet. When Dr Annaccone joined them again, he turned on the computer high on the wall above, so that they could all watch the workings of Kennedy's brain. They watched as the tracer circulated through Kennedy's blood, emitting positrons, particles of anti-matter which collided with electrons and produced explosions of gamma-ray energy.

They watched as the radioactive blood rushed to Kennedy's visual cortex creating streams of gamma rays immediately picked up by the ring of radioactive detectors. All the time Kennedy kept staring at the white cross as instructed.

Then, through the microphone piped directly into the scanner, Kennedy heard the question from Dr Annaccone, 'Did you in any way conspire to have the atom bomb explode in New York? Did you have any knowledge that could have prevented its explosion?'

Kennedy answered, 'No, I didn't.' And inside the black cylinder his words seemed to fall back like the wind on his face.

Dr Annaccone watched the computer screen above his head.

The computer showed the patterns form in the blue mass of the brain so elegantly formed in Kennedy's curving skull.

The staff watched apprehensively.

But no telltale yellow dot, no red circle appeared.

'He's telling the truth,' Dr Annaccone said, and he sounded exhilarated.

Christian Klee felt his knees buckling. He knew he could not pass such a test.

24

On the day after President Francis Kennedy passed his PET Scan Verification Test, Christian Klee went to visit the Oracle.

After dinner, they went to the library which was darker, more confidential. Christian was supplied with brandy and cigars, and the Oracle dozed in his padded wheelchair.

The Oracle said, 'Christian, I think you should get off your ass. Today it has been all over the TV that Kennedy passed that test, and he's innocent in the atom bomb scandal. He's sitting pretty. So when the hell am I going to have my birthday party?'

He was relentless, Christian thought. He could not tell the Oracle that everyone had forgotten about the birthday party.

'We have it all planned,' he told the Oracle. 'After the President's Inauguration next month, we'll have a great party in the Rose Garden of the White House. The Prime Minister of England will be there, his father was one of your best friends. You'll love it. Is this OK? The theme is that you are the symbol of America Past, the Grand Old Man of our country, the very incarnation of our virtues of thrift, hard work, and rise of the lowest to the highest, in short, that only in America could this happen. We get you one of those Stars and Stripes Uncle Sam hats.'

The Oracle gave his tiny cackle of heh, heh, heh's at this conceit. Christian smiled at him and emptied his brandy glass to keep up his own flow of good spirits.

'And what does your friend Kennedy get out of this?' the Oracle asked.

'Francis Kennedy will be presented as the spirit of the American future,' Christian said. 'All the people of America will have a stronger social contract, will be bound more tightly to each other. What you have planted, Kennedy nourishes to true greatness.'

The Oracle's eyes flashed in the darkness. 'Christian, how dare you bullshit me after all these years? Shove your symbolism up your ass. And what social contract? What kind of crap is that? Listen to me. You have those who govern and those who are governed. That's your social contract. The rest is negotiation.'

Christian laughed. He said, 'I'll speak to Dazzy and the Vice President. Kennedy will go along, he knows he owes you.'

'Old men have no debtors,' the Oracle said. 'Now, let's talk about you. You are in very deep shit, my boy.'

'Yes, I am,' Christian said. 'But I don't give a fuck.'

The Oracle said musingly, 'You're not even fifty years old and you don't give a fuck? That's really a very bad sign. Not giving a fuck is usually the symptom of the ignorant young. I'm a hundred, if I said I don't give a fuck, it's smart. When you're young and when you're old you don't have to give a fuck. But you, Christian, are at a very dangerous age not to give a fuck.' He was actually angry and leaned over to swipe the cigar out of Christian's hand.

At that moment Christian felt such an overwhelming affection for the old man that he was moved to tears. 'It's Francis,' he said. 'I think he's been conning me his whole life.'

'Ah,' the Oracle said. 'That lie detector test he passed. That brain scanning machine. What do they call it, the PET Scan Verification Test? The man who invented that title is a genius.'

'I don't understand how he passed it,' Christian Klee said.

The Oracle said with contempt that barely intonated because of his age, his signals, bodily and mental, fainter, but still unmistakable, 'So now our civilization has an infallible test, a scientific test mind you, for determining whether a man tells the truth. And they think they can solve the darkest riddles of innocence and guilt. What a laugh. Men and women deceive themselves continually. I'm a hundred years old and I still don't know whether my life was a truth or a lie. I really don't know.'

Christian had retrieved his cigar from the Oracle and now he lit it and that small circle of fire made the Oracle's face a mask in a museum.

'I let that atom bomb go off,' Christian said. 'I'm responsible for that. And when I take that PET Scan I will know the truth and so will the scanner. But I thought I understood Kennedy better than anybody. I could always read him. He wanted me *not* to interrogate Gresse and Tibbot. He wanted that explosion to happen. Then how the hell did he pass that test?'

'If the brain were that simple, we would be too simple to understand it,' the Oracle said. 'That was the wit of your Dr Annaccone and I suggest that is your answer. Kennedy's brain refused to acknowledge his guilt. Therefore, the computer in the scanner says he is innocent. You and I know better, for I believe what you say. But he will be forever innocent even in his own heart. Now let me ask you, you are scheduled to undergo the test next week, do you think that you can also trick the test? After all, it is a sin of omission.'

'No,' Christian said. 'Unlike Kennedy, I am forever guilty.'

'Cheer up,' the Oracle said. 'You only killed ten or was it twenty thousand people? Your only hope is to refuse to take the test.'

'I promised Francis,' Christian said. 'And the media will crucify me for refusing.'

'Then why the hell did you agree to take it?' the Oracle said.

'I thought Francis was bluffing,' Christian said. 'I thought

451

he couldn't afford to take the test and that he would back down. That's why I insisted he take it first.'

The Oracle showed his impatience by running the motor on his wheelchair. 'Climb up on the Statue of Liberty,' he said. 'Claim your civil rights and your human dignity. You'll get away with it. Nobody wants to see such infernal science become a legal instrument.'

'Sure,' Christian said. 'That's what I have to do. But Francis will know I'm guilty.'

The Oracle said, 'Christian, if that test asked you whether you were a villain, what would you answer, in all truthfulness?'

Christian laughed, genuinely laughed. 'I would answer that no, I wasn't a villain. And I'd pass. That's really funny.' Gratefully he pressed the Oracle's shoulder. 'I won't forget about your birthday party,' he said.

When Christian Klee told President Francis Kennedy and the assembled staff that he would not take the PET Scan Verification Test, they did not seem surprised. Klee cited his belief that such a test was a gross infringement of human rights. He promised that if a law were passed making the test legal but not mandatory he would volunteer again.

Christian Klee was reassured that his refusal to take the test was apparently received well. So much so that he was encouraged to ask Eugene Dazzy about the postponed birthday party for the Oracle.

'Shit,' Dazzy said. 'Francis never really liked the old guy. Maybe we should just forget it.'

'Bullshit,' Christian said. 'You and Kennedy don't like him because he's part of the Socrates Club. Christ, Eugene, how can you hold a grudge against a guy who is over a hundred years old?'

Dazzy smiled at him. 'So even a tough guy like you has a soft spot. When do you want this party?'

'Time is short,' Christian said dryly. 'He's a hundred.'

'OK,' Dazzy said. 'After the Inauguration.'

Just two days before his Inauguration President Francis Kennedy stunned the nation on his weekly television broadcast with three announcements.

First he announced he had conditionally pardoned Yabril. He explained that it had been vital to the nation to learn whether Yabril was linked to the atom bomb explosion and the attempt to assassinate him. He explained that by law neither Yabril nor Gresse and Tibbot could be forced to take the PET Verification Test. But that Yabril had agreed to take the test, on the urgings of the President, with the provision that if it proved he was not connected, he would be released after serving a five-year sentence in prison.

Yabril had passed the test. He was not linked to Gresse and Tibbot or to the assassination attempt.

Secondly, Francis Kennedy announced that after his Inauguration, he would do everything in his power to call a Constitutional Convention to amend the Constitution. Primarily to amend the sacred document. He cited the release of Gresse and Tibbot, after their great crime, as due to the faults in the Bill of Rights. He wanted the Constitution amended so that the important issues before the public would be decided not by the Congress or the President, but by the direct will of the people. That is, by referendum, a vote on the ballot.

Thirdly, on a minor note, he announced that to quiet the whole uproar about who was responsible for the explosion of the atom bomb, Attorney General Christian Klee would leave government service one month after the Inauguration. Kennedy reminded the audience that he himself had passed the PET Scan on that matter; and that he himself could vouch for Christian Klee's innocence, but that it was in the best interest of the country for Klee to resign. Now with these actions, the whole controversy would be resolved.

Kennedy promised that Gresse and Tibbot would be brought to justice. That once the Constitutional Convention revised the Bill of Rights, those criminals would be forced to take the PET Verification Scan.

Only the media controlled by the Socrates Club attacked this speech. It was pointed out that the President had used poor reasoning. That if Gresse and Tibbot had to be forced to take this test, why not Christian Klee? And then a more serious point was made. A Constitutional Convention had never once been called since the Constitution had been written. It would open up a Pandora's box. The media declared that one of the suggested amendments would be that a President could serve more than eight years in office.

It had not been easy for President Francis Kennedy to arrange these events and indeed to call a Constitutional Convention was a complicated task, but he had laid the groundwork and was sure of success. To persuade Yabril to take the brain test had been even more complicated. And to tell the man he loved most, Christian Klee, that he must resign as Attorney General, was the most painful. But it had been the struggle in his own mind that had been most difficult.

The Constitutional Convention he had planned meticulously. It would be necessary to consolidate his power, to give him the weapons he would need to make his dreams for America come true. That was settled.

He had planned with Christian that the case against Gresse and Tibbot would be weak and that they would be released. That made it ever harder to force Klee's resignation. But Kennedy knew that the critics would demand that the Attorney General take the brain test. With Klee out of the government, Kennedy knew he could keep it from being pursued.

It was the decision about Yabril that had given Kennedy the most trouble. It would be very tricky. First he had to convince Yabril to take the test voluntarily. Then he had to justify it to the American public. And then he had to struggle with himself about letting Yabril escape his punishment. Finally, he justified to himself the course of action he must take.

President Francis Kennedy summoned Theodore Tappey, the Central Intelligence Director, to a private meeting in the Yellow Oval Room. He excluded everyone, he wanted no witnesses, no recording.

He had to be careful with Theodore Tappey. The man had come up through the ranks, had been an operational chief, he was familiar with every strain of treachery. He had practiced long and hard in that business of betraying fellow human beings for the sake of his country. His patriotism was not in doubt. But there might be a line he would not cross.

Kennedy wasted no time on civilities. There was no window dressing of a leisurely tea. He spoke curtly to Tappey. 'Theo, we have a big problem that only you and I understand. And only you and I can solve.'

'I'll do my best, Mr President,' Tappey said. And Kennedy saw the feral look in his eyes. He scented blood.

'Everything we say here has the highest security classification, it has executive privilege,' Kennedy said. 'You are not to repeat this to anyone, not even members of my staff.' That was when Tappey knew the matter was extremely sensitive. Kennedy cut his staff in on everything.

'It's Yabril,' Kennedy said. 'I'm sure,' he smiled, 'I'm positive, you've thought this all out. Yabril will go on trial. That will rake up all the resentments against America. He will get convicted and sentenced to life imprisonment. But somewhere down the line there will be a terrorist action that takes important hostages. One demand will be to release Yabril. By that time, I won't be President and so Yabril will go free. Still a dangerous man.'

Kennedy had caught the scepticism in Tappey. The sign was no sign, Tappey was too experienced in deception. His face simply lost all expression, all animation in the eyes, the contour of the lips. He had made himself a blank so as not to be read.

But now Tappey smiled. 'You must have read the internal memos my counter Intelligence Chief has been giving me. That's exactly what he says.'

'So how do we prevent all this?' Kennedy asked. But it was a rhetorical question and Tappey did not answer. 'We still have a big question that hangs like a cloud over this administration. Is Yabril linked with Gresse and Tibbot? And is that link still an atomic danger? I'll be frank with you. We know they are not linked but we must make believers out of everyone.'

'You've lost me, Mr President,' Tappey said.

Kennedy decided the time had come. 'I will persuade Yabril to take the test. He knows once he goes to trial he's sure to be convicted. I'll tell him this, "Take the PET Scan. If the test proves you have no link to Gresse and Tibbot, or the assassination attempt, you will be sentenced to only five years in prison and then you'll be released." His lawyers will be overjoyed with such a deal. And here is how Yabril will think: "I know I can pass the test so why not take it? Only five years in prison and during that five years my fellow terrorists may get me released." He'll go for it.'

For the very first time in their relationship, Kennedy saw Tappey looking at him with the shrewd appraising eye of an opponent. He knew that Tappey thought things out far ahead but not necessarily in the same direction, as how could he? He let Tappey interrupt him.

Tappey said, and his words were not so much a question as a probing, 'So Yabril goes free after five years? That's not it. Is Christian in on this? He used to be very good when we were in Operations together. Does he do something?'

Francis Kennedy sighed, he was a little disappointed. He

had hoped Tappey would help him, would see a little further. This was difficult for him. And this was not even the hardest part. He said slowly, 'Christian doesn't do anything. Christian is going to resign. You and I have to do it because we are the only ones who see this problem clearly. Now listen very carefully. It must be proven that there is no link between those two boys and Yabril. The nation must know that. It needs the relief. Also, in a funny way it takes the pressure off Christian. OK. That can only happen if Yabril takes the test and proves he has no part in it. So we do that. But the problem remains. When Yabril is released he is still dangerous. That we can't allow'.

Now Tappey was on target. Tappey was with him. Tappey understood. Tappey was now looking at Kennedy as a servant might look at a master who was about to ask him a service which would bind them together for ever.

'I guess I don't get anything in writing,' Tappey said.

'No,' Kennedy said. 'I am going to give you specific instructions right now.'

'Be very specific,' Theodore Tappey said, 'if you will, Mr President.'

Kennedy smiled at the coolness of the response. 'Dr Annaccone would never do it,' he said. 'A year ago I myself would never have dreamed of doing it.'

'I understand, Mr President,' Tappey said.

Kennedy knew there could be no further hesitation. 'After Yabril agrees to take the test, I switch him to your CIA medical section. Your medical team does the scan. They give the test.' He could see the look in Tappey's eyes, the waver of doubt, not of moral outrage, but doubt of feasibility.

'We're not talking murder here,' Kennedy said impatiently. 'I'm not that stupid or that immoral. And if I wanted that done, I'd be talking to Christian.'

Tappey was waiting.

Kennedy knew he had to say the fatal words. 'I swear that I ask this for the protection of our country. When Yabril is

457

released after five years, he must no longer be a danger. I want your medical team to go to the extreme limit of the test. According to Dr Annaccone, it was under that protocol that the side effects occurred. And complete memory was erased. A man without memory, without beliefs and convictions, is harmless. He will live a peaceful life.'

Kennedy recognized the look in Tappey's eyes, it was the look of one predator who has discovered another strange species its equal in ferocity.

'Can you assemble a team that will do that?' Kennedy asked.

'When I explain the situation to them,' Tappey said. 'They would never have been recruited if they were not devoted to their country.' He paused for a moment and then said thoughtfully, 'And after five years in prison, we'll just say Yabril's mind deteriorated. Maybe we'll even give him an early release.'

'Of course,' Kennedy said.

In the dark hours of that night, Christian Klee escorted Yabril to Francis Kennedy's quarters. Again the meeting was short and Kennedy was all business. There was no tea, there were no civilities. Kennedy began immediately, he presented his proposal.

Yabril was silent. He looked wary.

Kennedy said, 'I see you have some doubts.'

Yabril shrugged and said, 'I find your offer too generous.'

Kennedy summoned all his strength to do what he had to do. He rememberd Yabril charming his daughter Theresa before putting a gun to her neck. Such charm would not work with Yabril. He could only persuade this man by convincing him of his own strict morality.

'I am doing this to erase fear from the mind of my country,' Kennedy said. 'That is my greatest concern. My pleasure would be to have you remain in prison for ever. So I make this offer out of my sense of duty.'

'Then why are you taking such pains to convince me?' Yabril asked.

'It's not in my nature to perform my duty as a matter of form,' Kennedy said and he could see that Yabril believed in this, believed that he was a moral man and could be trusted within that morality. Again he summoned the image of Theresa and her belief in Yabril's kindness. Then he said to Yabril, 'You were outraged at the suggestion that your people engineered the explosion of an atom bomb. Here is the chance to clear your name and the name of your comrades. Why not take it? Do you fear you will not pass the test? That is always a possibility, it occurs to me now though I don't really believe it.'

Yabril looked directly into Kennedy's eyes. 'I don't believe that any man can forgive what I have done to you,' he said.

Kennedy sighed. 'I don't forgive you. But I understand your actions. I understand you feel you did what you did to help our world. As I do what I do now. And it is within my powers. We are different men, I cannot do what you do, and you, I mean you no disrespect, cannot do what I am doing now. To let you go free.'

Almost with sorrow, he saw that he had convinced Yabril. He continued his persuasion, he used all his wit, all his charm, his appearance of integrity. He projected all the images of what he had once been, of what Yabril had known him to be, before he forfeited the whole of himself to convince Yabril. He knew he was finally successful when he saw the smile on Yabril's face was one of pity and contempt. He knew then that he had won Yabril's trust.

Four days later, after Yabril's PET medical interrogation, after he had been transferred back to FBI custody, he received two visitors. They were Francis Kennedy and Christian Klee.

Yabril was completely unrestrained, unshackled.

The three men spent a quiet hour drinking tea and eating

little sandwiches. Kennedy studied Yabril. The man's face seemed to have changed. It was a sensitive face, the eyes were slightly melancholy but good-humored. He spoke little but studied Kennedy and Klee as though trying to solve some mystery.

He seemed content. He seemed to know who he was. And he seemed to radiate such purity of soul that Kennedy could not bear to look at him and finally took his leave.

The decision about Christian Klee was even more painful to Francis Kennedy. It had been an unexpected surprise for Christian. Kennedy asked him into the Yellow Room for a private meeting, not even Eugene Dazzy was present.

But Francis Kennedy opened the meeting quietly by saying, 'Christian, I've been closer to you than anybody outside my family. I think we know each other better than anyone else knows us. So you will understand that I have to ask for your resignation to be effective after the Inauguration, at a time when I decide to accept it.'

Klee looked at that handsome face with its gentle smile. He could not believe that Kennedy was firing him without any explanation. He said quietly, 'I know I've cut a few corners here and there. But my ultimate aim was always to keep you from harm.'

'And you have done that job very well,' Francis Kennedy said. 'I would never have run for President if you hadn't made that promise to keep me safe. But I'm not afraid of that any more. I don't know why. I remember how scared I was in those old days and now I don't have that feeling.'

'Then why am I being fired?' Christian asked. He was feeling a little nauseous, he had never expected this blow, not from his friend, not from the man he admired more than anyone else in the world.

Kennedy smiled sadly. 'That atom bomb thing. I understand you did it for me, but I can't live with your doing it.'

Christian Klee said, 'You wanted me to do that.'

It was Kennedy's turn to be surprised. He said, 'Chris, you've known me almost thirty years. When have I been so immoral? You've always told me that you admired me and valued me because of my integrity. How could you think I would want you to do such a terrible thing?'

'Will we still be buddies?' Christian Klee asked jokingly.

'Of course,' Francis Kennedy said. And Christian knew that he would never be friends with Kennedy again.

The Socrates Club was summoned by the Oracle, and as rich and powerful as they were, they dared not refuse. Also their invitations indicated that the Oracle himself might solve their problem with Francis Kennedy.

The Oracle received them in his huge living room and despite his age was very lively. His motions seemed to be quicker, his motorized wheelchair scooted among them, he shook hands firmly, his eyes seemed to sparkle. He was impressive in his animation. But this animation, so unseemly in so old a man, was pleasing only because he was the richest man among them. The Oracle had percentages of all their empires.

George Greenwell was envious of the old man, to be so spry at a hundred years of age. Greenwell at eighty, in good health, wondered if he too could attain such blessed longevity. There was still plenty of life to enjoy, Greenwell thought, but he had to be careful.

The Oracle used the long table in his dining room for the conference. Servants were banished from the room but there was a stocked bar available and platters of English-tea sandwiches.

The Oracle addressed the meeting from the head of the table. But first he greeted each man by name. To George Greenwell he said with what was meant to be a humorous cackle, as one ancient to another, 'Well we're both still here.'

To Bert Audick, he said, 'You're out of arrest again?

461

Never mind, at the height of my career they indicted me five times and I never spent a day in jail.'

With Louis Inch, Martin Mutford, and Lawrence Salentine he merely said their names. Then he spoke to all of them. He spoke haltingly, as if the synapses of his brain, the deterioration of its neurotransmitters, caused a static in his vocalization, but his message was clear. 'Gentlemen,' he said, 'I hereby resign from the Socrates Club. And it is my duty to advise you, I will sell all of my holdings in all of your companies. We can make a pretty penny from that.' He gave one of his heh, heh, heh laughs. 'But most important of all I want to warn you, from all my long experience, that you must protect yourselves. Kennedy will destroy us all.'

In two days Lawrence Salentine had an appointment with President Francis Kennedy. The meeting was short and to the point. Kennedy informed him that no deal could be made for the others, that the whole structure of American society was to be changed. But Kennedy said that a deal could be made for Salentine and his people who owned the majority of media, newspapers, magazines, radio and TV in America. He needed their help to present his programs properly.

Salentine pointed out that the media could not really be controlled to an extreme degree. There were writers who followed their own ideas, there were TV newsmen who prided themselves on their independence in presenting the news. Many of these would criticize the legal reforms and amendments of the Bill of Rights that the President had on the drawing boards and were no secret. And that despite the power of the people who owned the media outlets, these independent working media people could not be controlled.

Kennedy assured him that he understood this. What he wanted was the overall support of the owners of the media.

Salentine finally agreed to the deal. In the spirit of free American enterprise, the others would have to look after themselves.

25

Christian Klee started making arrangements to leave government service. One of the most important things was to erase any traces of his circumventing the law in his protection of the President. He had to erase all the illegal computer surveillances of the members of the Socrates Club.

Sitting at his massive desk in the Attorney General's office, Christian Klee used his personal computer to erase incriminating files. Finally, he called up the file on David Jatney. He had been right on this guy, Klee thought, this guy was the joker in the deck. That darkly handsome face had the lopsided look of a mind unbalanced. Jatney's eyes were bright with the scattered electricity of a neural system at war with itself. And the latest information showed that he was on his way to Washington. Klee felt the thrill of a hunter closing in. This guy could be trouble. Then he remembered the Oracle's advice. He thought about it for a long time. And then he thought, let fate decide.

He pressed the delete key of the computer and David Jatney disappeared without trace from all government files. Whatever happened, he, Christian Klee, could not be blamed.

Just two weeks before President Francis Kennedy's Inauguration, David Jatney had become restless. He wanted to escape the eternal sunshine of California, the rich friendly voices everywhere, the moonlit balmy beaches. He felt himself drowning in the brown, syrupy air of its society, and

463

yet he did not want to go back home to Utah and be the daily witness to his father and mother's happiness.

Irene had moved in with him. She wanted to save on rent money, to go on a trip to India and study with a guru there. A group of her friends were pooling their resources to charter a plane and she wanted to join them with her little son, Campbell.

David Jatney was astonished when she told him her plans. She did not ask him if she could move in with him, she merely asserted her right to do so. That right was based on the fact that they now saw each other three times a week for a movie and to have sex. She had put it to him as one buddy to another, as if he were one of her California friends who routinely moved in with each other for periods of a week or more. It was done not as a cunning preliminary to marriage but as a casual act of comradeship. She had no sense of imposing, that his life would be disrupted with a strange woman and strange child made part of the daily fabric of his life.

Irene struck him as extraordinarily single-minded, in every facet of her life. She was politically to the left, she was untiring in her work for the Santa Monica Tenant League, she was immersed in the Eastern religions, passionate on making the trip to India and studying under her guru. With sex she was also direct and imperious, there was no foreplay, it had to be done and gotten over with and after the act she would pick up a book of Indian philosophy and begin to read.

What horrified David Jatney most of all was that she planned to bring her little boy with her to India. Irene was a woman who had absolute confidence that she could make her way in any world; certain that the fates would be good to her, that no calamity could befall her. David Jatney had visions of the little boy sleeping in the streets of Calcutta with the thousands of the diseased poor of that city. In a moment of anger he once told her he could not understand

464

anyone believing in a religion that spawned the hundreds of millions who were the most desperately poverty-stricken in the world. She had answered that what happened in this world was unimportant since what happened in the next life would be so much more interesting and so much more rewarding. David Jatney didn't see the logic of that. Where was the logic? If you were reincarnated, why wouldn't you be reincarnated in exactly the same miserable life that you had left?

Jatney was fascinated by Irene and how she treated her son. She often carried little Campbell to her political meetings because she could not always get her mother to babysit and was too proud to ask too often. At these political and spiritual meetings she put Campbell in a little sleeping bag at her feet. She took him with her sometimes even to work, when the special kindergarten he attended was closed for some reason.

There was no question that she was a devoted mother. But to David Jatney her attitude towards motherhood was bewildering. She did not have the usual concern to protect her child or worry about the psychological influences that could harm him. She treated him as one would treat a beloved pet, a dog or a cat. She seemed to care nothing for what the child thought or felt. She was determined that being the mother of a child would not limit her life in any way, that she would not make motherhood a bondage, that she would maintain her freedom. David thought she was a little crazy.

But she was a pretty girl, and when she concentrated on sex, she could be compellingly ardent. David enjoyed being with her. She was competent in the everyday details of her life and was really no trouble. And so he let her move in.

Two consequences were completely unforeseen by him. He became impotent. And he became fond of the little boy, Campbell.

He prepared for their moving in by buying a huge trunk

465

to lock up his guns, the cleaning materials and the ammo. He didn't want a four-year-old kid accidentally getting his hands on weapons. And by now, somehow, David Jatney had enough guns to deck out a superhero bandit; two rifles, a machine pistol and a collection of handguns. One, a very small twenty-two caliber handgun, he carried in his jacket pocket in a little leather case that was more like a glove. At night he usually put it beneath his bed. When Irene and Campbell moved in, he locked the .22 in the trunk with the other guns. He put a good padlock on the trunk. Even if the little kid found it open, there was no way he could figure out how to load it. Irene was another story. Not that he didn't trust her, but she was a little weird, and weirdness and guns didn't mix.

On the day they moved in, Jatney bought a few toys for Campbell so he wouldn't be too disorientated. That first night, when Irene was ready to go to bed, she arranged pillows and a blanket on the sofa for the little boy, undressed him in the bathroom and put him into pajamas. Jatney saw the little boy looking at him. There was in that look an old wariness, a glint of fear and very faintly what seemed to be a habitual bewilderment. In a flash Jatney translated that look to himself. As a little boy he knew his father and mother would desert him to make love in their room.

He said to Irene, 'Listen, I'll sleep on the sofa and the kid can sleep with you.'

'That's silly,' Irene said. 'He doesn't mind, do you Campbell?'

The boy shook his head. He rarely spoke.

Irene said proudly, 'He's a brave boy, aren't you Campbell?'

At that moment, David Jatney felt a moment of pure hatred for her. He repressed it and said, 'I have to do some writing and I'll be up late. I think he should sleep with you the first few nights.'

'If you have to work, OK,' Irene said cheerfully.

She held out her hand to Campbell and the little boy jumped off the sofa and ran into her arms. He hid his head in her breast. She said to him, 'Aren't you going to say goodnight to your Uncle Jat?' And she smiled brilliantly at David Jatney, a smile that made her beautiful. And he understood it was her own little joke, an honest joke, a way of telling him that this had been the mode of her address and introduction for her child when she lived with other lovers, delicate, fearful moments in her life, and that she was grateful to him for his thoughtfulness, her faith in the universe sustained.

The boy kept his head buried in her breasts and David Jatney patted him gently and said, 'Good night, Campbell.' The boy looked up and stared into Jatney's eyes. It was the peculiar questioning look of small children, the regard of an object that is absolutely unknown to their universe.

David Jatney was stricken by that look. As if he could be a source of danger. He saw that the boy had an unusually elegant face for one so young. A broad forehead, luminous gray eyes, a firm, almost stern mouth.

Campbell smiled at Jatney and the effect was miraculous. His whole face beamed with trust. He reached out a hand and touched Jatney's face. And then Irene took him with her into the bedroom.

A few minutes later she came out again and gave him a kiss. 'Thanks for being so thoughtful,' she said. 'We can have a quick screw before I go back in.' She made no seductive movement when she said this. It was simply a friendly offer.

David Jatney thought of the little boy behind the bedroom door waiting for his mother. 'No,' he said.

'OK,' she said cheerfully and went back into the bedroom.

For the next few weeks, Irene was furiously busy. She had taken an additional job for very little pay and long hours at night, to help in the re-election campaign, she was an ardent partisan of Francis Kennedy. She would talk about the social programs he favored, his fight against the rich in America, his struggle to reform the legal system. David thought she was in love with Kennedy's physical appearance, the magic of his voice. He believed that she worked at campaign headquarters because of infatuation rather than political belief.

Three days after she moved in, he dropped by campaign headquarters in Santa Monica and found her working on a computer with little Campbell at her feet. The boy was in a sleeping bag but was wide awake. Jatney could see his open eyes.

'I'll take him home and put him to bed,' David Jatney said.

'He's OK,' Irene said. 'I don't want to take advantage of you.'

Jatney pulled Campbell out of the sleeping bag, the boy was fully clothed except for his shoes. Jatney took him by the hand and he felt warm, soft skin, and for a moment he was happy.

'I'll take him for a pizza and ice cream first, is that OK?' Jatney said to Irene.

She was busy with her computer. 'Don't spoil him,' she said. 'When you're gone he gets health yogurt out of the fridge.' She took a moment to smile at him and then gave Campbell a kiss.

'Should I wait up for you?' he asked.

'What for?' she said quickly. Then added, 'I'll be late.' He went out, leading the little boy by the hand. He drove to Montana Avenue and stopped at a little Italian restaurant that made pizza on the side. He watched Campbell eat. One slice and he mangled that more than he ate it. But he was interested in eating and that made David Jatney happy. The kid really polished off the ice cream and when they left Jatney had the rest of the pizza in a doggie box.

In the apartment he put the pizza in the fridge and noted that the box of yogurt was encrusted with ice. He put

Campbell to bed, letting him wash and change into his pajamas by himself. He made his bed on the sofa, put on the TV very low and watched.

There was a lot of political talk on the air and interviews on the news programs. Francis Kennedy seemed to descend out of all the galaxies of cable. And Jatney had to admit that the man was overpowering on TV. Jatney dreamed of being a victorious hero like Kennedy. How the people of America loved him. What power he had. You could see the Secret Service men with their stone faces hovering in the background. How safe he was, how rich he was, how loved he was. Often David Jatney dreamed of being Francis Kennedy. How Rosemary would be in love with him. And he thought about Hock and Gibson Grange. And they would all be eating in the White House and they would all talk to him and Rosemary would talk to him in her excited way, touching his knee, telling him her innermost feelings.

He thought about Irene and what he felt about her. And he realized he was more bewildered than entranced. It seemed to him that with all her openness she was really completely closed to him. He could never really love her. He thought of Campbell, who had been named after the writer Joseph Campbell, famous for his books about myths, the boy so open and guileless with such an elegant innocence of countenance.

David Jatney did not have that adult desire to charm little children. But he felt it a comfort to the little boy to take him for drives through the Malibu canyons, both silent in the car, Campbell sometimes pointing out a coyote slinking away, observing and pondering, as children do. It was better than having Irene with him who talked so much he could barely resist putting his hands around her throat. He enjoyed stopping in a little café to feed the child. It was so simple. You put a hamburger in front of him with French fries and a glass of malted milk and he ate what he wanted and mashed the rest.

And sometimes David Jatney would take Campbell by the hand to walk along the public beaches of Malibu, up to the wire fence that walled off the Malibu Colony of the rich and powerful from the rest of the population, and they would peer through at the people who were loved by the gods. Where Rosemary Belair lived. He always looked hard to see if she was on the beach and once he thought he saw her far away.

After a few days, Campbell started calling him Uncle Jat and always put a little hand in his. Jatney accepted. He loved the innocent touches of affection the boy gave him that Irene never did. And it was during this two weeks that this extension of feeling to another human being sustained him.

David Jatney became impotent with Irene. It now became a permanent arrangement that he would sleep on the sofa and Campbell and Irene would sleep in the bedroom. From her constant chatter on every subject under the sun, she made clear that his impotence was a bourgeois hang-up because the little boy was living with them, she was in no way to blame. He thought that might be true, but he also thought that her lack of tenderness to him might have something to do with it. He would have left her, but he was worried about Campbell, he would miss Campbell.

And then he lost his job at the studio. He would have been in a jam if it had not been for Hock, his 'Uncle' Hock. When he was fired there was a message for him to come by Hock's office and because he thought that Campbell would enjoy visiting a movie studio, he brought the child. The boy was bewildered and delighted by the pictures shooting on the lot, the cameras, the shouted orders, the actors and actresses playing scenes, but Jatney saw that his sense of reality was distorted, that he could not tell apart the reality of the people on the sets acting, the everyday encounters of the people on the lot or the relationships of the people he knew from watching television. Finally Jatney held his hand and led him to Hock's office.

When Hock greeted him, David Jatney felt his overwhelming love for the man, Hock was so warm. Hock sent one of his secretaries immediately to the commissary to get ice cream for the little boy and then showed Campbell some props on his desk that would be used in the movie he was currently producing.

Campbell was enchanted by all this, and Jatney felt a twinge of jealousy that Hock was so charmed by the child. But then he could see it was Hock's way of clearing away an obstacle in their meeting. With Campbell busy playing with the props, Hock shook Jatney's hand and said, 'I'm sorry you got fired. They are cutting down the story-reading department and the others had seniority. But stay in touch, I'll get something for you.'

'I'll be OK,' David Jatney said.

Hock was studying him closely. 'You look awfully thin, David. Maybe you should go back home and visit a while. That good Utah air, that relaxing Mormon life. Is this kid your girlfriend's?'

'Yeah,' Jatney said. 'She's not exactly my girl, she's my friend. We live together but she's trying to save money on rent so she can make a trip to India.'

Hock frowned for a moment and started to say something. It was the first time he had ever seen a frown on Hock's face.

'If you financed every California girl who wanted to go to India you'd be broke,' Hock said, but cheerfully. 'And they all seem to have kids.'

He sat down at his desk, took a huge checkbook out of his drawer and wrote on it. He ripped a piece out of the book, and handed it to Jatney. 'This is for all the birthday presents and graduation presents I never had the time to send you.' He smiled at Jatney. Jatney looked at the check. He was astonished to see it was for five thousand dollars.

'Ah, c'mon, Hock, I can't take this,' he said. He felt tears coming into this eyes, tears of gratitude, humiliation and hatred.

'Sure you can,' Hock said. 'Listen, I want you to get some rest and have a good time. Maybe give this girl her air fare to India so she can get what she wants and you'll be free to do what you want. The trouble with being friends with a girl is that you get all the troubles of a lover and none of the advantages of a friend. But that's quite a little boy she has. I might have something for him some time if I ever have the balls to make a kid picture.'

Jatney pocketed the check. He understood everything that Hock had said. 'Yeah, he's a nice-looking kid.'

'It's more than that,' Hock said. 'Look, he has that elegant face, just made for tragedy. You look at him and you feel like crying.'

And Jatney thought how smart his friend Hock was for that was just what he felt. Elegant was just right and yet so odd to describe Campbell's face. Irene was an elemental force, like God she had constructed a future tragedy.

Hock hugged him and said, 'David, stay in touch. I mean it. Keep yourself together, times always get better when you're young.' He gave Campbell one of the props, a beautiful miniature futuristic airplane, and Campbell hugged it to him and said, 'Uncle Jat, can I keep it?' And Jatney saw a smile on Hock's face.

'Say hello to Rosemary for me,' David Jatney said. He had been trying to say this all through the meeting.

Hock gave him a startled look. 'I will,' he said. 'We've been invited to Kennedy's Inauguration in January, me and Gibson and Rosemary. I'll tell her then.'

And suddenly David Jatney felt he had been flung off a spinning world. Here were people he knew – he had had dinner with them, he had slept with Rosemary, no he had fucked her – and they were going to ascend the highest thrones of power without him. He took Campbell by the hand, the silken skin reassuring him.

472

'Thanks for everything, Hock,' he said. 'I'll keep in close touch. And maybe I will go back to Utah for a few weeks. For Christmas.'

'That's great,' Hock said warmly. 'You should call them more often. Kids don't know how much their mother and father miss them.'

And as Hock ushered them out of his office with repeated reassuring taps on Jatney's shoulder, Jatney thought with a sudden fury, what the hell does he know? He never had any kids.

Now lying on the sofa, waiting for Irene to come home, dawn showing its smoky light through the living room window, Jatney thought of Rosemary Belair. How she had turned to him in bed and lost herself in his body. He remembered the smell of her perfume, the curious heaviness, perhaps caused by the sleeping pills traumatizing the muscles in her flesh. He thought of her in the morning in her jogging clothes, her assurance and her assumption of power, how she had dismissed him. He lived over that moment when she offered to give him cash to tip the limo driver and how he had refused to take the money. But why had he insulted her, why had he said she knew better than him how much was needed, implying that she too had been sent home in such a fashion and in such a circumstance?

He found himself falling asleep in little short gaps of time, listening for Campbell, listening for Irene. He thought of his parents back in Utah, he knew they forgot about him, secure in their own happiness, their hypocritical angel pants fluttering outside as they joyfully and unceasingly fornicated in their bare skins. If he called them they would have to part.

David Jatney dreamed of how he would meet Rosemary Belair. How he would tell her he loved her. Listen, he would say, think if you had cancer. I would take your cancer from you into my own body. Listen, he would say, if some great star fell from the sky I would cover your body. Listen, he would say, if someone tried to kill you I would stop the blade with my heart, the bullet with my body. Listen, he would say, if I had one drop from the fountain of youth that would keep me young for ever and you were growing old, I would give you that drop so that you would never grow old.

And he perhaps understood that his memory of Rosemary Belair was haloed by her power. That he was praying to a God to make him something more than a common piece of clay. That he begged for power, unlimited riches, for beauty, for any and all the achievements so that his fellow man would mark his presence on this earth, and so he would not drown silently in the vast ocean that passed for man.

When he showed Hock's check to Irene, it was to impress her, to prove to her that someone cared enough about him to give him such a vast amount of money as a casual gift. She was not impressed, in her experience it was a commonplace that friends shared with each other and she even said that a man of Hock's vast wealth could have easily given away a bigger amount. When David Jatney offered to give her half the amount of the check so that she could go to India immediately, she refused. 'I always use my own money, I work for a living,' she said. 'If I took money from you, you would feel you have rights over me. Besides, you really want to do it for Campbell, not me.'

He was astounded by her refusal and her statement of his interest in Campbell. He had simply wanted to be rid of both of them. He wanted to be alone again to live with his dreams of the future.

Then she asked him what he would do if she took half the money and went to India, what would he do with his half. He noticed she did not suggest he go to India with her. He also noted that she had said 'your half of the money', so that in her mind she was accepting his offer.

Then he made the mistake of telling her what he would do with his twenty-five hundred.

'I want to see the country and I want to see Kennedy's

474

Inauguration,' he said. 'I thought it might be fun, something different. You know, take my car and drive through the whole country. See the whole United States. I even want to see the snow and ice and feel real cold.'

Irene seemed lost in thought for a moment. Then she went striding briskly through the apartment as if counting her possessions in it. 'That's a great idea,' she said. 'I want to see Kennedy too. I want to see him in person or I'll never really be able to know his karma. I'll put in for my vacation, they owe me tons of days. And it will be good for Campbell to see the country, all the different states. We'll take my van and save on motel bills.'

Irene owned a small van which she had fitted out with shelves to hold books and a small bunk for Campbell. The van was invaluable to her because even when Campbell was a little infant she had taken trips up and down the state of California to attend meetings and seminars on Eastern religions.

David Jatney felt trapped as they started off on their trip. Irene was driving, she liked to drive. Campbell was between them, one little hand in David Jatney's hand. Jatney had deposited half the check in Irene's bank account for her trip to India and now his twenty-five hundred would have to be used for three of them instead of only one. The only thing that comforted him was the .22 caliber handgun nestling in its leather glove, the glove in his jacket pocket. The East of America had too many robbers and muggers and he had Irene and Campbell to protect.

To Jatney's surprise they had a wonderful time the first four days of leisurely driving. Campbell and Irene slept in the van and he slept outside in the open fields until they hit cold weather in Arkansas; they had swung south to avoid the cold as long as possible. Then for a couple of nights they used a motel room, any motel on the route. It was in Kentucky that they first ran into trouble and in a way that surprised Jatney.

475

The weather had turned cold and they decided to go into a motel for the night. The next morning they drove into town for breakfast in a café newspaper store.

The counterman was about Jatney's age and very alert. In her egalitarian California way, Irene struck up a conversation with him. She did so because she was impressed by his quickness and efficiency. She often said it was such a pleasure to watch someone who was truly expert at the work they did, no matter how menial. She said this was a sign of good karma. Jatney never really understood the word karma.

But the counterman did. He too was a follower of the Eastern religions and he and Irene got into a long and involved discussion. Campbell became restless so Jatney paid the bill and took him outside to wait. It was a good fifteen minutes before Irene came out.

'He's a really sweet guy,' Irene said. 'His name is Christopher but he calls himself Krish.'

Jatney was annoyed by the wait but said nothing. On the walk back to the motel Irene said, 'I think we should stay here for a day. Campbell needs a rest. And it looks like a nice town to shop for Christmas presents. We might not have time to shop in Washington.'

'OK,' Jatney said. That had been the peculiar thing about their trip so far, how all the villages had been decorated for Christmas, colored lights across the main streets. A chain across America.

They spent the rest of the morning and afternoon shopping, though Irene bought very little. They had a very early supper in a Chinese restaurant. The plan was to go to bed early so that they could travel east before dark.

But they had only been in their motel room for a few hours, when Irene, who had been too restless to play checkers with Campbell, suddenly said she was going to take a little drive through town and maybe pick up a bite to eat. She left and David Jatney played checkers with the little boy

476

who beat him in every game. The boy was an amazing checker player, Irene had taught him when he was only two years old. At one point Campbell raised his elegant head with the broad brow and said, 'Uncle Jat, don't you like to play checkers?'

It was nearly midnight before Irene returned. The motel was on a little high ground and Jatney and the boy Campbell were looking out the window when the familiar van pulled into the parking lot, followed by another car.

Jatney was surprised to see Irene get out of the passenger side, since she always insisted on driving. From the driver's side the young counterman called Krish emerged and gave her the car keys. She gave a sisterly kiss in return. Two young men got out of the other car and she gave them sisterly little pecks. Irene started walking toward the motel entrance and the three young men put their arms around each other and serenaded her. 'Goodnight, Irene,' they sang, 'Goodnight, Irene.' When Irene entered the motel room and heard them still singing, she gave David Jatney a brilliant smile.

'They were so interesting to talk to I just forgot the time,' Irene said, and she went to the window to wave to them.

'I guess I'll have to go and tell them to stop,' David Jatney said. Through his mind ran flashes of him firing the handgun in his pocket. He could see the bullets flying through the night into their brains. 'Those guys are much less interesting when they sing.'

'Oh, you couldn't stop them,' Irene said. She picked up Campbell. Holding him in her arms she bowed to acknowledge their homage and then pointed to the child. The singing stopped immediately. And then David Jatney could hear the car moving out of the parking lot.

Irene never drank. But she sometimes took recreational drugs. Jatney could always tell. She had such a lovely brilliant smile on drugs. She had smiled that way one night when he had been waiting up for her in Santa Monica. In

477

that dawn light he had accused her of being in someone else's bed. She had replied calmly, 'Somebody had to fuck me, you won't.' And he had accepted the justice of that remark.

Christmas Eve they were still on the road and slept in another motel. It was cold now. They would not celebrate the Christmas season, Irene said that Christmas was false to the true spirit of religion. David Jatney did not want to bring back memories of an earlier, more innocent life. But he did buy Campbell a crystal ball with snow flurries, over the objections of Irene. Early Christmas morning he rose and watched the two of them sleep. He carried the handgun in his jacket always now and he touched the soft leather of its glove. How easy and kind it would be to kill them both now, he thought.

Three days later they were in the nation's capital. They only had to wait a short time until the Inauguration. David Jatney made up the itinerary of all the sights they would see. And then he made a map of the inaugural parade. They would all go see Francis Kennedy take the oath of office as President of the United States.

26

On Inauguration Day, the President of the United States, Francis Xavier Kennedy, was awakened at dawn by Jefferson to be groomed and dressed. The gray light of breaking day was actually cheery because a snow storm had begun. Huge white flakes pasted the city of Washington and in the bulletproofed tinted windows of his dressing room, Francis Kennedy saw himself imprisoned in those snowflakes, as if he were imprisoned in a glass ball. He said to Jefferson, 'Will you be in the parade?'

'No, Mr President,' Jefferson said. 'I have to hold the fort here in the White House.' He adjusted Kennedy's tie. 'Everybody is waiting for you downstairs in the Red Room.'

When Kennedy was ready, he shook Jefferson's hand. 'Wish me luck,' he said. And Jefferson went with him to the elevator. Two Secret Service men took him down to the ground floor.

In the Red Room they were all waiting for him. The Vice President, Helen DuPray, was stunningly regal in white satin, Lanetta Carr softly beautiful in pink. The President's staff were reflections of the President, all in white and black tuxedos, so startling against the walls and sofas of the Red Room. Arthur Wix, Oddblood Gray, Eugene Dazzy and Christian Klee formed their own little circle, solemn and tense with the importance of the day. Francis Kennedy smiled at them. The two women, these four men, were his family. It was amazing to him that he was a man in love, and that he would have a wife in the White House. That Lanetta Carr had agreed to marry him.

After his first dinner with Lanetta Carr, the dinner he had cooked so efficiently, Francis Kennedy had sunk into depression. The girl had so obviously not wanted him to woo her, had so desperately dreaded any amorous advance. He had invited her to other White House dinners, social occasions, where she would not have to worry that he would pursue a personal relationship.

He understood perfectly what she was feeling, that she was put off by his mantle of power. He had tried to allay that fear by going to her apartment dressed so casually and cooking her dinner with an apron tied around his waist. To disarm her; and it had partially succeeded. But it was only after she had seen the Presidential limousine blown up that she had weakened. That same night she had called Eugene Dazzy to ask when she could see the President. She had used those words. Dazzy had waited until the next morning to tell him of the call. Francis Kennedy still remembered the smile on Dazzy's face. It was the smile of an older brother fondly amused that his kid brother was finally being rewarded for a courtship. Francis Kennedy had called Lanetta Carr immediately.

There had been an awkward stilted conversation. Kennedy had invited her to have dinner with him in the White House, just the two of them. He explained that he could not leave, could not expose himself, that he would no longer be permitted to do so. And she had said that she would come to the White House whenever he wanted her to come. He told her to come that very night.

They had dinner in the residential apartment on the new fourth floor. Jefferson served them. They were very subdued while eating. And there was a moment as they left the dining room when Lanetta took his hand and he was startled by the warmth of her flesh. Blinded by long deprivation, by the lockings of his brain, he felt the different shape of her fingers, the shivery sleekness of her nails. And then he touched her shoulders and her neck, he felt a throbbing pulse and blindly touched the silken softness of her hair. Blindly he kissed her cheek, the corners of her eyes, all the warm flesh beneath the perfect skin. Transformed, delivered, his brain and body unlocked, he kissed her unshielded lips.

It was only when she responded that he dared to look at her face. It struck him to the heart, with amazement, with delight, with sorrow. She was so beautiful and her eyes surrendered her beauty to him out of love and her desire to make him happy. It was a look of trust, of belief in his humanity despite his trappings of power. He kissed her lips again and felt himself surrender, without compromise. Then almost as if in wonder, almost as if he had never discovered such strange land, he touched her breasts, the electric mysterious zones of her body beneath her dress. Remembered, cherished, he gave up his mind and body to her. And all the long years of dread and terror fled.

They became lovers and now Francis Kennedy had company when he roamed the rooms of the White House in the early hours of the morning when he could not sleep. And gradually he slept again through the night, eased into dreams by requited love. The nights he could not sleep, he drowsed happily, watched Lanetta Carr's sleeping face and nestled in her body. The nights became thoughts of joy rather than of dread. And like all true lovers he planned all the different ways to make his true love happy. And all the many ways he could make the people of America happy. And he thought how lucky he was that he was one of the few men in the world who could dream such dreams.

Two days before the Inauguration, Francis Kennedy and Lanetta agreed to marry. The wedding would take place the following April when the city of Washington would be celebrating spring.

*

Now that it was finally Inauguration Day, Francis Kennedy and his family emerged from the White House into a Washington made beautiful by great flakes of snow tinted gold by a cold winter sun.

Christian Klee watched Lanetta Carr and Francis Kennedy, the love on their faces. Christian thought there was no dignity in love, as there was no honor in politics, as there was no mercy in the struggles to rule this world. And what was mercy, after all, but a psychological insurance against total defeat? A subtle quid pro quo. He looked at the other men he had known so intimately for so many years. Eugene Dazzy, the President's Chief of Staff, Oddblood Gray, and Arthur Wix. They had, all of them, fought the battle for Francis Kennedy because it was their duty and he was their friend.

Then there was Theodore Tappey who dealt with evil on its own terms. Trick for trick, betrayal for betrayal. A simpler loyalty.

Dr Zed Annaccone was different from all of them. The star he followed shone clearly in the heavens. The irrevocable, unswerving truth of science, the only hope for man. He spurned evil, would have no truck with it. He would never coerce, never betray, he was bound in the immaculate conception of science. And good luck to him. As far as humanity was concerned he has his head, marvelous brain and all, stuck up his ass.

Or so Christian Klee thought as the Presidential party prepared to leave the White House for the swearing in of President Kennedy and the ride in the inaugural parade.

When President Francis Xavier Kennedy stepped out of the White House, he was astonished to see a vast sea of humanity that filled every thoroughfare, that seemed to blot out all the majestic buildings, overflowed all the TV vans and media people behind their special ropes and marked

482

grounds. He had never seen anything like it and he called to Eugene Dazzy, 'How many are out there?'

Dazzy said, 'A hell of a lot more than we figured. Maybe we need a battalion of Marines from the Naval Base to help us control traffic.'

'No,' the President said. He was surprised that Dazzy had responded to his question as if the multitudes were a danger. He thought it a triumph, a vindication of everything he had done since the tragedies of last Easter Sunday.

Francis Kennedy had never felt surer of himself. He had foreseen everything that would happen, the tragedies and the triumphs. He had made the right decisions and won his victory. He had vanquished his enemies. He looked over at the sea of humanity and felt an overwhelming love for the people of America. He would deliver them from their suffering, cleanse the earth itself.

Never had Francis Kennedy felt his mind so clear, his instincts so true. He had conquered his grief over the death of his wife, the murder of his daughter. The sorrow that had fogged his brain had cleared away. He was almost happy now.

It seemed to Francis Kennedy that he had conquered fate, suffered through its worst blows, and by his own perseverance and judgments had made possible this present glorious future. He stepped out in the snow-filled air to be sworn in, then lead the inaugural parade through Washington and start on his road to glory.

David Jatney had registered himself and Irene and Campbell in a motel a little over twenty miles from Washington DC. The capital itself was jammed. The day before the Inauguration, they drove into Washington to see the monuments, the White House, the Lincoln Memorial and all the other sights of the capital. David Jatney also scouted the route of the inaugural parade to discover the best place to stand.

On the great day, they rose at dawn and had breakfast at

483

a roadside diner. Then they went back to the motel to dress in their best clothes. Irene was uncharacteristically careful brushing and setting her hair. She wore her best faded jeans, a red shirt and a green floppy sweater over it that David Jatney had never seen before. Had she kept it hidden or had she bought it here in Washington, he wondered. She had gone off by herself for a few hours leaving Campbell with Jatney.

It had snowed all night and the ground was covered white. Big flakes were lazily drifting through the air. In California there was no need for winter clothing, but on the trip East they had bought windbreakers, a bright red one for Campbell because Irene claimed she could easily find him if he strayed, Jatney a serviceable bright blue, and Irene a creamy white which made her look very pretty. She also wore a knitted cap of white wool and a tasseled cap for Campbell in bright red. Jatney was bareheaded, he hated any kind of covering.

On this Inauguration morning, they had time to spare so they went out into the field behind the motel to build Campbell a snowman. Irene had a spasm of giddy happiness and threw snowballs at Campbell and Jatney. They both very gravely received her missiles but did not throw any back. Jatney wondered at this happiness in her. Could seeing Kennedy in the coming parade have caused it? Or was it the snow, so strange and magical to her California senses.

Campbell was entranced by the snow. He sifted it through his fingers watching it disappear and melt in the sunshine. Then he began cautiously destroying the snowman with his fists, punching tiny holes in it, knocking off the head. Jatney and Irene stood a little distance away, watching him. Irene took Jatney's hand in hers, an unusual physical intimacy on her part.

'I have to tell you something,' she said. 'I've visited some people here in Washington, my friends in California told me to look them up. And these people are going to India and

I'm going with them, me and Campbell. I've arranged to sell the van but I'll give you money out of it so you can fly back to Los Angeles.'

David Jatney let her hand go and put his hands in the pockets of his windbreaker. His right hand touched the leather glove which held the .22 handgun and for a moment he could see Irene lying on the ground, her blood eating up the snow.

When the anger came he was puzzled by it. After all he had decided to come to Washington in the pitiful hope that he might see Rosemary, or meet her and Hock and Gibson Grange. He had dreamed these past days that he might even be invited to another dinner with them. That his life might change, that he would get a foot in the door that opened into power and glory. So wasn't it natural for Irene to want to go to India to open the door into a world she yearned for, to make herself something more than an ordinary woman with a small child working at jobs that could never lead to anything? Let her go, he thought.

Irene said, 'Don't be mad. You don't even like me any more. You would have ditched me if it wasn't for Campbell.' She was smiling, a little mockingly but with a touch of sadness.

'That's right,' David Jatney said. 'You shouldn't take the little kid to wherever the hell you feel like going. You can barely look out for him here.'

That made her angry. 'Campbell is my child,' she said. 'I'll bring him up as I please. And I'll take him to the North Pole if I want to.'

She paused for a moment and then said, 'You don't know anything about it. And I think you're getting a little queer about Campbell.'

Again he saw the snow stained with her blood, little flashing rivers, a prickling of red dots. But he said with complete control, 'What exactly do you mean?'

'You're a little weird, you know,' Irene said. 'That's why

485

I liked you in the beginning. But I don't know exactly how weird you are. I worry about leaving Campbell with you sometimes.'

'You thought that, and then you left him with me anyway?' Jatney said.

'Oh, I know you wouldn't harm him,' Irene said. 'But I just thought me and Campbell should split and go on to India.'

'It's OK,' David Jatney said.

They let Campbell completely destroy the snowman, then they all got into the van and started the twenty-mile drive into Washington. When they pulled into the Interstate, they were astonished to see it full of cars and buses as far as the eye could see. They managed to inch into the traffic but it took four hours before the endless monstrous steel caterpillar spilled them into the capital.

The inaugural parade wound through the broad avenues of Washington, led by the Presidential cavalcade of limousines. It progressed slowly, the enormous crowd overflowing the police barricades at spots and impeding progress. The wall of uniformed police began to crumble under the millions of people who pushed against them.

Three cars full of Secret Service men preceded Kennedy's limousine with its bulletproof glass bubble. Inside that glass bubble Kennedy stood so that he could acknowledge the multitude as he rode through Washington. Little wavelets of people surged up to the limousine itself then were driven back by the inner circle of Secret Service men outside the car. But each little wavelet of frantic worshippers seemed to lap closer and closer. The inner circle of guards was pressed back against the Presidential limousine.

The car directly behind Francis Kennedy held more Secret Service men armed with heavy automatic weapons and other Secret Service men on foot ran alongside it. The next limousine carried Christian Klee, Oddblood Gray, Arthur

Wix and Eugene Dazzy. Also in this car was the Reverend Baxter Foxworth who had been given this place of honor on the urging of Oddblood Gray. The argument being that Foxworth had delivered the black vote, more than half the population in Washington was black and it was presumed that blacks would make up a good part of the inaugural crowd. Foxworth's presence signaled that the new Kennedy administration respected the black movement. Also, Oddblood Gray worried that the Reverend Baxter Foxworth might fight the Alaskan work camps. This gesture of riding in a place of honor might give him pause.

The Reverend Foxworth was well aware of all this reasoning and rejoiced in the fact that he was going to launch an all out attack on the Alaska work camps the very next day. He had observed that the crowd had a great many blacks in it but they were overwhelmed by the influx of people all over the United States who had come to worship Francis Kennedy on this great day. Foxworth observed everything very carefully but since the cavalcade was inching along so slowly he passed the time by needling Arthur Wix, the National Security Advisor.

'I've looked up the history,' Foxworth said. 'And you are the first Jew ever to boss the military forces of America. Do you realize what that tells us? Finally the Jews no longer need feel they are a minority group, or outside the political power structure. You give us blacks some hope.'

Arthur Wix found the Reverend Foxworth unamusing. He said coldly, 'The National Security Advisor does not control the armed forces.'

The Reverend Foxworth said amiably, 'But you know your appointment was very symbolic. Maybe President Kennedy will appoint a black man to head the FBI when Attorney General Klee takes off both his hats.' He grinned at Klee.

Christian Klee had always had a sneaking admiration for the Reverend Foxworth and also knew he was not the target.

He said, 'I hope so, Reverend. As you say it would be a great symbolic appointment. I'll mention it to the President.'

Eugene Dazzy had brought a briefcase of papers with him, the case locked to his wrist with a steel cuff. He looked up for a moment and said, 'When Christian resigns Peter Cloot will be reinstated. The FBI slot will likely go to him.'

They were all silent. Christian Klee was lost in admiration at Francis Kennedy's finesse. The appointment would shut Cloot up about the atom bomb thing and then Kennedy himself would sweep everything under the rug.

The limousine was barely moving, the broad avenue was becoming awash with the crowd, stopping the advance of the cavalcade.

The Reverend Foxworth said to Wix, 'You know Israel could use your talents. But then I guess you co-operate with them pretty much even now.' He was tickled at how red Wix's face got.

Arthur Wix rose to the bait but more cold-bloodedly than Foxworth wished. Wix said, 'My record shows that I have given Israel less influence in our foreign policy than any other National Security Advisor. But I understand your implication which is essentially why don't I go back where I came from? That eternal question put to minorities. The answer is, that I come from America. What is your answer when someone puts that question to you?'

The Reverend Foxworth laughed and said, 'I just tell them you took me out of Africa, you figure out where I should go back. But I don't mean to quarrel. After all we represent the two most important minority groups in America.' He paused for a moment then added, 'Of course your people are no longer treated with any prejudice in this country. But we hope to get there someday.' It was just for a moment but Foxworth saw it. Arthur Wix held him in absolute contempt. And what made it worse was that it was not the contempt of a white man for a black man, it was the contempt of a civilized man for a primitive.

At that moment the car came to a complete stop and Oddblood Gray looked out the window. 'Oh shit, the President is getting out and walking,' he said.

Eugene Dazzy put the papers in the briefcase and snapped shut the lock. Then he unlocked the briefcase from his wrist and handed it to the Secret Service man sitting beside the driver in the front seat. 'If *he's* walking we have to walk with him,' Eugene said.

Oddblood Gray looked at Christian Klee, and said, 'Chris, you have to stop him. Use that veto of yours.'

'I haven't got it any more,' Christian Klee said.

Arthur Wix said, 'I think you'd better call a whole lot more Secret Service men down here.'

They all got out of the car and formed a wall to march behind the President.

President Francis Kennedy decided to walk the last five hundred yards to the reviewing stand. For the first time he wanted to touch physically the people who loved him, who had stood in the snow for many hours just to see him in the mechanized bulletproof glass bubble. For the first time he believed he had nothing to fear from them. And he wanted, on this great day, to show that he trusted them.

The large snowflakes were still swirling in the air, but they felt no more substantial on the body of Francis Kennedy than the communion wafer had felt on the roof of his mouth when he was a child. He walked up the avenue and shook the hands of those people who pierced the police-manned barriers and then the ring of Secret Service men assembled around him. Every so often a tiny wave of spectators managed to wash through, pushed on by the mass of a million spectators behind them. They crested over the Secret Service men who had tried to form a wider circle around their President. Francis Kennedy shook the hands of these men and women and kept this pace. Far down the avenue he could see the specially erected viewing stand where Lanetta was waiting for him. He could feel his hair getting wet from the snow but the cold air exhilarated him as did the devotion of the crowd. He was not conscious of any tiredness, of any discomfort, though there was an alarming deadness in his right arm, his right hand swollen from being gripped so often and so harshly. Secret Service men were literally tearing the lucky spectators away from their President. A young pretty woman in a creamy windbreaker had tried to keep holding his hand and he had to wrench it back to safety.

David Jatney pushed out a space in the crowd that would shelter himself and Irene who held Campbell in her arms. The crowd kept shifting in waves like an ocean and Campbell would have been trampled otherwise.

They were no more than four hundred yards from the viewing stands when the Presidential limousine came into their line of sight. It was followed by official cars holding dignitaries. Behind them was the endless crowd that would pass before the viewing stand in the inaugural parade. David Jatney estimated that the Presidential limousine was a little more than the length of a football field away from his vantage point. Then he noticed that parts of the crowd lining the avenue had surged out into the avenue itself and forced the cavalcade to halt.

Irene screamed, 'He's getting out. He's walking. Oh, my God, I have to touch him.' She slung Campbell into Jatney's arms and tried to duck under the barrier but one of the long line of uniformed police stopped her. She ran along the curb and was through the initial picket line of policemen only to be stopped by the inner barrier of Secret Service men. David Jatney watched her, thinking, if only Irene was smarter she would have kept Campbell in her arms. The Secret Service men would have recognized that she was not a threat and she might have slipped through while they were thrusting back the others. He could see her being swept back to the curb and then another wave of people swept her up again and she was one of the few people who managed to slip through and shake the President's hand and then was kissing the President on the cheek before she was roughly pulled away.

David Jatney could see that Irene would never make it back to him and Campbell. She was just a tiny dot in the mass of people that was now threatening to engulf the broad expanse of the avenue. More and more people were pressing against the outer security rim of uniformed police and more and more were hitting up against the inner rim of Secret Service men. Both rims were showing cracks. Campbell was beginning to cry so Jatney reached into the pocket of his windbreaker for one of the candy bars he usually carried for the boy. His fingers felt the leather glove and inside it the cold steel of the .22.

And then David Jatney felt a suffusion of warmth through his body. He thought of the past few days in Washington, the sight of the many buildings erected to establish the authority of the state. The marble columns of the court and the memorials, the stately splendor of the façades; indestructible, irremovable. He thought of Hock's office in its splendor, guarded by his secretaries, he thought of the Mormon Church in Utah with its temples blessed by special and particularly discovered angels. All these to designate certain men as superior to their fellows. To keep ordinary men like himself in their place. And to direct all love on to themselves. Presidents, gurus, Mormon elders built their intimidating edifices to wall themselves away from the rest of humanity and, knowing well the envy of the world, guarded themselves against hate. Jatney remembered his glorious victory in the 'hunts' of the university, he had been a hero then, that one time in his life. Now he patted Campbell soothingly to make him stop crying. In his pocket, underneath the gun, his hand found the candy bar and gave it to Campbell. Then still holding the boy in his arms he stepped from the curb and ducked under the barriers.

*

The Reverend Baxter Foxworth didn't really like the idea of being on foot behind President Kennedy as they trudged up the avenue. It was boring, despite the multitude that cheered. He didn't like the wet snowflakes dropping, wetting and wrinkling his suit. But when members of the crowd broke through the two protecting rims, he quickened his step so that he would be beside the President. He shook the hands of the people who broke the barriers, trying to deflect them from Kennedy. He did this for two reasons. Primarily he wanted to be in the center of the TV coverage, secondly, he was worried about Kennedy. He prided himself on being streetwise, and this was a dangerous situation. But what the hell, he knew he would be walking near Kennedy, shaking hands, being hailed by the black brothers who recognized him. His spirits rose, this was one hell of a fine day. Then he saw running toward him a man with a small boy in his arms. He reached out to shake his hand.

David Jatney was filled with wonder and then a fierce elation. It would be easy. More of the crowd were overflowing the outer rim of uniformed police, more of those were piercing the inner rim of Secret Service agents and getting to shake the President's hand. Those two barriers were crumbling, the invaders marching alongside Kennedy and waving their arms to show their devotion. The street of the avenue looked like a marble floor covered with black insects. Jatney ran toward the oncoming President, a wave of spectators piercing the wooden barriers carrying him along. Now he was just outside the ring of Secret Service men who were trying to keep everyone away from the President. But there no longer were enough of them. And with a sort of glee he saw that they had discounted him. Cradling Campbell in his left arm, he put his right hand in the windbreaker, felt the leather glove, his fingers moved on to the trigger. At that moment the ring of Secret Service men crumbled and he was inside the magic circle. Just ten feet away he saw Francis

Kennedy shaking hands with a wild-looking ecstatic teenager. Kennedy seemed very slim, very tall, and older than he appeared on television. Still holding Campbell in his arms, Jatney took a step toward Kennedy.

At that moment a very handsome black man blocked him off. His hand was extended. For a frantic moment Jatney thought he had seen the gun in this pocket and was demanding it. Then he realized that the man looked familiar and that he was just offering a handshake. They stared at each other for a long moment, Jatney looked down at the extended black hand, the black face smiling above it. And then he saw the man's eyes gleam with suspicion, the hand suddenly withdrawn. Jatney with a convulsive wrenching of all his bodily muscles threw Campbell at the black man and drew his gun from the windbreaker.

The Reverend Baxter Foxworth had in that moment when Jatney stared into his face known that something terrible was going to happen. He let the boy fall to the ground and then with a quick shift of feet put his body in front of the slowly advancing Francis Kennedy. He saw the gun appear in Jatney's hand.

Christian Klee, walking to the right and a little behind Francis Kennedy, was using the cellular phone to call for more Secret Service men to help clear the crowd out of the President's path. He saw the man holding the child approach the phalanx guarding Kennedy. And then for just one second, he saw the man's face clearly.

It was some vague nightmare coming through, the reality did not sink in. The face he had called up on his computer screen these past nine months, the life he had monitored with computer and surveillance teams had suddenly sprung out of that shadowy jungle of mythology into the real world.

He saw the face, not in the repose of surveillance photos but in the throes of exalted emotion. And he was struck by how the handsome face became so ugly, as if seen through some distorted glass.

Christian Klee was already moving quickly toward Jatney, still not believing the image, trying to certify his nightmare, when he saw the Reverend Foxworth stretch out his hand. And Christian felt a tremendous feeling of relief. The man could not be Jatney, he was just a guy holding his kid and trying to touch a piece of history.

But then he saw the child in his red windbreaker and little woolen hat being hurled through the air. He saw the gun in Jatney's hand. And he saw Foxworth fall.

Unbelieving, he realized that he, himself, Christian Klee, had improperly directed fate by wiping David Jatney off the computer screen and canceling the surveillance. And in that same moment he saw that he, not Francis, must be sacrificed. Suddenly Christian Klee, in the sheer terror of his crime, ran towards Jatney and took the second bullet in the face. The bullet traveled thorugh his palate, making him choke on the blood, then there was a blinding pain in his left eye. He was still conscious when he fell. He tried to cry out but his mouth was full of shattered teeth and crumbled flesh. And he felt a great sense of loss and helplessness. In his shattered brain, his last neurons flashed with thoughts of Francis Kennedy, he wanted to warn him of death, to ask his forgiveness. Christian's brain then flicked out and his head with its deflowered eye socket came to rest in a light powdery pillow of snow.

In that same moment Francis Kennedy turned full toward David Jatney and heard the crack of the gun. He saw Foxworth fall. Then Klee. And in that moment, all his nightmares, all his memories of different death, all his terrors of malignant fate crystalized into a paralyzed astonishment and resignation. And in that moment he heard a tremendous vibration in the world, felt for a tiny fraction of a second only the explosion of steel in his brain. He fell.

David Jatney could not believe it all had happened. The black man lay where he had fallen. The white man alongside. The President of the United States was crumpling before his eyes, legs bent outward, arms flying up into the air as his knees finally hit the ground. David Jatney kept firing. Hands were tearing at his gun, at his body. He tried to run, and as he ran he saw the multitude rise and swarm like a great wave toward him and countless hands reached out to him. His face covered with blood, he felt his ear being ripped off the side of his head and saw it in one of the hands. Suddenly something happened to his eyes and he could not see. His body was racked with pain for one single moment and then he felt nothing.

The TV cameraman, his all-seeing eye on his shoulder, had recorded everything for the people of the world. When the gun flashed into sight, he had backed away just enough so that everyone would be included in the frame. He caught David Jatney raising the gun, he caught the Reverend Baxter Foxworth making his amazing supple jump in front of the President and go down, and then Klee receiving a bullet in his face and going down. He caught Francis Kennedy making his turn to face the killer and the killer firing, the bullet twisting Kennedy's head as if he were in a hammerlock. He caught Jatney's look of stern determination as Francis Kennedy fell and the Secret Service men frozen in that terrible moment, all their training for immediate response wiped out in shock. And then he saw Jatney trying to run and being overwhelmed by the multitude. But the cameraman did not get the final shot, which he would regret for the rest of his life. The crowd tearing David Jatney to pieces.

Over the city, washing through the marble buildings and the monuments of power, rose the great wail of millions of worshippers who had lost their dreams.

27

President Helen DuPray held the Oracle's one hundredth birthday party in the White House on Palm Sunday three months after the death of Francis Kennedy.

Dressed to understate her beauty, she stood in the Rose Garden, and surveyed her guests. Among them there were the former staff members of the Kennedy administration. Eugene Dazzy was chatting with Elizabeth Stone and Patsy Troyca.

Eugene Dazzy had already been told he was fired to take effect the next month. Helen DuPray had never really liked the man. And it had nothing to do with the fact that Eugene Dazzy had young mistresses and was indeed already being excessively charming to Elizabeth Stone.

President Helen DuPray had appointed Elizabeth Stone to her staff, Patsy Troyca came with the package. But Elizabeth was exactly what she needed. A woman with extraordinary energy, a brilliant administrator, and a feminist who understood political realities. And Patsy Troyca was not so bad, indeed he was a fortifying element with his knowledge of the trickeries of Congress, his lower branch of cunning which could sometimes be so valuable to more sophisticated intelligences such as Elizabeth Stone's and indeed, thought Helen DuPray, her own.

After Helen DuPray assumed the Presidency she had been briefed by Kennedy's staff and other insiders of the administration. She had studied all the proposed legislation that the new Congress would consider. She had ordered all the

496

secret memos be assembled for her, all the detailed plans, including the now infamous Alaska work camps.

After a month of study it became horrifyingly clear to her that Francis Kennedy, with the purest of motives, to better the lot of the people of the United States, would have, she believed, been the first dictator in American history.

From where she stood in the Rose Garden, the trees not yet in full leaf, President Helen DuPray could see the faraway Lincoln Memorial and the arching white of the Washington Monument, reminders of that city of massive stone and marble that was the capital of America. Here in the garden were all the representatives of America, at her special invitation. She had made peace with the enemies of the Kennedy administration.

Present were Louis Inch, a man she despised, but whose help she would need; George Greenwell; Martin Mutford and Bert Audick and Lawrence Salentine. The infamous Socrates Club. She would have to come to terms with all of them. Which was why she had invited them to the White House for the Oracle's birthday party. She would at least give them the option of helping build a new America, as Kennedy had not.

But Helen DuPray knew that America could not be rebuilt without accommodations on all sides. Also she knew that in a few years there would be a more conservative Congress elected. She could not hope to persuade the nation as Kennedy, with his charisma and personal romantic history, had done.

She saw Dr Zed Annaccone seated beside the Oracle's wheelchair. The doctor was probably trying to get the old man to donate his brain to science. And Dr Zed Annaccone was another problem. His PET Scan Verification Test was already being published in various scientific papers. Helen DuPray had always seen its virtues and its dangers. She felt it was a problem that should be carefully considered over a long period of time. A government with the capacity to find out the infallible truth could be very dangerous. True such a test would root out crime, political corruption, could reform the whole legal structure of society. But there were complicated truths, there were status quo truths and then was it not true that at certain moments in history, truth could bring a halt to certain evolutionary changes. And what about the psyche of a people who knew the various truths about themselves could be exposed?

She glanced at the corner of the Rose Garden where Oddblood Gray and the Reverend Foxworth were sitting in wicker chairs and talking animatedly. The Reverend Foxworth was wearing a flamboyant scarf bandage to remind people that he had miraculously recovered from the bullet that had torn his throat.

The Reverend Baxter Foxworth now spoke in a hoarse voice, but it was still vivacious, still enthusiastic about life in general and his own particular problems and ambitions. Helen DuPray could hear him distinctly.

'Otto, why the hell did I do it?' he said. 'I took that bullet for a white man. I didn't even think about it. I made my famous sideass move to get in front of Kennedy. He wasn't even a brother. Why, tell me why?'

Oddblood Gray, who was now seeing a psychiatrist every day for depression, said to him, 'Because you're a fucking born hero, Sideass.' The psychiatrist had told Gray that after the events of the past year it was perfectly normal for him to be suffering from depression. So why the hell was he going to a psychiatrist?

Foxworth contemplated the idea of being a hero. He said, 'I'm too competitive, that's all it was. And now that I'm going to run for Senator those fucking wishy-washy white niggers are calling me the ultimate Uncle Tom. They say only an Uncle Tom black man would take a bullet meant for a white man. How do you like that shit?'

'What do you care?' Oddblood Gray said. 'You'll be the

first black Senator from the state of New York. You can run their asses out of town.'

'The Ultimate Uncle Tom. Me,' Reverend Foxworth said. 'I broke the white man's balls for twenty years while they were combing out their Afros.' But he was smiling. 'What about you, Otto? Did the President ask for your resignation too?'

'No,' Otto gray said. 'I'm going to be a Cabinet Minister. HEW. Me and you will still be doing business.'

The Reverend Foxworth said. 'That's good. You know, Otto, now that a woman is President that sets a precedent. There's a chance for a black man to be Number One. If I were you, I'd stop going to that psychiatrist. You don't want that on your record if some day it happens you run for the highest office in the land. You can't be black and crazy both and expect to be elected President of the United States.'

In the Rose Garden, the Oracle was now the center of attraction. The birthday cake was being presented to him, a huge cake that covered the entire garden table. On the top, lettered in red, white and blue spun sugar, was the Stars and Stripes. The TV cameras moved in, they caught for the nation the sight of the Oracle blowing out the hundred birthday candles. And blowing with him were President Helen DuPray, Oddblood Gray, Eugene Dazzy, Arthur Wix and the members of the Socrates Club.

The Oracle accepted a piece of cake and then allowed himself to be interviewed by Cassandra Chutt who had managed this coup with the help of Lawrence Salentine. Cassandra Chutt had alrady made her introductory remarks while the candles were being blown out. Now she asked, 'How does it feel to be one hundred years old?'

The Oracle glared at her malevolently and at that moment he looked so evil that Cassandra Chutt was glad that this show was being taped for the evening. God the man was ugly, his head a mass of liver spots, the scaly skin as shiny as scar tissue, the mouth almost disappeared. For a moment she was afraid that he was deaf or ga ga so she repeated herself. She said, 'How does it feel to be a century old?'

The Oracle smiled, his face cracked into countless wrinkles. 'Are you a fucking idiot?' he said. He caught sight of his face in one of the TV monitors, and it broke his heart. Suddenly he hated his birthday party. He looked directly into the camera and said, 'Where's Christian?'

President Helen Dupray sat by the Oracle's wheelchair and held his hand. The Oracle was asleep, the very light sleep of old men waiting for death. The party in the Rose Garden went on without him.

Helen DuPray remembered herself as a young woman, one of the protégés of the Oracle. She had admired him so much. He had an intellectual grace, a turn of wit, a natural vivacity and joy in life that was everything she wanted herself to be. And of course not to be left out, to be honest, his extraordinary achievements in life, uncommon even in America.

Did in matter that he always tried to form a sexual liaison? She remembered the years before and how hurt she had been when his friendship had turned into lechery. She ran her fingers over the scaly skin of his withered hand. She had followed the destiny of power, most women followed the destiny of love, like poor Lanetta Carr who had returned to her native Louisiana. Were the victories of love sweeter?

Helen DuPray thought of her own destiny and that of America. She was still astonished that after all the terrible events of the past year, the country had settled down so peacefully. True, she had been partly responsible for that, her skill and intelligence had blanketed the fire in the country. But still.

She had wept at the death of Kennedy, in a small way she had loved him. She had loved the tragedy written into the bones of his beautifully planed face. She had loved his idealism, his vision of what America could be. She had loved his personal integrity, his purity and selflessness, his disinterest in material things. And yet despite all this she had come to know that he was a dangerous man.

Helen DuPray realized that now she had to guard against the belief in her own righteousness. She believed that in a world of such peril, humankind could not solve its problems with strife but only with a never-ending patience. She would do the best she could, and in her heart try not to feel hatred for her enemies.

At that moment the Oracle opened his eyes and smiled. He pressed her hand and began to speak. His voice was very low and she bent her head close to his wrinkled mouth. 'Don't worry,' the Oracle said. 'You will be a great President.'

Helen DuPray for a moment felt a desire to weep as a child might when praised, for fear of failure. She looked about her in the Rose Garden filled with the most powerful men and women of America. She would have their help, most of them, some she would have to guard herself against. But most of all she would have to guard against herself.

She thought again of Francis Kennedy. He lay now with his two famous uncles, loved as they had been. Well, Helen DuPray thought, I will be the best of what he was, I will do the best of what he hoped to do. And then, holding tightly to the Oracle's hand, she pondered on the simplicities of evil and the dangerous deviousness of good.